BOOKS BURN BADLY

Also by Manuel Rivas

Manuel Rivas

BOOKS BURN BADLY

Translated from the Galician by
Jonathan Dunne

Harvill *Secker*
LONDON

Published by Harvill Secker 2010

2 4 6 8 10 9 7 5 3 1

First published with the title *Os libros arden mal* in 2006 by
Edicións Xerais de Galicia

First published in Great Britain in 2010 by
HARVILL SECKER
Random House, 20 Vauxhall Bridge Road
London SW1V 2SA

www.rbooks.co.uk

Addresses for companies within The Random House Group Limited
can be found at: www.randomhouse.co.uk/offices.htm

The Random House Group Limited Reg. No. 954009

A CIP catalogue record for this book
is available from the British Library

ISBN 9781846551468

The publication of this work has been made possible through a subsidy
received from the Directorate General for Books, Archives
and Libraries of the Spanish Ministry of Culture

The Random House Group Limited supports The Forest Stewardship Council (FSC),
the leading international forest certification organisation. All our titles that are
printed on Greenpeace approved FSC certified paper carry the FSC logo. Our
paper procurement policy can be found at www.rbooks.co.uk/environment

Mixed Sources
Product group from well-managed
forests and other controlled sources
www.fsc.org Cert no. TT-COC-2139
© 1996 Forest Stewardship Council

Typeset in Quadraat by Palimpsest Book Production Limited,
Grangemouth, Stirlingshire

Printed and bound in the UK by
CPI Mackays, Chatham ME5 8TD

For Antón Patiño Regueira, naturalist and book-collector, in memoriam.

Burning of books by the Falangists, Coruña Docks, 19 August 1936

'The future is surely uncertain: who can say what will happen? But the past is also uncertain: who can say what happened?'
Antonio de Machado, *Juan de Mairena*

The Water Marks

At first, he bothers me. He's young. I don't know him. It happens sometimes. They get in the way. I was watching out for the tango singer who appeared on stage at the invitation of Pucho Boedo of the Oriental Orchestra. In a white suit and a red cravat. *Please welcome a friend of mine who sings like the sea rocked to sleep by the lighthouse: Luís Terranova . . .* A real looker. Even more so when he opened his mouth. All his childish features vanished and his bones stood out. It was 'Chessman', about someone who's been sentenced to death. I'd never heard a tango sung like that. It was as if he'd just composed it, was making it up. *It's ten and the clock chimes as I take a step into God's time.* Would you believe the time was right? That was at the dance in San Pedro de Nós. I don't remember now, but I think even the musicians stopped playing. That summer, I went with Ana and Amalia to the different fairs, hoping to hear him again, but he'd disappeared. I would sing the tango by the river – *My steps are books, the Lord's passion; my rest a chair the world put there* – and with a bit of effort I finally managed to compose his figure in the water. I know it's cheating. But I also have the right to evoke some images, not just to wait for those that turn up.

Like this one. This one came of its own accord.

He's a soldier. At first, I'm a little shocked. He seemed a bit of a monster. So young and in uniform. Smooth-faced. Baby-faced except for the lips, which are fleshy and more forward than his other features. Maybe the mouth hangs open like that when it's in the water, against the current. He looks at me with curiosity. And a sad smile. He has a round face, like those in our family. He's blond. The water is golden, not from the sun's

I

rays, but maybe because of his blondness. I enjoy the figures' company, but I don't like it when they stare. I drop the garment I'm washing in their direction, slowly, not to smash the image, but so that it fades away, lurks under a pebble, has a chance to hide in the reeds.

But this time I don't. This time, I let it be.

A baby-faced soldier with a man's look. A smooth-faced soldier. In a trenchcoat with big buttons and a stiff collar. Framed by a circle of water. His arms are crossed and he wears a badge on his left sleeve. A man's look, that's right. He looks at me without pride, but also without pity. It's what they do, the water figures, they come and see, look when you look.

I asked Mum about him.

I asked her about the young soldier.

She pretends not to hear me.

Slap, slap! Cloth on stone.

I think Mum would prefer not to know about my figures. Maybe she has enough with her own. I notice she avoids shaking the clothes out by the river when she sees me gazing into the water. I think they also move, change looks along the river, because they're extremely restless. When one disappears for a while, it's probably off somewhere in her circles. That's what happened to the boxer. The boxer hung around here for a while, on my part of the river, and then left. I reckon he went to where she washes since Polka told me the boxer liked women who worked in the local factories.

But she pretends not to see my figures, and I pretend not to see hers.

'What's that?'

'A soldier, a baby-faced soldier.'

'There's been more than one soldier,' she said. Slap, slap!

'Right. The one I'm talking about is smooth-faced and blond. And smiles. Or sort of, anyway.'

'You mean Domingos,' she finally replied, 'who died at Annual in 1921. The one with the tubes of laughter.'

The figure smiled. It was him, the one with the tubes of laughter.

'He always smiled,' said Olinda. 'Smart as garlic, but weak. Sickly. Our mother, Grandma Dansa, accompanied him to the recruiting office.

'"This lad's no good for war," she told them.

2

'And one of them replied, "Everyone's good for war, if not for killing, then for dying."

'One day he wrote a letter, saying he had responsibility for the tubes of laughter, the name they gave the radio operators' poles. He'd carry the radios on the back of a mule. And he learnt things. Said he could now understand the language of birds. All of his letters were a kind of joke. They seemed to have come not from a war, but from a comedy. They were such a joke grandma cried when we read them to her. At the end, he always put IKTH, which meant I Kiss The Hand Of My Mother. And grandma couldn't stop crying because of what he'd learnt at war.'

And then Olinda opened up. She talked about something she always avoided, about the soldiers in our family and our locality. The Philippines. Cuba. Morocco. 'Go forth and multiply as cannon fodder. An empire of bones, piled up year after year. Followed by those who died in the Civil War. What the army lost abroad they tried to reconquer at home.' That's what Olinda said. Slap, slap! The wet cloth striking against the stone seemed, in someone so taciturn, to be a way of expanding the story. Words with a layer of dusty sweat, iodine and blood, suddenly soaked, twisted, slapped, soaped, twisted, wrung out. Left in the sun. Clean. A white shirt drying. Some trousers. The wind filling the vacant clothing. At the washing place, in a crack in the wall that stops the north-easterly, there is always a robin. When the women fall silent, the robin sings. A tube of laughter. The old burying the young, according to Olinda. That's what war is.

Now there's something funny, and I don't know if it's normal or not, but I can't see myself in the water. I can see Olinda. I look sideways and see my mother both in and out of the water. She's on her knees, her body next to the washing stone. An angular woman's body. The stone seems to have been gradually worn down by the stroke of bellies. The axis in our bellies and the shape of the stone are what link the sky, the earth and the water. As she applies soap, I look sideways, first at her reflection in the water and then at her. The sun's behind her, her hair is gathered by a headscarf tied at the back of her neck, she again adopts an expression of hardness. She's hard on the inside. Her eyes give nothing away. You can see that better in the water.

3

The Night of the Moths

Oulton Cottage, night of 11 July 1881

'I asked the steersman if there was any hope of saving the vessel, or our lives.

'"None of us will see the morning," he replied.'

For the second night running, old Borrow recounted the storm off Cape Finisterre. Henrietta MacOubrey, his stepdaughter, decided that this time she'd listen for as long as it took a white moth to collide with the lamp. Two white moths if the first arrived too quickly. It seemed fair enough. He was a good narrator. When he told stories, his whole body became calligraphy in motion, from the flexing of his fingers to the dilatation of his pupils. Having been a Biblical propagandist, he knew the rules of suspense. And that's why he advanced in stages, subtly, without committing excesses, because he loved to invent, but he despised anything that smacked of implausibility as much as fanatical truth. So he wasn't telling the story for the second time, but getting a little closer, with inflamed accuracy, to that storm with hurricane winds on the night of 11 November 1836, off Cape Finisterre, the world's rockiest coastline.

He'd been excitable of late. Spring had been delayed, so summer came to Oulton Cottage like a frenzied agitator. The dwelling was festooned with the modest exuberance of fuchsias, gypsy flowers he called them, poking through the windows like prodigious Lepidoptera. An ardent atmosphere of drones and pollen made use of each crack and charged in, ready to deliver its message. Inside, everything seemed to hang on his renewed magnetism and to breathe a sigh of relief after the winter episode of a grumpy,

4

prostrate Borrow in the grip of a repulsive current he himself didn't recognise. Now things were different. He received a few visitors, the occasional gypsy friend who couldn't tell the time, a virtue Henrietta found annoying. But the old gypsies behaved as if Borrow, the tireless traveller, the polyglot, the youth who could cover a hundred and twenty miles in a day on a pint of beer and two apples, had come back to look after them. Lavengro they called him, which meant wordsmith. Spirited Lavengro never failed to return.

'Lavengro,' he whispered.

Henrietta glanced at the window in case something was moving beyond the fuchsias.

'There's no one there.'

'A terrible winter,' he said. 'Forgive my hedgehog's tenderness.'

Henrietta thought nothing is quite so tiring as an old person's excitability. More tiring than tiredness itself. Borrow bravely resisted the temptation to go to bed and spent most of the time tied to his desk, like a helmsman at the wheel, he said. He would read Scripture with the severity of someone threading the needle of eternity or start writing feverishly. But from time to time, which upset his stepdaughter, who suffered from what is sometimes termed caretaker's syndrome, Borrow would leap up in a fit of madness and take to the road, calling out for his gypsy friends, offering to let them camp in the garden, or begin to recite the poems of Iolo Goch and Dafydd ab Gwilym in the rain, natural prayers he himself had translated from the Welsh.

For the second night running, he went back to Finisterre. Henrietta had had a long day, but she still wanted to listen to the old man, who drew strength and a Biblical voice from the night. She didn't find such a description irreverent, something must have stuck after so many years travelling on the road with the Word of God. Though Borrow still joked about himself when he appeared to adopt too missionary a tone. 'Heavens above, I sound like a prophet of doom. Or a St Lupus!'

Henrietta could see the storm at Finisterre in the camera obscura of Borrow's eyes thanks to the light and shade in his voice. She saw herself as a moth attracted by the thunder and lightning of the story. The first moth.

George Borrow was convinced that the description of the storm, included in his book *The Bible in Spain*, was one of his finest literary achievements. The act of writing it had been like a second storm with gusts of wind and immense waves. He dipped his pen in the chaos of the inkpot, scratching the words in the belief that writing fast would create an inflammatory style. But now it was his translations, the murmur of youthful verses, that stirred his memory:

> The wild Death-raven, perch'd upon the mast,
> Scream'd 'mid the tumult, and awoke the blast.

The sickly steamer left London along the Thames, put in at Falmouth and finally departed with a crowd of passengers suffering from tuberculosis, fleeing from the cold blasts of England's winter in search of some sun further south. This time he gave the story an ironic twist Henrietta hadn't heard before, which referred to the state of the ship's engine: the boat was consumptive as well. This became obvious right from the start. Henrietta knew all the details, she'd heard the story before, but she still liked it when Borrow used the image of cathedrals to describe the clouds of spray and foam. 'The right ship for the time and place,' said Borrow ironically. And he added, 'With the ideal steersman.' The day before, he'd made mention of the captain, a person picked up in a hurry, who took the vessel too close to the shore, but to whom he attributed the utmost coolness and intrepidity, as he did to the rest of the crew. However, the only voice that speaks for itself in the story is that of the steersman. 'In less than an hour,' he says, 'the ship will have her broadside on Finisterre, where the strongest man-of-war ever built must go to shivers instantly.'

He had written, and was about to repeat, how a horrid convulsion of the elements took place and the dregs of the ocean seemed to be cast up, but in the end he said, 'Thank God for lightning. It's good for swearing!'

In a flash of lightning, he saw Cape Finisterre and swore he'd come back with a book of Holy Scripture in thanksgiving. Had the darkness been complete, there'd have been no way of reacting, of putting up resistance. Had the lightning not intervened, with the engine dead and the ship being tossed like a feather, the crew might not have committed the apparently absurd act of hoisting the sails in the face of impending destruction, just as the wind, without the slightest intimation, veered right about.

'I went back. I kept my promise. And there I met Antonio de la Trava, to whom I gave a copy of the New Testament, the only one I ever dedicated.'

The first moth collided with the lampshade. It had a white, hairy head and the uncannily human features of some moths. The savage, stubborn, suicidal collision gave Henrietta a start and she resolved not to stay beyond the second.

'Spain is not a fanatic country, but life there can hang on a single word.'

Henrietta forgot the moth and smiled. She loved this episode in which Borrow, being mistaken for the leader of the Spanish fanatics, Don Carlos himself, and on the verge of being shot by the liberals or *negros* of the Atlantic coast, was saved *in extremis* during questioning, when proof of his innocence was the way he pronounced the word 'knife'. '"Knife"? Did he say "knife"? The man's innocent,' declared Antonio de la Trava, the *valiente* of Finisterra, knife in hand. As Borrow went into details, Henrietta laughed so much she had to rub her eyes.

'In Madrid, we printed five thousand copies of the New Testament. Soon after I arrived, in May 1837. I distributed a large number myself through Spain by hand. Otherwise they'd have rotted in some dungeon, as some of them did a year later, when I was arrested and it was forbidden to sell or circulate the New Testament. The Papists didn't want the people reading the Gospel! The Vatican assigned Spain the role of butcher and always kept the people apart from the Word of God. A scandal that was never talked about. In the most Catholic country in the world, people were afraid to buy the Holy Scriptures. You could see their nostrils quivering when I put a book in their hands. They could smell the flames of the Inquisition.'

'There's one thing I didn't understand today or yesterday,' said Henrietta. 'Did you actually sign the Holy Scriptures?'

'Not sign. It was an act of thanksgiving, a bold step I never repeated. I wrote a dedication: "For Antonio de la Trava, the valiente of Finisterra". And then my signature. The man saved my life. And there's no denying that whoever saves a life saves mankind. You're inclined to agree with the Talmud, especially when it's you being saved. I presented him with the book on a night like this. He'd escorted me to the town of Corcuvion, to the house of the head alcalde, a conceited man who laughed at me for travelling with the New Testament. Antonio, however, was moved. He told me he would read the Word of God when the winds blew from the north-west, preventing their launches from putting to sea. I think he was a little merry. He'd been drinking brandy during my interview with the alcalde. He addressed me as captain and told me, when I next came to Finisterre, to come in a valiant English bark, with plenty of contrabando on board. He was clearly a liberal through and through.'

A second moth crashed into the lamp. A huge, white-haired saturniid. The moths first banged against the window and then found their way in with the breeze, together with the scent of lavender.

'I'm going to bed,' said Henrietta. 'You should do the same.'

It was the month of July 1881. Summer had irrupted into the old man's body. Now, having told the story of the storm at Finisterre, he seemed to have calmed down. He took a few unsteady steps towards his desk, wanting to translate some Armenian poems.

'Good night,' said Henrietta.

'Knife!' he answered.

The Newspaper Seller

16 June 1904

His. He thought it was his. Just as a new swarm, when it leaves the hive and takes to the air with the queen, belongs to whoever catches it. He'd caught a newspaper dated 16 June 1904. Today's newspaper. He was in the docks, on his way to the far end of the Iron Quay, it being about time he embarked, when the newspaper flew in front of him. The sluggish flight of newspapers that haven't been read yet, pursued by the seagulls' mocking calls. Not since his childhood had he been able to let a printed piece of paper take off like that. Others went after bird nests or bats, but he, Antonio Vidal, went after printed matter. Anything would do so long as it had writing on it. Even toilet paper, strips cut up with no respect for the columns' order, so he'd soon learnt not only to read, but to put the pieces back together. Which helped him to see the world. To spot what was missing.

Antonio Vidal trapped the newspaper by stepping on its wings. He then picked it up and folded it. Calmed it down. The newspaper was no longer alone, it now had someone to read it. It contained news of important events. A Greek freighter had sunk off the Lobeira Isles in the Corcuvion estuary. There'd been so much fog the members of the crew had been unable to see each other on deck. This was followed by reports of adulterated wine, fishing with dynamite . . . But his eyes were drawn to the section of Telegrams. He had an instinct for the latest news.

MADRID 15 (23 h.) *Parliament extremely dull today. Most MPs went to the bullfight.*

'What? You collecting stories from the ground?'

A strange apparition with a sunlike halo appeared before him. A woman carrying birds on her head. What in fact she was carrying in her basket were newspapers flapping their wings in the sea breeze. The young girl held out her arm, demanding what was hers, with a magnetism in her fingers. Who could say no, it doesn't belong to you, to someone carrying the weight of the news? He handed back the newspaper and was about to leave when she set down her basket and arranged all the headlines in an extraordinary fan. He stood there while she hawked the news. He'd heard all kinds of things being sold before, animals and fruit at fairgrounds. He'd heard a blind man sing. But never a girl hawking fresh news.

'What? You going to take the lot?'

His whole body started. He hadn't been expecting to run into a newspaper seller who was only a girl, early teens at the most, but who spoke like a fully grown woman. She spoke in a way that guarded her body and was dressed like the local fishwives. She might end up selling fish too. If he could contain his surprise, Antonio Vidal might end up seeing fish in that basket. A basket that could carry strawberries and cherries, sea urchins and sardines, depending on the season. But now she was hawking the news in a singsong voice that made her the city centre. If she changed position, the centre would also move.

'Is your hand stuck? Don't you know how to tell the time?'

Her last question brought Antonio Vidal back to reality. Over their heads was a scoffing sky, the seagulls' mocking calls. He counted on his fingertips in his pocket. He'd spent a large amount buying his uncle 'Doctor Ayala's Asian Tonic' and 'The Miraculous Zephyr', inventions that were supposed to stop you going bald. He felt he was being guided with a healthy vengeance by his mother's ghost because in Sucesores de Villar he also bought 'Carmela's Miraculous Waters', a lotion to prevent your hair going grey and to restore its natural colour. His mother insisted, 'As a boy, he had a receding hairline.' And added, 'A receding conscience as well.' There she stopped and he never wanted to find out more about Uncle Ernesto's receding conscience. In Havana, he had helped to set up a modern school in Cruceiro de Airas and from the pulpit it was rumoured the emigrants had turned into 'Masons, Atheists and Protestants' and were trying to corrupt children. 'You can't be all things at once,' observed Antonio Vidal. 'You can't be what?' 'A Mason, an Atheist and a Protestant, you can't be all three things at once.' 'You shut up, what do you know?' his mother, Matilde, told him. 'Say hello to Uncle Ernesto and then get on with your work, unless you want to end up with a receding hairline too. And don't go wasting your money.'

'Do you need a bullet extractor?' asked the newspaper seller.

'What for?'

'For your coins.'

Antonio Vidal scrabbled in his pocket. What he was really looking for were not coins, but some quick, light-footed, low-denomination words to get him out of a tight situation.

'I'll take one today,' he said. And then thought better, 'No, two. Give me the one that was flying away.'

'Lucky me!' she commented ironically. 'I found myself a tycoon to support me!'

'I'm off to Cuba, on the steamer *Lafayette*.'

'How I'd love to own a news-stand in Havana's Central Park.'

'What do you know about Havana?'

'Everything. Or almost everything. As if I'd been a rich lady sitting in the colonnade of the Inglaterra Hotel. When you get off the boat, don't go up Prado Avenue. People will laugh at you. And anyone laughing at your accent and beret is a Galician who arrived before and now has a white suit and a dandy white hat. Don't go up Prado Avenue at least until you've got yourself a white suit.'

The whippersnapper handing out advice. She really seemed like a chatterbox now. Talking nineteen to the dozen, words spilling out of her mouth. All that talking made her look smaller. Vidal decided he'd wasted quite enough time. He forgot about walking to the end of the Iron Quay.

He still had to visit his boarding-house and the General Transatlantic Company.

'I'm in a hurry,' said Antonio Vidal. He folded the two newspapers under his arm and left her gawping.

'Keep them, take them with you!' she shouted seriously, sensing his distrust. 'They'll each open a door for you, you'll see.'

She was going to add, 'I can't come tomorrow. Tomorrow I have to collect clay on Lapas Beach.' But she didn't, he was far away by now. Who cared whether she came tomorrow or not? He hadn't even asked her name.

Antonio Vidal felt ridiculous with his bottle of 'Asian Tonic' and other lotions to stop your hair falling out. Uncle Ernesto had a full head of hair and a stylish haircut. 'What you looking at? You like my hair?' He took it off. 'Here you go, a genuine wig imported from New York. The best there is. Made from the hair of a virgin Amazonian Indian.' Having arrived in Havana after a two-week crossing, he still wasn't sure when his uncle was joking or being serious. But the thick, black wig shone in his hands like jet. 'This is where progress is, don't forget,' Ernesto told him, 'you're the one coming from behind.' Yes, he was coming from behind. What's more, on the steamer *Lafayette*, having got over his seasickness, he spent almost all the time astern, watching the ship's wake and reading the newspapers the girl had sold him. He read them from top to bottom every day of the fourteen the journey lasted, enough to learn everything by heart, including the chapter in the literary supplement that came with El Noroeste. He'd read the supplement with the chapter from *Anna Karenina* so often it seemed the most real part of the whole newspaper. '"Here, if you please," he said, moving on one side with his nimble gait and pointing to his picture, "it's the exhortation to Pilate, Matthew, chapter xxvii," he said, feeling his lips were beginning to tremble with emotion. He moved away and stood behind them.' Everything he knew about the painter Mihailov was in that chapter, but it was enough, he thought. From this fragment, he'd built up a picture of the novel and was convinced it would be extremely similar to the one the Russian author, Leo Tolstoy, had written. Standing astern, he felt a bit like Mihailov. The newspaper, the ship's wake, mirrored his guilt.

He couldn't get the girl out of his mind, with her basket of newspapers flapping their wings in the sea breeze.

This newspaper would end up in the hands of an even more elegant friend of his uncle's. There was Fermín Varela in the portico of the Inglaterra Hotel, devouring the pages of El Noroeste. Uncle Ernesto was reading it over Varela's shoulder, a glint in his eyes. Artificial wine? Fishing with dynamite? MPs at a bullfight? He looked at him as if he were to blame. After all, Antonio was the last to arrive. 'Is ours a country or a scorpion?'

'What can you do?' asked Fermín Varela.

'A bit of everything.'

'I like the sound of that,' said Varela.

'That's the good thing about being born in the sticks,' observed Uncle Ernesto. 'You learn a bit of everything.'

'Can you fire a gun?'

He couldn't. But he said he could.

'Can you give orders?'

'Give orders?'

'I mean, can you tell other men what to do?'

He was asking very difficult questions. Antonio Vidal had never thought about that, about the possibility of telling others what to do. He'd come in search of a job. He could work hard, without stopping. But giving orders was something else.

'He'll soon learn, Varela,' Ernesto intervened. 'There's nothing that can't be learnt.'

'What do you want to do?'

He tried to suppress it, but a voice replied for him, 'Own a news-stand in Central Park.'

They burst out laughing. They hadn't been expecting such a remark. But then Varela said, 'It's not such a bad idea. I like it, Vidal, I like it. You've got potential. The future lies in Vedado, that's the golden rectangle. But for now your fate's a little further off. I can offer you a job in Mayarí. Go and work for my wife. A bit of everything, like you say. She'll teach you how to give orders. She's a real field marshal!'

Varela spoke with a mixture of irony and boredom.

'Are you not coming, sir?' asked Vidal.

'It's time for me to be dirty. I'm fed up of the provinces, my Galician friend. I feel like the people of Havana, now I can't stand the countryside. You'll feel the same one day.'

'I come from a village, Mr Varela, well, a crossroads actually.'

'There you go. But who do you think fills the music halls, gets their shoes cleaned twice a day here, in the colonnade of the Inglaterra, has a drink in the square? We all got off the Central Train, so to speak. And we don't want to go back. Work hard and you'll earn enough money to put a wrought-iron news-stand right in the middle of Central Park, next to the *Diario de la Marina*, and still have enough to build yourself a house on Seventeenth Street.'

'What kind of work is it?' he asked his uncle when they were alone.

'It's a large estate with wood and cattle in Mayarí,' replied Ernesto. 'Remember giving orders also means shutting up. His wife will expect you to give orders and to obey them. She's the really rich one. And there's something he didn't tell you. She's an educated woman. Reads books and the like. Even prefers them to Varela. What was that about a news-stand in Central Park?'

'I don't know. It just came out like that.'

He had a day to make up his mind. Antonio Vidal sat on a bench on Prado Avenue. He was wearing his new linen white suit for the first time and now belonged to the people of light. He'd looked at it from different angles, but realised his principal misgiving was this: he'd just arrived and didn't want to leave Havana. The second newspaper was spread out on his thighs. He started thinking again about the cynical painter Mihailov in *Anna Karenina* and the girl with the basket of newspapers on her head by the Iron Quay in Coruña Harbour.

'What?'

The dark boy's head had eclipsed the sun.

'Can you spare a sheet?'

'What do you want it for?'

'To make a hat.'

'Can you make paper hats?'

'I can't, but the teacher can,' said the boy, pointing to a bench further down, where there was a group of schoolchildren accompanied by a young woman who was waving to the boy to come back.

'Is that your teacher?'

'That's right. She's the one who makes hats. They're great, just like boats.'

'Here you go. Take the whole newspaper.'

From the bench, he watched the teacher make hats until there was no more paper. She folded the sheets in a special way. It was true, they did look more like boats than hats. When the schoolchildren came past, what he saw was a procession of figureheads.

'Thank you, sir,' said the teacher as she passed.

Sir? He bowed in reply. And then, without trying to stop it, he heard the voice say, 'Excuse me, madam! It's very hot today. You wouldn't have a spare paper boat, would you?'

'Here,' she smiled. 'Take mine.'

The Breadcrumb

12 July 1936

'Say Mass for us, Polka!'

The stone cavities looked like thrones, granite chairs. Francisco Crecente, or Polka, the only one who wasn't naked, climbed to the highest rock of the hill-fort's Ara Solis, with a nostalgic sigh spat out the last cherry pip, made the sign of the Cross and mumbled, '*In principio erat Verbum.*'

'Can't hear you!' protested Terranova. 'Louder!'

Polka felt the sun pricking his eyes. He shielded them with his hand and almost glimpsed what he was looking for. Down the slope, next to the stream, clothes were spread out like a happy graft of people on nature. He stretched out his arms and his preacher's voice rolled down the hillside on the sun's rays, '*Et lux in tenebris lucet et tenebrae eam non comprehenderunt, etc., etc.*'

The second Sunday in July was full of light. There was no trusting that vertiginous sky, the door of all the storms in the Azores, even in midsummer. But this time the mission had been successful. Polka was pleased and proud. They'd accepted his proposal. It was his village. And today it had the feel of paradise.

Everything was a gift of the sun and the landscape didn't seem to want to keep anything back. He was on top of the world. These ruins were the city's first settlement, a fortified mount, at a safe distance from the sea. Between Ara Solis and Hercules Lighthouse, up on the isthmus, there was a visual axis. Anyone in Polka's position could experience that geological view. The city had been reborn from the sea, had surrounded the great

Atlantic rock and become a palafitte on the sands and mudflats, making up ground on the bay's belly, with the sensuality of gardens and buildings whose foundations were glass. The sea today was a kind of mirror and Polka thought the second Sunday in July was a true gift and deserved a blessing.

'A divine office, Polka, if you please!'

Holando had read out the ten commandments of naturism. As they lay sunbathing, naked on the warm rocks, which were carpeted in velvet moss and golden lichen, the cherry pendulum hanging over their lips, measuring time from outside in, everything that was said sounded like the flowering of reason. The fourth commandment: 'Thou shalt not forget to bathe every day in cold water'. This got a boo. 'Where's the prophet from?' 'Dr Nigro Basciano is from Brazil.' 'That explains it.' As for the rest, they were in agreement. Until the tenth one: 'Thou shalt not eat meat or murder the poor animals, but be merciful to them. *Mens sana in corpore sano. Finis. Amen.*'

There was a pause, which lasted as long as the cherries.

'After the celebrations you mean!' exclaimed Polka finally.

'What?'

'All that being merciful to animals.'

'You treat everything as a joke,' said Holando. 'Slaughterhouses are a horrific spectacle. Go down to Orzán when there's a slaughter. The sea stained with the blood of animals. It's a prehistoric shame. Cows should be sacred here as well.'

'That's why we eat them,' intervened Anceis, who rarely spoke. Aurelio Anceis was serious and thoughtful. When he did speak, he seemed to regret it afterwards. He was about to leave for Pasai San Pedro to join a Basque cod-fishing trawler. He had only two days. He was also a poet. A secret poet. He'd started writing what he called 'SOS poems' in the wake of the seafaring poet Manoel Antonio, the avant-garde author of *From Four to Four*. He hadn't published any even in his friends' newspaper *Brazo y Cerebro*. One of the few people he showed them to was Arturo da Silva. He saw a connection between writing poems, as he understood it, and boxing.

'Just like Christ,' he added.

'I don't understand the comparison,' replied Holando.

'Why did people want Barabbas released and Christ crucified? It was, so to speak, a question of gastronomic quality. Who to eat. The divine tastes better. A kind of homoeopathy. The cult of the Sacred Heart of Jesus. Holy Week with its celebration of Calvary and the Crucifixion. The Sacrament of Communion. The need to feed on what's sacred. Greek singers ate crickets, the athletes ate grasshoppers.'

He heard them laugh and blinked. He'd made them laugh, no one had imitated his voice. His friends were laughing. They were good fun. They talked of revolution as if it were a party. For days now, they'd been preparing a trip to Caneiros. There was going to be a special train. Then they'd take boats up the Mandeo's sparkling waters to the heart of the forest. There'd be libertarian speeches, plenty of food and music, lots of music. It was a beautiful day, heaven on earth, it was a sin not to be happy. So he said:

'Sorry.'

Actually he was thinking about a poem in which words were crumbs of bread on an oilskin tablecloth. He hadn't slept all night; for the first time, his body seemed aware it would soon leave land on a long journey. The fingers of silence, working like moth wings, had polished rounded breadcrumbs with the inflamed accuracy of the beads of an astral rosary. One of those rounded crumbs was the sun on that second Sunday in July.

'Sorry, Holando.'

'You've nothing to be sorry about. What I'm saying is we don't have to sacrifice animals in order to survive. In a more civilised society, there'd be more than enough food. It's in the richest countries where most animals are sacrificed needlessly. Do you know why the buffalo almost died out on the great American prairies? Because of its tongue. The Indians used everything; wholesale slaughter was down to the whites. Buffalo tongue was a fashionable dish in New York restaurants. Buffalo Bill was a killing machine, an industrial-scale hunter. He's said to have killed more than three thousand buffaloes in a day singlehandedly.'

'Three thousand?'

They gazed out over the ripe Elviña valley and on to Granxa by the River Monelos. Three thousand were a lot of buffaloes. At that time, at the turn of the century, four million buffaloes were being slaughtered each year. Four million tongues. With the bones, they could have built another Wall of China. They lacked a monumental imagination.

'Holando's right,' said Arturo da Silva. 'That really would turn things upside down if we stopped being carnivorous. You know what the monks of Oseira used to do during Lent, when it was forbidden to eat meat. They'd drop pigs in the river and then fish them out with nets. The farmers, who couldn't get a whiff of bacon for fear of being excommunicated, went to the abbot to protest, but the abbot replied, "Anything in a net counts as fish!"'

Galicia's lightweight champion put his head and elbows on the mossy ground and stretched his legs athletically up in the air. Head down, he said, 'I need a steak for boxing.'

Terranova approaches him. He walks comically, like a barefoot Chaplin, carrying a stalk of hay like an imaginary stick, and points with it at the champ's penis while reciting a classic line from his dockside repertoire: 'I am that vast, secret promontory you Portuguese call the Cape of Storms.' Arturo can't stand being tickled with the straw and can't help laughing at the irony. He jumps to his feet and chases after Terranova, who's already cleared a gorse bush, scaled a crag and is standing on top like a statue on its plinth. He covers and uncovers himself with his hands, 'O thou, Great Prick, who art fallen low! *Lurdo di Columnata!* Poor bacon of mine cured in Carrara marble.'

His skin was so brown it gave the impression he'd spent his life naked in the sun. And he sprang about the rocks without having to watch his feet. The school of fishing for barnacles on Gaivoteira, Altar, Cabalo das Praderías, the great outcrops underneath the lighthouse. How he loved an attentive audience he could sing to, amuse with his dockside knowledge, this international wit that charmed old Master Amil during his evening classes at the Rationalist School! Terranova climbed a natural step. Covered and uncovered his sex.

'It's not my fault. Luba, the girl from the *Normandie*, told me, "If it's small, it's not your fault but Baba's." "Who's Baba?" "Who do you think? The devil. He used superhuman force against you, a potency greater than yours." Hearing that from a stewardess on board the largest steamship in the world left me a wreck. "Is there a cure, Luba?" "Of course there's a cure. Travel round the world." And she burst out laughing. You should have seen the teeth on that woman. They say, after the fire in Lino's Pavilion, only the organ keys remained intact. Well, that's what Luba's teeth were like. They should put her portrait as a figurehead on the bows of the *Normandie*. She's so cheerful it's frightening. "What do you mean, Luba," I said to her, "travel round the world?" You should see those teeth. The *Normandie*'s most valuable asset. It's thanks to them the steamship keeps moving.'

'Forget about that. What's the cure?'

'Read *Brazo y Cerebro*! And obey the commandments of naturism.'

Holando chucked a pebble at his belly-button. 'Don't be ridiculous.'

'I'm sorry, I can't say. It's against all my religions.'

'Even better then.'

'Luba said, "The woman should be sky and the man earth."'

'And that gives you a bigger penis?'

'It gives you a bigger everything, darling.'

'Here we are, drying out like gods.'

'Like eels. Don't talk to me about gods.'

'Greek gods,' said Holando. 'I like them. They spent the day ascending and descending between the two worlds. They weren't afraid of slipping on the fig-leaf. Prometheus was a libertarian. The first to break the chains. Dionysius too. We should take him to Caneiros as our patron saint. That's to say nothing about Aphrodite, Athene . . .'

'Minerva!'

'Not Minerva,' said Holando. 'She was Italian. Though she's also worth her salt.'

He peered round. They were all laughing. Even Arturo da Silva with his head on the ground. They were all thinking about Germinal's librarian, Arturo first of all.

'Worth her salt? You bet you!' exclaimed Dafonte. 'I wonder what she's up to.'

'They go to Pelamios, San Amaro and Cunchas Beach,' said Leica. 'Some of them bathe in the nude.'

'You've seen them!'

'I have. I've seen her on Cunchas Beach dressed in a pair of seaweeds. Divine!'

'Were you taking photos, Leica?'

'No, I was searching for the light. You have to learn to see.'

'What about your sister, Leica, does she bathe under the lighthouse?' asked Arturo da Silva.

'My sister's in France. They gave her a grant to do some painting.'

'Shame she can't come and do some painting with us in Caneiros.'

'I'm sure she'd have loved to.'

'The women go to the seaside and here we are, like sacred rams,' said Dafonte. 'On the Celtic mount. Next Sunday, we all have to go down to the sea, dress up in some seaweed and take a dip in classicism.'

Terranova started scratching at the moss and using his hands to dig with childish glee.

'There must be some treasure down here. Did you never come here with picks, Polka?'

'We did. When we were little. But we never found anything. Except for a siphon-bottle.'

'A Celtic siphon-bottle.'

'That's right. But what farmers find every time they plough the earth are trenchcoat buttons with *Liberté, Égalité, Fraternité* written on them. All this you see before you was the site of a terrible battle. The Battle of Elviña. As far as I know, the worst in Galicia's history. I myself have a button on my jacket. There, on the sleeve.'

And it was true. His jacket was hanging from the branch of a tree next to the hill-fort wall.

'It smells of treasure,' said Terranova. 'I reckon it's pretty close.' His digging had become comical as he imitated a dog searching for a buried bone.

'There was some treasure,' said Seoane. 'The treasure of the hill-forts and dolmens was routinely pillaged at the start of the seventeenth century. The king authorised one Vázquez de Orxas to excavate all the funerary monuments. He gave him exclusive rights so long as part of the profits found their way to the royal coffers. What's surprising is that they hadn't been looted before. The gold in America had run out and unfortunately someone thought of the truth behind the legends. People had disguised the treasure in stories. It was protected by dwarfs, Moorish princesses, winged serpents. The dwarfs were fluent in several languages, knew Latin, just like Polka, and if you spoke their secret language, they opened the door to the treasure. Old Carré told us the story of someone who stuttered and was very successful at finding treasure because the dwarfs thought he was multilingual. But Galicia's treasure went to pot thanks to an explorer who believed in books no one else believed in and paid attention to old people's stories. The stories were full of gold. And he wasn't wrong. In one dolmen, he even unearthed a solid-gold duck.'

'Something will be left. There's always something left,' said Terranova. 'What was the name of that old treasure guide?'

'*The Great Book of St Cyprian*,' replied Seoane. 'Probably the most widely read book in Galician history.'

'You anarchists should edit another Book of St Cyprian. A book of treasures. There's bound to be a wild gold duck around here.'

'The original book was pretty anarchic,' said Seoane. 'Apparently you had to be able to read backwards in order to understand it.'

Polka gazed in the direction of his village.

In some way, people carried light. In words, in clothes, in gestures. Sounds belonged to the light. He'd been born there. He listened to the conversation about treasure without taking part. He recalled the legend old Mariñán had told him, the most sensible thing he'd heard on the subject of treasure. You had to be on the lookout on sunny days because the dwarfs who guarded the gems and precious metals underground sooner or later had to bring them out to dry so that they wouldn't go rusty. Polka wasn't interested in what was buried, but in the surface. He surveyed the view. Some sheets were spread out and acted like a mirror. What he was really looking for was Olinda, the matchstick-maker. The bit from the legends of treasure that mattered to him now was where it said you don't find the treasure, the treasure finds you.

'Look'ee here!' shouted Terranova.

He began pulling out shells. He'd found an oyster bed. There were scallops too. 'How about that,' said Terranova. And he solemnly held up the skeleton of a sea urchin in the palm of his hand. A hypnotic sphere.

'They obviously enjoyed sea urchins as much as your mother, Curtis.'

'What about Mass, Polka? Who taught you the divine office?'

'I didn't play as a child. My only game was going to church. What I really wanted to be was a bagpiper. But I could only play at being a priest. All day in church. That was my school, my playground, my work, rolled into one. I started helping during Mass when I was very small. I was sent to be an altar boy because I was the poorest. Servers are not rich. That must be all that's left from the time before Constantine, when the Church was virgin. If you want to be a server, it's good to be poor. My father worked in a quarry. He died young, shortly after I was born. No, it wasn't a rock that killed him. It's never a rock. Some damp got inside his chest and he never recovered. Anyway, the fact is I started serving when I was aged six. Masses, novenas, rosaries, weddings, baptisms, communions, unctions . . . I almost spoke Latin before Galician. My mother tongue, pardon me, was that of the Vatican. All day shut up inside. I can't dissect Latin, but I know it off by heart. Mine was an immersion, in at the deep end. Besides, something important happened. The parish priest, Don Benigno, started losing his memory. Not gradually, the odd letter or word, but whole chunks and sentences. They left and never came back. He seemed to lose both the sentence and where it went. The space was swallowed up and then it couldn't come back. So I was his second memory. I was supplier of misplaced sentences, so to speak, which meant I had to pay attention during the services. I was his prompt. I was a real professional. I always tried to do my best. But then Don Benigno passed away, a new priest arrived and we didn't get on. That was the end of my serving. Don Benigno didn't mind me being bishop during Carnival. As you know, on Ash Wednesday there's a masked procession, when we bury the Carnival by throwing it into the River Monelos. And before letting go, we say a prayer for the soul of the deceased, a funeral Mass we call a funeral *mess*. Well, Don Benigno didn't mind. I think he even found it funny. An Easter laugh. "So long as you don't take my customers from me," he said to me. "Carnival is soon followed by Lent." But the new priest kicked up a fuss. No Easter funnies!'

'Carnival is like Caneiros,' said Holando. 'A democratic celebration, the world turned topsy-turvy.'

'You don't hear the bagpipes at burials any more. When I was small, I used to serve at funerals. And that's where I became a bagpiper. I learnt music like Latin, in one whole piece. I could have considered entering a seminary, becoming a priest, but no, it was being a bagpiper that got me excited. The bagpipes can rival the greatest bassoon. I'd go to funerals just to listen to a bagpipe requiem.'

'The bagpipes have no future, Polka, admit it,' Terranova intervened.

'Who said that? I didn't hear anything.'

'They've been kicked out of the dance halls. And they're no good for jazz or any of that. You'll end up on your own, on the mountain, playing the bagpipes for the treasure dwarfs and their Moorish princesses.'

'What do you mean, no good for jazz? You're dumber than a baritone. Wind . . .'

'A trumpet, a saxophone . . . That's music, Polka. The music of the future.'

'One day, you'll hear the bagpipes in a jazz piece, you fool,' replied Polka. He was really annoyed now. Everyone knew Polka was annoyed when he called someone a fool.

'Polka's right,' said Seoane. 'Mozart included a knife-grinder's whistle in The Magic Flute.'

Luís Terranova danced on top of a rock, moving his pubis in voluptuous parody of a folk-dance:

> All those steps
> they're now doin'
> inside out
> outside in!

'Shame Curtis can't sing,' observed Arturo da Silva. 'We'd have ourselves a Paul Robeson instead of a Luís Terranova.'

'Paul Robeson! He's the best,' said the violinist Seoane with enthusiasm.

'The voice of humanity, the earth and cosmos. Once, when he sang in New York, all the buildings of the banks on Wall Street started shaking. Supposing Robeson were to sing in Hercules Lighthouse, we'd be able to hear him over here, on Ara Solis . . .'

> Ol' man river
> Dat ol' man river
> He mus' know sumpin'
> But don't say nuthin'

'The length of the strings and the vibration of sound are in proportion. Robeson's strings are made from gut. What we need is a Paul Robeson. A voice that'll make bankers shake and stones wail.'

'With or without Robeson, we can't go to Caneiros without the bagpipes,' declared Holando. 'They're our cosmic egg! The mother of all airs. Come on, Polka!'

'I don't know,' said Polka. 'I'm not sure I'll take them.'

Luís Terranova slipped off the crag and knelt in front of Polka.

'Your blessing, father.'

Polka made the sign of the Cross and murmured, 'Verbum caro factum est et habitavit in nobis, etc. Now say three Our Fathers.'

Terranova stood up and wiped the earth and grass from his knees. 'Three Our Fathers?' he replied. 'I only know one.'

While the others were getting dressed, Polka shielded his eyes and once again scanned the valley. On the other side of San Cristovo, beyond Agrela, was Fontenova. That glint had to be the quicksilver glass sign of Shining Light, which Isolino Díaz had made in the Rubine glassworks. It had been a good idea to put up a sign. A sun in the middle of a fire.

He was going to say this, proclaim it out loud. But the others were giggling about something. So he mentioned it to the person nearest to him, Arturo da Silva. After all, it had been his idea.

'You see? That mirror over there is Shining Light.' The glint caused a smile to spread across the boxer's hardened features.

Look how easy it is to make a man happy, thought Polka. A glint in the distance.

They were laughing because of Holando, who'd sunbathed on a rock, but left the book of naturist commandments lying on his chest. This part of his skin had remained white and pallid while the rest of him was bronzed and done to a turn around the edges. The mark of a book on his skin. A natural print.

'Minerva'll be shocked,' said Seoane. 'Now you'll have to add a title with a hot iron.' He then announced, 'Next Sunday, the 19th of July, we're all going to that beach where the girls get dressed up in seaweed. And on the 2nd of August, it's the trip to Caneiros. Anyone without a ticket for the special train, talk to Hercules.'

'Here he comes again,' said Polka. 'Training for his first communion.'

There he was, running back along the paths in between the maize fields: Vicente Curtis, Papagaio's own Hercules and Arturo da Silva's sparring partner.

'Yep, his first fight's on the 17th,' said Arturo. 'He'll need your support. This lad'll be the glory of Galicia. He's as much air in his lungs as the rest of us put together. He lets his fists do the talking.'

'You know what I think of boxing,' said Holando. 'To defend yourself, you'd do better to learn how to shoe a donkey back to front.'

'That as well,' Arturo answered.

'You did it deliberately,' said Terranova to Holando. 'A book tattoo to impress all the Minervas.'

'Not at all.' Holando showed off his chest with the book's framed window. 'It's the instinct of culture choosing the best wood, nature achieving self-consciousness.'

Self-consciousness. Polka felt like a common criminal. He had to return that other book to the library as soon as possible. No later than next week. Every time he opened the book, he read it with greater devotion and guilt.

The Matador

17 July 1936

Curtis listens. 'Everything he owns is in that canvas bag, that sailor's bag.'
He's standing with Arturo da Silva next to the Obelisk. There are lots of
people outside the Oriental Café, the Palace Hotel and a little further back,
outside the Galicia Café. They're handing out leaflets advertising an anti-
Fascist meeting to be held in the bullring. One of those who take a leaflet
gives them a friendly wave. Curtis notices the contrast between what he's
wearing, a suit and tie, and his luggage. A simple canvas bag.

'That's Sito Marconi. He knows more about radios than anyone.
Everything he needs is in that sailor's bag. Give him a screwdriver and
he'll locate the voice of stones.'

Curtis is standing with Arturo next to the Obelisk. The boxer's way of
handing out information sheets is very formal. It's as if he's handing out
a parchment. He doesn't distribute them haphazardly, but frugally, as if
their message were decisive in the life of both giver and recipient. It reminds
Curtis of his mother's relationship with electric light. She can't stand a
light being on when there's no one in the room. Arturo looks each person
in the eye. Perhaps he's wondering what their fortune and direction will
be, as if it's not a scrap of paper but a rare papyrus. On the flyers, the
largest letters are those stating where the meeting is to be held. IN THE
BULLRING.

'Bulls? What you got against bulls? I shall summon the head matador
immediately!'

He's a tall man with a Cossack's moustache. His voice is threatening, carefully modulated to be intimidating. But while Curtis' reaction is to take a defensive leap backwards, Arturo's is to go forwards. In search of a warm embrace. This is how Curtis met Fernando Sada. He told them how he'd just played the ogre for the Barraca Theatre and the pedagogical missions. He'd done other things, of course, some of them more complicated, but it was his dragon's voice that had made him famous. Arturo introduced him as an artist, but Sada emphasised he was also a spokesperson for the International Union of Puppeteers.

'They won't get past Africa,' he said in such a thunderous voice it really did remind Curtis of a dragon's. 'They'll fall flat on their faces, just like General Sanjurjo four years ago.'

He showed Curtis the clock on top of the Obelisk. 'There's his lordship, Time. Wouldn't it be better if there was a cuckoo? My childhood hours were struck by Mr Tettamancy's cuckoo clock. The cuckoo's song. The knife-grinder's whistle. And the ships' sirens. All under the sweeping light, the luminescent fan, of Hercules Lighthouse. Those were the foundations of jazz in my life. When I fall over, it's that liberal cuckoo's song that keeps me going. That's right! *Cuckoo in the Clock.* A big cuckoo telling the time on top of the Obelisk. Or a ship's siren. Every time we hear the word "sea", we should all fall on our knees.'

He turned around and stretched out his arms like an orator's. 'People of Coruña, kneel before the sea! Neptune, Poseidon, Andrés de Teixido, these should be our gods, forever at the feet of the scallop-shell goddess. All the best things arrived by sea. Saints and virgins on stone boats. Who but King Lear is buried in Santiago?'

Sada looked at Arturo. The boxer's anxious silence. He changed voice and abandoned his declamatory tone.

'Truth is I'm a very good prophet. When it comes to predicting the past, I always get it right.'

He then had a look at the flyer and adopted a more confidential tone, 'ANTI-FASCIST MEETING IN THE BULLRING? Take care who you hand these leaflets to in case you end up giving one to the head matador. Sewn in here,' he said, pointing to his earlobe, 'is Juan Luis Vives' warning to Erasmus: "You can't talk or be silent without risk."'

He told them how when he was a boy, something happened he always interpreted as a bad omen. His father had been campaigning against bullfighting, demanding an end to all bullfights, which were described as a horrifying spectacle, a display of cruelty, a sacrifice held as a national festival in which the so-called 'moment of truth' was nothing more than the 'art of killing'. It was during the summer holidays, the city was a kind of ocean liner with all hands on deck. Sada set out with a pile of leaflets protesting against the maltreatment of animals. It was a radiant day in Ensanche Gardens. A perfect synthesis of nature and civilisation. There, at the entrance, was Lino's old merry-go-round, revolving in time to the Marseillaise, the harmonica so worn down it sounded as if the horses were snorting. 'And off I went.' *Allons enfants!* Children in sailor suits playing with a hoop. Couples walking arm-in-arm under the magnolias. And Sada fell to imagining what would happen. The shows of support. The voices of encouragement. *About time, lad. It was about time someone denounced such carnage, such barbarism.* He thought to himself, Give me a seed and I'll change the world. He believed the will could move mountains as Lino moved the roundabout, the children their hoop and those with the ball a planet. Perhaps he could bring about such a wondrous change all by himself. It must have occurred before in the history of humankind. We know the wars that took place, but how many men and women managed to stop one? You never know. He imagined his father in the café early the next day, unaware of the previous evening's commotion. Sada Senior unfolds the newspaper and finds the following headline plastered across the front page:

ALL BULLFIGHTS IN CORUÑA CANCELLED

And below, the details:

A triumph of civilisation. A boy's protest yesterday shakes the city. The authorities heed the public outcry against cruelty to animals.

'And off I went,' said Sada, 'straight to the crowded terrace of Alfonso's Kiosk, where the pleasant atmosphere suggested a state of grace among the citizens and consequently a brave acceptance of civilising proposals.'

29

Suddenly he saw the face he was looking for. His Touchman. The link in the chain that would spread the immense anti-bullfighting wave, the unstoppable current, which that same afternoon, by the decree of fate, would reach the governor's office and force him to cancel such an infamous event. The chosen one, in his white linen suit, had a kind appearance. Sada walked confidently towards him and Touchman noticed that the boy had recognised him as a superior being. And it was so. He smiled when he saw it had to do with bulls. It must be a programme. Or some advertising. But Sada observed a sea change as he continued reading. Not just in his face, but in all his being. He seemed to emit the odour of a resinous liquid. The piece of paper was burning in his hands. Metaphorically to begin with, without a flame, as if he'd lit it through the stunned magnifying glass of his eyes. Then he asked one of his companions for a lighter and really did burn it.

The man was a bullfighter, Master Celita, and topped the bill for the next bullfight.

'You remember Bela Lugosi in *Dracula* and the terrifying light in his eyes? They showed it not long ago in the same place, Alfonso's Kiosk. Well, that was how Touchman looked,' recalled Sada. 'It's as if he's never moved from there and is waiting for me to this day.

'A particular feature Celita had was a slight limp. So he wasn't brandishing a sword, but a terrible stick. Is there anything more frightening than a child being pursued by a lame matador with a thrusting-stick? Give me a bull any time!'

Since then, he'd been watching his back. In a state of permanent alert. He'd acquired the visual field of a woodcock, the wood's guardian, with eyes in the back of his head. 'I feel destiny running after me,' said Sada. 'A lame destiny with a wooden sword or sabre. That's how things are in Spain, ever on the lookout for the matador. I should have been a descendant of the blessed, a child of the generation that advocated a federalist Utopia. My mother taught me to walk to the music of *Le Temps des cerises* and all my life I heard my freethinking father tell his friends, "Don't ever let me falter." An entire life, almost, taking care not to fall into the hands of the soul hunter – bam! – with his last breath. And it was a moment's negligence. We stopped hearing the harmonica and heard instead the bells of the viaticum and the confessor triumphantly leaving his bedside, proclaiming, "Today I converted a heretic!" My poor father's soul turned into a trophy. A bull's ear in the hand.'

His expression, his voice, even the size of his body had changed again. Curtis thought this man's words were linked not only to his mind, but to everything going on in his body. His breathing. The circulation of blood. Incredible, but true. From where he was, he could hear his heart beating.

'Now I'm going to paint windows,' said Sada. 'Never sleep with the windows closed, Widows' Wind permitting. And if there aren't any windows, paint them. Invite the sea in!'

'That's a good one,' said Arturo da Silva. 'The window revolution.'

'I'm into the naturist revolution. Another commandment is to bathe every day in the sea. I wouldn't mind having your determination, Arturo, swimming in the sea in winter and summer. Galicia will discover her karma the day this custom spreads. I'm waiting for my own personal bathyscaphe and for when Scandinavian diving suits go on sale in Espuma. Or better still, one of those waterbeds invented by the glorious William Hooper. If this were a practical country, we'd develop an industry of waterbeds. I have to talk to Mr Senra from the shoe factory. Why can't I be an industrial artist?'

'I only wish I could paint a starfish the way you do,' said Arturo. 'A single starfish is enough to justify a life.'

'Why paint them if you can go down and collect them in fistfuls from the bottom of Ánimas? I paint the sea because I can't dive. I have to make do with the starfish that fall from the sky. They escape from the seagull's beak by amputating the arm it's holding them by. Did that never happen to you?'

'It did once. It fell on my head. I was petrified. I thought the Universal Architect had got hold of me.'

'A mythological sign, Arturo!'

'It's Hercules here who needs one of those,' Arturo says for Curtis. 'He's got his first boxing match tonight.'

The Burning Books

19 August 1936

The books were burning badly. One of them stirred in the nearest bonfire and Hercules thought he saw it suddenly fan out its fresh pollack's red gills. An incandescent piece came off another and rolled like a neon sea urchin down the steps of a fire staircase. Then he thought a trapped hare was moving in the fire, and that a gust of wind, which kindled the flames, was scattering in sparks each and every one of the hairs on its burnt skin. So the hare kept its form in a graph of smoke and stretched its legs to bound off down the glazed diagonal of the Atlantic avenue's sky.

The first book fires had been built by the docks, on the way to Parrote, on the urban belly so to speak, where the sea gave birth to the city, the first cluster of fishermen. Much grass had grown since then, even on the roofs, whose vocation is to be the brow of a hill, in the area where today the bay's passenger boats, the city's trams and national coaches all meet. The other fires are placed alongside, in the main square, which is named after María Pita, the heroine who led the defence of the city during one of the many attacks by sea at the head of a commando of fishing women, and now contains the town hall with its inscription 'Head, Guard, Key and Antemural of the Kingdom of Galicia'. Curtis had heard of the heroine María Pita at the Dance Academy as if she were still alive, in that undying present that is to be a rumour on people's lips, not just because she'd stood up to the sea dog/admiral Francis Drake, but because she'd been married four times and the judge had had to warn her that she'd been widowed enough and should see that no more men died in the battle of her bed.

There's a pauper called Zamorana who lives and sleeps among the tombs and pantheons in the city of the dead, in the seaside cemetery of San Amaro. She once gave Hercules a fright when she stepped out from behind a grave and, holding up a cigarette butt, asked him:

'Got a light, boy?'

Zamorana is not really a beggar. She has a job paid for by tips that is very important for the city. Coruña's late departed look out to sea. Near the shore by the cemetery are the Ánimas shoals, the best breeding grounds, with more starfish on the bottom than can be seen in the sky. Though they can also be spotted falling from on high. Seagulls and cormorants fly with starfish in their beaks, so the starfish jettison their captive limb and return to the sea an arm short. The cemetery affords the best view of the mouth of the bay. And this has something to do with Zamorana, who asked Curtis for a light the night he spent by the graveyard. The beggar-woman is a sentinel. When a liner comes into sight, she goes down Torre Street, warning of the boat's arrival. A liner is full of rich pickings. Zamorana's voice sounds like a husky conch shell. 'Boat's coming, Mr Ferreiro, boat's coming . . . Boat's coming, Mr Ben, boat's coming . . . Boat's coming.'

Zamorana emerges with her ditty about a boat's arrival, and she emerges from the cemetery, not from any old place. Curtis recalls how when he was a boy, Zamorana was already old, already announced boats in her husky voice. He thought she and others like her lasted for ever. María Pita, for example. The procession of country dead remained at the city gates. And the seaside cemetery's occupants delegated the lighthouse and Zamorana's husky conch to rouse the city: 'Boat's coming.'

The reason Vicente Curtis, otherwise known as Hercules, is thinking about Zamorana is because she's standing by the Parrote viewpoint. Besides the arsonists, she's the only discernible presence. She's unmistakable. She's wearing all the skirts she owns, the skirts of a lifetime, one on top of the other, so she looks like a female bell. Some ships arrived yesterday. Warships. They're moored next to the yacht club and are part of the Third Reich's fleet. She saw them coming, but didn't go down Torre Street, singing her ditty, 'Boat's coming, boat's coming!' She watches. She's seen

33

many things. But not that kind of fire. She's never read a book. There was a time, perhaps her happiest, when she sold newspapers. She hawked news though she couldn't read. That's why she thinks they're hurting her. Going against her. They're burning what she never had, what she always needed. There's something strange about the smoke, it stings, gets behind the eyes. Reminds her of a time she'd rather forget. The day a stranger set fire to the blanket she was sleeping rough under, the day she put out her flaming hair with her hands. And now her hands are scars healed by the sea. That's why she decided to sleep among the tombs. Where are the readers of books? Why are they taking so long?

'Oy you, old witch, what you looking at? Get out of here!' shouts one of the soldiers. 'Go find yourself a billy-goat on Mount Alto!'

She never kept quiet. This Cain had better listen up. She was going to tell him a thing or two. Put a few things straight. Have it out with him, face to face.

This strange smoke that gets behind the eyes. This itching. The smoky torch. The fire. The smell of fire in her hair. She burnt once already. The skin's memory. The scars' itching. She moves off. Better to keep the peace. She returns to her tombs, trailing her bell of cloth. All the skirts of a lifetime.

The book fires are not part of the city's memory. They're happening now. So this burning of books isn't taking place in some distant past or in secret. Nor is it a fictional nightmare thought up by some apocalyptic. It's not a novel. This is why the fire progresses slowly, because it has to overcome resistance, the arsonists' incompetence, the unusualness of burning books. The absentees' incredulity. It's obvious the city has no memory of this lazy, stubborn smoke moving through the air's surprise. Even what's not been written has to burn. Someone arrives from the local tourist office, carrying a pile of leaflets with the programme of festivities, 'fresh meat' they call it, possibly in reference to the woman bathing on the front cover under the heading *Ideal Climate* and the town's official coat of arms, the lighthouse with an open book on top acting as a lamp giving off beams of light. All this will burn slowly, the design as well, which won't make it back on to the city's escutcheon.

'Plato's *Republic*. About time! What's this? *An Encyclopedia of Meat!*' Bam!

It's a thick volume that sends embers flying and eats away the angles of ruins like the sudden collapse of a seam on lower buildings. The word 'meat' was enough to activate the throw. The head imagines a treatise on lust, pictures of orgies, shame not to have had a peek. When the volume reaches the end of its fall, the Falangist gives it a little kick on the corner with the toecap of his boot. As it opens, with a new eruption of smoke and cinders and the first flames, what meets the eyes is a two-page map of the peninsula with the different provinces shown in colours. The effect is too causal, an accidental jerk of the boot, which the eyes hasten to correct. No, they're not the provinces of Spain. It soon becomes obvious it's really an illustration of the different parts of a cow. Loin, sirloin, hock, coccyx, rump, rib, brisket . . .

'What you've thrown in there is a book of recipes!' comes a mocking voice from behind.

'Then it'll make a nice barbecue.'

The fires are in the most public part of the city, opposite the symbolic seat of civil power. Hercules shouldn't head in that direction because Hercules is far better known than he thinks. But for now he's in luck. He approaches the fires and none of the operators, all of them armed and dressed in the Falange's uniform, pays him any attention, taken up as they are with the problem of books burning badly. One of them likens them to bricks. And then attaches a geometrical clarification even he finds strange:

'They're parallelepipeds!'

Next to him, the youngest soldier wishes to repeat the long word, but realises it isn't easy and tries whispering it. It sounds like the name of a very rare species of bird. More complicated than palmipedes. He doesn't have any problems with that, with palmipedes, and looks at the pyre without reading the titles, like an abstraction, like the model of an Aztec pyramid.

'Pa-ra-lle-le-pi-peds! That's it. Parallelepipeds.'

He finally got it. He feels better now.

'Parallelepiped!' says the sergeant, slapping him on the back.

'Parallelepiped,' he replies proudly, following the trail of smoke and gazing up at the sky. Encouraged by his success, he tries to remember the names of clouds he studied at school. All he remembers is nimbus. What's a nimbus? What kind of cloud is made by the smoke rising from the pyres? But he stops thinking about clouds because the one who likened the resistance of the books to bricks and pronounced the word 'parallelepiped' with incredible ease is preparing to fan the fire with some sheets of newspaper. One of them slips out of his hands and flies like a palmiped. A strange bird, the beginnings of a collage in the sky. Curtis also follows the sheet through the air. The soldier who lost it runs after it, jumps and traps it in the claw of his hand. Looks smug. Calls the others over. There they are with arms upraised in a photo taken yesterday, when they lit the first fires, which the clerical daily El *Ideal Gallego* printed today, 19 August 1936: 'On the seashore, so that the sea can carry off the remains of so much misery and corruption, the Falange is burning heaps of books.'

It's a strange kind of fire, this, Curtis thinks to himself. Its tongue is invisible. It's a fire that chews, with canines.

Not long before, at the end of June, huge festive bonfires had been erected in the city to celebrate St John's Eve. Curtis had been one of a group of boys and young men from Sol Street who collected dried branches, worm-eaten pieces of furniture that held themselves together with the dignity of geometrical spectres and the usual donation of wooden remains, broken planks, disjointed limbs, from the highly active Orzán window factory. The structure they raised around the central post was reminiscent of the large stacks of maize that could be seen in winter, conical formations like those in Indian settlements, in the villages of Mariñas and Bergantiños, the countryside that opened up as soon as you left the city's isthmus, from San Roque de Afóra, San Cristovo das Viñas, San Vicente de Elviña and Santa María de Oza to the fertile valleys of the River Monelos and Meicende, Eirís, Castro, Mesoiro, Feáns, Cabana, Someso, Agrela, Gramalleira, Silva and Fontenova. But these stacks were never burnt. Once the maize had been husked, it was used as fodder for the cattle during the long, hard winter and for the warp of the land. The image of American Indian settlements belonged to Curtis, who associated tepees with the way the maize stalks were arranged after the harvest. But burning books was new to him. The bonfires this year had burnt well and the fire's final smell had been of sardine fat soaking maize bread, for such was the fire's destiny, to cook fish and ward off evil spirits. Which is why you had to leap over it seven times.

But this fire is different. It's not for leaping over. There aren't any children around it. This also is a way of distinguishing fires, whether they're for jumping over or not.

Curtis wasn't sure he'd jumped over the fire on Sol Street seven times on St John's Eve. He'd certainly jumped more than once. Now he was sorry he hadn't counted. He had been in a good mood and felt like talking. Not just because his first fight was coming soon. His opponent was someone called Manlle. He had also informed anyone who wanted to listen of two important pieces of news. The first, that his friend, Arturo da Silva, Galicia's flamboyant lightweight champion, had found him a job as an apprentice climatic electrician.

'Climatic?'

'That's right, climatic. Heat the cinemas in winter and then cool them in the summer. And install large fridges up and down the country so that there's always something to eat.'

'That's fantastic, Curtis. A real revolution.'

But equally important to Curtis had been the second piece of news. This year, he let it be known, on Sunday 2 August, a special train would depart for the Caneiros festivities. And everyone there, their mouths trimmed with sardine scales, listened intently because a trip upriver, to Caneiros, in the heart of the forest, was the most enthralling excursion for miles around, in a country that knew how to celebrate. Leica said that Curtis had a photographic memory. A shutterless camera. And now he was focusing on life. That's right, he added, he himself had tickets for the special train, which included the trip by boat and a buffet.

'A buffet?' asked someone who'd drawn close to the Sol Street bonfire. 'What the hell is a buffet?'

Curtis had a photographic memory so, given his role as impromptu spokesperson for the event, he decided to borrow a phrase Holando had used.

'It's a sort of Pantagruelian meal.'

'And what's in that alien meal?'

Curtis wasn't entirely sure what Holando had meant. But he'd liked the phrase and understood what he was trying to say not just from his ruddy expression, but because of the word itself, which was fulsome and whose meaning seemed to dance on top of its letters.

'Pantagruelian is Pantagruelian, as its name indicates.'

'Lots of it?'

'Absolutely.'

'Well, why don't you say so, so that people can understand?'

'It's a question of culture, right, Curtis?'

'That's right, culture. And there'll be lectures too.'

'Lectures? Hmmm. Don't scare everybody off! A party's a party.'

'They're before the meal. To give you an appetite.'

'All right then. It's not just the rich who'll partake of a bit of culture.'

'Caneiros is an excursion the dead would go on if they could,' underlined another.

'That's right,' Curtis agreed, 'and I can get you tickets. This year, there's a special train. That's right, a special train.' He liked to repeat it because he thought, as he gave the information, he could hear the departing whistle and the engine's eager optimism as it pulled out. And then they were on the boat, the Atlantic tide returning the river to its sources and the bagpiper Polka playing an aubade on the stern.

Three pesetas each. And he could get them tickets for the special train to Caneiros.

Vicente Curtis realised he'd never wondered where the material books are made of came from. No, he wasn't thinking about ideas, doctrines and dreams. He knew that books had something to do with trees. There was a relation. It could be said somehow or other – and as he walked towards the pyres, he clarified his thoughts – that's right, we could say that books come from nature. It might not even be false or exaggerated to say that books are a kind of graft. Though that would be to speak in metaphors. This was one of the things that had impressed him about Arturo da Silva, Galicia's lightweight champion, that his head was full of metaphors.

He wasn't known for this, he was known for his hook, feared like a cobra, and for how he moved, his tireless dancing during fights. His celebrated jig. At this point in his recollections, as the first gust from the fires reached him, so similar it seemed to the leaves in autumn, a smile flickered across Curtis' face as he heard Arturo da Silva reply to a journalist's question in a teasing voice, 'My jig? Don't tell me you're one of those who come to see a boxer's legs!' The second wave was the smell of untimely smoke, the mournful, afflicted smell of things that won't burn, it reminded him of the damp, discordant smoke of green wood or the unwilling smoke of sawdust and the remnants of formwork, a fire that hides, grows cold. He knew it well because it signified bad weather and drowning. But he carried on. He knew how much Arturo da Silva loved those books. The people carrying and throwing them called out the source of their spoils, as if a guarantee of origin would give the flames the stimulus they needed, 'Germinal Library! Hercules Cultural Association! New Era Libertarian Association! Galician Torch of Free Thinking!' The soldier who seemed to be in charge of the fires, since he was the one others consulted, who from time to time read out titles and origins with gusto but also with nuances, like someone pronouncing a final judgement or a last word, is a man who is devoted to his mission, focused on the sacrifice, who eagerly accepts a copy a joyfully exultant colleague has run across to give him, holding it open by the flyleaves, open, that's it, and pinned down like someone who's just caught a rare lepidopteron and is taking it to the leader of the expedition. Time runs around like a stiff breeze, flaps its wings over the pyres and then stops. Everything now hangs on the decree. Finally the supervisor cries out, 'My word, it's a Casaritos!'

He pores over the guarantee of authenticity, the distinguishing mark, the ex-libris that matches the owner's signature.

'Yes, well done. It's a genuine Casaritos!'

Curtis knows who he's talking about. He knows who the supervisor is referring to by this diminutive he relishes with pleasurable disdain. On one occasion, on Panadeiras Street, next to the Capuchins' myrtle, his mother pointed out Santiago Casares Quiroga, the Republican leader, to him and then boasted, 'We're practically neighbours.' Then, however,

Curtis had paid attention not to Casares, whom he already knew as the Man with the Red Buick and the yacht *Mosquito*, but to the woman and girl accompanying him. The woman wore her hair down in a mahogany blaze while the girl, unusually for her age, wore a white velvet cap with a hairnet, which covered her dancing curls. The Woman with the Mahogany Hair smiled, adopting a pose Terranova would have termed 'a natural close-up', while the Girl with the Hairnet seemed preoccupied, her presence austere and even surly. She kept looking back as if she feared that some of those applauding, since many of the people on the pavement had burst into spontaneous applause, would turn into a mob, snatch her cap and abduct her parents. The rest of the time, she stared at the ground absent-mindedly. Casares' shoes were black and white like a tap-dancer's. Curtis was convinced that if he showed the soles for a moment, they'd be as shiny as the rest, polished like an upside-down mirror. It wasn't long before they became the object of the couple and their daughter's attention. Curtis' mother was carrying a rolled-up mattress on her head. The mattress had a red damask cover and Curtis' mother was content. She smiled at the couple and their daughter. This gesture had the effect of cheering the girl, who was surprised, intrigued by a woman smiling with such a load on top of her head. Curtis was also content. He was carrying a blue damask mattress. But he was used to that. The first thing he'd learnt in the street was that he was the son of a whore.

'Hercules, son of a whore!'

There was Hercules Lighthouse, Hercules Cinema, Hercules Café, Hercules Transport, Hercules Insurance. The city had a myriad Hercules. Why did he have to be precisely Hercules son of a whore?

No sooner had he emerged into the street than he heard the drone of that nickname. He heard insults and would have liked them to pass on by, to fly far away from him. But the nicknames clustered around him like wasps. And sometimes they stung him. Died, stuck to his skin. So as a small boy Vicente Curtis understood that, just as his mother carried a mattress on her head, he carried another being on his shoulders. His nickname. Hercules, son of a whore. The difference between one Curtis and the other was that Curtis the carrier looked permanently mystified while

Hercules, the other Curtis, was indomitable. Years later, when he was a travelling photographer and had a wooden horse, the mystified and indomitable took turns to be cameraman or invisible horseman. Which is why Hercules sometimes didn't talk or talked to himself. Before the war, when he was a promising boxer, the boy who held the champ of Galicia's gloves for him, his friends couldn't understand why he minded being called 'Hercules'. He would have preferred 'Maxim' or 'The Corner'. Even 'Tough Guy' was better, which is what Terranova the singer called him. But not Hercules. He didn't like it. 'What do you mean, you don't like *Hercules*, you fool?' they said to him. 'That's how you were born. You know nothing about honour. Just imagine the poster: "Today, Saturday, in Coruña Bullring, star combat: Vicente Curtis 'Hercules' versus . . ."'

'He has another daughter,' said Milagres suddenly. 'He has another daughter studying abroad. He's a good man.'

He had another daughter and was a good man. Curtis felt as if he were missing part of the story. So he waited for Milagres to catch her breath. When you're carrying a mattress on top of your head, even if the cover is damask, it's not easy to go into great detail.

Milagres finally told the story:

'When he was studying to be a lawyer in Madrid, he had an affair, apparently with his landlady. And the result was a daughter. Do you know what happened? He kept the child. He didn't just give her his name and some maintenance money. He turned up in Coruña with the child. On his own. The child in his arms on the train. He didn't give a damn what people might think. Oh, no. How many men in the world would do that?'

Milagres was very discreet. She had a reputation for being tight-lipped. But she asked that question on the pavement of Panadeiras Street as if she were directing it to the whole universe. The answer as well, accompanied by a flourish, 'I could count them on the fingers of this hand!'

From the skylight, the back of 12 Panadeiras Street looked something like a toy garden surrounded by walls clad in ivy and passion flowers. On holidays, the girl, helped by a maid, would bring out the cages with budgerigars on to the balcony. And conduct the orchestra of birds with a stick. The garden had cats, a numerous family, and Curtis can see the Casares' daughter telling them to sit down and listen to the concert. Some of the older, more worldly-wise toms pretend to obey and park their bottoms.

'Hey you, what's your name?'

The girl had interrupted the concert, pointed towards him with the stick and shouted out her question. At that point in time, Curtis was a sort of alien. A head with a body in the shape of a three-storey house. He replied and asked her the same question.

'María Vitoria!'

'You what?'

'Vitola,' she said. 'My name's Vitola.'

She put down the stick and, with her hands as a speaking-trumpet, shouted out some news that echoed in the backyards, across the border separating the well-to-do from the seedy district of Papagaio, 'My father's just come out of prison.'

Of prison? Curtis was shocked. What had Mr Casares been doing in prison? In Madrid as well. In the capital city. It must have been something serious if they'd taken him there. He was an educated man. Rich too! He had a Buick, he had his yacht Mosquito. He wore a tie and shoes that were so polished they reflected the clouds. He was also a lawyer. One of those who got people out of jail. It was even said he'd defended free thinkers and anarchists and stopped them going to jail. He also had tuberculosis. It was difficult to understand what Mr Casares had been doing behind bars in Madrid when he was supposed to keep people out of prison.

Vitola turned up one day dressed as an Indian. With plaits. Somebody had managed to restrain her curls, those waves Curtis liked so much. It wasn't any old outfit. She looked like a woman. A little woman. She sounded like one too.

'Curtis!' she cried. 'Get down here!'

His head was sticking out of the skylight. What did she mean, get down? Impossible. He'd kill himself.

'The other way, silly. Come down through the front door.'

Curtis didn't tell anyone where he was rushing off to, nor could they have imagined. It was the first time he'd set foot in 12 Panadeiras Street. What surprised him most was that the walls of the house were made of books. That and the outfits of Vitola and her friends, who were all wearing exotic costumes.

'Curtis is the only native,' said Gloria, the mother who looked like a film star, with those large, daring eyes and mahogany hair. Native, Curtis mused. Another alias. Hmmm. Gloria spent most of the party next to the window, smoking and looking out on to Panadeiras Street. Occasionally she would change the Bakelite record on the electric gramophone. Many years later, whenever he passed that way with his camera and Cariri, his horse, Curtis sought out the window and the glass, like a plate, sent back the image of Vitola's mother. It was simple. You had to photograph back to front. Instead of capturing images, release them.

He enjoyed that party he could never have dreamt of being invited to. He was the only man. A native, that's right. He danced with women of all races. The adults may have thought it was only a game. But for them it was something more. He understood the importance for people of getting dressed up. He was older than Vitola, but the Vitola who stared at him while she danced did so from a new face, from make-up. Shortly afterwards, her father was appointed a minister of the Second Republic. At the end of the summer of 1931, the family moved to Madrid. But at Christmas the lights on the tree in 12 Panadeiras Street came on again.

It was midnight already. Too late for Christmas Eve dinner. It was his now inseparable companion Luís Terranova who rang the changes. And Luís Terranova didn't want to spend that evening at home. He didn't want to see his mother cry. He didn't want to eat cod and cauliflower. It was like biting into his father's memory. The cod so pale and fleshy. The flower-heads like funeral bouquets.

'You're lucky,' he told Curtis. 'Christmas Eve at the Dance Academy is much more fun. Lots more people crying together around a pile of sweets. I wish I had that many aunts!'

At that point, they watched a carriage arrive, pulled by two horses, and heard a gong sound in 12 Panadeiras Street. The Christmas tree lights were reflected in the ground-floor windows. Father Christmas got out of the carriage with a sack.

The two of them stood on the pavement, their hands in their pockets, a puff of breath around their mouths, like cartoon figures who remain speechless.

Father Christmas looked around.

'Good evening!'

'Evening, Mr Casares!'

Father Christmas went inside 12 Panadeiras Street and Terranova gave Curtis a nudge. 'Casares? That Father Christmas was the minister?'

'That's right.'

'He could have left us a present. Shared the weight out.'

'I think he was carrying books. Books for the most part. Books are heavy.'

'Well, he could have given us one!' exclaimed Terranova. 'Even if it was a book. To say the least!'

One of Curtis' part-time jobs had been to cart books for the Faith bookshop. He brought them in a barrow from the railway station. They were kept in boxes. One of them, the biggest, had a label which read *Man and the Earth* (Reclus). Another big one contained *The White Magazine-The Ideal Novel*. Smaller ones were marked *Mother* (Maxim Gorky), *The Story of the Heavens* (Stawell Ball), *Metamorphosis* (Franz Kafka), *How to Become a Good Electrician* (T. Corner). As he pushed the iron-wheeled barrow, he stared at the labels. 'Maxim'. He liked that name as a possible alias for the day he became a boxer. 'Kid Kafka' wasn't bad either. And 'The Corner'. That was perfect. But he liked 'Maxim' as well. The books were heavy. Tobacco weighs a lot less. As do condoms. Terranova was into the international trade of liners. Whatever he could hide under his coat. He was paid in kind by the crew members he took on a tour of the city. An easy job. Many of them stopped not far from port, in Luisa Fernanda's cabaret or the Méndez Núñez, charmed by the Garotas variety show. The way they came out half naked, singing with a puppet between their legs, 'Mummy, buy me a negro, buy me a negro from the bazaar, who dances the Charleston and plays the Jazzman.' Terranova imitated their performance with a boxing glove between his legs. What a clown he was and how well he did it. As when he pushed the barrow and stopped. Read the labels on the boxes one by one. 'Man, earth, heavens, mother . . . What you doing with all this weight, Curtis? You got the whole world in here.' 'I'm going to the Faith bookshop.' 'That's right,' he replied, 'always trying to help. To carry all this, you'd need the barrow of faith.' There were days he spoke like an old man.

'Maxim' wasn't bad, 'Kid Kafka' was unsettling, but he liked 'The Corner' best.

A gong sounded again inside 12 Panadeiras Street. It was louder this time. Came from deep inside the house. Cut straight through them. Like the cold. Like the moon.

'A book at least,' murmured Terranova, 'would be something.'

'You want a book?' Curtis asked him. 'You really want a book?'

Both of them had their hands in their pockets. Terranova's feet were half off the kerb and he was leaning forwards. The same game that annoyed Curtis so much when he played it on the edge of the cliffs. His insistence on always walking along the edge, hanging out over the abyss.

He pretended to fall. Did a somersault. 'Yes, I want a book!'

'Come on then. I know where we can find some books.'

It was Christmas Eve 1931. They met no one on the way. The sea in Orzán redoubled its efforts when it saw them. Threw foam, drowned in its own roars. They were counting on this. On certain dates, the sea has a tendency to be vainglorious. The more witnesses there are, the more powerful the waves. They advance sideways against the wind. The water runs down their faces. They laugh and curse. In a corner of the Coiraza wall, which acts as a breakwater, the fashioned stone of the quarries is piled up with natural rocks. Kneeling down, with his back to the sea, Curtis moves a stone and puts his hand in the gap. He knows Flora has a store of *The Ideal Novel* in there. She goes there to sunbathe. And sometimes smokes what she calls an aromatic. These, she says, are her two square metres of paradise. The naked body revives in the open air. Here she reads her short novels. Keeps a stack of them under the stones.

'*The Ideal Novel?* These aren't books, they're handkerchiefs. Look what's here: *Sister Light in Hell, My Misfortune, Last Love, Decent Prostitutes, The Executioner's Daughter, Nancy's Tragedy* . . .'

'You can only pick one,' says Curtis, impervious to his remarks. 'They're Flora's. They're OK. I like them.'

'I'm not in the mood for crying. I already have to have dinner with my mother and an empty plate. What's the son of the orphan's father going to have for dinner? Cod. *Corpus meum.*'

'Why don't you tell her not to lay three places?'

'She won't listen. She goes crazy. You don't know what she's like. Poor Mummy Cauliflower! She'd accepted it. What does it matter whether he died in St John's or here? But someone went and said something, and now she's got this idea a dead man could have been stored in salt. If cod is stored in salt, why not a salted man? Some cod are as big as a man.'

Curtis stared at him in disbelief. Stretched out his arms to measure an imaginary leaf.

'I'm not joking,' said Terranova. 'Some cod are like men.'

Water was pouring down his face. Not all of it from the sea. He took a sip. Spat it out. 'I'll take this one. *The Decline of the Gods* by Federica Montseny. Judging from the title, it'll go against the world, be a little funny.'

That's it. A 'Casaritos'! The supervisor wouldn't look at the book in the same way if it didn't have that signature, the ex-libris of his name in artistic handwriting. He feels the excitement of having captured something of its owner. He feels that somewhere in Madrid, wherever he may be, Casares is aware two claws have just grabbed him by the lapels and are prising apart his weakened ribs. He examines the signature. He's not an expert in calligraphy, but he can see the portrait of the man in it. His signature is really a drawing. With its angles and curves. The second 'a' of 'Santiago' and the first 'a' of 'Casares' are eyes. The most peculiar stroke is that linking the 'g' of 'Santiago' with the 'C' of 'Casares', as if the missing letter, the final 'o' of 'Santiago', had given its skein to join them. In this case, the second surname, 'Quiroga', is represented by the digraph 'Qu' and a full stop. Like this: 'Santiagcasares Qu.' There is a slanting line underneath, which rather than underlining his name, acts as a gently sloping ramp which the signature ascends.

Weren't there any more?

Santiago Casares was known to have owned the city's finest private library. 12 Panadeiras Street had two kinds of superimposed walls: the external wall and the internal bookshelves. Having inherited the library from his father, he received new publications from some of the best bookshops in Europe. Many such books arrived by sea. The supervisor remembered having read an interview in which Casares explained how sailors brought his father books by hand that were forbidden or unavailable in Spain. And how one of his happiest childhood memories was opening the packages 'brought by the sea.' He remembered that bit perfectly. He also knew something about packages brought by the sea.

'Brought by the sea,' he murmured.

'What?'

'More, there must be lots more.'

'There's a pile of them burning over there, in the main square. And a bunch were arrested and taken to the Palace of Justice. There are also some in the bullpen.'

The supervisor acknowledges his subordinate's intention with a smile. Books as defendants, under arrest, against the wall. With their backs to people. In a line, squeezed tight, unable to move, in mute silence. They were the lucky ones. Days, months, years will go by and the arrested books will gradually disappear. A slip of the hand. A determined grip. Book by book, the dismantling of the library, what's not burnt, in the Palace of Justice. And the same thing will happen to the man's entire credentials. Everything will be the object of pillaging. Possessions great and small. Even little, intimate things. Not just his books, but the carved wooden shelves that hold them. The collections of the amateur scientist, the curious naturalist, have been carried off or destroyed. The lenses, measuring instruments, appliances for seeing what's invisible. His herbaria and entomological boxes. All his effects, all his fingerprints. Here's the last of the pillagers, one who was there in the beginning and returned as if to a wreckage. He'd already made off with a stack of books and optical instruments. This time all he found in the hallway, lying on the floor, was one of the entomological boxes containing labelled insects. What he saw were some repugnant bugs that looked like beetles. He kicked it away with disgust. Why weren't there any large butterflies? He then went to what must have been the girls' bedroom. There was a china doll. Broken. On the window sill, a dried starfish and some sea urchin skeletons. He decided to shake the skeletons and out fell some jet earrings. That was something at least. From the window, he could see the garden with a large lemon tree in the middle. The garden's back wall formed a border. On the other side: sin city. The dividing walls of Papagaio. He looked carefully. Something was stuck to the wall, in among the weeds. Something black. Possibly a ball. But balls weren't usually black. He went downstairs and descended the garden steps. Swore again. The ball was a strange, oval shape, glistening from the rain. A head. But a head that wasn't a head. He picked it up. Made of wood. It looked like a head. Eyes, mouth, nose barely discernible in thin lines. And a hole as of a bullet. You never know. Perhaps it's meant to be like this. It could be a sculpture. Something valuable. The Casares were fashionable people. À la mode. He'd take it. It wasn't bad, the black woman's head. Something at least. And as he pondered the mysterious value of things, he glanced at the entomological box and read *Coleoptera*. If they're Coleoptera, maybe they're not beetles. Who knows? There are some strange folk around. Someone might even pay for them. This one, for example. What's it say? *Coccinella septempunctata*.

Another book fell next to the scaffold. He picks it up by the back. A little higher. By the neck. That's life. He steps aside and again opens the book. The supervisor, still a young man, turns the page. Starts reading slowly as he paces around the fire. He may have found an unconscious discipline in reading, a comma or a full stop on the bottom of his boot. He suddenly stops, closes the book and holds it to his chest, in his left hand, like someone carrying a missal, while with his right hand he removes his spectacles, rubs his eyes with the back of his hand and blinks like someone emerging from a cinema. He takes the book and places it on a small pile away from the fires. 'This one's staying with me,' he says. 'Under house arrest!'

* * *

'On the Fertilisation of Orchids . . .'

One of them, the youngest, who to start with looked lazy, but gradually grew more enthusiastic, especially when he managed to repeat the impossible word, that abracadabra, to say 'para-lle-le-pipeds', which made him feel as happy as if he'd just vaulted a horse, three jumps in the air, after various unsuccessful attempts, is the one having fun reading out the titles. House arrest? He also has a peek at the pile of books the supervisor's making.

'On the Fertilisation of Orchids by Insects! By Charles Darwin.'

Parallelepiped sniffs three times as he reads. Fertilisation? Orchids? Insects? Something's not quite right. Something bothers him. The idea of orchids being fertilised by insects.

'That's disgusting!'

He drops the book in the fire, fucking insects, orchid whores, spits and starts to move faster, using his jokes as a kind of manual lever.

'Quo vadis? Straight for the flames! Another Conquest of Bread! How many Conquests is that?'

He lifts the book and shouts, 'More bread! Make bread, ye baking women!' He manages to attract a few sarcastic smiles. He then goes full out in search of a belly laugh, 'If you're not up the duff already!' He chucks the book, which falls not like a parallelepiped, but like a concertina. A flame comes in search of this light being and he feels encouraged, as if there's an understanding between them and the fire also likes his jokes. Where is everybody? Why isn't there more of an audience? Has he got to organise the party and let off the fireworks?

'What a lot of bread! Germinal, come on, Germinal! Spread your germs. Another Germinal in the pot. The Ex-Men by Gorky. You soon will be. L'art et la révolte by Fernand Pe-llou-ti-er. Well, I never, monsieur! Coruña Corsair Library. Corsair? Coarse air, more like. And what have we here? New Bellies on Strike, Sun Library. Bellies on strike? You mean not working! The Numancia Rising as Told by One of Its Protagonists, Coruña Workers Press. I've had about all I can take of that. Does God Exist? Aurora Library. No more questions, Aurora, darling! Victor Hugo, Les Misérables. Hell's not miserable. Madame Bovary. One less ovary! What's this? O divino sainete . . . Boss, what do we do with this one? The Divine Comedy or something.'

49

'The Divine Sketch is by Curros!' said the supervisor without having to look, which impressed his subordinate.

The queries were few and far between. There wasn't much selection. Books were unloaded in heaps or thrown haphazardly from boxes. When one did emerge from anonymity, like a face emerging from a common grave, the reading aloud of its title conferred on it a dying distinction, the ultimate proof that the title was actually a good one, since there was that cretin, in his own words, Parallelepiped, with certain pomp, asking about it. Here perhaps, unlike with others that gave rise to jokes, the allusion to the divine made his hands itch. Until that moment, he hadn't paid a great deal of attention to the meaning of the titles, only to the humour in them. He hadn't discriminated between them. So it was no surprise he should now think there was something strange in his having picked up one that spoke of 'the divine' alongside 'sketch.' The one that referred to God to ask if he existed shouldn't be allowed to exist for another second. But this one, The Divine Sketch, suggested the idea of a superior laugh. And he liked to laugh. To laugh at danger as well. He had guts, you might even say he was hardened. Before the military uprising achieved its purpose, he'd been involved with a group of trained gunmen in acts of provocation aimed at destabilising the Republic. On one occasion, they'd broken up a meeting and someone had been shot. It took him some time to believe that he'd done it. And he never really accepted the fact. He'd been shocked. In his view, the amount of blood a wounded man can lose bore no relation to the simple act of pulling a trigger. After a few days, it became less important. Now it wasn't important at all. Now even winning the war wasn't enough. The idea of war itself had little to say. Things had advanced to another stage. Beyond war.

'Manuel Curros Enríquez, that's right.'

The Falangist, whom everyone now calls Parallelepiped, remembers why the name sounds familiar. The city's largest sculpture is dedicated to Curros. He must have done something. In the gardens, surrounded by a lake. Very near there. He noticed it because on top of the monument is a naked woman rising triumphantly into the sky. Now that's a monument. Were it not for the new Post Office, the woman could see the fires. Amazing what you can do with stone. Afterwards he'll have to go and have another look. At the stone slut.

'What? What shall I do with this one? Under house arrest?'

Curtis guessed that the authority of the man who decided the destiny of books derived not just from his position in the hierarchy, but from the fact he read a lot and was what is generally termed 'a man of culture'. In fact, he didn't stop reading and consulting books, some of them rescued from the flames. While his subordinates carried out the burning, egging each other on with jokes and directing insults at particularly obnoxious titles, their boss circulated. He went from group to group, issuing the same instruction under his breath, 'Any copies of Scripture, in particular the New Testament, let me know at once.'

Now he frowns.

'You can throw *The Divine Sketch* in the fire!'

Parallelepiped moves his arm like a lever, releases his fingers and drops the book without further ado. Then unconsciously, either because his last memory of the sculpture is of water bubbling on stone or because his skin senses rather than feels an itch, what the boy in uniform does is shake his hands and rub them on his trousers. And then he falls quiet.

With the passing of time, the initial funeral procession of mockery turns into a routine, an industrial-scale burning, which must have something to do with the increasingly thick smoke, a tactile, sticky stench that suggests to Curtis one last metaphor. The books had come down from the trees and fallen into the trap of some men with viscous arms. So, from close up, the embers at the bottom of the fire resembled a cluster of birds reduced to ashen silhouettes and glowing yellow or orange beaks. Had Arturo da Silva been here, the books wouldn't be burning, thought Curtis. Or perhaps they were burning because he wasn't here. The fact they were burning was further proof of his loss. And Curtis' mind, which in Arturo's words was a spiral staircase, ascended, or descended, another step. It was the boxer from Shining Light, the writer of *Brazo y Cerebro*, who was burning. The books' last smell was of flesh.

'*Revista de Occidente*. Federico García Lorca. New York (Office and Denunciation). What have we here?'

51

The name sounded familiar to Parallelepiped. He hadn't read anything by him, but he'd heard lots of jokes about him under the heading 'red queens'. In a Fascist publication, one of those papers he did read, there was always a stubborn misprint in the second surname: García Loca or 'madwoman'.

He opened it up. Adopted a humorous tone:

> Under the multiplications
> is a drop of duck's blood

Shit! He didn't read any more. The drop of duck's blood changed his voice. He looked away and made an effort to shout:

'Boss! There's a Lorca here.'

He threw it with obvious hatred into the middle of the volcano, which spewed out black smoke and shiny sparks.

He took another handful. Meanwhile his boss had approached. The first of the new lot was a slim volume, the only illustration a single scallop shell in the centre.

'Six Galician Poems! Fe-de-ri-co . . . What's this? Can't they leave each other alone?'

He turned to face his boss with the book held out and a look of disgust.

'Samos! Did this faggot also write in Galician?'

His boss lingered over the cover, though young Parallelepiped thought there was hardly much to read. Six Galician Poems by Federico García Lorca. Foreword E. B. A. Nós Publishing House. Compostela. Samos may have been investigating those dots after the letters. Deciphering those initials. He leafed through it slowly, page by page. Parallelepiped tossed the other books while watching Samos. What's he up to? Is he going to read the whole thing?

> Locks that go out to sea,
> where the clouds their glittering dovecot keep

The book danced in his hands. He looked at the boy observing him steadily, waiting for some informed remark.

'He spent some time here,' said the supervisor, 'with a theatre company, Barraca. Yes, he was right here. I think he made a lot of friends. The book's recent. Under a year.'

'That was another age, Comrade Samos,' declared the young boy.

A year. The phrase Parallelepiped used was of someone measuring an astronomical distance. The look of someone abolishing time. He was right. After all, he knew how to measure what was happening. It was a month to the day since the war had started. The first month of Year I.

The war had changed all concept of time. The war had changed many things, but above all measures of duration. Nós Publishing House. He could have given him a lecture, but it didn't exist any more. It had no future and it wouldn't have any past either. That was where Galicianist Republicans hung out, those who had this stupid idea of a federal Spain. The publisher was Ánxel Casal. Mayor of Santiago de Compostela. Or rather ex-mayor. In a dungeon right now. Like Coruña's mayor, Alfredo Suárez Ferrín. He felt something like vertigo to think that these two figures of the Republic, democratically elected mayors, had been imprisoned as enemies of the nation. But the vertigo was exciting, intoxicating. He'd finally arisen from inaction, from a bland form of Christianity. He could shout as during the Crusades, 'God wills it!' And in fact this is how, with a warlike cry, he'd ended a short speech at the local branch of the Falange, which now had a large skull painted on the wall. Yes, he felt the telepathic force of Carl Schmitt, his new, revered master. It was naive to believe in a telepathy of words, but not of ideas. In the thesis he was preparing on Donoso Cortés, concerning the dictatorship, he'd noted down an idea he later discovered in one of Schmitt's texts: a state of emergency was to law what a miracle was for theology. Since the machinery of conspiracy had been set in motion and above all since he'd felt the itching in his brain that came from holding a weapon in his hand that afternoon when Dez invited him to military training on the beach, since then he'd been accompanied every day by the image of Heidegger, the Nazi Rector of Freiburg University, giving the order to descend to Plato's cave to requisition the projector of ideas. Yes, he knew them. He knew Casal. Compostela's mayor had been born in Coruña and founded his publishing house there. His wife, María Miramontes, was a well-known designer. His mother, Pilar, had even ordered her famous dress of black chiffon with black velvet grapes from her. The mother's final act of daring. Needless to say, Casal and Miramontes were friends with Luís Huici, the artistic tailor, the inventor of incredible

53

double-breasted waistcoats and broad-shouldered jackets which were so popular with Coruña's Bohemians. Waistcoats, ideas. He'd got the young drunk with his speeches at Germinal. Right now, Huici was probably tasting castor oil in the barracks of the Falange.

He gave the book back to Parallelepiped, 'You can throw it!' Parallelepiped might have wondered why he didn't throw it himself though, given the circumstances, that would have been a strange thought. So he just carried out the order. Should somebody ever write a history of the burning of books in Coruña, they could add a non-gratuitous detail: Ánxel Casal and Federico García Lorca were murdered that same morning. The Galician publisher in a ditch outside Santiago, in Cacheiras, and the Granadine poet in the gully of Víznar, Granada. At about the same time, six hundred miles apart.

The book landed on some copies of *Man and the Earth* by the geographer Élisée Reclus. It was still there, safe for the moment, on those sort of rocks which formed a mountain range the fire ascended. Samos kept looking at it. He was sometimes superstitious and trusted his instinct. Now he was thinking this little book could one day be a rarity. A work printed in the Galician language might become a relic. A first edition of the *Six Poems* would be as valuable as a medieval parchment.

'What? Feeling sorry for it?' Parallelepiped asked him.

Prattler, thought Samos. But right now he didn't mind him being so nosy.

'Not sorry,' he said. 'Those initials! I've just remembered why they could be useful to me. See if you can fetch it . . .'

'Here it is, boss. Just in time.'

'In extremis,' said Samos with a sigh.

'In extremis,' whispered Parallelepiped. He was learning lots, he thought, while the books burnt. That's it, in extremis.

'Wells, Wells, Wells!'

There's a flurry of activity.

'Wells, Wells, Wells!' shouts the one we already know as Parallelepiped, throwing a book each time he imitates a dog's bark.

'More Wells! There's lots of him. Wells, Wells, Wells!'

For a moment, for the briefest of moments, when he heard that mocking onomatopoeia – 'Wells, Wells, Wells!' three books into the fire – there was an acidic reaction somewhere in Samos' digestive system, which caused him a slight indisposition, a rumbling in the bowels, part of which involved remembering fragments from *The War of the Worlds*, not as they were, but in Héctor Ríos' penetrating voice, '*Does time pass when there are no human hands left to wind the clocks?*' It's Easter 1931. They're in the Craftsmen's Circle, in a group of declamation and amateur theatre directed by Ríos, who is studying already at Santiago University, in the Faculty of Law. Two years older, he's in front of Samos, but they still work together at weekends on that project that so excited them to begin with. A radio version of *The War of the Worlds*. 'The radio's an extraordinary invention,' asserts Ríos. 'It'll transform communication, culture, everything. It'll cross borders through the air. Coruña Radio is due to start broadcasting soon.'

'Wells, Wells, Wells! Out the door, and you're not coming back.'

Samos felt bad and was about to say something. Pull him up. Why did he have to be so uncouth? He was going to ask him to be a little more polite. A bit of culture, please. You don't have to bark. But he realised the absurdity of such an order at that time. They'd all burst out laughing. That's a good one. Some of the older soldiers might recall the impresario Lino's historic intervention in his Pavilion of Spectacles when, at a charity performance in the presence of some nuns, he attempted to subdue the top gallery, 'Manners, gentlemen! Manners! There are ladies in the audience, some of whom are even decent. Ho, ho, ho. Your manners, please!'

But he didn't say anything. The gripes were building like an inner storm. He had to suppress his body's rebellion. The upset of some scruples. He addressed Parallelepiped in an energetic voice, 'Throw them all in at once, for fuck's sake. Without consideration. I've had it up to here with Wells!'

And then he seized the moment, sidled up to Parallelepiped, who had a good eye. A bit of culture and he'd make a good hunter of books. He said, 'Don't forget the New Testament.' Went further, 'It's not any old book. It's of great historical value, got it?'

'How will I know which one it is, Comrade Samos? Scripture, there's plenty. Even the Masons on Nakens Street had a stack of Bibles, more than in my parish.'

Samos suddenly hesitated whether or not to carry on giving information to that numskull. 'You have to be discreet,' he said to him. 'Find the book, talk to me. Only to me. You'll get your reward.'

'Right, but how will I know which one it is?'

'It's easy. It's the only one with . . . a dedication.'

Samos bit his lips. There was no going back.

'What's the key, boss?'

'It says: "For Antonio de la Trava, the valiente of Finisterra".'

'I like that,' said Parallelepiped. 'I've got relatives in Finisterre.'

'Good then. But be discreet. Don't start shouting. Bring it to me by hand. No noise, no fireworks.'

Parallelepiped was a bit annoyed by Samos' superior tone. There was a coldness about him. But he replied seriously, 'Not to worry. I also know how to get on in the world, comrade.'

Next to the first fire, Curtis took another step forwards.

To be more exact, the burning books smell of leather mashed with flesh. Of boxing gloves.

'Hey you with the cap! You like books? Can't take your eyes off them!'

'He probably likes the fire. If he's here, he must be one of us.'

Curtis pretended not to hear. He'd spotted a living book which the flames were just starting on. *A Popular Guide to Electricity*. Arturo da Silva wasn't a professional boxer. You couldn't live from boxing unless you made the jump to Madrid or Barcelona. And he hadn't wanted to. He was a plumber by trade. His job, directing the forces of water, had something in common with the way he behaved inside the ring. He'd convinced Curtis his future was in electricity. More specifically, in air conditioning. So Curtis had gradually become the champ's right hand. 'You'll succeed him. Hercules of Shining Light', Abelenda in the gym had told him. He was sure of it. On the poster for his first fight, he could see the words 'Hercules of Shining Light versus . . .' But there was no poster for his first fight. There wasn't time. It would be on 17 July. His debut as an

56

amateur boxer then would be with another youngster called Manlle. There'd been a cancellation and they'd agreed to include them. The typical warm-up fight while the spectators found their seats. But for Curtis it was the most important event of his life. He'd trained hard with Arturo. 'On one condition.' 'What?' 'You'll start as an apprentice in a workshop for climatic installations, soon to be opened by the Chavín factory, which makes Wayne refrigerators. I've a friend there. But to get in, you'll have to know something about electricity. You'll have to study. What do you think?' He thought it was great. If he ever had a business card like the ones he'd seen travelling salesmen use at the Dance Academy, he could write: 'Boxer and Climatic Electrician.'

Arturo da Silva had told him that sometimes the safest place was the middle of the ring. The harpooner had talked to him of the calm at the centre of a hurricane. Maybe it was that instinct which had brought him here, to the city centre, after thirty days in hiding. A whole month stuck in the attic of the Dance Academy, also known as Un-deux-trois, his only company a mannequin the harpooner Mr Lens had given his mother. A headless mannequin. A very tall woman, the mannequin, which the sea had thrown up unharmed among a multitude of cripples, maimed figures, loose heads, broken busts and odd extremities. The ship that lost them when it listed violently in a storm off Rostro wouldn't come back for cast-aways like these. Mr Lens scoured the beach, slung the tall woman, the only one who was complete, over his shoulder and also picked up three wooden female legs. These were gratefully received by hosiers across the city. They were long, very slim, and were soon on display in the windows of Crisálida, Gran Corsetería Francesa and Botón de Oro. But he couldn't place the mannequin. The ebony woman was simply too tall. 'If the country progresses, if we advance, there may yet be room for such tall women,' said the clothes manager in the Espuma department store on San Andrés Street, who was considerate enough to offer Mr Lens a blanket to wrap her up a bit since, while it was a liberal city, people had their own views and susceptibilities and Mr Lens didn't want to run into the procession coming from St Nicholas', bearing Our Lady of Sorrow, being in possession of this tall, black woman.

'It must be heavy,' said the clothes manager. 'Though beauty weighs less.'

For the first time, Mr Lens took a close look at his discovery. When he'd found it, it had been half buried in the sand. What the sea had made with the scattered bodies and mangled limbs was a horrifying pastiche. He thought that now, not before. On the beach, he'd gone in search of useful items. The sea wasn't going to surprise him. The tall woman's head was like a highly polished large wooden egg. As he turned it around, he observed there were no eyes, mouth or nose. So what was there to look at? And yet now, in the shop, before he slung it over his shoulder, he examined the head carefully and noticed some very delicate features, the beginnings of a face. First of all, he saw some cheekbones and then, below the cheeks, the melancholy protrusion of some lips. He stroked the head and decided it wasn't quite smooth. He could feel a few invisible hairs pushing through. This woman was coming into being. He took a fancy to it. He'd take it to the Dance Academy to see if Milagres would keep it for him. He wouldn't say anything about the life in the wood. They might think he was bringing them a monster. She'd already been scared the last time, when he showed her a small but ferocious-looking revolver. A Bulldog.

'Where did you get that?'

'It arrived in a whale.'

'You find everything inside a whale.'

'Almost everything.'

'Bring it here,' said Samantha. She gripped the revolver. The madame had turned up unexpectedly, without them realising. She had a cigarette holder in one hand and the revolver in the other. 'It's about my size. Today's my birthday. Will you give it to me? I need a friend I can trust.'

On 20 July, Curtis was with Arturo da Silva and others from Shining Light, helping to erect one of the barricades protecting the Civil Government by the Rosalía de Castro Theatre on the side of the docks. They'd carried sacks of sand from Orzán. As on Saturday and Sunday, to the sound of ships' sirens and horns, thousands of people had occupied the city centre in support of the Republic. Early in the afternoon, the insurgent troops placed pieces of artillery on Parrote. Curtis recalled where he'd seen a weapon.

A small revolver, but at least it was something. He rushed to Papagaio. Pombo only opened the door when he recognised his voice. He was on a mission, to find the Bulldog revolver, and ignored what they were trying to tell him. He started rummaging in Samantha's room until he heard, 'Your mother's ill. The least you could do is go and see her.'

That was the ruse. That was when they barred the door. He shouted. Called his mother a traitor a thousand times.

'Traitor? You'll all get killed. Who ever saw a war of fists versus guns? And you'll be one of the first. Just so they can have a laugh about who killed Papagaio's Hercules.'

He was left alone. With the mannequin, the tall, black woman the harpooner had brought. Punching the old leather bag Arturo had given him. Thumping the handcrafted sack of sand he himself had hung from the beam. At it all day long. The house's lament on account of his rage. 'Stop it!' shouted Pombo from the other side of the door. 'You're making the whole city groan.'

'Let me out, Pombo!' he pleaded. 'On the roofs, they're shooting to kill.'

'It's worse on the ground. Wait until the hunting season's over.'

He thought the mannequin didn't have eyes. Or a mouth. The head, an oval sphere. But it's funny. In the half-light, he begins to discern features. Subtle lines appear on the wooden egg. He opens the skylight and leans out with the Tall Woman. A cat approaches along the edge. Looks towards the Casares' garden and starts to meow. For a moment, the shots fall silent, as if to respect the night, and other animal sounds are heard. The seagulls' scandalised calls, the cats' detailed inventory, the dogs' distant denunciation. At night, in the beams from the lighthouse, Curtis perceives beauty in the mannequin's face. The intermittent beams bring it to life. The cat comes and goes, but doesn't make up its mind to climb down to the Casares' garden. There are voices. It's not clear if they're coming from inside. There's no light on, but the windows the pillagers have broken disturb the domestic darkness. From time to time, torch beams flicker from the other side, the front of the house on Panadeiras Street. The darkness is also in pieces. Translucent, empty. They must have taken the doors, curtains and lamps as well. Secrets, he thought, have nothing to do with darkness. Secrets belong to the light. What was going on in Madrid, what had happened to the Casares? The darkness of the house was translucent. Dangerous. The cats refused to climb down to the garden. Skirted their old haunt cautiously, warily. Eyeing the crater. What had happened to the girl with the rebellious hair of Orzán waves?

He'd also like to have known what had happened to Flora. During the day in the Academy, he listened to all the voices, interpreted all the noises. He heard what the voices said about others. But he didn't hear Flora or anything about her. He'd like to have heard her energetic dance, the telegraph of her heels. He thinks about her when the shots start up again. Tries to understand their meaning.

And then single reports, cartridge by cartridge. Someone trying not to waste any ammunition. Each shot sounding like the last.

He remembered Arturo da Silva the day he threw a succession of euphoric punches, which the champ answered one by one, cartridge by cartridge, he said. But now the sound of automatic gunfire silences the handcrafted shots. Showers the sky. And when it grows tired, there is the stubborn response of a fugitive on the tiles, counting his cartridges, one by one, the space between each clap of the bell allowing time to imagine where they're coming from, where they're going. The automatic gunfire starts up again with renewed vigour. Bites pieces off the tiles. Silences once and for all the fugitive who was saving his cartridges.

The Tall Woman's head rolls down into the gutter, where it is stopped by the foxgloves, their tall spikes in flower like carillons of rosy bells. The roofs here are like meadows. The Tall Woman's head has been hit. In contrast to the hole, now it is possible to imagine some eyes. In the beams of light, he observes the oval beauty he can no longer hold on to. The foxgloves eventually give way. The head rocks in the gutter. Falls down into the Casares' garden. Everything is quiet. The moon full and astonished on the Mera coast. What a beautiful summer, sewn with bullets.

Among the attractions at the festivities in Recheo Gardens were distorting mirrors and a Travelling Theatre of Live Impalpable Spectres. Luís Terranova had taken him to hear the voice of Mirco, the amazing queen with a glass eye. The German Circus had set up shop on the Western Quay, near the Wooden Jetty. To advertise the fact, a chimpanzee was driving in stakes, tightening ropes and, dressed as a field marshal, appeared to be in charge of erecting the big top. The beaches were crowded. Swimwear this year was more colourful, brilliant hues that enamelled bodies, but also smaller, revealing shoulders, stretches of thigh, hitherto unseen. Ancient and modern wonders filled the gardens on canvases photographers hung like stage sets and completed with wooden or papier mâché props. You could have your portrait taken in front of images from all over the world. The pyramids of Egypt, the skyscrapers of Manhattan, the Eiffel Tower, the Alhambra in Granada, the Statue of Liberty, Gaudí's Sagrada Família, a winter landscape in Dalecarlia, the Plus Ultra hydroplane in Buenos Aires, riders at the Seville Fair, Machu Picchu, the Taj Mahal, the entrance to the Paris Métro at Porte Dauphine, the Pórtico da Gloria, Hercules Lighthouse, a picture of garlanded boats at Caneiros. Lots of people wanted a portrait in front of the snowy landscape of Dalecarlia in Sweden, with its sleighs and wooden cabins, but the longest queue was for Manhattan. Curtis and Terranova stood staring at the canvas of the river and a model boat with the sign 'Caneiros'.

'Do you want one of the Excursion to Caneiros?' asked the idle photographer.

'No thanks. We're going on that universal cruise this year,' said Terranova. 'We've a ticket and everything.'

'Nature imitates art,' said the photographer. 'Go on, as a kind of advertisement. A free photo. Everyone's mad about skyscrapers today. That's it, look this way, pretend you're rowing, see if anyone wants a boat. Manhattan, they all want Manhattan. How folkloric!'

Apart from the soldiers, the place was empty, but Curtis thought about the attractions at the festivities as a way of protecting his back. Everything he'd experienced had come from behind, on the lookout, cautiously following in his footsteps. The spectres. Mirco's glass eye. The people and their portraits in front of landscapes from around the world. Some in Swedish Dalecarlia, others queuing up for Manhattan. Luís Terranova imitates Mirco, waves a fig leaf as a loincloth while reciting 'I am that vast, secret promontory . . .' No. Luís Terranova isn't there. He knows nothing about him. Feels guilty for letting him down. Because he's got both their tickets. The tickets for the special train to Caneiros.

From time to time, as a leaf curled up, he saw words that were burning. He tried to reach, to catch them before they turned into smoke. He realised now why there were so few flames. The fire burnt inwards, down the furrows of printed words. Rooted in paper, words can be like heather. It can rain on the book, but the words still give off heat. There are some that take longer to burn than others. Which explains why they end up on their own in the ashes, on the surface of small membranes like those of crickets, cicadas and grasshoppers. He'd heard this from Polka. A mountain fire in summer smells of a mixture of vegetation and cricket and cicada wings, burnt song.

It was night still. He opened the skylight. Clambered over the roofs. At last felt the foxgloves' rosy touch. His jealousy of cats and seagulls. When he dropped down on to one of the lower roofs and managed to land in Hospital Street, he walked in a daze. Walked in his sleep. This wasn't a recent state. He'd been like this for quite some time.

He'd spent the days hiding in the Academy's attic, his only company the headless Tall Woman, deprived of her oval beauty. Anxious to start with, waiting for news, which swept under the door like a cold current, however warm the voice of the one conveying the news. He'd occasionally peep out of the skylight. It was then Curtis discovered the true meaning of fear. Fear is a beach that is deserted on a sunny day. Or almost deserted, which is worse. Figures in black with large, black umbrellas to keep off the sun. Some *catalinas*, the name given to peasant women who came to bathe in skirts made of matting. They kept watch on the sea like fish caught in a net. They may have been disturbed by the solitary bather who ran up and down, wearing a strange black-and-yellow-striped costume. And passed between them like a gigantic wasp. There was a new, terrifying silence. Each silence conveyed some kind of horror. He looked at the headless Tall Woman and began to feel the same, like someone who's lost his head. Only at night did the beams from the lighthouse give it back to him.

He ended up at dawn on Riazor Beach. He looked around insistently, in case the bather in the black-and-yellow-striped costume appeared, buzzing like a wasp. He didn't see anyone. He heard the murmur of the sea, which reminded him of the notion of stuttering speech.

He climbed up through Peruleiro and Ventorillo. He sleepwalked to Fontenova and the Shining Light building in the Abyss. He was thinking about the tickets for the special train and the excursion to Caneiros. He had to hand in the money he'd collected. He had to settle accounts. It had become an obsession. What would Arturo and his friends think?

It was he who noticed the fear in things. The discomfort of houses under construction, intimidated by the irritation of their elders. The distrust shown by doorways. The frown of windows. The premises of the libertarian association were in Fontenova. They looked completely dispossessed. Even of their name. The quicksilver glass sign on the front had been smashed. Isolino had made it in the Rubine glassworks, with an emery design reminiscent of a roadside shrine. A sun surrounded by flames. Curtis picked up a stela of sun. It was cold. The confiscators had padlocked the door. Curtis went round the back and broke in through a window. The first thing his eyes sought out was the Ideal typewriter. One of the reasons that had driven him there was the hope no one would have remembered that small centre for social studies in humble premises, in a distant quarter. His most intimate hope was to find the typewriter. He heard the keys like Morse. He blocked his ears to the night's reports, shut his eyes. And then he felt the keys on the pads of his fingers, Arturo da Silva's voice as he dictated:

EXTRAORDINARY EXCURSION TO
CANEIROS-BETANZOS BY SPECIAL TRAIN

'Leave two blank lines. That's it. Now continue.'

The two of them slowly caressing the keys, making a caravan of letters. The whole night in front of them.

Curtis was in a dark room. He'd forced an entry, opened the windows, but the light seemed reluctant to return. They'd taken everything. Even the electric current. He went to switch on a bulb hanging from interlaced

63

wires in a cloth casing, but they'd cut off the supply, so from the inter-laced wires hung the absence of light. If he found the typewriter, he could make the train to Caneiros go. Hear the stationmaster's whistle. The move-ment of connecting rods. He'd sold a lot of tickets for that train. He'd heard so much about it, but never been to Caneiros, on that trip upriver to the heart of the forest. After leaving the train, you had to walk a bit and then board some boats. 'The boats,' Arturo da Silva had told him, 'are all decorated with garlands and covered in laurel branches.' Although he'd never been to Caneiros, he adopted the project as his own. With the titbits of information he picked up along the way, he composed an enthusiastic proclamation, as if the one selling the tickets came from the fairground, had been conceived there and was speaking in the name not of the organisation, but of the river.

Since his childhood, he'd been given errands, odd jobs. Almost always as a carrier or messenger. Pombo had talked of putting a telephone in the Dance Academy.

'In case of need, Samantha. We have to modernise. What if you receive a call from King Alfonso?'

'Come on!'

'Or from a millionaire like Juan March?'

'Put him through. Start drawing up an estimate.'

While they were waiting for the telephone, which would take some time, there was young Hercules with his nimble legs and telegraphic races. Once, when he was still a little boy, he'd sat down in the Dance Academy's kitchen and fallen asleep with his head on the table. Flora came in, saw his eyes were open and spoke to him. She got frightened. Shook him. He blinked and woke up. She was on the verge of tears. Embraced him. 'Are you all right, are you all right?' 'Sure I am, I was just asleep.' 'But your eyes were open!' 'I know, but I was just asleep.'

The Shining Light premises were empty. Huddled in a corner, he fell asleep like the last time. With his eyes open. He'd acted as a messenger for the special train, but the train was unable to arrive. They'd taken every-thing. The furniture, the posters, the Ideal typewriter. All the books. It was so dark, so empty, it seemed they'd taken the place itself, the painting on

64

the walls, the words that had been spoken there. They'd taken the special train, the garlanded boats, the buffet, the orchestra. The river.

He'd managed to persuade Milagres, who never got out, even of her own self. She'd come with Mr Lens the harpooner. He'd also sold Flora a ticket. Of course they'd all travel in the carriage with Arturo da Silva and Holando. The bagpiper Polka with Olinda, his Spark. And the carriage would attract attention, on the way there and on the way back, because no less a personage than Luís Terranova had a ticket. On 18 July, they'd still been able to go and see *Melodía de Arrabal* together at Linares Cinema in Catro Camiños. Luís needed Curtis' company in the films of Carlos Gardel because Curtis had the gift of memory. Three showings were enough for him to learn the lyrics to the songs. And what's more, sometimes, at the request of the audience, the projectionist would rewind so that they could listen to the song again. Applause.

> Old quarter . . .
> Forgive me if when I evoke you
> a tear dwops

'Let's see. Try again.'

He tested him on the songs, quips and gibes but in the last department Curtis was so calm you had to wind him up constantly to get a response. Arturo da Silva, Galicia's lightweight champion, trained with him in the ring. For Terranova, Curtis was a kind of sentimental sparring partner. Luís kept throwing the double meaning of language at him because Curtis, however alert he might be, always believed what they were saying. He paid attention to the smallest things. There were times Terranova couldn't bear such confidence. He wanted to break this unbreakable friendship. But in the end he loved him like no other. Curtis looked after the best of himself. To start with, he carried the songs, all the songs, in his head. Luís' memory lived inside his friend's. And he didn't hold back on the adjectives. Portentous. Curtis' memory was truly portentous. He said it in syllables, por-ten-tous, and with his right hand rotated an imaginary bulb in the air. Or, with both hands, his fingers were orbits, a celestial globe. Such gestures were precious gifts to Curtis. He felt his memory. Was aware of carrying it and that it was comfortable. Arturo had taught him always to protect his head. His head worked for his body and so his body should protect his head. Even his legs, dancing in the ring, were taking his head into account. And there was his memory, like a child with wide open eyes, riding on him.

The idea of a child on his back was something that stuck in his mind, an image his memory had of itself after a visit.

Neto, a friend of Arturo da Silva's, had had a fight the day before in the bullring and the words hurt as they came out. His eyebrow had split open and they'd stitched it up there and then, without anaesthetic. He also had knocks and bruises and bloody ribs at each commissure of the lips and eyelids. And his nose displayed the enormous surprise of prominent things that have survived an unexpected catastrophe.

Curtis and Luís Terranova had come with Arturo and another boy from Shining Light who was a boxing fan, Pepe Boedo. They'd come to see the victor. And now they were feeling a little disappointed. According to local legend, Neto was a kind of gladiator. So they'd been expecting to hear a description of the fight, a glowing account of his exploits, but instead they were shown into a poorly lit room. The boxer had his feet in a bucket of hot water. Around his ankles, the bubbles looked like a flower arrangement, which was the only concession the scene allowed the hero. Even Carmiña, his wife, appeared to be forging the seven swords of Our Lady of Sorrow, though what she was in fact doing was hammering at a slab of ice in the kitchen. She'd bring in handfuls of irregular pieces, some like rocks, others like nails, for him to choose.

A newspaper was lying on the floor. It seemed to have been written there. Printed in that very room. The matrices of the letters scattered by Neto's broken anatomy.

CHAMPION'S CALVARY

Good headline, thought Curtis. That newspaper was a bit like a mirror. He watched Arturo da Silva pick it up off the floor and casually put it out of sight.

Neto spoke through the cut in his eyebrow. Monosyllables, short

66

sentences that pushed their way through the stitches. The rasping of words. Craters in some sentences where syllables had been punched out. Arturo da Silva administered the necessary dose. They now understood the reason for their visit was to cure, not celebrate, his victory.

'All I can see are clouds. Your face looks like a storm's coming.'

'Every cloud has a silver lining. Who was it told me that rubbish?'

'Could have been me,' said Arturo with the same irony.

'Culture'll be the end of you, Arturo. Silver lining, my foot! Are you still attending the Rationalist School?'

'In the evenings. Occasionally.'

'I liked it, but I'd doze off. Without my knowledge, as I lay snoring on the desk, old Amil would use me to talk of the evolution of species.'

Curtis and Terranova also attend Master Amil's evening classes. Arturo persuaded them. Curtis' first teacher had been Flora, the Girl, the Conception Girl. She hated being interrupted when she was teaching him letters and numbers, but then she still held her tongue. Looking back at his life, in front of the pyres, Curtis remembered the last time he'd seen Flora, when she caused an earthquake in the Academy.

'I'm leaving,' she said in the dining-room.

No one seemed to have heard anything. They carried on eating. The suspense of spoons striking the bottom of plates.

'What are you leaving?' asked Samantha.

'This. All of this. It's nothing personal.'

'Are you not happy? Do you want a bigger share?'

'It's not a question of how much. I won't sell myself any more.'

Samantha exploded, brought her fist down on the table, 'There isn't much to sell!'

'Well, what's left of me.' Flora didn't take her eyes off Samantha and spoke surprisingly calmly, 'Don't be daft. I already said it wasn't personal.'

'Who converted you? The boxer? You think he's going to change your life?'

'Don't bring him into this. You don't have to drill holes with your tongue.'

'Plenty of beach now. What happens when winter comes?'

'Carry on with your sums,' Flora would tell Curtis when she was teaching him how to multiply and had to go at the request of a client. 'Remember how many you've counted. I'll be right back.' He counted by piles. She'd taught him using beans, chickpeas, grains of rice. Whatever there was. Numbers had colour and value. But now he had nothing to hand, they'd taken Flora and he had to replace real things with downstrokes. Two by four. Two piles of four. He then discovered she'd come back as he was finishing his sums. He thought if I'm quicker at doing the sums or writing out the sentences, she'll come back sooner, she'll get rid of that untimely client sticking his nose in where he's not wanted. And so it was. The power of letters and numbers.

When he laughed, Neto complained most about the space around his eyes. It hurt him to look. So they had to be grateful to him for looking at them, and this is where he made a heroic effort. Curtis learnt that day that winning in questions of merit involves extra work. Had he lost the fight, Neto wouldn't have been under any obligation to view them with sympathy. He wouldn't have had to look at anyone and so he could have given his eyes a rest.

He had a white towel around his shoulders, his feet in a zinc bucket, while the upper light slid down the seated man to the foam's flower arrangement. They'd arrived during the afternoon. It was December. The slats of the blinds began to contain the darkness. Dampness stretched, leapt out of the bar of soap and licked the pale cracks in Neto's fingers.

Many of the scenes Arturo moved in, like the boxer Neto's house, shared one characteristic. You could witness the waking and falling quiet of things. The water in the tub was quiet. An example of sad water.

In one of the talks at Shining Light, Curtis had heard a painter called Huici refer to things falling quiet. He was distracted, thinking about the special train and the tickets he hadn't sold yet, but his memory was alert and reminded him. The falling quiet of things. Things fell quiet and spoke. A thought put simply, but not easily reached. There it was, like a buoy under the water, but you had to pull on it.

Things spoke and things fell quiet. Here were two perceptions that made a picture or a poem special. One, the speaking of things. Capturing the speaking of things, their expansive aura, their meaning, and translating it into the language of light or sounds. The other, the falling quiet of things. Their hiding. Their being absent. Their emptying. Their loss. Relating or reflecting that was another shudder. The first art caused a frontal shudder. The second, a lumbar tremor.

Just a moment. Even when things fall quiet, there are two classes of silence. A friendly silence that keeps us company, where words can be at leisure, and another silence. One that frightens. One that Rosalía de Castro, Huici told them, called 'mute silence.'

The warm water in the tub was quiet, a friendly silence. Curtis thought about the special train, the boat, the trip to Caneiros. Which would be on 2 August. The procession upriver. The waking of water.

Neto called to his wife and whispered, 'Bring the child, will you, Carmiña?'

And then they saw it. The head with the same slight lean of a globe and the relief of bruises, the physical geography of nightmares. The girl had emerged from the painful falling quiet of things. Neto took the child in his hands and gently placed her like a live poultice on the cuts and bruises.

'Her fontanel, her little head, is the most soothing.'

'Do you feel relief?'

'Relief? It's the best cure,' said Neto. 'I can't explain it. Like a skin graft.'

He rocked forwards with the child on his lap. Gestured to say something. Curtis had the feeling he was about to float an original thought, but the boxer held back the words in the reservoir of a half smile. A position his wounds copied.

At Santa Margarida Fountain, Curtis took a sip of water. An obligatory rite. Arturo da Silva said it was the best water in Coruña. There were women with buckets and children with jugs. He only wanted a sip and they let him through so he could use a spout. It seemed to him they also suddenly fell quiet. Not the water, though. The water sang out its tango.

'Go, go in front.'

He wiped his face on the back of his hand and said thanks. It was then they spoke.

'I'm not going in today.'

'Why not?'

'There's a fire in the centre. Something's happening. Can't you see the smoke?'

'What can happen that hasn't happened already?'

'Now they're burning books.'

The others' thoughtful silence next to the water's bubbling. The boy who brought the news, who's come to fill a jug for some workmen, blurts out, 'My mouth's dry!' Cups his hands, fills, sips, gurgles and then spits out. Places the jug under the spout.

They all had their reasons for being there. Something to fill. Barrels, buckets, jugs. Curtis had nothing. Only his cap of green rhombuses and dishevelled clothes that mark him out as an erratic person. This may be why the boy who told them books were burning looked at him, then at the spirals of smoke, and announced:

'They've taken the books from Shining Light as well. In a van.'

'These look good. They'll go up in no time. Shining Light!' He was looking at the bookplates, a stamp of the sun in flames. 'Hey boss! What do you think? Shining Light Centre for Studies in the Abyss.'

'Those idiots in Fontenova,' said Samos. 'That's what I call a rendezvous with destiny!'

Parallelepiped laughed. He liked it when his boss was more talkative.

'Into the abyss!'

Hercules listened without looking in their direction. Went right up to the fire, stepping on thin air, ready to jump into the ring. Saw a living book the flames were starting on. *A Popular Guide to Electricity.*

When he told her, when he explained he was going to train as a climatic electrician, she would burst into tears. Curtis wasn't sure whether to tell his mother the good news because good news made her very nervous.

She wasn't used to such things. They lived in a garret in the house in Papagaio where she worked. If she works in Papagaio, Coruña's seediest district, his mother must be a whore. No, he'd learnt to reply with great assurance, my mother's the one who fluffs up the mattresses. Later on, he learnt from Arturo da Silva there's a similar response in boxing: opening up side spaces. Throwing off balance. Empty corridors. 'My mother's not a whore. She fluffs up the mattresses. Sews the damask covers.'

'Hercules, son of a whore!'

They really lived in the attic, which had been converted into four rooms with wooden partitioning. The attic was almost too low to walk straight, but had the advantage of being the quietest place in the house. Hercules occupied one of the rooms with his mother, while three women he called aunts lived in the others. As a child, he was very well looked after, being passed from lap to lap. Afterwards, in the street, another Hercules came to life, the one he carried on his shoulders, who only came down to fight. When he was born, they'd put a skylight in the roof, in his room in the attic, and the time came when his head knocked against the glass and opened the window. Before he escaped, this was the only way Hercules had of standing up straight, with his head above the roof. He was a partial inhabitant of the skies. He sometimes stayed still for ages, sharing the condition of seagulls and cats as an architectural plume.

At night, he would open the skylight, stick out his head and not only see the beams from Hercules Lighthouse, but feel them as well. The touch of a lighthouse beam is similar to the turndown of a sheet. The circle of Hercules' life widened, he only went up to the attic to sleep, but he always had the impression this was where the centre was. He'd bring his mother sea urchins he'd collected in Orzán Creek or barnacles he'd prised off the lighthouse cliffs. These presents also made his mother nervous since she was very afraid of the sea, the sea that had swallowed the father of her son's best friend, Luís. 'He's going to be an artist,' he says. 'You should hear him sing. And imitate. Anyone from Charlie Chaplin to Josephine Baker.' *Your attention, distinguished audience. Society note. This city has just received the visit, on a liner of course, of the dancer Josephine Baker, known as the Black Pearl, and the architect Monsieur Le Corbusier, whom we shall affectionately refer to*

71

as Corbu. She changed the history of the body. He, the history of the house apparently. So you see, architects will also be famous one day. What happens, people of
the sea, if you make a body out of a house? A boat! The talented couple never left
their cabin on the Lutetia, with the complete understanding of the people of Coruña,
ever respectful of humanity's star-studded moments, meaning no disrespect to yours
truly, an expert in dockside activity, who managed to peep through the porthole. The
whole day in Josephine and Corbu's nautical suite. The dance of architecture, the
architecture of dance. Oh, I'm dizzy! He can also do the Man of a Thousand
Faces. Though he makes his own mother laugh and cry when he dresses
up as Mrs Monte and acts out the Fascinating Widow. He grows thin and
fat, like Laurel and Hardy. In order to sing, he sometimes goes to rehearse
on the hill by Hercules Lighthouse, with Curtis as sound technician.

'Sound technician?'

'You have to say whether you can hear OK when I sing. I'll gradually
go further away. Oh, and work with your right ear. It's a little bigger.'

'No, it's not. They're the same,' said Curtis, distrustful for once.

'A gift from the Universal Architect, Vicente. When I triumph, I shall
hire you. You'll be my ears. You'll earn a fortune just for listening. You'll
only have to move your hand up and down. Louder, softer. Like this.'

The last time they carried out a sound check was for Carlos Gardel's
Melodía de Arrabal.

'I'll redo that part,' said Terranova. 'Move back a bit.'

'Listen,' said Curtis. 'It's not "tear drops". It's "tear dwops", got it?
Tear dwops.'

'Got it, "tear dwops". There it goes! One tear. Goodbye, tear!'

Curtis moves off. With the sea behind him. His silhouette on the ocean's
horizon.

'Louder, louder!' shouts Curtis.

'I haven't started yet!' mumbles Terranova. Then he shouts out, 'Wait
a minute, Tough Guy, you dummy.'

'Louder!'

That night, seated on the roof under the vanes of light.

Quarter silvered by the moon

Quarter silvered by the moon

Milonga murmurs
Milonga murmurs
All my fortune

'All my fortune. Hear that, Tough Guy? Today, when we were rehearsing, I noticed something. The city has a triangle.'

'A triangle.'

'A triangle that's connected with us, where we've always played. If you look to the right, there's San Amaro Cemetery. The first vertex. If you look to the left, there's the provincial prison. The second vertex. There's no future either to the left or to the right. That leaves only one vertex. The lighthouse. The beams from the lighthouse. And what do they say?'

He already has an answer, 'They say goodbye. Goodbye! The light of emigration. Our light, Hercules!'

'To me, they don't say goodbye,' grumbles Hercules, who doesn't like to contradict his friend.

'You don't understand, Vicente. You just don't understand when you don't want to.'

They fell quiet. The intermittent beams moved the emotions like cartoons.

'You already have a legend, Curtis. You're Arturo da Silva's sparring partner. You're Papagaio's Hercules. In the first round of your first fight, you knocked your opponent over. Floored him. What was it? A side corridor? People laughing. And when he got up, you did Arturo's one-two. End of story. That's what I call creating a legend, Curtis. The tooth stuck in your glove. Which you gave back to him. "Here you go, Manlle, your tooth." You even wanted to sell him a ticket for the special train! That won't be forgotten. That'll go down in history. But as for me, I don't have a legend.'

'Yes, you do.'

'What is it?'

'That you were born in a fish basket. Among scales.'

'That's an embarrassment, not a legend.'

'I like it,' said Curtis. 'My mother too. And Flora. Everyone does.'

His father at sea. His mother, a fishwife. Alone on her rounds, she gave

73

birth down a lane and placed the child on the softest thing she had. Among hake, wrasse, sail-fluke, horse-mackerel, sardines. His mother would leave Muro Fishmarket early to sell cheap fish in the outlying villages. Horse-mackerel is humble, even in its colour. But Luís couldn't understand how wrasse could be so cheap, having all those colours. It's rainbow meat. He used to make a pause for the fish basket's contents and crack jokes like the one in the Academy, 'I'm just a poor sail-fluke, but don't think I was lucky!' Milagres, like everyone else, thought he'd made up the story about being born in a fish basket. He was certainly imaginative enough. Until one day she bumped into his mother, Aurora, the fishwife, who confirmed it was true. She'd been to Cabana and Someso and taken the path that leads to Castro by the River Lagar. There was nobody about. It was some time before anyone saw her.

'What better place for him than among the fish?'

When Milagres cracked open a sea urchin, it made her life worthwhile. Curtis knew this and at low tide he'd collect sea urchins, since he knew where they hid in the rocks, where there were likely to be lots of them, though he preferred the risk of fishing for barnacles on Gaivoteira. If there was something that worried him about sea urchins, it was getting their spines stuck in his skin. He'd made his best friends there, on the sea's stormiest coast. You didn't have to pretend. Next to the stormy sea, you had no enemies. One of those rock friends was Luís, who taught him how to treat the spines. The problem is their thickness. Unlike other prickles, such as a horse chestnut's, they don't have a sharp point. When trying to remove them, people become desperate and carve out deep flesh wounds.

'No craters,' said Luís. 'A sea urchin's spines come out by themselves. They work their way through the flesh together with the tides. Go down to the sea at low tide and they'll come out on their own.'

This was partly a joke, partly true, as always with Luís. He was almost always playing with something. With the sea as well. He played with the sea most of all. When it was calm, he'd leapfrog Cabalo das Praderías or hang off the side of Robaleira Point and provoke it, 'Oy you, beardie, Neptune, stupid dummy! Look who's here! The ghost of Terranova! The son's father. The father who died on a Portuguese doris.' 'It's a big boat,' he'd told Curtis, 'full of small vessels. Each old fisherman boards his own green launch and comes or doesn't come back.' Once a pair of Basque cod trawlers called to pick up Galician crewmen and Terranova mounted a bollard with an empty bottle as an aspergillum and in a priestly voice mimicked the words he'd once heard predicated from a pulpit, 'Work, fisherman, work! Only work dignifies a man. Do not fear the biting wind or rising sea, for death respects the brave. More men die in wine than at sea.' The crane operator felt sorry for him and moved the hook towards him. Luís hung on and the operator raised him, lowered him, swung him to the left and to the right until he began to laugh. The crane had a wooden cabin with windows and was like a house in the air, with a bed and everything. The operator had painted the name 'Carmiña' on the outside. All the cranes were named after women. There was a 'Belle Otero', an 'Eve' and, on the Wooden Jetty, a 'Pasionaria'. 'Carmiña's' operator had a shelf of books in the cabin. One section labelled 'The Day', with scientific texts, and another labelled 'The Night', with novels. The operator didn't just read. He wanted to be a scientific writer.

'Not literature. Entertaining, yes, but scientific.'

Apart from reference books, he had a folder where for years he'd stored notes and drawings he'd made and grouped together under the title 'Intimacy of the Sea'. The work in progress had to be kept a secret. The folder was concealed behind a false leather cover, which said 'Liverpool Telephone Directory'. One of those things that land up in ports. But Ramón Ponte partook of that special kind of pleasure which comes from sharing things that are supposed to be top secret. And he didn't stop smiling from the moment he opened the folder, having revealed its contents, to the moment he closed it. It had to do with the sex life of marine creatures. 'People are always talking about the sea,' he said, 'but no one's noticed the main thing. The sea is the largest nursery on the planet and possibly in the universe. One huge orgiastic bed. The scene of the most unusual acts of copulation. The most surprising arts of insemination.' He admired Élisée Reclus, his anarchic science, the union of branches of knowledge towards an understanding of natural history. To start with, you'd have to combine zoology and geography. Why do animals live in one place and

75

not another? He was appalled by people's ignorance, in this case the ignorance of many in Coruña, a maritime city, about the creatures of the sea. He read widely, there were times he spent the whole night in the cabin with an oil lamp, but the questions he returned to inevitably had to do with the reproduction of sea creatures, the same questions he'd asked himself as a child when he went fishing with his father. His fascination for octopuses. The superior intelligence in their eyes, the wisest of all invertebrates, the endless functions provided by their eight tentacles bearing suckers, from propulsion to building stone walls, ink as a defensive weapon, camouflage and mimicry.

'What you'd really like to know is how octopuses do it, right?'

'Right.'

The kind of question that, once asked, ends up involving a lot of people. Somebody in Odilo's Bar on Torre Street brought up the third arm.

'That's the octopus' penis. The third arm. As for the female, well, she has herself a good glove for that arm.'

'Yeah, but how do you know which the third arm is if there are eight of them?'

The kind of question Terranova and Curtis would end up asking when they visited the cabin on 'Carmiña' and Ponte showed them the progress he'd made as a self-taught enthusiast on his treatise entitled 'Intimacy of the Sea'. Thanks to his contacts in port, he obtained books and international publications that were translated for him at the Rationalist School. He also received illustrations and engravings he endeavoured to reproduce. Of current interest were not the techniques of reproduction, but amatory forms.

'The ones making love in a cross, at right angles to each other, are lampreys.'

'And which get the most satisfaction?' asked Terranova.

'How should I know, dumbhead? Some people are never satisfied and one day discover the third arm so to speak. I knew a woman who was only ever happy with an ear of maize. Her husband was difficult and clumsy. One thing is satisfaction, another time. As far as I'm aware, cuttlefish have the greatest stamina in the sea. Once they mate, that's it, they never stop making love. They only part for the female to spawn and then they die.'

Both Luís Terranova and Curtis were listening very carefully because they'd caught cuttlefish in their hands and now they understood why there were times these extraordinary beings with ten jet-propelled arms didn't try to escape, but gave themselves up so easily. The trouble is the well of knowledge, once opened, is never filled and Luís and Curtis wanted to know how crabs and sea cows do it, with their armour-plated bodies and legs that are pincers. 'Here's an interesting detail,' said Ponte, searching in the folder for the notes he'd made based on the experience of the Sea Club's divers, whom he called the Phosphorescents.

'Crustaceans also mate for a long time, the difference being the males carry the females on their back, take them for an amorous walk on the bottom of the bay.'

'And sea urchins?' Curtis suddenly remembered. 'How do they do it?'

'Sea urchins live together, but love at a distance,' said Ponte somewhat mysteriously as he closed the folder. 'I don't know! At this rate, I'll have to put the scientific texts under "The Night" with my novels.' He had *Haunted Shipwrecks* and *Captain Nemo's Lovers* together with copies of 'The Ideal Novel'.

All the same, the most precious object in the cabin on 'Carmiña', which the operator had set up on a kind of pedestal, was the ball from the *Diligent*. According to legend, which it would be sacrilege to question in the operator's presence, the first leather football to arrive in Coruña. The *Diligent* was a British ship. Some crewmen started a game up on deck and the ball fell on to the quay. 'As soon as it bounced off the ship, it was obvious the *Diligent*'s ball wasn't coming back. It seemed to want to stay on dry land,' said Ponte ironically. There it was, on the altar of 'Carmiña', like the orb of a strange planet.

'That's enough science for one day,' said the operator. 'Let's see, Luís, sing us that carnival tango, the one about the Columbine who put smoke from the fire of her heart under her eyes.'

Terranova was at home there. He felt relaxed in the cabin on 'Carmiña', the house that moved without ever leaving, which was simultaneously on land, at sea and in the sky. Very rarely, the wind would get up inside his head and he'd battle with the world. He seemed to be collecting all the nicknames pumped out of all the ships' bilges. You had to let him wander alone, with his hands in his pockets. When Curtis learnt this from Arturo, it was the first thing he passed on to Terranova. A human's best training is with his shadow. You have to fight with your shadow.

'Who told you that?'

'Arturo da Silva. When he was in prison, years ago, he said he spent the time fighting his shadow. It taught him a lot.'

They were on Atocha Alta, on their way to Hercules Cinema. They took up combat positions by the wall next to the entrance. Each of them ready to fight his shadow.

'But I don't have a shadow,' said Terranova in surprise.

It was true. They stood staring at Hercules' shadow, which was squat and broad-shouldered.

'Let me fight yours for a bit.'

'You're not allowed to kick. Look, like this. One two. One two.'

It was when he moved that Luís Terranova saw his slippery shadow take off from the kerb.

'There it is, there's my shadow!'

He ran and danced along the kerb, one two three, one two three, trying to stamp on it.

'Don't be stupid. You can't tread on a shadow. It won't let you.'

'With my shadow, I'll do what I feel like.'

He was also the Man of a Thousand Voices. This voice that expressed irritation, the one he'd just used with Curtis, was what he called his impulsive voice. The one his mother used when discussing price or quality. A fishwife's voice. Her firm conclusion, which there was no going back on, was that the fish was fresh so long as a woman was carrying it on top of her head.

Luís twisted around, keeping an eye on his shadow, until he saw its profile on the wall, next to the stills.

'A talented shadow! A film star.'

He picked up whatever he could find in port, most of all information.

When he earned a few coins guiding sailors around the city's lesser known parts, one of his favourite destinations was the Dance Academy. Luís had the nerve Curtis lacked. He'd promised his mother he'd take her to make a dress in the Paris-Coruña-New York style of the designer María Miramontes. He'd been there, spying on the seamstresses, having helped Vicente collect a stack of books for the Faith bookshop. María Miramontes' husband was the publisher Ánxel Casal. Rumour had it the printing machine kept working thanks largely to her needle. It was true, the day they went, the designer and seamstresses were sewing books. But Luís Terranova was interested in the models. There was one, a rayon dress with a red silk bow around the waist. Imagine wearing that! It'd make anyone look cultured.

Luís had fun in the Dance Academy. The two extremes of a nomadic existence were the cabin on the crane 'Carmiña', with Ponte the operator, and the premises in Papagaio. Sometimes, when the madame, Samantha, previously known as Porch, was having a bad day, she would treat him like a mosquito that had come inside, trying to get away from the clouds and attracted by the lights. But other times she was the one who demanded silence and asked him to sing, one of those child prodigies born with the gift of voices, a thousand voices, who could sing like a man, a woman. Or a eunuch.

'Why don't you sing *The Flea*, Samantha? Where's the flea, Samantha? It must have bred by now!'

A foul-mouthed spectator, reminding her of times that for her had not been better. Distant. Like Chelito after her stint in Lino's Pavilion. But Samantha knew how to gain respect.

'Well, now, I haven't seen the flea for some time. It must have slipped down your mother's fanny.'

It was like dropping a stone into a well. He wouldn't be back. The others laughing.

'Quiet! Manners, gentlemen, you're like a bunch of Bolsheviks! Allow me to introduce a new Gardel with all the elegance of Miguel de Molina. When he came into the world, he was taking it like an adult. Come on, boy, shut those bores up!'

He was smart as garlic. He'd already found out what a eunuch was, it wasn't the first time he'd been called one. And then he sang, not the tango Samantha had asked for, but a classic foxtrot in honour of his gracious hostess currently in her second or possibly third youth.

> There was a time woman was feminine,
> but fashion put paid to that

When Luís had a go at her, making fun of her boyish haircut, Samantha was the first to laugh. A seismic laugh that shook the whole building. Sometimes Luís would stay the night in the attic room Curtis shared with his mother. Curtis had the size and strength of two Luíses. He'd open the skylight and lift Luís up by the elbows.

'The lighthouse is shining on me! Hey, it's me, Terranova! Look, Curtis, the great spotlight of the universe is searching for me on the rooftops.'

He was next to the fire, watching the flames close in on A Popular Guide to Electricity. He missed the contact of sea urchins, all the sea urchins he'd ever touched, in his hands. He'd like to have had at least three so that he could juggle, as Arturo did during training.

'Oy you! Who's that giant in the cap?'

Some pedestrians who came across the fires on their way from Parrote or the Old City changed direction, though not abruptly, which would have been suspicious, but by walking instinctively sideways towards the arcade. In search of the identity of some shade.

The same thing was happening in María Pita Square. Anyone coming down Porta de Aires and stumbling on the fires had seconds to react in the face of something new, since they never could have imagined the smoke was coming from books. No, the city had no memory of smoke like this. A hasty or fearful walk had implications. Seen from one of the terraces or the balcony of the town hall, pedestrians traced obtuse angles in relation to the fires. A fearful walk had a certain controlled speed that deliberately avoided acceleration. The square was the same, but there'd been a change in the history of walking. In that space taken over by the flames, it was no longer possible to walk curiously or indifferently or, as one might say, normally, having a destination, but with time to spare. Or as the Italians say, *andare a zonzo*, to go for a stroll. What defines a fearful walk is that it would like to go back, but has to continue. If only there was a line the victors had drawn that could be followed. On one of the terraces is a man who can consider these things while the books are burning because he's thinking about a newspaper article he's going to write, which has nothing to do with burning books or fear, but with chironomy, the art of moving the hands melodiously and of elegant body movements in general. He's going to write about the School of Pages in Vienna, which had a Chair of Walking. And has to come up with a suitable quote. A finishing touch. A classical flourish. Lope perhaps. How was it? 'Spaniards, sons of the air'. The air of walking. He should include a local reference. Are people distinguished by the way they walk? Of course they are. Classes of walking, walking with class. Sometimes the same person changes the way they walk depending on where they are. Depending on the street. Seamstresses walking on Cantóns! Better not to be too specific. Cantón ladies. Coruña ladies on Cantóns. That is the excellence of walking. A place among the walks of the world, together with the Parisian, etc., etc. If he thinks about it, he's terrified, but he has to write an article today as if nothing had happened. So he doesn't think about it. Watching from the terrace, with this bird's eye view almost, he feels for a moment detached from what's going on right next to him, as if his legs were removed from such conflicts of walking. But suddenly one of the soldiers burning books looks up and stares at him. The journalist, a cultivated man who's going to write an article on elegance, has the strange sensation he's being watched over his shoulder. So he decides to beat a retreat. But he's not quite sure how to do it. Whether to walk backwards or to turn around.

In the docks on the other side of the square, attention is focused instead on someone who isn't moving. On that boy wearing a cap with green and white rhombuses, leafing through a book he's just salvaged from the flames.

Among those who've turned their attention to Curtis is one who's stockier than the rest. His constitution might have been called gymnastic were it not for his sagging belly. Urged on by his physique or the fact he's also wearing a cap, though his is a bonnet with a Carlist pompon, he decides to take the initiative:

'Oy you, Chocolate! Are you deaf or something?'

What he cannot know is that the use of this nickname causes a jolt to pass through Curtis, who looks to the side and then backwards. There he sees Marcelino, the black seller of ties, always elegant, always with his samples on his outstretched arm. Huici used to say the town council should pay him a salary for touring the city with that range of colours and his smile. What's the seller of ties doing by the fires? Chocolate? Chocolate's dead, one of the first to be murdered. This news had reached Curtis when he was still receiving news the first days he was shut up in the attic. That's why he looks backwards, in the hope that Antonio Naya, who worked in the Chocolate Factory and was also nicknamed Chocolate, has come to set the record straight.

'What you looking at? Hey you with the cap! You also at the circus?'

This time, Curtis feels the insults approaching like lassos. His experience from when he was a boy and first set foot in the street tells him the first and second nicknames lead to a third with greater precision.

Two come together. Two orang-utans. A black and a white one. Aaaaoouuuu! Aaou!

The big one begins to imitate the shouts and gestures of a monkey. The pompon swings on his forehead like a loose pendulum. The soldiers around him burst out laughing. Start joining in the fun. Walking on all fours. Beating their chests. Bending and waving their arms with their hands in their armpits. Egging each other on. They look as if they're dancing.

Flora, the Girl, whom Samantha out of envy rather than spite calls the Curl, even the Conception Curl, is performing an unusual dance in the Academy. On the sign, it says Un-deux-trois, but people still use the old name, the Dance Academy. All of Flora's body is involved. The stamping of her feet tells a suspense story on the drum of the stage. It seems they only stop to listen. They could be saying what's happening tonight under the same roof. For some time now, attentive spectators have known Flora's dance ceased to be part of the entertainment as her body became more refined. Though when she dances, according to Samantha, her hands trace the outline of the bodies she used to have before her body got thinner, when she was more voluptuous. She's not sickly. It's not that. When it's not raining, all day long stuck to the Coiraza wall. In the Orzán sea breeze. Like an eel drying out. In the sun, like a stone animal. And now she's fallen in with those boxing types, who could at least come and spend some money. She won't get thin! Not for nothing did the poet call her and Kif 'the Coiraza sirens, the storm's hetaeras'.

'You're happy, no doubt, but I don't like the sound of hetaeras,' said Samantha when she read *Orzán Odyssey*.

'Well, the poet, an assumed name of course,' said Flora, knowing how much Samantha went in for qualifications, 'is a doctor, no less. A proctologist!'

'Meaning?'

Flora winked. 'An arse doctor, Samantha. An expert in humanity's rarest centimetre.'

'That must be a gold mine,' said Samantha, having worked out whether she was pulling her leg or not.

'Now I knew you'd be interested.'

'I suppose poetry's not so bad,' the madame decided. 'Storm's hetaeras. Well, I've heard worse.'

The madame doesn't like Flora being so obvious, dressing up as a flamenco dancer in black and white, wearing trousers, with her hair tied up, trying out a *farruca*. All her life doing *bulerías* and now she does this. To stand out. Despite the knowledge in Coruña, where they even understand about jazz.

She's become interested in art in her old age.

But now she listens. She's up in the attic, helping Milagres give birth, and she understands the heels' Morse code.

'Isn't that Hercules, Arturo da Silva's pupil?'

'If it is, Manlle would know. Isn't Manlle here?'

'Not today. He said if it's books, he wouldn't even burn them.'

'Well, I think it is Hercules. So the son of a whore's still alive.'

'Milagres? That's not a serious name for a whore.'

'I'm not a whore. I've come for the mattresses.'

'The mattresses?'

'Yes, madam. To wash them and fluff up the wool.'

Samantha almost burst out laughing. Milagres was like a ghost repeating a password. She'd said something similar when she arrived in town. She'd come to fluff up the mattresses as well. She was going to say somebody already did that. Down on Panadeiras Street was a store with a large garden, which in summer transformed into a huge blanket of wool fermenting in the sun, with the joy of wool when it fluffs out all the weight and tiredness. The stiff fatigue of wool. It's just that Samantha, when she wasn't Samantha, what she had to fluff up was herself, her body, ferment it and mash it, on a mattress of maize husks or wood chips. Fluff and spread her legs.

'So it's Milagres. Well, I'm not exactly the Pope. Call yourself what you like.'

When she arrived, she thought about kicking her out. She seemed more dim-witted than innocent. But soon she realised she was really afraid. Samantha had lost or thought she'd lost the notion of fear some time ago, but Milagres' arrival made it obvious she hadn't. A remote, familiar thread linked them. That's why she'd been sent, with this reference. Which made Samantha furious inside. It was this detail that awoke her fear of the long anaesthesia, as if a ferret had been let loose in the burrow of her mind. There was this girl with a woman's body. A girl who'd already carried all sorts on top of her head. A girl who'd come from fear of the village to fear of the town. From one form of slavery to another. She needed some time. That was her excuse for not sending her back at the first sign of fear.

'Yes, madam. I've come to fluff up the mattresses.'

'The mattresses? The mattresses and everything else. You'll have to work from noon to night. Come on.'

She recalled the attic. Lifted the trap-door and said in the dark, 'We'll make a place for you up here. A cave in the sky.'

Here she is, biting a white cloth, exuding a dew that coats the bulb and the candle Pretty Mary, the girl who sometimes sings fados, has put in front of St Raymond Nonnatus with a coloured ribbon. Her fearful eyes are fixed on Samantha's. Her sweat is cold because she's giving all her heat to warm the room. Samantha remembers and keeps quiet. Lucky for you you're here because you'd probably be alone in the village, bleeding to death, while the house blocks its ears, with no one to watch over you, no one to give your body back its heat.

The house beats to Flora's heels, transmitting a code of dots and lines that echo up the stucco walls, climb the stairs and open the trap-doors. The dance is so close, so intense, it thunders on the roof, as if Flora were dancing in the beams from the lighthouse, which helps Milagres take her mind off the pangs inside, because the body that's coming, by all that's holy, is bigger than she is.

Milagres doesn't know, but Samantha put a key under her pillow to help during the delivery, to help open the door of life, her vagina to be more precise, though she has more faith in the infusion of rue recommended by the midwife. Because that good woman is a midwife today, but three months earlier had come as an abortionist. She couldn't believe the girl was pregnant. When she found out, when she realised that she wasn't walking strange, but was pregnant, or both things at once, strange and pregnant, the madame was amazed. Milagres had managed to conceal it under various skirts and a woollen girdle she wrapped around her body several times. Quiet, elusive, working all day, with her back turned, cooking, making the beds and going early to sleep in the attic.

'Are you cold, girl?'

'It's the dampness.'

Samantha made a lavish gesture that incorporated the length of her wardrobe for all seasons: silk dressing gown, necklace, earrings and holder for smoking Egyptians.

'Find someone who'll give you a gold necklace. Keeps you very warm.'

No doubt some of the others, those rats, knew about it. If that was so, she didn't understand the need for secrecy. What favour were they doing her by helping her to hide it? Putting a crown of thorns on her head. Samantha took any kind of disturbance in the house as a personal insult. A conspiracy against her. But she'd grown her nails. This wasn't the first eye she'd scratched out of a setback. She'd come out on top. She no longer let herself be mounted. She was the one who chose, who did the mounting, for pleasure, for money or for the hell of it. Recently she only did it for all three reasons together. Why had that silly girl done it? Why had Milagres done it?

'Call the Widow.'

They couldn't get a word out of her. The Widow, whom in private, only in private, they called the Abortionist, though she was also known as the Good Woman or the Midwife depending on the nature of her errand, well, the Widow said the child was well formed, was at least six months, and the best they could do now was lift the future mother's spirits, since they were clearly low. One arm longer than the other. By three fingers. And not give her hare to eat, otherwise the child would always sleep with open eyes. She'd said this as a joke. She didn't often joke. Every remark she addressed to the women was a fathom in length and always meant something it was worth remembering. One day, she told them very seriously that the womb was a 'sacred chamber'. Infections were the cause of great mortality. So she spoke of hygiene as of a creed.

'You've a surprise coming your way, Samantha.'

'What surprise?'

'Ah!'

It was Pombo who said this. He was her confidant, the one who made her laugh, who never engaged in conspiracies and who made a fuss of her, because one thing she could not allow was a drop in her spirits. He also looked after the Academy's money and kept an eye on things. He liked to say he was their *arma mater*. He loved crêpe shirts, bracelets and shoes with a raised insole, though his speech was more aesthetic than his dress sense or he dressed his wardrobe up in language, so his shoes always came from the Kingdom of Morocco or the Republic of Dongola, the names he gave the two shoeshops in Orzán. If anyone called him a queen, if it was a friend, he'd correct them by telling them he had both sexes, María Pita's and Hercules'.

'You mean you're a hermaphrodite, like snails?'

'You don't know much about snails. Snails are only hermaphrodites when they're on their own.'

'Rumpy-Pumpy!' Samantha said to him in a reproachful tone, a name only she was allowed to use.

Pombo's eyes and ears were an extension of Samantha's senses. He swore the same thing had happened to him. He hadn't known Milagres was pregnant. It was he who then took care of her, following the Widow's advice. The last days before the delivery, he cooked for her. He went to the Chocolate Factory on San Andrés Street and returned with some bars of Pereiro chocolate and some dried cacao husks for making tea. So he was the one who lifted Milagres' spirits. Who, on the night of the birth, prepared the concoctions of rue and marshmallow, just when Flora was winding up her clock of intestines, the clack of her heels on the Academy's stage.

'You miss out on everything and now you come to me with this nonsense. Tell me, what's the surprise?'

'A surprise, Samantha, darling, a surprise.'

She murmured, 'You exhausted my capacity for surprise.' And he made off down the corridor, wagging his hips from side to side. 'They say that tango goes to great lengths, which is why it was forbidden by Pius the Tenth.'

As if the dance enabled her to escape, guided by her chiselling heels, Flora left the stage, crossed the small hall of the Dance Academy and ran up the stairs to the first floor, where the clients' reception rooms were; then up a narrow staircase to the second floor with Samantha's suite, Pombo's room and another two rooms which the eight permanent women shared. At night, when there was a show, Pombo would give way to anyone accompanied by a man and to any on their own whom he called *nymphs*. Finally up a stepladder. Leading to the attic. The trap-door was open and it reminded Flora of a window into another, more intimate room with the veiled light of lamps and botanical shades, where people confessed to

87

indiscretions, since she could hear laughter and whispers, when what she'd been expecting was torn flesh and fresh lamentation.

Flora goes up to Milagres. She'd tried to help her by dancing. She's not alone, but her eyes are closed, her eyelids swollen, with bluish rings around them.

The child, in the Widow's hands, resembles another fragment of solitude. The Widow doesn't like him being so quiet. Hangs him upside down and slaps him to get him crying.

'What are you doing?' asks Pombo, who's more nervous than the rest.

'What I have to,' replies the Widow.

The child cries calmly, at measured intervals, as if he thought about each one. The cries sound distant, in the orbit of the seagulls' calls and the mew of cats climbing down from the roof. The fauna of the lighthouse beams. For seconds. People aren't generally prepared to let the onomatopoeias of night fill the void. And there's lots to say.

'Is he like that?' asks Samantha.

'Like what?'

'That big. And that ugly.'

'No. He'll change with the light,' answers the midwife ironically.

'No. It depends on the day. Honestly, Samantha, for a worldly woman you do ask some silly questions,' says the Widow, holding the child now with a look of satisfaction, as if she'd modelled him with her large, miniaturist's hands.

'He's a chocolate-coloured mark on his back. The cacao husks!' remarks Pombo, stroking the child with his fingertips. 'A Coruñan through and through, Samantha.'

'Give the child to his mother,' Flora intervenes. 'You're like a bunch of parrots.'

'Popinjays,' Pombo corrects her.

'That's what you get for not bringing her proper chocolate.'

Flora was too late.

'Proper? Wasn't the chocolate good, Milagres? Was it or was it not good?'

'That's what you get for staring at posters of the Charleston dancer

Harry Fleming,' added Samantha, fishing for information, to see if anyone would say something about the child's father.

'You're not wrong,' said the Widow with a knowing wink.

'What was the name of that jazz orchestra?' Samantha suddenly asked. 'The one that played with kitchen utensils in Marineda Hall.'

'What kitchen utensils? You're still on about Monti's *Cardash*.'

'*Csárdás* actually,' Flora pointed out.

'Don't spoil my lapsus, Miss Academy,' said Pombo, who was always at odds with Flora. 'And forget about who the boogie-woogie was, Samantha. The question now is whether or not to take the child to the orphanage before daybreak.'

'I do believe I recognise that giant. Isn't that . . . ? Didn't he carry Arturo da Silva's gloves for him?'

Some of them only hear the crack of a proper name. A name that causes a certain commotion. The Falangists next to their stocky companion, the one who asked the question, copy him and place their hand like a visor against the sun to see better, though they're not all looking in the same direction, where Curtis has stopped, but are turning, taking in the panorama, the roofs as well, as if that name evoked a vague feeling. Not a person exactly, but something in the air. Curtis knows he mustn't move. He's the hare. He's the one with the wider field of vision. He's helped by the sun, which has put the others in a blind spot. That's why he does well not to move. A sudden movement would give him away and hasten events. 'If you're going to fight in the open air, with natural light,' Arturo da Silva had told him, 'the first thing you have to do is seek the sun's help. Make sure the sun is on your side.'

Samos comes up and also shields his eyes.

'What's that about Da Silva?'

'No. I'm not talking about Da Silva. I'm talking about that guy over there, next to the first fire. He seemed to me to look a bit like . . . Isn't that Papagaio's Hercules? The one who floored Manlle. Da Silva's sparring partner. At least, I thought so.'

'Fear everything and you'll believe anything.' Samos pats his robust colleague, the one who's permanently on the lookout. 'Fear everything and you'll believe anything.'

'You know what, Samos? Confidence died of old age, but suspicion is still alive.'

One of the places Coruña's boxers used to train was called the Sunhouse. It was built as a TB clinic and, for a time, also had a small surgery where women working as prostitutes could go for a check-up. The Sunhouse, next to Orzán Sea and very near Germinal Library. On stormy days, foam from the waves would beat against the windows of the gym. The first time Curtis set foot in the Sunhouse, the sea was up, it was a grey day, he had the contradictory sensation he was entering a dark place, a large whale's belly, where men seemed to lash out at each other blindly. He didn't think of a cave that day, but of a whale. And what made him think of a whale's belly were the gloves. Seeing a pair of gloves in the dark, lying on the edge of the ring.

They were calling to him. Calling to his hands. Made of leather-coloured leather. An animal shine. He didn't make any calculations. He went for them as for a find that belonged to him. He grabbed them and took to his heels. Ran first along Orzán Beach. His legs joined in the fun with his hands, which were carrying something that would be for them and for them alone. They'd get inside the gloves and never let go of them. To start with, all he could hear was the sea, the waves lapping his feet. This helped him to run, it was a familiar sound of encouragement. He chose not to look back. When he reached the cliffs, he'd hide the gloves and act all innocent, as if he were fishing for sea urchins. Which is why he was surprised when he heard, but did not see, someone coming up beside him, on the side that wasn't the sea. Without breaking into a sweat, without apparent effort, with enough breath left over to ask, 'Where are you off to with my gloves, boy?'

His hands fizzled out. Now the gloves were heavy, an unbearable weight, and his legs turned to jelly as they sank in the sand. He threw the gloves into his pursuer's face and jumped over the rocks until he reached the pools left by the sea at low tide.

'What did you want them for?' shouted the boxer.

'To go fishing for sea urchins,' he replied. And muttered, 'What a question! The worst of all failures, having to provide explanations.'

The other fell about laughing, 'That's the best joke about boxing gloves I've heard. Gloves for fishing. Get down from there!'

'No. I made a fool of myself. That's punishment enough.'

'Not to fight. Boxers don't fight. At least not with sea urchins. What's your name?'

He was annoyed with himself, 'Some people call me Hercules.' And he felt like adding, 'I'm from Papagaio,' for the other to see he was of wild stock and not just a turd on the staircase.

'Hercules? How about trying on the gloves?'

'No. Not today. Another day perhaps.'

'Well, if you come, ask for Arturo da Silva.'

Arturo da Silva? Curtis didn't wait until the following day. He gave Arturo a twenty-yard head start and then followed him to the Sunhouse. When he arrived at the gym, he saw the gloves where they were before, in the corner of the ring. Waiting.

Vicente Curtis had heard lots of stories from sailors. Not just from sailors, but theirs were his favourites. And he was their favourite as well. In time, Curtis learnt to distinguish between the trades and occupations of those visiting the Dance Academy. On Sundays, some stockbreeders came, possibly in the same suit they'd wear to a wedding or funeral. Several details in their appearance soon gave them away. One above all. The rebellious nature of the knots in their ties. Stockbreeders' ties had a life of their own and they, not their owners' hands, seemed to decide when to loosen or tighten. Then there were their nails. Their sideburns and moustaches, if they had them, were carefully groomed, yes, but appeared to shy away from precise measurements and leave a gap, like a furrow, between fallow and arable land. As for their nails, they seemed resigned to belonging to themselves and to the earth as well. They were unlike any others and what Curtis found most strange is that they were unlike each other, the nails of one hand, like small stone axes or slates embedded in flesh. They didn't wear a suit, the suit wore them. Curtis didn't like these men who came from villages with a false modesty, a grimy shyness. A state that didn't last long. Alcohol soon transformed them into braggarts and produced a mean, greedy monster. In the case of sailors, speech came before presence. Words hauled them in on threads. People who listen are a blessing for sailors on land. And Hercules was there to listen.

During the afternoon, in the long summer hours, when the Academy's only client was Monsieur Le Clock, the odd sailor would drop by. Most of the women used the afternoon break to sleep in time's embrace, under a quilt of shadows. And the sailor would look around in search of someone to listen and light on Hercules' open eyes. Because while he also was in time's embrace, even when he slept, his eyes stayed open.

'Not completely, but a little bit, yes.'

'That's good,' declared Pombo. 'For someone like him, that's good. He needs them on both sides, like a hare, all the better to see with.'

'You've got them on both sides,' said Flora, 'like a sentry.'

'Get over it, girl. At a certain age, you become invisible. Transparent. They can't see you.'

'Even with raised insoles?'

'Hey Samantha! Will you go and see if that pussy's laid an egg?'

'The orphanage? No one's leaving here for the orphanage,' said Samantha and for once her authority and sentiment seemed to coincide. 'The only thing I'm sorry about is I promised Grande Obra a baby Jesus for their nativity scene.'

'And what's wrong with the child?' asked Flora.

'You're impossible to talk to,' said Samantha. 'He's ugly. And that mark on his back . . .'

'It's no problem,' said Flora suddenly, looking very serious. 'He's been offered to the Union as well.'

'The Union has a nativity scene?'

'And an Epiphany parade.'

'Grande Obra asked first,' said Samantha. 'The Bolshies have enough with their revolution.'

'They're not Bolsheviks. They're anarchists.'

'Like me. From here on down.'

'You're a brute the size of a plough.'

'I'm from the village, like you. And proud of it.'

'I'm not from the village,' said Flora. 'I was washed up by the sea.'

'Now listen here, you . . .'

'The important thing,' the Widow intervened, 'is to have a godfather who can say the Creed. So the child doesn't stammer.'

'In Italy, there's a baby Jesus who's a girl.'

'And in Vinhó he's dressed up as Napoleon.'

'Aren't we international!' Samantha exclaimed, while Pombo started singing a Peruvian carol:

> Here comes the Mayor's child
> Here comes the Christ-child

It may have been the effect of having to draw back an entrance curtain, but many of the stories the sailors told Curtis or, to be more precise, told his open, attentive eyes were about things that turned up in whales' bellies. Some brought not only the stories, but the things as well. Like the harpooner Mr Lens.

There were two big whaling companies in Galicia, the Spanish Whaling Company and the Spanish Crown Society. Behind both of them was the influential industrialist Massó. One of the factories was in Caneliñas, in Cee, with the whaling ships based in Coruña Harbour. Lens of Arou, the harpooner, knew nothing about Massó, but a lot about whales. They were his life. The first time he saw a whale was on top of a rock on Lobeira Beach. He was fishing for octopuses with an ear of maize. The rope, the stone, were an extension of his arm. Despite all their intelligence, and Lens' father said they were like people, octopuses had a weakness, an irrepressible desire to latch on to an ear of maize. And that ear was part of Lens' body, a third arm. He once caught an octopus as big as himself. When it saw itself out of the water, betrayed by that alluring, golden ear of maize, the octopus, which was huge on the Lens scale, infuriated by such skulduggery, enveloped the boy's body, and face as well, with its eight arms. But Lens wouldn't let himself be dragged out to sea. With the octopus stuck to his head, he ran to where his father was and when he finally got rid of it, little Lens bore the mark of its suckers and had been completely drained. 'It was the octopus' revenge,' he told Hercules. 'It sucked out everything I had. I didn't have much education, but what I did know, I lost. I had to start from scratch. Put it all back. The names of people and things. Every single word. The whole lot.' A whale was his unit of measurement. Especially when talking about emotions. Joy, when great, was of whale-like proportions.

'How many whales have you killed?'

'The joy is not in killing them, but in watching them emerge. Seeing a whale emerge. It's the kind of joy that doesn't fit inside your body. Pain's like that as well. The trouble with a great sadness is that it doesn't fit inside your body.'

Hercules remembered this unit of measurement the harpooner taught him on afternoons in the Academy. Real joy and pain were too big to fit inside your body. It can be very painful to see a giant man cry. He'd seen this. Harpooners collapsing with sadness on the table, smashing glasses and bottles. Their pain was as heavy as a whale. But a weak, scared woman can also carry tons of pain on top of her head. A premonition. A whale.

'And your mother?' asked Lens of Arou.

'My mother? My mother cooks,' replied Curtis hastily, 'sews and fluffs up the wool inside the mattresses.'

'I know that. But where is she?'

'She went to buy some damask,' Hercules lied.

'Some damask?'

'For the covers. She has a thing about damask.'

Vicente Curtis liked the harpooner. But when it came to his mother, he tried to keep men at a distance. The harpooner was twice the size of Milagres. Even Curtis had been too big for her. When he emerged from her belly, he left an empty space in what the Widow called her 'sacred chamber'.

'The birth,' warned the Widow, 'will be followed by a melancholy air. An insatiable wind that preys on newly delivered mothers.'

'What do we have to do?'

'It's a crafty, human wind that searches out gaps in people and likes to plant sadness in the space left by the baby. Keep the child always close at hand. What the wind wants is for her to hate the child so that it can take his place. You have to love her. And the child as well.'

'And who's going to love me?' asked Samantha.

'Some questions in life just don't have an answer,' said Flora.

'That was a good one,' said the madame. 'I won't hold it against you.'

Milagres had the child always with her. Not just tied, grafted on to her body. On her back or front, in a series of girdles. When he started walking and disappeared from view, she let out a whine that was like a cat or seagull mewing. Later, when they made the skylight and Curtis embarked on his existence as a head popping out of the roof, the cats and seagulls were like distant company, suspicious residents. He realised how similar they were at night. A crossbreed of feline gulls and cats about to fly. Sleepwalking fauna for a sleepless city.

Curtis would have liked the roof fauna to come down and sniff around the books' remains. Something to fill the void. Even the books burning badly, slowly being consumed, seemed to be waiting for somebody. Cats and gulls, rooftop plumes, gull-like cats and cat-like gulls remained still, taxidermic, as in an experiment to dispense with the atmosphere.

If only Milagres was with the harpooner now. Curtis had discovered that Mr Lens' size was proportional to the stories he stored inside. If anyone could exorcise the void, it was the harpooner. To start with, following his mother's instructions, Curtis provided a barrier. The harpooner would arrive in the Academy at some sleepy hour of the afternoon, when even Pombo took a break, leaving Curtis in charge, practising his scrawl in the light of a green lamp. He would ask after Milagres, the boy would come out with some excuse, sounding increasingly unconvinced, but the harpooner never kicked against the pricks. He'd deposit part of his store of stories in the boy, leading his body to become normal while Curtis' grew. There was not a drop of fat in the harpooner's storytelling, it was all lean meat.

'Do you know where all the umbrellas the wind takes in Galicia end up? On the same boat.'

'Always the same one?'

'That's right. An old container ship, which acts like a magnet for umbrellas. About two hundred miles out to sea. It's called the *Mara Hope*. From here, it goes to Rotterdam and sells them on in bulk.'

He then told him how things from the sea rain on earth and things from the earth rain at sea. In Galicia, in the middle of winter, a shower of pilchards had fallen inland from a cloud of seaweed. The cloud had burst, like someone opening a net in mid-air. Thousands of small, silvery sardines falling on the rye. Which is why the fields of Courel sometimes smell of the sea. While the woods are covered in a moss of seaweed with starfish hanging from the treetops. These are the so-called animate waves which rise in gale-force winds, turning into pregnant clouds. 'Don't tell me you haven't heard of animate waves and pregnant clouds. Isn't there an old newspaper lying around?'

'It's true what he says about umbrellas,' intervened Pombo, who'd finished his break. 'The other way round too. Have you never seen a flock of cod heading in the direction of Terra Cha? And in Riazor Stadium the other day it bucketed down caps with the name "Numancia" embroidered on them.'

'I can only talk about what I've seen,' said Mr Lens a tad suspiciously.

'Honest to cod,' insisted Pombo.

Curtis enjoyed this duel. Things to-ing and fro-ing by air and sea. They vied not to tell the truth, but to invent the biggest story. Before working as a harpooner in the North Atlantic, Lens had spent many years in the Gulf of Mexico and the Caribbean.

'Never trust the calm,' he said unexpectedly. 'It's what I'm most afraid of. The calm. You know, when nothing happens, there's a dead calm, the sea like a plate.'

Curtis shook his head.

'At the centre of a hurricane! What they call the area of calm. Don't forget it. In the area of calm, be alert, in a state of emergency.'

Curtis thought he heard Pombo blink. Alert. His tongue tickling.

'You can be on the boat with nothing moving. Everything completely still. When suddenly, swept offshore by the hurricane, something falls. What you'd least expect. Because it's one thing,' he said sarcastically, 'for it to rain a tin of sardines in the mountains the day Pombo goes for a picnic and quite another for it to rain, as I have seen – I have seen! – a flock of sheep on board a ship, carried along by a hurricane.'

'Sheep with umbrellas, I suppose,' commented Pombo ironically.

'Only when the flock has a shepherd. Then they fall with a large umbrella, of the type called "seven parishes". In the Caribbean, I've seen it rain a whole chapter, a Mexican chapter.'

'It's normal for a flock to have a shepherd of souls,' added Pombo, 'and fall right on top of a pagan from Death Coast.'

'What's frightening is to be in the area of calm and think the worst is over,' said Lens seriously, ignoring Pombo's jokes. 'That's it, you think the worst is over when in fact it's just beginning. You think the hurricane's gone and you're in the eye of the storm.'

His tone now smacked undeniably of the truth. The ship's name was right. The *Mara Hope*.

As they listened, even Pombo's mocking hemisphere was eclipsed. Whether in suspense or under the force of Lens' memory, the silence in the Dance Academy had acquired the sound of an electric hum, of sultry heat, around the green lamp, which Pombo's long eyelashes had been drawn to.

'It's terrible what you've endured,' Lens continued. 'Everything's in disarray, the boat and your bones. And then you find yourself under the illusion that it's all over. Because the other boats you thought had foundered in the storm are coming towards you, safe and sound. A horizon of ships. You're dumbstruck by such a miracle. Merde! Shit! Verdammt und zugenäht!'

The harpooner, like many other maritime residents and guests, practised the art of saying ugly words in foreign languages for them to sound a little distinguished. A kind of crude elegance.

'What happened?' asked Pombo on tenterhooks, he who'd heard so much.

'Not a single ship. It was a decapitated forest. Bits of forest torn to shreds which, after the storm, came together at sea and interlaced roots to hold up trunks and crowns like the masts of sailing ships, with nature's will for weaving tapestries out of tatters. It's normal in shipwrecks to find a brotherhood of remains. But this was as big as the horizon itself.'

The harpooner's enormous hands ordered the geology of earth on the table's tectonic plates. He took a slice out of the table with the corner of his right hand and lifted up a chunk of Yucatan. 'It was this wooded territory coming towards us, towards our ship in the area of central calm.'

'Was that before or after you had cataracts?' asked Pombo at last, unable to control himself.

'What?'

'The wood moving at sea.'

'I'm talking here to Hercules. Anyone else can shut up or provide tobacco.'

'Portuguese blond,' said Pombo in a conciliatory tone, holding out a cigarette.

'To start with, we thought no,' Lens continued, 'they were boats, an entire fleet that had been reunited. Because we could hear shouts as well. Isolated, distant. Unintelligible. Sometimes they sounded like hurrahs of joy carried on the wind, others like cries of agony and anguish filling the sea with fear. We approached with our hearts in our mouths. No, they weren't boats. This was no vast fleet of salvaged ships. As we got closer, our eyes were forced to accept something even more fantastical. What was coming towards us was the forest. The sea had gathered strips of wood, drifting timbers. The masts we descried in the distance were in fact large trees, huge mahoganies. Then we heard an orchestral guffaw. A spine-chilling peal of laughter. All of that nature was making fun of us. Laughter can be truly terrifying when you don't know where it's coming from. Until the mystery was revealed. The trees had their birds in them. A colourful display of parrots, orioles and long-crested cockatoos. Someone shouted, "The birds are warning us!"

But it was too late. When we tried to turn around, the boat was surrounded by the forest.'

'And what happened?' asked Curtis uneasily.

'The forest gobbled us up. Swallowed us whole.'

'That's more or less what happened to me with the wolf,' said Pombo after the requisite pause to take a swig.

'What happened to you if you never left this hole?'

'I'm from the mountains, and proud of it. Bloody mountains! One freezing winter's day with a lot of snow, the height of a man at least, I was sent with a message down by the border and bumped into the wolf on my way. It stared at me. I stared at it.'

Everyone remained silent. Pombo marked a bony kind of time by rapping the bar with his knuckles.

'And what happened?' asked Lens finally.

'It ate me.'

Pombo adjusted the knot of his necktie and stared at the harpooner artistically. 'What did you expect? It ate me! That's right. The wolf ate me.' And he waited before delivering the final blow, 'Just as the forest ate that ship of yours.'

'You don't know what the area of calm is,' replied the harpooner painfully.

Some of the fishing boats still have their festive pennants. The vessels haven't left port for a month. Haven't been back out to sea. The sirens sounded on the feast of Our Lady of Mount Carmel. A few days later, with the military coup, they sounded again. A day and a night. Without stopping. In the Academy's attic, Curtis heard them one after the other. He couldn't see. He could hear. He heard shots and sirens. Shots against sirens. For a time, the shots stuttered, as if sliding down the sirens' greasy hair. The shots increased, the sirens diminished. The sound of the sirens was round, slow, fleshy, labial. The shots were straight lines which multiplied, pulling on each other, sieving space. Eventually there was only one siren left. Very clear. In long hoots. The shots fell silent. Seemed to be listening as well, in surprise. Then there was a loud volley. The death throes

99

of the last sound being riddled with bullets. Lots of the pennants are frayed, bitten. The atmosphere around the burning books is full of holes. Perforated.

The smoke was looking for somewhere to hold on to, to clamber up. In the upper part of his body, Curtis felt the tickle of its creepers and suckers. Climbing up his face. Invading his nose. Catching on his eyes. Sealing his mouth.

Another day, the harpooner had told him how a sandstorm had consumed paradise in a single night. A place called Tatajuba in Brazil. Curtis realised he wasn't making it up, he'd been there as he said, from the way he went into details. He even made a pencil drawing on the marble of the kitchen table. How well the harpooner could draw America! His map of Europe was pretty good too. On the Iberian Peninsula, he took great care over the twists and turns of the Galician coast. But America came out from north to south as if by memory. He put a cross to show where paradise had disappeared overnight, eaten up by the sand. This is Tatajuba. This is Camusin. He'd been walking from Camusin, all along the beach, because he'd heard what a paradise it was. On the way, he slept on the beach and woke up to see a sow with piglets bathing in the sea. Or else they were eating fish. Because the fish there could be caught by hand. Skate, swordfish, mullet and porpoise, all jumping about. A Galician fisherman's dream. Pigs swimming and fish jumping in the air. When he reached Tatajuba, it really was paradise. The following day, it no longer existed. A sandstorm had swallowed it up overnight. What Curtis remembered best about the sandstorm that buried paradise in one night was how the harpooner told him people stopped talking. The sand set their teeth chattering and drowned out their words. And that's when the men and women who'd worked so hard, with such devotion, gave up.

Curtis hadn't read many books. All the burning books had something to do with him. They were books he hadn't yet read. But this one had clearly belonged to him since he'd set foot on the scene. In the end, he picked up *A Popular Guide to Electricity*.

'Hey you, put that back!' The stocky soldier hadn't let him out of his sight and this time he really did take out his pistol.

'Now, now, calm down!' said Samos. 'It's just a clown looking for some Tarzan comics. Which one of them would dare show his face?'

Arturo da Silva used first to write out his texts by hand. He had curious handwriting. It was very neat, as if the act of writing, though it called for action, or perhaps because of this, was incompatible with speed. Given the size of his fingers and the heavy machinery of his hands, it must have been a real effort. And the truth is Dafonte, Holando, Félix Ramón, Varela, Curtis, Terranova, Marconi, Leica, Seoane, all the new group of boys who visited the Shining Light premises, some of whom contributed to *Brazo y Cerebro*, tried to make room when he was using the table to write, forging a territory with his bulk, his head close to the paper and his whole body focused on moving that caravan of words like beasts of burden forwards against all the odds. To start with, the paper had the texture of rocky ground or was treacherous as a marsh. A few words opened the way, like tracks, sleepers or stepping-stones. They were the eyes and feet of those running behind.

It helped him to hear a voice, a voice like that of Amil, the teacher at the Rationalist School, tugging at his fingers.

Amil, who always talked to them of Heraclitus and Parmenides. Life, the course of the universe, all explained as a river. A river which is never the same, which is always changing. You cannot step into the same river twice. A changeless river, a river which is always the same. Heraclitus and Parmenides are so familiar he's surprised no one in the city is named after them. They're in the ring. Heraclitus constantly on the go. Parmenides solid as a rock.

You cannot step into the same river twice, he wrote. It wasn't highly original, but he was pleased with this beginning. It would allow him to talk of that point in history, of everything that was happening, based on the trip upriver due to take place on 2 August.

Reality is constantly changing. We can say it's never the same, as Heraclitus said of the river. Heraclitus was right, but Parmenides wasn't wrong. He maintained the river was always the same. Humanity flows like a river. We think everything's changing, moving, progress is driving history. But it may be an illusion. Parts of the river are stagnant and lifeless.

He created a circle with his arms. And out of that circle an article slowly took shape. As he typed it up, his body imitated its movements.

'I'm going to call it "The River of Life and Death".'

'What river's that? The Nile? The Ganges?'

'No, stupid. The river that passes through my village.'

He typed on the Ideal, using a couple of fingers. Above it, a bare bulb hung from interlaced wires in a cloth casing. As his fingers danced over the keys, Curtis couldn't help seeing Arturo's exploratory movements inside the ring. On tiptoe, as if he were skipping. His whole body behind the fingers that were typing. Gradually warming up. Now jumping by themselves. When the metal bars got caught up, he took a deep breath. He lived the construction of each sentence in its literalness. As he sought each letter, his fingers an extension of his eyes, what registered on the paper was for the first time. For example, when he wrote 'elevation', what Arturo did as he pressed the key was add everything the word could lift. And so, when he moved on to another sentence, his final flourish, the one he'd thought long and hard about, the one that said 'The river flows inside of us and life is the art of hydrokinetics', then he got a little nervous, excited, and pressed down hard with the fingers of a dowser searching for a spring. He found a patch of hard ground, the bars got entangled, the carriage got stuck.

'It's no problem,' said Dafonte, who understood the Ideal best. As he repaired the machine, he looked at what he'd written. 'What's hydrokinetics?'

'Something to do with reading in water. I came across it in *The White Magazine*. It's a naturist idea.'

'You'd better explain it.'

He nodded in time to his index finger pressing the 'x' key and deleting what he'd written. At first, he didn't like to delete things, but then he started to enjoy it. The 'x' was a curlew leaving its footprints on the sand. He thought as well about the pleasure of stepping in others' footprints, filling their mould on the beach. He deleted. X xxxxxxxxxx. Curlews. Sandpipers. Plovers. Redshank. Bunting.

* * *

Curtis looks up from the book. He's already learnt there are different kinds of heat. Sensible heat, latent heat and specific heat. Specific heat is the most important, technically speaking . . .

'Well, blow me down if that isn't Papagaio's Hercules. Arturo da Silva's pupil. Of course it is.'

They move towards him, with diligence, forming a circle.

The silence is broken by the sound of turning wheels. Everything seems to be waiting. The gulls adorning the pinnacles of roofs and masts. The sound increases, turning on the stones. Curtis and the Falangists look towards the Rey building on Porta Real. There are the caryatids with flowers in their hair, supporting the balconies. Women's heads holding the house up.

Then the horse appears. It was a wooden horse making all that noise. The horse Leica kept in his studio on Nakens Street. His father walks in front, with the travelling photographer's tripod camera over his left shoulder and his inseparable cane in his other hand. Leica pulls on the pretty piebald horse, which today looks like a natural animal, part of the caryatids' modernist landscape.

'When are you taking that horse out?' Curtis had asked him not long before. He couldn't understand why he kept it shut up in his studio. It would draw the crowds in Recheo Gardens. The finest photographer's horse. And Coruña was a city that had lots of wooden and papier-mâché horses. It even had a horse factory at the bottom of the hill of Our Lady of the Rosary. But the horse Carirí, the horse that had come all the way from Cuba, was quite a horse. 'When are you taking it to Recheo?'

'I'm not. It was my father who brought it from Cuba. The whole lot came together. Cameras and horse. I think it was the horse he liked most. But I don't want to be an instant photographer. I want to take artistic photos. Why don't you have it?'

The page of an illustrated magazine nestled at Antonio Vidal's feet the day of his departure in July 1933 on the quay in Havana. This lost, flying page, which had reached the end of the pier, along the ground, and was about to fall into the sea, but suddenly gained height, spun in the air and came towards him as if it had found a direction. It landed at his feet, he didn't have to harpoon it, spear it with the tip of his cane.

Spirals of smoke rising from their coquettish lips

He felt the smoke had nothing to do with tobacco or the picture of a happy life, but was a message in itself, aimed at him, rising from the paper like a swift climbing plant. He could read so well because a large part of the surface was taken up with photos of women's faces. He couldn't tell them apart. They were smiling, but each one seemed to contain a mystery. At this distance, for a man who, to walk, had to overcome his legs' resistance and whom others were beginning to regard as a watch running slow, all the smiles were as one before disappearing into the cone of the paper wrapped around the cane.

Farewell, Havana.

The page searching for him now in Coruña has other concerns. Mayarí shakes the sheet in an effort to get rid of it. While he finds it difficult to resist paper flying in front of him, today he's on another mission. To reach the coach as soon as possible and save his son. The son pulling on the wooden horse. Ever since he set eyes on that horse, he's always trusted it.

He tries to shake it off, but now it's the page that doesn't want to let go and enfolds him. Antonio Vidal's attempt to shake it off, the rotatory movement of his arm, a slap in reverse, seems to provoke the large sheet, which sticks to him, holds on with the desperation of someone who doesn't know how to escape. So he has to stop. Put down the camera.

'Come here,' he says to the sheet of paper. 'Calm down. The world's such a big place, didn't you have anywhere else to go?'

A photo. It catches his eye because it's the only photo and the scene is very real. It looks as if it's been taken from where he's standing. And what can be seen in the background of the photo is what he can see as well. The fires. The burning books, but also the Falangists who are burning them, making the Fascist salute. He now understands why the sheet clung to him. It was fleeing from the flames.

'Hey you, photographer!'

*   *   *

On seeing the cameras and horse, everyone seemed to lose all interest in the boy next to the fire.

Hercules, meanwhile, was focused on something else.

Yes, he'd swear it was him, Terranova, with his hands in his pockets. Now he takes out his hands and puts them to his mouth. For God's sake, don't shout, don't give yourself away. What's he doing? Whistling with his fingers. Yes, it could only be him. The whistle attracts the Falangists' attention again, puts them on their guard. They peer through the clouds of smoke to see where it's coming from. What's that idiot up to? Now he wears the horn in the artistic style of Lucho, maker of Andalusian costumes. This apparition, whistle, ornamental gesture with the horn, upsets everything. Curtis takes a few steps back and performs an unusual manoeuvre. He takes to the air, jumps over the largest fire and enters the open corridor.

'Have you got my ticket?' shouts Terranova.

'Run! They're shooting.'

They leg it up Luchana Alley, Rego de Auga, Anxo Alley, Florida Street. If they can reach Ovos Square, they'll be safe. Curtis has thought of a hiding place. The store on Panadeiras Street. It's summer. The garden will be covered in fluffy wool.

'Who are they shooting at?'

'Us!'

'These bastards can't take a joke.'

They didn't find those two. They disappeared after Ovos Square. What does it matter? All that fuss over a couple of clowns! The stocky soldier likes to boss everyone around and is ready for anything. Trigger-happy. Dagger-happy too. The one who's going to be a judge is smarter, but he's a bit soft next to the other, the big guy, always on the lookout. Who knows what he'll get up to tonight with that vocation? Because tonight, you can tell, is going to be terrible. Apparently they've got Huici, the inventor of coloured waistcoats, in the barracks of the Falange. But rumour has it tonight they're going after the last Republican governor's wife. The librarian Juana Capdevielle. They shot him on 25 July and they already sent her death flies. She lost a child in her womb. It's her turn tonight.

They're going with the intention of killing her several times over. It's something that has to come from the top, from the so-called Invisible Tribunal, the Delegation of Public Order, whose director is Mr González Vallés. This evening, Mr Vallés' daughter will preside over a friendly football match to be played in Riazor between a team of Falangists and another of crewmen from a Third Reich warship. They'll go for the librarian early in the morning. It's not his turn to go out hunting tonight, so Parallelepiped is going to try to slip away, to skip it. He gave the river something to eat from Castellana Bridge. Yep, tonight he'll skip it. Now, for instance. The others were busy having their photographs taken. Their portraits had already appeared in two newspapers, with them saluting like Romans in front of the fires. Well, now they wanted more photos. The one who's going to be a judge, Samos, spoke on behalf of the old man in a straw hat and the boy with the wooden horse, 'Let them go! They're like family. I might still ask for your daughter's hand, Mr Vidal!' He was distracted, had a lot to think about. So Parallelepiped could finally put the book under his blue shirt, very surreptitiously. And leave without saying goodbye, in the shadows, down the corridors of smoke, while they stood tall and proud in front of the pyres. Shame not to have a librarian to hand, someone to consult about the value of this book to the valiente of Finisterra. Better to keep it under wraps for a while. Not tell anybody. Samos said it was very valuable. He might be cultivated, but he wasn't very observant. You have to dirty your hands if you want to get something. Now it belonged to him. The emotion of nicking something. The emotion of reading 'For Antonio de la Trava, the valiente of Finisterra'.

Parallelepiped walked along the Western Quay. He lived in Garás. He looked at his hands. They were blackened. He was happy, pleased with his booty. It was about time he found something valuable. Dead men's pockets don't even carry air. Judging from Samos' anxiety, this book must be worth a fortune.

It was then he felt a slap on the back that made him stumble. A paw that had little to do with greeting or friendship. He knew the effect of this surprise impact. Intimidation. He himself was an expert in the surprise blow to the back of the neck, which terrorised poor souls scurrying away, hoping to avoid making the Fascist salute. With his elbow, he held on tightly to the New Testament hidden under his shirt and this immobilised one arm. He turned around. Ren, his robust colleague, grabbed him by the collar. His hands were iron claws. He unarmed him.

'What you got there, Parallelepiped?'

'A novel, comrade. A Frenchy to read in the toilet.'

'I'd better read it myself first. Hand it over.'

The Books' Burial

'You.' 'Me?' 'You too.' Ten men he pointed to. With rakes and shovels. Rakes? It was August, but I wouldn't have been surprised to learn the leaves were falling off the trees. That was the first thing I did. As soon as we entered Cantóns, I looked to the right to see if the beech still had leaves. It was beautiful, in season, like the bust underneath belonging to Mr Pondal. I mean the bust was also in season, with the dark age of bearded men in white marble. If we have to collect leaves, then I hope they're the beech's. That beech's. But the lorry went straight past at an improper speed. Even if all the men in the back of the lorry were disaffected, the speed was still improper. We'd heard the order. To pick men who were disaffected. There we were, park and garden employees, and the new manager pointed to ten men. 'You, you, you,' and so on, up to ten. That finger stung like a horse-fly. It doesn't matter what it's for, who likes suddenly to be called 'disaffected'? Because just now, a few days ago, there weren't any dis-affected. I mean I was unfamiliar with that label. Had I had to introduce myself to the world, I wouldn't have started: 'Ladies and gentlemen, my name's Francisco Crecente, Polka to my friends, municipal gardener, specialist in pruning palms, oh and by the way I'm disaffected.' It was like an oedema appearing that hadn't been there before. Or a tic. He pointed with his index finger, 'You! You! You!' And with the same reflex action of pointing to ourselves, we replied, 'Me? Me? Me?' Like that. As if we all had tics, which we didn't. On the lorry, swaying from side to side, the disaffected, clinging to the rakes, more than that, physically attached to the rakes, which have the solid shape of tools that put down roots even on a violently unstable lorry. The lorry had acquired the arrogant attitude,

108

the cheek of heavy machinery that's been relieved of its scruples. The soldier who gave the order and the new manager who carried it out travelled in the motorcycle and sidecar combination behind. We disaffected, with tics, dancing around for them. Stuck to our rakes. Estremil looked to see which way we were going and then tried to explain something, something important, but couldn't make himself understood because it was like riding a horse, your teeth cut the words short.

'What?'

The lorry turned sharply. The wheels creaked. It braked suddenly.

We were next to the port in a kind of low, grimy mist. I now understood the reckless driving and the hollow feeling in the stomach. We hadn't travelled horizontally, we'd fallen. Now I could hear Estremil, the echo of what Estremil had been trying to say. He was cursing. 'Blasted mouth of hell!'

'Out!'

The ground was giving off a thick, sticky smoke that, rather than leaving, seemed to return. Sniffed around the embers. A smoke that, instead of disappearing, came back to the trail left by the rakes' teeth. It wasn't until we were down by the docks that we realised why we were there. To rake up the ashes and smoking remains of books. Some of those who'd burnt them hung about, sifting through the pyres, kicking at the bones of books. This gesture reminded me of the first image I had of death. Not the first time I saw a dead person, when I was small, which didn't frighten me since it was my grandfather, who looked very peaceful, cradled by women's prayers, his arms over the sheet, one hand on top of the other as if he'd caught death with his fingers, but the first time I saw death out of a box, another image. There'd been a fight between two men after a party. They got on badly, but that night, strangely enough, they'd been drinking together like lifelong friends. I remember my father interpreted it as a bad sign. Afterwards he was annoyed with himself for getting it right, 'If it's a bad sign, son, don't say so, because words hanker after what they've said.' Someone woke us early the next morning with the news. One of them was badly wounded, the other dead. They'd come to blows at the crossroads. We children ran to have a look. The corpse had been piously draped in a sheet, awaiting the magistrate's arrival. All we could see was the outline. A woman told us to go away. She called us 'death flies'. 'You're like flies that won't leave. I should drive you off like flies.' This also impressed me. There was something about the label that was right. So I was about to leave, but then one of the deceased's brothers appeared on horseback. He got down and, without letting go of the reins, approached the body. He was wearing boots with spurs and had a thick, blond moustache like a covering of hay on his upper lip. He didn't pay us any attention. With the toe of his boot, he pulled back the sheet to reveal the dead man's face. That was the first time I saw the horror of death, a pointless, ugly death. This may have had something to do with what the brother said. 'That's it,' he spoke to him reproachfully. 'The time has come for you to sleep out in the open.'

The one stirring the badly burnt books with the toe of his boot had a resinous voice. Part of the smoke had got inside his throat. The action of his toecap lifted layers of ash. He flicked out orders in an effort to speed things up. And warned us, 'If you see a book which says New Testament or Holy Scripture or something like that, give it to me, understood? It doesn't matter if it's damaged or charred. I want it!' The bitterness with which he spoke made our work even more irksome, as if we were partly to blame. I wish he hadn't said anything at all. Now everything had a sacred feel. Even the smoke weighed down on our shovels. If those who wore the Sacred Heart as a symbol went so far as to burn Holy Scripture, then my father was absolutely right, 'Better not to predict what's coming next'. Everything that had burnt was in that sleepwalking smoke. I thought about the governor's wife, the librarian. She'd turned up dead yesterday in a field next to the road to Lugo, having been raped and riddled with bullets. She was walking barefoot on the coals, her skin entirely blackened, naked and sleepless among the piles of night.

There was lots of cleaning to do. Here and in María Pita Square. Lots of burnt books. We'd heard they were burning books by the sea. There'd been fires before, when the coup started. But this was something else. Whole libraries going up in flames. Apart from the resinous voice of the one in charge, echoed by the new manager, the only sound was of rakes scratching the ground and shovels loading the lorry.

The one in charge wanted us to go faster. But this wasn't something you could do any old how. All jobs follow certain rules and none of us could remember how to load the remains of burnt books. Nor could the tools. We were both used to collecting fallen leaves, to the scent of autumn bonfires, which lent the city a medicinal aroma. More than smoke, it was that, an aroma. Nature whose time had come. What was burning today, however, was time itself. I realised that. I didn't say anything, but I thought it. Estremil, my friend, time is burning. Not hours or days or years. Time. All the books I never read, Estremil, are burning. He was a good reader. One of those who stopped to read, and did so conscientiously. Estremil did everything conscientiously. I bet some of the books he'd read were there, in the ashes being raked up, in the shovel-loads filling the lorry.

I picked up a spadeful. There were plates of ash retaining the form of pages and the 'black shadow' of printed lines. Some of those plates hadn't burnt completely. The flames had gone in a circle and left bits of paper intact. My fingers reached out to one of those wafers quivering on the surface.

'Look, Estremil, "a drop of duck's blood".'

'What's that? You're crazy. You treat everything as a joke.'

I wanted to give it to him. Gave it. As the plate fell apart, the piece of paper was no bigger than a samara wing.

When he trained me, Estremil used to say of autumn leaves, 'Don't kill yourself running after them, they'll come to you. It looks as if they're falling haphazardly, but they have a direction. See? The flurry bends a certain way. Build a good bonfire, find a good place, and then wait. They'll soon come.' He was pulling my leg, testing me, I could tell from the glint in his eyes, but there was meaning in what he said. That was some time ago. Now Estremil was quiet, uneasy. Gritting his teeth. Like me. To stop them banging together. That day, something happened to me that had never happened before. The sway of the lorry stayed in my body. Wouldn't leave. I couldn't stop my teeth chattering. I listened to them resounding inside, behind my eyes. Maybe the same thing was happening to Estremil.

If he gritted his teeth, he could hold his body together better and concentrate on his pulse to keep the spade steady and not spill the ash, the folds and tips of toasted skin, the nervous resistance of gut-string, the bony splinters of shrivelled paper. The books' remains.

The Invisible Man

On Cantóns, Curtis can clearly see the thick, ashen, earthy clouds, the breath of ruminant fire, coming from the docks. The sky above María Pita Square is also overcast. He knows he can't turn back. Has to continue to see it with his own eyes.

He looks at the clock on top of the Obelisk. Remembers, 'His lordship, Time!' It looks as if it's always been there, marking centuries, as if the hands had yet to make a circuit. Sada was right. A cuckoo clock would have been better. If a cuckoo were to come out now, thought Curtis, maybe everything would be different. It'd raise the heads of those walking uneasily, counting questions on the slabs of stone like someone stepping on the squares of a chessboard. It might alter the march of those following a straight line. The cuckoo might hinder that soldier in the bonnet galloping astride a straight line.

He thought he saw him, Sada, on his way through Pontevedra Square, where troops were starting to enlist. The rebel army had taken over the city and had control of Galicia, which would be a rearguard territory for what the insurgents called the 'new reconquest of Spain'. Yes, he thought it was Sada. So tall and burly, he was difficult to miss. He thought he recognised other faces, though recently not only had people's mood changed, but their faces, presence, physical features as well. This was one of the things that had most surprised him on his walk. A kind of winter had suppressed the summer season. From the skylight, he'd seen the desolation of Riazor Beach. It was the sight of an urban beach deserted in summer, on a beautiful sunny day, that made him afraid. Unfamiliar fear caught up with him. There were days only the Headless Man seemed to emerge from the city's shell, sitting on the breakwater with a book in his lap. When he decided to escape through the skylight, when he tricked his mother and aunts in the Dance Academy, he discovered years had gone by in days. Hairdos had disappeared, colours had darkened, skirts and dresses lengthened. People had changed their way of looking. Of walking.

He realised there were people and things asking not to be named. To be spared words. Which is why he stopped scrutinising the soldiers. He knew he shouldn't do it. For his own good and for theirs.

If they asked him who Sada was, he'd say, 'I don't know, I can't see him.' And Sada would call him to one side, 'Can you really not see me, Curtis? Praise be to God, long live the Umbrella Maker of the Universe!'

'If you want to stay safe, become invisible.'

He was told this plainly by a well-informed man. A Navy legal officer who admired his painting and had a certain sense of humour. 'I like most of all the way you paint echinoderms and gastropods.' 'Now listen here, you,' replied Sada, 'there's no need to insult them.' The officer was kind enough to warn him. He wasn't interested in war. His hobby was studying the first world circumnavigation. By Magellan, Elcano and what he called the enigma of the third name. Sada would have liked to return the favour at once and become immediately invisible.

But although he was up to date with Franz Roh's theory about magic realism in art, Sada didn't know how to become invisible. He was just too big for escapism. He had magician friends he was unable to help in rehearsals or performances because all the swords wounded him, all the saws sawed him and, in the disappearing act, when the magician announced he'd vanished and was no longer there, he'd appear, ruining the spectacle, like a heavy load that doesn't know how to transform into spirit.

His informant was clear. He was on the list. Sooner or later, they'd kill him. To be invisible was to become a soldier, to join the conquering army and go to war.

No sooner did Sada's enormous bulk reach the front in Asturias, no sooner did it slowly stand up in the trench, than he was shot three times. You'd have thought this is what he wanted. But his fellow soldiers told their bosses he'd been talking all the time about being invisible. He considered himself an invisible man. And this is what they called him: The Invisible. One soldier kept quiet. The one whom he'd told about the child and the matador the night before.

In metaphysical art or in magic realism, there as well, the lame matador pursued him. Pointed with his stick, 'That's him, that's the one, the Invisible.'

I'll Just Go and See Who It Is

They're killing all his friends. One by one. He has to send them to a safe place.

'Safe? Where's a safe place?'

'The land of wolves. That's the safest place nowadays.'

When Pombo talked about the land of wolves, he knew what he was talking about.

From the beam in the shepherd's hut, Curtis had hung a sack full of sand from the river. A gunny sack which, every time Curtis hit it, gave off a fine spray. Terranova encouraged him with that refrain 'Yamba, yambo, yambambe!' But sometimes he fell into a melancholy trance and watched the sack swing from side to side. Seeing him stuck in the station of sadness was something new, since Curtis thought he had a permanent spring in his mind protecting him from nostalgia. He'd sing to the sack. 'The Moorslayer's not working!'

Underneath the outer roof, the hut had a second ceiling of large cobwebs, not as resistant as gunny, but thick and well made, like a large canopy. 'There are no spiders,' said Terranova one night in the light of an oil lamp. 'Have you seen a spider? Who's making these webs, Curtis? They must be tireless spiders, but I haven't seen any. One day, they'll envelop us and gobble us up. We have to eat them first. Remember what Holando used to say about the French astronomer who only ate spiders? They're the messengers of time. We can't see them because they're spinning with our eyes, with the threads of light. If we eat them, we might see the stars. Otherwise they'll eat us. Or the bats will.

'I should be eating skylark pâté, like the soloist of a French cathedral choir. As Picadillo once said, "Nightingale pie, ladies and gentlemen, for the singers."'

He's losing his mind. The spiders have got inside his head, thought Curtis. He left the hut. Was going to make him a present. To lift his spirits. He knew where there was food. In the roadside shrine, up at the crossroads. There was a stone relief showing prelates and pontiffs in the flames of purgatory. And a saint with scales for weighing souls, probably St Michael, whom he'd heard about in the Dance Academy's kitchen from his mother and Pretty Mary. The weighing of souls would take place at the Last Judgement. How much would a good soul weigh? 'The scales must be pretty accurate,' said Milagres, 'like the ones they use on Galera Street for spices.' She added, 'Souls must be like saffron. A gram is worth a fortune.'

In the niche, behind the little lights of burning wicks floating on oil, among flowers, he found the present. The dead didn't care! Terranova was a spirit as well. He also needed an offering. His spirits needed lifting so that he could sing. Curtis didn't mind what it was. What he wanted was for him to sing. Never to stop singing or pretending to be his trainer as he laid into the sandbag, the sack of time, with his fists.

'Yamba, yambo, yambambe!'

He found food. More than on previous occasions. At the end of August, gusts of furtive, northerly wind were already scouring the fields of hay. Winter could be very long and swallow up autumn and spring. Eyes open in the back of his head, Curtis cautiously felt inside the niche and, aside from foodstuffs, found an unexpected treasure. A bottle of brandy and half a dozen Farias wisely wrapped in a cabbage leaf that had been tied with a straw plait. He smelt the tobacco inside the cabbage, that rude, precious package, and the mixture seemed to him strong and evocative, even though he didn't smoke, or perhaps because of this, like the fragrance in the corridor leading from the Dance Academy's sitting-room to the kitchen, where Milagres kept the factory of tastes and smells working round the clock, with the humble, captivating vapour of soup in the background, visible like a family heirloom. Sometimes he thought it couldn't be. The girl with the budgies from 12 Panadeiras Street had never set foot in that kitchen. But it was the image of a bowl of cabbage soup, her anxiety as she eats it, that made the memory plausible. Milagres' laugh, a laugh of popular satisfaction at the joy of eating, eating from hunger, of a rich girl, daughter of a cultivated man she admires, who's turned up out of the blue, from across the border. Yes, it must be true. Can't you hear them calling for her, Vitola, María, Vitola, thinking she's hidden in the garden?

'Look at her eat,' says Milagres with pride. And with pleasure, 'Poor girl, she must have been hungry!'

'No,' she replies. 'I wasn't hungry. It's the smell of cabbage. Ever since I was little, I've always been desperate to try it.'

So that's what it was. The fragrance of Milagres' cooking crossing the border between two cities.

He didn't smoke, but Terranova did. Despite having a small chest, he liked Havana cigars. They sometimes formed part of his payment in kind, his dockside business activities. He'd drink brandy whenever he could before singing. Two glasses better than one to clear his voice. Who'd have thought that today in far-flung Xurés, working as a shepherd in a mountain hut, he'd have good tobacco and brandy as well as food in abundance?

He unwrapped the cigars and savoured the smell. Took a swig of brandy. Looked at him with theatrical eyes, 'Now I know who you are, Curtis, after so many years. The souls' mafia boss! You kept that quiet! I'm at your service. I'll be whatever you want me to be. Your butler. Your servant. Your shepherd. My captain of souls!'

The weather was changing. One morning, the swifts stopped drawing lines in the sky. Curtis crushed a furiously stinging horse-fly behind his ear and then didn't feel another. The cicadas suddenly fell quiet and the mountains reverberated. The flocks and herds returned to their stalls.

As they were tucking into the salami from the roadside treasure, there came a knock at the door, a tender rap of the thunder's knuckles.

It was the three seamstresses, each with a sewing machine on top of her head. They'd dropped in before. They travelled from village to village, carrying their little Singers. They stopped in a place for a while, depending on the jobs that needed doing. As well as a bed and food, they received a day's wages in cash or kind.

The youngest and liveliest was called Silvia.

'Let us in. The lightning is chasing our sewing machines and it's pouring down!'

They knew how in this weather the Atlantic climbed up the mountain ridge. Scores of miles inland, the clouds carried a bellyful of sea. Which is why they had specks of Irish moss in their hair and smelt of salt.

Terranova stroked the back of a Singer. 'I can sew as well,' he said. 'Lucho from Mount Alto taught me. He had a little theatre and used to dress up as an Andalusian woman. At night, he'd sew his polka-dotted costumes. He had a brother, a tough guy, who wouldn't let him. This brother was a stevedore. So Lucho would sew his Andalusian costume at night, when his brother was down on the wharf. He sewed pretty well. Not like me.'

The seamstresses gave him a suspicious look. He could be making fun of them.

'The thing Lucho taught me best was how to make rude gestures, including wearing the horn. He was very good at wearing the horn. He'd go down Independencia Street and the women who lived there would deliberately come out to watch him declare his allegiance to the Fraternity of St Cornelius. No one in Coruña wore the horn better than he did. Watch.'

Then he made them laugh. They'd never seen horns lifted in this way, with hands reversed, on buttocks, and cheeky fingers dancing obscenely.

They invite them to eat. Silvia becomes serious and steps forward. Appears to speak for all three of them. No, they don't want to. They're not hungry. They already ate on the way.

'Then let's have a dance,' says Terranova. He's feeling happy, replenished. 'I'll sing. You three can dance with him, let me tell you, with Hercules himself. Mystical roses, you have the opportunity to dance with a prince from Un-deux-trois, on a tour of the mountain ranges. Dance cheek to cheek, Spain's perdition, no peeping!'

> The light burning in your eyes
> dawns if you open them,
> as you close them
> dusk seems to fall . . .

When it's Silvia's turn, she comes up close, embraces him. The other two laugh, pretend not to watch. Terranova jokes, 'Don't get burnt!' Changes tune. 'What do you care, my love, if you no longer feel the same?' Silvia talks to Curtis, whispers in his ear, 'Don't you dare touch the food in the shrine again.'

He looks at her in surprise. Why?

'It's not for the dead, it's for my father. Understand? My father's hunger is not like that of souls. It's the hunger of a hungry fugitive. Do you understand or not?'

He understood all right. Terranova always said there was an invisible man in those parts. An ex-man. Who must be living in Barxas Wood. In the eye of the water. The trees had long, ancient beards. The Invisible as well.

Some guards once passed the cabin. In cloaks. The barrels of their guns sticking out. They were obviously in a hurry, but made enquiries. And then Terranova gave them the spiel. They were Portuguese, from across the border, hired as shepherds, when they were young they'd been offered to Our Lady of the Rock, the tallest stone staircase in the world, etc. Curtis was amazed by Terranova's skill at accents, his palatal pattering speech.

'Has the cat got his tongue?'

'He's dumb. Name's Hercules. Lots of brawn and no brains.'

'Lucky him,' said the corporal. 'Seen anybody about?'

'Not a soul.'

'If someone comes asking, don't give him a thing, any bread or water.'

'Even if he's a Christian?'

'He's not a beggar, you know. He's a fugitive. A bandit. A red. A descendant of the one in Anamán who shouted the poor don't have and the rich won't give.'

'How can we tell?'

'Because he doesn't know how to curse. Whoever heard of a Christian that can't curse?'

'Change of partner. Dance by ear!' announces Terranova. 'If you see your father, tell him when he doesn't receive alms, he has to curse. Blaspheme.

They're on to him because he speaks properly. Words are the most visible footprints.'

'The thing is he doesn't believe, so he doesn't blaspheme. When he gets really worked up, the worst insult he comes out with is "Papist".'

'I could teach him to say, "I pick my teeth on a fragment of the Holy Cross". I could make a list and leave it in the shrine. I had a thorough education. My mother's a saint. He has to ask like a chaplain and curse when he doesn't get. He believes in souls, doesn't he? They say if you bump into a soul, you have to make the following request, "If you're a soul from the other world, say what it is you want." My mother and Curtis' are always getting bogged down with souls, because they ask them what they want. The best thing is to send them packing, as priests do, "Christian soul, off to heaven with you!"'

When the storm had passed, the seamstresses put their sewing machines back on their heads and asked Curtis and Terranova to go with them for a bit.

'We're headed for Barroso,' said Silvia. Adding mysteriously, 'Come with us to see how goats fly!'

'There are more crazy people in this world than in the world of spirits,' said Terranova. 'Lead on!'

Several hours later, Terranova asked, 'Where are the flying goats?'

'Not far to go now.'

Nightfall. The gloaming hour. They were on the edge of an inland cliff. In front of them, a huge marsh giving off mists. They'd clearly reached a limit. Then they heard bleats falling from the sky, spine-chilling cries that drew lines, wrote acrobatics two by two. Bleats joining in a serpentine drawing.

'They're woodcocks,' said Silvia. 'In these parts, they're called goats.'

'I never heard birds make such a sound.'

'They make it not with the throat,' said the seamstress, 'but with their feathers. With the wind and their bodies.'

'Louder!' shouted Curtis. 'Louder!'

'He can speak!' exclaimed Silvia in surprise.

'He has his days,' replied Terranova. 'Only when he gets emotional.'

The weather changed from one day to the next. It wasn't a summer storm any more. The clouds were full of stones and dark sea. They creaked and crushed brutally, with adult gearing, having lost the artifice of summer storms suitable for all ages. They had to think of returning. In mid-September, they'd take the sheep back to the village on the border. They'd still have time for a quick trip to the feast of the Acclaimer, the virgin who won't keep quiet, music booming over the mountains all night. And then back into the Salgueiros' basement, the house of the Stone Man and the Woman with the Black-beaded Rosary, to make baskets out of chestnut branches as the Stone Man had taught them. The village was good at this trade and the merchandise was sold at markets along the border. That was the deal. In summer, shepherds in the mountains; in winter, basket weavers hidden in the shade. Why was he called the Stone Man? Because he was made of stone. He'd sometimes move, stick his finger up his nose and pull out navelwort of the sort that takes root in between stones, on the edge of roofs. That's what Terranova would say to make Curtis laugh. The Stone Man had navelwort up his nose, in his ears and all his body's various orifices. 'The point is they're good folk. We don't know what they think, but we know what they do. They fulfilled their side of the bargain. Gave us shelter. Never asked questions. How long's it been, Curtis?'

On 2 August, the day the special train was due to leave for Caneiros, Terranova had been circling the station. Waiting for Curtis. He was sure he'd come, because Curtis had his ticket. Days before, he'd gone to the Academy during the night. Pombo half-opened the door and told him neither Curtis nor anybody else was in, he himself did not exist, and what Terranova had to do was stay in his mother's house and not go wandering about, which was like wearing a cowbell around his neck. When he went to the station, he couldn't get in. It was heavily guarded. He peered through the fence from Gaiteira. All the trains were still, a silence of engines that seemed to him resounding. The train to Caneiros never left. It transformed into a phantom locomotive. When they did start up again, all the convoys, somehow or other, were headed for war. Anyone who knew about trains realised they'd changed sound. The engines and tracks were still the same, but the sound had changed.

He found Curtis the day they burnt books. Following Pombo's plan, they finally boarded a train, but this time as corpses, inside coffins, using real dead people's identities. As far as Ourense. From there, by road. The driver stopped in Maus de Baños at night. Which is when they dropped their coffins into the River Limia.

'You're dumb,' their contact said to Curtis. 'You say no to everything. It doesn't matter what they ask you. Unless they say Guiné. If they say Guiné, you say yes. It's a code, see? You,' he said to Terranova, 'you're a gypsy.'

'A gypsy?'

'A Portuguese gypsy.'

'All right then.'

Curtis was reading his *Popular Guide to Electricity* in the smoky light of a carbide lamp. The printed lines trembled in the shadows, as if marching over the yellow surface towards the charred margins, telling a capnomancy, the matter of an ancient divination. The flickering light and spirals of smoke, reflected against the book, appeared to rise from the pages and not from the carbide's death throes. The Stone Man slept next to the hearth. The woman's litany sounded like a radio. *Domus aurea.* Broadcasting at night. *Foederis arca.* Once he'd heard her sigh over the airwaves. *Janua coeli.* Salgueiros would die if they didn't bring the light. *Stella matutina.* At this point, the Stone Man stirred, opened and shut his eyes. It really was like this, thought Terranova. The woman's voice was a radio, a connection he'd found. He listened to it as when he used to search for tangos on the crane operator's Atwater Kent at night and out came uncertain voices. This is how he discovered Paul Robeson. At times, he seemed to fade, to go, to leave them behind. At others, he sounded stronger, with renewed intensity, and you could light a match in his breath. *Rosa mystica, Turris Davidica, Turris eburnea.* But there was always a distance, as if she were one thing, her voice another, and she also were listening. The woman stopped praying, stopped telling the beads of her rosary. Her fingers, however, kept going. They left the jet and started making beads out of breadcrumbs. One to start with, slowly, it looked as if it would be the only one. Then more and more quickly, small spheres filling the blue and white squares of the oilskin tablecloth. Terranova copied her. The two of them rolling stars. Something had changed in her as their departure approached. She'd thrown off her mourning. Let down her hair. When they went back to the city, he'd send her an Atwater Kent. With batteries and accumulators.

She lifted her eyes, which were damp, glistening. Her shaky hand felt under the table. A rosary of years to make that movement. Finally to whisper an invitation.

'The dogs are barking. Shall we go and see who it is?'

The Rabble and Providence

Something happened which upset him and left him speechless. One of his colleagues, who'd later occupy an important post, started urinating on one of the pyres. There'd just been an incident. Someone, that huge lad they called Papagaio's Hercules, had unexpectedly jumped over the fire the way they do on St John's Eve to ward off evil spirits. They'd gone after him without success. He ran as if he had wings on his feet. The point is this colleague, back from the chase, went and pissed on one of the pyres. And all the others in their squad, without prior agreement, automatically went and pissed with him. Though he was one of those in charge, Samos was incapable of expressing his disgust. On the contrary, he reacted with a nervous smile. Exempt. This lowly act ruined the picture he'd composed of having an archangelic sword to hand. The books stank more than ever, a mixture of urine and smoke, animal remains. He could make out the folds and tips of Dutch binding, Valencian boards. The horse-nerve twines. That warm piss, spattering on the remains, gave off an unfamiliar smell. They may not have noticed it. The breeze lifted the pestilence to his nose.

When they were out hunting, there was a moment in which the group, already somewhat inebriated by nightfall, would obey a kind of natural order and the hunters would line up to piss in manly formation, with rude, brazen jokes. A disgusting scene. An ugly, base form of Fascism. One of his Portuguese colleagues, his host in Coimbra, who'd taken part in the Viriato Legion of volunteers backing Franco's army, had been amazed by what he'd seen among fellow troops. Teutónio confided in him, 'Samos, Spain's a dangerous country. Are you not afraid to have such colleagues?'

When in 1940 he'd visited Milan and Berlin, he'd been impressed.

There was an aesthetics, another dimension, an athletic kind of futurism, he'd said. A harmony of bodies and weapons. Ren was an example of coarseness. León Degrelle, another Fascist who'd sought refuge in Spain, after the war went on the Road to Santiago and complained about the fleas and lice in the towns' boarding-houses. Ren, who'd gone to welcome him in Portomarín, as a government representative, laughed about him, 'Very refined, don't you know!' Samos the judge had later heard the Minister say, 'We have to plough with the oxen we have.' The stink came and went. As for the hunting squad, he and one or two others, Father Munio when he came of course, would try to hold it in or, if they had to, do it a little apart, at a discreet distance, not so far apart as to attract attention, but without joining the common flood. Lofty thoughts don't come when you want them to. What gave the regime real meaning was not bravado, but the idea of divine leadership. 'Forget about the vulgar nature of the rabble and think about history,' Dez had said to him one day. He was the most refined in their circle, spoke with nostalgia of Primo de Rivera's poetic court and shared his sentiment, 'What we need is culture.' Their leader was an envoy of Providence. They had to maintain the link: follow our leader, follow Providence, keep the enemy at bay. That was the important thing. What was written on the face of coins being used by every single citizen: 'Caudillo by the grace of God'. What was on the reverse, not written, but in everyone's mind, like a tonsure clipped with scissors of fear, could well be the title adopted by the Assyrian king Tiglath: 'He who subdued his enemies'. A historical reference he resorted to with delight. In his lectures and seminars, and above all in his involvement with *Arbor* in Compostela and Coimbra, were those two special moments when he released his Christian Epimetheus, opened Pandora's box or descended with Heidegger to Plato's cave in order to arouse the soft, comfortable descendants of the Victory elites. He knew how to wake them. Nothing better than a bolt of lightning from his revered master Schmitt: 'And Cain killed Abel. This is how the history of mankind begins . . .'

At that point, he'd got their attention. The judge would then turn to another hammer-blow from another of his most distinguished colleagues, the future Minister: 'Without war, there would be no history.' He'd then take a good look at the Old Testament, where God is known as the Lord of Hosts. 'The Lord is on my side. Whom shall I fear? The day of the Lord is great and terrible.'

Natura Est Maxima in Minimis

He's going to examine a sample of his blood. Having coughed. His blood on the slide. The new world he's going to discover today was inside his chest. If a drop of water is the first sphere, that drop of blood is a final sphere, since in it are life and death, the two of them working for each other. It's one of the extraordinary moments in 12 Panadeiras Street. He recalls the eye's expectation as it approaches the microscope, blinks, sings *Natura est maxima in minimis*, drawn by the universal exhibition contained in a drop of blood, his own blood. They've plundered his cabinet of curiosities, his amateur scientist instruments, appliances for finally seeing what's invisible, this and the other side contained in a drop of blood. In every drop of blood. Speaking of spheres, they've plundered that as well, his wooden globe made in England. The first thing he noticed on that globe, like strange, unnamed territories, were the roses of the winds and the drawings of unusual sea creatures. The one he liked most, and continued to like as time went by, was a half sea-serpent, half-man, playing the lute by the Seychelles. After that, he ventured into the large patches of colour. On the seas and oceans, the globe was marked with sailing ships tracing historical routes. The first his father's finger pointed out to him was the *Beagle*, next to the Galapagos. Darwin's ship. A stubborn finger. It always went back there. The *Beagle*, the Darwin finger. Later, when it was his own finger doing the pointing and his daughter reading, the thing that captivated her most, the great discovery, were the names of places. These words were the globe's greatest charm. The Pacific, for example, was populated with words. The dots showing the islands were barely visible, but what really came across were the names. Nanumea. Nanumano. Nanumanga.

Nukononu. Pukapuka. In November 1937, in his native city of Coruña, Governor Arellano sends a letter to the president of the Tribunal, proposing that the sheet in the official register recording the birth of Santiago Casares Quiroga be torn out and destroyed. A hitherto untried punishment. The eradication of his name.

Which is on page 447. There the magistrate, one Pérez Arias, certifies that at half past ten in the morning of 8 May 1884, at number 6 San Andrés Street, a child was born, named Santiago. Page 446 belongs to a child called José Suárez Campos and 448 to a girl by the name of María de la Concepción Vaamonde. The secretary, Mr Patiño's handwriting is very neat, reminiscent of a musical score with quavered letters, a fountain pen like the crest of a golden oriole.

Natura est maxima in minimis. Come, Vitola, come. See what's inside a drop of water. The whole seed of the universe. Come, come. See what's inside a drop of blood. The composition of life. It's all there. Hate as well. We can approach the mystery of life, but it's impossible to understand the mystery of hate. The kind of hate that causes people not only to kill, but to want to erase you from the census of births. I have to concentrate on that mystery. Read everything there is. It has to be in a drop of blood. It has to have its chemistry.

No, he doesn't say anything. He's motionless. Watching himself. Trying to burn up as little oxygen as possible. When he has a relapse, María Casares, Vitola to her parents, thinks of the image of someone carrying an invisible bucket of water on their head. Not a single drop of water is allowed to fall under pain of death. There was a time he hoped he'd beaten it. As a young man, in the sanatorium in Durtol. He always had that bucket. Always had the scythe nearby. Death was part of the way he lived. What he never imagined was that one day they'd try to make him non-existent.

He'd never met this Arellano, the governor who officially declared him a pest and ordered that the name of Santiago Casares Quiroga be removed from the register of the College of Lawyers and any other book for 'future generations to find no more trace than the record of him as a fugitive'. For many years, Casares, who at one point was Prime Minister, did not appear in Spanish encyclopedias. María Casares knows that Spanish

Fascism largely achieved its aim of erasing him from the map of mental geography. He was a symbol of the Republic and now he's a crater. They've plundered all his things. His books, furniture, home. Microscope. Herbaria. Entomological boxes. There's something on the tip of her tongue. A round, reddish word with seven black dots on its wings.

One of the first songs he taught her. A song for learning how to count. A folk-song, a scientific song.

> King-king, how long will I be?
> Twenty-five? Could be.
> One, two, three . . .

'The seven-spot ladybird, *Coccinella septempunctata*,' he explains, 'is, together with the glow-worm, the creature with the most names in Galicia. Why is that? Why those two? It's called "king-king". "Little Maria". "Sunsucker". "Spotty". "Seamstress". "Little Joanna". Little things have the most names. As Jules Renard says, "truth is of small dimensions".'

In November 1944, in Paris, they received the news that 12 Panadeiras Street and the rest of the Casares' property now belonged to the Fascist State. Pillage became law. He was in London at the time, to avoid falling into the hands of the Gestapo. She stopped playing the game that if she closed her eyes at the door of 168 Rue de Vaugirard, she'd turn up on the stairs of 12 Panadeiras Street. On his return, the atmosphere of a liberated Paris helped him to breathe better. As he said, on account of his consumptive optimism, he could see every molecule, taste the air: *Natura est maxima in minimis.*

A few months later, Gloria died of a cancer that had appeared suddenly like the dagger of an efficient assassin. He was able to close her eyes. María was stunned at the sight of her dead mother. All her previous faces returned to her. Daughter of an unmarried factory worker, seamstress, melancholy woman at the window of 12 Panadeiras Street, minister's wife, nurse in a military hospital. The word that came to María's lips, forced a way through her suffering, was beauty. What beauty! And her father said, 'She always was pretty, whatever she did.'

He felt the crises arrive in the barometer of his chest. They were increasingly strong. He'd adopt the lotus position without moving, like a diver running out of oxygen.

The worst thing was when his temperature rose, because then he'd consume oxygen in his dreams, his nightmares.

One day, he emerged from his delirium, looking wide-eyed and mutilated, as if he'd lost all his teeth. He said he'd been pulled out. He felt in his flesh how he'd been pulled out of the register. Of the book of births.

'Don't think about it, Daddy. They'd never do that.'

'I don't even know who he is, this governor who wants to tear out my birth certificate. I have to study this, the nature of hate.'

'Don't think about it now, Daddy.'

'You're right. It uses up lots of oxygen.'

And then he spoke with his hands. If she gave him a finger to hold on to, he'd grab it with the strength of a newborn baby.

Live Phosphorus

Polka had stopped playing the bagpipes long before. He hadn't played them since the war. When he was freed, after labouring in a wolfram mine, it was some time before he could even hold the instrument, let alone play it. While he was away, Olinda would occasionally allow their daughter to blow and try to fill the bag, made of goatskin covered in dark blue velvet with a similar-coloured trim. The girl thought it was always on the verge of turning black as if night had sheltered in the bagpipes with the mystery of her father. But her father returned and the bagpipes remained hanging on the wall. As time passed and the bagpiper paid them no attention, O thought they got smaller, condemned to extinction, like an ancient creature in a forgotten legend, skin and bone of a rare, long-legged bird, with their melancholy colour and golden tassels which seemed to have lost their majesty, but for her were like coloured caresses. No, he couldn't touch them. Later maybe. Polka said he'd run out of air. His chest wasn't strong enough. But one Christmas Eve, when Olinda was pregnant with Pinche, he played them again. O was amazed and Olinda almost died laughing as she cradled her own belly. To start with, both Polka and the instrument looked as if they would burst. Polka's face was red from the effort of containing the air. But the bagpipes sounded again and it seemed to O they were finally letting go of all they'd been saving.

The bagpipes kept not only the light they'd saved up inside their black velvet, but a lot of silence. Silence must be kept. O soon distinguished two classes of silence. There was mute silence. The silence of suppressing what cannot or should not be said. A precautionary, fearful silence. And then there was friendly silence. The silence that makes you think. The silence that protects you and allows room for meditation. The silence of the bagpipes waiting for Polka.

She and her mother had also saved on joy. While Polka was away, they had to save on everything. Like women dressed in mourning. They saved as well. Not only did they wear the same dull clothing, but their nature changed. They spoke less, didn't laugh, hardly spent anything on looking at others. They saved on words, joy, light. And yet all the people in mourning, like O and Olinda, didn't feel any less, more perhaps, and they didn't have any less to say. More perhaps.

They saved.

Everything that had been saved at home, in all the homes, now emerged from Polka's bagpipes. Because once again he'd sized up those booming pipes, those snoring pipes, an inheritance, good for parties but also for accompanying choirs, processions and union marches.

On 1 May, the priest had said to him, 'You played the bagpipes in town for Sacco and Vanzetti and now you come here to play them for St Joseph.'

'I play *Saudade*, father, for all souls, yours included. This danceable requiem doesn't hurt anyone.'

No, it wasn't that priest who informed against him. This was something he'd never know. Some people died as a bet in a game of cards. They had no idea, were asleep perhaps, while their fate hung on a movement of cards or dice. After Polka was arrested, Olinda was sacked from Zaragüeta Matchstick Factory. In fact, all the employees were sacked, mostly matchstick-makers, about three hundred women, and their union was outlawed. The factory didn't work for several months. Then it opened again with staff specially selected by the Falange who had to belong to the Glorious Movement. Olinda didn't pass the test. She obtained a not unfavourable report by bribing one of the local bosses who'd multiplied in an ever increasing chain of command supervising the confiscations. But it was all for nothing, because another local boss decided the jobs would go to a group of highly recommended women who'd recently joined the Fascist Party. Within a few months, parallel power structures having quickly sprung up, this marginalised, fanatical group of pre-war gangsters took control of the city. As she staggered about from place to place,

Olinda was shocked. The governor had ordered the Roman salute to be obligatory. In any official building or even in the street, whoever should ask for it, you had to raise your arm and respond with the standard 'vivas'. In an atmosphere like that, Olinda witnessed a change in many people that went beyond political opportunism. Something like a biological mutation. Not just in appearance. Some people's voices changed. Some people didn't hear her. And, most upsetting of all, some people didn't see her. Despite the fact she was pregnant. She even wondered if she still existed. Lots of people had disappeared. Maybe she had too, without realising. Many workers from the Tobacco Factory in Palloza and the Matchstick Factory in Castiñeiras lived in the suburbs like Olinda. They'd get up early, when it was still dark, with oil lamps and candles to light the way. These luminous processions would converge. Get their bearings, see each other like lines of glow-worms in the night. These moving lines carried words as well as light. Constructed murmurs, songs, news, as each candle arrived. Sometimes one of the lights would be missing, there'd be an empty place, a gap in the sentence, murmur or song. This meant someone had disappeared. Olinda never missed the procession of lights until she gave birth. These lines of female workers reminded some of the Holy Company of Souls, but for Olinda it was just the opposite. With the death of Arturo da Silva, the arrest of Polka and the disappearance of all those young people who were supposed to board the special train to Caneiros, being there, being a candle, was a strange duty she had to fulfil while she could. The child she was carrying, the heavy load in her belly, was another certainty, you might have thought. The uncomfortable graft in her body was like an advertisement, a guarantee of reality. Or at least it should have been. But what worried her was that no one, on her bureaucratic rounds to safeguard her job, referred to her state. No one, even out of habit, used the phrase 'happy condition', as if in her case it would have been a mistake. No one congratulated her. You can have disappeared, thought Olinda, and be pregnant. The child be real, but not you. That's why she had to get up every morning and join the procession of candles.

Olinda did not get past the so-called 'period of purges'. As far as she could tell, there were at least two weighty arguments against her. Her husband was in prison and she had just given birth. She tried not to think with her mind so as not to lose it. At times, however, furtive thoughts would come to her, such as the belief that a situation like hers was a cause for mercy and not greater punishment. But she had to avert such thoughts, otherwise she'd go mad. This elementary law no longer applied. She also had to forget the word 'purges'. She had not got past the 'purges'. Those now holding power did so on the basis of hundreds of uncleared murders. Who raped, tortured to death and slashed the breasts of the librarian, the Republican governor's wife, having caused her to miscarry? Who were the purgers? She should feel honoured to be a purgee. She should take comfort in the whispers she heard as she passed, 'That's one of the purgees.' But no. Everything that was happening took its toll on her body. She found herself ugly. She'd lost the shine in her eyes and hair. Purged, impure. She hardly had any milk to give to the baby. How could she have been born so pretty?

The Matchstick Factory was surrounded by a tall wall. She'd worked in that enclosure for many years. She'd started when she was still a girl. She had to get up early, under cover of darkness. But in her memory it was a party. Like the day a street band came from the parish for her to carry the festive bouquet. She loved carrying her candle. She wasn't sorry to leave home, to be separated from her parents, as at other times. She worked in all the different departments. Started by counting matches. Her hands and mind were very alert and she got to count so quickly, by thirties, fifties, seventies, nineties, that her fingers ran ahead of her brain, danced attendance on the voices. She then took to sticking the strips of glass-paper that were used to rub and light the matches. The department she liked best, because of the work and company, was the one for cutting and assembling boxes. She was extremely skilled in making boxes. She knew the importance to a household of a good box of matches. She also knew these boxes, especially those bearing phototypes, could become small chests. For keeping someone's first tooth, a curl, a letter, a ticket for a special train. The women who cut and assembled boxes acquired a certain way of telling stories. Their stories, their secrets, were designed to fit inside a box. Which is why a box of matches, when it's empty, if you hold it half-open to your ear, will whisper to you.

135

This box doesn't say anything.

There were days the women were silent. And then the boxes had matches, but no voices.

She also spent time as an assistant in the laboratory, weighing and measuring live phosphorus, potassium chlorate, glue, ground glass and red aniline, the paste that contains a matchstick's true soul. Known as English paste. Fire's mystery. Smoking blood, they call it in the factory.

Olinda woke up in the middle of the night and looked through the window at the lines of candle-women.

In his hut in the labour camp, every time he lit a match, Polka would let it burn until the flame reached his fingers. A match was very important to him. To everybody, since they were hard to come by in the camp. This is the advantage of small things. A 'wagon-box', for example, containing ninety matches, with a little skill, passed from hand to hand, can store vital information, detailed plans, for a train not to arrive in port with tons of wolfram. A yellow 'economical box' contains seventy matches. Some are even smaller, pocket-sized, and contain fifty or thirty matches. The most attractive are those bearing coloured phototypes. The skill to turn a simple box of matches into a magnificent transmitter of secret information resides in one box in fact being two. But for this they have to be cut and assembled to perfection. The information can be walled up inside this delicate stucco work on rolling paper. In code. For this you need the people giving and receiving the information to be referring to the same book. One number identifies the letter, another the line, another the page. If you don't know or can't find the reference book, it's very difficult to decipher an intercepted message.

Polka held a new match in front of his eyes, closed his left eye and examined the head as a surveyor's reference point for measuring the world.

The matchstick head filled the mouth of the mine shaft.

'Let me tell you what it's made of, the formula for English paste, smoking blood: live phosphorus, potassium chlorate, gypsum glue, ground glass and red aniline.' He could add, 'And Olinda.'

'And Olinda as well.'

'What's Olinda?'

'A special ingredient in some matches. The ones that light straightaway have got Olinda in them.'

One of the technicians in the mine was a Portuguese engineer. He picked various prisoners to be his assistants, some of whom were highly competent. There was one, a Catalan, who'd been in Coruña in the summer of 1936, when war broke out, with some architect friends. Joan Sert got on well with Polka. Actually he followed him wherever he went because he'd never heard him complain. Polka carried the wounds of a failed escape. He said ants were left inside and then told him about the wasps that grow inside figs.

'They lay their eggs in a flower and then the fruit grows and the wasps have to bore a hole through the flesh. Which is why fig trees are always surrounded by wasps. The same thing happened to me. They tied me to a tree with open wounds and the ants used this opportunity to come inside me. Now, from time to time, they want to get out.'

Polka put his hand in his mouth and produced a handful of ants. 'See? See how they want to get out?'

Joan Sert looked at him in amazement and said, 'You're a surrealist!'

'Don't lay any more charges against me. How many years would I get for that?'

'For what?'

'For being a surrealist.'

Olinda was not allowed to return to the Matchstick Factory. There was always the river. The traditional occupation of women in Castro, washing for Coruña's middle classes. Washerwomen, for good or bad, were from another world. Even their shape, their figure in the street, was different. Bodies with bundles, with a huge globe on top of their heads. Amphibian creatures from villages by rivers and streams who took away dirty clothes and returned them clean. Sometimes even ironed and smelling of roses.

So Olinda joined the procession of women carrying things on top of their heads. A washerwoman living nearby gave her a job. Washing for the eye doctor's house and surgery. This was lucky. Because it gave her confidence. Reality. If she could wash for the eye doctor, then there was a certain amount of light. This was followed, she wasn't quite sure how, by the opportunity to wash for Chelo Vidal. One door opens another. She was not without matches. Invisible friends kept her supplied. She could throw a few boxes in the bundle and sell them. She could even take the odd box, the odd phosphorus box, to the doctor and painter.

Open Body

'A washerwoman has to be good at repartee. A quick retort, girl, otherwise they'll eat you alive. But keep it polite. Words and stones, once thrown, you can't recall.'

Olinda taught me the trade. I even know how to make lye using vegetable ashes. But it was Polka who taught me repartee.

He said, 'This girl has an open body. She won't have any problems. Her body's more open than Moeche's.'

'Moeche's?'

'A girl who one day started talking with the voice of a priest, and expert in dogmatics, who'd died over in Havana. On Sundays, she'd go out on to the balcony and deliver the most wonderful sermons in a Cuban accent. People came from all over the parish in their droves. Until one day she got fed up, went out onto the balcony and called them pagans and Corinthians. Among other things.'

'You're always pulling my leg.'

'It was in all the papers. Manuela Rodríguez. Back in 1925. This is what happens when people are bored. If you ever talk in a voice that isn't yours, don't worry. Don't panic. It's what you get for having an open body.'

The fact I had an open body calmed Olinda down. She suffered just to think I was no good at repartee and had inherited her silence. Not that Olinda stuttered or had a short tongue. She was very alert. When she was young, when she worked at Zaragüeta's, making matches, she could lift the roof all on her own, she was the life and soul of the box-room, 'the Spark of Castiñeiras', according to Polka, not a small thing in a matchstick factory. 'My spark,' he says when he's feeling romantic or wants to encourage her. Among the old, yellowed papers in the drawer of his night table is a cutting from *La Voz de Galicia* with the title 'A Trip to Castiñeiras' and a circled bit which says: 'The ones seen here chatting work at tables in a nearby room, sticking boxes and building crates for them. They're all women, lots of pretty women!' Polka repeats, '"They're all women, lots of pretty women!" Now that's what I call a good journalist.' Something happened to Olinda, silence entered her body. But that's another story.

She doesn't talk a lot now. Not that she's dumb. She's afraid of mute silence. Says it can get inside you and then doesn't want to come out. She had friends at the factory who suffered from this silence. But there's another silence she calls friendly silence, which helps. She says, 'Good words don't cost much and are worth a lot.' It's obvious she chooses her words. Which ones to say and which ones to hear. As when Polka's talking. She doesn't mind him being like a radio. But she doesn't listen to him all the time. Sometimes he can be broadcasting and she's immersed in silence. But suddenly she'll come out of her hole and pay attention or laugh out loud. Those are the words that matter. I wish I knew which ones they were.

Guillerme, or Pinche, my little brother, is a lot like her, like Olinda. He was born quiet. He was born a man. A little man. The first time I got to appreciate how similar they were was when I saw him help wind the tangled wool from an old sweater into a ball in order to knit a new one. Pinche with arms outstretched, straight, parallel, pulling the wool taut. The two of them joined by the moving thread. Not a word. Winding silence.

Speak, when it comes to speaking, he's not bad. Except for 'salicylic'. He can't say 'salicylic'.

'Not "sacilytic"!' shouts Polka. 'Salicylic.'

According to Polka, I could say 'salicylic' when I was only two. It was the first and last time Olinda took me to see him in the labour camp. A Sunday visit. A few minutes. The mine wasn't easy to get to! Couceiro, the seller of herbs and spices, took us in his sidecar. And Polka all the time making me say 'sa-li-cy-lic'. 'Salicylic acid'. I could not have known this was an expression of a father's great love for his daughter. Making her say 'salicylic'. I think I cried and everything. I had the impression when they came out of the mine shaft, they were possessed by strange words.

But I said it: 'salicylic'. And then he gave me a pair of clogs he'd made with his own hands. He said, 'They're for when you go to the river.' But the clogs, made of birchwood, were too small and could only be used as thimbles. Or for playing in the water. For making ladybird boats.

When he returned from the camp, one of the things that made him happy was listening to me read aloud.

'Shame you weren't born half a century earlier,' he said. 'You could have read in the Tobacco Factory.' He explained how the workers paid a colleague to read novels to them while they went about their tasks. 'Shame. You could have been an expert in Dickens!'

'Sure,' said Olinda, 'but if we gave her an extra half-century, she'd be an old woman by now.'

Polka became thoughtful. Took out the little book with the marks. The novel *The Invisible Man*. He'd hidden this one and a book by Élisée, together with some newspaper cuttings, in a leather pouch he buried under a large, chair-shaped stone. You could see he was emotional. To him, it was something important. Something like a treasure trove.

'Here. What's in it? What's in this book that twitched its ears in the ashes?'

I often read the story. For the three of them. For the neighbours who'd come on a Saturday evening in winter to eat roasted chestnuts or something. We laughed a lot when the invisible man had to watch what he ate. He was invisible, but the food wasn't. Milk at night, moving through his intestines like a luminous snake. The invisible man was much talked about in Castro. How we laughed at the poor man when a dog found and bit him! And at the cat's eyes when Griffin conducted his first experiment and managed to make the cat invisible, but with two exceptions: its eyes, which carried on shining, and its claws. This was one of the most successful episodes in the book. The listeners would search for those solitary eyes in the shadows. For an invisible man, snow is a problem. The snowflakes settle on and expose him. The great dream of being invisible has turned into a fatal condition. Which is why, after laughing so much at his misfortunes, people kept a respectful silence when the dead albino becomes visible and someone shouts, 'Cover his face! For Gawd's sake, cover that face!' I think at the time Griffin was more popular in Castro than in Iping. Perhaps because this was the disguise which had always been used during Carnival. Those who dressed up were, in effect, invisible men for a few days. They covered everything, mouth as well, using nylons, sheets, cloths and bandages. Part of the disguise involved not speaking or speaking very little with a distorted voice. At one point, I began to feel sorry for the invisible man. I stopped laughing and read with a pain in my stomach, as if my own cramps could be seen as well. What Griffin, the albino, experienced was the height of loneliness.

Years later, when I went to England to work as a domestic, I was sent to a house in Chichester, not far from Brighton. I went first and Pinche came a few months later to work as a gardener or whatever was needed. Before Pinche arrived, I had a terrible time, there were days I felt like an invisible woman, but I didn't think about Griffin at all until one Sunday in spring Pinche went for a bike and the owner of the house, a Mr Sutherland, pointed to the horizon with his pilot's arm and said, 'Let's see if you can get to Iping!'

'I wish you'd keep your fingers out of my eye,' the invisible man was forced to protest. A sentence I never forgot. And often used as a retort.

Not being good at repartee is like being born without hands. A washer-woman is unarmed if her tongue stops working. Like any woman who lives from what she does. You have to know how to defend yourself. If you've lost an item of clothing, well, you're in a tight spot and you've got to have what in crime films they call an alibi. Take unpaired socks, for instance. That's a problem. Socks have a nasty habit of getting separated. If you stutter, the other people laugh. If they laugh, you stutter even more. And then you're unarmed. You can't defend yourself. Polka disentangled me, undid the knots we all carry inside.

'You have to turn words slowly in your mouth. Think about it. A bird, a blackbird, for example, carries food in its mouth to give its chicks. What it's carrying is a measure. A beakful. You are both mother and chick. You have to have a beakful with which to defend yourself. Take the necessary words. Turn and re-turn them so that they'll sing to your tune. Know that you're not afraid of them.'

Polka also taught me to practise in front of the mirror.

'Don't always say you're right. That's no good. The first thing you have to tell the mirror is that you don't agree. Even if it isn't true. You say, "I don't agree". The first commandment is to have the courage to say no.'

When we tried it out, I was good at that part. Better than at re-turning words. I eyed up my opponent in the mirror and spoke from the heart, 'Well, I don't agree . . . My dog caught a fly, now how about that?'

'That's my girl! Keep going. Don't let her look over your shoulder.'

Of course not. I went and told my opponent in the mirror, 'I wish you'd keep your fingers out of my eye.'

'That's my girl! A perfect retort.'

I walked around the house with a small mirror. To start with, I'd object all the time. But I couldn't always be arguing. I looked pretty when I was annoyed, it suited me, but it wasn't my natural state. So, from time to time, I'd say some nice things. And when Polka appeared, I'd put her back in her place. I didn't want her taking liberties.

Everything changed when we began talking in the river. In the river, I couldn't argue with her because she wasn't exactly the same. She was different. For a start, we were both older.

And there were more people in the river. There were the water figures.

Dead Man's Slap

It was the Castrelos iron bridge over the Miño. The night enlarged its arched contours. The night enlarged everything. The dark mountainside as well, crowned by a church with its fortress-like structure. When there's no hope, everything seems to be on the side of the crime. The moon's projector. The barn owl's timed call. The metallic echo of footsteps. Everything grew bigger, the mouth of the river as well, the roar of its current, the yawning abyss, except for him. He felt smaller, the size he was when he visited the bridge for the first time with his father, who read out the inscription of the foundry, 'Zorroza Bilbao 1907', and talked to him of progress. The bridge was beautiful. 'An improvement on nature,' his father said. And he agreed that the riverbanks and mountains, even the church, looked better thanks to the bridge. Because there they were, in the middle, leaning on the parapet, seeing the river with the bridge's new eyes. If they made a postcard of Castrelos, it would have to show the bridge. Being there now, on the bridge, at night, he knew what it meant. There was no need to write anything. Just the sender's name. A sign of non-existence. Wherever the postcard went, they'd know he was no longer important to the force of gravity. What happened to him wouldn't even be death. The murderers, if they drank, would say, 'We took him for a walk by the river.' There is no killing, only the dead.

When the murderers threw him off the bridge, he weighed the same as that postcard he'd imagined on his first visit. Suddenly he regained his real body. He gripped the two iron bars with such strength his hands were made of iron, formed part of the foundry, 'Zorroza Bilbao 1907'. The landscape was not a hostile stage set. It was on tenterhooks, amazed, waiting for something other than that premeditated crime to happen. Perhaps the Castrelos iron bridge had also grown tired of being a place of horror in the hunt for humans. To start with, the murderers laughed. 'He doesn't want to fall,' said one of them, kicking at his hands with the toecap of his boot. Gradually getting annoyed because he wouldn't let go. 'Blasted eternity! Let me.' And the other rammed his fingers with the butt of his rifle.

'They're made of the same metal as the bridge! Considering he's a teacher, he's got a blacksmith's hands.'

'They're not iron,' said the other. 'You'll see.'

He took out a knife and flicked it open. For the victim hanging from the bridge, night again enlarged things. The voice of a face he couldn't see. A blade glinting in the moonlight.

'It'd be better if he let go,' said the one with the knife, cutting into his first finger, addressing his colleague, not him, as if the latter no longer responded to the world of words. 'Why won't he let go?'

The second in the group (there was a third with a rifle at one end of the bridge) stood watching two fingers, wondering why, having been cut, they didn't move. Like lizard tails. 'I don't think he's going to let go,' he said.

The group leader quickly sliced through the other fingers. He was furious and very offended by the victim causing all this mess. The normal thing would be for him to die as he fell against the rocks on the bottom and be carried off by the waters. When he did finally let go, the third soldier, feeling impatient, shot at the white shirt flying through the air as if it were the barn owl from before, enlarged and fallen. Then the three of them started shooting. At the human specimen, the river, the night. Another job for the Arnoia boatwoman, who'd have to recover another body from the water. Apparently the magistrate had said to her, 'No more dead, please.' But she rescued them for the families, who trudged up and down the river, searching for missing relatives. Besides, however careful they were, neither she nor the other boatmen downriver would ever find all of those who'd been sacrificed. Some bodies would end up going westwards, out to sea. Who knows where the ocean currents will take them? A man thrown off Castrelos bridge could end up off Rostro, or Galway, in Ireland. Or in the Atlantic trench by Cape Prior, at a depth of eight hundred fathoms, from where he'll never come back.

Or he'll come back on foot, upriver, to a bar in the Ribeiro region, in the self-same parish, twenty years later.

'What are you having?' asks the bar owner, a man they sometimes call Abisinio, sometimes Silvo. He has a bitter look. His wine isn't made from the finest grapes.

'A jug of wine,' says the outsider.

The barman serves him a jug and cup. Time goes by. The outsider remains silent and motionless. Staring at the jug. The barman comes and goes. Also glances at the jug from time to time.

He doesn't usually talk to his customers, especially if they're strangers. When he clears his throat, it sounds like a snarl.

'What? Not drinking?'

He doesn't like being a barman. Behind the bar, he feels shut up inside a cage.

'Not if you don't serve me,' replies the customer calmly.

He's in the same position he was in when he arrived.

'Customers here serve themselves,' says the barman, suppressing his anger. 'We're all on good terms.'

The outsider then takes his hands out of his pockets. With stunted fingers.

All on good terms.

'That's what a dead man's slap is like,' related Polka.

The Doorknocker

26 July 1952

All sorts of things are done for money, even killing, the value of life and all that, there are even some executioners on a State salary. When it came to Foucellas, the most wanted resistance leader, apparently they sent him their finest executioner, so he can't have been as bad as they made him out to be if they sent him an executioner from outside, from Salamanca, the best they had. Not the worst, the best killer. They kept the day and hour a secret, but people knew. Because the executioner got off the train in Teixeiro to have a coffee. And the one who served him realised it was the executioner as if he'd been wearing a badge or uniform. How did he know? From the hands. His hands were refined, manicured, hidden, peeping out of the burrow of their sleeves. And because he added a lot of sugar. No one had ever added so much sugar to their coffee in Teixeiro before. Some even said, 'He had a good death, they sent him the quickest.' Some consolation when you're being garrotted! He had a thirteen-year-old daughter, who went knocking at the governor's door to stop her father being killed. We were walking by, with our bundles of clothes, and my mother whispered to me, 'That's Foucellas' daughter at the governor's door.' Very early, it was cold. The only sound in the city was that of the doorknocker. Everyone walking by, all the office clerks, the squad lugging an enormous carpet, the workers taking down the hoarding from Colón Theatre, the brickies with their tile-coloured pots under their arms, everyone moved away from there, from that sound of a clapper. The sticky trail a broom leaves on the road. The knocker sounding like a clapper made of bone.

The Street Singer

He's on his way to the censor's office. Glances at the window of Camisería Inglesa on Real Street. There they are. The musicians' shirts. This is where all the orchestras and bands buy their costumes. Shirts with lace adornments. Frills, embroidery, tassels, flared sleeves, large collars with sickle-shaped corners. They even have mariachi outfits. A festive assortment of shirts. That zone of intense colours. With the fuchsia shirt. Blasted bees! He should go straight in and get that fuchsia shirt. Not think about it. The day is luminous. All the sea and city mirrors work towards the light. A sin, fuchsia.

Today he's in civilian clothes. No one's going to shout out, 'The censor, Commander Dez, has just bought the fuchsia shirt!' You can never tell. No, Commander Dez knew he wouldn't enter Camisería Inglesa this time either. He needed an assistant for such things. He'd already mentioned it at headquarters. Yes, like others, he needed a soldier for his domestic affairs. He carried on. Stopped outside Colón, previously the Faith bookshop. An avant-garde hang-out in the 1930s. With a name like Faith. Who'd have thought it? Words are like shirts. Here we go. He'd stopped to give his eyes a rest. To forget about the fuchsia. He certainly didn't feel like looking at books today. He had a stack of them waiting at the office, as yet unpublished. Recently he'd been lazy. And he had this problem with his fingers. This contagious dermatitis.

By the Obelisk. Now that's a good voice.

'It's ten and the clock chimes as I take a step into God's time.'

Good? Extraordinary. A true voice. A spring. And he dares to sing that tango about someone who's been sentenced to death right here, in the city centre. Coppery skin, clear eyes. What a guy!

He chucked him a coin. A big one. It fell outside his cap and rolled further along the pavement, as if making fun. The coin did a dance and finally settled near Curtis, the instant photographer, that tower of a man, thickset and silent, so still he seemed made of wood like the horse.

'Some money's fallen on the ground,' said Commander Dez to Terranova. 'Aren't you going to pick it up?'

'I didn't see it fall,' said Terranova, squinting comically up at the sky.

His reaction amused Dez. He was in a good mood. Anything this guy did had to have style. He put his hand in the inside pocket of his jacket, opened his wallet and produced a note which he held aloft, clinging to his fingers, and then released. The fall of the note seemed unreal. A period of slow motion which spread to all the movements on Cantóns. The note fell unwillingly. Landed near the cap and trembled uneasily on the ground like someone who, having been warm, is now uncomfortable.

The street singer glanced over. The note struggled, didn't want to stay put. Finally Terranova bent down for it.

'I sometimes make exceptions.'

'You sing well,' said Dez. 'You shouldn't be here, begging in the street.'

'I'm saving up to buy a suit. A white suit with a coloured shirt.'

Dez the censor smiled. He was going to ask what colour shirt he wanted, but felt a tingle inside his mouth.

He said, 'Is that what you're begging for? For a shirt?'

'And to buy my passage.'

'Where to?' asked Dez for the sake of asking. He knew where people bought passages to.

'Buenos Aires!'

'Buenos Aires, Buenos Aires!' the commander mocked him.

He turned around. Started to leave. Another bout of nausea. He looked back and shouted at him:

'Do what everyone else does, stupid! First leave and then buy a white suit and coloured shirt.'

'No. I want to board the ship in my suit and shirt. A shirt that's visible from the lighthouse!'

Tomás Dez retraced his footsteps. Glanced at the impassive cowboy photographer and produced another note.

'That should buy you a shirt. This is no place for you. You could be a prince.'

He was still there. Coppery skin, clear eyes. 'Chessman' again. When it came to tangos, he could always sing 'Street Gang' or 'For a Head'.

> For a head,
> all that madness . . .

This time, he was in uniform. The percussion of his military boots on the paving stones kept time with the song. He walked purposefully, martially, and when he did this, he had the impression the echo of his footsteps thundered in an imaginary bell-jar that contained the city.

He went straight up to him. Looked at him carefully. Took a coin out of his pocket and, tossing it in the air, caught it again. Only he saw whether it was heads or tails.

'You're not a gypsy,' said Commander Dez to Terranova. 'You're not a gypsy or a showman and you're certainly not Portuguese.'

Terranova fell silent. Looked like a squirrel at Curtis. Who looked like a woodcock at both sides of the street. Two military police jeeps had just pulled up and a black Opel parked behind them.

'I know who you are,' said Tomás Dez. 'I know more than you can imagine. I even know where you were in hiding.'

Terranova again sought Curtis' eyes, which had the same texture as the horse Cariri's.

'You're both deserters,' said Dez. 'You should have joined up. A long time ago, I grant you, but your papers are waiting for you in a file somewhere. Should someone open that file and find those papers, you'd be in for a bad time.'

'And who might you be?' asked Terranova.

'Someone who's going to give you an opportunity. And I'll tell you why.

Some voices are a divine gift. A gift that must be protected. Come with me. I've an office near here. There's no point in trying to escape, God himself won't save you.'

Luís Terranova pointed to Curtis, 'What about him?'

'Who? That clown? He can take his horse somewhere else!'

'An assistant. About time too, Dez. He'll have to train, I'm afraid. Three months and you'll have him permanently at your service. He'll have to show his face at the barracks every now and then. Is that the guy? Good-looking. Your parents' housekeeper's son? Of course you have to help out. And if he's an artist, as you say, if he's talented and does wonders with his voice and would have made an excellent falsetto, then it's quite right he shouldn't be on sentry or night duty. Of course you should have an assistant. If he needs domesticating, just send him back to the barracks and we'll do the rest. Everything in order, Dez.'

The Lead Locomotive and the Flying Boat

The lead locomotive climbed the ascending railway with all the twists and turns. A line of bodybuilders waited their turn. If it reached the top, a firework would go off with a lot of noise. But it never arrived. None of the hopefuls managed to push the lead locomotive to the summit, which was waiting to make a boom. Luís Terranova paid and asked Curtis to have a go, to accomplish that bodybuilder's mission. He did it without breaking into a sweat. The lead locomotive whizzed up the railway and crashed against the top. It was like a performance of lightning and thunder. The silence that ensued, rather than recognition or envy, seemed to contemplate the inexplicable. Luís raised Curtis' arm in triumph, as if he were his manager. He was wearing his white suit and darting around the fairground like someone who's both happy and worried.

He'd decided to break with Dez. He'd got involved to avoid going to prison, but it was now he felt like a deserter. He'd gone with Curtis to a remote part of the city, where he wouldn't look for him, but now he realised how sticky Dez's shadow really was. He never thought freedom could adopt such a stormy expression. Cause so much fear.

Two days earlier, he'd taken a decisive step. He'd gone looking for Curtis and invited him to eat in the restaurant Fornos. They'd stopped in front of the menu before. 'Shrimps, prawns, crab, clams in seafood sauce, Pontesampaio oysters, Andalusian tripe, stewed lamprey, Fornos kidneys.' They'd peered through the window at Sada's paintings. It was like opening a submarine door and discovering a mass of fish and seaweed. 'Come in, take a look,' Sada said to them, 'you can eat in your dreams as well.' But Terranova promised they'd return and eat in reality. And there they were, sitting down, asking for the menu. Terranova was happy. He'd finally kept a promise. Bad luck. It was Curtis who spotted Commander Dez as soon as they entered the restaurant. At the far end, at a table with three others. Dez, for his part, didn't just see them come in, part of his face did not recover its initial position, that of someone joining in a lively gathering coloured with vermouth. His face was split down the middle. This may not have been visible to the rest, but it was to Curtis. The part of his face that did not go back to its first position watched them with a mixture of surprise and rage. Luís adjusted Curtis' tie, laughing all the time, because, as he said, the knot had never become completely undone since the first time it was tied.

'Samantha's knot!' Luís proclaimed. 'You'd need an imperial sword to undo it.'

He either hadn't seen or was pretending not to have seen Tomás Dez. He had his back to him, so the line drawn by his guardian's rage through the air hit the back of his neck and bounced against Curtis' eyes. Luís summoned the waiter with all the ease of a regular and read the menu out loud, in the tone of a futuristic herald he adopted in high places.

'He's over there, at the far end,' warned Curtis when he'd finally calmed down.

'Who? Bela Luvoski? How terrifying!'

'Well, it is a bit,' whispered Curtis, moving his head as if his shirt collar was bothering him.

'That's his tactic,' said Terranova. 'The next stage is to threaten. Another tactic he has. Only he doesn't know that today I'm with Galicia's champ.'

They avoided the subject. Curtis swept it aside with a wave in the air. But he didn't lose sight of the danger. He was serious. Eyes in the back of his head.

'Do you know what you remind me of?'

He didn't. He hadn't seen Terranova like this for quite some time. He was both cheerful and vulnerable. In suspense. His eyes smiling, but about to break into pieces. Everything in his body was awake, as when they went fishing for barnacles and confronted the ocean's hydromechanics. The moment when terror and euphoria combined at their feet. In case of doubt, it was best to crouch down in single combat with the sea, never to turn around. When it came to it, the worst thing you could do was doubt. Luís always jumped. Everything had to be decided and carried out in the pause between each puff of the sea. He held his knife, prised off the best fruit and jumped again just as the foam covered the whole rock. All this in the time it took the sea to breathe. For him, it wasn't a heroic deed, but a joke. The veterans didn't like him fooling about in the middle of that warlike roar.

'Every single wave,' Mariñas told him one day to earn his respect, 'has an impact of thirty tons per square metre. This is the most powerful machine in the whole universe.'

'But the winkle hasn't even moved!'

There was no point arguing. Luís Terranova had the right to laugh at the sea if he wanted to. Everyone deals with fear as best they can.

To leave the restaurant, Dez passed next to them without saying hello. With a look of hostile indifference.

They'd talk about it at home. That was the message.

'Why did you have to take him there?'

'Why not? He's a friend of mine from childhood. There's no reason to be jealous.'

'Officially you're now my ward. You were my assistant and now you're my ward. That's a promotion! Which is why you're in this house, because I'm your guardian and you're my ward. You know what people will say. "You'll have to take Hercules in as well. And the horse. A large family. Who'll pay for it all, Dez, for fodder for the wooden horse?" And so on.'

'As you'd say, that's your fault for consorting with commoners.'

'And what was that about being jealous? Who do you think you are?'

The night was too warm for the Atlantic coast. As if waiting for people to let down their guard, a stormy armada had gathered behind the Sisargas. For anyone wanting to see it, the front of storm-clouds advanced in thick darkness, adding night to night. So the first bolt of lightning was mistaken for a breakdown in the firmament. The thunder, however, came from a magazine at sea. Everyone noticed the fleet of storm-clouds. And carried on dancing.

Part of the gleam landed on Luís Terranova's white suit. He let the shock go through him and then gave Curtis a friendly punch on the shoulder. 'Hey, that was you! You did it with the lead locomotive.'

The sea suddenly wanted to devour the houses, but the orchestra carried on playing. It sounded like an ancient dispute. Pucho Boedo was singing. Luís Terranova got on the flying boat. Singing the same song. Against the wind. Gusts that changed perspectives, tore off faces and left only expressions. Only the musicians' stage and the flying boat held on to the scene. And the fairground owner, who was removing the lead locomotive, because all hands were now fighting the sea, pulling boats out of its mouth, turned to Luís and went straight to the point, 'Ride's over!'

'A bit longer, please.'

Surprised that his thunderous voice had not had the desired effect, for the first time the fairground owner sought out the eyes of that figurine dressed in a white suit and a red cravat. Curtis had stopped pushing and the boat had slowed right down. He was dark, but his eyes were very clear, aquatic. The fairground owner felt like doing something he'd never done: letting off one of the lead locomotive's fireworks. But, on the other hand, he needed that boy to sing, now that the orchestra had stopped.

'The wind'll take everything.'

'I'm owed another ride,' said Luís.

The storm was carrying the sea inland.

'I'm not responsible,' said the fairground owner to Curtis. 'I'm not responsible for that boat your friend's in.'

It was then his three blond sons appeared. They'd been helping secure the boats and were drenched and out of breath, as if dressed in water and grease. One of them dismantled the railway with his father. The other two stopped the flying boat, ignoring Terranova's protests.

'I'm owed another!'

'Do you want to end up in the sea like Faustino?'

The other laughed at his brother's joke. Faustino was a very well-endowed straw man who was thrown into the sea during Carnival. Having fallen, he stayed floating for a while with his huge penis sticking up like a mast. A procession of mourning women wept over the loss, 'He was the best, the best!' Some men laughed, others didn't.

'I'm not afraid of you, little owl,' Terranova mocked them. 'Little owl, I'm not afraid of you.'

'Let him be,' said the flying boat's father. 'He can go as often as he likes, so long as he keeps on singing!'

He then spat on his hands, which were covered in grease from the lead locomotive's wheels. 'The night is whimsical indeed!'

Dez and Terranova

He turned on the light again and started reading without conviction. He only paid attention to the advertisements. The sleepless gaze does what it wants to. He noticed something he hadn't seen before. The large number of advertisements for electrical appliances, flexible mattresses and shampoos. Great emphasis was laid on the anti-dandruff properties of these last products. It seemed the whole of Spain had taken to washing its hair. He'd brought a stack of newspapers from the censor's office and was reading *ABC*, which was published in Madrid. He also had *Arriba*, the Falange's official mouthpiece. It was its newspaper, its doctrinal spokesperson, a necessary resource to know what was going on in the hierarchy, essential reading for a man in his position. He sometimes amused himself trawling for small differences. The relevance or absence of a news item. The language of silence. The conservative, monarchist daily had introduced the odd comment on Europe, was even in favour of Europeanism, a reviled concept in the press of the Movement, whose leading exponent was *Arriba*. Europeanism was the Trojan Horse of the opposition, the enemy, those in exile. In another time, a time that seemed to him now unreal, in which he hadn't quite managed to affirm his existence, he'd written a great deal on Europe, the rebuilding of a new Holy German-Roman Empire based on the triumphs of Hitler, Mussolini and Franco, with the Pope's blessing. An intellectual standpoint shared by many. The official line. Occasionally time played the dirty trick of returning with the sweaty, delirious thickness of an epidemic, making him believe the Holy Empire was something he'd imagined and in Spain, Europe, the world, only he had written such things. He then decided in his dream to board empty, phantasmagorical vehicles, which drove him through the night to every nook and cranny that had an archive or library. He'd break down the doors and expunge those pro-Nazi articles of his. But almost everything was pro-Nazi, an unending trail. The paper multiplied and grew. He would tear and tear. He'd written the same as everybody, hadn't he? The judge, for example, his friends at the magazine *Arbor*, Catholics from the Opus, the leading jurist, Carl Schmitt, weren't they still saying the same in a different way? In his nightmare, however, the judge Samos would turn to him, 'How could you have written those things, Dez?'

'What things?'

'What do you think? That praise of Nazism. You should have censured yourself, damn it! You have to know how to control yourself. Change style.'

'Look who's talking!'

'I was different. I was a Catholic, remember? The katechon. The one who draws the line. That's what I'm doing.'

'Hang on a minute! You're not the only one. I also draw the line. Mark words in red. It's not so easy to keep words in line. They're like cockroaches or rats. They live underground, in sewers, among tombs. They're like insects. Bacteria. It's easy to stop men in their tracks, but it's not so easy to contain words. Silences, pauses, are part of language. A man in silence, if he's honest, is dangerous.'

'You should have censured yourself, Dez.'

And so on. Banging on about it. There was something perverse about recommending control to a censor. He also could return to the past, if he wanted, like a dog to its vomit. Remind Samos of who he was. The university student who fancied himself as a Catholic intellectual, beholden to the idea of a benevolent God, still reluctant and hesitant on the eve of the coup, like that day in Pontevedra Square when he trembled in front of Arturo da Silva, the boxing plumber, who grabbed his pistol from his hand and chucked it into the sea in Orzán. 'Weapons are not toys, young man,' he told him and threw it over the heads of bathers, a parabola seen by everyone, how embarrassing, though he took his revenge, how a man can change in one month, the sudden stimulation of the cultivated Catholic, aesthete, orator, bibliographer, how the blood rises to his eyes and the once cowardly student is ready for anything, even he, Dez, was surprised, what resolve, what firm steps, his pulse is steady, armed and in uniform he looks taller, stronger, his subtle voice has become more daring. He's now in charge. He's standing with him, in front of the pyres of books, down by the docks.

'The Divine Sketch!'

'Manuel Curros Enríquez. Straight in the fire!'

'Remember, Samos?'

He didn't know why he chose Samos as his rival in that nightmare, that night of sticky hours, of a melting clock. Why he conducted such a tense dialogue, since they were on the same side and of the same opinion. The ending, however, never changed. The mere mention of burning books dissipated the scene. All the characters fell silent. Disappeared. The nightmare was officially over. There was no specific instruction. They hadn't assembled on purpose to agree on perpetual silence, nor had it been suggested at some meeting. The burning of books had simply ceased to exist. The pact of silence applied to the subconscious as well.

No. 5 Chanel Paris.

Everything was contained in that bottle.

It took up an entire page of ABC.

It was like a strange event that captivated his eyes. He realised they were being disobedient, weren't the slightest bit interested in the articles or reports on the mournful, doctrinal pages of Arriba. All the news and charm were in the emerging publicity.

The censor would have liked to hold that bottle in his hand.

Yes, ABC had much more publicity and its superior, glossy pages showed off the advertisements and emitted the tinkle of money being paid for large spaces: the plots of land in Torrelodones, attention, girlfriends of doctors, engineers, professionals, come and visit the flats being built in the Pilar district. More shampoos, more flexible mattresses, more electrical appliances. On the leisure pages, the eyes were drawn to the large advertisements for fashionable nightclubs in Madrid, such as Black Swan and Moulin Rouge. One of the advertisements was for a Kelvinator refrigerator, which had a smiling woman next to it with an American flag in one hand and a Spanish flag in the other. He got up. In the fridge, there was only a cauliflower and a plate with flakes of cod on it. Both things looked yellow, as if stained by the interior light of a prison. He'd been 'on night duty', what in military terms he called not having slept, tossing and turning. He slammed the fridge door shut and started pacing up and down the corridor, a manic-depressive walk in which he went from a sorrowful, reflective state, practising something as difficult as a seductive excuse, to a progressive state of war. The way he walked matched his mood. There was a pause. He put on the record of 'La favorita' and sat down on the edge of the sofa to wait, in the secret hope that the thickness of the music would give way to the sound of Luís Terranova arriving, a key turning, a door opening that changes everything. He murmured sounds of regret. Felt happy. Fine. His singing kept the romance company. *Vien, Leonora, a' piedi tuoi serto e soglio* . . . Of what importance was the time? Who could be disturbed by the sublime? Rest, sleep, all you cuck- olds, while bel canto's High Command on permanent night duty discusses a prince's fate in a room of curtains with turbulent folds, like Sotomayor's sumptuous, warlike sky in his paintings of enhanced bigwigs. That's what I call having a painter to hand. Taking midgets to the heights. He got up at the end of the music and went over to the window. He could easily imagine himself in a portrait by Sotomayor. Conquerors painted with conquering paint. Successful outcome guaranteed. Needless to say, Sotomayor, Director- General of Fine Arts, was out of his reach. The ranks of painting. What about his pupils? Of the ones he knew, there was none he liked, who was up to the task, without being decadent or abstract. Chelo Vidal was, without doubt, a good painter. Nothing in common with the school of Sotomayor, of course, her art was semi-naive like Chagall's. Her realism had mystery. That was the word. Now that he thought about it, she put aura on the canvas. The judge was right. She should be better known. Leave the provinces. Change theme. She couldn't spend her whole life painting those women with things on top of their heads. Even if she had a special way of doing it. No, they weren't typical scenes. It wasn't folk-art. The women she captured out and about turned into goddesses on the canvas. That chap from the shipping company who bought everything of hers was smart. Before she finished a painting, he'd already bagged it. 'Jews,' Ren said to him one day laconically. He did look a bit like a Jew. His surname was Loureiro. Laurel, the name of a tree. Apparently anyone named after a tree is of Jewish ancestry: Maceiras, Carballo, Pexegueiro, Nespereira, Freixo, Salgueiro . . . Apple, Oak, Peach, Medlar, Ash, Willow . . . But that would make half of Galicia Jewish! Lots to think about. That Ren doesn't even trust his shadow. You can't live like that. Doesn't even trust the dead. He told him he had to calm down. 'You won't have a single enemy left, Ren. Leave a cripple for the museum at least. Don't take your duty so seriously.' He said it as a joke. But the humorous side of Ren's brain wasn't very well developed. 'I don't do it out of duty,' he replied. 'I do it because I want to. We all have our pleasures and this is mine.' One day, he had to cut him short. Because of Luís Terranova, who else? 'That assistant of yours, that singer . . .'

'That's my business, Ren. He's my ward. Didn't I tell you he was my ward, Ren? I think I made it clear.'

He was going to add, 'Gilda has a ward.' Because nothing is hidden and Commander Dez also has his spies. Out and about. One of whom informed him. Too much drink and even mutes loosen their tongue. Which is what happened to him. He referred to Gilda when talking about the staff working in censorship. He quickly pointed out he didn't mean anyone in particular, but it was too late for that.

'We all have our things, Ren. I have an assistant, like so many others. He's clean and attentive. And if I ask him to sing, he sings. Even "Amado Mio", like Gilda, like Rita Hayworth doing a striptease. He sings very well, but I don't have to force him. Got it, Ren?'

Ren grunted and fell silent. He understood.

Yes. The judge and he were old friends. He'd picked up one of the most beautiful women in Coruña. Not that it was obvious, you had to spot her beauty and he'd spotted it. Good shot, Ricardo Samos. A woman who was both artistic and sporty. Modern, but not in the modern style. A futuristic woman, he thought, and chuckled. He also had been a futuristic poet. For a few months, like Eugenio Montes. What had happened to futurism? In fridges. He found it in the advertisements for electrical appliances. Yes. Artist and swimmer. He'd known Chelo Vidal before the war. She was one of the sirens who swam from Coruña to Ferrol. The judge was a Triton.

Dez too, in his own way. He laughed to himself. So the judge spotted her, if you like, at sea. Next they coincided at an exhibition. A retrospective of women painters. The Republic encouraged all that stuff about free women. It included María Corredoira, Maruja Mallo, Elena Olmos, Lola Díaz Baliño and others. Chelo Vidal was one of those unknown others. She used a pseudonym back then, what was it? Oh, it doesn't matter. She was there. Samos spent more time looking at her than at the paintings. And the paintings weren't bad. What Dez noticed was Chelo's outfit. Each to his own. Now, in censorship, he enjoyed going to measure the cabaret singers' skirts and necklines. Chelo Vidal was wearing a black rayon suit, with wide trouser legs like two hybrid skirts. Around her waist, an esparto belt like a sailor's rope. The shape of the sleeves accentuated her slim arms. The whole effect was boyish. So natural, so simple, that was what made it so provocative. Whatever happened to that black rayon suit? The war had quashed such pleasures and it would be many years before a woman, even Chelo Vidal, dared to wear a trouser suit again in public. He used to say, as a provocation, that he liked women in trousers. Women dressed as men. It upset his machos. What the hell, he could afford to take such liberties. After all, he was one of the conquerors. From censorship, I grant you, but I have my tastes. And closet intimacies. He didn't say this, of course. If he didn't do what he did, he could have been an expert in fashion. The point is Ricardo Samos and Chelo Vidal were distant relations through her father and his mother. Half cousins. Yes, he remembers Samos' eyes and impassioned words when he fell for the rayon artist, 'This cousin of mine is worthy of a crime!' A real compliment. The war found her in France on a scholarship awarded by the government to a group of young artists. But, unlike many others, she came back after the Victory. She was an artist but without blemish. None that could be uncovered. Except for her brother. That good-for-nothing photographer. This Leica was friends with Huici, who turned his tailor's shop into an avant-garde hang-out and ended the way he did. Leica saved his skin thanks to his sister and her marriage. He's not a bad lad. He married a local boss's daughter, who was crazy about him. He must have something. She won't let him out whatever the weather. Enough to make any stone warm, so I'm told. He went to photograph a couple who'd just got married, straight out of church, in Mariñán Gardens. First, photos of the two of them, like that, smiling. Now the bride on her own. He takes his time, adjusts the white tulle dress without spoiling the train. That's right. The bridegroom gets bored, heads off to see to the reception. The photographer and bride are left alone to work with the light. The expression, look at me, don't look at me. They touch, hair better like that, he moves the bouquet, neckline far prettier, and of course it was a hot day, filled with aromas, on the banks of the Mandeo, a day for Caneiros, anything could happen and it did. They thought they were alone. He stood with her on top, wrapped in tulle, her back pressing against the trunk of the old Jupiter tree, shaking the heavy clusters of pink flowers. The photo they made. A good one, unforgettable. It may not have been next to the Jupiter tree, but under the large canopy of the Caucasian fir. Or the showy cedar. It worked well with any tree, though he preferred the one with the pink flowers. The point is they shook their bodies and the branches. This story Dez had embroidered, which was based on unconfirmed rumours, met with great success on evenings out, especially among well-to-do couples. He avoided rude words, using instead French delicacies copied from out-of-print erotic novels, the *coup de foudre*, *coup de folie*, the *coup* created an atmosphere. He gave particular emphasis to his description of the combined movements of pink flowers and tulle and could see the jubilant perturbation, the colour in their cheeks. He took pleasure in their pleasure at being shocked. Listening to the censor, with a bard's qualities, giving a *coup sur coup* account of the *s'accoupler* under the tree of the wedding photographer and newly-wed bride.

Of course he never told his elaborate story if Ricardo Samos and Chelo Vidal were present. He felt great admiration for her, the painter. She had all the presence of a great lady with the charm of a young girl who's come from Cuba and a slight touch, like eye shadow, of having had contact with Bohemian life in the Republican city. But she always put art first. Minded her own business. Her most revolutionary act, thought Dez, had been to wear that rayon suit and dazzle Samos, it wasn't easy for a woman to quicken his heartbeat. Samos had confided in him. First he'd made that unusual declaration, 'This cousin of mine is worthy of a crime!' Then he'd affirmed, 'She'll be my wife.' Dez, at the time, was already a Falangist, but Samos, the future judge, still moved in the world of ideas, fancied himself as an intellectual and contributed to the magazines *Acción Española* and *Integralismo Lusitano*, fostered by two monarchist, Catholic groups whose goal was a conservative Iberian league. Back then, Samos claimed the City of God went against the Falange's 'primitive aggression', though he conceded a certain 'barbaric charm'. So Dez made fun of him, 'If it's action you're after, real action, then you know whom you have to talk to.' But it was books, not Dez's perseverance, which led Samos to become a Fascist and join the conspiracy against the Republic. The discovery of Carl Schmitt, that Don Carlos. When they walked through Mina Square, with the huge flag bearing a swastika hanging outside the German consulate, Dez would deliberately make the Roman salute, which bothered Samos to start with. He had that Catholic prejudice against the Nazis. But he got over this after reading Schmitt. This Don Carlos took him back to Donoso Cortés and Joseph de Maistre. A concoction that transformed Samos.

Commander Dez stood up and went over to the record player. 'La favorita' had ended, but the record kept on turning. A fault that annoyed him, as did the disobedience of faulty machines in general. The listless, practically inaudible creak grew louder like the groan of an axle in the thick of night. He'd already told Luís Terranova to take it to be repaired.

'It's nothing.'

'What do you mean, nothing?'

'You just have to lift the arm and put it back on its rest.'

'Why must you always contradict me?'

'I'm not contradicting you. I just think differently.'

It had been, he thought, an electrical attraction, an attraction of opposites. For him at least. What bothered him made Terranova laugh. It would always be a mystery. Simple and irresistible. A magnetic body. Electricity. Bodies went about their own business, ignored each other, played at distances or struggled to enter each other, to fit, curves and angles, bones, muscles, gaps, vents. A forging of symmetry. *Ad libitum.*

'What was that?'

'*Ad libitum.*'

'You're crazy, degenerate.'

Degenerate. How he liked to be called that. It was one of the 'official' words he used daily in an attempt to classify what was unacceptable. Degenerate. With what pleasure he'd spoken of the degenerate artistic avant-garde as a symptom of social unrest and western decadence. He liked to adopt a virile tone in cultural meetings, especially in a lacklustre environment of schoolmistresses who'd secretly be reading God knows what by Pardo Bazán or Pérez Galdós and small-time artists with the informalist devil inside them, the dangerous look of hunger in those who dream of eating the world of forms. When the order came to close the magazine *Atlántida*, not long before, around the time Dionisio Ridruejo and others who'd gone soft in the head were disgraced in Madrid, he was one of those who informed the editorial board of the decision and how he enjoyed passing on the head censor's anathema, 'Existentialist claptrap!' He did, however, make it clear this wasn't his opinion. Sada was there, among others. Now he was a great painter, could even be described as painting itself, shame he didn't do portraits, but fell into the sea, never to resurface. Someone else who didn't know how to catapult themselves. And he'd been asked to paint the inside of Franco's yacht, the *Azor*. Even so. There he was, catalogued under 'existentialist claptrap'. When the alarm sounded, words came first. Standing firm, in line. He'd already warned them, after the last issue devoted to Valle-Inclán, that they were on the red line. No, these schoolmistresses and artists had no idea how much he enjoyed condemning 'degenerate art'. He wore an expression of disgust, but inside he felt a tingling. The same tingling he felt when he heard about the 'existentialist claptrap' of *Atlántida* from head office. He chewed on these hostile words. Words he then poured with saliva, salted, leavened balls, into Terranova's ear: degenerate, existentialist, unruly.

They shared a fascination for music. It was something that moved him, he had to confess. Arriving to find Luís Terranova listening to Schubert's lieder, *Die Forelle*, that song about the trout, his eyes wide open, without eyelids, like a fish watching sounds in the flooded house. Absorbed, motionless, breathing music through his skin. And then there was his voice. His voice drove him crazy. And Dez was demanding, very demanding. He knew a real voice when he heard one. Some time ago, when Terranova came to live with him, he found him two good teachers, one for music theory and another for singing. The two of them were agreed. He had what it took, voice and talent, to triumph. But, deep down, Terranova made fun of bel canto. He always had that glint in his eyes. He lacked ambition. Wasn't up to the task. Dez should have realised sooner. Perhaps it had been absurd to lead him in that direction. He'd got him some performances. Christmas charity concerts and the like. He could have got him more if he'd been more determined. But it wasn't an unmitigated disaster. No one could accuse him of doing the same as the tycoon Kane with his beloved, of trying to turn that pipsqueak into an opera star. Luís Terranova was good. People liked him. Dez shuddered just to see him walk out on stage in that bow-tie. He particularly enjoyed his performances at private functions in hotels or expensive villas. He shared the applause. Was congratulated on his protégé. He wasn't interested in rumours any more. He never bothered to clarify Terranova's move from assistant to ward or nephew and finally to artistic protégé. He was proud. Luís Terranova was popular with both men and women. But he belonged to Dez. That much was clear. Dez would allow flirting, small seductive adventures, adulterous games at those glamorous parties. Terranova was sweet, kind and attractive, a perfect target for bored rich people during crazy nights. The censor didn't mind such games. He took an irate pleasure in the thorns of jealousy, savoured them as the prelude to what he called training sessions, sessions of taming and conquest.

The years went by. Both leading a double life, but Dez felt sure he was in control of the situation. Terranova was used to the role he'd been given. And there was something very important, which almost no one knew, a closely guarded secret. Terranova had been taken as a slave. Terrible to say, but it was true. Terranova knew he had no life beyond Dez's reach. And like a frightened sheep, he was being strangled by his own halter.

'Houses have a tendency not to fall,' says a humorous aphorism he'd used in patriotic discussions after the United Nations had condemned the regime. He was now reminded of it. Paradoxically. Because his house, his building, was in a state of collapse. Terranova had come to his office one day, looked him in the eye and told him he wanted to lead his own life. Dez wasn't sure how to react. Luís was wearing his blue bow-tie with the silver filaments. 'You shouldn't wear that during the day, it loses its charm,' he replied. 'My own life. Starting with work. I'm not doing any more of those ulcerous performances. No more bel canto, Tomás. I'm going to sing at dances.' Yes. What he wanted was to sing at open-air dances, for his friend, the singer Pucho Boedo, to invite him on stage, for people to ask who that guy was and for someone to say, 'One with a voice like Pucho Boedo.' That for him was to triumph. To be compared to Pucho Boedo. To triumph in dance halls or in the open air. To excel at a tango one Sunday evening at Chaparrita over in Ponte da Pasaxe. He'd got it into his head he was going to enter and win that radio competition, 'Parade of Stars', which was so popular.

'You're so childish! What are you going to do in "Parade of Stars"?'

'Don't worry. I won't sing Violetta's cabaletta.'

He may have overreacted. It was just a punch. The trouble is Luís was fragile. He had a glass nose and it spewed blood. He was doing it for him. So that he'd lose some of his coarseness and aim a little higher. He also overdid it the day Luís came home with that friend of his, the cowboy photographer, Papagaio's Hercules.

'I don't want to see that hick here again.'

A house has a tendency not to fall. He'd turned up elegantly dressed in his office. His first visit since the time Dez had summoned him to expound his delicate situation. Years had gone by. He'd achieved his objective. He'd taken possession of him. He governed his life and enjoyed his body. Without losing face, power or position. Why'd he come? To tell him his house was in ruins?

'What a wretch you are. I'll crush you like a worm. You'll end up in a prison for queens or with a bullet up your arse.'

'I just want to lead my own life. Follow my own path.'

'A goat always heads for the mountain, right?'

Tomás Dez went over to the window. The roofs of the Old City seemed to be squeaking like mice in the storm. The wind drove the clouds, torn from the sea's straw mattress, to cover the first cracks of dawn.

If only he hadn't been so inconsiderate, so wild, so . . . He finally found the word a silent part of his mind had been searching for during his vigil. So ungrateful. He repeated it in a fairly loud voice to make amends to himself. So ungrateful! What was he doing awake all night, being martyred, while that pimp was out and about? Martyrdom, martyrdom, martyrdom, that was the word. From then on, his passage through the house, at the slow pace of a procession, turned into a summary trial. His walk regained its measure, his body its figure. Every step he took was a new charge laid against Luís Terranova. He finally felt well. The boss had taken over that weak, crude, unruly body. He felt well all right. As when he took the stage, alerted the audience, silenced the rustling of Sunday poems and brought not emotion, but fear to the literary festival organised by the group Amanecer. It was a spring festival and everything was going like spring. The atmosphere was relaxed, even joky. One of the participants read a poem with a questioning refrain, 'Where's the key?' Until someone in the audience shouted out, 'Here, between my balls!' The organisation was linked to the regime, but clearly the time for ardent patriotic hymns had passed. He was nervous, he also had some 'spring' sheets in his hand. He'd been invited by a childhood acquaintance, a simple woman turned poet who one day had been naive enough to declare herself 'pregnant with poetry', having been possessed on an evening stroll in Bárbaras Square by the ghost of Gustavo Adolfo Bécquer. The point is she'd agreed to act as messenger and invite him to the festival. She said, 'Ah, Dez! Censor and poet. How thrilling!' Yes, she found everything thrilling. But he'd see fear on her face too. Because, when he was announced, as a poet, of course, not as censor, someone inside him forgot his 'spring' sheets and deadened his nerves. The boss had taken over. His voice thundered like a cannon. Put an end to smiles and rustling.

> My mind has become exact, defined, sure,
> from the mist of vague reality far removed.
> The War is hard and pure,
> as hard and pure is truth.

It was the *Poem of the Beast and the Angel*, José María Pemán's contribution to the 'holy war' against the satanic Republic. A poem belonging to them, to the victors filling the auditorium. But they were still confused. Confused in spring. Stunned. Unsure whether to clap or not. How he enjoyed that lyrical upheaval.

He made some coffee. He felt well all right. The verdict was clear. That bastard would remember Tomás Dez for ever. He'd stuff night down his throat. He just had to make a call. Ren answered immediately. He must still sleep like that. As he said, next to both his bugs. The telephone and the pistol. Yes, it was a service, a favour after so many years. Yes, with the car. And a blanket for the upholstery. He then went to get dressed. At least his shoes were shiny. He smiled as if looking in the mirror. 'No, no, no,' he told his shoes, 'don't come to me asking for mercy!' His walk now was martial. He felt well, stepping firmly. He looked around. The whole house was under Terranova's charm and he'd have to reconquer it. Luís had weaved his spell on things. It was obvious. He spent more time with them. Tolerated their faults. Now, at daybreak, they were sleepless and wary. Distant. They'd be waiting for him to leave so that they could start having some fun. No doubt Terranova was thinking the same. That he'd leave early. Have his coffee and read the papers in the Oriental Café or Alcázar, next to the censor's office. Well, no. He wasn't going to leave.

He heard the lock muffle its own mechanism. They were in cahoots. He'd have found it impossible to open the door so quietly.

Luís Terranova was carrying a sailor's canvas bag. Empty. He saw Dez standing erect, with his arms crossed, on the brink of dawn. Funny, he thought. In the dark, the first thing he made out were his black shoes. The shoes he'd polished. Good work. He did it almost as well as the shoeshiner in Cantón Bar.

He decided to go to his room and do what he'd planned. Take his things and leave. His belongings would easily fit in the canvas bag. He wouldn't take any presents, not even a cravat. He could have not come back. Now that he thought about it, saw the ghost of Dez like a skeleton next to the hat-stand, it might have been better. But he wanted to show that he was leaving. As I came, I went.

'Where are you off to? To sing in the street?'

'Goodbye, Dez. I'm not your assistant any more. Or your ward. Or your housekeeper's son. Or your nephew. Or your protégé. No more being a slave. No more second clown Toni. I've paid back the favour by now.'

Dez seized his shoulder.

'Slavery? Hardly a sublime farewell, Terranova. After all these years, a castrato's song at least.'

Luís was two feet away from the door. He wheeled around suddenly and hit him with the canvas bag. Not enough to stop Dez's well-oiled machinery. Dez grabbed his hair just as he was about to leave.

'I told you you should cut your hair as men do. Remember what I taught you? The pulmonary strength of a man for a child's voice. You know how to imitate them. Do Gaetano Caffarelli in the Sistine Chapel!'

The pressure on his head and neck forced him on to his knees. Dez slammed the door shut. The first punch was aimed at disfigurement. Luís heard his nose crack as if part of a collapse in which the roof caved in. Perhaps all that blood was from the splintering beams. It spattered the lapels of his light-coloured jacket.

'Now you won't be able to do the castrato number. Give us something local. What was that song, Terranova? The one you sang to make me jealous. Don't look at me like that. You're far too ugly.'

'Let go of my hair, will you, Dez? It hurts more than my nose.'

He pulled harder. A tuft of hair in his hand.

'That really hurts,' stuttered Terranova.

'"I fell in love with a thorn . . ." What was that song, Terranova? Sing it again. "The flower that was". No. That wasn't it. Do you remember? You were full of yourself. "A Pontevedran Alalá!"'

'You shouldn't set your heart . . .'

'That's it, that's it.'

'on things that belong to the wind'.

'Good, good. That's our sublime farewell. Now I can really smash your face in.'

'If you hurt me any more, I won't be able to enter the radio competition and sing the cabaletta.'

There was an innocent, defenceless glint in Luís Terranova's eyes. Dez watched the blood pouring out of his nostrils. It was the colour of lava.

'I'll take you to have that seen to,' he said without letting go.

'No, no. I'll go on my own.'

'On your own? You won't go anywhere on your own. Do you think I'm crazy, Terranova?'

'Don't worry, Dez. I won't talk to anyone. I'll disappear into a hole and won't come out until I'm healed. I promise. Let go of me, Dez.'

'I like it when you're meek and mild. Not another word. I'll take you to a bonesetter, my little dove. Who'll fix that cherub's nose.'

Luís Terranova made one final attempt to escape when he saw the black car parked in the street and the stocky guy in an ashen hat and raincoat opening the back door. The two of them held on to him, laid him on the back seat and he stopped moving when he felt the barrel nuzzling under his ear. It was as if a bullet had gone into him without needing to be fired.

They beat him up on the far side of the lighthouse. The last thing he remembers hearing was a sound of his coming from outside. The crunching of teeth. Of his teeth. He then heard a voice from a state of unconsciousness, 'You'll never sing again, Terranova!' And the first thing he heard when he woke up was actually a vision: the beams of light from the lighthouse.

'Louder! Can't hear you. Louder!'

Curtis' Second Fight

Terror was crystallised on Luís Terranova's face. The frost of night on top of the beating. Curtis ran to open the door when he heard the knocker's Morse. He sat him in the middle of the room, under the lamp. This was his house on Atocha Baixa, a single room with a kitchen and bathroom, a kind of boxing ring which had grown walls and a roof. Even though he was sitting down, Luís carried on bending over under the lamp. His hands between his thighs, on his groin. The instinct to protect his private parts. He was barely able to speak. He gurgled words spattered with blood through the gaps of his broken teeth. But he didn't stop. He knew Curtis understood every single trill of his. Could mend the onomatopoeias, the badly injured syllables. His face was swollen, the bald patches where they'd torn out his hair covered in scabs, his lips split open. They'd really given his mouth a hammering. Which is maybe why Luís Terranova didn't stop trying to speak. He was checking to see if he was alive. He spluttered out a tango, a song he put together with disconnected bits from different pieces, scraps of 'Downhill', 'Laugh Clown' and 'Chessman' which began to make sense. He didn't need to articulate them clearly. Curtis understood. He could see the words pushing through the clots, splashing in his saliva. He gave him a swig. Arturo da Silva was right. The terrestrial globe changes place, but there's always one in Luís Terranova's mouth.

'Don't drink it. It's for rinsing and spitting out. Spit it out slowly.'

'More champagne, if you please, boy . . .'

He knew what to sing all right.

'Now I really look like a boxer, don't I, Curtis? If Arturo da Silva saw me, he'd give me a ticking-off. He'd say, "Your face is the colour of raw flesh. How could they beat you up like that? Why didn't you keep your distance? Make a feint, open a side corridor?"

'"There wasn't time, Arturo." That's what I'd tell him if he came round here. "I was going to open a side corridor, Arturo, I just needed a fraction of time."

'"A fraction is everything," Arturo would say. "A fraction is the difference between life and death."'

Curtis had filled a zinc bathtub with warm water. He prepared the brazier and placed it next to him. He took off his shoes and helped him to undress. Cleaned his wounds. Applied iodine. Cut his hair so that he could cure his head better. Sewed up an eyebrow. Three stitches without anaesthetic. And while he did this, Curtis made plans. He knew Terranova was hard behind his fragile appearance. He was the one who'd taught him to let a sea urchin's spines come out by themselves without carving deep flesh wounds.

Terranova recognised the wooden horse in a corner of the room, in the shadows. 'There you are, Cariri!' And the horse replied with the affection of inanimate things when they're called by name. It made Terranova get rid of that crystallised fear and smile for a photo. He remembered another travelling photographer who was hit by a tram and fell to the ground with his wooden horse. 'To hospital, to hospital!' cried a witness who'd come to help the injured man. The photographer raised his head with difficulty and said, 'Not hospital! To the horse factory!'

'Take me to the workshop for horses,' mumbled Luís Terranova. 'A bonesetter with cardboard and paste.' Curtis smiled. He knew the story. They'd often stopped in front of the horse factory between Troncoso and Our Lady of the Rosary. The horses came in all shapes and sizes. From a little horse for a keyring to a fairground or photographer's horse. This also would make a good business card: *Vicente Curtis 'Hercules', Boxer and Horse Manufacturer*. He tried to straighten the fingers on his hands, but the right middle and index fingers wouldn't respond. They'd bent them back until they snapped. 'A horse repairer,' he said. 'Or even better one of those who dissect animals. A taxidermist. Can I sleep there, Curtis, next to the horse? Wait for all of this to be over. It'll never be over, will it, Curtis? Now I really must look interesting. All the colours of raw flesh. A Cubist painting. I'll make better use of the mirror now, Curtis.'

In the house on Atocha Baixa, there was only a small mirror, which Curtis used to shave. It was broken and was joined by a plaster, though the whole piece was big enough. The size of the blade of a cut-throat razor.

Manlle moved in little light. He smoked a Havana cigar and seemed not to be in a hurry, like the smoke, which gathered slowly, forming a pale bell on the mezzanine of the dockside warehouse. He had a philosophy. So he then took time to explain his philosophy. He wasn't a man for whom business was just business. It was a personal matter. He'd never do business with someone if he couldn't shake their hand. That's what he was explaining to Curtis. He wasn't in a hurry. Money: the more you run after it, the further away it gets.

'See, Curtis? Course you do. A man's a man. I respect people who've nothing but day and night. I know what it is not to have enough to make a blind man sing. I can't stand people who fill their pockets just by lifting the receiver and dialling a number. That's how money's being made now, Curtis, in shedloads. There's corruption all over the shop. You just got to have contacts. Doesn't matter whether you put a building in front of Hercules Lighthouse. With contacts, you can do it and who gives a shit about the panoramic view, the perfect location, the city's smile? Big business is like that, Curtis. Those who make money don't touch a brick, don't touch a fish, don't touch anything. Contacts, information. That's what counts. I got my contacts, I got my information. But I like to touch things, the merchandise. Touch what I'm selling. Whisky, tobacco. Women. I like to see it all. That's my pleasure. See how it works, right? If there's a shipment, be where it's happening. Watch the movement, watch how the merchandise changes value each step of the way. Same with people, Curtis. I'm glad you came. You moved. I know you're an honest man. We met in the wrong circumstances, what to do? It's history. I was wanting to talk to someone about Arturo da Silva. A shame, Curtis. He was a champ in and out of the ring. I saw him that day, just before the war, when he unarmed that guy who's now a judge

174

in Pontevedra Square. He went straight up to him. Took the pistol out of his hands and threw it in the sea. Now he no longer exists. There's no one to talk to about him. Just the guys who killed him. I met one or two of them. You know, you bump into all sorts of people in this life. And there I was, with one of his murderers, discussing Arturo da Silva's style of boxing. He had to admit he was the best in the ring, another reason for taking him out. The things you have to hear. I could have ate him up right there and shat him in the toilet. But I can't be St Clare, Curtis. I got to look after my interests. I can't go walking about without shoes or clogs.

'Arturo da Silva, that's right. You were lucky enough to train with the best. Do you know what I liked about him? The way he took up all the space. You have to feel well in the place you move in. The ring was his country and the other had to conquer it. That's it. I know he used to visit the ring beforehand.'

'Yep, he always liked to be the first to arrive,' said Curtis.

He could see him now. When there was no one about, he'd walk around the ring. Still in his clothes. His hands in his pockets. He'd stand there for a while, deep in thought, and complete a circuit.

'He always had that idea about the globe.'

'The globe?'

'The terrestrial globe is on the move. You have to try to know all the time where its point of support is.'

That's right, he thought, the globe's support.

Manlle blew a cloud of smoke through the left side of his mouth as if making space for what he listened to carefully. He was a sponge. And proud of it.

'Everyone,' he said sententiously, 'has at least one brilliant idea in their life. Maybe no more. But they have one.'

The phone rang. Three times. He didn't answer. It rang again, twice. He waited. The third time, he picked up the receiver. Said, 'You're not feeling well? No problem.' He hung up and then dialled a number. 'Falcón? Tell Mother we won't be coming to dinner tonight.'

He looked at his watch and then at Curtis. 'My ideas never reached my fists. I could hit hard. But it's one thing to hit hard and another to hit with ideas. You had ideas, Curtis. You belonged to Arturo's school. Your left was a cobra. That one-two, a killer. You see, Curtis, I never forgot that fight. You didn't give me time to breathe. I hit hard, but my idea didn't make it to my fist. You didn't give me time.'

'I was in a hurry,' said Curtis. 'It was a special day.'

'Unbelievable, eh, Curtis? We made our debut the day a war started. You would have been champion. You know, I'm glad you knocked me out. I soon learnt my place in boxing wasn't inside the ring. My brilliant idea was something else. So I lost a tooth and discovered a mine. What I had was good eyesight, but I didn't know it yet.'

He opened his mouth and pointed to a gold canine. 'They could at least have given us a gumshield! Here it is. Pure gold. But I kept the other. I'm glad you gave it back to me. It was a fine trophy. Stuck in your glove like that. Man, you could hit hard. I'm sorry they didn't let you compete again.'

He scratched his throat as if he'd found a bitter-tasting vein. Stamped his cigarette out in the ashtray. Curtis knew what had happened. The guy was a wheeler-dealer. There was no one else.

'I'm in a hurry right now, champ. Some urgent business to attend to. I'll do what I can. What is it you want, Curtis?'

'A passport and passage to Argentina.'

'You're finally leaving, are you, Curtis? You do well. I always said walking about with a photographer's horse was no job for a champ.'

'It's for someone else. A friend.'

'A mighty good friend.'

'That's right, a good friend.'

'Makes no difference. If you don't escape, you leave. It's what our country does. Export people. I said to a local boss, "At this rate, we won't have any clients left. You, the priests and me." He said, "If they're not happy, better that they leave. One less to deal with." Unbelievable! They don't care if they're put in charge of a cemetery. Exporting's easy. It's importing that's difficult. You don't smoke, right?'

'Sometimes,' said Curtis.

'Here you go. Genuine Sport A. Passage and passport with visa? Done. You know what you have to do, right?'

'I brought everything with me,' said Curtis, handing over Luís Terranova's photograph and documents.

'Sure. You know what you have to do, right?'

A slaggish smoke rose from the ashtray.

'Fight without gloves for an unlimited number of rounds. Few people, but with lots of money. Bets taken along the way. This Saturday night. There's no address. Someone'll pick you up and give you the agreed after the fight. Trust me. And I'll trust you.'

Curtis looked at his hands. He was rubbing them slowly.

'But none of your Hercules, right? No fateful one-two. You got to keep back the cobra, Curtis, understand? You got to lose. That's all there is. You fight as if you were going to win, but you got to lose. It's up to you when you go down, but make it look convincing. Lots of them will be betting for you. We need to see some raw flesh. And if it's in a pool of blood, so much the better.'

There was a knock at the door of the house on Atocha Baixa. Terranova got up with great difficulty and swore. Someone had locked it from the outside, he couldn't open.

He heard a voice, 'Pay attention to what's coming under the door.'

He then saw an envelope.

'That's your ticket,' said Curtis outside the door.

'What's up, Curtis? Why don't you come in?'

'It couldn't be Buenos Aires. It's for La Guaira. The next ship, got it? I suppose they'll sing tangos there too.'

'Where've you been, Curtis?'

'Listen. When you go through customs in Venezuela and they ask you your profession, you have to say you're an electrical engineer, got it?'

'Got it, Curtis.'

'Go on, repeat it.'

'Electrical engineer, electrical engineer, electrical engineer.'

He went over to the window. It was reinforced. He removed the bar and slid open the bolt. Stuck his head out. There was no one there.

The White Roses

The wild, white roses on the road from Castro to Elviña are small and seem to be putting all their effort not into growth, but into their fragrance. You can miss them, hidden, shy as they are against a backdrop of myrtle, but then they lift their heads and fill the place. Polka says the most envied bees visit those rosebushes.

'Some bees go in front to look for the flower and then keep quiet about it back in the hive.'

'That means they're selfish, not envied.'

'No. When you and Olinda stop looking for wild roses, there won't be any.'

In the bundle of clothes and the basket, she'd put white roses, everlastings, fennel, marjoram, rosemary, aromatic herbs for the house of the painter. The knowledge she'd inherited from Olinda. And on her return, Neves, the maid, would hide fashion magazines she liked to read sitting on the toilet.

The Prickles of Words

He didn't remember when he started getting tongue-tied, but he remembered the day his father noticed. It was the first time he'd received the warning, something inside him had said here comes a word with problems. A word dragging its own skeleton. A spicule without a sponge. A mushroom in the shade. A wounded crab. This warning, this alert, caught him by surprise in front of his father. He couldn't let the word out, he felt its traction, its attempt to climb, its prickles, but couldn't let it out because it was crippled, maimed, trembling and possibly beside itself.

'What is it, Gabriel?'

The way he asked. The way he looked. A catastrophe. Everything was happening not inside him, but on his father's face. He knew the fear he had of trembling or precipitate words was as nothing compared to the fear his father's fear gave him. And he sensed his father's fear was fear of what they'd say in the city. Occasionally, very rarely, he'd heard him say this. 'What'll they say, what'll they think in the city?' But when he referred to the city, he wasn't talking about the whole city. Gabriel knew by now what his father meant when he referred to the city.

'What were you going to say, Gabriel?'

He shook his head.

His father insisted. Rationalised what had happened. His ears tried to remember. Not one, not two, but more. Gabriel was stammering. His son. A child who was . . . perfect. That was the word. In short. He wanted to make sure it wasn't a nightmare.

'You were going to say something, Gabriel. Go on. What is it? Are you not well? Say something. Speak. Tell me about the trolleybus.' His imaginary journeys with Chelo, his mother. Every Tuesday, they'd depart from Porta Real. The red, double-decker buses had been brought from London, second-hand. What fun it was to go upstairs, to sit in the first row, the large front window like a screen in the city's real cinema. 'Where did you go yesterday? To Montevideo. Come on, say Montevideo. You sometimes go to Lisbon, don't you? Lisbon's easy to say. Say Lisbon.'

'Lisbon.'

'That's good, Gabriel. Another city you go to is Paris. Let's see if you can say Montevideo, Lisbon, Paris, Berlin, Barcelona. It's just a joke. A game. I know you can say all of this. But say it to me now.'

'Montevideo, Lisbon, Paris . . .'

Things always happened somewhere. On the beach this summer, he'd learnt to dive. A little. But for him these first experiences were like underwater journeys. He couldn't believe it when he opened his eyes and saw Chelo's feet, enormous under the water, the toes like rock creatures with pearly shells. Now he'd like to dive and go between his father's legs. He felt the presence of Grand Mother Circa, the grandfather clock, behind him. It had come from Cuba, like the wooden horse Carirí, and been a wedding present from Chelo's father. He'd always end up there when he started to walk. He'd use it as a support, watch the pendulum. It was a fantastic creature, alive, with its own way of speaking day and night. He used to dream something was happening and this is where he'd hide. The grandfather clock leant against the room's central pillar. The sunlight coming in from the balcony – it was a winter's day, but there was a magnificent sun, a 'Catholic sun', someone at court had said – drew a dividing line with the pillar's shadow. So Grand Mother Circa was also, in its own way, a light mechanism. He listened to it up close. He listened to it inside. It calmed the words and ordered them for him. This time, they'd gone on a boat to the Xubias. They'd gone up and down the beach, from the jetty to the estuary channel. On the sandbank, from a neighbouring dune, they could see the two waters fighting it out. Blue and green. They then climbed some rocks to reach a chalet. He tripped several times. Chelo took his hand and helped him up that steep shortcut. The house was closed, except for one of the shutters. How strange. Look. It was a house full of books.

Inhabited by books. A house without books must be sad. Even sadder a house of books without people. Brambles and roses intertwined on the pergola. He protested, 'What are we doing? Why did we come here?'

'It's a boat-house. Isn't it beautiful?'

'Where did you go, Gabriel?'

'To Santa Cristina.'

His father's concern abruptly switched objective. Abandoned him to focus instead on this other place.

'To Santa Cristina? To that beach in this weather?'

Grandpa Mayarí's Cane

Grandpa Mayarí hunted down items of news with the iron tip of his cane. He preferred the yellow ones, dipped in sun and frost, swept along the same paths as the dry leaves, though newspaper stays one step behind, on its own. The leaves of trees and newspapers, freed from the date, move westwards in flocks of crazy melancholy. They sometimes crouch in an abandoned doorway, all mucky, like the hair of a pet which has come back from its nocturnal outing with a dead man's cold slap and been unable to locate the cat-flap. On Mount Alto, the hill on which Hercules Lighthouse stands, some of these itinerant leaves catch on prickly thickets and turn into dry meat. But a few go into a trance and are carried this way and that, tattooing the wind.

These are the ones sought out by the tip of Antonio Vidal, Grandpa Mayarí's cane.

Here's one now. The cane pretends not to see. Suddenly darts through the air and harpoons the piece of news on the sea lane opened by feet in the soft grass. We're on the high cliffs of Gaivoteiro, in the direction of Fura do Touciño, and there's something of the sea bird in the piece of paper. A final flapping of navigational wings.

Mayarí vacated his position at Aristotle's Lantern, grocer's, and chose the start of summer, the best he could remember, to spend a period of time in Coruña. He came to see the boats. This was no excuse, no figure of speech. It was true. Absolutely true. He'd get up very early to go to Muro Fishmarket, which is where fishing boats, *bacas* and *bous* from the Great Sole, unloaded. Although all sales there were by auction and in large quantities, he'd always get some fish, if possible scad and sail-fluke, and sometimes bring one of those large hakes people of the sea call 'Baby Lola', perhaps because of their resemblance to baby mermaids, something he accepted because it fell into his hands and he couldn't say no to the patter of a fishwife, like anyone in the din of a fishmarket who was born a farmer. He never ate it. He liked boats, not fish. In time, I reached the conclusion he bought it for the news, in this case wet and scaly news, since it was usually wrapped in newspaper. He soon got rid of the fish, like someone finally surrendering an infinite, innocent sadness into safe hands, those of Neves, maid and cook, though for a few moments he'd read those sheets of newspaper serving as a shroud. This observation of mine shouldn't sound strange. What was strange, hence it caught my attention, was that Grandpa Mayarí didn't read normal, whole newspapers, there being several, including the two that arrived a couple of days late by subscription from Madrid.

From this first visit to the fishmarket, he'd return when dawn was straining at the oars on the other side of the bay, in Mera. He'd come home when the sun was the height of a man in the east. He'd then have breakfast and, happy as a frog in a puddle, take in a view of the port from the gallery. He adored his daughter and maintained a solemn silence in front of her paintings. His daughter, Chelo, respected this silence. I don't recall her ever asking for his opinion, in search of an adjective, though she could so easily have elicited praise from someone who loved her so much. I'm sure Antonio Vidal liked those paintings, I'm in no doubt, I think I knew him quite well, but I suppose, like almost everyone else, he wondered why Chelo didn't paint landscapes and, above all, why she didn't paint seascapes.

I possessed the answer to the question grandpa never asked, but to the one who did ask, I didn't want to give it.

Chelo painted landscapes on the palm of my hand. Souvenirs, she called them. When she was satisfied, she'd sign them: *Souvenir* by Corot. So this name was always familiar to me, like someone tickling my hand. A name that went from my hand to my eyes with an easel on its back.

When I couldn't speak, when I stumbled on a word and she saw that this struggle with language was filling me with icy horror, that of an inner being whose teeth are chattering in the cold, teeth and a cold which got inside, behind my eyes, under my tongue, she'd say, 'Come.' And paint a souvenir on my hand. 'White, blue, grey and silver today.'

The habit of opening and closing my hand.

'Hey, what's that?' Grandpa Mayarí would ask.

In the afternoon, we'd go out to Mount Alto, as far as Hercules Lighthouse. But first we'd stop at the Grapevine bar and sit under the trellis. He'd say to me, 'You watch her laugh.' When the woman came, he'd order a fizzy water for me. 'And for the old man,' he'd say, meaning himself, 'an electric Ribeiro.' And it was true, the woman did laugh.

'Now let me see what you've got in there.'

I opened my hand very, very slowly.

'A boat, eh? A boat in the mist. Lucky you.'

But there was something else Chelo did to help me with language. Teach me how to read and write as soon as possible. Long before I went to school. Chelo's idea was that I had to transfer my thoughts to my hand. 'Your mouth,' she'd say, 'will speak through your fingers. And what you do with your fingers will demand sound.' It was true. A straight line had a sound. A wavy line demanded a sound. A curved line, another. You had to write them down. Play with sounds. Not be afraid of them.

I started writing by drawing. Before letters, forms. Zigzags, spirals, crosses. And it's true that forms produce a sound, a sound that's already inside you, lying in wait, in the gorge of your throat. I realised this the first time I drew a large triangle. A large triangle demands the sound of a large triangle. In this way, my voice followed the line drawn by my hand. So that letters, when they arrived, were also forms of nature, as t is the mast of a boat and l a cypress. O can be lots of things. An o can be the sun or moon. We had a washerwoman called O. In the calendar of saints, there was Our Lady of Expectation, Mary of the O. I used to laugh when my mother saw her in the distance and exclaimed, 'Here comes Our Lady of Expectation!' She was easy to spot since she carried a huge O on top of her head. An O full of clothes. When she arrived, her face was also a smiley O, with two clear eyes, so that her presence recalled the sun and circles of water.

'Hello, O.'

O, the washerwoman, was one of the women Chelo painted. A series that seemed unending, and in fact was, which she called *Women Carrying Things on Top of Their Heads*.

O and Harmony

He wasn't a baby any more. When he was five or six, he wet the bed. Not before. It was around that time. It wasn't something to shout about. You didn't come for the clothes, only to be told, 'I'm afraid the boy's wet the sheets, he can't control himself.' The thing is clothes tell their own stories, like a book. Not that I go about repeating what they say. It's our secret. The clothes' and ours. Which is why the bit I like most about washing is laying the clothes in the sun. The point when the sun puts colour back in the clothes and things, the way it shines you'd think you washed the whole place. Puts colour back. In clothes, right, but also in the landscape, in objects, in people's expressions. So you're the one who puts black and canary yellow in ears of maize and the football shirts of Elviña Wanderers. Purple in heather. We sometimes think of happiness as being impossible. Between you and me, the closest thing to an unhappy person is someone who's happy. I've heard Brevo, not a bright lad, I've heard Brevo called happy and unhappy. What does it matter? The children just call him stupid. Children. Who'd believe it? I'm not surprised some people get stuck on words. Some words are like insects, they change, they seem one thing and in fact they're another. Polka reckons we've got it wrong. Words did not come into being to name things. Words existed first and things came later. So someone said 'centipede' and out came the insect. I know it doesn't have a hundred feet. It's the intention that counts. Whoever invents the word sets the trap. I wouldn't want to think of a name for something bad. Imagine you say it and it works. You have to watch what you say. Or not. Maybe the boy, the painter and judge's boy, maybe he wanted to take the words inside and they turned into a ball, a plug. Because words are like crumbs. When I'm alone with my thoughts, sitting quietly at the table, my fingers make beads with the breadcrumbs on the oilskin tablecloth. By the time you realise, snap out of it, those spherical forms, polished like stars, are watching you. I don't know about you, but what I do is eat them, the words of bread, of silence, very slowly so as not to choke. Lucky for me I had Polka. Papa. Had it not been for him, I don't think I'd have got off the ground. I'd be happy. Unhappy. Dumb. I'd still wet the bed. I'll have to take him to see the boy, Gabriel, one of these days. I bet he'll know what to do. The painter smiles more than she talks. Not that I like to gossip. About other people. You won't hear me saying, 'This boy wets his bed!' I suppose this business of wetting the bed, this incontinence, has something to do with his stutter. His mother told me it was a nervous thing, some fear inside his head. Which got worse when he started speaking. Stuttering. The body's full of channels and sluice-gates, I'm well aware of that. What I can't handle is laughter. If I burst out laughing and can't stop myself, however tight I squeeze my legs, this joy comes pouring out of my organism. Polka tells the story of a colleague who'd been drinking and stopped to pee at the side of the road, without realising there was a fountain on the other side of the wall. The man had released a whole ocean, but he carried on standing there, his member confused with the spout, until finally he grew anxious, 'Holy smoke! I'm weeing to death!'

Harmony tells me off, 'There you go again! You think everything's a joke.'

No. I don't agree. The thing is I like talking to myself. Sometimes I can't wait to be alone, so that I can talk to myself. I start walking and talking and feel a special joy in my legs. My whole body is talking. There are times when I'm about to invent a word and have to stop. Not a good idea. There was one I saw that looked invented to me. A brickie was carrying a sack of cement, which said PORTLAND in big letters. I thought that word was invented. Hadn't existed before. I could have asked him. He was pretty dishy in that skimpy T-shirt. After that, I saw lots of them, who weren't bad-looking either, all carrying that word on their shoulders. PORTLAND cement, I mean.

The only one I have to explain myself to is Harmony. Harmony, you see. I know I have to pay her attention.

The painter told me she'd found an alarm mechanism which warns you when the boy is going to pee in his sleep. A mechanism from abroad. I think that's good. We all need an alarm, whatever the fault. When I saw it, I realised the world was changing. The importance of machines. And those yet to come. Some people are opposed to medicines. For the head. It's easy to say, but if I get ill, they can give me anything. Acetylsalicylic acid straight off. Whatever's necessary. I don't mind being left alone, but not without something to take against a migraine. Sometimes, when I go too far, when I stand against the world, I'm afraid she who organises things will get upset and leave me. Because, of all the women inside, Harmony's the most affable. She's great at tidying up the mess, at picking up the pieces, all the scattered rubbish, at putting the mouth back on its hinges and above all at pairing socks. Because if there's something that bothers me, come nightfall, it's having odd socks. Not one, not three, but up to half a dozen socks without a partner, which on their own are a question: what happened to the other? It's one thing for that to happen in a room, quite another at the washing place, where it's cold, damp, and you're searching for socks which, when they're loose, are like insects with a mind of their own. They like to be unpaired. It's the same inside your head. You're about to go to sleep when you notice there's a mess, the things you thought or said are missing a sock. One's caught on a bramble bush, in a corner behind your eyes, and you have to go and look for it. That's where Harmony comes in. And she still has time to talk to you with the voice of a bonesetter putting the bones of words in their place, so that you can sleep without pain, without itching, without the cold that makes you lose your hands and feet. That can really happen. Suddenly you don't feel your hands. You're washing, but you can't feel them. They're the colour of elder wood. You smack them to get the blood running. You breathe on them, as much as you can, like an ox in the crib. Though the best solution is to pop them up your skirt, between your thighs, in the nest. There they warm up. There they revive. But it's much worse when you lose your hands in a dream. Then it's Harmony who comes to the rescue and gives you some new hands, like those of a mannequin. What a relief!

Harmony, Harmony. How I love Harmony! There are lots of other women stuck in my head, each doing her own thing. Each with her own tics and peculiarities. There are some that disappear one day and come back when you're least expecting it. Some you don't miss so much, but Harmony I can't let out of my sight. When I lose her, when I'm desperate about something, when the socks are unpaired, the first thing I have to do is find Harmony. Which I almost always do in shop windows. I don't know why. But there she is. The last time was at Bonilla Chocolates. 'Bonilla in sight!' it says on the sign with its little sailing boat. First of all, I saw my reflection in the glass. I looked bad. The bundle on top of my head was shaped like a crag. I'd left Grumpy in Pontevedra Square, in the place for animals. That day I'd had a run-in with a local policeman. With old cross-eyed shorty. There are some, the shorter they are, the more they look over your shoulder.

A policeman who said to me on Falperra, on the way to Santa Lucía, 'Get that starlet out of here.' I knew he meant Grumpy, but I didn't like his superior tone. He must have noticed my surprise because he added, 'Sometimes it's difficult to tell who's more stupid, the one on top or the one underneath.' Who was he to call me names? So I replied, 'To have authority, the first thing you need to be is polite.' I lost all the fear inside me. I reacted and out came Griffin's voice, 'I wish you'd keep your fingers out of my eye.' Those in authority in these parts are always resorting to physical or verbal violence. Torture. Inflicted on so many. 'Those in authority,' says Polka, 'are like Judas. The world upside down. In this country, we're ploughing on the bones of the dead, girl.'

'Have you any idea who you're talking to?'

'Not if you don't stand on a stool.'

'For that quip, I'm going to give you a fine, so that you'll remember me for the rest of your life.'

The milkmaid was the first to protest, 'What's that, dummy?' Then another woman, who put down her basket of sea urchins and made the sign of Capricorn, 'Colonel, colonel!'

He must have felt alarmed because there were lots of women showing him the horn and calling him Beelzebub, pervert, goatee, so he soon changed his tune.

'Enough's enough. On you go now. End of story!'

And they say that words don't help.

All the same, that man spoiled my day. My mood. I was going to leave the clothes at the house of the judge and painter. My words were in disarray. I started getting nervous. I'd lost Harmony. That made me afraid. Because along came The Horror, my worst memory.

It was back at school. When she came in, like a virgin, with her child. OK, it was a doll, but what did they care if it was a doll or a baby? She carried it in her arms like a baby, came into school and sat down at a desk. I think she came in there because she thought who's going to hurt me in a school. Well, in a school, if you want my opinion, the first who can hurt you are the children. She unbuttoned her dress and pulled out a breast to feed the baby. Yes, I know, it was a doll. It wasn't even a china doll. It was stuffed with sawdust and had a head made of maize husks. But she behaved like a Madonna. Every gesture she made was genuine. She'd come into school because it was winter and children were there. And because she'd run away from home. Who could possibly hurt her in a school? She came in slowly, without a sound, I reckon she was barefoot, and we only realised she'd occupied an empty desk, the one at the back, from the look of shock on our teacher's face. Our teacher was frightened. She didn't know what to do. You could see in her eyes she'd never been taught what you have to do when a woman carrying a doll in her arms, pretending it's a baby, comes into school in search of refuge. Until her husband showed up. Took off his belt. Whipped the floor with it as if whipping the school's back. The roof and beams. He hit the floor, but we looked up at the ceiling since it seemed everything was falling down. I never thought a leather belt could make so much noise. That day, I saw everything was unpaired. Including the teacher's eyes.

'Stop that now!'

'Stop what? What am I supposed to do? Blasted night and day!'

Again and again. He whipped the floor. The back of the earth.

In front of the chocolate shop, with Harmony sitting down, drinking her chocolate, pretending not to see me, not to know me even, I must look bad, I must have unpaired eyes, a bundle of unpaired thoughts, the taste of that school comes back to me. It was the taste of powdered milk. A yellow taste. I couldn't say if it was bitter or sweet. It was yellow.

The powdered milk arrived in sacks sent by the Americans. To start with, seeing so many sacks, a few beggars turned up, but they didn't come back. They didn't like the taste at all. Or the colour, maybe it was the colour. Which makes me think, sometimes, if you're poor, it's almost better to be completely poor, because then you have the freedom to have nothing at all. And to reject what you don't like. The pale yellow taste included. Nobody forced them back. 'Even if you don't like it, you still have to drink it.' That's what our teacher said initially though, to tell the truth, she didn't sound very convinced. They should have sent something else. Coca-Cola, for example. Because people couldn't understand why the milk was powdered. They were happy to receive things, they opened their arms. But it's one thing to be polite, quite another to drink powdered milk when you're surrounded by cows. As the first planes flew over, we'd shout, 'Sweets, sweets!' Older people were suspicious of the planes, but we trusted them. We had a lot of faith in aviation. They then told us the potato plague arrived by air, not like a Biblical plague, in an unhealthy cloud, but in light aircraft, brought on purpose. So, according to this, when we were asking for sweets with our arms stretched heavenwards, what in fact came down were beetles. Beetles are pretty, even those of the potato plague, which are golden, with black stripes. They look like tiny toys made of tinfoil. They're strong enough when they're chewing. But then they die in that modern way, in heaps, from insecticide. Polka reckons plagues are a business. He says he won't give a penny to the people who invented DDT. He won't have anything to do with them. Mama inherited a plot of land, the Field of the Twelve Sisters, as it's called. When Polka wants to wind her up, he has a go at the name. 'Twelve Sisters? Is that because it's long enough for a dozen cabbages?' She doesn't like him joking like that. She's really very fond of her inheritance. The twelve cabbages. Which grow by hand, as it were. Cabbage by cabbage. Each fully grown cabbage is a step upwards. Cabbages. Amazing. Such determination. A piece of land, the only one, that is so remote, so rock hard, beetles don't make it that far. Or planes for that matter.

Chimpanzee Language

19 August 1957

On the cliff, next to the lighthouse, Antonio Vidal thrust his cane like a quick harpoon. Swish! There, pinned to the ground, still breathing, wagging its tail and beating its navigational wings, was the sheet of newspaper.

The two of them looked in amazement. Grandpa Mayarí still nervous about having caught a living being.

'What's it say?'

Gabriel read aloud, 'Before furnishing your home, visit the Mist.'

'"Visit the Mist?"'

And he stared down at the rocks, at the sea grottoes belching forth mist.

'It's a furniture shop.'

'Go on. What next?'

Gabriel read slowly, 'Northwestern Tie Industries. Manufacturer of fine ties and unique underwear with no stitching behind, more comfortable than anything you've worn before (American model).'

'"American model"?' asked Mayarí in surprise. And after a pause, as if speech had just returned from a reconnaissance mission, he added another unanswerable question, '"No stitching behind"?'

'It's just an advert, grandpa.'

'You never trip up when you're reading. Did you realise?'

He moved the tip of his cane. 'What's it say there?'

Gabriel read carefully, 'Lumumba says he'll ask "the devil" for help if necessary to get rid of the Belgians.'

The two of them, mesmerised. As if a porthole had opened up in the ground.

'The first thing you have to know when dealing with the devil,' said Mayarí, 'is that it's best not to call him by his name. If you're speaking Spanish, you can address him as Sir or *Caballero*, he rather likes that. He also doesn't mind Prince. Prince of Darkness, Prince of the Air and so on. And then there's Your Excellency, Your Eminence, Your Lordship. He's terribly keen on protocol. If you address him as Don, he'll even whistle for you. Not that he whistles well. A fault of the devil's. What to do? I shouldn't worry if I were you.'

The sheet of newspaper stayed still. Overhead, with an eye on the cane's prey, the seagulls and their mocking calls.

'It's best to talk to him in languages he doesn't understand,' added Mayarí.

Gabriel suddenly felt courage, the need to share what's inside. Only once had he spoken to somebody in chimpanzee language. A lanky girl with long, skinny legs and a flat chest. From a distance, she looked like a cut-out piece of cardboard. On the dunes in Santa Cristina. When the tide came in, the huge beach became like an archipelago. The huts for selling drinks and snacks stood over the flat part, which was now underwater, like wooden palafittes with roofs of straw, palm leaves or broom, supported on stakes driven into the sand. The softly invading waters brought foam trimmings and strips of sun soaked in green shadows. This unreal oil painting surrounded the buildings, cut the adults off in the colonnade of a happy settlement, as if nature obeyed floating Sunday orders. Gabriel had his back to them, looking westwards over a fairly extensive territory, where freedom meant above all not running into other beings who, like him, were digging holes in the sand and excavating wells they then fortified. It was time to talk to himself in the secret language he was fluent in.

'*Kagoda, sord ab?*'

'*Kagoda!*'

He felt the chill of a wet shadow. He was leaning over and digging. The shadow passed over him and stretched along the dune's valley. He thought of a Mau Mau. Everyone was talking about the Mau Mau rebels in Africa. Perhaps the Mau Mau, outside their territory, spoke Tarzan's language.

'Tand-ramba!'

Should he obey? His survival instinct told him yes, he should stand up. He did so with trepidation, not daring to look back.

'Tand-unk!'

He obeyed. No, he wasn't going to move.

'Tand-utor!'

Followed by a guffaw. The shadow slipped away and turned into a body rolling in the sand, in a fit of laughter. He ran towards her in an unfamiliar rage. But she got up, started running and climbed the other side of the dune with feline agility. Now he'd reached the top and was trying to catch his breath while she was down the bottom. She was very thin and taller than him. Her skin was very white, a little sunburnt on the shoulders, as if she'd been let loose on the beach for the first time, her bones jutting out so much it seemed her skeleton had just been hastily assembled. She had blond, curly hair and freckles. Her big mouth maintained a smile, like a tic to protect her from the sun, which was now right in front of her. But what most disturbed Gabriel was that she wasn't wearing a swimsuit like all the other girls. Just a pair of knickers. Her chest was practically flat, but her nipples, in Gabriel's eyes, were circles of confusion in both colour and size. They contained all the imagination he'd stored up on the subject of sex, including Zonzo's biro. The first day he saw it, he'd have swapped all the items in his cabinet of curiosities for that biro shaped like a transparent tube, full of liquid, except for a bubble of air, which allowed a naked woman to swim up and down. Even were it confiscated in customs, it was almost impossible for such an item to make it into his father's hands. Something like that would always fall by the wayside. It could only be a present from Manlle, the owner of La Boîte de Pandora. One of Zonzo's privileges. One of the things everyone envied and he appeared to attach little importance to. Because he had one overriding feeling. His hatred towards Manlle.

'Where are you from?' Gabriel asked the girl who spoke Tarzan's language.

193

'*Dan-do!*' she shouted, very annoyed.

Gabriel obeyed. He stayed rooted to the spot. He'd have liked to go after her, but he didn't move. And she vanished.

'*Zu-dak-lul!*' shouted Gabriel, encompassing the vastness of the sea with a sweep of his arm.

'What does that mean?' asked Mayarí.

'Ocean. It means ocean.'

'In what language?'

Gabriel hesitated. The shout had come from deep inside him and now he was afraid of appearing ridiculous. Mayarí said, 'Don't you worry. People who stammer are the best singers. There was one in Cuba who was the king of boleros.'

'In chimpanzee language,' said Gabriel.

'It's good to know languages.'

Mayarí released the sheet of newspaper and covered up the hole in the ground as if closing the indiscretion of an eye into the earth.

The Strategy of Light

On the rocks facing the island was a fisher of wrasse. Gabriel remembers this because the man with the rod emphasised, almost boasted, that what he wanted was to fish for wrasse, ballan wrasse, and treated with contempt any other fish he hooked. Some didn't even make it into the basket, but were scattered over the rocks. To tell the truth, ballan wrasse were masterpieces with their sudden green and red glint and the added excitement in fisherman and spectators of seeing the extraction of something precious from the sea. Aside from their colour, before they landed in the basket, the trace they left in the air was of fleshy lips. A flash of sensuality. The fisherman with the automatic rod, who was dressed impeccably, like a statue on the rocks, sometimes named the fish he threw away with contempt.

'Another musician!

'Here's a clown!'

Gabriel thought he was making it up and rejected them because of their names, creatures that weren't to his liking. Gabriel and Mayarí focused primarily on the way they gawped or still convulsed. He didn't know exactly what his grandpa was thinking. He didn't say anything. But the fact they stared at the same spot, at these creatures writhing in agony, shaking with mute silence, was something Gabriel would always remember as a moment of confused fraternity.

His father, the judge, was a hunter. This was no passing or temporary hobby. As he himself said, it was a constitutional passion. At home, especially in the large study, an Italian room with a small alcove, and the adjoining part of the main sitting-room, there were several trophies. The biggest was the head of a stag with large antlers. There was also a boar's head, which his father was particularly proud of, not just because of how he'd caught it, but because of the way the head had been mounted, a work of art in his view that had preserved all the animal's wildness and spirit, so that when you looked at it up on the wall of the study, in semi-darkness, a glint of black sun in its eyes, you could see the exact moment the end appeared. The judge had a special way of rounding off that story.

'Forgive the boast, but a large specimen measures up its opponent, chooses a superior,' he'd maintain. 'Only he who knows it better than it knows itself can hunt a prey.'

The same could be said of the woodcock. Another prize specimen. Not because of its size, but because of its intelligence.

'The wood's guardian. A master at camouflage. Better than the partridge any day. A living detector, a periscope in amidst the bracken and leaves. It hears and sees everything that's going on in the forest. Even with a good dog, it's very difficult to flush a woodcock. And we had the best, Eusebio's pointer. A fine companion, yes indeed. We put a little bell around his neck. When it stopped tinkling, this was the sign he'd found the woodcock. I can still hear that silence now!'

The judge gave pride of place to that specimen. You could see it was of great personal value. But a few years later, in the spring of 1963, a capercaillie became the star attraction. Because it had an illustrious partner. The judge had gone hunting with his friend the Minister in the Ancares. As he said, it was a trophy with history. The Minister had shot one specimen and he'd shot the other.

Both the woodcock and later the capercaillie stood on a shelf, flanked by thick volumes, in the most visible part of the judge's extensive library, that on the wall of the sitting-room next to his study. All four walls of the study were also covered in shelves full of books. It was what he called, with ironic pride, 'my Crypt'. Soon this was the name everyone used, just as that part of the sitting-room Chelo used for painting ended up being known as the Chinese Pavilion, a name inspired by a folding screen from Macao ('exquisitely designed,' they'd taught Gabriel to say as an oral exercise) which the judge had bought in Portugal, on one of his trips as visiting lecturer to Coimbra University, and which soon became an inevitable border point in the house. The name created the space. A landscape of paintings and plants, which seemed to be constantly on the go. In one corner, an exotic touch: a large pot of bamboos, together with ferns and herbaceous plants such as Aureola. In the eastern part of the house, there was a clear preference for plants. Different species all over, on the floor, on the furniture, all along the gallery of course, there were the begonias responding with conviction, even more in winter, to Chelo's warmth: its leaves went further than the flowers in intensity of colour.

So the sitting-room had two, almost symmetrical hemispheres, though there was a second dimension, that of the line of shadow from the central pillar, which showed the sun's daily orbit, so that, mornings, the library side was left in shade and the sun illuminated the so-called Pavilion whose inner circle, the nucleus, contained the painter with her easel and a table like the trough found in rural homes. Her Technicolor Table. Instead of bread, the trough held a mine of tubes, jars, pigments, resins, varnishes, lacquers, bottles and the odd rock with plates of mica and other minerals. On top of the table, aside from bowls, plates, tins and boxes which served as palettes, was a pile of soiled cloths. Which grew and grew. Chelo didn't need someone to make a quip about this. She herself said it was her finest work. She only got rid of the cloths when they overflowed the trough and started invading the outer circle, which went beyond the bamboos. It was then that O, the washerwoman, stuffed the colour-stained cloths into gunny sacks.

When they reached Lapas Beach, they saw a *gamela* walking. Out of the water, crossing the sand. With the stubborn air of riverboats, even when they're sailing. Its upturned bottom had the exact curvature of someone leaning over a balcony. A strange being, the boat, a kind of enormous, comical creature painted the colours of dawn, a product of the sea's imagination. The boat suddenly turned towards them. Under its large shell of white and coloured planks was a smiling, toothless man. The gaps in his teeth made him look more like Mayarí. When Chelo insisted he use his stay in Coruña to order a set of false teeth, he'd always make excuses and crack one of his favourite jokes, which Gabriel didn't understand immediately, because he pointed to his eyes, not his mouth, 'I'm bidentate, you see.'

Except when he was talking to himself, Mayarí was pretty quiet. He seemed to understand his silence as a way of taking up as little space as possible. At the same time, however, when he was asked a question, especially by his son-in-law, the judge, he made every effort to satisfy the other, which in his view meant seasoning seriousness with a pinch of humour, the closest thing to a sweet taste. Their relationship was formal; conversation, if it existed, was restricted to dinnertime. Gabriel, if he was paying attention, couldn't help noticing the difference between his father's and grandfather's teeth. The difference was . . . monumental. His father's teeth, apart from being perfect, were made of marble. His grandfather's teeth, the few there were, were made of granite. Stone slabs. Years later, he could be more precise. His father's teeth were neoclassical, Mayarí's dolmenic. From the evening before, he remembered part of the conversation, Mayarí's intervention, which was celebrated with laughter and seemed to him to contain secret information. The judge had asked him why so many people were abandoning work in the countryside. Why they were leaving the villages. Mayarí thought about it for a moment, adopted a more solemn air and said, 'When it comes to it, your honour, the problem with the countryside is a problem of height.' Everyone looked at him in bewilderment, especially Chelo, who'd already asked him not to refer to a member of the family, his daughter's husband, as 'your honour'. On this occasion, however, she kept quiet since, like everyone else, she was waiting for the answer to the mystery of the countryside's height.

'What height do you mean, sir?' asked the judge very seriously.

'I mean the countryside is very low,' said Mayarí, opening his arms as if stating the obvious.

'Yes, but not that low,' said the judge, uncertain why he was being so forthright. 'Things are getting better after all.'

'The countryside is very low, so you have to bend down,' Mayarí explained. 'The earth should be a little higher, the height of this table at least.'

Everyone ended up laughing, though the laughter was slow. It was the kind of laughter Mayarí set in motion. A slow laughter. Put another way, a comical seriousness.

In one of the books Gabriel was reading in the alcove, mostly because he enjoyed the illustrations, there was a full-page photo he'd have liked to rip out and take with him or put in a frame on his bedroom wall, though it had nothing on Zonzo's biro with the naked woman. It was an image with the title 'Eskimo Beauty'. The girl's features were very similar to those of O, the washerwoman. She wore a Greenlander's festive costume, the most unusual part of which were the trousers, made of leather on the thighs and down to the knees and then, on the calves and over the boots, of a thin, white, embroidered material. The whole was reminiscent of a well-clad, free-spirited harlequin. Mayarí and the sailor carrying the boat seemed to belong to that moment, on Lapas Beach, to a race omitted by Pericot in his inventory. The race of smiling, bidentate men. In his life, Gabriel would come to realise this is one of the most pleasant smiles a human being can give. Mayarí tipped his hat and bowed his head slightly, and the sailor did the same with the boat.

The boat man walked towards the water. Having set it down, the old man tugged at the boat as at a large, blind, docile animal. When everything was ready, he jumped in the boat, put the oars in the tholepins and started rowing. It was strange. He rowed with his back towards where he was going. His infallible means of orientation. He watched what he was leaving behind, a view that grew wider and wider. His tiny presence transformed the whole sea. Even though he was far off, you could still see the door and jambs of his bidentate smile.

'Now,' said Mayarí to Gabriel, 'let's go and see the horse Cariri. It's supposed to have kept Hercules the photographer good company. Shame Leica, your uncle, didn't understand. I tried to tell him. Animals always liked the city.'

The Urchin Woman

Fine. All right then. He wouldn't have to make a speech. The judge himself was aware of this limitation. The children's show was due to take place in María Pita Square. A forbidding scene. As were the circumstances. It was billed as a public tribute paid by the city's children to the Caudillo's grandchildren and would include music and traditional dances. Followed by a performance of The Mountain Goat. They'd suggested giving his son a secondary role. He'd have to be there. No, he wouldn't have to speak. That's what the actors were for. It would be filmed by the cameras of NO-DO, the documentary news programme. Even if it was for children, nothing would be left to chance. Everything would be carefully planned. The Head of State would not be present, but his wife would be there, Mrs Carmen Polo. The idea was to make the Caudillo and his family look warmer, more human. The judge said of course, it would be an honour, thank you for thinking of him, of his son, he meant, he would thank the deputy mayor in person, and so on. Was he sure the boy didn't have to say anything? Yes, quite sure. Not to worry. They wanted children they could trust on the stage. Get closer to the people, yes, but everyone in his place. They'd discussed it with other local authorities. For example, the public prosecutor's son would also be there. Would he now? That's right. Maybe Gabriel could have a role in The Mountain Goat after all. It'll depend on the show's director. And that's how Gabriel was assigned to special effects. He'd be one of the Boreads, the sons of Boreas, god of the north wind. But with an angel's wings. In one corner of the stage, on a platform, at the top of a hill, with a tuba and a sheet of copper, there are the Boreads. At a prearranged signal, they blow down the tuba, shake the copper.

'Wasn't the storm just splendid?'

He heard this himself from the Caudillo's wife, Mrs Carmen Polo, who was presiding over the show with her grandchildren. He'd been fore-warned, however, about instigating speech and didn't say anything, not even thank you. The whole week concentrating on onomatopoeias and galeforce winds. How to blow down a tuba and shake a sheet of metal. But it didn't matter that he kept his mouth shut. Quite the opposite. It was clear the Head of State's family were used to the bewilderment of their subjects. Besides, it was time for the presents. Gabriel got a sheriff's outfit with a revolver on a belt and a star with the letters USA. And there was Leica, Uncle Sebastian, taking photos, looking rather sozzled, as the judge would say, since he always drank before an official engagement. You never knew what Leica's photos would be like, though the worst of them weren't bad. He linked the end result with the camera's mood. He had a reputa-tion for conquering with his camera, which made it easier to work with both men and women, since whoever posed for him did so with a ques-tion mark and this always makes for a better pose. Or does it? Leica stroked his head and murmured, 'Wonderful, Gabriel!' And then to himself, in a whisper, 'Wonderful, grotesque, wonderful.' When the judge came over, relieved and happy, Leica took a photo of them together. To get a smile, he'd always ask the judge to say thirty-three, 'Say thirty-three,' but the judge never heeded his petition. It was a joke or something Gabriel didn't understand. All the photos Leica took were very serious. But this time he said, 'The storm was the best!' And the judge smiled for the photo.

His father had rehearsed with him. Asked Chelo to teach him. 'Teach him what?' 'To do a storm well.' 'I'll teach you something else first,' Chelo agreed. 'To walk like a leading actor. When you cross the stage and go to your corner, you have to walk as if you were Boreas himself, god of the wind. And forget the wings. Either you're a god of the wind or you're an angel. An angel doesn't go about frightening sheep.' 'This is The Mountain Goat,' the judge pointed out. 'I'm the mountain goat up on the moun-tainside and I'll eat whoever should dare to cross this line!' The two of them burst out laughing. Perhaps the last time they laughed together like that, openly, freely, Gabriel remembers.

'It may not be right,' said the judge, 'but he has to wear wings. Those are the instructions and we're not going to change them now. The important thing is to sound like a storm, like a strong wind. You have to blow down the tuba and shake the sheet of copper for the whole city to hear.'

'You'd better take him to the lighthouse,' suggested Chelo seriously. 'Singers used to go there, to the rocks at the foot of Hercules Lighthouse, to fight with the air and expand their capacity.'

'We get to the lighthouse and what'll we do there? Start shouting?'

Outside his usual haunts – his study, court, the game preserve – the judge was a man on the defensive, on permanent alert. 'Besides, it's August, the weather's good. There'll be loads of people. They're going to say . . .'

'What are they going to say?'

'A madman shouting and a child playing the tuba. I'm not Dalí. I'm a judge.'

The three of them went to the lighthouse in the Hispano-Suiza. Samos first looked for a remote place. Gazed out to sea. Tried to make out the Sisarga Isles, but it wasn't a clear day. There was a lazy, stubborn mist. By the time he realised, he could hear the sound of Gabriel's tuba and Chelo's shouts telling him, 'Louder, louder!' But he couldn't see them. He thought he'd find them all right. By walking in that direction. He went around a few gorse bushes. Heard a ship's siren. The tuba. Or was it another siren? It was some time since he'd heard ships' sirens so close without being sure. He felt very uneasy. The mist, the siren. The fear this mix gave him, though he didn't know why. He shouted out Chelo's name. And got the same response:

'Louder, louder!'

The two of them crouching behind a rock, by the cliff face, crying, 'Louder, louder!'

On the way back, driving along the lighthouse road, he seemed comforted. In a magnificent voice, he recited that fragment they hadn't heard for a while:

And I who love modern civilisation, I who kiss machines with my soul,
I the engineer, I the civilised, I the educated abroad,
Would like beneath my eyes to have just sailing ships and wooden boats again,
To know no other maritime life than the ancient life of the seas!

'Enough,' he told Gabriel, 'for Grandpa Samos to forgive all sins. He's a devotee of the *Maritime Ode*. And I who get seasick, go weak at the knees with these verses.'

When the day arrived, Gabriel played the wind with all the conviction of a raging northerly, a ventriloquist of the air. The judge was on tenterhooks. Had Gabriel been able to see him, he'd have seen how his father half-opened his mouth to reinforce the effect of the wind. Had it been down to him, he'd have stood behind the curtain, churning out thunder and lightning. Despite being a judge. A judge who doesn't suffer fools gladly. Not long before, next to Gran Antilla, the confectioner's, a woman came up to him in a black shawl, carrying a basket on her head. He was taller, much taller. When she addressed him, he didn't look at her, but seemed to be peering down and sniffing around inside the basket.

'Your honour, if he goes to prison, that'll be the end of him. He's like a crystal vase. He'll break.'

Gabriel noticed her apron was covered in scales he hadn't seen before.

'Quiet, woman. This is not the place,' said the judge, walking off. 'It is not the place.'

She stepped forwards, intervened, 'Where then can I see you?'

'Your lawyer. Talk to your lawyer.'

'My lawyer?'

She stared at the ground in fright. Seemed to be looking for something important she'd lost.

'My lawyer?'

'That's right. Talk to him. He'll tell you what to do.'

'He's the one who said there was nothing to do unless you wanted. He said you're the law, in such cases some judges have one yardstick and others, another, and it depends on you whether or not he goes to prison. It's the first time, your honour. He's not a criminal. He just has this thing.'

'Well, he's going to be cured of this thing. Put back on the straight and narrow.'

'You think? No. He's going to be smashed to pieces like a crystal vase.'

The judge suddenly wheeled around towards the woman carrying sea urchins on top of her head. Apart from height, apart from the fact that one was a man and the other, a woman, this was the principal, visible, undeniable difference between the two. He was wearing a hat, a wide-brimmed, cinnamon-coloured hat, while she had a basket. Gabriel was with his father. Next to him and on his side. This street, hour, were their space and time. The woman had disturbed their tranquillity, come from outside, with a basket full of sea urchins and problems. A basket she set down, exposing a kind of cloth crown on top of her head, which took the weight. She didn't even realise she'd left it there, her cloth crown.

'He's already considered to be a danger. A danger to society!' The woman raised her voice as she said this, and a few passers-by turned around, the kind of silent twist that imputes guilt to the object under scrutiny. 'That's punishment enough. He can't find work. He can't drive or get a passport. His life is ruined. A danger? People in the street call him "girlie". He's the one in danger.'

The woman's hand dipped inside a pocket of her apron, rummaged around and produced a newspaper cutting. Gabriel was reminded of Mayarí's strips. This printed piece of paper had a layer of blood and fish scales.

'He's already appeared in the paper. Take a look. His name and every-thing. He's already an outcast. Please don't send him to Badajoz, your honour.'

'He'll be cured there. He has an illness. And he'll be cured.'

'In prison? He'll be cured in prison? How? With beatings? Ice-cold water? Electricity?'

Her chest was heaving. She seemed about to burst and the judge took Gabriel by the shoulder and moved off. All she did was cry. Silently, not with sobs. Fat tears rolled down her cheeks.

'Please leave us alone.'

'Fools,' she said. 'You fools!'

The judge glanced angrily in all directions. Being called a fool infuriated him. Somebody in the crowd might know him. This stinking fishwife, with her basket like a picture hat, calling the judge a fool. That'd make them laugh. No doubt Black Eye was in the vicinity. That bastard. Gabriel also looked around. He found the woman disagreeable, especially when she started crying. Crying and talking about electricity. A strange woman with a strange son, who was bothering his father and spoiling their walk. But it was also true this destination, Badajoz Prison, didn't sound good next to Gran Antilla. On a pleasant Friday afternoon. With lots happening. On the crowded terraces, in their white jackets with anchor-like golden buttons, the waiters, instead of carrying drinks, resembled elegant sailors keeping their balance on the city's deck.

An impression that wasn't far away from the description the judge repeated like an advertising slogan, 'In summer, Coruña's an ocean liner.'

They'd walked down Real Street. As was their custom, they'd gone into Villar the chemist's and weighed themselves on the scales. It was a magnificent machine, its brand and origin in large letters, 'Toledo Scale Company (Ohio)', which turned weighing yourself into a serious act, your body's solemn incorporation into the industrial process. You stepped on to a platform and through the glass could watch the whole mechanism in action. Your weight activated it and, as you stood there, you couldn't help seeing the device as part of yourself, transported to Ohio. When the judge weighed himself, there was a detail. He took off his hat and gave it to his son. Gabriel never knew how much his father weighed. He was slim, but had a strong constitution. And was very serious about keeping his weight in check. One of the features that distinguished him from the common herd. A definite aim he shared with Chelo, which made them different from most of their colleagues. Whenever they conducted a 'review', the term they used for gossip, their comments seemed to be ruled by the Ohio scales' precise mechanism. For the most part, those under scrutiny were deemed to have put on weight.

The judge's felt hat was very light, or so it seemed when Gabriel was holding it while his father weighed himself. Now, as he got more and more angry at the Urchin Woman's interference, the hat appeared to be something more than an article of clothing. Something of weight. Calcareous. Part of the body.

They were at the junction of Real Street and Rego de Auga, between the Rosalía de Castro theatre and Gran Antilla. Every urban setting has its speciality and, in Gabriel's intimate topography, this was a warm, lively place meant for happy encounters and polite greetings. The sellers' balloons and little ships rose above the field of heads. A good spot for Curtis to stop the horse Carirí and the children to mount the horse and have their photo taken, holding on to its natural mane, which was black as jet. Which is why the unexpected reference to Badajoz, for Gabriel, suddenly caused an orographical accident. If she hadn't said anything, anything in particular, if she hadn't given it a name, he'd have wandered over to the window of Gran Antilla, the confectioner's, and so given his father an excuse to dispatch this plaintive woman with her cargo of prickles. But no. No. She had referred to that place which was the first hole in the GNM or Glorious National Movement's game of skill called 'The Reconquest of Spain', a present from Inspector Ren for his cabinet of curiosities, together with a game of bombardments called 'Victorious Wings'. So that when Gabriel heard Badajoz, the steel ball started rolling and, instead of getting past and continuing on its path of conquest, it went and fell in the hole. He then heard Ren's voice, as if it were part of the GNM's game of skill, singing out the localities and dates the steel ball rolled past on its triumphant way, if the move was skilful: Badajoz (14/8/36), Toledo (27/9/36), Málaga (8/2/37), Bilbao (19/6/37), Teruel (22/2/38), Lérida (3/4/38), Barcelona (26/1/39) and Madrid (28/3/39).

'Badajoz, 14th of August 1936.'

And he'd add mysteriously, 'Yagüe. Now that was a good one!'

Whenever the ball fell in Badajoz, didn't make it past the hole on to other scenes of conquest, he heard the refrain, 'Now that was a good one!' Even when an elated Ren was holding the game, it was still a sombre exclamation. Something that stuck to the city's name like an involuntary accent. It was, after all, a mistake. It would be many years before Gabriel found out what had happened in that hole the ball sometimes landed in. Before he discovered that hole in a game of skill contained a bullring piled high with corpses, in a warlike corrida where people were the victims. The ball was always the same, but when Ren had the game and was tensing his muscles to direct the ball, it didn't always carry on, but sometimes rolled its own way, fell in the hole labelled Badajoz and like an echo triggered that admiring 'Now that was a good one!' which the boy perceived as a rare distortion of meaning, since if the ball fell in the hole, you had in fact played badly.

Years later, Sofia, a love of Gabriel's, also failed to understand the look of amazement, panic even, she saw in him when she used such a collo-quial expression as 'Now that was a good one!' It was something trivial. She didn't even remember what they were talking about, she was so surprised by his reaction. She had to get used to this man who had a tense physical relationship, was permanently on edge, with words. Who lived in a state of extreme alert with language. She couldn't see what he was seeing. The GNM game. The direction of the ball. Badajoz. The bullring. Inspector Ren's exclamation, 'Now that was a good one!'

To start with, she thought the relationship wouldn't work. He moved between silence and an entomologist's precision when he used a word and she soon discovered there were lots that, for one reason or another, caused him commotion or conflict. He seemed to see the words. He attributed this extreme precaution to a particular phase of his training to be a judge. Anyone could betray the meaning of words. Starting with a writer. But not a judge.

'Even when it's a question of love?'

His eyes scribbled. Before opening his mouth, he'd sketch out what he was going to say, its implications, in his mind. He'd even move his fingers over a surface. Search instinctively for a blank sheet of paper.

'What you say is a state of emergency.'

Jolies Madames!

There came a time in Chelo's work when women entered the painting. Or was it the other way round?

She gave the tiredness of bodies a rest.

Sometimes the feet were left dancing and she painted them with dots and filigree, the ankles as well, as if putting on embroidered tights.

One leg from Chantilly, courtesy of Jacques Fath, another from Camariñas, courtesy of Chuchú.

Apart from moments of melancholy introversion, she was a cheerful woman. She liked to assume the frivolity of reading out far-fetched phrases in women's magazines or newspaper fashion supplements, which got bigger and bigger, especially on Sundays. New clothes and hairstyles to brighten up the papers.

'White cotton piqué with black dots!'

She paused. Stood up. Stretched her arms towards the sun and proclaimed to the begonias, 'Jolies Madames!'

One of the women entering and leaving the painting was the knitter.

'What I find most difficult,' she said, 'are children's socks. My mother's pretty good at making socks. We never wore them. When she was pregnant, she started knitting embroidered socks for doctors' children in Compostela. Making strips of *entredeux*, as we used to call it, in French. We're three sisters, each with her own father. The fathers were brothers, three blonds who turned up one day, looking like Vikings around a campfire. The eldest died at sea, and Mum married the next brother. The second drowned in another shipwreck, and Mum married the third. Who was my father. Mum said, "Each time I got married, I married the one I liked."

As a girl, she found a crucifix on the beach, being lapped by the sea. There was only the upright, the arms had disappeared. It must have been pretty ancient since the wood had been petrified, moulded and converted by the sea, like a bone or shell, and the body, instead of breaking off, as presumably had happened to the arms, had merged with the sacrificial wood, hinged like a shell, as if handcrafted like that, and Christ was covered in a layer of limestone and nacre from the valves, but more surprising was the hair he'd grown, which to start with they thought was a clump of seaweed, since it was all entangled in siren's string, a bunch of water-crowfoot, Irish moss and sea lettuce, but when they pulled, they saw the seaweed stuck, was entangled in real hair. They cut it with scissors and it grew again. I saw this with my own eyes.'

'What? You saw hair grow? You're more likely to see grass grow.'

'What she meant was . . .'

'Chelo, you act like a magnet for all the spirits of Galicia.'

And then, addressing the priest, 'She's like that, Don Munio. An epicentre.'

'It may be true,' said the priest. 'The hair, I mean. The Christ of Finisterre was the same. They used human hair and it seemed to carry on growing. The ones from the sea were called Protestant crosses. There were virgins as well, images that arrived by sea with hair that grew. Wooden virgins with real virgins' hair. When I was ordained and sent to that parish . . .'

'You didn't stay long, Don Munio. Such a pretty place. The rectory overlooking the sea.'

'No, I didn't stay long. I'm not a typical Catholic priest. I'm ambitious. As you are with art. Spiritually ambitious.'

Gabriel had told her what Father Munio had said recently, one morning he got the time wrong, 'I cannot and will not tolerate my children being late.'

'My children? Is that what he calls all the boys and girls?'

'No. It was the first time he said it. I was really annoyed. Some of them started giggling.'

'Don't pay any attention.'

Another strange thing Father Munio said to Gabriel, 'When I see you on your own, I'll whisper a repertoire in your ear.'

'A repertoire? Is that what he said?'

'I suppose now you're going to tell us it's true what happened to the Metro lion,' said the judge, enjoying the taste of irony.

'The Metro lion?'

'The lion in films, father. An informer of Chelo's, one of her spirits, told her the lion was on Death Coast, not on the screen. Was one of the wild animals the Nil was carrying to Dublin Zoo. The ship sank and lots of the fauna swam all the way to Traba Beach. Including the lion. Right, Chelo? You'll be wondering what happened to them. Well, they were frightened by the dogs and sat down to wait for the consul.'

'You didn't tell it well,' said Chelo. 'That's what I get for giving toothless here something to eat.'

They pretended still to be in love. Tried to find a balance. For a time, she played jokes on him, which the judge classified as dangerous. One example remained with him, the day some friends they'd arranged to meet knocked at the door, which was ajar, and she shouted from the sitting-room, 'Just a minute, we're making love!' She was in fact alone in the sitting-room. Painting. And she shouted this. The judge was in the hallway, heard Chelo shout they were making love and the chuckles that followed. He remembers the word that came into his head was 'indescribable', a word that related to him, to the expression on his face.

'You see, Father Munio, we've run out of wedding cake!'

The priest was enjoying himself, as in a skit, and surprised them with one of his modern metaphors, 'Come, come! Your marriage is like a pair of scissors. One blade can't function without the other.'

'How very touching, Father,' said Chelo, recovering from her astonishment. She knew Father Munio was primarily interested in the judge. He was the target, an influential and suitable candidate to join the Opus. She said, 'Well, you should know she worked with three pairs of scissors.'

'Who did?'

'The knitter's mother. With three brothers. And she had a daughter with each of them. Which makes three sisters.'

Chelo deliberately misquoted the knitter's mother.

'She married three times and said, "I liked them all, but the third was my favourite."'

The judge laughed, 'A magnet, Chelo. You're a magnet for Galicia's spirits.'

The Apprentice Taxidermist

The judge and master taxidermist were discussing how to mount the caper-caillie so that it looked more lifelike. As lifelike as possible. Its wings extended, showing the total span. Meanwhile the taxidermist's son, the apprentice, whispered to Gabriel, 'Come with me!' In a darker, adjoining room, illuminated by a lamp so dusty it seemed to have fur, the apprentice gestured proudly, 'See. I invented it. I invented an animal.'

Duck's body and hare's head. The creature's wings were outspread, but it crouched like a hare.

He smiled when he saw the boy's look of astonishment, 'They make the best pair. Wild duck and hare. I'm also working on a cat-gull, a cat with a seagull's body, lord of the rooftops.'

'What for?' Gabriel ventured to ask.

'My Dad's a taxidermist. I want to be an artist.'

In a wooden box with cells like the one for buttons at the haberdasher's, which Chelo loved so much and wanted to paint one day, or the box for type at the printer's, where she went with Leica and discovered words were made up of solid elements that sometimes stuck in the throat, in this first box were all sorts of glass and resinous beads. The taxidermist's son picked up a handful and poured them into his visitor's hands. 'How do you like eyes?'

He smiled with satisfaction at again causing a look of astonishment in Gabriel.

'Silly. Nature does it too. Likes to deceive. Come and have a look. I'll show you something the like of which you've never seen. And may not see again.

'Come on,' he repeated, gesturing mysteriously.

Windows on to a small, inner garden. Unkempt. Nettles. Several cats. Silent spectators in a museum turning into statues. Imitating the other, stuffed animals.

He drags him along, Gabriel is more confused by the air of mystery than anything else. They go up to a fridge door. The taxidermist's son gives him a stern look. 'Promise you won't tell anyone.' The apprentice grabs the handle with both hands. His last smile aimed at Gabriel seems to form part of the opening device, since it also rotates, turns into an expression of hardness, a feeling Gabriel recognises as contempt.

He opens.

Slams the door shut.

'D'you see it?'

Gabriel nods. It was only a second and he's frozen. He won't tell anybody. Ever.

'You're pretty amazed, huh? Want to see it again?'

In a whisper, 'Come on, let's have another look.'

He repeats the procedure. But doesn't close so quickly. There is the angel. Its white feathers. The cold blast is a kind of breath the body emits, an escape of colour.

'Want to touch it? It's a guardian angel.'

Gabriel preferred the apprentice's mysterious contempt to this sudden tasteless intimacy. Deep down, he regrets the change. Stretches out his arm. Touches the feathers so that slowly, between the wings, driven from its lair by the other's laugh, the swan's head slides out and hangs in the balance.

The judge was not in the habit of showing what he called 'internal documents'. His feelings. This lack of expressiveness was one of his main features. He considered it an obligation in his position to try to be dispassionate and to act always with discretion. This didn't mean detachment from his ideals or political power. On the contrary, his advice in legal matters was increasingly sought out by the authorities. He also wrote more for newspapers under his old pseudonym, Syllabus. Everyone – this was the word his friends in the Crypt used – 'everyone' knew that sooner rather than later he'd be promoted. Receive an appointment in Madrid. Perhaps – and why not? – what he most wanted. A place in the Supreme Court.

He was certainly very reserved. Professionally austere. But there were things he enthused about. A passion he'd long had, somehow inherited from his father. Collecting books. Another, hunting, he'd acquired later. He himself talked of a sudden conversion. He went on his first hunt for reasons of friendship, but what was supposed to be a hobby turned into a devotion. He recalls this happening not on the mountainside, but in a marsh, the day he brought down a wild goose. The swing after the specimen in the sky, the shot, the fall and, most of all, the tower of water it caused. The emotion was something else. The experience, unnarratable. The times spent hunting became an essential part of Ricardo Samos' life. Which is why he attached so much importance to the trophies. They weren't abstractions or symbols. In them, real nature had been overcome. Though he held in check the hunter's desire to exhibit. He chose which specimens to stuff very carefully. The heads of a boar, a stag, an Iberian goat. Birds. A woodcock. A ptarmigan he'd shot in the Pyrenees. Later on, his most valued specimen, a capercaillie from the Ancares. But now he's talking to Gabriel. That strange situation when it's the adult who's being childishly enthusiastic. Telling him his plans, adventures the boy finds illusory, albeit coming from a man who is seriousness itself. That afternoon, as they leave the taxidermist's workshop, Ricardo Samos talks to his son about the Carpathian bear. Feeling happy and satisfied, he goes and confesses to him, a secret between the two of them, that he has two wishes: to catch a Carpathian bear and to find a very special book. No, it's not an incunabulum. It's a New Testament printed in Spain in the middle of the nineteenth century. Yes, he does have Bibles and Gospels from that period. But this book is dedicated and signed. A whim. An obsession. Yes, it could be called an obsession.

On the subject of obsessions, it'll soon be time for hunting woodcocks. It'll soon be time for Eusebio.

This woodcock hunter was now Ricardo Samos' essential guide and companion. In his trips to the city, he almost always paid them a visit.

Apart from hunting, Eusebio was a mayor and had business. He almost always brought presents. Solid presents that forged a strong link. Fruits of the earth. Sometimes meat. As if he'd chopped nature up into cubes. But also books for the judge from some rectory or country estate fallen on hard times. Eusebio did all he could to avoid looking like a peasant. He dressed elegantly and sometimes overdid it.

Chelo would say, 'To be a fox, all he's missing is a tail.'

She who was always pleasant, flexible, able to turn into an art deco mask if necessary, was, however, brusque with this visitor. She didn't hide her antipathy. 'I can't help it,' she'd tell Samos. 'It's something physical.'

He turned up with a woodcock's feather in a glass case.

'The hunter's most prized trophy,' said the judge. He was clearly trying to mediate on behalf of his hunting companion. A historic assertion by the judge, 'You can go out on to the mountain without a dog, but not without Eusebio. He was born to hunt. I swear he has a pointer's scent. That's his dog, a pointer, when he's after woodcocks. They understand each other through a code of silent gestures. It's impossible to tell who supports who. He's always the first to spot the mirrors.'

'The mirrors?'

'Their excrement. White with a green centre. Their excrement is the only clue. The only thing that gives away the most secretive bird in Galician forests.'

Chelo, who's not at all interested in hunting, is curious about this bird. She asks the women who come with things on top of their heads. Turns into an expert. The woodcock. The wood's guardian. Its mission is not just to survive, but to warn the forest of danger. Its sudden flight is a signal to take cover, which all attend to. The earth's accomplice. It raises its young among bracken, lays light, ashen eggs on the ground. The perfect camouflage. Light cream or brown colours with a dark band on its wings. It has the best defensive weapon. The most extraordinary vision. Without a blind spot. Encompassing 360 degrees, all around.

Eusebio sets off with his pointer's scent to find the mirrors. He's a crafty enemy. Transforms into the mountain. Has his own camouflage. He can be like a rock. In fact, he is that rock. His face resembles bark. His field of vision is not like the woodcock's. He has a large blind spot. His field of vision is like the eagle's. Not being able to see behind can be a disadvantage. But all he cares about is hunting precision. Getting as close as possible. Within range. Hitting the target. Bagging the guardian.

At the tip of a woodcock's wing is a very fine feather. Of legendary quality for a painter's brush, better than horsehair. A unique feather only the eyes and fingers of an expert can tell apart.

'Amazing, Chelo! No hunter would give up such a trophy.'

Eusebio is wearing Ray-Ban sunglasses today, golden frames with dark green lenses. You can't see his eyes. He smiles. He really does have sharp canines.

The 666 Chestnuts

Old lazybones, if he was in prison or a labour camp, he must have done something. I can see he's got a limp. But even with a limp, a man's got to bring home a wage. He can't find work? Well, he should look in hell, God forgive me. They've been at it for hours, without a rest. What can they be talking about? There he is, like an equal, like a theologian with the priest. I don't know why he permits it. Why he doesn't shut him up with a spot of Latin. Though he knows Latin as well. He was Don Benigno's altar boy and when he started losing his memory, there was Polka to prompt him during Mass. He's not stupid, shame he got all those ideas. What does a poor man want ideas for? To complicate life, his own and his family's.

To start with, when she opened the door, she expected there to be a scene. She knew why he'd come. To demand an explanation after the incident with that girl. Well, not such a girl any more, a young lady, and what a tongue! No, it wasn't right, that punishment, all because of some chestnuts, but O, the girl, shouldn't have been so rebellious, so offensive, quoting the Bible at the priest, who ever heard such a thing? The girl, we'll call her that for now, came into the rectory's enclosure with some other children to collect chestnuts. They'd been warned. One or two of them had received a beating. They ought to have known by now Don Marcelo had a special devotion to Our Lady of the Fist. He'd preached about it in church, when there was that dispute about common land, that he wasn't a communist even when it came to chestnuts. And Polka in the Cuckoo's Feather bar went and said if anyone was a communist, it was Christ, he didn't even own the Cross, poor thing. Don Marcelo wasn't Don Benigno.

She knew that. He bore a grudge. Which may have had something to do with the girl's punishment, I can't say. The point is it was Sunday afternoon when they came to steal chestnuts. They reckoned on his taking a siesta. So they came in all confident, even put up a ladder to climb over the stone wall, which was high, pretty solid, with bits of glass along the top. But he can hear you thinking. He'd already suspected them of something during Mass. And he was waiting. He let them make a good pile of chestnuts. And when they'd finished, he turned up in his cassock, as vast as the night. Thundering out, 'Once a thief, always a thief!' And they all took to their heels, except for her. She just stood there and had the audacity to confront him, 'Whoever finds a nut is allowed to keep it.' Of course he couldn't believe his ears. He grabbed her by the arm and shook her. 'You're a proper little madam! You threw a stone at the roof and it's landed on your head.' And O replied, 'Make your own sermon, but don't bang on the pulpit.'

That girl ought to wash her mouth out.

No, the punishment wasn't fair, muttered the housemaid. To threaten her with the police, well, that much was to be expected. But not to make her collect that number of chestnuts. That wasn't right. It wasn't right to make her count up to 666 chestnuts. On her knees as well, in the damp grass, it being so cold. But you should have seen her! Seen her count! The chestnuts flew through her fingers. The way her mother used to count matchsticks.

666 chestnuts in a flash.

'Now go and tell your father about it.'

That wasn't necessary. That was adding insult to injury. Which is why, when there was a knock at the door and she opened and saw it was Polka, she expected the worst. After all, the tiniest spark can set fire to the whole house.

During the conversation, however, the priest beat his fist on the chestnut table in the rectory dining-room only once. The table was as big as a diocese, to use a parishioner's metaphor, since on feast days all the local priests could sit around it together. Don Marcelo beat his fist and said, 'Don't ask me what Lot got up to with his daughters again!'

We know this because it was the only thing the housemaid heard from the kitchen.

She was very worried, because she'd often heard about Lot's wife in that passage from Scripture which was read during Mass and seemed to serve as a warning to all women, about gossip, curiosity, that instinct for wanting to know what's happening, which is why she was punished and became a pillar of salt. She was lost while the angels went about the business of destruction, of burning and razing Sodom and Gomorrah, because there couldn't be witnesses to such destruction, they didn't want people talking about the terror inflicted by those angels. This is what crossed her mind, the lesson, applicable to all, that it was better to look the other way. But what confuses her now, what disturbs her as she plucks two pigeons for the priest's dinner is his warning to Polka not to ask what Lot got up to with his daughters, and his daughters with him, again. He's not in the mood for sermons. And if he doesn't tell the whole story, it's because he doesn't feel like it, the pillar of salt is enough. She pricks up her ears. Polka starts talking about a certain Elisha, prophet and disciple of Elijah, who lost his temper with some boys who called him baldhead as he was walking along. 'Go away, baldhead, go away!' So, bald as he was, he turned around and cursed them in the name of Jehovah and forty-two of the boys were mauled by two she-bears. How many? That's a lot of carnage for the Lord, I'd say. Anyhow he speaks well, can keep up with the priest, is better even. Little devil, he makes me laugh! The priest puts his hand on his head, which is shorn, and says, 'I went too far, OK, but you can't compare what I did with what the bald prophet did to those children.'

She can't resist, quickly wipes the layer of blood and down off her hands. She's nervous and heads out of the service entrance towards the chapel to see what it says about Lot and his daughters, there'll be something in those books, something about the forty-two boys mauled by she-bears on account of the prophet's temper. Which explains why the housemaid's expression changed, perhaps for ever, and why the priest asked her if something was wrong when she appeared with a face the colour of pure wax. She was so upset she said nothing about the negligence of serving him with bird down in the cracks of her fingernails.

'He's going to be the new gravedigger,' said the priest.

She wiped the pigeons' blood on her apron. She knew that rather than talking to someone he was trying to convince himself.

'Someone has to do it,' continued the priest. 'But I did stipulate one condition. No more Carnival procession. No more lame cardinal. No more goliard's sermons from the tavern's pulpit.'

And, without wanting to, she felt sorry. Polka was a wretch, but he was funny. She cursed him, but every year, during Carnival, she'd be waiting to see him dressed up as a cardinal, with his *Ora pro nobis*, sprinkling holy water with a watering can. Dressed in purple, he looked better than the priest. He led the procession in which they carried an effigy of the Carnival made of turnips in order to throw it into the River Monelos. Ever since the war, it had been forbidden to wear a disguise, but they'd come out at nightfall from under the stones. Two years ago, they had the audacity to tack photos of Franco, the Caudillo, to the turnip dummy and to give it an escort of revellers dressed up as Franco's Moorish Guard, riding donkeys. The police turned up and laid into the revellers. But the dummy had already sunk in the river.

She didn't reply. What could she say? Besides, there weren't so many to choose from. The young men were all emigrating. And the old men were more likely to die than dig graves.

'He'll get used to it,' said Don Marcelo. 'He'll end up being the most serious person around.'

'Yes,' she agreed. That was the trouble with that job. Everyone took to their role, treated the whole world as if it were a graveyard.

Rocío, the cook, suddenly remembered, 'Will he still be allowed to dress up as a woman?'

'Not in my parish. Certainly not. I don't care what he does outside it. I'm not going to take a peek at his legs.'

'Praise be to God!'

And the priest couldn't tell whether this was an expression of horror or relief.

The Gravedigger

'I've got a job for you, Crecente,' said the priest.

He stood up and went to switch on the light. A chandelier where electricity was a tired guest. In one corner, in a basket, were the chestnuts, polished now, with that luminous tint, that suppressed glee of a second life you find in fruit ripening inside houses. Like so many other chandeliers, grapes for sweet wine hung from mimosa branches. Apples, pregnant with aroma, occupied the planisphere of Zamoran blankets. Nuts were lost in thought. More than the solid furniture whose wood was mineral, petrified, extracted from the forest of night, Polka noticed this other presence of the fruit.

He worked as a labourer. Whatever was going. In summer, the odd aubade on the bagpipes. He'd have liked to go back to working for parks and gardens. But he was lame and had a record. Being lame, he used to say, was a record and a half.

You couldn't have a 'record'. A word you'd have thought was easier to pronounce than 'salicylic', but it had weight and sloped upwards.

Some men had a record and others did not.

He also seemed to have a stubborn destiny.

He was arrested during the war. When he thought they'd forgotten about him, they came to fetch him in a lorry carrying prisoners from Silva and San Cristovo. And they simulated something. They took them at night to Castro. To the ruins of the Celtic settlement. The moon was shining and he could see the shadows of memories, of nine months before, when Holando read out the commandments of naturism. They were told to dig. It was all very sinister, having to dig a ditch there, in Castro. The order was, 'Dig hard, in a straight line!' And he thought, Bloody hell, imagine I find Terranova's treasure now! It wasn't funny, come on, after all he was digging his own grave. 'Your mental current's back to front,' Holando had told him. 'When you have to cry, you laugh. You're a walking paradox.' The freethinker's gift. He had to bite his lips, make them bleed to turn the current around. Come on, dig. But one of the spades hit on some metal. 'What's this?' 'Some junk,' said one of the soldiers. 'Let me have a look,' said another, who was wearing a Cabaleiro cloak. He knocked the clay off against a stone and held the object up to the moon.

'Well, blow me down if we haven't got ourselves a torque!'

'Let me see. Are you sure it's not a horseshoe?'

Everybody examining the object in the moonlight, fondling the metal, in search of gold.

'We'll have to see what it looks like in the daytime. Now get digging!'

'Straight?'

'Sideways! One piece leads to another.'

Sideways is better, reflected Polka hopefully. You don't dig graves sideways.

They were there the whole night. The soldiers eagerly sifting each clod, examining each pebble, poking in holes.

'Here's something hard. Oh no, they're bones!'

'Bones? An animal's, I suppose.'

'Well, what else are they going to be?' said the big guy in charge of the squad. He then looked at the hole as if the question he'd asked were now turning over soil.

With the thirst for gold came dawn. Painting witnesses on the horizon. Men on bikes and mopeds, women carrying the first light of day. The whole hilltop between the rocks of Ara Solis riddled with holes. The idea was to kill at night. 'We're out of time,' said one of the squad of soldiers and it wasn't clear whether he meant for digging or killing. The point is they ordered them back on to the lorry and so it was that Polka went to prison. Having dug his own grave, first straight and then sideways.

*   *   *

'I've got a job for you, Crecente,' said the parish priest. He hadn't stopped turning the matter over since punishing O. It was obvious he felt remorse. 'A job for you. With two conditions. No more pagan processions with the lame cardinal and monumental women during Carnival. And no more competing with me by preaching in taverns. I know you do it well, you make people laugh, but it's time for you to shut up, Polka. That's the way it goes. You can't be priest,' he said ironically. 'Verger's taken. That leaves gravedigger. What do you think? As a gravedigger and a bagpiper, you'll get by, so to speak . . .'

'The man was very chatty,' Polka informed Olinda.

King Cintolo's Cockroach

It had to be said properly, not any old how. 'Acetylsalicylic acid'.

'Come on, Pinche, repeat it.'

'Acetylsacilytic acid.'

'Not "sacilytic"! Salicylic.'

Polka believed if you wanted to speak well, you had to be able to say 'acetylsalicylic acid'. An invention which was to be found in nature, like all others. It just had to be rescued from invisibility, as music is sound rescued in bagpipes. One of Polka's set phrases, though he was careful when to use it. Everything of importance had been rescued from invisibility. And aspirin was no exception. The best proof of the virtues of aspirin was in river rats if only you could see them. They were always healthy, clean, with shiny skin. Why? Because they gnawed at willow roots. And what was in a willow?

'Acetylsacilytic acid!'

'Salicylic!'

O liked the theory of invisibility, but not rats. They didn't strike her as a model of healthy beauty. She always tried to have a stone to hand in case they showed up along the river. But one day a rat stared at her from the other side, the first time she saw its eyes, and O came to the same conclusion as Polka. She decided it was beautiful. An unsettling beauty, as with all animals that live by the river and try not to be seen, like the praying mantis, easily confused with the grass, or water boatmen, which live on the surface of the water without ever getting wet, darning river marks with their long, slender legs. According to Polka, the most interesting creatures also formed part of what was not immediately visible.

And this was the solemn moment when he would contribute his own discovery.

'No,' Olinda would say, losing her patience. 'That's enough of that!'

'Where's the harm in it?'

O and Pinche would laugh. They'd heard it many times before. They already knew that the prettiest creature on earth was the cockroach that ate bat shit in King Cintolo's Cave.

Acetylsalicylic Acid

'What this boy needs is acetylsalicylic acid. Bring me an aspirin.'

Neves stands still. Rigid. She'd been expecting something else, some cure. A few divine words. Some animal's anatomy. A picture of saints. Of a cabaret singer. Herb tea. Something.

'Aren't you going to say something to him?'

'Listen, is there an aspirin?'

'There is. But take care, you'll make a hole in his stomach.'

'I know that, woman. Dissolve it in a spoonful of water. And make some coffee.'

'Coffee?'

'Yes, coffee. Coffee from the pot.

'OK. Now listen, Gabriel. Take the aspirin first and hold it in your mouth for a bit, without swallowing, so you get the taste. The bitter taste. Don't spit. Good. That's good. Now take a sip of coffee. Coffee's also bitter. Bitterness on the palate is the best thing to get you talking. Sweetness is far too conformist. That's it, my boy.

'Now what you have to say is "acetylsalicylic acid".'

Gabriel repeated it swiftly, perfectly.

'Good, that's good. Did you notice how the words contained what was spoken?'

Gabriel looked at Neves and O. They had large, wide open, beautiful eyes. He thought he'd like to be an ophthalmologist when he was older, as well as an underwater archaeologist. Be able to look into those eyes.

'Ophthalmologist,' he whispered, surprised that fear hadn't climbed the walls of his throat.

'What was that?' asked Polka.

'Ophthalmologist.'

'That's also valid,' said Polka with satisfaction, seeing an improvement in Gabriel's initiative. 'It's also scientific. Now let's re-turn a few other re-turnables. As if we were singing, but without singing. Say, "The drunken accordion speaks English, German . . ."'

It was then the kitchen door suddenly opened. The judge was wearing his hat and overcoat, he hadn't hung them up in the hallway as he usually did, which may have been why he looked bigger than the door. To Neves, the most nervous among them, he was like an enormous creature trying to enter a miniature house. The man with the sack of beans inside a bean. A cat, with whiskers as wide as the door, inside a mouse-hole. Behind his glasses, his eyes bespoke urgency. He glanced at Polka. A local. In his kitchen. The poor light at that time was like a continuation of a country storm.

'And my wife?'

'She received a call from Fine Arts, your honour. To take some foreigners on a tour,' Neves replied nervously, but quickly, without slipping up. 'She said if you called, you were not to worry. She'd be at the official dinner on time, just as you arranged.'

'I see.'

Before leaving, he looked again at Polka. It was a fleeting, wordless glance. He was waiting for Polka to gesture to him in greeting with his corduroy peaked cap. For his part, Polka thought the opposite. That the initiative should come from the man in the hat. He was the owner of the house. The one who had to welcome him.

'This is my father, your honour,' said O.

'Hello. How are we today?'

'Same as always, your . . .'

He was going to add what he always said with friendly humour, 'Working for eternity, making a bed for those who are going to sleep in the open.' But he didn't have time, he spoke like a mute, because the judge was already taking leave of his son. 'Don't forget your exercises.' An admonition that, from the tone, appeared to be directed towards everyone.

Neves accompanied the judge to the door. Polka, meanwhile, poured himself some coffee, which he sugared generously.

'But you're . . . having . . . sugar!' the boy protested.

Polka winked.

'My words are re-turned already.'

'Phew! I'm glad he didn't ask anything,' sighed Neves when she came back.

'I'd have explained it all to him,' said O. 'We weren't doing anything wrong.'

'He's very particular,' commented Neves in a low voice. 'When he gets all authoritative, there's nothing to be done. He walks with his bust on a pedestal.'

Polka savoured the last drop of sugary coffee. *La dolce vita*, he called those dregs. A phrase he'd heard from Luís Terranova. What had happened to Terranova, to that boy who was a diamond, a Gardel? He hoped he hadn't had dealings with eternity.

Polka savoured the last drop as if it were an undying pleasure and then clicked his tongue.

'What was the problem? He looked at me and didn't see me.'

He turned to face Gabriel.

'Now you know. What you have to do is look and see. Give eyes their vision. Words their meaning. Come on. Let's have another go. Say, "With each note he played, the bagpiper made a polished diamond".'

Gabriel recited the sentence without getting stuck on the jingle. He didn't choke on a single word. His voice sounded happy and singsong and the words contained everything they named.

'That's it. That's what I call many happy re-turns,' Polka congratulated himself. 'You have to find the right key for the lock.'

He was emotional. He took Gabriel's head in his hands as if he might lift it off his body and polish the sculpture. These were no sad verses, but the man's eyes were wet. He heard Luís Terranova's voice again. He was standing naked, a god in the nude, on top of Ara Solis. He mumbled that incomprehensible refrain *Yamba, yambo, yambambe!* as if it were Latin. Something Polka only did when he'd just killed a worm of fear.

The Witch's Kiss

'What? Isn't anyone going to die? There's no money to be made here!'

This is what Polka would say when he passed in front of the the Cuckoo's Feather bar. His jokes as parish gravedigger encouraged people to carry on living. Sometimes he'd switch refrain and say at the door:

'Anyone want a reference?'

And they'd shout to him from inside, 'What death needs is an open mouth. Wine for you, Polka!'

This was something he could always count on. An invitation to a round of wine. He liked it this way. One thing he couldn't stand was drinking on his own. There are lots of solitary drinkers. But Polka didn't go in for this wine of solitude. Wine deserved a story, a conversation. Of the Here and the Hereafter, in people's opinion, he knew more than the priest, who toed the official line. There were questions they didn't discuss in the vicar's presence, simply because he couldn't answer them. For example: 'Polka, tell us, who's in charge of the Holy Company, the procession of the dead?' 'As I understand it, the one who sets the Holy Company in motion is the first to be buried.' 'And who's the leader?' 'Why, Adam, I suppose.' 'And who buried Adam, Polka? Was it Eve?' 'No, it was a son, a third son who's rarely talked about and must have been a good sort. Here Cain and Abel get all the attention. The third man must have wanted to avoid any publicity. But it was he, Seth, who buried his father. And stuck an olive branch in the ground over the first corpse. From that olive tree, they took the wood for the Holy Cross.'

'That's quite a coincidence, Polka.'

'Life is like that, my friend, its vocation is to be a story. If you don't understand that, you don't understand anything. So I suppose it's Adam, in order of antiquity, who calls to the others, "Arise, ye dead, and come out together!" Which seems to me an important detail. The fact they decide to come out together, without distinction.'

Polka to O: 'Don't be afraid of the dead. What you have to watch out for are the living who spoil life. Old people used to say those who hate life belong to the Bone Society. Sowing terror is both ancient and modern. What they used to do was throw a bone at night against a window they saw illuminated. Which was their way of indicating the victim. But the dead know how to get their own back. Something these thugs don't realise. The dead find a way to defend themselves. Old people used to talk of a cold slap, which is a slap given by the dead who haven't been properly buried. I know lots of examples. Lots of examples of murderers who were never judged. Or worse than that. Murderers who even now are meting out justice, making laws. But there were lots who got a dead man's cold slap. Murderers who lost their mind. Like one who went around with Luís Huici's fountain pen. Do you know who Huici was? One of the most cultivated, most stylish men this city ever had. A forerunner, a shining star. Well, his assassin would swagger into the bar with the dead man's fountain pen. And one day he decided to write with it. But all he could write was Luís Huici's signature. Luís Huici's name. He died a little later from an illness. That's what they said. But I knew what it was. He got a cold slap.'

'Years ago, when I was small,' said O, 'I heard you say the dead in the Holy Company would sometimes take a black dog for a walk.'

'That's right. A black bitch with a little bell.'

'Oh, come on! Did you ever see it?'

'No, I didn't see it,' replied Polka, 'but I heard the tinkle of the bell and scarpered. Listen, O, the only one from that world I had dealings with was Antaruxa.'

'Get away with you!' said Olinda, who to thread a needle in the poor light of the lamp concentrated so hard she involved all her muscles, the whole house, every concentric ring from the village to its antipodes,

230

in such a way that, were she to fail said Olympic task, the pillars of the world would come crashing down.

Polka waited for the thread to pass through the eye of the needle. And then answered the question which was still hanging in the air, although Olinda had tried to swish it away with her hand.

'Antaruxa is a high-ranking witch. She's the one who kisses the devil.'

'Be quiet, Francisco!'

When Olinda addressed him by his proper name, it meant she was serious. Very annoyed. And Olinda, annoyed, was no joke. The women of Castro knew how to put you in your place and assert their authority. So Olinda said, 'Either you shut your mouth or I'll sew it for you.' To carry on talking, Polka moved off a little, sat on a stool and spoke from the shadows.

'She smacks his behind!' hissed Polka as if he'd revealed one of the greatest secrets of the night of spirits.

'She smacks what?' asked O.

Olinda reprimanded Polka with her look. They remained silent. The sea of trees, the dark purple waves of Zapateira Heath, roared. O wondered whether Olinda really would sew Polka's mouth for him. Suddenly the two of them, husband and wife, burst out laughing.

'She kisses his bottom,' hissed Olinda. She was laughing as well.

Pinche's Bike

Olinda said to Polka, 'We have to buy Pinche a bike.' For such a reticent person, this was quite something. A Biblical sentence. 'If he's going to work on site during the week and then, at the weekend, if he wants to go and play, he won't manage.' Pinche had taken up Polka's bagpipes and was making something. Polka would say to the boy, 'The good thing about this instrument is it already has the music inside.' Polka looked at Olinda, who was waiting for his approval, and said, 'You're absolutely right. He'll need a means of transport.' This definitely sounded convincing, dispelled any doubts, because it cost a lot of money at that time to buy a bike, even if it was secondhand.

The point is Polka made that judgement about the means of transport and was himself convinced and very proud, as if the words had come from a decisive voice of Providence which had happened by. There weren't many bikes around at that time and lest anyone should think it a senseless waste or a whim, careful what the neighbours might say, Pinche's father declared:

'It's a means of transport!'

This argument, however, so pleasing to local ears, was touted about only when they'd bought it and were coming back, father and son, leading the conveyance by the handlebars. It was a kind of tribute to its owner, an old friend, another disaffected worker by the name of Estremil. His widow said of man and machine, 'He liked to lead it by the hand. He rarely got on it, only on the flat, and, as you know, it's not very flat round these parts. So it's pretty new. He was very affectionate towards his things.' And what could have been a compliment paid to the dead turned out to be a splendid truth when they were shown the workshop and saw the order and cleanliness that reigned there, together with the heavy mourning of tools that are without their operative.

'Would you like to see his shoes?'

An unusual invitation, thought Polka, but who could refuse to see a dead man's shoes? So the widow opened the door of a wooden shed and there, arranged on shelves, were his shoes and boots. Not four or five pairs, but all the pairs of a lifetime. The widow pointed to the clogs he wore as a child, his football boots, his wedding shoes, a present from a brother who worked for Senra Footwear. Every Sunday morning, Estremil would take out his shoes, line them up and polish and shine them. In silence, he'd travel back down the road of existence.

'Would you like to see his radios? He painstakingly repaired half a dozen. I can't sell them to you because away from here they don't work. And his books? He had a thing about books. More than he could read.'

'Objects have a homing instinct, madam,' said Polka.

'And they're selfish too!' replied the widow. 'Careful with the bike, boy. He loved it like a sorrel mare.'

This was the image that stuck in Pinche's mind. As soon as he took possession of the machine, he felt the tug of a tetchy, resentful animal.

Surrounded by a pack of children, they stopped in front of the Cuckoo's Feather bar. In the face of night, in the burnt, smoky tavern light, the bike had an animal aura, a cervine air. The machine was waiting for some kind of communal recognition and people lent themselves to the task.

'You need to keep the chain well oiled. 'Tis the vehicle's soul.'

'The frame's heavy. It'll be tough to ride uphill.'

'What goes up must come down.'

'Who d'you buy it from if you don't mind me asking?'

And Polka let it out, 'From Estremil de Laz.' He realised too late. The information was inappropriate, then at least, and he tried unsuccessfully to correct his mistake, 'I mean, from the bike's widow.' This is what happens when you trip on your tongue, you lose your sense of direction.

'Wasn't he run over as he was wheeling it along?'

The others eyed the bike with suspicion. Some of them moved off, partly as a joke. And Pinche and Polka were left alone.

'You know what I think?' asked Polka aloud. 'You're a bunch of fools!'

Enough said. For Polka, being a fool was the gravest insult to a man's honour.

'It's just a bike,' he said to Pinche. 'Caress it, so it gets used to you.'

The Woman at the Window

Zonzo's mother was almost always at the window. Or rather she walked up and down the gallery as in a glass cage. Gabriel had never seen her outside the house and there came a time he couldn't imagine her away from the window. The large house they lived in was very similar to the Samoses', which was also near the marina, facing the bay. The entrances to these buildings, erected for the well-to-do in the space left vacant by the collapse of the Old City wall, give on to María Pita Square and Rego de Auga on the westward side. With regard to the architects' initial plans, what happened was a curious revolution involving light. The part that was going to be the back, with a stone wall and small windows, was transformed by means of a radical shift into an eastern front. Instead of the dour expression of smooth granite, they built large, glazed balconies. Boxes of light. A large area that gathered and harvested light. And gave it back a thousand times. Chelo Vidal was working on an essay for the forthcoming magazine *Oeste*, in which she described this as the most important act in 'the history of the city's body'. A serious essay with several drawings of 'Women at the Window'.

Zonzo's mother seemed never to leave the window. There she was whenever he accompanied him. Smoking. Doing her nails. Talking on the phone. Occasionally looking at the docks. And the bay beyond. On a small table for the phone were some binoculars. Zonzo barely mentioned his family. He sometimes let out the odd snippet. For example, his father was a musician on tour. He was always on tour. And if Zonzo said something, it was because Korea was there. Korea knew things.

He said, 'What's amazing is the mark your Dad has on his lips. A perfect circle.'

235

'That's because he plays the trumpet,' replied Zonzo.

'A brilliant musician,' said Korea. 'Have you ever heard him?'

'Course I have,' replied Zonzo, feeling offended.

'All right, keep your hair on,' said Korea.

That day, Zonzo had a fishing rod with an automatic reel. A brand-new fishing rod. From America. The three of them were going to fish for squid at night up by San Antón Castle.

'Keep your hair on, mate,' repeated Korea. 'Hey! That house with the light on, isn't that your place?'

'Could be,' said Zonzo almost without looking.

'Your mother's like a train,' said Korea. 'His mother, the painter, she's all right. But yours, Zonzo, yours is gorgeous. Did she really used to sing under the name Pretty Mary?'

'Piss off,' said Zonzo, leaving with his brand-new fishing rod.

'All right, I won't say anything else,' shouted Korea. 'We're not going to catch squid by hand. They'll all bite tonight, Zonzo. Look at that moon!'

'Watch it, Korea. One day, I'll kill you.'

Zonzo was special. He had no fear. No fear of Korea, and that was brave. He remembered one day he went to his house. His mother at the window. In came a man, wearing a smart suit. Tall and strong. He occupied the centre of the room with the absolute control of someone who conquers territory with an imposing look. No one heard a knock at the door for the simple reason he opened the door himself. 'Hello, boys.' He threw a package at Zonzo, who neither looked at it nor opened it.

'It's all arranged for you to sing at La Boîte. If you don't like Pretty Mary, we'll have to think of another name. How about Nostalgic Mary?'

'Nostalgic? I hardly feel nostalgic. I feel like something the cat brought in.'

He burst out laughing. Went over to the woman at the window. Embraced her and kissed her on the lips.

'Let's go,' suggested Zonzo. He didn't say goodbye. Outside, he opened the present. A pair of new, genuine football boots, which he dropped down the stairwell.

'One day, I'll kill him.'

'Temper, temper!' Korea exclaimed. 'This guy's hung up on his mum. Lucky I didn't say anything about Manlle.'

'Who's Manlle?'

'Ask Mr Justice,' said Korea ironically.

The Judge's Drawer

This drawer, the largest in the desk, on the bottom right, was where the judge kept the folders with his manuscripts, Syllabus' articles and the legal affairs he was currently involved in. He locked it. Always. But the hiding place was hardly a secret. He locked it and kept the key with others in what Chelo called his *potiche*, a present she had given him, a small rounded jar made of enamelled glass with vegetal designs. His *potiche* stood on a shelf to the left as you came in, flanked by thick volumes.

The judge never told Gabriel he wasn't allowed to open the drawer and rummage through the papers. The fact of opening, locking and then hiding the key was enough to let it be known this was a reserved space. What's more, despite what you might think if you saw him acting as judge, Samos was not in the habit of giving orders at home. Both he and Chelo were methodical in their own way. Gabriel would never mix his mother's colours in the Chinese Pavilion without her permission. Nor would he rummage through the drawer with his father's manuscripts. If he did rummage through the drawer, it was because of that surprising discovery. The day he saw him pull out a western novel.

When the opportunity presented itself, he opened the drawer and searched archaeologically through the different layers in among the folders. And found not one, but half a dozen western novels, all signed John Black Eye. And all looking as if they'd been read many times. With slips of paper marking pages where some passages had been underlined with a red pencil. Almost all these sentences, some of which seemed rather strange for a western novel, had a single protagonist: the Judge of Oklahoma.

So it was he read:

The Judge of Oklahoma always had the last word, which ended up convincing him he was always right.

Whenever they went to the river on a picnic, the Judge of Oklahoma would warn his nephews and nieces, Anyone drowns, I'll kill them!

On the subject of influences, the Judge of Oklahoma would fill his mouth with Cicero and other classics. One day, a visiting lawyer dared to reply, But it's not their fault, your honour.

Whenever in clay pigeon shooting he shouted 'Pull!' both the trap and the clay pigeon felt a certain kind of relief.

The Judge of Oklahoma, a great consumer of eggs, considered chicken farming an inferior occupation.

A smuggler who was arrested for breaking the prohibition law made the following statement, They've outlawed shit and turned it into gold. The Judge of Oklahoma interpreted this as an act of contempt.

The Judge of Oklahoma explained the different ways of applying the death penalty: hanging, firing squad, garrotte . . . One of those present in the courtroom couldn't help commenting admiringly, What a versatile lot you are!

The Judge of Oklahoma pronounced sentence with the same inclination with which the painter Castiglione sketched his Young Man with Lowered Head.

In order to avoid protests in the courtroom, he had the public divided into three halves.

Return to the source! Look in the source! exclaimed the Judge of Oklahoma when indoctrinating future judges. Everyone thought he meant Roman Law, but he had in mind the blonde, northern mermaid splashing about in the Trevi Fountain.

In the field of law, had he been the only judge in the world, he'd have known no rival.

In his time as a member of the special tribunal, the Judge of Oklahoma would take pity on those who'd been sentenced to death and tell them, Not to worry. The day you die will be the last of your life.

Let the trial begin! declared the Judge of Oklahoma solemnly. And then he added, Show the culprit in!

On one of the folders, he saw the name John Black Eye. Inside was a carbon copy of one letter and the original of another. The first was dated in Coruña and addressed to the publisher of the Far Off West series.

The person writing introduced themselves as 'an unconditional follower of John Black Eye' and quoted some of his titles as examples of 'masterpieces in the western genre'.

'Such galloping prose,' it said, 'is only possible against the backdrop of a vast culture, whose qualities are stressed in the learned historical and ethnographical references and detailed geographical descriptions. What stands out, however, is the ironic style, the great subtlety, the unmistakable talent that suggest the presence of a great and hidden artist.'

Finally the letter's author enquired about John Black Eye's real identity or, if this were not possible, his address so that he could send him 'an admirer's humble tribute'.

There was one surprising detail in the letter. It was signed R. Mandivi and it took Gabriel some time to realise this was his father's initial and second surname. He wasn't the one who asked questions. The questions came to him. Why not put his own name?

The other letter, written at a later date, came from Barcelona. The typed text was brief:

Dear Mr Mandivi,

We passed on your request to John Black Eye, who in turn expressed his heartfelt gratitude for your comments. It is his rule not to enter into correspondence with readers. He was delighted, however, to comply with another of your requests, for which we enclose a signed copy of *Word of Colt*. Please accept our apologies and our own thanks for your interest.

Yours, Salomé Senra

He carried on excavating. The title of one novel in the Far Off West series was indeed *The Judge of Oklahoma*. There was also *The Mysterious Outsider*, *The Yoke Collector*, *The Peace of Graveyards* . . . But what he anxiously sought, and could not find, was *Word of Colt*. There was something else, however, a folder that had nothing to do with westerns, marked '12 Panadeiras Street'.

The Mysterious Outsider

On one occasion, just one, the judge lost his effigy's composure, his immutable presence that paralysed so many defendants and only the odd mischief-maker would parody in a whisper, far away from the Palace of Justice, recalling that monumental slip-up, 'Let the trial begin! Show the culprit in!'

The one time his face fell, and he couldn't help thumping the palm of his left hand with his right fist like a mallet, was when the defendant in question, who was up on charges of 'disorderly conduct' and 'being a public nuisance', turned out to be someone who looked like his twin. An exact copy, as if out of a mould. His first impulse, having ordered him to stand up and give his name, was to demand an explanation. He felt a chill on seeing that they were exactly the same. Not even a marked difference in their clothes could detract from their awful similarity. He glanced at the people in the courtroom. No one seemed to have spotted what for the judge was a case of mistaken physiognomy. And it wasn't that they were blind, since he himself agreed with the local saying to define the sort of character you find roaming around courthouses: gait of an ox, eyes of a fox, teeth of a wolf.

The defendant was very daring. He seemed to be imitating him. To be staring at him and in a way so that others wouldn't notice, with tiny movements of his eyebrows and lips, to be constructing a caricature. He blinked and the defendant did the same. He winked and the defendant repeated the gesture.

'Stop doing that!'

'I can't, your honour. I've got something in my eye.'

'You should have thought about that.'

'You don't think about something in your eye, your honour,' reasoned the defendant, surprised at having to explain such a basic law of nature to a judge.

He really was the spitting image.

While a female witness gave evidence, the defendant pulled out a book he had hidden under his shirt and started reading.

'Behave!' said the judge. 'This isn't a reading-room.'

The defendant was about to put the book away when the judge ordered it to be handed over. 'My word, this looks interesting! The Spirit of the Laws by Montesquieu. I'll have to read it. It's been confiscated . . . By the way, what were you before you turned up here?'

'I was a judge, but I meted out justice.'

The outsider's reply caused a wave of consternation to spread through the courtroom.

'I sentence you to life in exile,' pronounced the judge. 'I don't want to see you in Oklahoma again.'

From The Mysterious Outsider by John Black Eye, Far Off West series.

The Yoke Collector

The director, publicist, only editor and typographer of the newspaper Maritime Awakening, Ernest Botana, walked in a daze, having received the order to close issued by the Judge of Oklahoma and carried out by the sheriff, Trigger Happy, and his not very bright sidekick, Light Weight.

'Why?' he asked the judge in the short interview he was allowed with the door ajar.

'In the law, there are no whys,' replied the somewhat oblique voice of Large White, the Judge of Oklahoma. Adding from a dark room, 'The point of the law is to be the law, not to be just.'

He'd heard this before and had felt a mixture of fear and disgust, something akin to what a goldfinch must feel when it lands on a limy twig.

'And don't lodge any more appeals. I've ordered the building to be razed to the ground. I already told you there's no sea in Oklahoma.'

Suddenly, on the main street, he bumped into a poorly paved shadow. He rolled his newspaper into the shape in his passionate columns he called 'the Winchester of freedom' and looked up to find the flinty profile of the supremo. His heart told him to express contempt. That the lives of people in Oklahoma should be in the hands of individuals like the judge at this stage of civilisation made him feel a fatigue he defined as 'reticulate drowning'. There was a time his optimism knew no bounds and grew on top of itself, step by step, like a cabbage. It was then he'd written a brave and memorable denunciation of State abuse and corruption: The Yoke Collector.

Memorable especially for the judge. The day, no doubt, he swore to get his revenge. And summoned him. He was really annoyed.

'You'll feel all the weight of the law . . . and a little something extra from me.'

What was published in Maritime Awakening was true. The judge did collect

yokes, which he hung in the hallway. He had three particularly interesting specimens:
a Texas yoke, a Kansas yoke and a yoke from Oklahoma.

From *The Yoke Collector* by John Black Eye, Far Off West series.

Sulfe looked around. Between the stag's antlers was a crucifix. The vision of St Eustace, patron saint of hunters. Three yokes hung in the hallway like coat-racks. One of each of the local kinds, called Galician, Portuguese and Castilian. Why had the judge summoned them? Did he suspect one of them of feeding information to a writer of western novels? What was his name? Black Eye.

'There are the three yokes, but it's not a collection. One good yoke is enough,' said the judge with studied humour that made the others laugh. 'As you well know, what I collect are Bibles. Tell me if the man isn't mad!'

'Who could it be?' asked Father Munio. 'Do you suspect anyone?'

He had the novel now. Everything in those hands, clad in a pair of soft white gloves, took on the appearance of remains waiting to be expunged.

'All I know,' said Samos, 'is that someone wishes to malign me in this twisted, abject way. Without naming names, in a world of fiction that is vulgar and remote . . . Cast me as the bad guy. A perverse judge of Oklahoma! The trouble is you never know where such a ridiculous, infamous game might end up. Imagine this judge, practising in Oklahoma, is blamed for things, atrocities . . . Some people are obsessed with the past.'

'They're coincidences,' said Tomás Dez. 'That's all it is, Ricardo, chance.'

The judge and censor exchanged glances. Dez realised this meeting was an indirect way of forcing him to act more diligently. They'd always been close. He couldn't understand why Samos, who was usually so calm, had lost his nerve over something so trivial. The worst thing he could do was show his fear. Imagine . . . There was no need to imagine anything.

Samos, however, regained his composure, adding a touch of humour, 'I just wanted, friends, to fill you in on this rather picturesque situation. Even in a country as secure as ours, there's no escaping the evil eye.'

'There's something artistic, deeply human, about yokes,' said Sulfe after a pause. 'And about halters, those wire and wicker art pieces for muzzling mouths.'

Sulfe stopped abruptly. He had a passion for 'alighting on the classics'. Being one of them. Each of them. Cultivating his chosen model to the end. Not just knowing what they thought, but how they expressed it. Assuming their voice, as he said. In short, copying them. So his relationship with knowledge was a form of possession. The secret of his moments of brilliance was this identification that led him to act in his lectures, though he was generally a shy man who spat out monosyllables. Recently the process had been reversed. He began to feel possessed by those he studied and delved into. There was no telling when it might happen, no warning. It was like having a ventriloquist who spoke for him, without permission. Who controlled not only the levers of thought, but the threads of speech as well, until turning him, in the most unfortunate circumstances, into a comedian, a satirist or a gossip. Some people lost their memory. Sulfe acquired new memories. He started consuming what he'd always reviled. From Catullus and Sappho to Afonso Eanes do Coton and María Balteira, the last to mention two members of the most obscene school of Galician-Portuguese *cancioneiros* or songbooks. The discovery of this branch of wild eroticism, words fornicating like bodies, in medieval lyric poetry, together with his interest in Rabelais, had caused not only a mental upheaval but a shift in his organism similar to a radical change of diet. Possibly to defend herself in a conservative environment or else to justify the daring act of absorbing and disseminating universal poetry's most obscene creations, Carolina Michaëlis talks of this 'the most dissolute carnivalesque pasquinades', of compositions whose language is on a par with that of 'brawlers and gamblers'. Another leading authority on the medieval treasures that lay hidden for centuries, Rodrigues Lapa, talks of a spirited willingness to confront 'certain verbal sewage'. Dissolute pasquinades! Verbal sewage! When having to refer to these compositions, Sulfe himself didn't hesitate to talk of 'a vulgar and immoral branch on a golden tree'. And as he recovered his health, he'd think of a poem by João Soares:

Miss Lucy, Lucy Sánchez, for God's sake,
if fuck you I could, fuck you I would!

'Finally,' he heard the familiar voices of Gargantua and Falstaff, 'you can tell the difference between pleasure and enjoyment, you're poking your nose in where you should.' There was indeed 'a second world and a second life outside officialdom', to quote his now revered Mikhail Bakhtin, but not just in Antiquity and the Middle Ages. It was a secret, but he was living a second life in a second world. Yes, he was an amphibian in the new Spanish Middle Ages. On the outside, he was the same old doctor. 'See these fingers yellowed not from tobacco, but from alighting on the classics.' He was capable of vehemently, even angrily, defending what he called 'the grammar of power'. The essential superiority of some languages over others. The mystical, warlike quality of Spanish, which made it more suitable for talking to God. The relevance of Nebrija's warlike grammar, the Empire's companion language, as a contemporary apothegm. And so on. But anyone who knew him from before, when he came offstage, would observe an ironical form of boasting, an obvious horror of any kind of ambition for public notoriety, be it in the academic sphere or the sphere of official culture and journalism, where he'd attained the stature of a golden personality. When called on to give his opinion on special occasions, he had a sixth sense which enabled him consistently to match 'the grammar of power', the taste of mandarins, which he seasoned with a culture they lacked. There were things he couldn't even mention. Once he bumped into the mayor and greeted him in his most colloquial Latin, '*Quo vadis*, your worship?' The mayor answered him with sickled face, 'There you go again, Sulfe, spouting German.' He now enjoyed himself as never before. He'd crossed 'the threshold of invisibility'. He was a secret being. He worshipped one, mortal God, the great Dionysius, whose feet the dog Cerberus licked at the gates of hell. It was through him, through Dionysius' eyes, he saw the world now, without others knowing. He was particularly bold when it came to those he'd always avoided. He turned his reading hours into a nocturnal spree in search of 'dissolute carnivalesque pasquinades' and 'verbal sewage'. It had all started as a funny paradox.

He'd been asked by the chapter of Santiago Cathedral to study expressions of *risus paschalis*, paschal laughter, and the so-called *festa stultorum*, feast of fools, as well as the existence or not of a 'feast of the donkey' in the Compostelan Church's tradition. He didn't get very far. He couldn't cope with the fields that suddenly opened. All those books waiting for him on inveterate shelves, in locked cupboards, buried alive in filthy attics and basements. He started poking his finger in cracks he'd previously despised. His warrior philologist's yellow fingers smelt now of sex and shone like tasty word-slops. What he'd run away from became his bread and butter. As he read, he heard, as if in prayer, the emotional, excited chorus of Bacchantes, 'When Dionysius leads, the earth will dance.'

He could claim to have been a bibliophile ever since he was a child. He'd certainly grown up with ordered reading, tutored by a pack of Carlist clerics, who kept an eye even on the Spanish mystics and allowed access to enlightened fathers such as Feijoo and Sarmiento only in tiny measures served with little spoons. But somehow he'd become an expert. Books were his most treasured property. When he thought of the old family seat in Ribeiro, he pictured not the land, but the volumes. This set him apart from many other professors and ecclesiastical friends and Compostelan theologians, who were leading authorities on property registers and lawsuits over land inheritance and ownership. And extremely concerned about the culture of rents and the number of feet in a granary. He'd alighted on the classics. And if he'd been given a chair, it was as a result of his knowledge, not of booty or contacts. He was very conservative. A traditionalist. He'd never hidden the fact. Even as a boy, he'd come to the conclusion it was something biological, in his nature. He remembered this with horror when the Dean of Sciences in Santiago conferred a doctorate *honoris causa* on Franco, comparing his warlike activity to 'a biological, scientific experience'. In his second life, Sulfe had a stock response, 'I'm conservative, not inhuman.' A message that was so simple, constantly repeated as it was in the endless post-war period, it sounded like a bizarre riddle.

Hardly anyone knew about Professor Alfonso Sulfe's second existence. They may have set out from a similar port, but he'd long since veered off on a course that had nothing to do with the judge Samos or those others who were convinced they had a direct link with God. If he'd renewed a friendship dating back to the 1940s and accepted Samos' recent invitation to join their conversations in the so-called Crypt (which the judge, with intellectual coquetry, also termed his San Casciano in reference to Machiavelli's retreat), it was for a reason he kept secret. To start with, he'd replied to the invitation with grateful politeness, alleging, however, that his teaching commitments and his own studies made it difficult for him to attend. He'd be delighted to do so occasionally. But then the embers of a memory revived, turning into a fire that blazed day and night in his brain.

'It being a madman . . .'

Dez was not happy with the meeting. He failed to understand how Samos, who was intelligent, sly when necessary, could have exhibited his paranoia with that western novelist so publicly, albeit among friends. He appeared now to be taking it lightly, but Dez knew how much it bothered him.

'Strange the way it continues,' said Father Munio, who with his white gloves turned every book that fell into his hands into an object for dissection.

> Ernest Botana the journalist tipped his hat to the pruned, skeletal, naked poplars:
> 'Courage, old friends!'
> Then he saw the judge coming and stretched out his hand:
> 'I absolutely will not allow you to consider me an enemy.'
> The servant of the law was confused and blushed. He left, irritated by the weight of that pious affront.

The judge held out his hand to retrieve the novel. He'd have preferred it if Father Munio hadn't chosen that particular passage to read aloud. It had quite upset him, which is why the page was marked. And now hearing someone else read it aloud finally revealed the source of the unsettling echo in his head. There was the memory of a similar sentence addressed to him.

It was the last time he'd talked to Héctor Ríos in Mazarelos Square, Santiago, outside the Law Faculty, that Christmas Eve in 1935. The day he refused the gift of a book by Wells and Ríos had the audacity, the unbearable goodwill, to comment, 'I absolutely will not allow you to consider me an enemy.'

A fine *coup de théâtre*.

That's right, he refused the book from Ríos, with whom he'd shared a passion for bibliography ever since they were children. He refused the book by Wells, an essay on *The Salvaging of Civilisation*.

'I already read it,' Samos lied.

'And I read your article,' said Ríos eventually. '"Germany's Scholars Align Themselves with the Führer". I think you've forgotten one or two . . .'

There was Héctor Ríos, saying goodbye to Professor Del Riego on the steps of the Law Faculty and then jovially turning towards him, with his Kantian categorical imperative spectacles, a bundle of books in one hand and bulging jacket pockets. Who knows? He may still have been carrying his notes on cards from Xohán Vicente Viqueira's lectures in Coruña on ethics, which the pupils of the Free Teaching Institute exchanged with lay devotion, like prayers. 'Listen, Samos, to what Viqueira has to say: "Conscience is the mental activity of esteeming the good". Could anyone have put it better?' Once, in the spring of 1931, Ríos had persuaded him to attend a tribute to Viqueira in Ouces Cemetery. One of the participants, Bieito Varela, knocked on the gravestone and said, 'Mr Viqueira, the Republic has arrived!' The atmosphere was pleasant and effusive, with lots of cultured people, but Samos felt uncomfortable. Viqueira's grave was outside the Catholic cemetery. Why was he buried outside? Ríos looked at him the way he did sometimes, through ironic spectacles that made him feel a fool, and said, 'He's outside because they wouldn't let him in.'

Now, in 1935, Héctor Ríos is on his way to Madrid, to the hall of residence, with his brilliant academic record and plans to become, with the help of the prestigious penologist Luis Jiménez de Asúa, one of the youngest public prosecutors in the Spanish Republic. Héctor Ríos, with whom he'd shared children's games on Parrote Beach, secondary studies, declamation classes in the Craftsmen's Circle and a youthful passion for Herbert George Wells.

'You're not going to consider me an enemy, Mr Samos?' His Kantian glasses looked at him with irony and Samos again felt small. 'If you are,' declaimed Ríos on the faculty steps, 'I will not allow it.'

He came down the steps.

Held out his hand.

Samos was slow to accept the gesture, but did so in the end, unwillingly. He knew this meant carrying on the conversation. He now despised what he had once thought of as a virtue. Héctor Ríos enjoyed a polemic. Never gave in. So he didn't pass up the opportunity to suggest, for his forthcoming thesis on Juan Donoso Cortés' influence on contemporary thought and more especially on the prominent German jurist Carl Schmitt, he'd do well to read the Austrian jurist Hans Kelsen, to which Samos replied he'd already read a bit and he wouldn't last a round with Schmitt. 'With the rise of Nazism,' answered Ríos, 'while most jurists went into hiding, Hans Kelsen had the courage and the clarity to say there were only two possible kinds of State: a democracy or an autocracy. That is to last not just a round, but the whole fight. Kelsen is no wizard, but he's right. It'd be crazy to put the terrestrial globe on your Mr Schmitt's head.'

Right? There was no point arguing now. The sun's gone past the door already, Ríos. No, he didn't say that. It wasn't the right time. Héctor still lived in his old liberal world, full of ideas. Nor was he going to answer the question Ríos then asked, begged him to think about. 'Can you be a Christian, a Catholic conservative, and approve of Fascism? Isn't tyranny the ultimate moral failure?'

In conversation, Samos was usually cautious. Not in writing. Recently, under the pseudonym Syllabus, he'd been expressing himself more and more freely, getting more and more excited. He converted this ardour into speech. He felt like talking with ferocity.

He had nothing to think about. That was his answer.

'I've nothing to think about,' he said suddenly.

It felt good, addressing him like this, boldly. Ríos had always been up front, but now he'd taken over his position. It was a strange, thrilling sensation. Ríos, the mature young man, struck him now as naive. His revered Schmitt talked of a 'providential' meeting with Donoso Cortés' *Speech on Dictatorship*. He felt the same 'providential' moment with Schmitt. He gave Ríos some information he lacked: history was preparing to move with steely ferocity. Ríos still trusted in Wells' fiction in one pocket and Viqueira's cards on ethics in the other. On his way to the hall of residence in Madrid, with his jacket worn out at the elbows.

'No, I've nothing to think about. And since you ask, I have an answer to that, which Donoso Cortés gave me in 1849.'

Héctor knew what he meant, he was talking about a dictatorship. He jokingly pulled a pocket watch out of his waistcoat. '1849? I haven't time to go so far back, Ricardo. I've a train ticket for tomorrow.'

Samos looked at him in such a way it was clear he never wished to see him again. 'That's not an answer, it's a frivolity.' He then turned his back on him and strode off. He didn't mind if Ríos thought he was running backwards.

'Your priest, Mr Schmitt, is wrong when he affirms the history of the world begins with Cain. After that, everything in him is mistaken.'

Ricardo Samos turned around for a moment. He felt invincible, stimulated by the idea of steely speech. He could speak boldly. Now Héctor Ríos would be the fool. '*Auctoritas non veritas facit legem.*'

'Come back, Ricardo!' shouted Ríos. 'You're a couple of centuries past 1849. Come back for the book, for civilisation!'

He spoke theatrically, but was really sorry Samos had refused the book by Wells. He felt a pain in his stomach. Poor Wells. It's lunchtime. I'll look after you.

'I still don't think you should take it so seriously,' insisted the censor. 'You have to be above all this.' It seemed like a good way of both calming and complimenting the judge. 'We're talking here about western novels, trashy literature. Even if the author meant it, who's going to connect you with the Judge of Oklahoma? Who reads it, Ricardo? Ask at a bookstall and you'll see. Sailors from the Great Sole, unemployed youths, prisoners . . .'

He stopped because this seemed to worry the judge. He could see what he was thinking: Prisoners? So they read John Black Eye too?

'You may think I'm exaggerating, Dez,' said Samos after a pause, 'but I have my reasons. I want a muzzle on that mouth.'

He opened the drawer, put *The Yoke Collector* inside and locked it.

'Bring me that Black Eye's head on a platter!'

The Supplier of Bibles

19 August 1957

Bibles were the library's main attraction. Copies from different periods and in different languages. They filled the central shelves in the Italian room where Samos had his study. This collection of various editions of Scripture was the most obvious reason the judge's office had been given the name the Crypt. The room, with its alcove, had the air of a reserved space. And time was disciplined and acted in accordance with this designation, placing religious objects, hunting trophies, photographs and prints in silver frames in gaps between books or on the mantelpiece. As for the library itself, it contained the collection of Bibles, which was always growing, and books the judge would consult in matters of law, together with reference works concerning history and thought. The alcove was the home of classical literature and, to use the judge's expression, 'a resting-place for all sorts of flotsam' he'd picked up along the way in his foremost bibliographical search for copies of the Old and New Testaments. The alcove was altered slightly when it was decided Gabriel might use it, not that he was forced to do so, rather he was the one who took it over as a study, to the great surprise of his parents, especially Chelo, his mother. 'It's a good place for bats,' she said to Gabriel. This is partly why he liked it. Because it was dark and secret, like a lair, in such a luminous house, a kind of bell-jar facing the bay. On the other side of the street, there were no houses. On the other side was the sea. Boats. The docks. Into the recess, into his cave, Gabriel carried his cabinet of curiosities.

★ ★ ★

He wasn't very outgoing. He was almost always silent, bad-tempered, thought Gabriel, but then he decided it was something permanent, nothing to do with his mood, since when he laughed he looked bad-tempered as well. His body seethed slowly. It was one of those large bodies which want to offload things, starting with his suit. Perhaps it was because of his physique, thought Gabriel, that he couldn't help being brusque in his movements and speech. He was brusque when he expressed his opinion in conversations in the Crypt, those meetings that were held in the judge's office almost every Thursday evening. He had a tendency to exclaim and come out with short, cutting sentences. His manner of speaking caught Gabriel's attention at a time he was having his own struggle with language. Whenever he greeted Chelo, he tried to change attitude completely. He was brusque in this too. He did so with such exaggerated politeness his body seemed on the verge of violence.

Such was Ren. Inspector Ren.

They were utterly different. But Gabriel soon realised there was a strong link between Ren and the judge. He was one of his suppliers of Bibles. Of old books. Whenever he came to make a delivery, they met alone.

One afternoon, inside the alcove, Gabriel was privileged enough to witness an act of transfer performed by Ren and the judge with certain ceremony. Ren, who was usually very abrupt, on this occasion moved in a measured way, very cautiously. He placed a large leather and suede travelling bag on the desk and unfastened the zip in slow motion. He then very carefully pulled out six volumes. The judge leafed through them with reverence. His hands verified. And took possession.

'A jewel, your honour. Look at the prints.'

'Gabriel, come here! La Sainte Bible published by the Garnier brothers, Paris, 1867. Observe the quality of the illustrations, the perfection that came off steel plates.'

Gabriel, however, really was observing the illustrations, what was in them. All the prints showed women, female Biblical figures. There was the Queen of Sheba with her bowl of pearls. Rahab, waiting at the window. The Pharaoh's daughter. Judith with her curved sword, next to the bed where Holofernes lies. Sarah, Tobias' wife, with gaudy earrings and a bracelet. Eve. He'd never seen such a beautiful Eve. It was in fact the first time he'd wondered what she looked like.

'You like it, right? One day, I'll tell you about all the Bibles in here. It's still too soon, but you'll have to add to this treasure in the future.'

Gabriel was taken with the figures. This would be his favourite Bible for a long time. He'd love them all. Even Judith with her curved sword. The Garnier brothers' *Sainte Bible* was one of his best erotic books, together with those he found in the section of charred remains, such as *Le Nu de Rabelais*. Opening each volume was like opening one of the six gates in a feminine city.

But today the judge would only allow him to touch. He was the one who opened the gates.

'Chelo will be fascinated,' he said.

She'd be late today. Gabriel was already in bed. He'd like to have seen her fingers on this new Bible's illustrations. For him, they were his mother's most peculiar feature. The shape of her hands, the length of her fingers. He thought, even though he was a man, his would never reach that size. Her toes were in proportion. She looked after and painted the nails of both her hands and her feet. The latter, visible when she wore sandals or could step on the grass or sand, distinguished her from other women. At home, she went barefoot whenever she was painting, which was most of the time. Occasionally she'd receive a call from Fine Arts to take some special visitors on a tour. She spoke French well and got by in English. But most of all she could read the book of the city. She understood its art, architecture and history. Today she was with two French women writing their doctoral theses on Emilia Pardo Bazán. They were also going to visit one of Rosalía de Castro's daughters, her only surviving descendant, named Gala. Rosalía had been born of unknown parents, so it said on her baptism certificate, though it was well known her father was a priest. She married the librarian and historian Manuel Murguía and they had five children. Gala, who is eighty-six, explains she's not only the last surviving daughter, but the end of the line. She suddenly falls quiet. The expression on her face is of horror more than pain. Chelo had visited her before, acting as ambassador, but had never seen her like this. Josette and Nelly, the two French women, exchange anxious glances. Their courtesy call is turning into something else. Gala then tells them something she claims never to have told before. Her twin brother, Ovidio Murguía, a painter, had a sweetheart in Madrid, a young woman by the name of Visitación Oliva. Ovidio became ill with tuberculosis, the biggest killer of youth in those days, and returned to Coruña to recover. In fact, he came to die. But what Gala is telling them is that she burnt the love letters that arrived from Madrid for her sick brother. She burnt them one by one. Including the letter with the happy news that Visitación Oliva was with child. This gesture of dropping the letter into the fire somehow put an end to their line. Ovidio Murguía died, thinking he'd been totally forgotten. Why? Why did she do this? Why is she telling them now? This is what their looks say, but no one asks questions. No one says anything. Gala murmurs, 'I'm sorry for what happened.' In the night, in the brazier, in a corner of the room, Chelo watches words burning.

Back home, Chelo finds her husband ecstatic. He has a new Bible, an extraordinary Parisian edition illustrated by European print masters of the nineteenth century. Chelo says she's not in the mood. It was a tiring day. Everything's fine, it's just she's exhausted. Even so, she'll take a look. 'The illustrations are of the most remarkable women in the Bible,' says the judge. He knew she'd be interested. She sits down. Is captivated. Then says she's changed her mind. She's awake now. This is what happens after a tiring day. She's going to paint. 'Excuse me. I'm going to paint. Paint the night,' she says, pointing to the picture of a female worker resting her oil lamp on a colleague's head as a joke.

That afternoon, before Ren left, they talked about anonymous letters. The judge showed him an envelope with no return address and the sheet that came inside. A typed text. A carbon copy.

'Same as always,' said the judge. 'Same poem. Third canto of *The Divine Sketch* by Manuel Curros Enríquez. Same date at the bottom. 19th of August 1936.'

With rude gnashing of teeth . . .

Rather than reading, Ren seemed to be searching for fingerprints on the sheet.

He offered me some and said,
'It's not exactly the best,
but you're welcome.' 'What is it?'
'A morsel of human flesh.'

'Can't we find the typewriter and typist?' asked the judge, giving Ren a deliberate look.

'I also got a copy,' said Ren. 'Dez as well.' He moved his moustache uneasily, as if searching somewhere outside the Crypt. 'Who can the bastard be? It's the same typewriter as every year. I checked it against clandestine pamphlets, leaflets, writing samples from prisoners, people under surveillance, but found nothing out of the ordinary. What the hell happened that day, Samos? I know something must have happened. Something almost always did. But what was so special this nutter can't keep quiet about it? I don't remember.'

The judge looked at him and was silent. There'd been several things. He didn't remember either, but his memory did. The advantages and disadvantages of having such a good memory. Memory sometimes does its own thing, thought the judge. By the time you realise, without wanting to, you've a book in your hands from the alcove, with burnt edges. He could have gone in search of others, other bibliographical jewels that were in there, English editions with gilt edges and watercolours, wonderful editions. But no, by the time he realised, what the memory of his hands had done was pull out the little book with burnt edges and the symbol of a scallop shell in the centre, the little book with the Six Galician Poems. The way things happened, both poet and publisher had to go and die on that day, 19 August, the day they burnt books. He had to study this law that wasn't in the code. The law of chance. Change, chance, words are so mixed up. Which is why it was important to be precise. Did they come from the same family of words? He'd have to check that.

'Something must have happened.' Inspector Ren re-examined the letter. *With rude gnashing of teeth.* He dropped it casually on the desk. Well, he was convinced it had been typed on an Underwood Universal. But there were lots of those. 'What we need is a register of every typewriter there is. The day I find that Underwood Universal, I'll show him rude gnashing of teeth.'

The judge smiled. He knew about Ren's obsession for typewriters. Ren had told him he had a collection at home, about twenty of them, including some that had been confiscated when war broke out. He also had a few from secret resistance groups. Sometimes, after a day's work, he'd sit down and type. 'Nothing that makes any sense. I just bash the keys.' Biff, bang, wallop. It made him feel good, hitting those machines.

'All this in confidence, right, your honour? Strictly between ourselves.'

'One day, you'll have to invite me to your sanctuary, Ren.'

One day. One day he'd have to extend an invitation. 'It's all a mess. You can imagine what it's like living on your own.'

'You know what the Portuguese say? "Desire of solitude leads to great virtue or wickedness."'

'All my vice is taken up with eating.'

Samos was clearly talking through one side of his mouth, but thinking something different. He'd grabbed the mallet. And was thumping the palm of his hand.

'Thanks for the Bible, Ren. A good price too.'

Yeah. Thumping away at the palm of his hand.

He asked, 'Any other news?'

Beating the palm of his hand. Looking elsewhere. At the mystery of the leather bag.

'I'd tell you, Samos, if there were.'

'Nothing about the valiente of Finisterra?'

'Nothing, your honour. I've done all I could. Been through all the lists. The Falange. The knights militia. Those who transferred Casares Quiroga's library. Those posted to his house. Those at the docks and in María Pita. The squad of workmen who disposed of the remains. I've been through it all. Conducted searches. Nothing. Better forget that book, your honour. I'm after another, by that Irishman, you said belonged to Huici. I don't think it's far off. That's what my nose tells me. When you're least expecting something is when it knocks at the door. That's the way of old things.'

I Was Forsook

He saw Hercules go by, that crazy photographer with the horse. Terranova's friend. He couldn't help it. His orbital look upset things. Not for him, but for his memory. Blasted memory, always up to no good. Going off like that without his permission. Now following the photographer and his horse. He knew their story. The horse was from Cuba, Vidal had brought it with his son's photographic equipment. But Leica had kept it in his studio. He wanted to be an artist. Not lead a horse about. So he rented it to Hercules, or lent it, whatever the arrangement was, you never know, they belonged to the same group, did him a favour, lent him the horse and instant camera. The horse's eyes were well done. The point is horse and photographer made him nervous. It was too much. Why hadn't he gone as well, that colossus, cowboy, hick, subnormal, champ, son of a whore, why hadn't he left instead of wandering around the city like a ghost complete with wooden quadruped?

Tomás Dez was so distracted, distracted and disturbed, as if he'd heard 'Chessman' carried on the breeze, was so preoccupied he didn't notice his secretary's warning signs when he reached the censor's office. So this stranger coming up to him, dressed like a sailor from a spectral boat, caught him by surprise.

'Are you the censor?'

Censor? It was true. He was one of the censors. He gave him a supercilious look. 'I'm very busy.' And carried straight on to the door of his office.

'I was forsook!'

He turned around as if he'd heard a strange, inescapable code.

'You what?'

'I've been waiting for months for a reply. My book. A book of poems. Called *I Was Forsook*.'

'What's it about?'

'The Most Mysterious of the Mysterious.'

Interesting. I was forsook? I was forsook? Part of his memory identified the echo.

'Just a minute,' said Dez. 'I've some matters to attend to and then I'll come back to you.'

He was feeling generous. Time to redeem yourself, Dez, said his ironic side. Possibly the taste on his palate after chewing 'Chessman', the condemned man's song. Why be despotic with this old sailor in a worn overcoat, invoking the Most Mysterious? He shut the door and rummaged through the pile of originals waiting for a report. It had been some time since he'd read or processed anything. His problem with dermatitis was getting worse. Other times, it cleared up completely. Like now.

There it was: *I Was Forsook*. Signed: Aurelio Anceis.

He opened the book. Was hit by the unforeseeable. By way of a preface, two lines from a medieval poem by Pero Guterres:

> They all say God never sinned,
> but mortally I see him sin.

What was this? He turned the page. Read:

> CRUMBS
> Word-crumbs
> rounded and
> polished
> by the fingers of silence,
> with the inflamed accuracy of
> beads in a rosary
> on the star-map of
> an oilskin tablecloth.

> Crumbs like these
> can save hands.

He read:

> CRUSADE
> I the warrior thank you,
> my God,
> for crippling me.
> I was a good shot,
> but you, Lord,
> direct a bullet with your eyes:
> in the rifle's soul,
> an hallelujah caws.

Commander Dez would recite the poem 'Crusade' that evening at a literary gathering in Rita Angélica's home. Everyone was amazed. Somebody had just dedicated a piece of nonsense to Christopher Columbus. They were all sitting around in armchairs decorated with chintz. They knew he was forthright. They still remembered the day he read Pemán's 'Beast and the Angel', which sounded like a further declaration of war. But this poem . . .

They were stunned. Rita suggested, 'It's very different from your previous work.'

You could say that again! He read:

> CONCENTRATION CAMP (I)
> Your rays
> this beautiful Sunday morning
> are like a divine roving eye
> moments before the attack.

He read:

> CONCENTRATION CAMP (II)
> You're like the house-cat, Lord,
> which doesn't go out to hunt,

but makes corpses
to play with.

He read:

BURNING BOOKS
As the fruit falls,
the emptiness is not left alone.
Why else
this itching of the eyes?

He lifts the receiver. Dials an internal number. He can't picture the visitor. Can't see his face. He's too anxious. Tells his secretary, 'The guy waiting in a sailor's hat and coat, don't let him leave.'

'Why are you so angry with God?'

The cough that exploded violently from his chest, which Anceis suppressed by placing a handkerchief over his mouth, didn't make him any weaker. Rather it suggested he had little to lose. Dez the censor finally understood the unusual precision, the physiological composition, of certain passages. Like this one from 'The Fisherman Remembers the Matchstick-maker':

The ball of spit won't come out,
strikes against glass-paper lips
and ignites like failed phosphorus
in the white Nova Scotia night.

After the coughing fit, he was again strong enough to speak.

'What do you think? I censured myself before coming here,' said Aurelio Anceis suddenly. 'Imagine a verse that simply reproduced the legend on official coins: "Caudillo of Spain by the grace of God". This excess is overt blasphemy. The total lack of God is an excess and excess, a terrible lack. Which leads to a second verse, an elementary question: "Could I speak to the Boss, please?"'

'You did well to censure that,' said Dez ironically. 'It would have been unpublishable. But the sense of unease, the constant allusions to defeat. This poem entitled "News of Defeat" . . . You could have found another date that wasn't the 1st of April. You discourage the victors, so imagine the losers. This other one that speaks of the 18th of July. You should be more careful. Coming here. Talking about it.'

Aurelio Anceis' face had a knotty seriousness. He didn't move and his breathing, a loud, inner bubbling, sounded like that of someone living inside him. His eyes, half-closed, seemed to have landed on gaps in his rough skin, like shiny beetles attracted by his elongated eyelashes.

'In the poem about a doris, there's some respite at least: "The lonely fisherman constructs a place with his oars . . . Constructing somewhere with a lonely fisherman from Halifax."'

'You think? Do you know what a doris is?'

'I do now. I asked. Thanks to you. Poetry's mission is also to inform.'

Dez the censor stood up and went over to the window. He referred to the labourers, all the people in the street, 'Everybody keeps a safe distance. Everybody except for the poets. Those who reveal the inner sanctuary, get to say the unspeakable.'

Aurelio Anceis watched his hand moving like a baton.

'They're unaware,' Dez continued, 'of a metaphysical change in history. From being to time, and from time to being. Off with time!' He rubbed his hands. A way of applauding himself, thought Anceis. And then lamented, 'They think I'm talking about watchmaking. Makes no difference. Your poems, Mr Anceis, are extraordinary!'

He fell silent. Looked at him. He was waiting for some kind of reaction. That was a real compliment, thought Anceis. But he didn't say anything.

'In short, I'll do whatever it takes to publish them.' And he added jokingly, 'If necessary, we'll move heaven and earth!'

Then Anceis had a sense of foreboding. Something that sprang up in his intestines like a biological warning and affected his poems. Suddenly the reason he was there ceased to be relevant. He held his sailor's hat, turning it slowly, not always in the same direction, but like someone steering. He stood up, put on his hat and made to take back the original.

Dez got there first. 'Extraordinary.' He opened the folder and read an extract he didn't know, but pretended he did. He recited the last bit as if he knew it off by heart.

> Silent woman of Godthab,
> I can hear the purple pigment of your eyes,
> the thread of your murmur
> linking a long, luminous word I don't understand.
> Blessing on the kayak leading this needle through the sheets of ice.

'Mysterious,' said Dez. 'There's something moving.'

Anceis watched him silently.

'Godthab?' asked the censor. 'Somewhere to do with God?'

'It's a port in Greenland.'

Not wanting to be subjected to a poetic interrogation, he volunteered a few bare details.

'Most of the cod-fishing fleet refuels in St Pierre, St John's or Nova Scotia. I spent time on a ship that went a little further, to the Davis Strait, on the edge of the Arctic Polar Circle. We stopped over in Godthab.'

'Just once?'

'That's right.'

'So the Godthab woman really existed? Was she an Eskimo?'

'She was an Inuit. They say Inuit. It means person. Eskimo is an eater of raw flesh. Inuit is a person.'

'What happened? I imagine you can say. Did you take her on board ship?'

Anceis became thoughtful. One hand explored the other. Dez couldn't know, but the old sailor was slotting breadcrumbs between his fingers. They headed and cleaned the cod, using canvas gloves. The fish from the sea were covered in slime that filtered through the canvas and, with the cold, caused cracks around the finger-joints, which were very difficult to heal and withstand. The best way to avoid the fingers rubbing together was to sleep with breadcrumbs between them.

But these were intimate, insignificant details. What did they matter to this bureaucrat who wouldn't let go of his texts, whom books had to ask for permission to exist and who was suddenly on heat because of the Godthab woman?

Aurelio Anceis said, 'All the information you need is in the poem. It's a poem with a lot of information.'

And added, 'Sorry, but I have to leave.'

The Bramble Sphere

Ferns were her merchandise. Green ferns. She carried a huge bundle.

'Half the mountain, my dear.'

She sold them at Muro Fishmarket as a way of bedding and protecting the fish that were exported in pinewood boxes. In the case of women carrying ferns on top of their heads, there was a strange coincidence. They brought the largest burden and took away the fewest coins. One day, Lola, painted by Chelo, made some extra income. She came with the whole mountain on top of her head. On St John's Eve, she brought posies containing seven aromatic herbs. They were soaked in water overnight for the healing bath of the morning, since this herbal water washed inside and out. The posy was then kept at home and a year later, dried out, thrown on to the St John bonfires. Which is why there were three paintings by Chelo Vidal of that woman from Orro. *Woman with Ferns*. *Woman with St John Posies*. And *Woman with Bramble Sphere*.

If you calmly study the woman carrying ferns, who looks the most humble, she eventually acquires a noble bearing. As if she held a large, natural basket, a mysterious heart of the forest, a green monstrance. Talking of wild plants, it was she who one day said, 'For me, brambles make the best rope.'

'Brambles?'

'They're as flexible as string and as tough as leather. It's just a shame about the prickles.'

Chelo was stunned by her description. She'd always thought of brambles as aggressive and intractable, only letting up during the blackberry season. Even then, you had to pick the fruit as if your fingers were a blackbird's beak.

A blackbird hopped between Chelo's head and the Woman with Ferns.

'Of course life is full of blackberries and prickles,' said Lola, the Woman with Ferns. 'It's a brier from start to finish.'

This conversation gave rise to what today is one of Chelo Vidal's most famous works. In many reviews, it is given as the pinnacle of a new symbolism, being in this sense the most direct painting in the series 'Women Carrying Things on Top of Their Heads'. But this doesn't stop it being one of her most enigmatic works because of what some have termed 'the unsettling calm' of the *Woman with Bramble Sphere*.

'Is it possible to make a ball of brambles?'

'Why not? You just have to scrape off the prickles and weave the stems together.'

'No, I mean without leaves, but with prickles.'

The ball of brambles resembles an armillary sphere. The woman in the portrait, like many others who carry weights, has a cloth crown to support the weight, but in her case the cloth is a silvery grey and really does look like a crown, perhaps because what it supports is more overtly symbolical. From a distance, it resembles a sphere. From close up, the coarse skein is like a labyrinth, made more dramatic by the prickles. The portrait would be very severe were it not for the gesture of the woman looking to her left, slightly foreshortened, half smiling, thought Chelo, and unaware of the weight she's carrying, as if it were an extravagant hat. Why's she smiling?

'What's so funny?' asked Chelo.

'It'll sound strange to you, but I was thinking about the day of my first communion. We were all dressed up, looking very smart. The best we could do, by borrowing things or whatever, but smart. The boys in a suit and tie, like little men, and us in white. An aunt of mine worked as a maid in a house in Sigrás and the lady of the house lent me a tiara with a tulle veil. So there we were, kneeling in front of the altar, at the most solemn moment, waiting for the Sacred Form, when I went and glanced at Daniel. He was like a squirrel, never stayed still. It was funny seeing him looking so formal, with cropped hair and hands held together in prayer. He suddenly looked back, without losing his composure, and . . .'

The Woman with Bramble Sphere pursed her lips. Blinked. Tears of laughter were bubbling up in her eyes. It was Chelo's turn to smile in the face of mystery.

'What happened with Daniel?'

'He moved his ears!'

'His ears?'

'Yes, madam. He moved them as if they were wings. He could do that, move them without having to touch them. What he called "doing the ding-dong". But only I saw him do it that day. The day of our First Communion. In church. That day, he did it just for me.'

This is the secret of why the Woman with Bramble Sphere is smiling in Chelo Vidal's painting. Because she can see Daniel beating his pointed ears like wings.

Nothing more disturbing than the following painting.

That of the Woman Carrying a Secret. It was not known what was in that basket covered with a cloth. The cloth's contours suggested small, irregular spheres. But the strange thing was the cloth itself. A black cloth. Nobody covered their merchandise in Santo Agostiño or Leña Field with a black cloth. Their head, OK. But never their merchandise.

'You've painted me with a bad look,' said the Woman Carrying a Secret.

'No, it's not bad. That's the way you look. It's fine. Adds a touch of mystery.'

'Not like that, it doesn't. I may be a bit cross-eyed, but not that much. And it's one thing to be like that for a moment, another to be like that for the rest of your life. Paintings are for life. I don't know why you want to make me look cross-eyed.'

'That is your look. That is beauty. The real thing, emotion.'

'Well, it looks to me as if those eyes you painted aren't working properly when they should be beautiful.'

'In those eyes can be seen all that you contain inside,' responded Chelo passionately.

'I'd rather nothing could be seen.'

She's now the Woman with Lowered Eyelids.

'Is that better?'

'Much better.'

Gabriel remembers passing her on the back staircase. He'd often use it to reach the kitchen more quickly. Neves always had a surprise for him. A little beakful, as she called it. He bumped into the Woman in Mourning, whose head-cloth matched the cloth on her basket. She seemed very pleased. When she saw him, she pulled back the cloth and gave him a handful of her secrets.

The Unfalling Leaves

His name's Antón, I think, but what stuck in my mind was what Mr Sada said: this country doesn't deserve its poets, look how it treats them, working as building labourers, carrying sacks of Portland cement. Every time I see a man with a sack on his back, I think of him. Of my poet. My Portland.

That day, her wish to find him in the painter's house was fulfilled. She was taking their clothes. On the way from Castro to Elviña, she plucked a few white roses and sprigs of mint and fennel. To give the clothes a nice smell.

Neves received her in the hallway. She heard voices coming from the more open side of the sitting-room, what they called the Chinese Pavilion, and, being on good terms with the maid, she let herself go a little, just enough to see the group of people. All of them deep in thought. Each looking in a different direction. Listening. To him recite. And she still had time to hear about the leaves that don't fall in San Carlos Gardens, they burn, that's what he said, on a low heat, at the top of the elms. And he said something about the hanging clusters' spectral elegance. But she wasn't quite sure about this.

She went there that afternoon. And others.

In San Carlos Gardens, at the top of the elms, she did indeed see a few coppery leaves that hadn't fallen. She knew there were some trees that didn't shed their old leaves until they'd grown new ones. But this was very different. In the whole remarkable plantation, the branches' austere elevation, fat charcoal markings in the sky, ending in a filigree of twigs, shoots and buds, pure, unsullied lines, well, up there were these copper-coloured leaves on a low heat, burning at dusk without being consumed.

It was one of the happiest moments in her visits to the city. It was unthinkable that she, of all people, should be able to see the black elms' unfalling winter leaves in the so-called Romantic Garden. Not only did they not fall, they burnt in the plantation's sober lattice. The more you looked at them, the more they burnt. She was far away, but she could feel the heat on her cheeks.

So when she came back, many years later, one of the first things O did was go and see the unfalling leaves in San Carlos Gardens.

But O's here right now. She's twelve years old and is starting to go to the river to wash. She likes the river, but not washing so much. At the cross-roads, one road leads to school, another to the river. If she didn't have to wash, she'd always choose to go to the river. Which is where she's in the process of discovering the water figures.

Polka suffers as a result of ignorance. Yesterday he was very hurt because he rode side-saddle on Grumpy, the donkey that carries the clothes Olinda and I wash, and some people had a go at him for not riding normally, like a man. All because of ignorance. The animal suffers less if you sit like a woman. Everything that itches is because of ignorance. Ignorance itches. That's what Polka thinks. He used to have a lot of friends he could talk to against ignorance. One of them was Arturo, Galicia's lightweight cham-pion. I know there are rumours, some say Arturo could be my Dad. He was killed before I was born, but if he's in the water, if the river brought him to me, maybe there's something in it. They loved him a lot. He always had his gloves and books.

'But if he was a boxer, didn't he have to hit people?'

'Yes,' said Polka. 'But boxing isn't quite the same as hitting. With his boxer's hands, he would write in a magazine called *Brazo y Cerebro*. In Fontenova, he and others founded a cultural association with a library called Shining Light in the Abyss. It had a glass sign showing a sun. It's so cold in Fontenova it must have helped having a sign like that.'

'And what happened?'

'They killed him like Christ. There was no war here, girl, what they call a war was a hunt and they hunted him down. Before he died, he managed to write on a piece of paper, "The worshippers of Christ make a new Christ every day."'

'What happened to the sign with the sun?'

'They smashed it.'

'And the cultural association, the books?'

'They burnt them.'

'Burnt books?'

'That's right.'

Polka talks of him as a hero, a champ the world forgot.

'The future's uncertain,' said Polka. 'Who can say what will happen? There may come a time, girl, only you know who Arturo da Silva was and that Shining Light existed in a place that is now so gloomy. Hold on to this word as well. Arturo da Silva was an anarchist.'

'An anarchist? But . . .'

'Yes, I know. I've said it now. It's a frightening word. Just let it be. It can look after itself. It's all I ask. Hold on to it. Find a little space for it, you don't have to go back. It won't bother you.'

He muttered something about invincible resignation. Talking to himself. Polka, Polka. Papa. Olinda says nothing. Almost nothing about her life. She likes radio novels, she becomes absorbed, unaware of time. I know this because, at Amparo the fashion designer's, there's a radio in the workshop and when they listen to the novel, read by Pedro Pablo Ayuso and Matilde Conesa, it's as if the machines are making tears and the pedal is pushing them up the nerves of their legs to their eyes, well, once my mother became absorbed, lost in her friendly silence. Which can happen to anyone. There's a young lady, Ana told me, who writes poetry and claims to have received this gift from the spirit of Bécquer, we learnt about him at school, 'the dark swallows will return', I liked him a lot, she must have done so too, they met in Bárbaras Square, the spirit possessed her and apparently she got pregnant. Pregnant with poetry. Ana and Amalia laughing about it, the spirit's spunk, ooh, spirit, ooh!

'Will we go to Bárbaras, O, see if we can find the spirit of that no-good Gustavo Adolfo?'

'I've already been,' I told them. They were speechless, unable to laugh, I was so quick.

'You what?'

'I rather prefer another in San Carlos Gardens. He doesn't get you pregnant.'

Amalia, pretending to be shocked, 'Oh, my girl! You've turned into a spiritual slut now, haven't you?'

And there I was, pulling at Olinda, who'd got into the novel and wouldn't come out. She only came out when the sewing machines stopped. When they're all going together, they're like a special train. But when they all stop at once . . . 'What happened?' asked Olinda in surprise, when they all stopped at the same time.

The Star and Romantic the Horse

He thought of a joke of destiny. Mislaid poems with wings. Moved by a spiritual medium. What were they doing there, among the originals for the first issue of *Oeste* waiting for the censor's approval? What were those snippets from *I Was Forsook* doing there? The inclusion of the medieval poem by Guterres at the start could have been a coincidence, some coincidence, but where had three poems by Aurelio Anceis come from? He went back. Annoyed and upset.

There they were, in the table of contents. Three unpublished poems from the anonymous collection *I Was Forsook*: 'Zero', 'Infinite' and 'Standard Vivas'.

He returned to the texts. There was a noticeable detail. The triumphal dates had disappeared. Aurelio Anceis' game with the regime's calendar of celebrations. He, Tomás Dez, had also made a change in the book that was now being printed. But a different one. He'd replaced the Fascist anniversaries with others that were either neutral or delicately dressed up as cultural obsequies. Whoever was responsible for including Anceis' poems in *Oeste* had simply eliminated the dates and left only the final irony in the poem *Zero*:

> But no one is as wise as Leonardo Fibonacci
> who in the crucible of emptiness made zero.

His fingers like claws grasping their prey. He raked through the pages. In 'Standard Vivas', he'd removed the pagan calendar of saints that made reference to Apache, Half-tit, Syra, Samantha Galatea and other renowned hetaeras who would never appear in the city's chronicles. However, he'd left other, more enigmatic names to give critics a headache that not improbable day the work turned into a classic. International names of an ocean-going cosmos. Cape Town's Storm in a Chinese, or Starry Simona from St Pierre and Miquelon. That's right, Simona, Pouting, Snubnose, Hunchie. He'd asked Anceis who he was referring to and he'd replied, 'Sirens. It's always said there are no more ancient sea myths in Galicia. It's not true. At least as far as sirens go. Sirens are sirens.'

'Do you mean whores?'

'I mean sirens. For that, I turn to Mr Thomas Stearns Eliot and his idea about heights of sensibility. It depends on the height.'

'What height?'

'The height you're writing and reading at. Or depth, if you like. Your vision is only partial. Think of men breaking up ice on deck. Not blocks of ice, ice covering the whole ship, every nook and cranny. And imagine then the skipper decides to head for St Pierre. They haven't seen or stepped on land for months. Going to St Pierre, which is only a small harbour with a slope of wooden houses, is like a trip to paradise. They're so happy lots of them start drinking in order to celebrate and, by the time they reach St Pierre, they can't disembark. They can barely walk. For them, without the need to cite Mr Eliot, the simple fact of saying St Pierre, the decision to go, meant already being there. In paradise. That's the power of simply saying words, they make a place, change bodies. But let me tell you about those who disembark. Lots of them queue up outside L'Étoile, which is soon Anglicised as the Star, the dance hall owned by St Pierre's only professional diver, also known as the Communist, and they queue up, do you know why? No, it's not what you're thinking. Dozens of men waiting in a line, in the snow, to dance, just to dance with the one they call Hunchie, La Bossue, Miss Hunchback. To put their hand on her hump while they dance. Skippers will pay her up to a thousand francs to go on board ship and pee on the nets. A kind of magic charm. Dancing, washerwomen, lucky sirens.'

The censor Dez couldn't help cracking his fingers in a sign of sudden discomfort.

'Well, I'm glad, Anceis, you met Eliot and whoever else out at sea.'

Those of the G, dancing around the axis mundi,
in the Flaming Star . . .

'I know something about Freemasonry, Anceis. The G, the axis mundi, the flaming star, the next bit about the liber mundi. I'm not a complete fool. What's it got to do with fishing for cod in Newfoundland?'

'Very simple. The geometry of a dance. The most popular dance hall among fishermen in St Pierre was the Star. The stage was a wooden table. On top of the table was a chair. On top of the chair, an accordionist, the Diver. On top of the accordionist, a lamp. This is the axis mundi. The accordion is the liber mundi, which is both open and shut, virgin, fertilised matter.'

'After all that,' said Dez, 'it's no surprise my ecclesiastical colleague, with his divine eye, should be confused before what he terms "a muddy mare magnum".'

'I like that,' said Anceis. '"A muddy mare magnum". A realistic reading.'
He again made to retrieve the manuscript.

'I'd better take it. Truth is,' said Anceis, 'I'm not sure I want to publish it.'

But Tomás Dez's hand, swift as a claw, grabbed the folder containing two handwritten copies of I *Was Forsook.*

'No, leave it. I'm going to defend this book as if it were my own. We have an obligation to try.'

He said this with a vehemence that took Anceis by surprise. That word as well. An obligation. It was true. To him, the only reason for writing and publishing it was because he felt a strange obligation, something akin to fate.

'I'm going to defend this book,' repeated Dez. 'Do you know why? Because, talking of heights, above all I'm a poet, Mr Anceis. I haven't a civil servant's soul. You'll think it contradicts my role, but being contradictory is part of the human condition.'

'You said before the ecclesiastical censor wouldn't change his negative opinion. Wouldn't give his *nihil obstat.* Had it in for my book.'

'Yes, he does. He's set against it. We'll see what he puts down in writing. He told me he considers I *Was Forsook* a case of overt blasphemy. I told him God can look after himself. But this is a man who goes around with the *Index Librorum Prohibitorum* in his pocket. Don't think he's particularly fond of me. What to do? For me, fanaticism is to religion what hypocrisy is to virtue. In short, we're up against a wall, but there may be a key. We have to find it. I'll see what I can do. Where there's excommunication, there's absolution. It may take months. Even years. But I swear to you I *Was Forsook* will see the light of day.'

He'd redone the bit about sirens in 'Standard Vivas' as a separate text, whose language, being explicit, was provocative but infused with the moral lesson of a cruel fate awaiting transgressors. An edifying scandal. Aurelio Anceis talked of 'God's punches' as the blind blows of an arbitrary, brutal force, a sworn enemy of beauty, enjoyment and happiness. In Tomás Dez's version, God's punches were always well aimed and even the misfortunes of the righteous or innocent had a positive purpose: the quality of their laments, the height of their tragedies.

In *Oeste*, the poem was kept the same.

He banged his fist on the table. On that worm that had wormed its way out of the table. He'd kill *Oeste*. He'd kill that bug any which way.

The application to publish the magazine, which was described as 'An Independent Cultural Weekly', was signed by Chelo Vidal, Ricardo Samos' wife. 'Playing the prima donna,' he snarled. Its director, who had to be an accredited journalist, was the guy from the evening *Expreso*. On the editorial board were Sada the painter, that young poet friend of his, Avilés, Dr Abril, the teachers Eloísa Garza and Dora Castells and the two Vidals, Chelo and Sebastián the photographer. There was then a long list of contributors, a mixed bag among whom, with his magnifying glass, he could detect the odd liberal survivor, youngsters who were suspicious from the moment they started writing, and a few exotica, who were above suspicion, travelling companions, like that pretty girl in National Formation, Laura. But he had Ren's report. And pretty Laura, the Carlist, so beautiful in her traditionalist uniform, was now keeping company with 'existentialist claptrap'. It had all been carefully planned to lend an air of respectability to the invention, which showed all the signs of being a second *Atlántida*, closed years before by a specific order from Madrid based on a report he'd never publicly acknowledge as his own, the terms of which he only had to repeat to cause excitement on his palate: 'A group of degenerate, existentialist Bohemians.'

Among the promoters of *Oeste*, the young poet would soon be out of play. Ren had in mind a simple operation to intimidate him and force him out of the country. He would open his post, make it clear he was being watched. Or issue one of his favourite warnings by phone, 'You're living by permission.' Dez centred his suspicions on Sada. He was the oldest and had the constitution of a cobweb. He seemed to hang in the air, like a dream, but with moorings everywhere. He had to confirm it. He had to locate the source as soon as possible. *I Was Forsook*, with its new title *The Moment of Truth*, was about to appear in his name. Yes, *The Moment of Truth*. That was his contribution, his touch, and he liked it. He felt the paternity of the title somehow justified his appropriation of the work. It was like an adoption, he thought. And the title was perfect.

Eight months after this final attempt to have *I Was Forsook* authorised for publication, Aurelio Anceis died. It was a poetic death. He threw himself into the sea from the Coiraza wall in Orzán on a day of swell.

Dez had already decided, before Anceis' death, that *I Was Forsook* had to exist. But in his own way. It would now be Tomás Dez's second book, the sequel to his literary debut, *From Mars to Daphne*. A decade had gone by. It was a prudish book, but he had to be grateful to a work he was deeply ashamed of. It had enabled him to make contacts, there'd been a few reviews in which the book was described in agreeable terms and, since then, he'd appeared as a poet in the wake of the so-called 'creative youth', those who after the war had followed the banner of Garcilaso de la Vega, poet and soldier. Not unintentionally had he begun his work with a quote from Garcilaso's Second Elegy: *O crude, o rigorous, o fierce Mars, clad in diamonds for a tunic and always so hard!* His strategy worked. An initial review in the local press, which was unsigned, talked of 'poems of virile race', a formula that was repeated in other commentaries. He'd also sent the book to Agustín de Foxá, with a humble dedication in which he deliberately used Foxá's own verses evoking Madrid: *From my eucalyptic shadows, these poems travel in a landau with cinnamon horses to visit the master and kneel while he drinks from the pink shell with rainbow veins.* He was a real admirer of Foxá. He'd memorised the two centaur sonnets, the young and the old. Reciting them was one of his *coups de théâtre* among friends. But Foxá never answered. He may not have liked the image of someone kneeling while he drank from the pink shell. The truth is it was a ridiculous dedication. He realised this as soon as he'd posted it. As often happens with extreme eulogies, it smacked of parody. Nor did he reply to a second attempt, when Dez sent a copy of *Tableau of the Middle Ages*, asking for it to be signed, for which he enclosed an envelope with the necessary stamps. He had better luck with Eugenio Montes, when he did the same with his book *The Star and Trail*, published by Ediciones del Movimiento. He went straight to the point and paraphrased Sánchez Mazas' preface in a spirit of Fascist camaraderie: 'With thanks for placing human letters at the Falange's service.'

I Was Forsook, that is *The Moment of Truth*, would signify a radical change. A literary bomb. 'Garcilasistic', my foot! He was going to shock the literary world beyond this oyster city, stuck in its own shell. And then this had to happen. He had to do something about it. Right away.

He again visited the Sahara boarding-house, where Anceis had stayed during his last two years as a grounded sailor. No, said Miss Dalia, the owner, no one had asked after Aurelio Anceis. No relative had turned up. No one had made any claim.

'No one?'

She didn't find it so strange. In a boarding-house like hers, with a majority of long-term guests, the world was seen differently. Some people, some sane people, who were like hermit crabs, only ever came out of their rooms to eat. Talked to nobody. Lived like zeroes.

'Zeroes? Why do you say zeroes?'

'Don't get me wrong,' replied Miss Dalia. 'What I mean is nobody missed him. Nobody came looking for him before you.'

Dez would remember this visit. It was the last time he saw him alive.

Anceis barely said anything. He complained of a strong migraine. He was dressed under the bedspread, with his sailor's hat pulled down as if he wanted to hold on to the pain rather than letting it go. He asked him, out of courtesy, how he felt and unexpectedly Aurelio Anceis replied he felt guilty.

'Guilty for what?'

'For having survived. Don't you feel guilty?'

'No, not really,' said Dez.

'I'd like you to return *I Was Forsook*.'

'Why?'

'You heard me. All the paperwork. The poems, applications. Everything. It's my last wish. I can't demand it of you, so I'm asking you as a final wish, as a plea. If it doesn't reach me in time, burn it. I was going to burn it anyway.'

'What do you mean?'

'I wanted the poems to come out as a book so that I could burn them. Make a bonfire down by the docks. They were written to be burnt.'

He was seized by a violent cough he quickly tried to stifle with a handkerchief, though all it did was redden his face. Dez associated Anceis' words with that cough and the abrasive change in the colour of his skin.

He stood up, turning away, averting his eyes from him. This was not the proper way to behave. To hell with it. He was in the company of an ex-man.

He turned back at the door. 'Goodbye, Mr Anceis. I hope you get better soon.'

When he reached the censor's office, he told his secretary, 'If that seafaring poet turns up again, I'm not in and I'm not expected. Get rid of him straightaway.'

'Yes, Commander Dez.'

Commander. He liked it when his secretary called him that.

'Anything to report concerning Aurelio Anceis?' Tomás Dez now asked the owner of the Sahara boarding-house. Dalia had shown him into that lounge which still had a gramophone. Mute, but there it was, lending a certain style. The woman also looked more ancient and more attractive than the first time, with those painted nails dancing like dragonflies. 'Anything new turn up, any request?'

'You know what he wanted. Everything of his to be burnt. What a fright he gave me when he tried to do it in the kitchen. He wasn't very good at handling fire. At the end, this became his obsession. In the lounge, he'd start writing verses on scraps of paper and then set fire to them in an ashtray. It was the only time I had to ask him to be careful.'

It was better to confront your ghosts than to carry them on your back, thought Dez. There was a certain matter rolling around in his mind. He realised he was talking to a smart woman, who maybe didn't just read the fashion magazines with faded covers scattered about the small lounge of the Sahara boarding-house like holidaymakers caught out by winter. The same could be said of Miss Dalia. Her hairstyle, jewels, make-up, nails, everything about her shared a family likeness with the gramophone and those illustrations in *Belle époque* summer programmes.

'I wonder if you share my opinion,' said Dez. 'There was something wrong with Aurelio Anceis. I mean apart from his illness. Recently he'd become very suspicious, don't you think?'

'I know people who spend their lives at sea and come ashore to die, Mr Dez. They can't accept things. They find us strange. But he never used to complain. On the contrary, to him almost everything was wonderful. In his last days . . .'

'The man was a wretch!' Dez blurted out in a loud voice that was petulant and accusing.

'Did he never tell you about the dance in L'Étoile?'

Now it seemed to be the characters in the cover photos listening to her narrative. Dez guessed she wasn't the kind of woman to start crying, but she blinked and rubbed her hands, 'In his last days, of course we didn't know it, he'd pay tribute to the smallest things. I'd give him an apple for dessert and he'd carry on looking at it for hours. He'd say to me, "Isn't it wonderful, Miss Dalia?"'

Dez glanced in the same direction as the Sahara lady, but found nothing that could be described as wonderful. She abruptly shook her head and said, 'If what you mean is whether Mr Anceis had a secret, I'd have to reply

I don't know. If he had any secrets, he took them with him. All he left me was a Festina watch.'

'That's all very interesting from the point of view of Anceis as a poet. But right now I was thinking about something else. Do you think there's any possibility Aurelio Anceis hasn't died?'

She was stunned. Dez would have liked to know whether her contemplation had to do with him, an assessment of his sanity, or whether she was really considering the hypothesis Anceis might not be dead.

'Listen, sir. It was very polite of him to die the way he did.'

The Sahara lady had adopted a hard tone that sounded quite genuine.

'He spent the nights coughing,' said Dalia. 'I even considered throwing him out, fond as I was of him. "Mr Anceis, why don't you go to a hospital or some home?" When I said this to him, he fell quiet. He got over his cough for a time. Either that or he smothered it, who knows? He then had the decency to go and die outside. Without bothering anyone. He even made his own bed. He wrote a farewell letter, which I gave to the police. But first he made his bed. He'd smooth out the creases in his quilt with his hand, like an iron. It was very kind of him to die like this. One thing about sailors, they can fend for themselves.'

Her expression hardened further as she addressed Dez. What questions was he asking? Wasn't he his friend? She said, 'Mr Anceis was a correct man. Didn't they find his polished shoes neatly placed together on the Coiraza wall in Orzán as if he'd gone and lain down on the sea?'

The next step was to go in search of Sada. When he found him, on the terrace of the Galicia Café, he spoke with the utmost caution. He had to obtain information, discover what he knew, but not slip up. Sada was either in another world or pretending to be mad. Or both. But, if he did know the truth, he had plenty of reasons to plot his revenge.

'Anceis?'

'It's not an official matter, Sada, my friend. I'm acting as intermediary. They've expressed interest in him from the *Index* in Madrid. He sent some poems. They're impressed and want to publish them with a fanfare. Funny thing is he only wrote his name and the following address: Orzán Sea, Coruña.'

'Orzancy is a poet. That's right.'

'Not Orzancy. I'm talking about Aurelio Anceis. He hasn't published a book. I said I'd look into it. Try and remember, Sada. Is there a hidden Parnassus among the bars of Orzán?'

'Anceis? Never heard of him. There was an Aurelio, the great Aguirre, who drowned in the wildness of Orzán, not in a bar. He'd go around with his head uncovered during God's storms. *Wie wenn am Feiertage . . .*'

Dez the censor was aware that words, even those pulled out of a hat by chance, had a purpose. 'As on a Holiday . . .' He knew the poem, he'd heard it before, but what was the point of quoting Hölderlin? Sada was starting to rise. Ascending through clouds of expressionist Atlantic thunder. He was getting away and the mystery hadn't been solved yet.

'But that, Mr Dez, was another time, when shells were still coated in nacre.'

He made a final attempt.

'He may not still be alive,' said Dez. 'Is there anyone whose absence has been noted? If not in Orzán, then on other seaside Parnassuses. The heroic route of the Star, Elms, the Galley, the Strip . . . To say nothing of the islands in Coruña's Aegean: Enrique's, Leonardo's, Delicacies, Nautilus, the Cribs . . .'

'Don't torture me now, Dez. I was born yesterday in the Cuckoo's Song, resuscitated in the Ship's Lantern and died in the Cuckoo's Feather. There are abstemious poets too. Go and find one. After all, it never rains but it pours.'

'Don't try to be difficult, master. Geniuses like you are not allowed to indulge in such flaws. Please. Take a trip around the world of spirits. If there's any news, give me a call.'

'I'll toast you with Ferrero Tonic. And the soul of the loin of pork in Enrique's. By the way . . .'

Tomás Dez realised he'd kept the conversation going too long. There were seconds that got stuck in time like bits of dust in the eye.

'What is it, Sada?'

'How's it going with *Oeste*?'

He was about to say, 'It's fine, being processed.' But the dust had taken its toll and Dez replied carelessly:

'Between you and me, there is a problem. Have you read it all?'

'No, not all of it. I did the cover and a few illustrations. What I can tell you is that magazine is more innocent than Carral bread, Mr Dez.'

'In the strictest confidence. My report was favourable, but authorisation has been withheld somewhere up the line. The Madrid offices are in disarray. The Julián Grimau case has made a mess of things. We have to be patient.'

'Patient? Do you know why there are so many seagulls and mullets in this city? Because they feed on patience. The drains are full of patience.'

He made as if to summon the waiter and said, 'A foie gras of patience, if you please.'

'Remember, Sada, that was in confidence. *Oeste* will be published. We may have to pull some strings. Prune it back a bit. But you can trust me. Whatever the circumstances, I'll always be on the side of art, you know. Which reminds me, I've a new work on the way. *The Moment of Truth*. That's the title.'

'Very good,' said Sada. 'Very bullish.'

Dez left without looking at the seagulls, but he heard their calls like a soundtrack of suspense on the way to his office. Very bullish. What to make of that? The bastard. He had things to do, the sooner the better.

He hatched his plan. He would have to shake up, send tremors towards, the director of the *Expreso*. They'd never been close. His professional style, the way he kept his distance.

The other key figure was Samos.

He gave him a call. There was a problem with *Oeste* and he preferred to discuss it with him out of friendship and to avoid disturbing Chelo Vidal. He then made another call. To the printer's. He'd decided to withdraw three poems he wasn't quite sure about: 'Zero', 'Infinite' and 'Standard Vivas'.

He met the judge that same afternoon in the Union Café. *Oeste*, he explained, was being considered by the General Direction in Madrid. He'd been favourable, even enthusiastic, in his report. Everything was going well until the fishing line, so to speak, unexpectedly got caught and became knotted. Someone had noticed some poems which were described as

284

perverse and the fact of being anonymous made them even more insidious. In confidence, it was a senior official. He couldn't say the name, the judge would understand.

'Yes, I understand. In my situation, as you well know, I also understand how uncomfortable one can feel in front of texts that are anonymous or written under a pseudonym.'

Yes, of course. They'd come to that later, said Dez. He had some news. But going back to the problem of *Oeste*, circumstances had something to do with it. The state of emergency declared for two years, the Grimau case, the international campaign . . . It all had an impact and at such times controls were tightened. Each to his own. As for the poems, they may have been a little heated, he couldn't say. He'd pulled some strings and been given a solution. The magazine could come out if those poems were omitted. But there was another demand he wished to discuss with the utmost discretion. The authorities wanted to know who'd written the poems. In short, he had to put together a confidential report. Their personal details and public conduct. The authorities had thought to go through the usual channels and seek information from the Brigade of Politico-Social Investigation, but he'd persuaded them that wasn't necessary, at the head of the magazine were some highly respected individuals who were close to the regime and could be trusted, first among them his honour's wife. This reference had sufficed, explained Dez. So he'd offered to look into the matter himself. Which is why he'd called and here they were. It was a question of avoiding any damages and making sure *Oeste* came out.

'The most important thing for us all is that none of this has a knock-on effect.'

'I understand, Dez. I'll talk to Chelo. There won't be a problem. She may seem to have her head in the clouds, but she's rooted in reality.'

'I know. That's why I came to you. I thought it had something to do with Sada. A pseudonym. I spoke to him before, without telling him the truth. You know how it is, he needs feeding separately.'

'We'll solve the case of the perverse verses,' said the judge ironically. 'I mean it. Perversity is a concept of great importance in our legal history.'

'As for the other matter,' continued Dez, 'I thought you'd want to know. Something's come up in the case of Black Eye.'

The censor saw yet again how the mere mention of that name, for whatever reason, had an epidermal effect on the judge. It altered his disposition. To help him relax, he added, 'I've taken a liking to western novels and brought you a present.'

To the judge's surprise, he pulled a western novel out of his pocket. Samos went along with the joke and accepted it. It was called *Romantic the Horse*. And signed John Black Eye. Showing he already knew it, even though it had only just been published, he searched for the chapter where there was a trial and discovered that Dez had already underlined the relevant paragraph. The judge nodded in acknowledgement. He read, 'Even after the verdict, the lawyer Henry Botana had the courage to tell the Judge of Oklahoma that the death penalty was a form of premeditated killing.'

'Of course we couldn't just leave that alone,' said Dez. 'With all this fuss about Grimau being shot! But in the censor's office there's a dislike for trashy literature. My colleagues are highly academic. Who'd have looked at *Romantic the Horse* past the first paragraph? Even that would have been a lot. There are more readers of sentimental stories.'

Dez opened the novel at the beginning and adopted the tone of a radio series, 'Henry Botana was six feet tall, had a girlfriend who loved him, a horse named Romantic and a head the judge had set a humiliatingly low price on. He hoped, on the day of the Last Judgement, Archangel Michael would be fairer about his soul's weight.'

Dez smiled ironically and closed the book.

'Not bad, eh? Listen, Ricardo, I wasn't inactive. If you thought that at some point, you were mistaken. The truth is it wasn't a difficult mystery to solve. There was some confusion because, at his publisher's in Barcelona, our man was known as Dr Montevideo, actually an alias. Force of habit. That is until, after my insistence, you might say warning, they uncovered his real identity. Héctor Ríos. He's our man.'

Dez had known all of this for quite some time, without having to read *Romantic the Horse*. But he thought the judge would enjoy the dramatic denouement. Samos' expression wasn't exactly the look of someone who's finally trapped their prey. He seemed to grow pale.

'Do you know that name?'

'Yes, a bit.'

'Was it who you suspected?'

In the storm, the Orzán waves attempt to regain their ancient channel, the memory of the isthmus, before the great Recheo put a stop to the union of two seas, the wild side and the calm bay. The former attempts to force an entry, climbs up Riazor and manages with its tassels of foam to get as far as the giant eucalyptus in Pontevedra Square, the spot where day labourers wait to be hired. And where saleswomen from the suburbs and washerwomen moor their beasts of burden. It's raining with seaside conviction. They're young. Héctor's a little older. He's been in Santiago for two years, studying law, but at weekends he still works with the group of theatre and declamation in the Craftsmen's Instructive and Recreational Circle. Thanks to him, Samos read in public for the first time in the hall there. They recited the scene with the two gravediggers in Act V of *Hamlet*. He played the part of the First Clown. How often had they weighed up the curve of that question! 'What is he that builds stronger than either the mason, the shipwright, or the carpenter?' Now Héctor's planning a new project. An adaptation for Coruña Radio, which is due to start broadcasting, of Herbert George Wells' most popular works. Samos has to help. They share a passion for this author. A series called *Wells, Wells, Wells*. With a signature tune in Morse code. They're on their way to rehearsal, in the rain. It doesn't matter. Ríos pulls out a book from under his coat. Reads, '"From Castro to Mount Alto, the face of Coruña was grimy with powder of the Black Smoke". Yep, the first radio broadcast will be a version of *The War of the Worlds*. What do you say? Then we'll move on to the adventures of *The Invisible Man*.'

Héctor doesn't let up. He's optimism personified. In the summer, he helps out in the family academy. Since he was a child, he's been good at both skills, typing and shorthand. He always says they were his childhood games and he finds it difficult to write normally. He's a devotee of

Esperanto, which he's fluent in, having studied it at nights. His passion for a universal language is based on the ideals of rational socialism, for which he drew inspiration from Ramón de la Sagra, a Coruñan of the nineteenth century who, in his opinion, is on a par with the Frenchman Proudhon or the Welshman Owen. He's also always flicking through his notes on ethics by Xohán Vicente Viqueira. To start with, Ricardo Samos likes the sound of this message of faith in humanity. They're heading towards the Craftsmen's Circle, down San Andrés Street. Héctor Ríos, as always, is carrying a book in his hand. He alternates between speaking and reading, with fervour, as if it were a musical score. They bump into Dr Hervada, who points out he's walking with one foot in the road and the other on the pavement. Héctor replies with quick wit, 'Thank you, doctor, I thought I'd suddenly gone lame.'

'In the time of the Spanish Republic, were you never tempted?' Schmitt asked Samos one day when they met in Casalonga during the summer of 1962.

'I was a rational socialist for a few hours of crazy joy,' he replied ironically.

His attraction for Ríos lasted a little longer than that. Samos had been brought up in an atmosphere of traditional, monarchist Catholicism. A few months earlier, in April, the Republic had been declared. The swift course of events made him dizzy. To start with, he shared the other students' joy. The Republic had arisen like spring, a creative impulse in society. In that vote in 1931, of the thirty-nine members of Coruña Town Hall, only five were monarchist. But gradually he felt the distrust that dominated in the family home, where the fall of the monarchy was labelled a disaster. There was an air of tension at home. His mother's apprehension about laicism led her to pray for the salvation of Spain, sometimes on her own, other times with groups of female friends. His father, a Navy legal officer and historian by vocation, seemed to be distant from it all, including his marriage, though he'd occasionally let fly about the Philippines, Cuba, Puerto Rico, Morocco and the Statute of Catalonia. Whether he liked it or not, Ricardo Samos was subject at home to a constant sense of apocalyptic doom. During this time, Héctor Ríos provided a balance. It was he who embodied the charming side of current events. Ricardo was also going to study law. If they coincided in Santiago, could Ríos teach him Esperanto? Of course he could. But when that meeting took place, a year later, Samos expressed no interest and Héctor was no longer absorbed in the task of disseminating a universal language.

'There's one priority for which we need all languages. We have to talk about the League of Human Rights.'

Samos was unhappy about the boarding-house. Perhaps because he was a freshman, he'd been given a small, dark room with damp patches on the ceiling. He still hadn't decided whether he was going to fulfil his promise to his mother to attend first Mass in the cathedral the next morning.

'Why's that?'

When he got enthusiastic, Héctor had a tendency to construct paragraphs. 'The only way to oppose totalitarianism is to aim for a World Federation governed by just principles of universal law. These human rights, without borders, will be the framework for a common language, the real Esperanto.'

They'd known each other as children. They were neighbours in the Old City. Playing on the beach. They can't see. It's a game of gangsters in the Wild West. You have to crouch down, move stealthily and find your enemy without being seen. You shoot with your mouth.

'Bang, Ríos!'

'Where am I then?'

'What you say about the League of Human Rights sounds Masonic,' Samos blurted out. His mother had said his voice was finally dropping and he'd have sworn it happened on that day, at that moment.

Héctor felt the blow. Was confused. Samos' voice, which sounded so different, may have had something to do with it.

'Masonic? Is that good or bad?'

Samos preferred not to reply. He emphasised his silence. He knew this silence was the sign of a definitive parting of the ways. Months later, he'd come into contact with those at *Acción Española*. In the Law Faculty, there was also a very active group of traditionalist teachers openly conspiring against the Republic.

'Now you've a voice of thunder. You'd be terrific playing the part of the Last Martian. Remember? Instead of Regent's Park, we'll choose Mount Alto, next to Hercules Lighthouse. That superhuman note. Ulla, ulla!'

They laughed.

'Ulla, ulla, ulla!'

It was burning. The flames were licking at the cover. The books had been released by the blasted time machine. He hears a voice. That guy who's taken to reading out the titles and their authors on the pyres by the docks.

'Wells!'

He turns towards him.

'Wells, Wells!'

Though he looks at him seriously, the guy is smiling, 'He certainly wrote a lot!' He's holding a third book in his hand. Why does he have to try and be funny? Why is he imitating a dog's bark?

'Wells, Wells, Wells!'

The books are burning. Ricardo Samos is about to raise his arm, mumble something. He coughs. His body bends over. The young Parallelepiped approaches with concern, dumb camaraderie. 'Is anything wrong, boss? It's all this horrible smoke. Why don't you go down to the beach for a breath of fresh air? Or drink some coffee.'

'I'm fine,' says Samos to Tomás Dez. 'Don't worry.'

'Coffee. With lots of sugar. It's the best thing for stress.'

The Prohibited

There was a secret person inside Sulfe. It was well known he was a loner. And single. 'Celibate, you mean,' his father would say. 'Married to his books.' Not any old books. His motto was, 'He who alights on the classics'. Gabriel had heard his father say this several times and always solemnly. Now he knew the phrase came from Alfonso Sulfe and was peculiar to him.

'I've nothing to hand, Gabriel, but I'm going to give you a word for your cabinet of curiosities. Take note. OK. Are you ready? The word is "colophon". An example: "The book had no colophon". In this case, it refers to the final notes, and this is its general meaning. "Colophon" is the end of something. But the strange thing is where it comes from. It's connected with the life of a Greek fortune-teller called Calchas. An important person in the history of war, which is to say in history. It was he who invented the greatest trick this world has ever seen, the Trojan horse. But he had to cope with a terrible prophecy. That he would die when he met a more powerful fortune-teller. And that's exactly what happened in a place called Colophon.'

'What did the other foretell?'

'We don't know.'

Gabriel thought it would make an interesting story for a postcard from Durtol Sanatorium.

'Do you like reading? It's the best thing that can happen to you in life. Writing has other implications. Another word, my favourite. "Scruple". From *scrupulus*. This was the name for a small, pointed stone. It could also be used as a bargaining chip. But then came the meaning you're already familiar with. Rather than knowing what a scruple is, you feel it, don't you? *Injeci scrupulum homini.* I put a scruple in the man, I put him in a quandary. Funny. It's still a sharp, pointed stone. The difference now is it's inside the body. What's yours? A word you like. Come on. Quickly.'

Gabriel wondered whether or not to say his word. The man seemed kind enough and, whenever he said it, he felt the pleasure of someone playing a prank on a sage.

'"Acetylsalicylic", sir.'

'Not bad.'

Samos the judge would occasionally refer to Alfonso Sulfe as one of the most talented men in the country. Shame he shut himself up so much in his hole. He clearly enjoyed the other's etymological expeditions. 'Sulfe, tell us the origin of the word "jacket".' His friend's wisdom was thus put on show during conversations in the Crypt. To start with, Alfonso Sulfe would blush, but then he'd succumb to a few minutes of glory.

'We could say the word "jacket" comes from the Road to Santiago. St Jacques in France. There's the germ of the word. Jacques. There were so many peasants who had this name it became a generic term for a local and the article of clothing he wore. In that way . . .'

'Did you know that, Don Munio?'

'No. Another miracle performed by the Apostle.'

Apart from that, Alfonso Sulfe barely intervened in the conversation when it had to do with 'the current state of affairs', meaning politics. He'd been friends with the judge for a long time, ever since the 1940s. The 1940s! He talked of those years as of a distant age, with dark melancholy. Now a colleague from that period had reappeared. They met in Santiago at a tribute to Álvaro D'Ors and discussed renewing lost ties. The judge invited him to the Crypt. Sulfe was grateful, but couldn't. As well as his lectures, he was stuck in the belly of a medieval whale, he said enigmatically.

'Are there any Bibles in that whale?' asked Samos. A game of allusions. Alfonso Sulfe exerted a kind of esoteric influence on him. The first person he knew who'd studied in detail the Coruña Bible, now known as the Kennicott Bible, kept in the Bodleian Library in Oxford. Sulfe had been there in 1935 and he described it as if he'd impressed a copy of that treasure on his memory. The Sephardi script, the colourful illustrations in burnished gold and silver leaf, the strange morocco goatskin box binding, blind-embossed on all six sides. Yes, he could see it now. One of the unforgettable illustrations showed the moment Jonah was swallowed by a whale. And you simply had to see that of the astrologer Balaam consulting an astrolabe. This miniature alone was worth a civilisation. Samos had asked a question Sulfe found a little naive. How had they let such a treasure get away? The Bible was made in 1476, Sulfe explained, shortly before the expulsion of the Jews from Spain in 1492. Samos should not forget the Coruña Bible was commissioned by a Jewish family and illuminated by a very talented Coruñan Jew, Joseph Ibn Hayyim. 'I don't mean that, I mean the book,' said Samos. 'Shame such a treasure got away.'

He was surprised by Sulfe's call the day after the tribute to D'Ors. Jonah's whale would let him out of house arrest in the case of such a stimulating proposal. He'd be there. Samos was pleased about this re-encounter. They'd shared an interest in Lusitania and for the poet Teixeira de Pascoaes, though one day they'd had a lively disagreement on the subject of *saudade* or longing. The judge had even raised his voice and got quite angry. He'd kept using the word *outrage*. 'An outrage, Sulfe. Teixeira's proposal to declare a metaphysical concept such as *saudade* a tenet of the New State. A State is something very serious. You're not a jurist, so you can't know. Without wishing to boast, I'd say there's a moment for the soldier and a moment for the jurist. An act of victory has to be translated into law. But what's *saudade*? It has no juridical worth. You can't sustain a State with a wooden sword.'

'A wooden sword?'

'Yes, all that about *saudade* is a wooden sword for floral games.'

'And when they talk about the grace of God? Caudillo by the grace of God? The New State as *creatio a Deo?*'

The judge glanced in amazement at the others who were present.

'Such a comparison is improper,' said Samos. 'Between God and *saudade*.'

'Of course it is. Floral games! Like that, on its own, doesn't it sound

293

funny?' asked Sulfe, adopting a conciliatory tone. 'So too does the grace of God.'

And they all laughed with jovial relief.

Alfonso Sulfe stayed behind. He clearly wanted to see Ricardo Samos on his own. Not quite on his own. Gabriel was there, in the alcove, camouflaged in a green skin from the desk-lamp, as he liked to think, and focused on the text from Durtol Château Sanatorium. It described New Year's Eve, 1913. How much he missed his family. It also said how much he'd weighed that day, though in his case he'd used data from the Toledo-Ohio scales in Villar the chemist's.

'Dear Samos, I wanted to ask you for a special favour.'

'What is it, Sulfe?'

'At university, shortly after the war, you mentioned some very interesting books that had come your way by a stroke of fate.'

Ricardo Samos raised his guard. The tension of being with an acquaintance who you fear is about to commit an act of folly. Not a simple slip-up, but a grave mistake.

'One of those books was called *Le Nu de Rabelais* . . .'

'What?'

'*Le Nu de Rabelais*. In French. Highly illustrated. Drawings and photographs of extraordinary erotic grace . . .'

'No, I don't have that book.'

Sulfe didn't seem to register the negative. He rubbed his hands together and his eyes gleamed. 'You'll wonder why I'm bringing this up after so many years,' he said. 'It was, for me, a very special night of friendship. The evening before the trip to Paris, Milan and Berlin. There was something that separated us from the rest of the group. A passion for books. You then had the kindness to share a secret.'

Samos had remained rigidly silent, but at this point he interrupted the story with coldness, 'I don't have it. Are there any other books you'd like to see?'

'I understand if, for you, this meeting has been lost in the mists of time, but it's still very fresh for me, for reasons I will explain. I'm immersed in a study that began with the paschal laughter of the Middle Ages. *Risus paschalis*. After that, I moved on to a second world we could call the rituals of laughter. The *festa stultorum*, Mardi gras . . . When something becomes an obsession, you never know where it's going to lead. It'll sound absurd, even puerile, Samos, but I can't stop thinking about that book . . .'

He was about to add, Of naked queens riding donkeys and rams, dragon-fly women in a sacred grove, siren women in Lusignan, playful, warrior women armed with sensual spears, parodying war through amorous combat. Silenus advances in the vanguard of Bacchus' army. Wine from bars in Franco Street and Algalia had undone locks, loosened their tongues. He could recall Samos' words as he savoured his treasures, the fruits, he himself had admitted, of pillage.

He said, 'I'm on Rabelais, in the sixteenth century, immersed in a feast of words. This is something of what I've discovered in the belly of that whale. And the more I rummage through its entrails, the more I think about that unknown book with its pioneering photographs.'

'Whoever told you about that book must have been very passionate, very convincing. But it wasn't me, Sulfe.'

'Don't you remember anything?' asked the professor in dismay.

'*Le Nu de Rabelais*? Is there such a book? I haven't the faintest.' Samos' voice was hard, cutting. 'It's the first I've heard of it. You're mistaken, Sulfe. Completely and utterly. You've got the wrong man, the wrong night. And if I did share a secret, something I don't recall, I trust you'll know how to keep it.'

It was his father's reply, the sudden change of tone, that alerted Gabriel. He looked at them without changing position. The intimate smoke of convivial jokes hadn't entirely dissipated. For a time, the atmosphere was the same and reminded him of a cartoon. Balloons hanging in the air, containing words and thoughts.

'That must be it, a mistake. It was so long ago. I'm sorry to have bothered you,' said Alfonso Sulfe tentatively, surprised by Samos' response. 'It's turned into an obsession. The others don't realise how important it is. But you know what happens with obsessions. You end up like Captain Ahab chasing Moby Dick.'

He stared at him. 'Moby Dick must be around here somewhere. Benito Cereno too. But not your whale, Sulfe. None of the books you've mentioned.'

He stood up so that Alfonso Sulfe had no choice but to do the same. Sulfe glanced at the dark corners, richly bound lands, of the walls. Gabriel sensed his agitation. He had no doubt the professor would have liked to leapfrog the judge and scour those bookshelves. In silence and at a distance, he somehow shared their tension, participated in their duel. It might be said he knew more than either of them, like someone watching a game of cards who's seen the players' hands. But he held his breath. Were his father to pay him attention or Sulfe to look in his direction, he'd have to abandon the battlefield.

'At least clarify one thing for me, Samos. Didn't you have a first edition of The Prohibited?'

'The Prohibited?'

For the first time, the judge seemed to realise his son was there, in the alcove, writing, contained in the circle of light from the desk-lamp, which, rather than bringing him closer, kept him apart with the astral effect of torches in the night.

'Yes, it belonged to Santiago Casares. As did Le Nu de Rabelais. We talked about a set of teeth,' insisted Sulfe. 'About the eroticism in Galdós' description of a woman's set of teeth.'

'The Prohibited?' repeated the judge. 'I've got the Episodes somewhere. But I was never very keen on Galdós. I always found him rather vulgar. Whether or not I've books that once belonged to Casares.'

'That's it,' said Sulfe. 'Those were exactly my words. Mistaken, obviously.'

The professor's response upset and confused the judge even more. What was all this about a set of teeth? What was he really after?

'A set of teeth, you say? What a good memory, Sulfe! You'd make a fine instructor.'

'A fine pathologist,' joked Sulfe.

The judge's tone grew impatient and contemptuous, 'Maybe. It could be here or up in the attic. That book with the teeth.'

It was. Without its partner, but it was there. As was the one about nudes. Women with moth and dragonfly wings fluttered about the lamp. Gabriel knew this. He could feel the first part trembling in his hands, the wrinkled wound where the corner of the book had been burnt. He remembered the signature like a password or greeting: Santiagcasares Qu. And then, as he turned the pages, an exasperated scent of smoke and human beings.

'In two volumes. We also discussed *The Future of Death* if my memory does not fail me. Talking of obsessions, I recall you were struck by Casares' interest in the beyond. His library . . .'

'I really don't remember any such conversation. His library is as unknown to me as Popefigs' Island.'

'You also were after something, Ricardo. Did you find Borrow's book? Did it escape the flames?'

The judge gave Sulfe a look he reserved for ex-men and sought out his son's face behind the green light of the lamp.

'Mr Sulfe's leaving, Gabriel. Go with him to the door.'

It was as if Sulfe had suddenly woken up in a storm. He knew the door was closing for good. 'I don't think I'll be back any time soon,' he said, half smiling. 'Goodbye, acetylsalicylic.'

When Gabriel returned to the study, the judge was spitting out curses. 'Whale's belly?' he fumed. 'He really went too far!' He drummed his fingers on the desk's padded surface. Then grabbed the magnifying glass and examined the geography of the palm of his hand. A habit he had that seemed to calm him. He turned towards Gabriel. 'A rare bird,' he said. 'You watch him. A professor who spends all his time trying to lay his hands on books he's after. A professor and a kleptomaniac! Who'd have thought it?'

'Kleptomaniac?'

'Biblioklept, to be more precise. That's the word he used years ago, when he told me about his urge to steal books. I was kind enough not to remind him of it. This urge has got him into trouble. He's lucky it's not much of a sin around here. I don't remember anyone being found guilty of stealing books. But this time he went too far. He won't enter this house again.'

He drummed his fingers on the desk as if pressing imaginary keys and

297

smiled with irony, 'Colophon! Jacket! Scruple! Who does he think he is? Pointed stone!'

Finally he got up and Gabriel followed him. Nightfall had turned the large sitting-room into conquered land and all that remained of colours in the Chinese Pavilion was a scent of oils and solvent and the damp breath of plants. Grand Mother Circa raced through time.

'If Mummy comes, tell her to drop by the Oriental. You also should get out. Clear your head. We don't want you turning into another Sulfe.'

'I've got to study today. Tomorrow we've Father Munio's championship for God.'

He never stuttered when he had a lie prepared.

'Championship for God? Now that you have to win. *Ego sum qui sum.*'

'It has to be in three words.'

Gabriel wanted him to leave. What he'd said about being another Sulfe made his hands tingle with a mixture of excitement and guilt. As soon as his father had closed the door, he ran towards the study. Climbed the library steps and there, in the zone of charred remains, sought out *The Prohibited* by Galdós. Pulled down the first volume. Remembered how sleepy he'd been on a previous attempt. But now he knew the most interesting thing about that rather gullible character, José María, was not what happened to him, but what he desired. He read it inquisitively. And particularly enjoyed it when the prose became voracious, rudely attractive, as when Camila's perfect set of teeth bit into his heart.

The Championship for God

'In three words, God.'

Father Munio was a fan of such competitions that gave classes of Religion what he termed 'a competitive cheerfulness'. He moved about the classroom with great dynamism. In his cassock and white gloves, which he never took off, he had a certain hypnotic effect on his pupils, especially the first few days. His was a spectacular, telegenic style, which contrasted with the severe and often bitter or intimidatory seriousness of most teachers. In fact, he was the only one who talked about television in class without treating it like a diabolical or despicable appliance. He created a bond with pupils whenever he referred to programmes or characters that were gaining notoriety, such as the family of ranchers in *Bonanza* with their model father, or the most popular advertisements. His comparisons not only were celebrated by those who had televisions, but immediately won over the others. His televisual colloquialism placed Father Munio firmly on the side of screen-lovers, which meant everybody, but especially those who were subject to a regime of rationing, verging on prohibition, as was the case with the boarders. The latter, on the odd Saturday evening, had even been forced to occupy the lounge in front of a disconnected television. One of Father Pedrosa's disciplinary ideas. They'd used their afternoon break to go and play at bullfighting with the waves in Orzán and, when they came back, there was Father Pedrosa waiting for them with the dramatic special effects of his wreaths of breath as he strode across the darkening quad. The television, not switched on, was a petrified piece of grey, wintry sky that Saturday evening. And there was a correlation between the overcast sky, the tutor's warm vapour and the imageless screen.

From where they were, they could hear the hoarse sound of the waves, they were, so to speak, inside the submarine, but deprived of the journey to the ocean bed being undertaken around that time by all whose television was working. The boarders sat there in silence, condemned not to see.

Which is why, to begin with, they liked this Father Munio who was on their side, that of the illuminated screen. This priest who wrote the order of the day on the blackboard: 'I want you to be happy on earth' (*The Way*, 217). Or: 'There you have light, to help you discover the reasons for your gloominess' (*The Way*, 666). And then the daily exercise, the spiritual gymnastics of his so-called Heroic Minute. 'Attention. It's time now to stand up. No hesitation. A supernatural thought and . . . up you get!' The whole class on its feet, with raised arms like wings, copying him as he flapped his white gloves. Yes, this priest who was such fun he gave himself a round of applause.

'Allez-hop! Now don't you feel better?

'Books, men who accumulate knowledge, are OK, but what we need are publicists for God. Just as merchandise is put on offer, material goods from detergents to fridges, and the person responsible is not afraid to show his face, to repeat the jingle, how much more then should we be engaged in publicity for God? No, we should have no scruples about turning into Walking Advertisements.' And he'd make them laugh by referring to 'the spark of life', Coca-Cola's slogan. Then he'd hush the amused murmurs with the studied, winged gesture of his gloves and the voice of a liturgical illusionist. 'If this is how we talk about a beverage that mysteriously contains sugar and caffeine, what invincible force can we extract from our faith?' He then pointed to the order of the day on the blackboard, a phrase he wrote in large letters as soon as he arrived, which was meant for them to think about and which today sounded like a contradictory, unsettling proclamation: 'Holy Shamelessness'. Now did they understand?

'Another go at Heroic Minute. Attention. It's time now to stand up. No hesitation. A supernatural thought and . . . up you get!'

He sneered at the class. 'What faces! I don't see a supernatural thought anywhere.'

Zonzo was always at the back, in the shelter of the wall. He was a bad student with bad marks, but everyone knew he wasn't sluggish. Nor was he unruly. Almost always mute, even though they threatened to fail him for ever, he made it clear what his attitude was. He was there, at school, under pressure, meeting an obligation that, unlike the others, he didn't need. Whenever a teacher called his name or said something to him, he became uncomfortable and alert, glancing sideways as if asking, Why me? He had a problem. He was very tall, very slim, and had thick eyebrows which, rather than shading his expression, magnified the slightest ocular movement. Zonzo wished to pass unnoticed, but the more he tried, the more he resembled an intruder dressed up as a pupil.

'Except for Zonzo,' said Father Munio, knowing he'd get a laugh. 'On him, I see the savage sincerity of silence.'

Which is why the surprise was complete when Zonzo raised his hand the day of the championship for God.

'In three words, God.'

'The Great Champ,' said Zonzo. A ripple of nervous laughter spread across the three rows of desks.

Father Munio, standing on the rostrum, held his chalk aloft. His eyes bounced off various heads until reaching the back of the classroom and landing on Zonzo like a discovery. He blinked. With a winged gesture of his gloves, he quietened the murmurs.

'Could you repeat that?'

'The Great Champ,' said Zonzo in a powerful voice.

'Magnificent,' said Father Munio. He wrote on the blackboard in capital letters THE GREAT CHAMP. Remarked, 'Extraordinary.'

Zonzo, amid applause, came and occupied the front desk. It was the first time he'd emerged from the shadows.

'More answers.'

'The Most High.'

'Lord God Omnipotent.'

'In three words, God. Gabriel?'

Gabriel had spent the previous evening jotting down notes for the competition for God. He'd found two images, two references to the Creator, inspired by postcards sent by Santiago Casares from Durtol Sanatorium, to be precise, accurate: the Universal Architect and the Most Mysterious. But he had been warned. His mouth would refuse to say these words. He'd get tongue-tied.

'Father, Son, Spirit.'

'That is true. Three distinct persons and only one true God. Classic,' his white gloves moved like the doves of a magician, 'but I'm after something new, an updated message. And today's biggest contribution came from our new ace.'

He lifted Zonzo's hand like a boxer's.

'We'll make a mural in the quad.'

GOD,
THE GREAT CHAMP

There it was after so long, visible for all to see, Zonzo's biro. In his hand. He was sitting at the front desk and holding it. He was writing his Religion exam in Father Munio's class and using that special biro with the naked woman. They couldn't detect the details, but any of the pupils could imagine the movements of that Swedish woman, Zonzo had said she was a Swede, completely naked, riding up and down the biro, in the chamber of water, as he wrote. He'd always been careful only to show it outside school. And not to everybody. But the biro, bandied from mouth to mouth, had become famous. It was a legend that had almost been forgotten until it reappeared the day of the exam in Zonzo's hand. Zonzo, who had just been promoted and was now occupying the position of class captain.

Yes, the first time he saw it, Gabriel would have swapped all the items in his cabinet of curiosities for that transparent biro, full of liquid, with the naked woman swimming to and fro. He also had a water biro, which was pretty and Swedish, but there was no comparison. A present from Grandpa Samos. What moved up and down was the royal flagship Vasa, partly coated in gold, which was going to stun the seas with its radiance, but got its real reputation for sinking on the day it was launched. His Vasa biro was curious, but it paled into insignificance next to Zonzo's naked swimmer. Something they all wanted to possess. Something out of reach.

Zonzo's biro carried on writing and seemed to grow in front of everyone.

302

It shook like a mast. He hesitated over the question which God created first, the lion or the swallow. He hazarded a guess. First the lion. No. Reason told him the lighter would come first. He thought a lion would never be able to catch a swallow. He went on to the next question. What words did Our Lord utter when he prepared to create man? Zonzo stuck the end of the biro in his mouth. They were on the tip of his tongue, but he couldn't quite remember them.

Father Munio realised first that the class had become excessively silent. Then that everyone was trying not to look in exactly the same direction.

He followed that direction. It led to Zonzo's hand.

They all stuck to their seats in amazement. It wasn't the first time they'd seen a priest hit a pupil. Harsh treatment was a mark of prestige in this school whose motto was to give each pupil a sense of being one of the elect, on a road without softness. Lots of the boarders were sons of emigrants who invested a large part of their savings in fees for this private, religious school, believing this was the best way for them to ascend in the social scale. Other pupils came from the upper classes, who valued the educational demands and rigorous discipline. So there was nothing strange about a priest hitting a pupil in class. Even laying into him. What was surprising was that the priest should be the jolly Father Munio. That he should lay into Zonzo with such anger. That the knuckles of his right glove should be stained with blood. That the pupil should resist and absolutely refuse to let go of the biro with the naked Swede.

The Photos

He had a mental image of Schmitt before their visit to Casalonga on the outskirts of Compostela. He appeared in two photos which occupied a preferential place on his father's bookshelves. It was a beautiful summer's day. His father told him, 'Say good morning, "Good morning, Mr Schmitt," and nothing else. Wait to see if he says or asks you something and then clear off. Go with people your own age.' Several times, he'd heard the judge use the expression 'power of presence' to describe someone he regarded as a master. So, having got out of the car, he was a little flustered as he crossed the lawn. He was helped, as almost always, by the calm temperament of Chelo, who took him by the arm. She was wearing a white dress with lace. Mr Schmitt was sitting in the garden and the guests went up to greet him with an attitude of reverence.

'What are you going to be when you grow up?'

'An archaeologist,' he replied. Perhaps. He'd been toying with the idea for some time. He'd read an article and been attracted not so much by the purpose of finding something as by the method. It was silent work, where first you had to divide an area into squares and carry out the excavation. A method that was valid for all time. Not just for the ruins of the past.

'Good! Another Schliemann in search of Troy!' exclaimed Schmitt. He looked not at him, but at Chelo Vidal. In the luminosity of that summer's morning in 1962, she was the one who had 'power of presence'.

Of Schmitt, all he particularly remembers is when, in the evening, he raised a glass of red wine and said by way of a toast, 'May the fat . . . never dance on my grave!' After 'fat', he spat out a name. The judge didn't usually drink, but this time he accompanied his revered master. Back home, Gabriel asked his father who the fat man was who would never dance on Mr Schmitt's grave. His father laughed and replied, 'Don't worry, it's not Oliver Hardy. He was talking about the German chancellor, Adenauer.'

'I don't think anyone will dance on his grave,' said Chelo on the return journey. 'He's in a good state. He looks after himself. By the way, it was almost impossible to take a photograph of him.'

'That's right, he's not a fan of photos,' replied the judge.

'Who was that Barry Goldwater he likes so much?'

'A senator from Arizona. Supposedly from McCarthy's school, but a lot cleverer. A thorn in the side of the Kennedys. A good, strong conservative, he called him. Funny. It's the first time he's been nice about an American politician.'

It would take Gabriel longer to see a portrait of Santiago Casares. He had a look in Espasa, an extensive encyclopedia that joined forces on the walls with the volumes of Aranzadi. It didn't even give his name, despite the fact he'd been Prime Minister. A pamphlet his father kept had a caricature signed by Rogelio Rivero. A terrible drawing which said something about the quality of the text. The portrait was followed by a kind of introduction in rhyme: *Even knowing God's might, / I still don't understand / how it is he might / turn into such a blight / such a miserable man.* There it was, at the bottom of the large drawer in his desk. The folder for Santiago Casares, underneath the marked, underlined novels by John Black Eye.

The comments in the Crypt were few and far between, and always along the same lines. A general condemnation expressed with utter rage, a contempt that took in all the letters of that name with which Gabriel maintained a hidden relationship. Because the man himself did not exist. The link was with his name. Santiagcasares Qu. What he heard, when he heard something, was talk of a Dandy, Señorito, Mason, Hyena, Murderer, Consumptive Nuisance. A strange mix, words that made it difficult to compose an image. Then there were snippets of information that complicated it all. The yacht Mosquito. The red Buick. The Atlantic Hotel. The villa in Montrove. His mother-in-law, who worked in a factory. His wife, a fashion designer. At this point, the cryptic comments became transparent, jovial, regarding the love affairs of his attractive wife. 'Attractive?

She's a bitch on heat,' was all they would say. He had two daughters. One, Esther, was in prison and then under constant surveillance until she managed to escape to Mexico. The other, María, had a triumphant career in the Comédie-Française. Given how reviled he was, it was amazing the number of followers that were attributed to him in the Crypt. Artists, teachers, the guy from the shoe factory, the foundry, the glassworks . . . traders, most of those who were discussed in the past tense, that sunken city, almost all of whom were branded Republican supporters of Casares, who was stuck with an adjective that accompanied him, even after his death in exile, like another first surname: Pernicious Casares.

Gabriel heard everything in the alcove as if he'd been, like it or not, in a room in Durtol Sanatorium. He'd come across postcards, letters. He aimed to go through all the books in the zone of charred remains. There were almost always surprises, notes, quotations, verses, postcards from Durtol. They weren't all like this, but those that were burnt acted as bookmarks. He identified with what the signature said, what this young man wrote. The way he addressed his parents with affectionate openness, the references to literary works and scientific discoveries, the observations on meteorological changes and their effects on the landscape and his body, the way he linked his physical condition with what was going on around him in nature. Most of all, however, he was impressed by his sense of humour when he talked about his illness, his habit of watching and noting his ailments and the state of his health.

He felt archaeological joy the day he found a photo inside an English edition of a book by Wells, The Time Machine, dated 1895. It was a photo from his youth. On the back was written 'Winter 1900' followed by 'Panadeiras, Coruña'. Gabriel was sitting on a stool, reading. He quickly put it in his cabinet of curiosities, the small, wooden box which contained, among other things, his family's most valuable donations. The tin Lisbon tram that goes to Prazeres, number 28. The postcard from Mozambique. Grandpa Mayarí's cigar bands, which he called little brands: Flower of Havana Cigars, St Damiana, The Imperious, Havana Eden, all with beautiful drawings, especially the Alhambra, which showed two women, one white and one black, the only curiosity that stood a chance of competing

306

with Zonzo's Swedish swimmer. Grandpa Mayarí had also given him a ten-peso note from the Spanish Bank of Cuba, dated Havana, 1918, showing a yoke of oxen with sugarcane. Among the coins, his favourite was a sol from Peru which, on the palm of his hand, resembled a solar nugget. A share in the Spanish Hydroelectric Society, a present from his father, showing three horses in a waterfall, which Archangel Gabriel held by the reins. Picture cards from bars of chocolate, showing aviation heroes and monuments. A few stamps as well. Grandpa Pedro Samos had presented him with a Portuguese stamp from 1898 celebrating the fourth centenary of the discovery of a maritime route to India. A dark blue stamp worth fifty reis. He kept it in an envelope with a description saying it represented 'a Manueline window with the galleon behind and, above it, the inscription "If there were more world, there I would arrive" and two medallions of Vasco da Gama and Camões'. The judge had insisted it was very valuable and would be much more so when he grew up and the thirty odd years had gone by until the fifth centenary in 1998, with him in possession of this marvel, this stamp that by then would be a secular relic. What would its value be? Who could say? With a grandiose gesture, 'Incalculable!'

Fernando Sada, his mother's painter friend, had given him what he claimed to be a mako shark's tooth. He said, 'The most perfect, successful predator ever to have lived!' With the passing of time, as he got to know Sada better, he began to doubt the tooth belonged to a mako shark or to any shark at all. But, if it wasn't a shark's, what was it? One day, he met him in the street and Sada asked, 'Have you still got that tooth belonging to the dog Cerberus?'

'Let me see,' said Korea on the Wooden Jetty. Gabriel had started going there with Zonzo occasionally, protracting the journey home from school. Besides, the doctor's advice to his parents was that Gabriel should get out more. Spend as much time as possible with people his own age. Why go any further? There, next to his home, was the most alluring space in the city, the docks. So Korea played at sticking the shark's tooth in his mouth like a false canine.

'Be careful,' said Gabriel, afraid he might steal it, go off with it in his mouth. 'It's very, very . . .'

Korea spat it out on the ground.

'Yes, you already told us it was very ancient. Well, I don't like things that are ancient, especially teeth.'

Ren had given him the GNM game and *Victorious Wings* when he took part in conversations in the Crypt. He also visited the judge on his own sometimes, bringing old books and antiquities. They'd have heated discussions as to their value and the judge would almost always end up buying the items. The visits were more or less spaced out, but Gabriel remembers them from his childhood. For a long time, he thought Ren sold fragments of history and he associated his presence with a leather bag or a sturdy suitcase with metal rivets. On one of these visits, one of the last Gabriel witnessed, when the two men had wrapped up the day's business, the inspector called him over.

'How's your cabinet of curiosities?'

Gabriel shrugged his shoulders. The most recent additions had been a planisphere and a small telescope. But he soon grew tired of observation. At night, if they let him, he preferred to go fishing for squid with Zonzo up by San Antón Castle. Together with his fishing apparatus, Zonzo brought something probably no one in the city had ever seen before. A portable, battery-operated television. A television you carried under your arm. Not any old piece of junk, the genuine article. While they tried to entice squid with a torch and mirror, most of the other night fishermen would take in a gangster movie, the fearless and incorruptible Eliot Ness versus Al Capone. Everybody adjusting the aerial whenever they lost the picture on the only channel. The mini-television was a present Manlle had brought back from Rotterdam. No, there was no competing with Zonzo in the field of curiosities.

'Well, I understand you like things that have to do with nature. Serious stuff, I mean.'

'Yes, that's right. Absolutely.'

Ren, swollen with pride, solemnly extracts an entomological box from the suitcase with metal rivets. 'For you. They're Coleoptera. To start with, they all look the same, but then you realise they're different. I never thought there was so much in them.'

308

Gabriel read the label: *Coccinella septempunctata*.

Around the lighthouse, in his memory, the tip of Grandpa Mayarí's cane starts moving, calling out names: little Maria, little Joanna, little Teresa, king-king, sunsucker, seamstress, blond cow, little reed, God's bug.

Coccinella septempunctata came into the house shortly after Santiago Casares' photo turned up inside *The Time Machine*. Now he knew what the young man from Durtol and 12 Panadeiras Street looked like, he could imagine him growing up.

As for Mr Schmitt, he was there, on one of the main bookshelves, behind his father's chair, sharing the stage, so to speak, with other notables the judge admired. He was there for ages. Gabriel couldn't say when Mr Schmitt, Don Carlos, vanished from between the tomes of Aranzadi. It was in 1994, on one of his furtive visits just before the trip to Paris, he noticed he was no longer in the portrait gallery. The two photos of the judge with Schmitt had disappeared. The ones he's looking at now, because there they are for all to see, in the inner sanctuary, a motive of pride, an honour for the judge to be portrayed next to his revered master, both photographs having been dedicated and signed: *Katechon*. There's a symmetry in the dates. The first photograph flanked by juridical volumes is dated 1942 in Madrid. The more recent of the two was taken twenty years later, in 1962. It's strange, despite the time that's gone by, there's not much difference, perhaps because the latter's quality is no better than the first. There's a certain imperative urgency in Schmitt's eyes. Gabriel recalls the judge saying it was unusual since his master generally tried to avoid having his photograph taken. On both occasions, the two of them look serious. The second portrait is dated in Madrid and gives the day and month as well. 21 March 1962. Which is when Carl Schmitt received his decoration. Showing the photograph allowed the judge to describe this great event, to which he had the good fortune to be invited by the master of ceremonies, who would later, in July, be appointed Minister of Information. And there was another signed photograph. From the Minister himself. His father knew him, they even went hunting together, but, after the appointment, he simply referred to him as the Minister. There are the two of them. The Minister and he. Smiling at the camera.

The Paúl Santos Smile

'Paúl Santos Unknown. But you can call me Unknown.'

He said it as if he'd read his name on a poster. An exercise in esteem, control, but also in fathoming out his interlocutor. Simply saying his full name provoked a reaction he measured according to what he ironically termed 'the Unknown scale'. It immediately helped him to discover if the person he was introducing himself or being introduced to knew something about life, the existence of a very special door in the city, the wheel, a kind of turnstile, where almost every night newborn babies were left, who knows how many, thousands since Charity Hospital opened back in 1791, before which date all Galicia's unknowns, if they went somewhere, ended up in Santiago's Royal Hospital.

This is what a priest had written on the baptism certificate. 'Father's name: unknown. Mother's name: not given.'

When Catherine Laboure finally agreed to go with him and show him the document, he read it with care and serenity. Had he been asked, he'd have said he felt well, really well. His only reaction was to gaze at Mother Laboure and smile. This smile that was as slow to form as it was to leave. One of the features that made him so popular inside the grounds of Charity Hospital. The Paúl Santos smile. In short, Paúl Santos smiled when least expected. For example, when something went wrong. When he dropped a plate in the middle of the dining-hall and it smashed into pieces. When . . . Some older children conducted a secret experiment. They inflicted small tortures on him, which increased the more he smiled. He knew they weren't bad, not especially wicked, they just wanted to see how long his smile would last. And there was nothing he could do. He didn't know how to erase it.

'It's a tic,' said Laboure one day, 'that smile of yours. The tic of the frozen smile.'

'One moment, Santos. Allow me to introduce you to an impregnable fortress. Chief Ren!'

Paúl Santos had heard about Chief Ren. He'd come from Barcelona. Two years' intense work experience in Crime. Every police station had an unusual character who became famous further afield and Chief Ren was one of those veterans. The only reference he had was the inspector's name. Nothing else. 'You're from Galicia? Then you'll know Chief Ren.' 'No, I don't.' 'Well, you'll meet him.' 'What's so special about him?' 'You'll meet him soon enough.'

What did surprise him was that the station chief should call Ren chief, albeit colloquially. People on top don't tend to fool about when it comes to hierarchy. But Santos soon learnt that Ren moved in a different orbit. Had his own circle of power. Which he carried with him. The chief, that is the station chief, had been right when he described him as a fortress. Aside from a few details of clothing, such as his hat and his tie, which he wore tight as a hangman's rope, splitting his neck in two, and which Santos would have loved to pull loose, apart from such details, Ren looked like a large, medieval defence work.

'Chief Ren, this is Paúl Santos Unknown, who's joining Crime. The first year to graduate in Modern Criminology. We're getting old, Ren.'

'You just got out of school?'

Santos knew he was walking a tightrope. There was no way he was going to call him chief.

'I've come from Barcelona, Ren. Two years on the streets.'

'Listen, Santos,' said the station chief. 'In this building, Chief Ren carries a lot of responsibility. He's in charge of the Brigade of Politico-Social Investigation. But you should also know he's one of the greats. This is one of the greats, Santos. Hierarchies aside, in our view he's the best. In terms of information and in terms of application. Did you hear what the Minister said when he was decorated?'

'That's enough, boss! I'm getting overweight.'

'He called him Great Captain. A great captain of State security. Now what do you say?'

'It's a great honour.'

'It is. He called him something else. A soldier of God and the State. Sometimes you have to recognise things for what they are. Listen to this, Santos. If our archives ever disappeared, there'd be no problem. We'd have Chief Ren's brain.'

'Thank you, that's enough. I think Mr Unknown is like me. He's not easily impressed. Doesn't give words great importance.'

'No, no. I give them every importance.'

Ren's head was very wide. So was his body. But not his eyes. His eyes were small, didn't stop moving in their sockets, seemed to suffer from a deliberate squint in contrast to the amimia of his podgy face. The boss's deference went beyond mere courtesy and momentarily pulled in his large body, which was wide and asymmetrical. The structure of his torso was still that of a strong man, but taken together, Paúl Santos reached the conclusion he was in the presence of a body that was seriously dysfunctional, starting with a belly that had long since stopped trying to be discreet. As for his face, it was noticeably swollen. Santos was meeting him for the first time, but it was a work in progress and he assumed it had something to do with the abuse of alcoholic drinks. It could also be a physical strategy since, when they shook hands, Ren's face revealed a hard kernel, the scrutinising look of those sunken eyes. His hand was almost twice as big as Santos', but he didn't hold back on the handshake.

'At your service, Mr Ren.'

'I'm in a dilemma. I'm not sure which you like better, Santos or Unknown.'

'My friends call me Unknown.'

'Then I'll call you Santos. Let me tell you what a confessor told my rather gullible spinster aunt, "Listen, Milucha, even saints have pricks."'

They burst out laughing. Santos felt his colleague's slap. A slap of intimacy, which knocked him forwards. Ren seemed to feel better, having got this off his chest. He crossed his arms and his body regained a certain symmetry.

'Till now, the only Unknowns I've met were criminals. Santos, right? So you went to university. Got yourself an education.'

'I studied law, Mr Ren,' said Santos, who couldn't help varnishing his words with a hint of pride.

'Yeah, me too,' said Inspector Ren, looking at the station chief. 'It was lawful.' They again burst out laughing as if they'd played a joke on a novice.

Santos went along with it. Forced a smile. His first impressions were confirmed. The tone used by the station chief to refer to Ren wasn't just one of loyalty, even friendship. It pointed to the mental position of a subordinate.

'I'm called Unknown because I grew up in Charity Hospital, Mr Ren,' said Santos politely.

'I know that,' Ren replied gruffly.

'His head contains our finest archive,' said the station chief. 'All the city's secrets.'

'You're exaggerating. But we have picked up something along the way. Now things will improve. Our friend Santos here will incorporate new methods. Long live scientific police work! I always wished I'd had a scientific training.'

'The departments are different, but you'll have to work together when necessary,' said the station chief. 'So welcome and don't hesitate to seek help from a master like him.'

Ren couldn't hide the fact he enjoyed adulation. Paúl Santos measured his proportions. Ren's ego was large, physiological. It had increased in size. Ren took up more space now than when they'd first been introduced.

'Tell me something, Santos,' Ren intervened. 'How did you get to Charity Hospital? Did someone take you in their arms? Were you left at night at the wheel? What's your story? Have you looked into who your parents were?'

The man was wide. That was the word. Strong, robust, but above all wide. His manner of speaking was also expansive. With his arms crossed, he heaped rubble at the other's feet, without caring if it landed on top of him. The only thing that was different were his eyes. They were lively and small calibre.

'I was born in the Room for Secret Deliveries.'

Ren fell quiet. He'd be searching through the Archive for Secret

Deliveries. This is where rich women gave birth to their indiscretions, so it was said. Santos thought Laboure had trained him to deal with just such people. People like Ren. Laboure's pauses were not meant to transmit calm, but greater speed to the engine. First she'd drink some coffee. Light a cigarette, inhale deeply and seem to wait for the smoke to go to her head. Then she'd stand up and blow a plume of smoke, *'Courage!'*

It wasn't easy to explain. A nun who gave him strength. Not with tales of martyrs. Her motto was, 'No excuses'.

'You weren't born just anywhere. You were born in the Room for Secret Deliveries. You've been called. You're a chosen one. You have to fight against evil. *Il faut tuer le mal!'* She spoke with drunken clarity. Catherine Laboure visited every corner of the city. Went down alleyways. Knocked at doors. Left a trail of black tobacco, her Gauloises. She'd go down to the port, where she had some local skippers who kept her supplied. But today she was smoking thanks to a legionnaire who'd gone blind and sometimes dealt in cannabis.

'You can tell good by looking at it.'

She was half crazy. Perhaps the only way to gain respect in such an enclosed space.

'Ah, *que tu es beau!'*

Then very seriously, 'You were born in the Room for Secret Deliveries.'

'So what?'

'Never be inhuman.'

When they were left alone, the boss said about Ren, 'He's not a bad person, it's just he has a problem with people. There was a British king, George I, a Hanoverian, who was said to be an extraordinary person because he hated only three people in this world: his mother, his wife and his son. Ren's mother died long ago and he doesn't have a wife or child. So he's plenty to choose from.'

Santos smiled the Paúl Santos smile.

'I think he includes you in that category.'

'What category?'

'Humankind.'

314

On leaving the office, Santos had formed a different idea about the boss's character. He was one of those who, instead of taking your hand, let theirs hang loosely and quickly withdraw it like a slippery concession. He wondered now whether this sharp observation he'd made about Ren, to his surprise and in confidence, wasn't in fact a message. A warning from on high.

The Inhabitants of Emptiness

The inexplicable hadn't changed with the passing of time. Sometimes the crane's arm wasn't long enough to reach an object lying on the bottom. But it was long enough to reach the bike. Which became visible at low tide and still seemed, on its own, to be quickly turning its wheels without moving, as if it had acquired the existence of a mechanical echinoderm. The boy with the lazy eye who lost control, Pinche, was saved by one of the Phosphorescents.

'They killed him. I told you a thousand times,' the crane operator sighed impotently. 'So don't ask me why they killed him if he was champ.'

'Why'd they kill him if he was champ?'

'What does it matter if he was champ? Dumb boy. They were out to kill and they got him.'

He had to be discreet. Some people were impenetrable. Memory acts like a mollusc, secretes a protective shell. But sometimes he came across ugly, disgusting scabs that were in denial. With Korea, it was different. He felt strangely obliged to try and explain the inexplicable.

He'd tell him what happened to the Montoyas, the gypsy basket-makers.

There's a night brigade in the car, the black Opel. September 1936. They're not out to see what they can get. They're obeying the orders of the so-called Invisible Tribunal, which is where terror, the decimation of the adult population, is planned. The Falangists are out searching for someone from San Pedro de Nós to 'give him coffee'. That's the expression they used. They were sitting in the Union Café, in Pontevedra Square, and the one in charge said, 'Today we're giving so-and-so coffee.' The Delegate of Public Order had agreed, using the same expression, 'Coffee!'

316

The radio broadcasts of a nationalist general, Queipo de Llano, had made it fashionable to talk about death in this way. The gypsy basket-makers are in Ponte da Pasaxe, heading west. So they've all the pyrotechnics of dusk in front of them. The sun will be sizzling like hot iron in Bens Sea. It's the end of summer. Nightfall. They can feel it on their backs, almost hear its wickerwork shadows. But what they see are the purple dyes, from reddy blue to clot-like, in the woolly clouds. The Montoyas like colours, prints, wherever they may be, on the landscape or bodies. But today this is also their direction. They're heading westwards for the simple reason they're going home, to Gaiteira, next to the railway station. After Ponte da Pasaxe, they'll turn right along Xubias Road and then dusk won't be in front of them, but on their left, behind Eirís Mountains. But they haven't turned yet. The Montoyas are spellbound by the range of purples and one of them bursts into song. As is only natural. He should have started earlier, think the other two. The oldest of the three basket-makers is Manuel, aged forty-five, married to Guadalupe, with whom he has eight children. And then there are his two nephews, Antonio, sixteen, and Manolo, fourteen. It's Antonio who starts singing. Singing for all of them. Singing a fandango with a grown-up's voice. Manuel is silent. He thinks when Antonio sings, he's doing it with his voice, the way he'd sing were he to have the gift of expressing what's inside. 'And my sorrow is your sorrow. Your pain is my pain. Your happiness is my joy.' Merchandise on their backs, purples in the sky, Antonio's fandango, the smell of sex at low tide. None of the three notices the black Opel coming the other way, from the city. The black Opel's occupants, however, with the sun behind them, spot the three gypsy basket-makers from far away.

'Gypsies?' asks the one who's co-pilot.

The driver nods.

'You know something? We still haven't given it to one of them.'

And adds, 'That other rabbit can wait.'

No one inside the black Opel says anything else. The third occupant is sitting in the back. Playing with a ring he twiddles around his wedding finger. The ring bears a skull and the inscription 'Knights of Coruña'. One of the names used by the paramilitaries. The back seats fold down, so the car can be used for transporting cargo and people. Ideal if you've a large family. They confiscated two cars from the same owner. The black and the cherry Opel. The cherry Opel, a soft-top, is a beauty. Not that the owner was a tycoon. He made his money in America and, on his return, set up a garage and car-wash. He was crazy about cars. Now he prefers to walk. Avoids cars if he can. When they went to take them, he stuttered, said he'd already given money, paid what they'd asked. He was obviously fond of the cherry Opel. That summer, he'd taken his daughters and their friends for a ride along the coastal road. The driver of the death outing remembers it well. It happened by chance. They'd just been practising their shots in Bastiagueiro, greasing and warming their weapons for the military coup that was close. Having finished their training, they returned to the road, openly dressed in Fascist uniform, and one of the cars that passed by was the cherry soft-top with Mr Alvedro and the four girls wearing white silk chiffon with floral patterns. The driver remembers it with a kaleidoscopic memory. Their eyes were used to aiming at the target, concentrating so hard that all the rest – the ocean, the city grafted on to sea rock – disappeared behind the small black sign with white circles. So their eyes reacted like bees that have found their way out of darkness through the eye of a bullet when they saw the cherry soft-top come into view with those girls wearing floral patterns, their hair trailing in the breeze. They shouted. Or rather they burst in unison into a sound that might also be described as a return bullet. A visual onomatopoeia: their eyes snarled in the wake of the car accelerating down the road to Santa Cruz lined with plane trees.

Confused, perplexed, stuttering, his voice trembling, Mr Alvedro tried to stop them taking them.

'You can see they're no cars for war,' he said.

He knew they were going to take them anyway. They hadn't come to discuss mechanics, but to hop in the cars and leave. However, he felt he had to speak for them. To intercede. Say something. For the cars. He loved so much. It was a moral obligation. When they were returned, if that ever happened, they wouldn't be the same. The vehicles stood waiting, in the shadows, lost in thought. Heads bowed.

'The cherry's just for outings.'

Since everyone remained silent, what he'd said swept around the corners. He realised the terrible import of the word 'outings'. When they changed hands, things acquired a different meaning. As if he'd unwittingly said, 'The cherry's just for killing.'

'That's why we're taking it, Mr Alvedro,' said one of the confiscators. 'To go on outings.'

The driver smacks his lips as if he were chewing gum, but he isn't. He simply accumulates saliva, which he then chews. He comes to a halt just in front of the Montoyas. In the short distance that's left, Antonio stops singing and the night's dark breeze whirls around the Opel. The driver chews his ball of spit. The other two get out of the car, holding their pistols, aim at the basket-makers and force the Montoyas to lie down in the back, without heeding their protests. The youngest doesn't want to let go of the baskets or maybe it's the other way around. He's learning the trade and fingers and osiers still form part of the weaving. The Opel pulls off. The Montoyas turn up dead in Montrove the next morning. Each with a bullet hole in their head. 'Meningeal haemorrhage', it says on the death certificates.

Coffee. Meningeal haemorrhage.

They were passing by.

'They killed three basket-makers who were passing by. One of them was your age.'

'Passing by where? Where they killed the champ?'

'No. Wherever it happened to be. They came across the murderers' car and were given coffee.'

As soon as he spoke, he regretted using that expression. The unreality of euphemisms. A petty, macabre genre.

'Coffee?'

'They killed them.'

'Were they anarchists as well?'

'They were just some basket-making gypsies. One of them was fourteen, another sixteen. Your age, more or less.'

'Did they kill them because they were gypsies?'

This boy, Korea, had a hard head. Other times, it was in the clouds. You never knew if he'd heard you or not, though he did repeat snippets of conversation. As with the difference in age, there were very few similarities. He was vain, always worried about what he was wearing. One of the reasons he came down to the port. He bartered with sailors from other countries. He was crazy about jackets and weird trousers, like the bell-bottoms he's wearing today, which are orange and covered in zips for non-existent pockets. The crane operator wasn't particularly fussy about clothes, but what was the point of having zips if there was nothing to close? Korea had abandoned his studies and had no fixed occupation. He said he wanted to be a boxer. That's what he said. When he turned up with his gang, it was obvious he could rule the roost, but he wasn't normally in a group. Occasionally he'd arrive on a motorbike he'd borrowed, almost always with a girl behind. For a time, he'd often turn up with the same girl. She would be dressed in her convent school uniform. White socks, tartan skirt, green V-necked jumper and white shirt. The contrast between Korea's style and the teenager's uniform was funny. But all this was, so to speak, at the service of sublime nature. What was unforgettable was the girl's long, blond hair flapping like a head on the seas. Together they looked like a fearless, beautiful human machine. They'd circle the crane a few times and then zoom off. There was a reason Korea behaved like this. The crane operator appreciated these fleeting appearances of the blonde Amazon in a schoolgirl's white socks, as if he'd been offered a sequence from a dream. One day, Korea turned up without a motorbike, on foot, with his cap pulled down.

'Now you can see what's inside my head.'

He removed the cap. His head was so shaven it looked transparent, pale white, like tripe that's just been washed.

'What's this?'

'Station house style. A number zero. Have a look inside.'

He'd been arrested. Two days in the clink. He hadn't been taken before the magistrate, there were no specific charges. But he knew why.

'You know why you're here, don't you?'

He shook his head. Which they'd yanked backwards. And were holding by the hair.

'You're a step away from the reformatory, Goldilocks.'

It wasn't the first time he'd heard this joke. The one about destiny. He lived next door to the remand home. They asked him about the gang of Red Devils. A fight in Vigo Square, outside the Equitativa Cinema, where he'd been seen carrying a bicycle chain as a weapon.

'That's history,' he said. 'I left it. I'm not a devil any more.'

'When d'you leave it?'

'Ages ago. I don't know. A day perhaps.'

Why wouldn't they let go of his hair? Each tug pulled out a handful, but also chippings from inside his head, bits of thought.

'It hurts, doesn't it? That's your fault for having hair like a girl's. Where'd this fashion come from, that you look like a bunch of queens? If it were short, we wouldn't be able to pull on it like this . . . and this . . . and this.'

Girl's. A queen's. It really hurt. Each root was a girl or queen.

Like counting hairs on a dog.

He'd always been told there was a good guy and a bad guy. Where was the good guy then? He finally arrived. An inspector who only talked. Talked to him about outings. Outings on a motorbike. A blonde girl. A blonde girl's father.

'Don't you go pissing outside your pot any more. Listen to me. You ride that girl again, they'll slap a clamp on your balls you'll regret for the rest of your life. Do you know what it is to be accused of fucking a minor?'

'I'm a minor as well. We used a condom. Next to the lighthouse.'

'A condom? Tell the magistrate that and he'll make it an aggravating factor. You used a condom next to the city's main monument. Have you any idea what country you're living in? Whose daughter she is? You can't go in there. They think you're a goat. A bum. A zero.'

A zero?

He liked the way this cop talked. He sounded like he was self-taught.

'She's the one who's in love with me. I don't give a damn.'

'Said the cat walking over the coals. Remember this. Water doesn't mix with oil, Spain doesn't mix with France. Stay away from that convent school. The further, the better. Or they'll separate your body from your soul. What's the name of that other gang?'

'What other gang?'

'Don't act dumb with me. The ones you fight to see who can make it to Charon's boat first.'

Whose boat? Charon's? He was definitely self-taught.

'Those pricks are the Mau Mau.'

'Then watch out. Think you're clever and you'll find the worst Mau Mau is an angel next to a senior official whose daughter is being fucked by a red devil.'

He didn't wait to be asked.

'Take a good look,' he said to the crane operator. 'You can see every-thing inside my head. Now is it or is it not empty?'

A shiver. He didn't like the locks, but right now he missed the boy with long hair. He was tempted to cover it so that Curtis wouldn't see. Curtis was very sensitive about blows to the head.

'It looks like a sphere. The terrestrial globe.'

'And you're the one who says I'm not self-taught. That champion you keep talking about, no one's heard of him. There's no memory of him. At the snooker club or gym. Arturo da Silva? No fucking idea!'

He liked to visit the crane operator's cabin. You climbed a ladder and were in another country. The crane was on the jetty, but in a floating world. Over there, the crowns of trees with starlings fluttering about like winter leaves. In front, the decks of ships, their masts, the piles or mountains of material waiting to be loaded, stripped of their old reality, as was the case with goods that had been unloaded. There were the red, double-decker buses, which had been pensioned off in London. Korea had also witnessed the landing of studs from Canada whose purpose it was to improve the Galician race. One of the bulls had got hurt on the journey and had to be lowered on the crane, tied in with leather straps. It hung in the air for a time, calm as a totem, with the starlings flying around. Another crane operator, a friend of Ponte's, had lifted an American plane rescued with its pilot by a Galician fishing boat in the Great Sole, on the Irish Sea. What most amazed him, an operation he watched in silence for hours, was when Ponte loaded a ship with three hundred coffins for export, 'Made in Galicia'.

'They're for a rich country. Chestnut wood. Immortal.'

Korea thought there was a link between things hanging in the air, a kind of sustained vulnerability. The Canadian stud with the broken horns, the plane with the detached wings, the old London buses, the empty coffins.

Inside the cabin, Miguel or Korea could handle a historic jewel. The first football to reach the city. The genuine article. Made of English leather. It had fallen off a ship, the Diligent, and not made it back on board. The crew scoured the port, but of course they didn't find it. When someone's looking lost, it's said they're searching for the Diligent's ball. And somehow or other, Ramón Ponte had inherited the ball from his father.

He also had a pair of boxing gloves.

Hercules' gloves. From his first and only official fight.

'Look. This is where the tooth was. Back then, they never wore a gumshield. Not on that day. And here's where the tooth got embedded. Not any old tooth. Manlle's tooth.'

'Manlle's?'

'You think I'm lying? Do you think he could lie?'

The 'he' in question was Vicente Curtis, Hercules. Down below, at the foot of the crane's ladder, his horse was waiting. Cariri.

'Because he was a champ. Those who lost against him in the ring added their own bullet, their own bit of torment. One of the shots went through the palm of his left hand. A mark left by the murderers. Lots of corpses turned up with a shot in the left hand. But the thing is he was also left-handed. Apparently they made him box. Crippled, lame and blind. His face smashed in. Who knows what they said to him. "Go on, hit, dance! Let's see you dance, champ!" Like cowards. It was over there, on the other side of the bay. A few farmers went down to the beach to collect seaweed with which to fertilise the land. They took pity on the dead man and loaded him on to the ox-cart, in amongst the seaweed, so that they could give him a decent burial.'

'I still don't understand,' insisted Korea.

'How could you understand?' replied the crane operator angrily. 'Your brain's in a mess. You spend your whole day getting into fights, like someone who's playing, and you're incapable of seeing what real violence is. A dictatorship is permanent war. The whole country has been conquered.'

'Conquered? Who conquered it?'

'Cain and the god who made him! You are dumb. You've no sense of history. You've no . . . no visual angle.'

'I can see very well, thank you,' said Korea. And he span around like a crane. 'History was the only subject I passed. History and Religion. So you see. I know all about conquest, reconquest and Cain.'

'You spend your whole day in the snooker club and you've a brain the size of a snooker ball. Imagine Al Capone was appointed governor to keep order.'

'I can imagine that, see?'

'We all have to start somewhere.'

The one called Korea became thoughtful. He wanted to say something about snooker, but couldn't put his finger on the idea. He knew the other was taking the mickey, as if he'd hung him on the crane's hook by a nappy. He jumped in and said to the crane operator, 'I don't like what you're insinuating.' He was subtle in his own way and the bit about the snooker ball sounded humiliating. He wouldn't have allowed anyone else to treat him like that, but the operator was special. An Autodidact. There were two guys in the world Korea respected, the actor Robert Mitchum and the crane operator. If he was self-taught, then surely the actor was as well. They looked almost identical. Yes. Being an Autodidact was something different from, and more important than, a profession.

It affects your whole being, from top to bottom, head to toe. You can't be an Autodidact only in part.

'Aren't I an Autodidact? Everything I know is self-taught,' alleged Korea. He glanced at his hands. A tribute to Mitchum, in The Night of the Hunter, who had LOVE tattooed on one hand and HATE on the other.

Stringer, to a certain extent, was also self-taught. Curtis was an Autodidact. So was Mr Gantes. But he wasn't.

'Why not?'

'You could be, but you've a branch of madness.'

He said it as if he really did have a vegetal appendix, a climber sprouting out of his head. There were things only a genuine Autodidact could know. And he gave him an example.

'Where does the word "sport" come from? From "port", right? When the sailors were at sea, they were at sea. When they were on leave, they were *ex portus*.'

The operator joined his index fingers and spoke slowly as if describing a graft of universal import, '*Ex portus*. Sport. Sporting. Deportivo Coruña.'

Korea's real name was Miguel. He was sometimes escorted, like a boss, by a group of other boys from Casas Baratas. They called themselves the Red Devils. Today he was alone. Wearing a black jumper with two yellow horizontal stripes and the trousers with zips for non-existent pockets. He'd arrived there by tracking Curtis, the photographer, and his wooden horse, Cariri. He was, for some reason, intrigued by him and followed him down through the port. Very intrigued.

'What was that champ's name?'

'Arturo da Silva,' said the crane operator. 'You know where Silva is, don't you?'

'Yeah. The ends of the earth. So what makes him a champ too?' he asked, looking in the direction of the horse photographer.

'I told you a thousand times,' replied Ramón Ponte. 'That's Hercules. He's called the champ of Galicia because he was the one who carried the champ's gloves for him. They were friends. Went everywhere together. Arturo died without losing. Which means he's still champ. Isn't that right, Curtis?'

Curtis nodded without speaking, a forced, polite movement. He had two cherry stones in his mouth, which he moved patiently around like a set of gears, as if he were chewing a clock's escape mechanism.

'Arturo da Silva,' said Korea, again addressing Curtis and adopting a boxer's stance. 'What was he good at, eh, Hercules? How did he fight?'

It looks as if Curtis won't reply this time either. Across his big, open eyes, like a hare's, pass large films. Not fuzzy patches, but real forests. Through the clouds, the eyes watch the legendary cranes, the irresistible machines of Maritime Awakening's operators. In the past, they each had a name on the cabin: 'Carmiña', 'Greta', 'Eve', 'Belle Otero', 'Pasionaria'. These had also gone, though Ramón Ponte still had the name *Carmiña*, given by his father, on his cabin. Inside he still kept, and had added to, a small library, some stills and his cabinet of curiosities, whose prize exhibit was the *Diligent*'s ball.

Curtis' eyes reflect what's outside and the view outside behaves like a thought. The hundred thousand starlings drawing a giddy cloud, a protective bird in the city's firmament. The mullets joining in a single marine muscle that snakes between the pontoons. The jumps of the Sea Club's Tritons and sirens, magnificent dancers of the tango too. Three sea urchins that Arturo da Silva throws in the air in a risky piece of juggling.

'Nothing. He's got stuck again,' says Korea. 'Hey, champ! Hey, Hercules! Nothing.'

Marconi goes by, quickly, in a pair of espadrilles. He keeps making a sound, a constant hum. Ommmmmm. Occasionally he bursts into onomatopoeias. As if he were spitting out screws into the oily waters of the port. A few mullets leap up to snatch a kataplum. A plof. A pliss plam boom. Tackateee! The crane operator calls out to him. Marconi panics when he hears his own name. Who's calling? Why? What for? At first, he remains upright. Rigid. Even his eyes are so frightened they don't move. He's hoping a mute let slip a word. But the operator again bawls out his name, 'Hey, Marconi!' And then he jumps in the air, doesn't look back and accelerates on the back of his hum. Ommmmmm. All he remembers from the last time they took him – 'It's nothing, just routine' – is he'd decided to stop being who he was. He explained to his captors that beating affected his skin a lot because he was diabetic. He had the innocence of people who watch the operation of cause and effect. 'What union do you belong to?' 'The Union of Light.' That was the name of the electrical workers' union. He shouldn't have said that. When he regained consciousness, his body was no longer bruised, it was almost rotten. They did it badly. They hit him so hard, in the barracks of the Falange, instead of killing him, they took him past death. They smashed his insides. Realised he'd gone crazy. All that came out of his mouth was a rasp of words. Disconnected phrases, bits hanging off his lips, which he only got rid of with his onomatopoeias, blisters bursting with language. Shhhhhh, kataplum! Maybe they didn't kill him out of superstition. Or because they'd gone a step past death. As he strode through the city, his humming was a broadcast, a constant reminder. He'd opened a door into fear. So he had to find a solution. Live in another sphere. At an ultrasonic frequency. It was on that wavelength he came into syntony with Galatea of the Seaweed and Shells, spokesperson for the Hypernauts of Infinite Space and the Inhabitants of Emptiness. He searches again with the dial. Finally locates the point. Ommmmmm.

There's Marconi. Everything he owns is in that sailor's canvas bag. All his belongings. Valves, cables, coils, washers, bulbs, all kinds of screws, stuff he's collected to build the decisive machine, a transmitter and receiver of Souls to communicate with the Inhabitants of Emptiness and transform their signals into cosmozoons, invisible spores like pollen, words with a translucent samara or wings like the pine-seed, carriers of a different life. He wanders around the city at night, rummaging through the rubbish from electrical repair shops, ironmongers, mechanical workshops. Apparently his house is full of faulty equipment. A house full of faults. During the day, he puts a new prototype of the Soulder into his bag and heads for Hercules Lighthouse. He always tests the machine in the same place. Sitting on the same stone. With a little exaggeration, it might be said the rock is gradually taking the shape of a chair where Marconi sits. It was there he was interviewed by Stringer, who introduced him as a Galician Roswell. The Hercules Man, a human body carrying an extraterrestrial being. The first time a UFO incident had been recorded in Galicia.

'Where are you from?'

'I belong to an astral diaspora, the Inhabitants of Emptiness.'

'What are you doing next to Hercules Lighthouse?'

'It's a point of cosmic convergence. It appears in the genetic information of the Explorers of Infinite Space. Among extraterrestrials, it's vox populi. This is where I hope to start the Soulder, an apparatus for receiving cosmozoons.'

'What are cosmozoons?'

'Particles of life from other systems.'

327

Marconi always sitting on the same stone.

'Why do you always sit on this stone?'

'It's not a stone. It's the Soulder's stator.'

'What exactly is a Soulder?'

'A space vehicle I'm trying out, which one day will move as a result of the energy accumulated in this ancient lighthouse. The historians of antiquity talk of a Large Mirror in this lighthouse of Brigantia which shows a reflection of Ireland. What are we talking about? A cosmic observation point, an equally old UFO base.'

It was the first time an article had been written about UFOs in Galicia. Stringer highlighted the similarities between the Roswell Man, who appeared in 1947 near Corona (New Mexico, USA), and the Hercules Man, who landed for the first time in Coruña in 1957, as he himself has confessed. They're both pale. Both completely bald. Only that the famous one died and disappeared while the other, who so far has escaped notice, lives on among us with an assumed identity. In his own words. An exclusive interview in the evening *Expreso*.

'See, it made the front page!'

Tito Balboa or Stringer is elated. It's his first piece. A report that will set tongues wagging. His first journalistic scoop.

Curtis blinks as he reads the news item.

'But that's Marconi!'

The travelling photographer eyes Stringer differently, with disappointment, distrust. 'So you think you're clever?'

'I have to do another report on you, Mr Curtis. Imagine the headline: "FOUND: HERCULES".'

'Right,' said Curtis. 'On one condition. You have to put, "FOUND: HERCULES, SON OF A WHORE".'

That seemed to shut him up.

Marconi, sitting on his stone chair, the stator, gazes at his own portrait in the paper's photomontage, next to a strange, membranous being. Emits murmurs. If the question is whether the earth is a shadow of the sky, the answer is yes.

The Diligent's Ball

On one occasion, he let them play with it, the first football. It fell off the deck of the British ship the Diligent. Some crewmen jumped down, but couldn't catch the boy who took it. He ran and ran down Luchana Alley, across Rego de Auga, until he reached Ovos Square, where his pursuers realised there was nothing they could do. The fugitive was safe among the stalls and the forest of skirts belonging to women selling birds and eggs. The ball was part of the city's secret.

There must have been a grain of truth in this epic story. When you held the ball in your hands, if you brought it close to your body, you could hear a beating that wasn't yours. The boy's race. The hero's heart.

'Who was it?'

'One of my grandfathers,' answered Ramón Ponte proudly. 'He was self-taught. Had his own scales for weighing the value of historical events. And you know what? That boat, the Diligent, went and sank in the entrance to the bay. Must have been as a result of losing the ball.'

'Can I report it? Make an interview with you?' asked Tito Balboa.

'No way. It might lead to an international protest. It's not a stone, boy. This is history.'

They were playing on the Western Quay. A place where, between nets and stacks of wood, you learnt how to control your pass, given the limits of the sea. Which may explain why Coruñan footballers such as Chacho, Cheché Martín, Amancio and Luis Suárez were so good at it. At passing accurately.

Ramón Ponte was there, watching. Suffering on account of the Diligent's ball and at the same time moved, as if this were a Biblical game being played with the terrestrial globe. The stacks of wood, like large blinds, enclosed the area and acted like barriers to stop the ball embarking. But even so, between the piles of wood, there were corridors, gaping mouths, down which the ball would sometimes disappear together with friends Gabriel had made in this dockside universe, which as a child he'd only been able to contemplate from the gallery. They left the field and didn't come back. As if they'd been swallowed up by the ghost of the *Diligent* returning for its ball. When they picked the teams the next day, one would be missing and someone would casually exclaim, 'He's gone!' Which didn't mean he'd gone for a walk. It meant he'd gone for ever. There was no need to explain. On that border, those who were leaving played with those who weren't leaving. And Gabriel realised that his family would never have to emigrate. An inequality that bothered him.

'You can't have everything,' whispered Destiny's Irony in his ear.

That summer, the day after the match with the Father of Footballs, they picked the teams and one called César was missing.

'César's gone!'

Another carried off by the ghost of the *Diligent*.

'Where to?'

'Burgos. To see his Dad in prison.'

'In prison? What's he doing there?'

'What do you think?' asked the crane operator. 'He's inside.'

'What for? Why's he in prison?'

He felt the others' silence and looks were directed towards him. He received a word warning, but this time the fear was external, not internal. It was the others being careful with their words. Keeping them in the dark.

The Roswell Man

'You can write about the Holy Company and all that. Beings at night. Holding a cross or whatever. Whether they're superstitions or not, these fears help religion. Happenings go well with faith. But extraterrestrials cause alarm, widespread panic. It's as if God and his representatives aren't protecting us. After almost twenty-five years of peace since Franco's victory, such stories create insecurity, the impression we're vulnerable. So forget about the Lighthouse Man, the Galician Roswell and all those fantasies about Hercules Lighthouse being a cosmic meeting place and write about ordinary people, ordinary people doing ordinary things, other-worldly things, but normal otherworldly things, got it? If you like this stuff, OK, go after it. You've got Corpus, where there are women expelling demons. Apparently there was one last year, all hairy, seen running down the rows of maize, followed by a bunch of children. Shame there's no photo. We've got all these devils in Galicia and no graphical evidence. Vicente Risco wrote reams. But he didn't have a Bolex camera, what to do? Then you've got the pilgrimage to Santa Marta de Ribarteme, with devotees being carried to the chapel in coffins. Don't tell me there's a lack of material. Right next to the city, you've possessed women going to Pastoriza, spitting out iron nails against the door. You've a brilliant future if you'll take some advice. What do we want with extraterrestrials in Galicia? What are we going to do with them? Encourage tourism? They'll attract a few loonies. Just what we need! To become the world capital for raving lunatics. Now, if we had a Loch Ness monster, that would be different. Then we'd be talking!

'We've enough with witches. Witches, imps, the Holy Company and,

331

at a push, between you and me, in confidence, the apostle James' white horse. Every country has its limit. And, as for spatial matters, we've the Betanzos hot-air balloon. Now that's a civilised superproduction. Compare it with those who chuck goats off a bell-tower! Whatever next? I understand we have to keep up with the times, the fashion. I'm on your side, I feel the beating of the teleprinter in my blood, I understand what you're saying. Nowadays a country without aliens, well, it's second-division. All right, don't tell me about the teleprinter again, I know it's informed about a UFO sighting in Gaintxurizketa, Errenteria, Euskadi. I tried to explain this to the Delegate of Information and Tourism, we've as much right to spot UFOs as anyone else. But we live where we live and we're not going to change it, me with my gastronomic dishes, you with your cosmic theory.

'In short, Balboa, what I mean is the governor doesn't want extra-terrestrials in his province. Nor does he want Hercules Lighthouse being presented as a cosmic reference point, an operations base, where, if I didn't misunderstand you, sowers of cosmozoons are planning a landing. So there's an end to aliens in the *Expreso*. A whole squadron of UFOs with Hypernauts and Inhabitants of Emptiness can turn up, we're not reporting it even in brief.'

'I still don't understand why.'

'Take my advice. Stop asking why! We're journalists, that's all. We're not philosophers or . . . selenotropes? Did you ever see a newspaper with question marks? This is not an industry of whys. Why's the US conducting a war in Vietnam? Why'd they demolish the Cooperative, one of the city's most beautiful buildings? Why'd they pull down Primitive Baths and the Health Spa, which is a lot of pulling down? Well, my friend, to build a garage. No more Primitive or Health, that's what great words have in store for them. We could print a full-page WHY? A local, universal, cosmic WHY? It'd be a great day for Spanish journalism. And our evening paper's last.'

He stood up. He looked fatter when he was annoyed. Today Stringer attributed this abdominal enlargement to his theory on the restriction of whys. He brandished the newspaper in front of him.

'See this photo? Who is it? Yes, it says so in the headline. It's Carmencita, Franco's daughter, water-skiing. Right here, in Coruña Bay. You ever see

332

someone water-ski in a long skirt? No, of course not. Well, she wasn't wearing one either. Her legs were bare as they should have been. So why's she in a skirt? Because we received an *indication*, got it? Someone upstairs picks up the phone and *indicates* the Caudillo's daughter has to appear in a skirt, so her legs can't be seen. You don't ask why. You just cover her legs. See this article. There's a quote from a song where it should say, 'Leaning against the jamb of the brothel'. What does it say? Go on, tell me.'

Stringer read the bit he was pointing to, 'Leaning against the jamb of the hostel'.

'Nonsense, right? Why? What for? You want to know why? The guy in charge of words is in charge of us, inside and out. I'll tell you something else, but I don't want it leaving this office.'

His habit of glancing to the sides. He looked as if he was going to withdraw his offer. He believed in oaths. He repeated in a deep voice, 'I don't want it leaving this office.'

'You have my word, sir.'

'I was thinking of publishing a childhood memoir by Salvador de Madariaga. No politics. Memories of a Coruñan child. An intimate piece with a strong regional flavour. Quite innocent. There weren't even any chlorocephalids.'

'Chlorocephalids?' enquired Balboa. The director of the *Expreso*, who was often reserved, had these expansive moments when he even invented new words.

'Yeah, those little men with green heads eating astropops, like the ones you saw around the lighthouse. Anyway, I was thinking of printing this piece by the Spanish historian, which would require authorisation since, as you know, the illustrious Coruñan may not be an extremist, but he does live in exile. For this reason, I went to Madrid, to the Ministry. Naively I thought the fact the three of us – the Minister, the writer and me – were all Galician would make it easy. But remember one thing, Balboa. All this pretence about being from the same country is a letter of credence, a visa, for someone who's planning to stab you in the back. The Minister received me in person and I thought no problem. I explained what it was about and he asked to see the document. He read it right there, in front of me.

Very calmly. He was obviously interested. He knew the areas where the child had spent his life. And the fact he was showing some interest dispelled any lingering doubts, any fear I may have had of needlessly stirring up trouble. Then the Minister raised his head, looked at me and said, "No, there's no way you can publish this."'

'No?'

Stringer imagined the story would have some surprise, but he hadn't expected this abrupt ending. He was shocked. Until recently, his only job had been to record the arrival and departure of boats and the price of fish. Obviously he'd heard about the censor's office, he knew there was a building on Cantóns with various censors. What's more, before starting to write, one of his errands had been to take the galley proofs to that building to be approved before they were printed. But normally nothing happened. He'd once heard the administrator who returned the proofs comment ironically, 'The pages devoted to the glorious 18th of July are exactly the same as last year and the year before that. A newspaper that repeats itself! These layabouts haven't even bothered to change the headlines.' Another time, he was given an envelope for the director. Someone had written 'Confidential' with a red pencil. But the envelope was half open or half closed and he couldn't resist the temptation. It said any information relating to Korea was to be treated with the utmost caution. Of course, he knew they meant the Asiatic country, but what he saw was the face of the guy down in the docks, Miguel, otherwise known as Korea. He'd received a beating. His shaven head was a globe with oedemas and scabs representing the poor countries.

'No?'

'That's what he said, "You can't publish this." And then I . . .'

He blinked. Too much light in his clear eyes. It was something that infuriated him, his glands' disobedience, 'Dacryocystitis! A journalist's nightmare. Would you please lower those blinds!'

Stringer quickly complied. He was afraid the lowering of the blinds would delay the story. So, as he was doing it, he asked, 'And then what, sir?'

'I was prepared to plead with him, to beg. It was all so absurd. And it seemed to me such arbitrariness was a defeat for the whole of humanity.

I said, "They're memories of when he was a child, sir. An old man recalling his childhood. That's all. Why not publish them?" The Minister rummaged through some papers and, without looking at me, pointed to the door and said, "Why? I'll tell you why. Because where there's a skipper, a sailor's not in charge. That's why."'

The director of the evening *Expreso* thumped the table as the Minister had done before him. Aldán was someone who couldn't say no. It grated on him internally like an ulcer of the soul. In his hypochondriac state, he sometimes thought about this, his soul's duodenum perforated like a sieve. He admired Benito Ferreiro from the shipping company, who'd just attended a dinner which should have formed part of the city's honourable history. A tribute to Valentín Paz-Andrade, ex-Republican MP, who'd come back from working as an expert for the United Nations in Mexico. The act was authorised under surveillance, so long as it was presided over by a stooge of the regime. Perhaps one of those who one day urinated on some burning books? Eyes sunken in the fat of time. Anyway, there was lots of talk about Paz-Andrade's knowledge of the sea. At which point the stooge stood up and proposed a toast, 'To the Caudillo, Spain's first fisherman!'

Benito Ferreiro refused to join in the toast. He got up and left the table.

'Where are you off to, Ferreiro?' barked the stooge.

Ferreiro turned calmly around and replied, 'To take a piss.'

'Let me tell you something else about the censor's office. Something you can take away with you. Certain scenes can contain tools and instruments of torture. But what can't appear is their sound. You can see the executioner as he prepares to use the garrotte, but not hear him. That's the soundtrack.'

It occurred to Stringer there was another man inside the director, a restless creature who was always coming and going. Perhaps a Hypernaut of Infinite Space or an Inhabitant of Emptiness. What he said next had a deliberately obscure meaning, he couldn't tell whether it was good or bad, 'What you learn here in a day you won't learn anywhere else.' He sat lost in thought, but Stringer knew he was counting to ten with his fingers like beads. An economical way of calming down. He then adopted a confidential tone, 'The governor called the censor and the censor called me. They're really upset about this report, as if they'd lost their mind. It seems this lunatic you interviewed has a bag of crossed cables on his back, but also a story inside that can't be told. Don't ask me anything else. No extraterrestrials, no boogie-woogie, no Hypernauts of Infinite Space or long-haired musicians, even if they're English. That's the final word. So now you know. Stay positive. Don't go upsetting the boat.'

'Mr Aldán . . .'

'What is it?'

'Nothing.'

'You don't have to keep secrets from me. I'll read you the script. Tell you what there is.' He added something Stringer didn't necessarily take as a warning, 'It's then up to you to get by.'

'I was thinking, about the Loch Ness monster, I was thinking we also had a sea monster.'

'Yeah, right. Leviathan and all that. Where there's sea . . .'

'I'm serious, Don Ovidio. You know the painter Sada?'

'I know him.'

'He painted it in his own way. More like a serpent than a whale. He calls it Antaruxa. Because of something he experienced as a child. It turned up in Coruña Bay, after a storm during which the waves, to use the popular expression, climbed the clouds of the sky. They say it whizzed up the Gulf Stream, first went round and round Marola Isle like a big wheel and, on the second day, entered the docks. People could touch it. It was very calm. Actually it was more like a whale than a sea serpent. A snow-white whale. Its eyes were two luminous slits, an emerald green. With two large black stains like sickle-shaped leaves on top of them. It never broke anything. It acted as if it had come to visit the city. According to the eye-witness accounts I've seen, it spent all its time gazing at the windows. But some considered it a kind of Kronosaurus, with huge canines a metre long, which would mash up the whole Sea Club's team. Not at all. It was very artistic. Most people applauded the miracle. But those who thought it a monster got their own way. A company of carabineers was dispatched and an officer gave the order to fire. They shot it. Right here, in the heart of the city, they blew our myth to smithereens.'

'That's a terrible story. I never heard anything like it. What can that inebriated boat, Sada, have been drinking?'

'A cup of red wine, but he barely touched it. He'd wet his fingers and paint with them on the marble table. As the girls in Two Cities say, it's a shame these masterpieces only last a day. Though this was a cruel painting. All the wine turned into blood. You should have seen it. He'd come to, stand up and shout, "Ready! Aim! Fire! Destroy the miracle!" That's right. He'd shout there were no sirens left in Galicia because we'd eaten them all. He claimed one of the first canneries was for siren meat.'

'That's horrible. Grotesque. Pure showmanship. He should have stayed in his magical world.'

'I didn't believe him either, Mr Aldán. I thought it had to be an invention, all this about a whale in the docks, next to the glass galleries. But I was curious. I sifted through some papers and there it was. There was a strange whale, more albino than white, shot to pieces in the very docks of this city. It happened during the toughest part of the war, on the 6th of September 1938. People applauded when it appeared, causing waves that pushed back the guards. It must have sensed the popular support. Until the soldiers, in spite of the wave of boos, shot at it. It ejected water through its monumental siphon. They shot it again. And again. The docks were stained with cetacean blood. People were shocked, dismayed. I thought we could do a report. Create a legend. That of the whale which came to live in the heart of our city.'

'And didn't they say why?' asked the director of the evening *Expreso*. 'Why they killed it in this way.'

He suddenly realised he'd fallen into a trap. 'Forget I asked. And forget about extraterrestrials, the Beatles . . . and endearing sea monsters riddled with bullets.'

Stringer decided to carry on. 'No, Mr Aldán. They didn't say why. But we could bring the story back to life, create a legend. Have our own monster. Almost all civilisations have imagined a colossal creature. The Scandinavians have the Kraken, with its luminous eyes and gigantic tentacles. There's Bigfoot in North America. The Yeti in the Himalayas. There are even souvenirs with photos of its footprints in the snow. I think they're made up, like dragons, unicorns or sirens. But ours is real. This mysterious and intelligent sea creature, the size of an enormous whale, actually existed. Paid us a visit. Wanted to stay. People clapped when it arrived.'

'What's the point of a myth if we killed it? Maybe if someone else had killed it. Almanzor, Napoleon, Hitler, Stalin . . . But like this, that's some propaganda!'

'What if it never died?'

'Did it die or didn't it?'

'We could write the story. With their applause, their cheers, the people managed to stop the shooting. A sensible officer, wary of public opinion and himself amazed by the creature, its mythical deportment, revoked the order and granted a pardon. The whale healed. Doctor Rodríguez from the Tobacco Factory came and healed it.'

'Now we're out of reality.'

As Stringer told the story, so he began to believe it. He understood Sada's passionate recreation, the vision in his eyes of Antaruxa, that sea-witch, that stylised cetacean the narwhals escorted to the invisible line drawn by Marola Isle and Hercules Lighthouse. Sada could paint it because he'd seen it. As he talked at the furthest table in the Supply bar, he traced its erotic lines in the ephemeral nobility of red wine on marble:

'That's it. The curve, our great contribution to the history of the line, the curve that even stuck to the tongue, as Unamuno said, of Ramón María del Valle-Inclán, who wrote with curves as Don Miguel wrote with frets. This is memory talking and writing in waves, curls, loops, spirals, heli-coid, sigmoid literature, the songbooks' leixapren, the fingers, ah, where are the fingers of the one "sitting at St Simon's Chapel, caught by the waves, how tall they seem", Sapphic fingers drawing concentric circles, inward spirals? All rock-carvings are really astrographs. The first writing, the first art, the first topography, the first house: always circles, groups of circles. Hill-forts. Huts. The inner curve, Mogor's labyrinth, humanity's first neural incision. The whole monoecious coast, phallic vulva, porno-graphic nation fertilising shoals underwater . . . When was Galicia fucked? The terrible day of the square, more or less.'

Sada fell quiet. He had bursts of energy and bouts of melancholy, like a speech warrior suffering from cyclothymia. In the way he talked, there was something of a phosphorescent diver's movements since he'd emerge in a sea of pyrotechnics, then suddenly mist. The curtain falls.

Why not create the legend of a city born from a whale? There were historical data. Evidence, proof, that didn't exist in the case of the tenant of Loch Ness. And the whale was female.

The director of the evening *Expreso* stood up to stretch his legs. What did this novice know about monsters and monstrosities? Right here in the docks, where the soldiers shot the whale the people applauded during the toughest part of the war, two years earlier, at the start of a new dictatorship, they'd burnt books from cultural associations and public libraries. He remembered that. The memory was accompanied by the smell of old, bound smoke. A sudden mist had entered his office. The director criticised his secretary for using a ventilator – 'A ventilator in the city of winds!' – and continued by attacking the country's capricious climate, partly to blame, so he believed, for the problems of circulation. On days of rain, sales dropped off dramatically. Culture versus nature. He rapped the table. Suddenly viewed Stringer suspiciously, like someone who's woken from a nightmare to find the culprit standing there. 'That's horrible. Listen to me. Forget about that story. It never happened and can't appear.' In a whisper, 'Have you any idea how the Caudillo catches cetaceans from his yacht? Not with a harpoon exactly. Forget about such battlefields. How are we going to run with a story about a whale that's been shot at? You have to start to distinguish between what you can and cannot tell. My dear friend, allow me to give you a word of advice, if not as an expert, then as a veteran. There are times a good journalist must separate the grain from the straw, so that he can publish the straw. Don't make the reader suffer. He knows he's living in a valley of tears. So cheer us up a little. Here. Tell us about the day the town hall dressed up rugged Coruñan sailors as Venetian gondoliers to welcome the Duke and Duchess of Lancaster. How they sang sweet, rhythmical barcaroles, rowing on their feet without even breaking into a sweat.'

Quickly the boats
surround the whole sea.

He went over to the window. Barcaroles. Atlantic sea-wolves dressed up as gondoliers to welcome royalty. Someone should write a comical history of the city. Lino's Pavilion packed for the charity concert, the nuns in the front row. The general public trying to hasten the first acts so that they can get to the number they're waiting for. Chelito, who's just arrived for the occasion from Barcelona's Parallel Avenue. Will she or will she not sing *The Flea*? Part of the public is worried. Views the nuns with suspicion, even if they are Sisters of Charity.

'The Flea! The Flea!'

The host, Mr Lino, appeals for calm. Reminds them of their manners.

'Why doesn't Lino sing *The Flea*!'

'Why doesn't your mother?'

And so on. He only had a photographic memory of the Pavilion with its sensual façade. Shame it burnt. It was one of the temples in that architecture, a peculiar form of Atlantic art nouveau, which spread from the Fishmarket to Recheo Gardens, reclaimed land, and which seemed to have been conceived as a permanent flirt, a joyful plan in which both people and materials took part, the wood's voluptuousness, the metals' erotic rebirth, the iron's sudden vegetal will, the dominant colour of glass everywhere, a second nature of mirrors, spaces to see and be seen, the glass's second life, at night, somnambulant, electric. The next, splendid wave, which not by chance coincided with Corbu and the Black Pearl's dockside visit, was of boat-houses. After the war, architectural horror. The violation of modernist carnality. The intimidation of property. The corrosion of the city's character. The dictatorship's main feature was ugliness. An unpublishable conclusion. Everything had got uglier. He himself had. So had handwriting.

Lino also owned a merry-go-round, a form of entertainment for a younger audience, which lasted slightly longer than the Pavilion. It arrived by boat from France. Played the 'Marseillaise' on the harmonica. Children sat on horses in time to the hymn of the Revolution. But it happened the other way round too. When the municipal band played the 'Marseillaise', a popular piece in their repertoire, children thought the band was paying tribute to Lino's merry-go-round with its wooden horses. As the years went by, music and machinery got out of sync. César Alvajar called it 'the twanging harmonica'. Coruña, perched on Atlantic rock, is a windy city. Not just visited, but inhabited by winds. There were days, especially if the roundabout was empty, the horses riderless, the wind, at least the wind in the gardens, would sway on the lonely mounts snorting bits of a nasal 'Marseillaise'.

He closes his eyes. For him, that sound, that twanging roundabout's wind, has to cross the walls of time. Some things that have disappeared are remembered by lots of people. But only he remembers the merry-go-round, its childish, nasal 'Marseillaise'. 'Are you sure it was the "Marseillaise"?' asked one of the newspaper's veterans in the conde-scending tone used with those who have craters or distortions in their memory. Better not to repeat it. Maybe there are memories that choose only one witness. The whale, Sada. Books, him.

When he recalls the burning of books, it all comes back to him with sensorial precision. He had a complete, aerial view from the terrace in María Pita Square. He thought he was well concealed, the perfect place for a spy. The smell reached him, but not the smoke. This was something that caught his attention. The way the smoke from the books hung about. He was watching how people reacted, this was his main focus. He had to write an article and was planning to write one on the art of walking. So he used the terrace as a vantage point. Paid particular attention to the soldiers' determined, lineal movements and the different movements of people who'd turned up there by chance. How they quickened their pace or took strange, curved, furtive detours. You could recognise a fearful walk. Invent a chironomy of power and fear. He could tell it all with accuracy, but not write about it. Perhaps the idea of an article on the ways of walking came later. A tactic on the part of his imagination aimed at forgetting. Because now he remembers it differently. With that inflamed accuracy. The resinous smell reached him in slow spirals, but lots of it was thick, stubborn smoke that hung around lazy volumes. He realised now what was happening. Something he'd never thought about. The smoke had forms. Fashioned scenes, characters, backdrops.

There was something vengeful about this melancholy. He couldn't write about it. The soldiers, the pillagers, were there. In charge of the city. Their leader was the Head of State. When could he explain how Cornide House, the most valuable historic building in Coruña's Old City, was bought for the dictator's family for the price of a pack of cigarettes? Never. He'd never be able to publish this headline:

FIVE PESETAS

Now we know what price
the authorities put on our dignity

If he didn't fight against this melancholy, he'd become mute, agraphic. Wouldn't be able to write or say another thing.

Stringer picked up the cuttings referring to that great Venetian day of joyful torment. The director of the evening *Expreso* had something to add:

'Pass this test, please. I've an important mission for you this summer.'

Stringer had an intuition. The future rowed like a merry gondolier.

'This summer?'

'How do you feel about taking charge of the festival supplements?'

Stringer was nervous. This was something he would never have dared to dream of. He wasn't envious of editors who spent their whole day constructing news items from the teleprinters, which almost always came from the same source, the state-owned news agency EFE, so named after Franco's initial.

'All of it?'

'Galán will look after publicity. You'll write like a tachygraphic lion. Interview beauty queens, mayors, the official chronicler, the most important businessman. You can also throw in the odd social poet or Bohemian artist. Get them to chat a bit about California.'

He tried to stop cynicism ruining his humorous intentions. 'Real journalism, my boy! And you'll earn a few pesetas. I don't want to hear again that you've been sleeping at night in the phone box, wrapped in newspapers. You'll have to invent something for the supplement on Caneiros, the Mandeo festivities. Forget about that novel, Balboa. You'll get home one day and find it's finished.'

'Thank you, sir. I'll do my best.'

Aldán considered asking Stringer for a favour. To see if anyone knew what had happened to an old roundabout. The twanging roundabout that belonged to Lino of the modernist Pavilion and played the 'Marseillaise'. But he looked at his watch instead and let out a kind of password in farewell:

'The Flea!'

The Chemin Creux

They thought he wasn't going to reply. That he too, Hercules, the travelling photographer, the Galician champ's old sparring partner, had stopped
listening. Was moving the dial. Was possibly tuning in to a radio station
from the past. They didn't realise he was walking towards the flames, clad
in smoke that made his eyes itch.

'His one-two. His one-two was very special, wasn't it, Curtis?' said the
crane operator ardently, trying to rouse him from his reverie. 'First, his
right would go for the face, give the impression it was serious. But it was
the left hook that was serious. As if a cobra had leapt off the ground. The
one receiving the blow didn't know where it had come from.'

He looked at Curtis, waiting for a nod, a nuance. Something.

'His one-two. That's what they talk about. And the way his legs moved.
My Dad used to say he was a dancer in the ring.'

'Back then, I suppose he had a good pair of legs,' commented Korea
ironically.

Gabriel, Zonzo and Stringer giggled nervously. They'd heard this conversation before. They knew what Curtis said about the champ of Galicia and
what he told a journalist one day, "I thought you'd come to watch me box,
not to see my legs!"'

'He had a good pair of legs,' said Curtis suddenly, fixing Korea with
his gaze. 'What wouldn't you give for such a pair of legs?'

When Curtis laughed, he did so with the whole of his body. Which may
explain why he didn't laugh very often. Not because of his character, but
because of the weight of moving his whole geography.

'He was good at making a feint. And at opening a side corridor.'

344

'Opening a side corridor?' asked Korea with a hint of mockery.

'Don't you know what it is to open a side corridor? When the other finds himself in a vacuum, punching the air. If you don't know the difference between equilibrium and disequilibrium, you've a long way to go.'

Korea started paying attention. Equilibrium, nice word. He wanted to ask something else. Suddenly looked in the other direction. Who said he had no visual field? Deformed and attractive, her body slightly bent, Medusa entered his wide-angle lens. Carrying a large fish on her head. On top of a cloth that had been so well coiled it resembled a crown. On top of the crown was a bluefin tuna. Equilibrium. Korea remembered seeing her with a dogfish, like a small shark, on her head. But today it was a tuna. A bluefin tuna on top of Medusa, who was wearing red tights. Payment for services rendered. She'd relieved the Chocho Kid of his virginity. And the Chocho Kid had paid her with his share of the catch.

'It seems to me a boxer doesn't have to think much,' said Korea abruptly. 'Hit as hard, as quickly and as accurately as possible. The rest is chitter-chatter.'

'You're right,' replied Curtis to Korea's surprise. 'If boxing were just a fight, you'd be absolutely right.'

He was going to say, 'Actually it's the opposite. The whole time, your whole body's thinking. Your hand is thinking about your head. Your eyes are dancing on the tips of your toes.'

He was going to tell them about Neto. He'd never told them before. About Neto's cure. How to soothe and deaden pain, heal wounds, lower bumps, touch up bruises. Neto, Arturo da Silva's fighting friend. Then he thought about it. Put the two cherry stones in his mouth. Pulled the cap of green rhombuses over his forehead. And fell silent.

Korea watched Medusa move off with the bluefin tuna on top of her head. The Chocho Kid in the other direction. His shirt was hanging out. He tucked it in and tied his belt, which was a piece of string. He breathed in and filled his chest to bursting. He felt he was being observed. Noticed he'd grown. Which was true. His tattered trousers had shortened and were clinging to his calves, as if he'd raised his head. The length of a bluefin tuna. Korea asked the crane operator, 'How much is a swordfish?'

'For that, you have to work like a man,' said the operator reprovingly.

'Who said anything about working?' Korea replied. 'All I did was ask about a swordfish.'

The *Chemin Creux* berthed at the Western Quay. Moored against the light. Seemed to be bringing a cargo of sun from the East. It was welcome. The stones on the quay were still covered in hues of rain, an oily water forming pools in the joins with bits of rainbow. It felt as if something was happening, perhaps because Tito Balboa rushed forwards and took a few fast notes.

There, on deck, with a smile as wide as his outstretched arms, was Roque Gantes. Who conducted a dialogue with the absentee. Heard Luís Terranova's singsong voice. His way of exorcising the pain of arrival.

'In French?'

'*Le zizi et la foufoune.*'

'In Italian?'

'*Il cazzo, la fessa.*'

'It's bloody cold?'

'*Fa un cazzo di freddo!*'

'Now I like a bit of cosmopolitanism.'

'*Prick, cunt! Schwanz, Möse!*'

'How about Esperanto?'

'*Foki . . .*'

'Enough!' he said to his memory. 'Just a moment, please.'

Pulling the wooden horse, with the tripod camera on his back, his old friend Hercules approached.

'Well, blow me down.'

'Mr Gantes!'

He blinked. The sun could do that, place a moment in a passing eternity. Grant a healing pardon to all things.

'Heard anything?' asked the travelling photographer.

'Not a thing, Curtis. The odd echo, that's all.'

The city's urban intelligence consisted of working with the light, its long, glass façades, and following the line drawn by the sea. Roque Gantes still became emotional when he saw the lighthouse and his whole body floundered in organic confusion whenever he entered a Spanish port. But he'd decided not to disembark. Never to set foot on native soil so long as the tyrant lived.

'Come on board, Curtis. I've spoken to the captain. We need people. Experts in cold. That was your thing, wasn't it?'

'Thermal electricity, Gantes.'

He went up to Cariri and dug around in the saddle-bags. 'Germinal's was a good one, Mr Casares' too,' he murmured. They'd taken an age to burn. People always supposed the saddle-bags were empty, were an adornment on the photographer's wooden horse. But Curtis had a few special belongings.

'I studied this book. Arturo told me, "If you want to train with me, you'll have to get a profession." I said, "I can be a shoeshiner. I've a shoeshiner's box." And he replied, "Anyone who wants polish can stick his fingers up his bum. There's something that has a future, Curtis. Will change lives. Thermal electricity." So, that summer, first I'd go to Germinal to read books on electricity and then to train in the gym on Sol Street.'

'It looks burnt!' exclaimed Balboa, Stringer, when he saw *A Popular Guide to Electricity*.

'It is burnt,' replied Curtis laconically. 'The edges are burnt.'

Gabriel felt a jump in his gut. A tingle in his fingers.

Korea was quick, 'If that's a book about electricity, all the fuses will start blowing.'

'The boy's not stupid,' said Gantes to the crane operator. 'He's got a causal sense of humour.'

'No, he's no fool. The thing is books give him cramps in his hands. Even if they're not about electricity.'

'That's not true,' retorted Korea. 'I like western novels.'

'It's a start,' affirmed Gantes. 'A watered-down version of Shakespeare!'

Curtis held the book like a relic, without opening it, afraid that it might fall apart.

'Cold is the absence of heat,' he said in contact with the book. 'You have to know that. And then there are different kinds of heat. Sensible

347

heat, latent heat . . . but, practically speaking, perhaps it's most important to understand the mechanics of specific heat, which is to say the
amount of heat per unit mass required to raise the temperature by one
degree Celsius.'

Everyone listened in silence, reverentially, as if a prayer had been spoken
on the quay from a hitherto unknown religion. At that moment, Curtis' look
had a slight iridescence. Between the dark refrains of the sea on the pontoons,
he seemed to hear Luís Terranova's startled laugh when he heard him recite
the definition of specific heat for the first time, aloud, from memory, without
getting a single word wrong. It was by the lighthouse at the start of summer.
Curtis was acting as Earman for Luís. He was his memory, his supplier of
lyrics and his ears. Luís was finally going to audition as a vocalist for a festive
orchestra. Terranova would sing and Curtis had to measure his voice. 'Can
you hear?' 'I can now. Go a bit further, to that rock.' 'Can you hear?' 'Louder,
louder!' 'Can you hear?' 'Not any more.'

'Come with us, Curtis,' said Gantes the engineer. 'With your knowledge, you should take a trip around the world. And there's a library on
board. We've *Spartacus* and everything. Come on. Who knows? We may
even find him.'

Curtis had his right hand on the horse Cariri's head and was stroking
its mane.

'I can't, Mr Gantes.'

'Why can't you? All you have to do is get on board. Bring the horse with
you.'

'I have to wait here, in case he comes.'

'What if he doesn't come? What if he never returns?'

'He'll send a message. We agreed. He was always late, Mr Gantes, as
you'll remember, he was like that, but he came. And when he came, the
rest was forgotten. He'd come and that was it. If he said he'd come, he'd
come. OK, he was always late. But once he arrived, the party was a given.
He was like a magnet for sweet iron filings.'

'When did he leave, Curtis?'

Curtis didn't want to answer that question. Didn't want to make that
calculation.

'What year did he leave, Curtis?'

'. . .'

'Years ago, wasn't it?'

'. . .'

'It's rained since then. Grass has grown on the roofs.'

'Time passes and it doesn't, Mr Gantes.'

For Korea, an eternity had gone by since these two had started their conversation. Time had no meaning for him if there wasn't movement. There they were – men, boat and horse – stuck. The sun projected the *Chemin Creux*'s prow like a giant needle or a cypress crown in search of hours on the stones. Korea jumped over the line of shade. Yawned and stretched like a cat.

'Luís Terranova? Who is this phenomenon who was always late?'

'I told you a thousand times,' growled the crane operator. 'A marvellous singer. People stopped dancing to listen to him. His voice still echoes in the air if you can hear it. He took "Parade of Stars" by storm with that tango, "Chessman", about someone who's been sentenced to death.'

Korea noticed the last part of Ramón Ponte's intervention was aimed at Curtis and Gantes on the boat. Korea didn't like the tone the crane operator used when addressing him. He treated him, sometimes, like a village idiot. But they were from the same district. Which, for Korea, was a sacred bond. Besides, the operator was somehow strong and cultivated. He had a small library in the cabin of his crane. And he had the first regulation football to reach Coruña, which fell off the back of a British ship, so to speak. Korea was proud of the operator, it's just that they moved to different rhythms. He was aware he wouldn't last long operating a crane, though he was impressed by the skill with which he could load a large block of granite, move it through the air like a bale of compressed mist, and by the elegance with which he unloaded those studs from Canada, the ease with which they flew off the boat and landed to effect improvements in the Galician cow's genetics. When one of the studs was in the air, the operator said, 'See, all this talk about Spanish bulls and bullfighting, but when it comes down to it, they bring in a Canadian stud to mate with our cows.' Yes. Being a crane operator was not without merit, but everything they did

349

happened slowly, with an animal's resistance. And Korea needed something to happen fast. It was late already. He stuck his hands in his jacket pockets and felt the emptiness.

'Why won't he come down?'

'Who?'

'The ship's admiral.'

'That's Mr Gantes, you fool. The engineer. Maritime Awakening's engineer.'

He didn't know quite how to interpret this information. According to Ponte, he must be some kind of local celebrity. All the more reason to descend from there.

'Is he going to stay on the ship? Why won't he come down?'

'Ask him.'

'Hey, Mr Engineer. Why won't you come down?'

Curtis had put the cherry stones back in his mouth and was grinding time between his molars.

'You know something, boy? The day I come down, I'll do it barefoot,' said Mr Gantes from the deck. 'I'll step on the sawteeth of rock barnacles till my feet bleed. From Portiño to Pedra das Ánimas, in bare feet.'

The *Chemin Creux*'s engineer was tense and in pain, as if he'd expelled a hermit crab through his throat.

Only Korea, recovering from the shock with wit, was able to break the silence, 'I like what you say. There's action in it.'

'Where's there action?' asked Gantes.

'In walking over rocks with bloody feet.'

'Have you any idea what I'm talking about, boy?'

'I'm not such a boy,' said Korea sternly. 'I've unmade a few beds, including a marital one.'

'He's no historical vision, Mr Gantes. He's a bit crazy,' said the crane operator.

'By the way, Mr Engineer,' said Korea, suddenly expressing great interest, 'did you ever know the champ of Galicia, Arturo da Silva?'

'What do you want to know?'

'Everything.'

'For that, you'll need a trip around the world. Come on board.'

'I can't right now. I've things to do.'

'Shame. When I get back, you'll be old, boy.'

'Then you're going to be a long time?'

'No more than a year.'

Stringer jots down notes with tachygraphic speed.

'What's your cargo, sir?'

'Who's this?'

'Tito Balboa. Maritime chronicler for the evening *Expreso*, sir.'

'Maritime chronicler?'

'Acting, sir.'

'This ship's called the *Chemin Creux*.'

'Yes, I noted it down. What cargo's on board?'

'General cargo.'

'Are you in transit?'

'That's it. In transit.'

'When will you leave?'

'Depends.'

'Depends? I can't put that in the newspaper, sir.'

Mr Gantes wasn't listening. He was paying attention to the phosphorescent diver who'd just climbed up the steps of the Western Quay with a bicycle. The bicycle's wheels were moving in the air on their own, giving off reddish-green flecks of Irish moss.

'What kind of fish you got there?'

'Mr Gantes! It's a devilish machine. Throws itself into the sea. Not like Clemente's, which threw itself in for a peso. This one does it for free.'

'Let me take it for a spin,' said Korea. 'I'll soon tame it.'

'The bicycle has an owner. Where's Pinche?'

'Hiding behind Fabero's stacks of wood,' replied Korea. 'He's in for a hiding. He was supposed to warm the pots of workmen's food and made a fire with planks of teakwood. That's because he only has one eye. And there were quite a few pots. I counted them. Twenty-five.'

'That's a lot of pots. It's not easy to warm them at the same time. You have to understand about fire,' said Mr Gantes.

351

The engineer looked at Curtis. They were both thinking about the type of specific heat. Twenty-five pots. All together, like large, tile-coloured mushrooms on the burning ground. Teakwood makes a good fire. Exquisite for workmen's pots.

'The builder's a tough guy in white shoes,' said Korea. 'By the name of Manlle. Doesn't show up much, pays surprise visits, but when he does, sends a shiver down your spine. He's a real bastard!'

White shoes next to twenty-five tile-coloured workmen's pots, warming their broth, potatoes with bacon and cabbage, the odd stew. That shout containing accusation and verdict, 'Who made a fire with teakwood? Blasted pallet of the world! I know someone I'm going to hang off a pontoon so that, when the tide comes in, the fish'll eat his balls.'

'What do you do then?' asked Roque Gantes the engineer.

'I'm an Autodidact,' replied Korea ironically.

'It's full of triggerfish,' said the phosphorescent diver. 'This'll turn into an invasion. They'll end up driving the other fish away. They're just like pigs. Cheeky. Fearless. They come up to you, going "Oink, oink, oink!"'

Balboa wrote with tachygraphic speed, imagining the headline:

INVASION OF TRIGGERFISH

And then, so as not to forget, the onomatopoeia. Oink!

O and Famous Men

Don't think the fact he was a writer impressed me so much. For a time, a writer came to live in a house in Souto. A little house that had recently been left vacant when Hortensia died and a niece let it out, so that everything was still alive when the tenant moved in. Except for the fire. To start with, there was lots of interest. It was the end of summer. The writer went for a few walks. He wore a sailor's hat, which made him stand out. Was very polite. He'd stop at the washing place, sit down and delicately enquire about the lives of the women and the stories they knew. When he finally left, the washerwomen would ask themselves what kind of writer this was that they had to tell him stories. Olinda would just say, 'He asks in order to know. He does well. Some ask in order not to know.' The worst thing was the fire. The writer couldn't get the iron stove to work. The house ejected smoke through every crack, every hole, except for the chimney. Sometimes he'd emerge from the doorway and take a few steps, coughing, with watery eyes. His incompetence was secretly observed from other windows with a sense of shame. Not even the most frenzied of ideas could resist such a sacrifice. 'Poor Anceis,' said Polka, 'when's he going to write if he spends all day fighting with the stove?' And one of the washerwomen asked, 'What's a man who can't light a fire going to write anyway?' There was more excitement when the Asphalt Man came. Now that was an unusual event. The tarmacking of the road to Grand Avenue. Years later, when I saw the Americans land on the moon, I recalled the Asphalt Man's arrival in Castro. It was all very similar, but Castro happened first. He came in a white suit with diving goggles, wearing large, metal-soled boots, and we realised – you only had to see the faces – that each step he took was going down in history. He walked very slowly over the gravel, spraying tar with a sprinkler and hose. He was obviously very good since he barely stained his white suit. When he finished, he removed one of his large, leather gloves and went and shook Polka's hand. I felt very proud. That, among all the inhabitants of the planet, the Asphalt Man should greet Polka.

My favourite, however, was the Poster Man. He'd arrive by bike. The roll of posters and long-handled brush on his back and the bucket with glue hanging off the handlebars. When he brought programmes, people would come from all around. That's what he'd say with his rabbit's smile, 'I suppose you were hiding under the stones?' The truth is it seemed not only living children turned up, but children from down through the ages. I swear there were lots I didn't know, had never seen. So the programmes for Portazgo Cinema soon ran out. One day, when I was late, the Poster Man winked at me and said, 'In the kingdom of heaven, my love, the last will be first.' With that rabbit's smile. Thin as a strand of spaghetti. Like the bicycle frame. And then he unfolded a poster, one of the big ones he stuck on the wall, and gave it to me. 'Here, for being Polka's daughter. Tell him it's from Eirís.' A poster for me! The Poster Man came on Thursdays to advertise the film for Saturday night and Sunday afternoon. So I had time to practise the film in the river.

Polka knew some pretty special people. Like the photographer with the wooden horse he called the champ of Galicia. One day, we were walking past the football stadium in Riazor and he greeted a man he said had also been champ of Galicia. 'Look, O, Tasende, champion of Galicia in cross-country running. He's now the owner of Riazor Stadium.' 'Don't you believe your Daddy?' asked the man with a smile. He then lifted two enormous rings with dozens of keys. 'These are the keys to every door in the stadium.'

Polka was also friends with the writer. He taught him how to light the iron stove without his eyes watering. He took a blank piece of paper from the typewriter, lit it with his lighter and put it under the flue. The sheet went up in flames and all the smoke went after it, never to return. This was followed by the sound of typing and one of the washerwomen said to Olinda, 'Poor writer, he's happy now, punching keys.'

The Phosphorescent Diver

The phosphorescent diver and the crane operator were agreed that the most fascinating pieces of scenery were not those in view, but those at the bottom of the sea, and there was no greater happiness for a human being than the moment he felt like a fish again. A bodily form of happiness. 'But the surface,' said the diver, 'can also be interesting.'

He gazed at Korea's shaven head and started to make out countries where the blows had landed.

'Give me a globe like this one and I'll tell you I wasn't here or here, the two places I haven't been, and we'll finish sooner. A friend of mine in the Merchant Navy I coincided with on the *Viking* used to write his name on the doors of toilets in dockside bars, "Carnocho I was here". He went through life pretending he was a king from Mount Alto. Had I done the same, I'd be more famous than Captain Nemo, since I've travelled a fair bit more than Carnocho I. But I prefer to avoid the publicity. One night I was on board, on duty, I read a book called *The Invisible Man* from beginning to end. That's an ideal state. Not normal or abnormal. Paranormal. A few years ago in South Africa, in Cape Town, I was walking down a long avenue, feeling exhausted, and was relieved to see a bench. The bench was perfect, in the right place, under a tree, for a quick snooze. When I went over to it, I found a large notice on the back. "Europeans Only". Blasted bench. An abnormal bench. I circled it a few times. Paranormally. Should I or should I not sit down? Was my bum European? Only the blacks seemed normal. They walked as if they hadn't seen us, the bench or me. They'd obviously decided they couldn't sit down. I again circled the bench paranormally and found an inscription on the other side,

"Carnocho I was here". I've been to more ports than I can remember. I could relate many different adventures, sexual exploits and the rest, but the funniest thing that happened to me was in Korea.'

'There's a North and a South Korea,' said Miguel.

'Precisely. The captain explained that the city we were going to, Incheon, was in the south, but the port was on the border, right between the north and the south, on what they call the demarcation line.' He pointed to a spot on Korea's head and said, 'Incheon must be here, right here. A line was painted on the ground. I was in a hurry to get out. As I disembarked, the captain said to me, "Stick to the line, don't leave the line for any reason." There were soldiers on both sides of the border, two rows facing each other. With me in the middle. You could hear the grinding of silent weapons. On board the ship, someone had said more than nine million people had died in the Korean War. That's a lot of dead. I never thought there were so many. There was that comic book, *Hazañas Bélicas*, whose hero was an American called Sergeant Gorilla. He'd kill Koreans four at a time. I thought to myself, well, it must be true. All the dead on both sides seemed to be looking at me. I advanced slowly along the line, feeling dizzy, as if the line was in fact a tightrope. One false move on my part and a world war could break out. That's when I understood what it is to be on the edge of the invisible. At one point, I froze. I couldn't move forwards or backwards. The horror! How I would have liked to read on the ground: "Carnocho I, second engineer", was here. But there was nothing. Just a line.'

He moved Miguel's head like a globe, 'Here you can't see the line so well.'

The phosphorescent diver is very impressed by the underwater rifle Manlle bought for Zonzo on his travels. 'Blimey, this could kill someone!'

Your Name

All Olinda remembered was my name. That's a lot if you're the one being named. Of all the names, the thousands of words, the only sound that comes out of her mouth (because she doesn't complain, sob, groan or moan) is your name. What's that? And she says your name. Like a stone figure suddenly calling out for you. She rounds her lips. Draws your name. That's a lot of weight. Like carrying someone on top of you. Not inside or around, but on top of you. Only your name. She could have said anything. She could have howled. I'd have understood that, a howl rising from deep inside her. But no. She says your, my name. All she gives out is my name. A wee-wee, a slight trickle. Droppings, chestnuts, quails' eggs, balls that get harder and smaller, like the pips of watermelons or morello cherries. Pips of life. You feel like planting them to see if they'll grow like seeds. Putting them in damp cotton. They might just sprout. Lentils. Finally a few jewels, precious, shiny droppings like ladybirds. Spit, no. All that comes out of her mouth is my name. She eats a beakful, the amount a bird gives to its chick. That's enough. She shrank. Withered. I could lift her in my arms like a baby. 'There we go! When you're better, we'll count matches. We'll fill box after box with matches.' I found her lying on the carpet, bent double, just another geometrical drawing. 'Leave me here,' said Olinda on the carpet. 'I'm popping out for a while.' This was the last thing she said with any of the old, coherent meaning. After that, only my name. O. She'd say O and I'd use the O to give her something. She keeps going on a beakful. The line of her body. Wee-wee. Jewels. Seed. My name. A circle on her lips, a sigh. So it's true she, what she was at least, left that day on the carpet.

357

The Price

'What if you lose an eye in one of those fights?' asked the engineer Roque Gantes from the deck.

'If I lose an eye,' replied Korea ironically, 'then they'll have to pay for it.'

'Why do you fight over neighbourhoods, between Mau Mau and Red Devils?'

'Why? You don't ask why.'

'You're an idiot. An idiot, gentlemen, an idiot!' shouted the crane operator.

'If I lose an eye,' continued Korea, 'they'll have to cough up for it. You bet they will.'

'Ten thousand pesetas,' said Gabriel suddenly.

'You sure about that, judge?'

Korea thought about Medusa with her red tights.

'And if a relative does the damage, your father, for instance, how much?'

'Nothing.'

Everyone was talking about a boy who'd been kidnapped in the city. Pepito Mendoza. A crazy woman who'd wanted a child of her own had taken him.

'Hey, judge, how much they pay for a slave?' Korea asked Gabriel.

'For cotton, in Virginia and those parts, three hundred and sixty dollars per head.'

Pinche became thoughtful. In Ovos Square and Santa Catarina, you could change dollars, pounds, pesos, bolivars. In secret. Under the eggs.

'How much is three hundred and sixty dollars?' asked Pinche absent-mindedly.

'You wouldn't fetch that much,' said Korea, 'if that's what you mean. Besides, you're boss-eyed. That lowers the price. You couldn't even fight.'

Pinche did not reply. He had two eyes. Trouble is one of them was lazy and they were using a patch to correct it. If the guy in white shoes caught him for making a fire with planks of teakwood to warm twenty-five workmen's pots, he really might take out his good eye. But he wasn't going to catch him. Despite having a lazy eye, he could see much better than Korea. Which is why he was the first to sound the alert and start running:

'Mau Mau!'

Élisée's Book

'We were going to the festivities on the 2nd of August. First by special train to Betanzos, from Coruña Station, then by boat up the River Mandeo to Caneiros Field. We'd spent ages preparing for it. This festive journey, this trip on boats with laurel awnings, swaying in time to the accordions, propelled by bagpipe airs, was like going to a place you'd dreamt of. So many turns and there it was, Libertaria. A day like that was worth a year. With a bit of luck, you'd set off empty-handed and come back in an embrace.'

Polka stood up and went in search of *Man and the Earth*, Volume I, by Élisée Reclus. With this book in his hand, Polka adopted the look of someone serious. The look of Élisée Reclus. Not that he couldn't be serious without this book. But in this case, he'd say, his seriousness was well documented. It took a lot of effort to convince him to go to the eye doctor, as he called the ophthalmologist. He hated admitting physical failure. They then spent hours talking. The doctor told him he had presbyopia, which is why little words vanished on the page. Polka then listed the seven deadly sins. The ministers, he said, in the government of Carnival. The doctor was still a child, but he remembered the costumes on Cantóns. It had been a special Carnival, the best, following the elections in February 1936. Processions came with bands of musicians from every single neighbourhood. The child's eyesight may have magnified the memory. Perhaps. It was the last great Carnival. After that came war, prohibition.

Yes, he remembered them well. The Ministers of Pride, Covetousness, Lust, Envy, Gluttony, Anger and Sloth. The sins were all very stylish, wearing frock coats and top hats, each with a big cigar and ceremonial staff.

Arm in arm with them, in very short, low-cut Charleston dresses embroidered with bugles and beads, with cigarette holders and boyish haircuts, came the virtues, the girls from Germinal, the eye doctor, though only a child, had a good look at them, at Humility, Charity, Chastity, Kindness, Temperance, Patience and Diligence. Diligence struck him as particularly beautiful. What he didn't know, said Polka, is that there was an eighth sin. Presbyopia.

Polka put on his presbyopics and, before turning and becoming really serious, made a gesture he learnt from Pepe Pazos, a sailor who was caught by the revolution of October 1917 in the port of St Petersburg and saw the *Aurora* fire cannon shots at the Winter Palace, who was also in Madrid in July 1936 – a sailor! – and asked, 'Where are you going?' 'To Montana.' 'What for?' 'To storm the barracks.' 'OK then.' Pazos, who was an expert in icebergs for the convoys that went to the Arctic during the Second World War. Pazos, who steered a support ship during the Normandy Landings. Well, this Pazos, before talking, made a humble gesture that Polka imitated, 'What can I tell you that will be lasting?'

Polka had gone off in search of Volume I of *Man and the Earth* by Élisée Reclus because it contained a key to what he wanted to say, to what that trip upriver, the festivities of that year, actually meant. But, as so often happened, he forgot what he was looking for and ended up staring at a globe in the book held by two hands. If he looked over his presbyopics, the globe moved, became hazy like a strange being. Through his glasses, it became crystal clear, in its place. He wasn't quite sure how he preferred it, whether crystal clear or blurred.

'You were going to read me something, Papa,' said O.

Unlike his natural state, Polka's seriousness was very dramatic. 'You've got to leave, girl. As soon as possible. Without delay. Before the years trap you and nothing changes. Everything here smells musty. The air. Time itself.'

She knew what was happening. The River Mandeo, the festive river, was running down his spine. It was the same when he recalled the quicksilver glass sign of the Shining Light in the Abyss association in Silva district. That emery design with a sun in flames. The Fascists smashed it to pieces and replaced it with a sign that said 'Winter Aid'. One night, somebody broke off the second part, leaving the word 'Winter' forever engraved on the façade. 'Winter,' like that, with a capital letter. So now the River Mandeo was coming back. Because the special train never left. Nor did the boats. And on 2 August they didn't travel upriver to the field of festivities, Libertaria, for a day. Instead, lots of them travelled as corpses that August, thrown a little further up, from Castellana Bridge, on the Coruña-Madrid road. The dead who washed up in pools were collected by locals and buried. Dead dispossessed of life and identity. The Unknown. In Vilarraso, Aranga and Coirós. Those who were supposed to go upriver, on an outing to Libertaria, ended up travelling downriver. Having been murdered. None of these crimes was ever investigated. The terror of the families, if any were left, was such they didn't dare look into the dead.

'You were going to read me something, Papa. You were talking about a trip upriver. And were going to read me something.'

'I was after a book about animal electricity, it was a bit of joke, to see what she'd say, the others were watching. And she, Minerva, the librarian Holando called Minerva, told me very seriously there was a book called *Hypnotism and Animal Magnetism*, so I told her the story about the duck. The day my mother took it and cut its neck, she was the only one at home brave enough to do that, to sacrifice an animal so that we could eat. The duck put up such a resistance it took to the air. Flew over us without a head. And my mother said, "That's because it had a lot of electricity stored up inside." Minerva listened with wide open eyes. She was obviously amazed by the story. She had a book on the desk. "If you're interested in nature," she said, "I recommend you read this one." It was *Man and the Earth* by Élisée Reclus.

'"Can I take it out on loan?"

'" No, you can't. There are six volumes. This is the first. You can start with this one. Here, in the library."'

When it came to closing time in Germinal, on Sol Street, which leads into Orzán Bay, Polka was so absorbed by the book he decided to commit a transgression and take it with him, hidden under his jacket. That was at the end of June, just before St John's Eve. He saw her at the bonfires and turned pale in front of the flames. He went to the library on several occasions, intending to return it, but on reaching the door, he saw Minerva there and was unable to enter out of guilt and shame. He, a park and garden employee, a bagpiper from Castro who could play as well in a tribute to Sacco and Vanzetti as in a procession for Our Lady of Mount Carmel, patron of the sea, shelter for castaways, he, member of the Shining Light in the Abyss association, reader of *Brazo y Cerebro* and *The Ideal Novel* – to have stolen a book like a petty thief! But he'd made up his mind. Without further ado, when he left work on Friday the 17th, before attending Curtis' first fight, he would go to Germinal and return it. Very seriously, he would offer his apologies to Minerva. Volunteer to help out. He could do a bit of everything. That was the advantage of living on the border between city and field. But it wasn't possible. That evening was the first time the ships' sirens sounded on news of the military uprising in North Africa and people flocked down to the city centre. He spent all night with the book under his arm. There were demonstrations for people to be given arms in defence of the Republic. And he went as well, feeling a little crestfallen.

'Don't lose your sense of humour now, Polka,' said Arturo da Silva. 'Without weapons, what'll we do if you're out of sorts? Come on, pray for us in Latin, it's quicker.'

It was nothing to do with his mood. Or fear at what was happening. How to explain to Arturo the burden of guilt? Guilt for Man and guilt for the Earth. Guilty guilt. He couldn't tell him. In the middle of a military coup, at a time of life and death, he couldn't say he'd kept a book by Élisée Reclus. It was a trifle, but the guilt was enormous and weighed on him.

He opened Volume I and saw the terrestrial globe held by two hands: 'Man is Nature achieving self-consciousness'.

'Would you believe it? That was how the first volume of *Man and the Earth* escaped the flames. The rest burnt. The guy in charge was desperate to lay his hands on a New Testament. Kept asking us. First he burnt the books, then he wanted to act as firefighter for Christ. But there was nothing he could do. What he didn't know was the pain I felt as I turned over the ashes to see if anything remained of Élisée Reclus. Even Olinda didn't know how I got this book. That's war for you. You're left with an encyclopedic volume whose brothers are missing. I sometimes dream the library's open. I go to return the book and Minerva says, "Now, as a punishment, you'll have to read all the volumes." So I have to read all the volumes and I can because we're not at war.'

'You were going to read me something, Papa.'

'That's right. Just a moment.'

Polka was unsure whether it was better to look at the globe through his presbyopics or to see it blurred. He now had problems with the sight of his hands. When the globe became well, sort of global, they trembled.

Nel blu dipinto di blu

Korea disappeared for a year from the Western Quay. He came back shaven, without that showy hair he wore like a mane. Very serious. Having lost weight. Everything in him had got smaller, except for his eyebrows, which cast a shadow on the gullies of his face, as if time had rushed past, carrying with it the vegetation, the flesh on the terraces, the laughter mechanism. Not his teeth. But it looked as if they'd grown like unearthed dolmens. He was holding hands with María Medusa.

He remembered the last time he'd seen them, between planks of wood, with sacks of salt for a bed. She'd been sitting, caressing Korea's crown, while he'd been lying with his head in the girl's lap. They'd seemed to him very beautiful. He'd never felt the desire to paint a scene before and that's what he'd thought he was doing when he looked at them. The stacks of wood framed the couple and at the same time filtered the light in slats like a large blind.

Close up, he's able to appreciate the patches on his face better. Has the feeling he's painted them before. Is familiar with the shades of flesh.

'Hello, your honour,' said Korea.

There was nothing threatening about him. His frank look was not one of revenge. Chelo would sometimes mark squares so that she could draw the oval of a face. Korea's was like this. A serenity marked off by scars. Medusa stroked his ponytail with her smooth, white hand. A fibrous hand with long fingers and prominent veins, which caressed slowly, as if it was going to stay.

'You had a record player, right?'

Gabriel was about to come out with a list of excuses. It wasn't his.

It belonged to his mother. It was portable, but very heavy. If he was caught bringing it down, he wouldn't know what to say. And the judge. The judge can hurt you, Korea, don't you realise? Wasn't it enough? But he didn't say anything. He nodded. Yes, they had a record player. In the Chinese Pavilion, Chelo used the radiogram, a piece of furniture that in Gabriel's mind, he wasn't sure why, went with the grandfather clock Grand Mother Circa. The record player had been a present from Leica for his sister. The result of one of his futuristic deals with the Wizard of Oz, as he called the owner of Hexámetro, in the field of publicity and window dressing. He'd heard his father comment that Leica was made of mercury. He thought he was referring to his ups and downs, but on this occasion he meant his ideas, as slippery as beads of mercury on a fork. It seemed the judge had forever been studying Leica and still wouldn't be able to pick him out at an identity parade. He was a mutant, capricious creature, in his opinion, who gave the lie to his idea of a catalogue of personalities and behaviours. At court, he could tell who somebody was at the first *coup d'œil*, the first *olhadela* . . . Leica had for some time been carried away by what he called the window revolution, which would transform the face of the city, create a new landscape, a second nature. The way had been prepared by a pioneer, Armando Liñeira, who'd had the sensational idea of parading models inside the shop window of La Palma. This was how things stood at the start of summer 1963, when Korea reappeared on the Western Quay and asked Gabriel to bring down the record player which Leica had given Chelo and he'd acquired. It worked on batteries. Why not? Why not bring it down? Why not give this hero of the Western Quay that pleasure? He'd even taken it the first Sunday they went to the beach in Santa Cristina. The day he waited for the girl to arrive who spoke chimpanzee language with a strange accent, had fair skin, greenish-brown freckles, was tall and lanky, but with hardly any breasts, despite the large, pink nipples.

'Go and fetch it, why don't you? And bring a record. "Volare" will do.'

He looked at Medusa and made her smile on one side of her face: *Nel blu dipinto di blu.*

When Gabriel and Zonzo came back with the equipment, he pointed to a space between the stacks of wood, where they'd so often played football.

'Our very own dance hall. The Seixal, the Moderno, the Monelos Liceo!' There were frayed, tattered clouds travelling slowly out to sea, as if heading back in search of a loom for some lost fabric.

It was the second to last time he saw them. They danced close together. Zonzo, as a joke, had deliberately chosen a record with opera. A soprano's quavering voice. He checked the credits. *Ach, ich fühl's.* But they didn't care. They danced cheek to cheek, the song of their life. Medusa twirled on tiptoe, her heels lifting from the boat of her flat shoes, which gave the impression of drunken abandonment. The space created by the planks of wood moved with her. The rest, sea and sky, remained calm. Medusa's long, shiny black hair fell like a mane over Korea's pale, shaven head. Gabriel felt a shudder he hadn't experienced before. To round off the composition, it needed Korea to kiss the woman's disfigurement.

The last time he saw them was a few days later. It was a kind of anniversary and the crane operator let them play with the ball from the *Diligent.* At one point, the ball disappeared down a corridor of wood for export. One of them went to get it. Then another. They didn't come back, so they all went. The operator started to get nervous. It wouldn't have fallen into the sea? No, no. Impossible. And then Korea and Medusa came out from behind one of the furthest stacks of wood, as if they'd been away on holiday. She was pregnant. Carrying the *Diligent*'s ball in her belly.

Ramón Ponte laughed as well. The last laughter heard that summer of 1963 on the Western Quay, when Medusa spread her legs and gave birth to the ball, which bounced until coming to rest at the crane operator's feet.

A police jeep careered around the corner. Ramón Ponte headed for the cabin with the historic football under his arm. The guards ordered the children back home. The port was not a playground any more. They should find somewhere else. The Caudillo's yacht, the *Azor,* would be here soon. 'As for you two, the chump with the ponytail and the disfigured whore, you can come with us. Show us your papers.'

Banana Split

The more impure your thoughts, the longer the cobra that comes out of your mouth. Going to confession as a child, I'd always say I'd had impure thoughts. All the time waiting for impure thoughts. Amalia and I liked to touch our breasts. In the attic, we'd try on clothes, pretend to be designers, copy the way they dressed in fashion magazines. And that was when we started stroking and measuring our breasts. I once had a thought that was sort of impure, fighting Rafa by the stream in Laranxeiro. I liked to fight. Not any old how. You had to provoke it, put a straw on your shoulder and say, 'Let's see which of you can get the straw.' The boys would ignore me, laugh, 'You're a brute, don't be such a brute.' But sometimes I'd manage it, they were so annoyed I'd got in the way. 'You're a fool,' said Rafa. He was holding me by the wrists, he'd floored me and was sitting on top of me, but I carried on twisting and turning. He was red in the face. 'Quieten down,' he'd say, 'or I'll have to smack you.' But all I thought about was winning, getting on top of him and making him ask for mercy. That was the sign of defeat, when they asked for mercy. I don't know if the thought was impure or not because I wasn't thinking about anything. Just winning and getting him to ask for mercy. Amalia and I had other thoughts. We'd cup our hands and stroke our breasts and see how they grew. They grew from one minute to the next, one day to the next, one year to the next. They can't have been impure thoughts, only men and women did that, but something must have happened because one day our tongues became like cobras. Polka said when they got older, cobras grew wings and took to the air, singing, 'I'm off to Babylon!' Sometimes, when we'd just been paid, we'd treat ourselves to hot chocolate and doughnuts at Bonilla.

368

Though the ultimate treat, the ultimate luxury, was to have a banana split at Linar. That came later. I think that's when we grew wings. We couldn't stop laughing. As if we'd been drugged. 'I'm going up the staircase,' Amalia would say after her ice cream. To go to the toilet, Linar had an impressive staircase, of the kind you wanted to go up or down. At a certain height, the staircase divided and in the middle was the cast of a large scallop shell. This trip to the toilet was an artistic outing. Step by step, you grew. 'With the one I like,' said Amalia one day, on her return from the staircase, 'I'll do everything.' 'What's that? Has the staircase driven you crazy?' 'Every single thought. Everything. From in front, from behind. Slowly, at a canter. He can do what he likes 'cos I'll eat him whole. Banana split.'

Montevideo's Cabin

He decided to live in exile without having to leave again. He went to bed in the old sailor's room. Where he wrote western novels signed by John Black Eye and gave shorthand classes using the Martí method. It was all painted for him by Sada, the *bateau ivre*, the double created by Urbano Lugrís, a man split in two. At the time, Lugrís was painting the inside of Franco's yacht. The dictator had taken a fancy to his marine paintings and commissioned him to decorate his boat. Like Hitler, he was a frustrated admirer of fine art. Power had enabled him to overcome other frustrations. As a young man, he'd failed to be admitted into the Naval Academy and had taken his revenge by regularly wearing an admiral's full-dress uniform. But the fact is this Supreme Commander of the Forces of Land, Sea and Air, named Sword of God during the holy year 1937, painted badly. Extremely badly. Above all, he painted the sea badly. Nobody told him this, of course. His flaccid seascapes received unanimous praise. On stage, they disguised his stature using wooden stools and platforms. Positioned the cameras to make him look tall. But he noticed how the sea invariably ran down his brush. One day, he realised he'd never manage to paint a sea urchin. He wanted to paint a *bodegón*, a still life, but the life was neither still nor moving. He had some fresh urchins brought from Orzán Sea, an intense dark red colour. Before fish, shells and starfish, he'd decided to try an urchin. Which seemed the easiest to do. A prickly sphere. No one would bother to count the prickles. He grew tired of struggling with the shape, each spine. This creature was both charming and deceitful. Rather than from the sea, it looked as if it had landed from space. There came a point he couldn't tell what colour it was, so he tried a simple solution, to paint it like a child. The result, however, was not a sea urchin. It was an unconvincing splodge. He felt annoyed and impotent. Remembered Lugrís' paintings. Had him sent for. He would paint all of this on his boat.

Urbano Lugrís was painting Franco's yacht. At the end of each day, he'd visit Enrique's and drink Palma del Condado wine accompanied by thin, almost transparent slices of pork loin, which, before eating, he'd raise to the condition of porcine soul. After that, feeling a little tipsy, like an aliped, he'd emerge on to Compostela Street, head home, change his clothes and then, dressed as Sada, take a roundabout route to the Tachygraphic Rose, kiss Catia Ríos, climb the narrow spiral staircase and enter another, twilight world, where he'd paint the old sailor's room, the refuge where his friend Héctor sailed in bed. The home of an enchanted castaway.

'Who goes there?'

'Sada, the drunken boat!'

He'd paint feverishly for periods he alternated with moments of complete absorption, in which he appeared to be gripped by mute silence. During one of these moments, he abruptly broke his silence and said to Héctor, 'You know? I'm painting the *Azor* with toxic paints, with lots of emerald green. It might even work.'

'Will it take long?'

'What does time matter? Didn't you hear what Carrero Blanco, his second-in-command, said, "Franco's mandate is for life!" We need to let the arsenic trioxide do its job.'

'Don't torture yourself.'

'Who ever got me to do magic realism? Shame I'm not a Cubist. You know what the Capitellum asked me? "Say, Lugrís, how do you paint those urchins?" That's what he asked me. "First I make room for them, your excellency, and then they grow alone, somewhere between the colour of stone and Patinir's blue."

'"Alone?"

'"With cobalts and by the grace of God, your excellency." I projected my voice, like Dalí. You can't be too careful.'

'You did well,' replied Ríos. 'People like that are susceptible to small insults. It's the big ones they don't notice.'

When the painter had finished, Héctor Ríos thought the four walls had disappeared. 'Here you'll hold out like Nemo,' said Sada. Adding, 'All you need is a waterbed.'

'Are you sure there is such a bed?'

'There was one in the Persians' paradise. Made of goatskin. They filled it daily with solar water.'

'That's the direction the science of the future should take in this wretched country,' commented Ríos, who was always inspired by Sada's ideographic speech. 'Technique with style. Mould dryers, boxes of light, waterbeds. Our poetry reveals, to those who can read, a lack of material resources. This permanent invocation of light is nature's simplest move-ment. Mystical obsession is the result of an absence of heating, a poor diet and sleeping badly.'

'Leaving paradise aside,' said Sada, 'I'm quite sure the great Verne sailed, so to speak, on one of those waterbeds Dr William Hooper invented during the last century. A belief that goes with the dates. I always thought Hooper was an invention of my father's. But this phenomenon of floating medicine really existed. As confirmed by the British consulate. Here's the address. The London Waterbed Company, 99 Crawford Street.'

'If you can get me a waterbed,' replied Montevideo, 'I'll write you a shortcut to Parnassus, an obituary in life that'll have necrophiliacs leaping for joy. You'll be immortal for twenty-five years at least.'

'Don't forget to include my sublime nickname, *bateau ivre*, in your obituary. Even if my first name, Urbano, sounds like a mode of transport.'

'Now sit down for a bit,' said Montevideo.

'Are you going to torment me?'

'Yep. I'm going to read you a fragment of present recalled.'

The Song of the Birds

He was the man who wanted to say no. Leica went to Rubén Lires, the cellist, for advice. But found someone else who didn't dare fill in the crossword. There he was, lost in thought, playing a sleepwalker's tune. The net had reached here also. On San Andrés Street, a group of workmen carried a large carpet from the Jesuits' church, which had been rolled up and lent for the state banquet. The bow sought a note of pain and fury on the strings, but the arm was disarmed. And fell.

'I'm going to have to play at the state banquet.'

The time for excuses had passed. Rubén had found protection, an underwater capsule, in music. Now his mastery had made him vulnerable. Visible. He wished he could be a travelling musician, one of those faceless musicians who congregate in Tacita de Plata and wait for village envoys and owners of dance halls. He wished he could be Papagaio's blind accordionist. He wished he could go back, all the notes return to nothing. Who'd been damn kind enough to think of him? Every year, the local authorities put on a state banquet for the Caudillo. This was followed by a session of classical music with chamber groups and select soloists. At what point, why, how, was his name mentioned? Who dropped it into the conversation? Who loved him so badly to do him such a favour? The praise, the applause, to him was a kind of conspiracy. No, he wouldn't be able to play. In that world, he considered his art a crime. He should be in prison. Under house arrest. Who was the music-loving provost, the flower-eating swine who thought of him? It was a mark of distinction, an honour, that a local artist would for the first time replace an established maestro at the reception. Rubén Lires spent the night writing anonymous notes about

373

Rubén Lires the cellist. About himself. He ripped them up, they were so precise they were comical, like those pre-communion confessions as a child: 'I had impure thoughts.' 'Did you now?' 'Rubén Lires, the cellist, is disaffected. Rubén the Jew. Rubén the Mason. Rubén the Communist.' He crossed this out, corrected it: 'Rubén the Trotskyite'. They won't understand that, better to put 'Rubén the Anarchist'. They know what that is. 'Rubén Lires is a degenerate artist.' That's it! Denouncing yourself also required a certain style. Then he thought of something more precise that really would set the cat among the pigeons: 'Despite appearances to the contrary, this man leads a dissolute life. He has no moral stamina, is subject to every vice. He is anti-Spanish, a revolutionary and a freethinker. We were quite surprised to see his name in the programme for this year's state banquet. Signed: an alert patriot. Long live Franco! Spain for ever!'

'What do you reckon? Do you think it'll work?'

He felt Leica's silence. The reason his photographer friend didn't say anything was that he was undergoing a similar trial. That of the man who can't say no. The Judge of Oklahoma talked to the provincial chief, the provincial chief talked to the governor, the governor to the Minister, the Minister to someone in His Excellency's household. 'There'll be photos. A photographic session with the Head of State. And who knows? Perhaps the new Official Portrait. Can you imagine? On all the walls of ministries, thousands of offices, official centres, schools, books. Triumph. Guess who the photographer's going to be, who'll have the honour.'

'I could always say my mother died. They might not ask me when. I'll say, "Listen, my mother died, I can't attend the state banquet." And that's it. She won't mind. She is dead, after all. And she always protected me. I can take her flowers. "See, Mum. I should have been playing for all those bigwigs, but I'm here instead, with my own."'

Rubén was distracted while he spoke. Next to the cello, he looked like a helpless child.

'I'll say I'm ill,' said the cellist suddenly, as if he'd finally hit on the right saving idea. 'The truth is I don't feel up to much. They'll hear the creaking of my bones, the rumbling of my intestines.'

He gazed at the instrument, which was ill as well. Today it resembled a hive that's been abandoned by the swarm. The cello, through its strings, gave him a bee's empty look.

'I've arthritis as well,' he added with a touch of glee. 'In my left arm. It sends my first and fourth fingers to sleep. These two.'

'I'm not sure that excuse will work, Rubén,' said Leica sceptically. He felt he should try to cheer him up, which was a way of addressing his own situation. The dilemma they were in, though Rubén knew nothing about the Great Portrait, wasn't so bad. They were just two professionals doing their job. Worse, he thought, they were scientists devising increasingly destructive weapons. What was Rubén going to do? Play the cello. That's all.

So he said, 'Here, Rubén, think of yourself as a bird that happens by. It's got nothing to do with the dictator. All the bird does is sing. What does it care if a saint or a criminal is listening?'

Rubén made an effort to imagine the bird. But the image wasn't so simple. He travelled back in time. There was a story that inspired him. In the palace of Ahmad I al-Muqtadir, king of Zaragoza, member of the Banu Hud dynasty, there was a tapestry showing a tree with eighteen branches, on which birds made of gold and silver threads alighted. The unusual thing about the tapestry was not its luxury, but the hidden mechanism that, when a breeze blew through the palace, caused the birds to move on the branches and sing. Closing his eyes, while he played the cello, Rubén had often entered there in the guise of a breeze. Time was measured by a clepsydra whose hours were represented by doors the water went round closing.

But the water opened the doors as well.

What was Muqtadir like? Was he an assassin listening to birds?

He could always play Pau Casals' 'Song of the Birds'.

Leica, from the window, instinctively followed the celestial gully of Santa Catarina Street. Beyond the massive structure of the Pastor headquarters, past the trees and industrial necks of cranes on the Western Quay, was the tapestry where, in winter, starlings flew in a cloud. This cloud was a cartoon composed of dots that took the shape of a formidable bird. The first time they saw them, arriving from Cuba in 1933, Leica and Chelo thought this aeronautical exhibition of hundreds of starlings was a kind of fado by fate, a one-off. There was no way so many birds could share a single aesthetic will, understand their place in the history of the line. It was Mayarí who told them, 'They're joining dots to make a huge bird that will scare off the birds of prey.'

But Coruña's starlings leave after Carnival, during Lent. Go back north. Someone had said they're the same birds pecking the crumbs of tourists at Stonehenge.

'They're not going to kill me,' said Rubén. 'They can hardly beat up the musician. They won't even know who Casals is.'

They'll know, thought Leica. Of course they'll know. But he didn't say anything. He was studying the starlings' space. If there's a history of the line, there's a history of the void as well. The starlings' absence in the sky was noticeable, just as the mark of a picture frame stays on the wall.

'Better not to say who it's by,' continued Rubén. 'These days, I can't get Manuel Seoane out of my head. I had a nightmare. I opened my instrument case and there he was. "What are you doing?" I asked him in horror. "Sssssssh!" he told me to be quiet. "I'm on the run. Protect me. I can't fit in the violin case." You could see the bullet holes, which were clean, as if a drill had made them. I couldn't speak. I couldn't tell him he was dead. "Is there something you'd like to tell me?" he asked. I nodded. "Something important?" I nodded again. But couldn't get the words out. So he passed me a piece of ruled paper and said, "Write it down on this."'

Leica knew Manuel Seoane, the violinist, well. He could see him through the viewfinder. He was taking his photo with a cravat tucked into his jacket like the swelling of an artist. His hair was slicked back, but staves rose up in an *allegro molto vivace*. He'd been shot in Rata Field with other young soldiers loyal to the Republic. An execution, that of eight soldiers, carried out in the light of day. They were accused of plotting a rebellion in Atocha Barracks. The whole city had been summoned to witness the execution. People were supposed to boo them. It would be a large public spectacle and final warning so that those who still hadn't come round would finally 'bite the dust'. But they weren't going out with a whimper. All the time, shouting, 'Long live the Republic! Freedom for ever!' The crowd falls quiet. This silence was the last great act of resistance.

In the studio, Leica lifted the needle without stopping the record. This way, he felt he could hear that piece he'd read and reread in the French cinema magazine: 'Following the release of The Testament of Dr Mabuse, Fritz Lang was summoned to the Ministry to take charge of German film-making. That same night, he took a train and fled to Paris.' Every evening, a train left Coruña for Irún, with a connection to Hendaye on the French border. It was full of Galician emigrants going to work in France. Rubén paid him attention. He'd leave on that train tonight.

'You have to leave right now,' Leica had told him suddenly. 'Don't think about it. Take your instrument and go on that train.'

How nice to hear that. To hear himself, albeit telling someone else. He gazed at the camera. He knew what the camera was thinking. It was jealous of the cello leaving on the train, with a seat all to itself.

Leica and Silvia

'It's the camera that takes the photos. Decides whether it likes the people. Picks them. Moves them. Makes them foggy. It's a good camera, sure enough, but most of the photos are pretty bad. When there's a good one, you could say an image has been born for humanity. It's down to the camera. The images it's been through! I'm not surprised it's a little manic, capricious. There was a time, in its youth, when it took photos with great pleasure. It was very clever. Found light where there wasn't any. And it's done a lot of things it didn't like, just for me. People sometimes do things against their will and end up feeling they like them. I haven't got that far. My problem is I don't know how to say no. So it's the camera that takes most of the decisions. Here, take a look. If you're that beautiful, blame the camera. It's the camera's fault.'

'Oh, come on!'

'No, it's true. There was a time I wanted to be an artist, photographer wasn't enough. Luís Huici, who was an artist and a tailor, told me one day, "The important thing in life, and in art, is not to bore people. To give or not to give, that's the measure of a piece of art. Here is a gift."'

The first time he entered his workshop on Cantóns, Huici handed him the magazine *Alfar*, a transatlantic undertaking to combat boredom. His workshop was a landing stage for avant-garde movements, its very own port. There were novelties, books or fabrics, you couldn't find anywhere else. There were people who went just to touch things. *Ulysses* by James Joyce, for example, that book that had everyone talking and had reached Huici's workshop by sea. There it was, a real, living being you could open and pluck words from: 'Those girls, those girls, those lovely seaside girls.'

Packages arrived, containing manifestos and publications: a gift. They'd open them and almost always come across a new species, an image, form or question that hadn't existed before. When he showed him *Alfar*, the copies were bound with an animal black ribbon. The artist and tailor was incredibly precise about colours. A jacket the colour of a fox's tail. A coat the colour of maize bread from Carral. A face as white as a sleepless night. This ribbon he said was animal black. Whenever Huici's name came into his mind, he saw those fingers untying the ribbon. As well as helping him to make a living, tailoring was, for Huici, a practical way of contributing to the city. People were the most active creators of landscape. They were like walking trees, mutating pieces of architecture. A man or a woman represented a nomadic nation. As they walked through the city, they wrote, drew and painted.

Every once in a while, something would happen to affect the composition. Suddenly the idea of nomadic culture ceased to have a figurative meaning. Lots of people, openly carrying their nomadic symbol, a suitcase, gathered in the port and disappeared from the landscape. This was a question Huici asked himself, 'When will we stop exporting sadness?'

Even though they accused him of being a snob, he used to talk about popular elegance. Elegance was to be found in the quality of the person, their style, and not necessarily in how much the piece cost. Coruña was a city of seamstresses. The ships that exported sadness also brought novelties. These seamstresses took photos with their imagination, copied or adjusted designs they saw on the first-class gangways of liners. They did haute couture, using humble fabrics. Huici visited popular markets and fairs in a daze. He admired the seamstresses. He once saw a group of them on Cantóns, each with a portable Singer on top of her head. There were lots of people on the city's busiest thoroughfare, but for a moment it seemed as if a corridor was opened to allow the sewing women through. He made lots of sketches of that image he described as an amusing Biblical interlude. Make way for the seamstresses!

He ties the pure, animal black ribbon. Goodbye, Huici. Looks at Silvia, the seamstress. We have the beauty of the face. Now what we've got to do is a session which shows all the beauty. That which exists, but is hidden.

'This portrait is wonderful, Silvia. Now what we need is a full-length portrait. What do you think?'

But Silvia was not the type to answer every question. She had moments of intriguing silence. Like now. Her eyes did the talking. A look that went from inside out and from outside in. Active melancholy with cinematographic curiosity.

'The portraits will be good,' said Leica. 'The camera loves you. We'll use the photos to persuade some advertisers. It's not easy making an advert with models from here. Everything comes from abroad. People believe everything from abroad is better. Everything modern has to come from abroad. I think otherwise. An optical revolution, you see? Publicity is one of the things that's going to change this country. We've been putting up with sad publicity for years. Digestive tonics, anti-dandruff lotions, restorative syrups. But now's the time for electrical appliances. Housework will no longer be thought of as a punishment. The home will become a paradise. The woman's smile when she opens the refrigerator. I know I'm exaggerating. But there's no publicity without exaggeration. No publicity, no art, nothing.'

'You can take photos of me,' she said suddenly. 'But not nude. Not without clothes.'

He gestured as if to protest. Was about to explain something. But, for some reason, decided to stay silent.

'I'm fragile,' said Silvia. 'I know where I am.'

She then surprised him by saying, 'I don't want your camera to feel guilty. If I take my clothes off, it'll be because I'm with you, not for a photo.'

None of the girls he'd taken to his studio had ever spoken to him like that. Some had got angry or cursed him, feeling duped. But they'd never spoken to him like that before.

'I have to protect myself because, if I don't, no one will. I know where I am. I prefer not to embarrass myself.'

'OK. Forget about the nude photos, but don't say that, that no one will protect you.'

'It's true. You might love me one day,' she said in a mysterious tone, 'but you'll never protect me.'

* * *

380

He was crazy about her. Just seeing her drove him crazy. I'm not surprised. As a girl, after she left hospital, she carried a portable sewing machine on top of her head. She went from village to village, over the mountains. With the sun and mists. Having to find shelter from the rains and storms. Easy to say, not so easy to do. That's what happened with Silvia, thought O. No, I'm not at all surprised Leica, Chelo Vidal's brother, was so captivated. I said to myself, If he takes a photo of that girl who's going by, if he takes a photo right now, she'll stick in his head, in the workshop of his head, and never leave. It seems to me, in the case of beauty, little is more. Perhaps because you have the impression it's close at hand. That's what happened to Leica, he lost his head for the little girl with locks sprawling down her back like a shawl.

He went crazy, he did. Some things are understood between women carrying things on top of their heads. And that's what happened, we knew he was head over heels. He took some photos of her for an advert. It wasn't like other times, no. This time, he gave himself. Went after her. Loved her more than that boys' bet he had with himself to bed every girl he used as a model. But one day Silvia left. We don't know the reason. She was refused papers for being the daughter of who she was, one who died up in the mountains. As a girl, she was taught invisible mending. Apparently there was no one who could do what she did: reconstruct an old garment. She worked with the memory of the clothes. In the folds, nooks, hidden places of vestments, she found threads with which to graft and renew. Thread by thread, she could mend a worn-out elbow or a twist of silk.

She was thin, small, with big eyes. Big eyes and big fingers. Her whole body seemed to be at the disposal of her eyes and fingers. Silvia's arms were very skinny. Which is why your attention was drawn to her hands, the long, pliant fingers that moved with the memory of movements.

She was given a special assignment. 'A very special assignment,' insisted the nuns in Domestic Service. Whoever it was had to be very important if they were being so secretive. The garment was destined for a museum, but there was a certain urgency because someone wanted it ready as soon as possible. Mother Asun gestured with her thumb, pointing very seriously upwards, but without raising her eyes. This meant whoever it was was high up, but not God. It wasn't God's stole or the Holy Spirit's alb that needed invisible mending. Silvia understood Mother Asun well. It might be said they understood each other with the inside of words. It was she who taught the girl her first stitches when she was confined to bed. Worse than that, when she was tied down to the bed with belts so that she couldn't move or get up during the night and most of the day. When she did get up, it was to eat and learn how to sew. She'd need something to do when she became a normal girl and her spine straightened. Thinking about that, about her backbone, she feels like an icicle. Lying down for years, in Oza, tied with belts, unable to walk. The diagnosis was that the deformed spine had to be controlled to stop a curve or a hump forming. All of which suffering could have been avoided with a simple treatment of penicillin. They also got up – there was a whole room of them, of 'imprisoned girls' – to receive communion on Sundays and feast days. With the priest came an acolyte who carried a tray with the wafers. He was the most charming boy Silvia had ever seen. Since she hadn't seen many, we might say he was the prettiest boy imaginable. What she felt when her body was untied for communion was real hunger, an overriding desire to prolong her mouth's movement and bite his hand and sew the boy with kisses. She knew they were not a girl's feelings. But she wasn't the age she was. Her enforced immobility made her live life so intensely that, when she finally got up, staggered to the window not only to see the sea she'd heard murmuring for months on end, but also to find a support, when she did this, she realised she'd already lived various lives and now had to try to rein them into her body or else go in search of them.

The sea entered her eyes with such force it made her cry. And a howl rose from inside her. Not a human shout, but a sea-howl. She thought at that moment she'd been tied not because of an incorrect diagnosis or the absurd idea of straightening her spine by force, but deliberately to keep her away from the sea. She couldn't stop crying. She'd spent years with dry eyes. The tears had to come with a swell from her body. Of all the lives she'd lived without moving, she chose one. To be the woman of invisible mending. Asun had taught her this art when she saw the skills of all her other senses were in her fingers. Silvia had long, thin fingers. After time spent in a hospital bed, her body was very skinny. Her arms were like elder branches. But her hands ran wild when sewing and embroidering. Played at shadow puppets, which played with her hands and made them longer.

'Big hands,' said Leica one day, interlocking fingers. 'A miniaturist's big hands.'

A group of worthies in the city wanted to give the dictator an unusual present. He was Supreme Commander of the Forces of Land, Sea and Air, he was described in the papers as Sword of the Most High, and yet he had a thorn stuck in his pride. The fact he had failed to enter the Naval Academy as a young man. His ambition was to be an admiral. So, when he achieved absolute power, his favourite outfit, which he wore on special days, was the Navy officer's full-dress uniform, worn by admirals in Ferrol only on Good Friday. It was in this uniform he had an important portrait done of himself wearing the Grand Laurelled Cross of St Ferdinand on his chest, holding some binoculars. The local authorities had already given him the manor of Meirás, which he travelled to Coruña in 1937, at the height of the war, to take possession of. He was then presented with the finest building in the Old City, Cornide House. The city's richest man, the banker Barrié, sold it to him for the sum of five pesetas. An emotional exchange, not without symbolism. Franco paid with one of those small coins bearing his face and the legend 'Caudillo of Spain by the grace of God'. The banker would later be named Count of the Electric Forces of the Northwest or Count of Fenosa. No, there was no point competing in new property values. Now that the twenty-fifth anniversary of providential leadership was coming, this new present had to be highly symbolic, something that would both surprise Franco and touch his heart. Why not go beyond the admiralty?

The idea came up at a dinner in the yacht club, hosted by the governor. They're all agreed. The governor is waiting to hear something so that he can assume the proposal as his own. One of the guests is Máximo Borrell, Franco's favourite fishing companion, described by him in front of everyone as 'an intimate friend', which gives his opinion the rank of placet. The proposal came from the judge Ricardo Samos, with his historical, one might say warlike knowledge, who, because of their parallel lives, is close to the governor, since they go hunting together. Samos has some very important information. A clue. He recalls an old conversation among Navy officers, at which his father was present. Yes, there was something of the stature required by history, which could move Franco, not an easy task.

'A majestic, royal cape.'

'Sounds good,' said the governor. 'Sounds wonderful.'

The judge explained. A festal cape had once been prepared for King Alfonso XIII to celebrate a planned visit to Galicia, which was meant to protect his royal highness during a naval display to be held in his honour. But such a portentous ceremony never took place. It was cancelled due to bad weather. The king never wore the cape. It wasn't even collected. As a result of bureaucratic intricacies, no one was willing to take charge of the commission. So the tailor decided he'd use it himself. It was a magnificent cape. And still is. Because that cape exists.

'And it's only been worn by the tailor?'

'That's right. You could say he was trying it on.'

The judge pulled a note from his inside pocket. Read the following: 'Festal cape for Alfonso XIII. Sea-blue armure fabric, night-blue velvet collar with golden-threaded soutache, red lining and a fastening of golden braid in cable-stitch. The vestment is in a reasonable state and can be recovered despite the intervening years. The fastening is a little frayed, the velvet soutache completely worn and there's a tear in the armure on the right shoulder as well as open seams in the fabric and lining. While of good quality, the velvet requires special treatment since it's been compressed. For the cape to return to its former splendour would need painstaking attention and invisible mending, since the use of new materials is out of the question, which would only detract from the garment's historical value.'

'Not exactly a piece of cake, Samos,' observed the governor with concern.

'The garment is unique. Historic. Don't think about the tears, think about the meaning. A royal cape is worn by Franco for the first time in public. "Your excellency, we humbly offer you this cape as Majesty of the Sea."'

'With those words! Those very words! Exactly. Write them down.'

'I won't forget them,' said Samos.

'Yes, but I will,' said the governor.

'Darning's no good. It's an extremely difficult, delicate task. That requires a surgeon. The only people who can do this,' the governor is informed, 'are the nuns in Domestic Service. They're the ones responsible for handing down the art of invisible mending.' When Mother Asun is shown the garment, she blinks and contorts her face. 'You'd have to work with tiny threads, use filaments the size of eyebrows.' She no longer has the eyes or hands for such a job.

'Who can do it with certainty?' asks the governor's secretary, who doesn't want to fail in this special mission. 'They can ask what they like.'

'Only Silvia can do this.'

'Silvia? Tell me where to find her.'

'No. We'll do it differently,' said the nun. 'I'll get in contact. She also is a special, sensitive case. Who's it for? It's important to know who will be using the garment.'

'It's an order from the governor, mother. A priority matter. It's a museum piece for which there's a special urgency. That's all I can say.'

Having spoken to Mother Asun, Silvia went for a long walk in the docks. It was midday. She saw the champion of Galicia with the horse Carirí and thought of Leica. This time, she said yes, she'd have her photo taken. Medusa was on the Wooden Jetty, sitting on an oak beam that would be used as a sleeper. She looked like the only inhabitant of a strange, empty city built on stakes behind her. Silvia couldn't help watching her. Whenever she went that way, the same thing happened. She was bewitched by that woman who only revealed half of her face, as if she were a black-and-white figure. Medusa stood up. The way they walked, they resembled two inter-linked people moving as one. One pulling the other. One forward, the other cautious, so that they walked with a mixture of brazenness and shyness. Or rather arrogance and fear.

She came up to her and asked for a cigarette.

'I haven't got any,' replied Silvia. 'It's true. I don't smoke.'

'I didn't ask whether you smoked or not,' said Medusa. 'What do I care whether you smoke or not? This is a city of chatterboxes. Ask for a cigarette and they start giving you their life story.'

Her hair was smooth, very black, and hung like a jet mane. When she talked, it swayed slightly and the shine created drawings that resembled brocade. Silvia would have paid her to carry on talking like this against the world.

'Why don't you give me something?'

She said this when Silvia was already rummaging through her purse.

'Do you want to see my face? I'll let you see it all for ten pesetas.'

Silvia paid up. And waited. But Medusa said, 'If you want to see it, you'll have to unveil it yourself.' Silvia held out her arm and stroked the smooth hair with her fingers, but didn't pull it back to see the hidden face.

'Go on. I'm not a monster, you know.'

Silvia withdrew her hand, turned around and quickly walked away.

That afternoon, a woman visited her in her rented room, as she and Mother Asun had agreed. A civil servant who carried out her instructions to the letter. She brought the cape with her in a protective covering. It was a garment of great historical value that needed restoring for an important exhibition. She could name her price. And conditions. There wouldn't be a problem.

Silvia explained that her work was measured by time. When she'd finished, she'd tell them how much it cost.

As she turned to leave, the woman said, 'Oh, I almost forgot! Greetings from Rocío.'

'Who's Rocío?'

'A colleague. She said she knew you.'

Silvia shrugged her shoulders, 'Well, say hello then.'

Silvia didn't want Leica to accompany her home or to visit her. Her rented room, in Gaiteira, was near the old railway station. She tried to avoid having contact with the other tenants or drawing attention. The people there were very silent and those that weren't old seemed to want to grow old before their time. The house, the solidity of the shadows, the taciturn furniture, the murmuring mattresses, the hysterical indiscretion of the cistern above the only toilet in a tiny, communal bathroom. She was there in passing and did not wish to leave any trace, even of the air that went through her lungs. She wanted to put everything, the air and the light, in a suitcase and take them with her when she left. Poor air, poor light. Her only joy was the sound of the trains as they stopped and pulled off. When she sewed, she tried to work her little Singer in time to the engines. But now she had an urgent task. She devoted all her free time to invisible mending. To that very special undertaking.

There was a ring at the doorbell and her sense of alert told her to go and open the front door but, when she entered the hallway, another tenant, Miss Elisa, had already answered. This woman smelt permanently of spices. Her hands were always stained. Her work, which was endless, was to wrap up pinches of cumin, saffron and paprika in tiny paper envelopes she folded at astonishing speed with her small hands and fat, sausage-like fingers. Silvia's invisible mending and Miss Elisa's work wrapping spices took place simultaneously, but belonged to two opposing hemispheres of time.

When she saw Leica in the hallway, politely thanking Miss Elisa for being so kind as to open the front door, Silvia was surprised not to feel bothered. She actually did something she would never have allowed herself to do, especially in that house. She embraced him and let him lift her off the floor. He was radiant.

'I know I shouldn't have, but I couldn't help it. We did it, Silvia! They're going to use your photo in the advert. In the window of Hexámetro! The first advert for electrical appliances with a local model. And Hercules Lighthouse in the background!'

He moved around the room like a master of ceremonies who opens his arms to turn on the lights. A master of ceremonies who plucks landscapes from the walls. Silvia witnessed her room's conversion. What had been behind the window came inside. Her room was a railway carriage in the station. She suddenly felt like hearing the sewing machine. A breath of animal and machine filtered through the joins between the floor tiles. The bed didn't sound embittered as usual. The bed listened to their bodies.

By the time they got up, the station was outside the room, without carriages, and the porter boys, the driver of the hire car, the florist, newsagent and shoeshiner seemed to be frozen. Painted. Only two figures moved up and down the platform. One was wearing a hat, both of them were wearing coats tied with a belt. One was short and fat, the other taller and thinner. They looked to Silvia like a comical, sinister pair. And seemed from time to time to glance over at her window. And perhaps they did.

'What's this cape?' asked Leica. The royal cape suddenly attained the status of a mysterious presence. He said, 'It looks like a garment with history.'

'Something the nuns asked me to do,' she replied. 'An urgent job for a museum. That's all I know.'

Silvia explained how the task was almost impossible. She could only use the garment's own threads. An extremely delicate operation. Rather than finding them, she would have to invent them one by one in order to reconstruct the warp.

'I'll be at it day and night.'

'Now that you're a publicity star? In this country, history always spoils everything.'

They again fell into an embrace. Something to do with their bodies. It's not easy to let go of the melancholy of bodies.

He had something to say, but he couldn't bring himself to do it. He hadn't even been able to tell Curtis, whom he trusted so much he'd lent him the horse Cariri so that he could earn a living. Curtis or the cellist. Deep down, he thought no one's going to realise. I'll just take Franco's photograph and that's it. What about the signature? 'Sebastián Vidal' won't pass unnoticed. He'd better put 'Sebastián V'. Or 'V. Photos' and leave it at that. That should do it. 'V. Photos'. People will identify Ángel Jalón with portrait photos and Sotomayor with paintings. Who's going to remember 'V. Photos'?

He was taken aback when she asked him, 'Is there anything else you'd like to tell me, Leica?' But, as always, he was quick to recover himself. He exaggerated his voice and gesture in what he called 'a Mastroianni moment'.

'Anything else? Isn't that enough? Our triumphal entrance into the future. We're inside the future, Silvia, inside the shop window.'

She can't actually know anything, he thought. It's a secret. Nobody, except for my brother-in-law, Judge Samos, and the governor, nobody else knows. Rocío? No. Rocío doesn't know Silvia exists. Nobody could have told her about Franco's portrait.

She hadn't expected him to say anything. She'd have had to force it out of him with a dentist's pliers. There was no way he was going to confess he'd been married for some time and the woman she'd once met in the studio wasn't the leaseholder and an old friend. He'd added the last bit with a hint of complicity, as if to say: There is, or there was, something between us, but you're much more important. What he actually whispered in her ear was, 'She's never happy with her portrait. I keep telling her it's not my problem or the camera's. Some people are never satisfied and confuse a photographer with a beautician.'

'He believes everything he says,' Rocío had told Silvia the day she accosted her. 'He's always confusing desires with realities. He lives inside a bubble. You're hardly the first. Ask him and he'll deny he's married. Go ahead and ask him. Go on, be brave. I could show you folders full of photos of all his attempted conquests. Maybe it's a kind of professional hazard. Maybe he has to fall in love in order to take good photos. I don't know. Could be. It's some time since I last looked good in a photo.'

Despite feeling dizzy, her senses on hold due to Rocío's sudden arrival, Silvia listened to her with interest. A woman who could express the idea that Leica's camera no longer loved her deserved to be heard.

But Rocío's tone soon changed, perhaps as a reaction to the surprising calm she observed on the map of Silvia's face.

'I want you to know I won't allow your relationship to continue. I'd crush you first. I can ruin your life, you've no idea how far I can go.'

As she said this, she pressed her thumb against the marble table of Delicacies, the café in Catro Camiños, whose display window had until then reflected Leica's cheerful greeting with one of his Mastroianni smiles.

'I've the means to do it.'

★　★　★

Are you married, Leica? Why didn't you tell me? No. She wasn't going to question him. Rocío's directness made her feel fragile again. Silvia often thought about Medusa's face. She also felt as if she'd been torn inside. She lived half a life and had noticed since being a girl that living a whole life was forbidden people like her in this patch of world. On days of sadness, she viewed the bay as a pool in which mullets fed on the dreams eyes threw into the sea.

'I've the means to do it. To crush you.'

All Silvia had was her invisible mending. Even feeling love was a problem. She realised one side of her, the enlightened part, had been deceiving the other, which was in shade, since she'd met Leica. And both sides knew it. Though they'd decided to carry on. To live that moment of truth. To go to the lighthouse, make love under the vanes of light, with the music of the sea in the background.

No. She wasn't going to use a dentist's pliers to force an unnecessary confession out of him.

When Rocío used words to strike her, in her fragile state, she glimpsed a way out. The day the civil servant came to pick up the cape, she said she hadn't quite finished yet, but she knew her price. Her papers. The papers she'd been refused a year earlier for being the daughter of who she was. This was her price for the invisible mending. A passport and a permit to work abroad.

'Are you pregnant?' asked the woman.

Silvia felt like a character in a radio serial that would never be broadcast. There were thousands of women trying to leave for this reason, because they were pregnant and unmarried or single mothers.

Seeing she remained silent, the civil servant said, 'You're not the first woman to be pregnant or the first to want to leave. But in your case,' she added, 'it'll be easy. You've Rocío on your side. Permission granted.'

And still he went on about his publicity dream.

When the advert was ready and the great photo had been mounted, they'd go together to look at the window of Hexámetro and to meet Mr Bendai. The shop owner and future sponsor would thus be able to see how much more beautiful she was in person. And he had the vague hope, though he didn't say this, that he'd give her a present. Possibly even a television.

She agreed, said she wanted to look at the advert, though she'd be embarrassed to be in the shop window for all Coruña to see. She imagined Miss Elisa standing there, proclaiming to all and sundry in a loud voice, 'But I know that woman! And she doesn't even have a fridge or a hoover! All she's got is a little sewing machine you carry on your head.'

They laughed. Imagined being together, holding hands, in front of the shop window. Mr Bendai waving to them from inside with his enterprising smile. This was the adjective Leica used to describe the shopkeeper's smile. Enterprising. Each smile was different and had to be described differently. The art of the photographer, like the great publicist he was, was to give each smile the correct photographic description.

Silvia's smile was that of the woman advertising electrical appliances. He liked it. A hidden smile hanging in the shop window. Happiness within reach. The future exists and it's in the window. Next they'd go to Paris. Live there for a while. Breathe another environment.

'Your smile is deceptive,' she said.

'Deceptive but true.'

She was the one who suggested going again. Making love next to Hercules Lighthouse. In Leica's car. On short wave, the music came and went. The beams of light from time to time illuminated the sea birds hovering like quavers in the night.

He didn't realise there wouldn't be any more nights.

'When you finish that important assignment, we'll have to take lessons in French. The foreigner and the florist. Every time I see that record in the studio, I crack up laughing. You were born with a French florist's accent!'

'Merde.'

'Oh! . . . et cette petite fleur . . . bleue?'

'La petite fleur . . . bleue: "Ne m'oubliez pas."'

'C'est merveilleux! On peut dire tout sans parler.'

'Everything.'

He didn't even know it was the last night when, the next day, he attended the photographic session to welcome the dictator to Meirás Manor. He followed instructions. Took part in the open session and then waited to be shown inside.

'Don't be long,' said an aide-de-camp. 'Have everything ready. He'll stand on that platform.'

'Yes, I'd already thought about the question of height,' he replied awkwardly.

But when Franco came in for a photo defined as that of a statesman in civilian clothes, Leica wasn't entirely ready. On the contrary, he was paralysed, with his head turned. There, on a coat-stand in a corner of the room, was the royal cape, staring at him.

A Dramatic History of Culture

Gabriel saw him come through the door painted green. There was one to go to the lavatory. That was painted white. The green door, however, only opened for students of advanced stenography. It was Stringer who appeared. Said something to Catia. Then approached Gabriel, who was practising his speed. Tito Balboa was in a hurry. He was ecstatic. The director of the evening *Expreso* had called him into his office to talk about his report on extraterrestrials by Hercules Lighthouse. He was proud to have instigated a new genre in Galician journalism. Sometimes, when they coincided at the academy, he'd wait for him so that they could walk together. Gabriel would accompany him to the offices of the *Expreso*. Gabriel envied Stringer the geography he moved in, as if he lived in a superimposed city. His room at the International boarding-house, his adult's place in the dining-room of the Tanagra restaurant, which included the right to cool down his gravy with red wine, his task of scouring the port and heralding the arrival of boats. Balboa would tell him about his literary projects. He was planning a great novel. Had what he needed. A space, a story to tell and a voice. Everything was important, everything had to be well struc-tured. But the essential thing was to find that voice. To decide who's doing the talking, that's the main decision. And he'd finally found the voice. A very special voice, since it was both the protagonist and the place where the events took place.

'I'm getting all muddled. Someone who relates their life, which is a mutation of space, a kind of nomadic home. A place which is a living being that stays the same, but changes every day.'

'A boat?' asked Gabriel.

'Well, almost. It's possible. It's not a bad idea. "My name is *Aurora* and this is my last journey . . ." If the trees of Cecebre Wood can talk, then why not a boat? There was once a fishing boat from the Great Sole on Lazareto Beach, waiting to be dismantled. Its last skipper, the one who'd moored it a year before, happened by and climbed up on deck out of curiosity. The boat was in ruins, but once the old skipper was on board, it started to shake furiously. Wouldn't let him go.'

'Could he not get off?'

'No. He was saved with broken bones like the ship's timbers.'

My name is Santa Cristina and I'm responsible for the transport of passengers in the bay. It's a summer's day, in the early evening. I'm crossing the bay. On the way back from the beach, at dusk, I'll be full of bathers, but now, on the way over, I'm almost empty. Astern, to starboard, leaning on the rail, watching the city we're leaving, there's a man in a white suit made of a light fabric that is so loose the wind forms part of his body and clothing. On the other side, to port, looking in the same direction, there's a woman in a dress of sea-blue silk gauze printed with bows. With her right hand, she's holding on to the skirt around her thighs, so the wind forms part of her hair. A little further back, sitting down, in shorts and a T-shirt with blue and white horizontal stripes, there's a boy who must be about eight years old, absorbed by the trembling of a compass needle. He looks up and shouts to the woman, 'We're going from West to East!' He smiles, proud of the information. This is the only time the man and the woman's eyes meet and they hold their gaze. They also smile. When I moor at the stone quay, the woman and the child disembark first and go past the paved ramp to the line of polychrome beach huts. The man walks at a distance. Carries his jacket folded over his arm. The short-sleeved white shirt, which is unbuttoned, makes his body real. There's a wooden kiosk with ice creams and refreshments. Here they rent out beach huts. The woman pays, takes the key and retraces her steps. It's the second time the man and the woman's eyes meet, while the boy's attention is still taken up with the compass needle. 'Now we're going back West!' he tells his mother. All the beach huts are painted in vertical stripes. With the colours that are most often used in maritime Galicia. On the hut the woman enters, they're red and white. On the hut the man's about to enter, they're white and green. The tide is low.

The woman, in a bathing suit, spreads out two towels, hers and the child's, on that part of the beach closest to the quay. The man comes out of his hut, looks around, places his folded towel on one of the paving stones and sits down. He's not the only bather to stay on the ramp. Here the sea is deeper and the water appears to be cleaner, with no suspended sand. It's also quieter. Almost all those who jump off the quay seem to prefer to dive rather than to swim on the surface. The woman swims and the man jumps off the ramp and disappears under the water. The boy looks at the compass, the trembling of the needle. He doesn't quite understand why it trembles when it's still. It's a good compass, no doubt about it. That's what everyone said when Laura gave it to him for his cabinet of curiosities. A Stanley London compass. On it is written The Road Not Taken. It must be good, there's no denying it, but he'd have preferred a compass with a quieter, less lively needle. Even when he puts it on the sand, the needle carries on trembling. He turns the compass from side to side. Half buries it in the sand. Funny how the needle always seeks out the North. He doesn't touch it for a long time. Now the needle floats gently. The boy looks up. Can't see his mother. But isn't afraid. She's a very good swimmer. He follows the line she was swimming along, her wake. And waits. Finally his mother's head emerges. At the same time, very close by, another head. His mother returns, swimming breaststroke towards the East. The man, diving every now and then, heads slowly back towards the West. As for me, I have to return to the docks. I'll come back for them on my last journey.

'In my case, the voice will be Hercules Lighthouse,' said Tito Balboa, Stringer. 'Who better to entrust a voice to? A novel in which the lighthouse will describe the things it's seen. Can you imagine everything the lighthouse has seen?'

'Over two thousand years,' mused Gabriel.

'Under this lighthouse, there'll be another. Or what do you think? That there weren't lighthouses and lighthouse keepers before the Romans?'

'You can talk about the first fight between Hercules and the giant Geryon, which gave rise to the city.'

'No, thanks. No mythology. The lighthouse will describe.' Balboa grins naughtily, 'I bet it's always been a good place for a quickie. Now couples do it in the car. Listening to foreign radio stations. Thing about the light-house is you can see without being seen.'

'How about you?' asked Gabriel. 'Have you seen that?'

'No. But the lighthouse has.'

The green door. Dr Montevideo's students of advanced stenography entered and left through there. In addition to Tito or Stringer, Gabriel paid particular attention to a man who reminded him of the actor Monty Clift. Because of his sunny and afflicted, scrupulous expression, with a curly fringe, and because of the changes in his appearance. He was almost always well dressed, even elegant. But other times he looked terrible, hadn't shaved, with creases in his clothes as if he'd slept in them. Dr Montevideo was never among those who came and went. Gabriel had never seen him, but knew he couldn't be one of them. When Catia agreed, said he could try, give it a go, he almost ran towards the green door.

Gabriel opened the green door, walked along a windowless corridor with the light on, and then climbed a spiral staircase which led to a room in the mezzanine. He knocked at a second green door with a pane of frosted glass. Thought he heard a kind of onomatopoeia, a verbal piece of stenography. Pushed open the door. Found himself immersed in a space that was both tiny and infinite. Whose four walls were covered in murals showing marine life. The style was unmistakably Sada's, and Gabriel remembered what this painter, his mother's friend, used to say about the sea's restless paradise, shoals that were now only to be found deep down. In this illusion of anemones, starfish, polyps, spirographs, sponges, gorgonians, sea-lilies, urchins, jellyfish, the bed where this smoky Poseidon was sitting seemed to be afloat. Gabriel noticed a colony of sea urchins in one corner of the room. They looked like a chromatic wheel containing all the passions. Among the lighter, pink violet urchins, he distinguished a scarlet urchin. The colour of Catia's nails.

Dr Montevideo was sitting up in bed, against some pillows, writing on sheets supported by a wooden book-rest. He was smoking a large cigar held more by his teeth than by his lips – a yellow, uneven, gap-filled set of teeth. To his right, on a night table, was a bottle of whisky and a glass.

The rest of the bed was strewn with papers, most of which had been covered in shorthand, though some had been typed and corrected by hand. To one side of the bed was a cardboard box wrapped in silver foil which served as a wastepaper basket. It was full of scrunched-up pieces of paper. Some had fallen to the floor like decomposed spheres.

His bulging eyes seemed to be held in place by thick-framed glasses. He rested his cigar on a ceramic plate. Still writing, without looking up, he asked, 'What would you think of someone who recites beautiful poems and sings melancholy songs before committing a crime? Does this affect the poems they recite and the songs they sing?'

'I don't see why it should,' answered Gabriel.

'You don't see why it should? Well, think about it. And tomorrow we'll talk. You know? A friend of mine, the argonautic painter, wants high literature from me. I'm currently tied up with the implications.' He coughed. 'Actually I just scrawl, it's poor Catia who does the writing. One day, there should be a tribute to the heroines of typing. Now help me bring a bit of order to this apocalypse. Put those planets back in the wastepaper basket and then pour me two glass-dilating fingers from the bottle. Make it three.'

Some time later, Gabriel Samos would know that what Dr Montevideo was writing was A Dramatic History of Culture. Being the first to arrive at the academy, he'd often find Catia immersed in the work of typing up the doctor's notes. He liked to act as Green Door Messenger between the classroom where Catia held sway and the doctor's sea-bed. He felt comfortable in the mezzanine and, though he abandoned his classes for much of the course, he didn't stop visiting the Tachygraphic Rose to see Catia, of course, and to climb the stairs to the cabin, to experience this strange ascent to the depths of the sea. He came back the following summer, in the middle of June 1963, with renewed anxiety. The transcription of the doctor's notes meant Catia was busier than ever and even devoted some class time to her labour. She typed with astonishing speed, without apparent effort. Her hands transformed the heavy Hispano-Olivetti into a fantastic machine. Her face had also changed. She typed the same or more quickly, but with a sense of urgency. Gabriel approached the corner where she worked one day to ask her something. She carried on typing. Said, 'Just a moment!'

397

He looked for the sake of looking. Peered over her shoulder. He liked to see how the words appeared. As if they'd been excavated rather than printed. As Catia's fingers galloped along, possessing the machine, he tapped his fingers against his thighs, keeping time. A reflex action. Except that now his fingers moved nervously like the Stanley compass needle. He read on the excavated page:

```
Who  was  this  German  jurist  Spain  paid  tribute  to
in  1962?  He  was  something  more  than  a  jurist.  He
was  once  considered  the  Kronjurist,  the  Third  Reich's
'official  jurist'.  The  architect . . .
```

'Yes, Gabriel, what is it?'

The lawyer Paúl Santos described Dr Montevideo's classes of advanced stenography as a chair of humanism. The man who resembled Monty Clift was, needless to say, his most attentive pupil. And more and more openly drawn to Catia. They – Stringer, Gabriel and the other pupils – were also admirers, but it was enough for them if she'd straighten their elbows. Sometimes they'd do it deliberately, get out of shape, so that she'd come and correct their posture.

'What's your job?'

'I'm a lawyer, Mr Montevideo. A lawyer.'

'A lawyer, eh? A man of law. That's good. A good lawyer has to be a good writer. Use words with the utmost propriety. Like a doctor. A good doctor is the one who puts together a story that will convince his patient. As for a pathologist, he has to be even more precise, since he has to convince a corpse, not a patient. High praise of a text is that it's as precise as a forensic report. Some writers aspire to this, to forensic precision. I've known pathologists, however, who were very competent in their field, but dissatisfied with their scientific language and envious of the precision of poetry. "Meadows sweet where flames are under." What do you think? "A Song of Opposites" by Mr Keats. Now isn't that an example of extraordinary precision concerning human beings? A good prosecutor should also be a good writer. And a judge. A judge has to rearrange all the pieces and construct a credible story for the future as well. Not make a mockery of justice. It sounds as if it's asking too much. But it isn't.'

'You don't think so?'

'For justice today, it's enough not to be unjust. Not as difficult as they make it out to be. You just have to let conscience do its thing. "Conscience is the mental activity of esteeming the good." Xohán Vicente Viqueira, yes siree! But there's something else very important. The police report. Which could be described as *materia prima*. The point of origin. The policeman who produces that report really does have to be a good writer. He's the one who investigates. The sniffer dog who follows the trail. Selects clues. Everything a policeman writes is politically committed literature. Don't you think so, Mr Santos?'

He knew he'd been detected. Peered through the doctor's thick lenses like a corpse trying to return the pathologist's searching gaze.

'I quite agree, Dr Montevideo.'

'Can I help?' asked Gabriel.

'Do you like western novels?'

Before alighting on the keys, his fingers trembled like the Stanley compass needle. After that, it was plain sailing.

'A Sacred Feast'

Madrid, 21 March 1962

It took place in the main auditorium of number 1 Marina Española Square, central headquarters of the only party, known as the National Movement. 'Large turnout,' it said in the newspaper reports. In the presence of ministers and numerous representatives of the regime, together with members of the judiciary and ecclesiastical hierarchy, the then director of the Institute of Political Studies, Manuel Fraga Iribarne, welcomed Carl Schmitt as an honorary member. The first time such an award had been made in this centre which was conceived as a factory of ideas during the dictatorship. Created in 1939, after Franco's victory and Hitler's rise to power, the Institute always gave Schmitt preferential treatment, as an intellectual, publishing his texts and commentaries on his works.

Who was this German jurist Spain paid tribute to in 1962? He was something more than a jurist. He was once considered the Kronjurist, the Third Reich's 'official jurist'. The architect of Nazi legality. The proponent of 'a state of emergency', for whom, after Hobbes, 'auctoritas non veritas facit legem'. Authority, not truth, makes law. The deviser of Decisionism, by which the 'providential' nature of absolute power was brought up to date, so that the monarch was now the Caudillo or the Führer. In practice, a futuristic formulation of tyranny for the masses. Unlike other periods, when the mark of a tyrant was his obscene contempt for the law, Schmitt's great conjuring trick was to transform the tyrant into Supreme Judge, the maker of law, the one who imprints the law with his footsteps.

After the fall of the Third Reich in 1945, Carl Schmitt spent a brief period in the internment camp of Berlin Lichterfelde-Süd and in Nuremberg as a defendant and witness, proceedings he managed to slip away from with customary ease. Regarding this experience, he wrote Ex Captivitate Salus, which contains a single show of repentance in the use of Macrobius' Latin phrase 'Non possum scribere in eum qui potest proscribere'. I cannot write against one who has the power to proscribe. An equivocal statement in a master of oblique expression. A surprising device in someone who read Melville and knew the scrivener Bartleby's response when asked to do something that went against his conscience, 'I would prefer not to.' Some were brave enough to say no. In the legal field, the courageous Hans Kelsen, for example, who had an argument with Schmitt about parliamentary democracy and, having been proscribed, branded 'an enemy', carried on defending freedom while in exile. Some at least resisted the crushing totalitarian machine in silence. Schmitt did not. On the contrary, his contribution to the rise of Nazism was enthusiastic and systematic during the crucial period 1933–1936. Before that, he had helped to undermine the Weimar Republic by proposing an abuse of presidential power that foreshadowed modern forms of dictatorship.

He had Donoso Cortés, the gleam of the sabre, in mind.

He was helped to join the Nazi party in 1933 by the philosopher Martin Heidegger, later Rector of Freiburg University, who also wanted to descend to Plato's cave and requisition the projector of ideas. 'Whoever loves storm and danger should listen to Heidegger!' he exclaimed on 30 November in Tübingen. Such rhetoric excited Schmitt, who also declared, 'When Heidegger speaks, the mist disappears from in front of our eyes.' This may not have been so important. For many, part of Schmitt's charm resided in his ability to use disguises. With a following wind, however, he would abandon his cryptic style and his prose would advance with perilous determination. On 1 August 1934, the then professor in Berlin wrote in the German jurists' newspaper, Deutsche Juristen-Zeitung, the most daring legal formulation of tyranny in modern times: 'Only the Führer is called to distinguish between friends and enemies. The Führer heeds the warnings of German history, which gives him the right and the necessary force to bring about a new State and a new order. It is the Führer who defends law against abuse when, at a moment of danger, through the powers invested in him as Supreme Judge, he directly creates Law.' This was not just an instrumental gift for Hitler's future. The text served to justify, a posteriori, the executions ordered by the Führer on 30 June that year, during the so-called Night of the Long Knives. Among those eliminated was an old friend of Schmitt's, the chancellor Schleicher. Later his contributions, which continued to be forthright, were aimed at legitimising the Third Reich's aggressive expansion. There is an idea that pervades his work, that of war as midwife.

'And Cain killed Abel. This is how the history of mankind begins.' Schmitt's lapidary statement. During a lecture at Cologne University in 1940, he instructed his students to convert ideas and concepts into 'pointed weapons'. His whole way of thinking is martial. Including 'true' politics, which he considers inseparable from the dialectic friend-enemy. Nor are the numerous images and metaphors inspired by religion disconnected from the idea of a theocratic totalitarianism which would influence his Spanish friends so strongly. It is no coincidence that his greatest affinity was with those who advocated 'holy intransigence, holy coercion and holy shamelessness'. Schmitt defined himself as 'a Christian Epimetheus'. Epimetheus ignored his brother Prometheus' advice and married Pandora, who opened the jar or box and unleashed devastating forces. 'I am a Catholic not just in accordance with my religion,' he wrote in 1948, 'but also in accordance with my historical origins and, if I might say so, with my race.' The most complete construction of his identity was the character of katechon. A concept taken from Christian apocalyptic writings, in particular the Second Letter to the Thessalonians, one of the most enigmatic texts in the New Testament. There is a power or person (ho katechon) who prevents the arrival of the lawless one (ho anomos) and restrains him. Anyone who assumes that role, as is the case with Schmitt, is performing a sacred, providential mission. Though there is another school of thought, which says the lawless one's most successful disguise would be to present himself as the katechon.

It is, therefore, no surprise that, at the tribute organised by leaders of Franco's regime on 21 March 1962, Don Carlos should invoke Providence and define the act as 'a sacred feast in the winter of life'. What had happened to him, the Kronjurist, the brains of Nazi legality, prior to celebrating the winter of life in Madrid?

A biographical error that is kind to Carl Schmitt has it that he was more or less sidelined at the end of 1936, having been criticised in an SS publication. And yet the all-powerful Göring supported him. He continued to be Professor of Law in Berlin until the end of the war. Nor was he otherwise silent. His activity as a lecturer and propagandist for the Nazi legal model was intense and continued almost until the end of the struggle for conquered or conspiring Europe. At the tribute in 1962, there was a veiled allusion to his visit to Madrid twenty years earlier, in 1942, the moment of greatest German pressure for Spain to throw in its lot with the Axis. It would seem he was then secretary of the German Cultural Institute in Madrid. 'Representing this centre and the German embassy' (Arriba, 22 April 1942), he attended a conference that opened with an address by the Italian Fascist Giuliano Mazzoni. Sidelined? So what was the 'providential' mission that brought Schmitt to Madrid at that time?

As always, the enemy.

'I never forget that my personal enemies are also Spain's enemies,' he wrote to Francisco J. Conde in a letter dated 15 April 1950. 'A coincidence that raises my private situation to the sphere of objective spirit.' Donoso Cortés (1809–1853) is the key to Carl Schmitt's early relationship with Spain or at least its more reactionary elements. The Marquis of Valdegamas was a happy Extremaduran liberal in his youth. Until, in his own words, he became 'a pilgrim of the Absolute'. Such an embittered pilgrim, who viewed sinful humans with such contempt, in the end he thought they deserved periodic cleansing. Donoso's was an orgy of reactionary bad temper which shocked the historian Menéndez Pelayo, a reactionary himself, but a more sober one, who was horrified by some of the marquis' statements. This one, for example: 'Jesus Christ did not conquer the world by the holiness of his doctrine or by miracles and prophecies, but in spite of those things.' Delirious, thought the orthodox Menéndez Pelayo. Later events in Spain, in particular the blessing by bishops of the 1936 war as a Holy Crusade, bear the stamp of this delirium.

For Carl Schmitt, the synarchist Joseph de Maistre, the traditionalist Louis de Bonald and the Catholic fundamentalist Donoso were the doctrinal trinity on which to build the 'new order'. The new version of the Holy Empire. Donoso Cortés wrote the only great speech nineteenth-century Spanish fundamentalism managed to export with a degree of success to the rest of Europe. Not surprising. The so-called Speech on Dictatorship, delivered on 4 January 1849 in the Congress of Deputies, must rank as one of the most horrifying interventions ever to have been pronounced in a parliamentary chamber. The conservative majority's whoops and applause are a vibrant part of the speech. Donoso does not hesitate to define dictatorship as a divine act, an order of Providence. The impact of the speech, whose content was nothing new, the reverberations it caused in conservative Europe, have something to do with its direct, apodictic style and intimidatory ending. It is probably the first Fascist discourse in the modern sense. Already, by the 1920s, it had captivated Schmitt, who was born in 1888 in Plettenberg, Westphalia, in a very conservative Catholic environment. In 1929, the German jurist and professor appeared in Madrid for the first time to deliver a lecture. What does he talk about? He reintroduces the Spanish to Donoso Cortés! Obviously 'it is a question of choosing between the dictatorship that comes from below and the dictatorship that comes from above. I choose the one that comes from above, because it comes from cleaner, more serene regions. It is a question, finally, of choosing between the dagger and the sabre. I choose the dictatorship of the sabre, because it is nobler.' (Bravo! Bravo!) An interest in the history of Spain has other useful reference points, such as the expulsion of the Jews under the Catholic Monarchs.

Such is the curious circle drawn by history. 'Decisionism' and a love of tyranny according to Schmitt, the demiurge who inspired Franco's jurists to turn their illegitimate new regime into a 'creatio a Deo' ('Franco, Caudillo of Spain by the grace of God'), were themselves inspired by a nineteenth-century Spanish reactionary's crazy ideology. Apart from shared ideals, here he finds the one quality that should characterise a Führer, Duce or Caudillo: 'ferocity of speech'. Although he was a liberal in his youth, Donoso's attacks on liberalism are expressed with extreme ferocity, which leads him to describe dictatorship as the form of government that corresponds to the divine, natural law.

There is one feature of political liberalism that is the focus of all his contempt and revulsion. Liberalism is . . . frivolous. Frivolous! My God! This is a mark left by Donoso on Schmitt, which the latter emphasises early on in his criticism of the liberal system and parliamentary democracies. Frivolity. This is the terrible sin, like relativism in religion, according to Syllabus. In 1934, a hybrid of Donoso and Schmitt, Eugenio Montes, first intellectual figurehead opposed to the Republic and then thurible for Franco's dictatorship, published his 'Speech to Spanish Catholicism', much vaunted by the right, in which he makes it clear there are to be no concessions regarding the form of government: 'All relativism is anti-Catholic per se. Turning relativity into an ideal norm or code of conduct is like yielding your soul to the devil.' Why does absolutism direct all its anger towards the scatterbrained idea of frivolity, making it the worst possible insult? Liberal 'frivolity' would have politics as a neutral field in an attempt to avoid confrontation. But 'serious' politics for the Donosos of yesterday and today is precisely that: confrontation with the enemy. And if there is no enemy, you just have to wait. One will turn up.

'It is a significant coincidence that a genuine interest in research has always led me to Spain,' says Don Carlos on 21 March 1962 before Franco's elites. And of course he talks about the war, 'In this almost providential coincidence, I see further proof that Spain's war of national liberation is a touchstone.' They understand each other. But such recognition was nothing out of the ordinary. In 1952, Arbor, a magazine dependent on the Council for Scientific Research and an important means of expression for Francoist intellectuals, published the essay 'Carl Schmitt in Compostela' written by Álvaro D'Ors, a leading member of Opus Dei and a professor in the Faculty of Law in Santiago. Which is where, in 1960, Porto y Cía published a Spanish version of Ex Captivitate Salus, a book that was well received, having been translated by his only daughter, Anima, married to a Professor of the History of Law, Alfonso Otero, whom she met in Germany.

This Spanish edition includes an interesting preface Schmitt wrote in Casalonga, a villa on the outskirts of Santiago, in the summer of 1958. Thirteen years after the collapse of the Third Reich, there is in this preface not a hint of regret, not a single allusion to the horrors of the war and the policy of racial extermination known as the Holocaust. The only concentration camp he mentions is the one where he was briefly interned after the war, the only lament is his denunciation of the criminalisation of defeated Germany. At the start of the 1960s, on Compostelan evenings, Carl Schmitt, who was always so critical of American democracy, begins to express unusual interest in a politician by the name of Barry Goldwater, a past collaborator of McCarthy in his so-called 'witch hunt' and current senator for Arizona. 'Watch Goldwater,' Don Carlos tells his Spanish friends. 'Goldwater represents an ultra-conservatism that wants to conquer the future.'

Let us go back to Madrid and 1 Marina Española Square in 1962. Manuel Fraga Iribarne praises Carl Schmitt's way of thinking, 'more relevant today than ever', and sums it up perfectly, 'Politics as a decision, the return of personalised power, an anti-formalist understanding of the Constitution, a superseding of the concept of legality . . . are scaled heights we cannot turn back from.' In his speech, the director of the Institute and master of ceremonies, who is himself a jurist, does nothing but defend the Kronjurist.

'The law can be likened to a long-range cannon,' wrote Manuel Fraga in the Revista General de Legislación y Jurisprudencia in 1944. Now this jurist with a gunner's vision, who is about to be named Minister of Information under the dictatorship, pins the decoration to the lapel of his 'revered master' Schmitt. Adds with emotion that this is 'a high point of his career'. After the round of applause, Don

405

Carlos, the man on the sidelines, takes centre stage. He is seventy-three, strong and in good health, and knows that the solemn use of language is going to make him grow in stature in front of a devoted audience. Emphasise the 'power of presence' his old friend and colleague Ernst Jünger attributed to him. He seems fully aware of what is happening. The unusual fact that somewhere in the world the Third Reich's leading jurist is being fêted and awarded.

With pleasure, he finally crosses the line he once drew for himself after the collapse of Nazism, that of taking shelter in the crypt of silence. In Spain, he finds his intellectual refuge and, to a large extent, living and triumphant, his model State. The stage on which to point to the defeat of parliamentary democracy. He is even able to take pleasure, when he meets cultivated reactionaries like D'Ors, in the rhetoric of an imaginary redoubt of the Holy Empire. Like his host, he emits not a word of self-criticism, not a hint of doubt or uncertainty. It is he who supplies his own best eulogy. Unlike his fiery predecessor, who is said sometimes to run out of control in his speeches, he talks slowly, enhances certain words to give way to that 'power of presence' described by Jünger. Makes use of liturgical gestures. 'What was that he said?' 'A sacred feast.' Yes, Carl Schmitt, Don Carlos, proclaims that this reunion with his Spanish friends is 'a sacred feast in the winter of life'. At that moment, exactly at that moment, according to the testimony of the ecstatic Falangist writer Jesús Fueyo, 'the lights went out'.

The press highlighted the event. Described the tribute to Carl Schmitt in large letters. Various media reproduced an interview first published in Arriba 'on account of its great interest', a euphemism, no doubt, for what was known as 'obligatory insertion'. 'It is possible that all European countries will have to justify themselves before Spain,' said Schmitt. But no medium, no newspaper, reported the blackout. Nobody explained that, when the hierarch was pinning a badge to the chest of Don Carlos, the auditorium in the headquarters of the National Movement went dark. Completely dark.

From A Dramatic History of Culture by Héctor Ríos, unpublished.

The Compulsive Writer

He filled his notebooks very quickly. He didn't just like to write, he had a passion for calligraphy. Which later became a passion for stenography after he learnt the Martí method in Dr Montevideo's version at Catia's academy. He noted down his thoughts. Noted down what he was going to say. Both Chelo and the judge, for different reasons, were proud of this premature writer's vocation. Chelo believed, rightly so, that it originated in those early lessons aimed at exorcising his fear of speech by means of graphic fluency and what she called 'the hand's sincerity'. She was pleased and deeply moved by the gifts of observation revealed by Gabriel's writing, since she still thought of him as a child. The judge Samos had forgotten about the years of despair, that complicated period when Gabriel was so fragile, always on the verge of cracking, like a nativity figure. One day, he'd even used the word 'defective' a little carelessly. At a time when Gabriel's stammer seemed to be getting worse. 'Defective,' he muttered, 'a defective son'. In search of a word that sounded neutral, an 'extenuating term', he later claimed, he chose one that, even in a whisper, banged like a tin can.

'You're thinking about yourself,' said Chelo. 'You're not thinking about him, you're thinking about yourself.'

There was a hint of horror underlying his wife's expression. She started muttering as well, in a sad tone, as if she'd picked the word 'defective' up off the floor and was trying to repair it.

'What do you mean?'

'You know very well what I mean. You're thinking about what they'll say. "Did you know the judge's son has a stutter, Samos' son can't get his words out?" That's what you're thinking.'

'Yes, that too. But most of all I'm thinking he can't be a judge if he stutters. Had you thought about that? There are many things you can't be in life if you're tongue-tied. You can't be a minister, or a general, or a bishop . . . No, you can't. You can't command an army, or say Mass, or pronounce sentence. You can't do the most important jobs in life. Right? You can't be a notary, secretary at the town hall, a policeman, a radio presenter. You can't even sing the lottery. Or commentate a goal.'

He suddenly felt well on this trip to the absurd. He was talking about getting tongue-tied while his was out enjoying a stroll down a shaded path.

'You can't even be a criminal. You can't hold up a bank and trip over your tongue.'

He stopped talking when he noticed Chelo's distorted face. A Cubist face on the verge of splintering. He didn't often see her cry, show her emotions. He'd thought about this, her phlegmatic qualities. A serenity whose immutability sometimes disturbed him. She seemed to contemplate the world in a frame, which allowed her to walk with curiosity, too much self-control. Her oriental calm in the Chinese Pavilion, where the only dramatic moments came from the grooves of the vinyl record, that Austrian soprano singing Pamina's amorous lament, *Ach, ich fühl's*, a sadness that forced its way into his study, made itself heard, stopped him doing anything else, despite the volume being turned down at its source, next to Chelo's quiet painting. This at least was the impression she gave when she thought she was alone and could be observed without her realising, that sweet, hypnotic movement of the brush. Perhaps all the drama coming from the vinyl grooves was meant for him. A personal matter with the Austrian soprano and her high notes. He took more comfort in the low ones. Actually he knew his sense of anxiety was proportional to the attraction he felt for this music. Now that he thought about it, he really liked it, though he couldn't have called it a passion. Aside from Chelo, he did know people who were passionate about opera. Something to do with the sea. There was a time great companies performed here on their way to America. Ships, however, no longer transported bel canto. What to do? A melancholy vision of things. It had been neglected. They had to agree that musical culture in the city had grown less. He'd mentioned this to various authorities. It's not just a question of trusting in the use of force and propaganda. A cultural vacuum is dangerous, etc., etc. But of course idiots abound . . . He hadn't said this, he'd kept it to himself. What he'd heard about the mayor. A spokesman for Friends of the Opera had gone to seek support for a festival and the mayor had replied with an intimidatory question, 'How many friends are you? We'll put you on a bus and . . . off to La Scala in Milan!'

What to do?

Chelo's face goes back to normal, but is somehow different. Her gaze has the unthinking hardness of someone who's managed to prevent a collapse, there is no collapse, and makes Ricardo decide to back down. Everything in him changes. He reveals the greatest discomfort, that of someone who's lost control.

'Excuse me. I was half joking. It doesn't matter anyway.'

'Of course it doesn't. Stop thinking about what can or cannot be and think about what is. Stop seeing it as a curse.'

Ricardo Samos was silent for a moment. The time it takes for a coin to be flipped in the air and land on the palm of the hand.

'I see it like that. I can't help it. As a curse. I want my son to be a judge one day. I've a right to want this. I want him to be the best. And yes, you're right. Do you know what they're saying? The look in their eyes when they ask, "How's your son? Can it be helped? Did you know about the orator Demosthenes?" And they keep cracking jokes. "When the judge finally passed sentence, the defendant was already in the street." And so on. The whole city cracking jokes.'

'The whole city?'

'Those who matter to us at least.'

He'd been sincere. Often, in his lectures, he'd defended the concept of *Dignitas non moritur*. According to this traditional viewpoint, having dignity meant wielding and handing down power. He wasn't going to discuss this now, the underlying coincidence between medieval political theology and his thought, a victor's thought, which made this unwritten law applicable. The old idea that 'dignity does not die' and is inherited, a justification of

409

privilege, 'corporation by succession'. But no. This was not the time to explain to Chelo what he thought and felt, there was probably no point.

'He may or may not become a judge,' said Chelo, 'but don't talk to me about a curse ever again.'

This time, Ricardo Samos took notice. No, he wouldn't use that word again. Besides, Gabriel's difficulty with speech soon entered a new phase. Of rapid improvement, it seemed.

During a visit to Madrid, Grandpa Samos, who was then a high-ranking Navy legal officer, had tried to convince the judge that Gabriel's problem was, in fact, the faltering expression of a sensitive and extremely gifted young boy. Ricardo didn't pay much attention. He didn't think his father an expert in such matters and, most of all, he couldn't marry the idea of being extremely gifted with tripping over your tongue, being unable to express yourself, having such a terrible fear of words.

But when he heard the same thing from others he held in high esteem, such as Gueldo the judge, Fasco the prosecutor, Professor Sulfe and even Father Munio, his old fears gave way to this new idea that sooner or later there would be a change in Gabriel when all his aptitude came to the fore.

What worried Chelo, who'd assumed the task of seeking out and consulting specialists, was how little was known about speech impediments. The pedagogical vacuum. The lack of treatments. And, what shocked her more than anything, the little importance they were given compared to the suffering they caused those who experienced them.

During this search that lasted years, she reached the conclusion that her idea of painting souvenirs on Gabriel's hands and making him practise his handwriting and drawing hadn't been so wide of the mark. It was also important he should enjoy words. She'd cried with laughter the day she arrived home and Gabriel came running up to her from the grandfather clock, shouting the formula for aspirin, 'Acetylsalicylic acid!'

Gabriel was getting better. He had periods of silence, when he withdrew into his shell, in a state of watchfulness, and appeared to be chewing over the whole of language.

He liked to read, would write things on his own initiative and put all his effort into practising his speech. This was beyond doubt. This was the best sign. His marks at school were excellent. He could spend days in almost total silence. This way, he avoided being laughed at and made fun of. The teachers knew this and didn't try to force him to talk. A few attempts had been successful. Others had ended in disaster. Gabriel stuck on a syllable for minutes. His face red. With an absent look.

Until there was a sudden change. A miraculous U-turn. It was when he started writing compulsively. The same summer he asked to attend typing classes. He was amazed by the skill of a student a little older than him, who was dockside reporter for the evening *Expreso*. He could type very fast, without looking, using all his fingers. And, even more amazingly, he was learning shorthand. Gabriel also could take this step. Acquire a technique that allowed you to transcribe speech at a natural rhythm.

'That's magnificent, Gabriel,' said Chelo. She was enthusiastic. 'It's a fantastic idea. Like drawing words.'

'How was it you became friends?' asked his father.

In the docks. Stringer is always down in the docks. Everyone calls him that, Stringer. He notes down the names of ships, where they're coming from, their next destination, the cargo on board. He sometimes conducts interviews. The other day, a ship arrived from the Great Sole, carrying a smaller boat inside, a sailing boat they'd found drifting without a crew. On board were the papers of a Dutchman who lived in the States. He was a photographer and artist.

'How do you know he was an artist?'

'Because it said so on his documents. He had the same name as Uncle. Bastian. It's a strange story. I was looking at his papers with Stringer, which said the voyage, the voyage he was making, was an art performance called *In Search of the Miraculous*.'

'You're talking very well, son,' said Samos, beaming.

Chelo, with a look, warned her husband to be prudent. Changed subject.

'You'll go to that academy, Gabriel. It's a fantastic idea. And we'll get out the immortal machine that hasn't been touched yet. Your father's dormant Hispano-Olivetti, on which he was going to continue Cicero's work.'

'I've decided to do it by hand,' said Samos, playing along. 'The way classical authors did. What's the name of that academy, Gabriel?'

'The Tachygraphic Rose. There's only one teacher.'

'Only one teacher?'

'Yes. I had a go with Stringer. And she positioned my fingers on the keys to teach me how to start. Her name's Catia. Catia's the one who positions your fingers on the keys so you can start. Each finger has its own keys. And the thumbs are for using the space-bar.'

He could hear Catia whispering instructions from behind him, close to his neck, like a breeze, 'Head and back straight. Elbows next to your body, like this. Try and keep your arms at right angles.'

'I've been practising,' he said, smiling, his eyes closed, his fingers pressing down on imaginary keys. 'I can find all the letters in the air from memory.'

The iron Hispano-Olivetti on its trolley occupied a central position in the alcove. The typewriter, its actions and constructive sound, implicated the whole area. It was the closest thing to making books. Now was not the time for calligraphy, imitating styles, English or Italian, decorating capital letters in the green light of the lamp, though, when his father had visitors and Gabriel couldn't move, he'd go back to handwriting. Almost always, he'd write a postcard dated 1913 to Santiago Casares c/o Durtol Sanatorium, telling him how he was solving his problems using an infallible technique, that of combining writing and speech.

His cabinet of curiosities, however, was relegated to a second level. Now, despite their value and meaning, they were more archaeological remains than anything. The typewriter was too big, too out of scale, and pulled him away from childhood, quickly through adolescence, to the doors of another age. That of secret, personal writing.

Eventually Neves, who was worried, decided to bring it up with Chelo. Gabriel had balls of paper in the pockets of his coat, jacket, trousers. He used to keep his notebooks tidy. Now he filled notebooks not only from school, but of different sizes. This may not have mattered. But sometimes, in the morning, his room would be full of loose sheets of paper covered in strange signs, as well as balls of paper, spherical forms that overflowed the wastepaper basket. Gabriel would rush out in the morning. If she'd come to have a word with Chelo, it wasn't to stick her nose into other people's business. She wasn't a meddler. Besides, she wouldn't have been able to understand anything even if she'd wanted to. They were scrawls. Unintelligible. She'd come because it seemed to her that Gabriel often didn't sleep at night. When she got up early, she noticed a crack of light under his door. All night with scrawls, shorthand or whatever they called it, couldn't be good.

'What are you writing?' his mother asked him that evening. With a smile, as if by chance. Without wanting to disturb him, without a hint of suspicion. (He's little; the door opens and it's her in a black felt hat with a white tulle veil almost covering her eyes; she bends down with open arms and he doesn't know whether to stay still or run towards her, crouching down with open arms: *doucement, doucement*; now he's the one wearing an invisible veil.)

He's momentarily taken aback. Why's she asking him this now precisely? He can't read her what he's writing.

My father entered the house in a rage. As he arrived, Medusa was leaving through the front door with a large fish, a bluefin tuna, on top of her head.

'I don't understand you, Chelo. Inviting her into the house. That *mere-trix*!'

Meretrix. Look it up in the dictionary. *Prostitute, a woman who engages in sexual activity in return for payment.*

'Do me a favour. Tell your models to use the service entrance. That's what it's there for. I'm a judge. I have to keep up appearances.'

'She's a woman. A human being.'

'I can see what she is. Did you know she was in prison for having an abortion? The stupid girl almost killed herself with a knitting needle. They left her outside the first-aid post. Blood was pouring down Palloza.'

'I see. There was a lot of blood. And, on top of that, she had to go to prison for it.'

413

'Not as long as she should have. She was lucky. The doctor who saw her used vague language in his report. You know what I think. It's possible to pity a criminal, but never a woman who aborts.'

'Do you know why half her face is covered?'

'What are you writing, Gabriel?'

'Everything.'

The Lighthouse's Novel

'Mr Montevideo . . .'

'Forget what I said. That joke about an inexperienced writer was a bit cruel. I'm always doing that. It's like a tic.'

In fact, Tito Balboa or Stringer wasn't worried about the joke. He'd heard it before. Santos, the one who turned out to be a policeman, may have been worried. Whatever the doctor might think, that policeman revered him. Catia as well, who didn't? But he also had great admiration for Dr Montevideo. Either that or he was very good at pretending. He'd listen to him with rapt attention. Take down all his notes. Do all the exercises. The doctor was convinced he was trying to catch him out, was accumulating evidence, investigating, so that he could then report him. Most of the time, he held himself in check. Other times, however, he started dictating excitedly, improvising a seemingly delirious text that left him exhausted: *The concentric circles leave the empty hand, go down a path with glow-worms, are the drops of rain in the blackbird's stave, quavers that catch on Virginia Woolf's cobweb covering Malevich's black square where all the colours await their day.* Full stop.

The result was a graphic hotchpotch in his pupils' notebooks. The nonsense of lines.

'Tell me, Balboa, what have you written?'

'I only had time to jot down, *Concentric circles await their day.*'

'Perfect. That's pure Dadaism. Gabriel?'

'Nothing, Mr Montevideo.'

'You're just beginning. Don't try to understand it all. Leave your ears free, let your hand do the work. Till you reach 'irreproachable traceability', as Don Alfredo Nadal de Mariezcurrena used to say. And you, lawyer?'

'Drops of rain in a black square.'

Having calmed down a little, Dr Montevideo sought out simple, self-contained sentences in among the sheets of material covering his bed. Fragments of humanistic stenography.

'Write down this by Éluard: *There are other worlds but all are in this one.* By Jules Renard: *Truth is of small dimensions.* Let's see if anyone can tell me who wrote the next one: *Therein no fairy's arm can transcend the Leviathan's tail.*'

'That's by Melville!'

'Well done, Balboa.'

On another sheet, he found something that made him thoughtful and he decided not to read. Then:

'*Farewell, my book. A single passenger, as I suppose you know, must not keep a vessel waiting.*'

'That's by Marcus Valerius Martialis,' said Santos immediately. 'The poet's about to return to Bilbilis in Hispania, his native city, after decades of absence.'

Dr Montevideo stared at him with the satirical astonishment of bulging eyes.

'Very good, lawyer, very good.'

A few days later, after class, Santos said to him, 'Doctor, I made so bold as to bring you some poems.'

'Who wrote them?'

'Who wrote them? I did, Mr Montevideo.'

'Why?'

What had been irony, a historical joke between poets, at that point became an implacable question, of the sort legal terminology defines as 'preliminary proceedings'. One of Dr Montevideo's commandments: *Every literary work should have a purpose in mind, like preliminary proceedings.*

'Why? Tell me why you wrote those poems.'

It was an embarrassing situation. His bulging eyes on the verge of firing off like gaucho bullets in search of an ostrich.

Santos had gone bright red. You could see the marks left by those whys like lashes on his cheeks.

'Reply. You write poems. Poems at such a time. Can you not tell me why?'

'Well, I suppose they're a kind of exercise.'

'An exercise? Respiratory? Typewritten?'

'To tell the truth, they're not mine. They're anonymous copies that fell into my hands. Why? I don't know why.'

Montevideo's eyes nestled back into their sockets. He had these outbursts, which he tried to lend a certain style to, but he wasn't organically equipped to abuse, sustain malicious pressure on somebody, 'Then forgive me. I'm actually very interested in those poems. You say they're anonymous? Leave them over there. They might even be fragments of dramatic history.'

Tito Balboa found it very difficult to admit to Dr Montevideo that he was going to abandon his project of writing a novel about the life of Hercules Lighthouse. Somehow it was he who'd helped give birth to the idea of *A Lighthouse's Autobiography*. They had certain set days when Balboa went on his own to note down stenographically (sorry about the -ly, Mr Montevideo), to note down in shorthand information about the city's hidden history: what the lighthouse could see at night. But he was leaving his literary dreams behind in order to devote himself to journalism. Who would have any interest in the story of a lighthouse told by itself, that theory about landscape's subjectivity, the scars of history on territory, bodies and words? Such a novel would be buried in this world's end. Maybe later. He had a stock of arguments. A horizon of professional opportunities was opening up before him. He had to mount the horse that was in front of him, not let the sun go past the door, etc., etc. In the cabin, when the two of them were alone, he got entangled in proverbs about the sun and horse.

'Festive supplements, eh?' exclaimed the doctor. 'Interviews with beauty queens?'

'Yes, I think that's one of the things.'

'And with the mayor. And with the president of housewives. And with the chair of the commerce of agriculture. The parish priest, blah, blah, blah.'

'That's right. That's supplements for you.'

'And with advertisers.'

'Yes, I think it's normal to interview those who place an advertisement.'

'Do you get paid for that?'

'I do, Mr Montevideo. I get a tip for each supplement.'

'A scruple? You get a scruple?'

'What do you mean, a scruple?'

'Are you the one who gets paid for the advertisements?'

'No. That's left to people with more experience.'

'You should get paid for publicity.'

Stringer wasn't sure if he was being serious, but decided to answer him with sincerity.

'That's something I aspire to, Mr Montevideo.'

'Good, my boy. Well, go ahead. You may meet a beauty queen who's also the mayor's daughter and your biggest advertiser's niece. Have a wedding list with Barros or Pote department stores. I'll send you a copy of Uruguayan divorce law.'

'I'm also planning to write a purely literary column, Mr Montevideo.'

'Purely? Pass me the back scratcher.'

Adverbs in -ly made his back itch. Asking for the boxwood scratcher was his most radical way of correcting, expressing the hurt, stylistic misdemeanours caused him. He was offended and sad.

'I'm sorry. A free-ranging column.'

'Just try not to use Espasa too much.'

'I'll bring you what I've written in case you want to bless it.'

'No. If you show your face around here again, bring tobacco and imported whisky.'

Balboa remembers the first time he demonstrated his trust and sent him on an errand. 'Go to Santa Lucía Market and perform the miracle of Cana, but with whisky.' He gave him a blue banknote. It was so strange, so valuable, it seemed to have come from another country.

As he was leaving, with his head down, dragging his heels, 'Don't let them trick you! Obituaries are much more profitable. They have to be paid for in cash. The rafters of the sky can come crashing down, only a good death notice will stop a rotary press from going around. If you have to weed festivals, weed festivals. But the first chance you get, boy, step into Charon's printing boat. Do obituaries. That's the future.'

'We don't have obituaries, Dr Montevideo. It's a market we can't get into.'

'Then your *Expreso* hasn't long to live. With no death notices abaft the beam, a newspaper's going nowhere fast.'

O and Animals

Hairs fall, fall separately, one by one, but then have a tendency to come together, they form an undulating skein on the water, they alight and are sometimes the warp that blocks the pipes. Mother Olympia told me one day that, in ancient stories, loose hairs turn into water snakes. She let it out: 'I once heard that . . .' And perhaps never returned to the story, which was left floating downstream like a fallen leaf. That's another one. Leaves look bigger when they're floating on the water, they're the rafts sometimes used by small, itinerant frogs or ladybirds, the ones they call God's bugs. How serene, how attentive they are on their makeshift boats! It's the same with large animals. They don't get restless. The horse carried off by the River Mandeo, as the tide was going out, which reached the sea and was fished out by some people from Malpica, who then exclaimed with reason, 'The things the sea comes up with, Blessed Mary, without the need for a shovelful of manure!' They brought the piebald horse to Coruña Docks, looking all formal in the bows. How pretty is a horse's mane. Like Grumpy's. How pretty are animals. I'd say there's not a single ugly animal. 'You're bewitched,' Ana tells me. And when she says that, I do the thing she likes that makes her laugh so much, I imitate Polka's voice in Latin: '*Lavabo inter innocentes manus meas.*' They're all pretty. Come on then, think of an animal, tell me an animal that isn't pretty. A rat? Take a good look. Look at the other side of the river. Don't let yourself be influenced by the word. What you don't like is the word. Besides, Polka said it was thanks to river rats we discovered aspirin. When other animals died in plagues, rats got off scot-free, looking all shiny, because they gnawed at willow roots. The eye doctor, Dr Abril, once said invisible animals, bacteria and the like, are even more beautiful. Like modern paintings. That's because bacteria are modern as well, I thought to myself. The Colorado beetle's also modern. And pretty. But, being modern, it can't be killed by hand. Modern armament is needed. Polka says they'll end up killing everything, the cure is worse than the disease. The poison also kills off snails and slugs. He won't go where there are dying snails. We must seem very strange to other animals. You can tell by the way they look at us. When I was little, I told Polka I was afraid of the wolf and he laughed, 'Well, imagine how afraid the wolf would be if he bumped into me. Wolves are terribly afraid of lame people!' He says that as a joke. Polka's not that bad. You can tell ancient animals are ancient because they've been around time and seem to have come from the future. Like octopuses and razorshells. Snails and slugs. Lampreys. Or eels. Maybe hairs turn into eels. That wouldn't surprise me. Eels are a bit like us. The way they live in the mud, are desperate to eat, slip away when there's trouble. They can move by land as well. At night, you find eels in the meadows, travelling inland. I'm not surprised. It's so damp there's sometimes not much difference between being in the water and out. You could stuff the mist in sacks like stive. People go slowly through the atmosphere not just because it gets in your bones and makes your body stiff, but because they have to clear a way through the mist, like divers in their suits, you have to pass through curtain after curtain. It all takes time and occasionally words, sentences, are imprinted on the air as when you write with your finger in condensation. That way, you find out things that weren't meant for you. As happened with the letters left in the pocket of trousers that were for washing.

The Portuguese Architect

Reading them was like looking through a keyhole of noble ancestry. The look didn't ask if it was good or bad. The look was greedy. An enigmatic character appeared first of all. Who was this Most Worthy?

> Most Worthy Judge
> My dear Dr Azevedo da Acosta,

That's how well they know how to address each other, the heights they reach. Imagine Polka receiving a letter like that: *Most Worthy Gravedigger*. He'd think it had come from another world. If that's the way you start, you're not going to write just anything. You've something important to say.

> I would be greatly interested to know your opinion concerning the work of the Portuguese architect António Soares, based in the city of Porto. I have the impression he is considered a bright hope on account of his boat-houses and is held in high regard in foreign countries, in particular France and Holland. I would ask for the greatest discretion in the likely event that you should have to request additional information. People of importance to me in the field of construction are studying the possibility of hiring his services, but I wish this initial exploration to be confidential and not to come to the said architect's notice. Before contacting him and taking a false step, my friends wish to count on the opinion of someone of sound judgement and exceptional meticulousness, knowing that he will be duly rewarded for his efforts. At your service as always.
>
> May God keep you for many years.

And there, at the end, was the typed name: Ricardo Samos Pego-Mandivi.

This is what sets hairs and letters apart. Hairs go in search of each other and re-form locks in the river. But letters in the water quickly disintegrate. Though it's true there are some letters that, if you dry them out, go stiff like survivors who've been put in plaster casts. These letters resist and help each other out. They snuggle up close, hold on to each other, to avoid being gnawed, pulped, consumed, burnt. Drowned. These two were saved. They're whole and alive. One protecting the other. The one signed by the judge Ricardo Samos is obviously a carbon copy. Protected by the other, enclosed in a folded envelope. On the stamp, there's a shield with a white horse and a rider dressed in red clothes and a headscarf. It says *Correios de Portugal*. And, under the horse, Timor 1963.

If they came to me, it must be for a reason. Shame not to read them.

Most Excellent Judge

My dear Dr Samos,

Having received your letter, I quickly sought out information concerning the architect António Soares. The investigation was carried out by people I trust implicitly and obviously I looked into the matter myself. The results could not be more surprising. We found no evidence of an architect by that name and I am in a position to affirm that there is not one in the whole of Porto. There must have been some kind of mistake. All our enquiries came back negative, in the sense that we received no news of such a person either as an architect or in any other notable profession. We could only find a baker of that name, a man with the habits of his trade, who sleeps during the day and works at night, and who eventually was kind enough to confess that he had travelled to Galicia only once and had no plans to return. When asked why, he simply said that he considered it, and the whole of Spain, 'dangerous land'. He went no further, since he spoke very little and was distrustful when silent. I only mention this episode because of its interest concerning the prejudices people hold.

With God, for many years.

P.S. How are your studies on the links between the thought of José Donoso Cortés and our own António Sardinha?

P.P.S. I remember now a strange detail. The architect's name is the same as that of a sculptor from Porto in the last century, António Soares dos Reis, who happened to receive first prize at the 1881 Exhibition in Madrid for his work The Exile.

She'd give them back to the judge. They were his. They were in a zipped pocket in his green hunting trousers. It wasn't usual to find something like that. She always went through the clothes. In case there was a banknote or something. She only ever found the odd coin, which are like nits. Who knows what the letters were doing in there, his carbon copy and the Porto judge's reply? To start with, she wondered what this Most Worthy would be like. But then she directed all her attention towards the Portuguese architect and his boat-houses. Until then, these letters had only been read by the two friends. If they'd fallen into her hands, there must be a reason. She shared the secret about that invisible man, the Portuguese architect. She stared at the film of water. Who was this António Soares?

No. She wouldn't hand them to the judge. All saints have their favourite. She didn't even tell Neves the maid about her find when she took back the clean clothes. She waited until she was alone with the painter. She posed in the Chinese Pavilion as every Thursday, just as they'd agreed. It seemed to her the portrait was progressing very slowly. That day, the two of them, painter and model, glanced at each other from time to time, but without talking. A woman's voice hung in the air. Chelo had put that record on again with the opera singer whose voice extended time. She definitely had an open body, thought O. She found her calming, said the painter, though on O she had the opposite effect. She made her alert, excited, there were even moments she felt anxious. Her voice came out of the flames and returned to the embers. It reminded her of moths around a lamp and, when the record came to an end, she thought she could hear and smell the scorching of wings. Wings that burnt badly. That day, she had the letters in her hands and felt as if she were holding people. The effect of the song, even though she only understood a few words, sparks of excommunion, was to complicate everything. Get in your life, in the life of anyone who happened to be nearby. The future was a mystery, but this blazing melancholy extended the mystery to the past. When they'd been looking at prints and, out of all the ones she'd seen, without hesitating, with the joy of someone who's found the picture of their life, O had chosen that portrait of a bride with a fan of flowers carrying her bridegroom on her shoulders in a red jacket with a glass of wine. The red wine is a continuation of the bridegroom's arm and the toast gives way to an angel who's also red.

'I'm not surprised,' the painter had said. '*Double Portrait with a Glass of Wine* by Chagall. I'd have chosen the same picture. It has something to do with happiness. And happiness is very difficult to paint.'

In this new session, Chelo Vidal devoted more of her attention to the figure taking shape on the canvas than to O. And, in the air, there was that other woman. It must be exhausting having a voice like that, thought O. It's a gift, of course, but also a concern. Every sound, every word, every sigh, laugh and lament, would have to be kept in a chest.

'She's got eyes now,' said Chelo. 'And a look.'

She talked about the woman in O's portrait in the third person. The washerwoman crept over. She knew she'd find another being and wondered whether it would be a new or an old O, whether it would be the woman in the picture uneasily making off in search of uneasy happiness. That stupid thing about the portrait taking your spirit. No, what she was afraid of was the opposite. She was afraid of being disappointed. She wanted it to be a new O. An O with desire and impulse. A better O.

Finally their eyes met. Chelo moved away towards the radiogram, as if wanting to leave them alone.

She was a fighter. She liked the O in the picture. In fact, the two Os in the picture, since there was one washing and her reflection in the river. They were, and were not, the same. The one who was kneeling down, washing, eyed the other with smiling curiosity. You could say she was laughing at her. The other, who rather than being on the surface of the water was at the bottom, had a pale, melancholy expression. O liked the picture. And, thanks to it, discovered that she was the new O. Chelo had painted her as well, the third O, the one outside the picture. It was she who had to go in search of uneasy happiness.

'What do you think?'

'They're a little ugly.'

'A little ugly?' Chelo looked at her in surprise. 'I don't think they're ugly.'

'The point is they're very well done.'

'You think they're genuine?'

'Absolutely.'

Now four of them were looking at each other. In recognition. Trying to prolong the moment. The portrait only needed one more session. And that day would also be the washerwoman's last. They'd discussed it. It was time the washing machine, currently covered by a white sheet in the utility room, started working. O knew from Neves they'd bought it together with some other appliances months before. It was something she'd foreseen. That sooner rather than later there'd be no more work washing for the well-to-do. They'd almost all got modern washing machines. In fact, O, Olinda's daughter, was one of the last washerwomen in Coruña. As Amalia, since the opening of Leyma Dairies, was one of the last milkmaids. She'd noticed this, how people had started to look at her when she was carrying a load. They hadn't done this before. Even if she'd been carrying a huge load on top of her head, big as a hot-air balloon, they still wouldn't have looked at her. But recently they'd taken a few photos of her in the street. And a group photo with Ana, the other washerwoman, and Amalia the milkmaid, the one who used to say, 'We'll soon be found only on antique postcards!'

No. She wasn't going to wait to be dismissed. She knew from Neves that Chelo Vidal had said the machine was only for emergencies. O would have work in that house for as long as she wanted. O understood. Neves the maid was a good carrier pigeon.

O knew everything or almost everything. The communications network between women carrying things on top of their heads. She even knew the price, how much she was worth, how much for a load, the river, the sun's detergent in the market of machines. O was familiar with the sky, but she didn't live in the clouds. She was a fast one. And she went round to Hexámetro to see the washing machines. There was a very special one that had a porthole like a ship's. In that dark circle, she could see all of the past the machine was about to – what's the word? – drain. She viewed them with sympathy, they were machines with which she had something in common, rivers moved by electricity. She recalled Polka's faith in electricity. He'd wanted to call her Electra. In honour of the Greeks? No, in honour of the New Coruñan Electricity Company founded by Pepe Miñones, the Republican who . . . And Olinda said the priest would refuse, they needed the baptism certificate and, with the war, they'd also lost those words, those names, that electricity. No, she didn't say that. She just said, 'The girl's going to be called O, Our Lady of Expectation.'

'Expectation?'

'Expectation.'

'All right then. Expectation.'

Now that the washerwoman in the picture and her reflection in the river had taken shape, O noticed how all the sadness went out of her. She'd given herself the portrait, the completion of the portrait, as a deadline. She'd work hard this summer. Wash for the Samoses, for Dr Abril and that temporary job she'd got, sheets for the Hotel of Mirrors. It was only for a few weeks, until they finished installing the machines. But it would help her to save something before she emigrated. Polka and Amalia were right. She didn't want to end up on a postcard.

'I've something for you too, madam.'

She handed her the letters.

'They were in the green hunting trousers,' she spoke very softly. 'In the zipped pocket.'

She didn't give any further explanations and Chelo didn't ask for them. As she left, from behind the door, she heard the urgent unfolding of papers. Before returning the clothes, along the way, she'd listened to different voices. One had said, 'Don't get involved in family affairs.' That was Polka's. But she preferred the other, 'Each to his own saint.' That was also Polka's.

She went down Cantóns. Stopped at the traffic lights outside Pastor Bank. While she was waiting, she glanced over at a table on the terrace of the Galicia Café where the judge was sitting with some other men. This situation had occurred before. The first time it happened, she'd expected

427

a small sign, a minimal greeting. She was then the most visible person in the whole of the city. She'd been carrying a load, a huge globe, on top of her head. But the judge hadn't seen her. Never mind. So where were these boat-houses?

The Hotel of Mirrors

'The Hotel of Mirrors?'

O had asked everywhere and people in the street didn't know, though some of them gave her a funny look, as if she'd been carrying a pink neon advertisement on top of her head. There must be a mistake with the address. She then dared to push open that door, the one with the neon sign for La Boîte de Pandora. There was a very steep staircase, a dark tunnel leading down to the basement. She felt the desire to go back outside, but the music climbed the steps and offered her its hand. The instruments were in conversation, sharing good and bad times, drawing and accompanying her footsteps. It was evening. When she reached the last step, there was a sudden movement of shadows and she felt with disgust a claw on her shoulder. She froze, unable to speak. The musicians carried on playing, as if they couldn't drop their notes so suddenly. She had the impression there were lots of them, huddling in a dark corner, around a piano's large set of teeth. She turned and stared into the small, bright eyes of the parrot which had landed on her shoulder. In fact, there were four musicians and the one who came over had a circle on his lips. The mark of the trumpet's mouthpiece. She looked at him, bewitched. Forgot about the bird's furtive presence. The trumpet player grabbed the parrot and returned it to its perch. As the darkness dissipated, she realised the establishment was full of exotic birds. And the wall at the end was made of water. Water that kept changing colour.

The trumpet player seemed to be watching her through the concentric mark of his lips. To avoid the circle becoming undone, O ran back upstairs.

She finally found the entrance she was looking for, on the other side of the building. There was no sign on the outside, not even the small, blue plaque indicating a boarding-house. But this did not mean it had been abandoned. The hotel had recently been refurbished and, already in reception, had the pride of decrepit premises that have suddenly grown chandeliers on the ceilings and mirrors on the walls. The reception desk clearly fancied itself as a bar, its counter having been clad in red imitation leather. To start with, O thought the receptionist had a tie which was also made of imitation leather. A man placed among the furniture and chandeliers. She could imagine this was a place for what Polka called 'women with schedules' – he was always very careful with his words. Polka was a great friend of women. One day, they'd laughed at him for calling Olinda 'sweetheart' in public. 'I'll be off now, sweetheart.' Since when it had been like a second nickname: Polka Sweetheart. He felt better with women. When he started working as a gravedigger, he used to pass in front of the Cuckoo's Feather bar, packed with men, many of them playing cards, and shout from the doorway, 'There's no money to be made here for a gravedigger!' He'd often go down to the river to help Olinda carry the clothes. O too, after Olinda died. And he loved to take part in conversation. He liked to play with words and make people laugh and think, like a comical priest: 'Let whoever is without a stone throw the first sin.'

Amalia came straight out with it, 'It's a brothel, darling, rooms by the hour, for fucking.' What did O care? She didn't mind what clothes she washed. It was only for a short period. Until she sorted out her papers, since she'd made up her mind to leave. What did she care? It was better even. No small, fiddly garments to wash. Just bedclothes. From beds for strangers with secret rendezvous. That'd give her something to think about while she was washing. There was a special room. A room full of mirrors. The ceiling itself was a mirror. The lady showing her around, who lived there and was a mysterious figure, it was unclear whether she was a guest or manager, explained in a whisper, as if she didn't want the mirror images to hear, that this was the suite used by Mr Manlle to unmake the bed with his little friends. Unmake the bed. Little friends. O found it funny the way she talked. She spun around, multiplying her image in the mirrors.

'Two people unmaking the bed here is like twenty people doing it twenty times.'

'Yes, it's more pleasurable.'

'Who's this Manlle?'

It was now the turn of Samantha, the Woman with the Feather Boa, to scan her multiple images in the mirrors. Despite being talkative, she seemed to have to weigh up her answer to that question.

'Don't you know who Manlle is? Better not to know. He's the owner of this and a lot more.'

She closed the door to the suite of mirrors.

'Come, come to my room,' she gestured.

It was a small room stuffed full of things. A strange mixture of luxury and second-hand. The walls were covered in photographs and portraits with the boa woman's unmistakable presence. Here there are no mirrors, but another kind of multiplication made with fragments of time. Everyone has their own air, which they always carry with them, thought O, but it was still surprising how much that woman resembled herself. She changed age, clothes, hairstyle. One thing remained the same in almost all of them and that was her sturdy physique. And yet in one of the larger photos she was extraordinarily thin, as if she'd wasted away. Strangely enough, she was more herself than ever. Because of that look she had.

The look she was giving her now. Hard and shocked at the same time.

'That Manlle's a bandit,' she said. 'He takes after Judas. Pretends to be a gentleman, but bites before he barks. He's never satisfied, the pig. He's bought off everyone, sealed their lips. But I've got it all in here, girl. Inside my noddle. I wish the rest of my body worked as well as my head. Do you know how he started? No, how could you?'

Anyone who stared at O for long enough felt like storing things inside those large, open eyes.

'He started with wolfram. Do you know what wolfram is? No, of course you don't!'

O nodded. She'd never actually seen it. She couldn't discuss its colour or appearance. But she knew everything about wolfram. There were three wolfram mine shafts in Polka's right leg. Two in his ankle and one in his

431

knee. He'd been forced to work as a prisoner in the River Deza mines. Had been wounded while trying to escape. A steady supply of this mineral, which was abundant in Galicia, was essential to the munition factories in Nazi Germany. Polka's scars changed colour according to the season. In summer, they were pink. In winter, they turned dark violet. Which was when he limped the most. He'd received poor treatment. Polka said it had given the ants time to come inside him.

'And why do you live here?' O dared to ask.

'I live here because it belongs to me. But now he wants to throw me out. Leave me in the street like a beggar. What am I supposed to do – sleep in a doorway? Trouble is he finds papers where there weren't any. He puts himself about and, wherever I go, buildings or offices, they look at me like I'm a scarecrow. I'm not stupid. He's taking everything. Making a mint with the old Dance Academy. I had it all, girl. Almost all. A lot. Something. I had something. You never heard of me, girl? Never heard of the Dance Academy? Look at that portrait. That's hardly a scarecrow, now, is it? That boyish haircut. You should have seen me dancing the Charleston, foxtrot, cuplé. And all the rest of it. I was always ahead of the fashion. I always loved life, girl, though it's a bitch. I got up to all kinds of things. But you won't catch me in a confessional. You have to have a little bit, just a little bit of shame.'

She pointed to another portrait on the wall, that of a thin woman wearing an Andalusian costume. 'Take her. Her name was Flora. She was a brave woman. Always contradicting me. She was almost always right. I was a bit bossy. And she did look better dressed as a flamenco dancer. She was right about that too. She disappeared during the first days of the war. That was the last I heard of her. I suppose, if she could, she died fighting.

'Others had a better time of it. Even during the war. That one there's Pretty Mary. She seemed very shy and delicate, like an eggshell. She was very devout back then, I suppose she still is, you can be both things at once, there are mystical women you had to see in order to believe when they let themselves go. They really could drive a man crazy. Pretty Mary is Manlle's sweetheart. She still sings from time to time, but her job is to stand at a window, OK, it's a luxury apartment, watching out for boats.

Customs patrol boats, if you get my meaning. All she has to do is sing down the phone. "They've just left, Daddy. They've just come back, Daddy." That way, the smugglers never get caught. There's a merchant ship which is always just inside international waters. Called Mother. With a bellyful of tobacco. That's the one that keeps everyone supplied. Manlle knows more about port traffic than the customs chief and police combined.

'You know why I know so many things? Because I'm also a Mother.' She draped the boa artistically over her shoulders, stroked her breasts and burst out laughing. 'I used to be more of a Mother than I am now. This boat's spent lots of time out in international waters. And some things only naughty mothers find out.'

O was curious about a smaller photo which was more worn than the others, had a serrated edge and showed a woman with a mattress on top of her head.

'That's Milagres. The cook who fluffed up the wool.' She again shrieked with laughter. 'The cook who fluffed up the wool! You probably know her son. He's a travelling photographer, large as a lighthouse, called Hercules. Goes around with a wooden piebald horse.'

O knew Hercules. Of course she did. He'd always enquire after Polka. One time, the photographer with the horse and O with the donkey met. 'What's the donkey's name?' 'Grumpy. And the horse?' 'Carirí.' 'They'd make a good couple, Grumpy and Carirí.'

'I was there at the son's birth. Curtis was already a lighthouse when he was born. He would have been champion of Galicia.'

Every time O went to the Hotel of Mirrors, she saw the Old Woman with the Feather Boa, who knew things others didn't. Sometimes she was frightened by what she heard. She'd leave the hotel with the exciting and dangerous sensation of knowing too much. On top of her head, she'd be carrying a load of clothes and another one of Samantha's secrets.

'Were you called Samantha as a child?'

She used a long holder to smoke scented cigarettes. O realised, whenever thorny episodes came up, Samantha created a cloud.

'I was never a child. I didn't have time to be a child. Childhood didn't exist when I was born.'

On such occasions, the smoke would pour out of her mouth's exhaust, in a grimace her make-up multiplied by three. O reached the following conclusion: everything in that woman was multiplied by three because of her superimposed faces. It wasn't farcical, it was real. When happy, very happy. When sad, three times dark.

'I had to run away from childhood. Hence my physique. I had to grow up quickly. Were you not maltreated when you were little?'

'By whom?'

Three times horror. Samantha blew out another cloud of smoke. Her face had turned deathly pale.

'I won't let them abuse me now I'm old.'

She went back to the subject of Manlle. He'd started making money transporting wolfram to the docks from the Carballo and Silleda mines. At the start of the Second World War, when the Nazis redoubled their efforts, wolfram became a precious mineral. 'Anyone with initiative and four wheels could make pots of money. He sought out vehicles wherever he could find them. Vehicles requisitioned during the war. Belonging to official organisations. To the army. Under wraps. He also covered up for others. Made lots of contacts. He can pull strings in the most unlikely places. But he's a spendthrift as well. He's like a spoilt child who's never had enough. To start with, I liked him for it. His background was poor, but he was open-handed. We came to an agreement. I'm not the peace of the world, its daily bread, but I keep my word. He's false. Like Judas. When he acquired the Dance Academy, he swore he'd give everyone work and he promised me the mirror suite for life. I trusted him. More fool me!

'Milagres, Hercules' mother, the woman with the mattress, eventually left for South America when her son came down from the mountains, having been on the run because of the war. She left with a harpooner who'd worked on a whaling ship in Cee. The harpooner had a cetacean's goodness. They went to Brazil. Opened a restaurant in Recife called the Whale's Belly. I'm not surprised. He was always giving Milagres things that had turned up in the bellies of whales.'

'What things?' O asked the Woman with the Feather Boa incredulously.

'You can find anything inside a whale's belly,' she replied. 'St Gonzalo

434

once entered a whale and came back with an image of the Virgin. So just imagine what it's like now!'

'For example?' insisted O.

'He gave her a beautiful doll whose hair grew because it was natural.'

'What else?'

'A revolver,' said Samantha, twirling her feather boa.

'He gave her a revolver and a doll?'

'No. He gave her the doll with the china face and goatskin body. I got the revolver, girl. Do you want to see it?'

'No way! Oh, go on then.'

O wanted to see what was used to kill men.

'It's called a Bulldog.'

And that's what the revolver was like. Snub-nosed and fierce.

The Lights Going Out

18 July 1963

The judge told the story again that evening in the main reception room of the Finis Terrae Hotel. Here a banquet was being held to celebrate 18 July, day of the National Movement, which had been declared a holiday in commemoration of the start of the military uprising against the Republic. It was attended by all the provincial and local authorities and leaders of the only party and trade union, arrayed in their uniforms, badges and medals. There were also select representatives of what was termed in official language 'the city's strata and kinetic energy'. This year, Franco's arrival had been postponed, but several prominent members of the regime had come from the capital to prepare the Caudillo, his family and entourage's summer visit. The main reception room, which had a mezzanine by way of a large interior balcony, was equipped on one side with tall windows which gave on to the port, but the scene that evening was dominated by majestic chandeliers and omnipresent marble, solid in the columns and stairs, shining on the surface of the walls, with a pastiche of festoons and honeysuckles. The guests occupied the main floor, the tables having been set out with exact, hierarchical precision. Despite the architectural consistency and a tendency towards uniformity of style in the guests, broken only by the bold anecdote of a few women's garments, there was this year a subdued murmur underpinning the tinkle of cutlery, which had to do with the delayed start to the Head of State's holidays and the spring's events.

He was feeling restless. The seat next to him was empty. He kept checking the time. But Samos' unease was not caused by the absence of his wife, Chelo, after whom the nearest guests, most of them judges and prosecutors, had enquired in order to be informed she would arrive a little late due to a pressing engagement. He'd considered giving a more detailed explanation, namely that she was taking her leave of a group of Portuguese teachers and students of architecture who'd come to study Coruña's boat-houses. But he kept quiet. He could imagine the collective sneer, 'What exactly do you mean by boat-houses?' However much he tried to put it to the back of his mind, he found a bitter taste in the phrase 'Portuguese architect'. Furthermore, despite Chelo's open enthusiasm, he still couldn't understand all this interest in boat-houses. Rationalist architecture inspired by Le Corbusier. A few days before, he'd done something unusual for him. He'd asked Chelo to draw up a route of boat-houses. Her favourite boat-houses. He wasn't greatly interested in modern architecture. If he had to admire something, he said provocatively, it was whatever had a vocation for permanence and magnificence, such as Santiago Cathedral with its baroque façade or Pastor Bank in Coruña with its neo-baroque entrance. These houses that did so much for Chelo and a few enlightened visitors struck him as simple and practical. They'd been inspired by the famous Le Corbusier. All right. What else? He didn't think they'd go down in history for their curved balconies that recalled a ship's bridge. Or for the ribbon windows, the synthesis of arts and the Modulor. The Modulor? A universal, harmonious measurement based on the proportions of the human body. But he still went and asked her for a map of rationalist build-ings because what he wanted was to observe her reaction. Her reaction was unexpected, much better, more calming than he could have hoped: 'Wouldn't you like me to be your personal guide? We could go and see them together.' And she added with a smile, 'Along the way, I'll explain to you Le Corbusier's five points of architecture.' Her reply cheered him up enormously. For some time, he'd been torturing himself with suspi-cions of infidelity. Of course it'd be wonderful if she accompanied him. If they went on one of those outings together they kept talking about and postponing. But in this instance he confessed he was curious to see them without her and to draw his own conclusions.

'You're resistant to any architectural charms,' said Chelo.

'No, I don't think so.'

'I'll give it a go in writing. I'll make you a map and some notes. It's best to start with the Atalaya building by Antonio Tenreiro in Recheo Gardens. Or else on Pardo Bazán, where there are several boat-houses, the best of which is number 6 Pardo Bazán. That has a façade which is reminiscent of a prow. You must have seen it.'

'You walk down the street and miss lots of interesting things.'

'Yes, our eyes are sometimes a little imprisoned.'

Chelo wrote while saying aloud, '6 Pardo Bazán. Architect: José Caridad Mateo.'

'Caridad Mateo,' he repeated. 'The son of General Caridad Pita.'

'That's right, one of them.'

They kept up the same tone, but to talk of the Caridad family normally was unusual. A pretence. In the city, its environment, even in private, you didn't talk about General Caridad Pita or his sons. It would have been an anomaly. His name was a taboo among the victors, even to be cursed or denigrated. General Caridad was the leading military authority at the time of the coup, he remained loyal to the constituted government and, in front of the firing squad, shouted, 'Long live the Republic!' No, it wasn't normal to talk about General Caridad. Or his son, the architect, who was in prison and then went into exile. Or the other, younger son who fled by ship. They disappeared, vanished. Ex-men.

'I understand the architect's in Mexico,' said the judge. In fact, he had this on good authority. Inspector Ren had told him so. But he didn't say this. He just added, 'I'll have to take a look at number 6 Pardo Bazán.'

'He was very talented. Did you ever meet him?'

'No,' replied Samos. 'Not him.'

They never spoke of the matter again. For him, the conversation had been reassuring. The mention of that name that had been struck off the census helped to banish his fears. The buildings were there, in the book of the city, with their styles, history and people who studied them. Hardly surprising they also had their ghosts, after what had happened.

Chelo did not deserve this suspicious, jealous state that had been gnawing away inside him for years. He couldn't exactly say when their relationship ceased to have to do with feelings. The balance of their marriage was a front sustained by interest and convenience. They didn't have problems because they were both polite and respected each other's space as you respect someone's furniture. The twin blades of a pair of scissors. It was Father Munio who had once compared marriage to a pair of scissors. One blade can't function without the other. The judge may have been the main cause of distance. This was something he'd started to consider after all these years. He hadn't paid her enough attention when her father, Mayarí, died. Depression? He didn't understand. Dying was one of the laws of life, wasn't it? He hadn't known how to respond in the case of Gabriel. He realised now his discomfort was caused not just by his speech impediment, that terrible stutter, but by any other sign of weakness or imperfection. Though he never would have recognised it – he believed a patriarch's sincerity was counterproductive in the home and the slightest Freudian concession gave him an itch – there may have been some truth in Chelo's theory that he was taking out his own frustrations on Gabriel. His serious character had lately veered towards taciturn melancholy. He easily got annoyed, especially in the Palace of Justice, be it in his office or in the courtroom. Where before he had felt firm and strong, now he frequently became despotic. His concern, his obsession with the 'Portuguese architect', had threatened to ruin their diplomatic entente. Stuck in the Crypt, driven by his reading of the man with fiery words, he fell into a kind of rugged fanaticism. When he received an answer from his Most Worthy colleague, he almost exploded with rage. The Portuguese architect didn't exist. Who was the other man? Finally he managed to control himself and enter a period of cold calculation. He went so far as to design the most sordid use possible of his powers as judge should it reach the point where he had to defend his honour. He went through the law and sentences with a fine-tooth comb. He could make Chelo Vidal go to prison, turn her into a social outcast. But his plan, the revenge that most satisfied him, was to pardon her and have her, self-confessed, at home. Watch the guilt drive her crazy. One day, he found her removing the dust from her opera records with a cloth. Her finger, in a velvet hood,

439

circled slowly around the vinyl grooves. Her finger like the needle of a bodily appliance. Her gaze distracted. That's how he'd like to see her all the time. Especially after discovering, in the false bottom of a wooden chest, a Getúlio-Vargas-style revolver with a pearly handle, perfect for what we might call an artistic denouement. All this had been in a fit of passion. He calmed down the day she herself mentioned the Portuguese architect. Without being asked, Chelo simply untied the knot that had so entangled him. She came to his study. Looking beautiful as always. Wiping her fingers on a colour-stained cloth. He adopted his recent glowering expression. Chelo said, 'Ricardo, the Portuguese architect called this morning. Remember? The one I took on a tour with students of boat-houses.'

'Yes. So what?'

'He's come back from Holland.'

'From Holland?'

'Yes, he lives and works in Holland. He's giving a seminar in Lisbon and has come with his students. I told you about it.'

It was quite possible she had, but for some time now he hadn't wanted to listen.

What was worrying him now had nothing to do with Chelo. It was the implementation of the newly created Tribunal of Public Order. Samos had been one of the advisers. Not the main one, but he'd made a contribution given his knowledge of political law. A state of emergency had just been declared for a period of two years. He'd written an article signed by Syllabus, in which he quoted Schmitt: 'A state of emergency is to law what a miracle is for theology.' As a result of the new tribunal, the state of emergency would no longer be a military matter, that burden on the regime that is a state of war, and instead would become a civil affair. Ricardo Samos had reason to believe that the creation of the tribunal would enable him to receive a promotion, finally to occupy a position of high authority. But he was concerned. The sentencing to death and execution of the rebel Julián Grimau for alleged crimes committed more than a quarter of a century earlier, in time of war, agreed by a military tribunal, had been accompanied by the irregularity of delaying the start of the new tribunal, which necessitated a legal artifice. Only a few knew about it, of course. And he was one of them. He wasn't quite sure what to think. He aspired to be a great jurist, but all that manoeuvring on their part . . . If only he could make it to the Supreme Court. Yes, the Supreme Court was where he should be.

The censor Dez arrived a little late and sat down next to him. Dez did know where he was going to be. After the summer, he'd finally make the move to Madrid. He was bored, he said laughingly, of his job as censor, of running after poets with a red pencil. Now he'd be on the front line. In the Ministry of Information. Instead of cutting bits out, he'd be adding them. There his publication was guaranteed.

'Don't say you're going to stop writing poetry?' asked Fasco the prosecutor. 'That new collection you promised us, *The Moment of Truth*, what will happen to it?'

'I'm going to let it sit for a while,' said Dez, diverting the conversation. 'Publish something different. A novel. You'll be surprised, I'm sure.' And he murmured enigmatically, 'I myself was surprised when I pulled that out of me.'

The judge had also pulled something out. He wasn't quite sure why or when or under what impulse the story had reared its head, but the fact is he again told the story of the tribute to Schmitt in Madrid a little over a year earlier, which he'd had the good fortune to attend as one of the jurist's Spanish disciples.

They egged him on. Some had not heard the story before and were greatly interested in Don Carlos, a living myth for jurists and practising judges, such an influential and mysterious figure.

As had happened in the Crypt, the initial reaction to the end of the story – Don Carlos' statement, 'This is a sacred feast in the winter of my life,' followed by the lights going out, a total blackout that immersed the headquarters of the National Movement in darkness – the initial reaction, Samos saw once again, was one of amazement, thoughtful silence. Despite the fact that, as Samos was fully aware, the ending invited spontaneous laughter. But his listeners hesitated between laughing, since the scene was particularly funny, and biding their time, since the people in it weren't particularly funny. Samos, the only one who'd witnessed the event, then made use of all his eloquence to turn that blackout into a kind of apotheosis of Schmitt's power of presence. A mystical ending.

He'd been there and counted it as one of the most memorable acts he'd been fortunate enough to attend. 'The master of ceremonies was wonderful and I'm not just saying that because he's now minister. What a minister he'll be! A long-range cannon. Did you see how he devoured the international media? And something that's important given the current situation. He's a man of law. He has our training.' He was sure the last bit would please his fellow guests. 'It was a lesson in oratory. Going back to the roots. A man with fiery words, as Donoso was said to be.'

They were serving the first course after some appetisers. The judge looked at his watch. Chelo would be here soon. Fasco the prosecutor raised his glass and proposed a toast, 'To next year!' He then addressed the judge, 'The lights going out must have been a pretty special moment. Weren't you afraid?'

In the hotel's main reception room, the lights did not go out, but Fasco the prosecutor and Samos the judge could not help feeling partially responsible for what happened next. A cloud of lampoons fell from the interior balcony, covering the chandeliers and causing momentary darkness. Rather than being a cloud, its form was of a flock of white birds gliding softly. On the one hand, the flock of lampoons silenced all the guests, who were astonished and raised their heads. On the other, their sound, that of the lampoons, had more in common with the idea of music than with noise, since their descent was in slow motion, autumnal.

Faces of shock, amazement, irritation. In short, blank lampoons.

'Well, they're not entirely blank,' said Fasco in an intriguing voice, feeling and examining the pieces of paper. 'They're in Braille!' He glanced at his fellow guests, stood up and went towards the top table, his annoyance at such an absurd event causing him to mutter, 'In Braille!'

The others did the same. Fingered the pieces of paper. He was right, they had raised points, they had perforations.

The language of the blind. Blind, blind, blind. Wells, Wells, Wells. The judge drank some water. The taste of water. It could do with some sugar. Yes, the gorilla who'd urinated on the pyre was there somewhere, in full-dress uniform, an authority now. They hadn't read Wells. They hadn't read his story, *The Country of the Blind*, about a man who fell into a valley where the faculty of sight was considered abnormal. Blast it! Why did this scandal, this act of subversion, make him think of Wells? There were days he became angry with his memory, his mind's insistence on going off alone.

After the initial commotion, pre-war posturing, the dinner guests of the National Movement returned to their ranks and were harangued by the governor. Meanwhile plain-clothes agents picked up every single blank lampoon.

Chelo ran as fast as she could down Tabernas Street. She knew she couldn't keep going for long. But she also knew she had an option. A refuge. Santiago Church. She'd been there often as a guide. And had often exchanged messages in missals. There was a place, a hollow under the altar of Our Lady of Milk, which a restorer friend had shown her and even the priests didn't know about. Long enough for the immediate danger to pass. She'd leave in the morning, as the first Mass was being said.

Shame about the shawl. She needed time. She had to think. An item of clothing could change everything. The situation struck her now as absurd, but absurdity is defined by bad luck. That bogey. When she entered the hotel through reception, where she was received with smiles, from the policemen as well, she'd seen the danger, that woman sitting alone at the bar. Reading a newspaper. A strong woman with lots up front, on the verge of bursting at the seams. She'd reminded her of the Feminine Section chief Sada always joked about because of the way she walked, 'There goes the National Movement!' But it wasn't her. Chelo hadn't seen her before. She carried on. Checked her watch. Soon it would be time for the governor and provincial chief's speeches. The best moment. She headed towards the mezzanine, as if to enjoy the views of the port. She propped the pack of lampoons against the balustrade. There was a timing device which would set it off. But as she was preparing it, she felt the shadow behind her. Coming after her. It couldn't catch her. But it grabbed her shawl.

Inspector Mancorvo discreetly approached the judge. Said, 'Please don't get up now, Samos. But before you leave, don't fail to talk to us. We'll wait for you at the exit.'

And there they were. Mancorvo, Ren and a third person, a woman he hadn't seen before, in a suit. Tall and strong.

'We have a serious problem, your honour,' said Ren.

They went to the far end. There really was a magnificent view of the bay. The twinkling of green and red lights. Their vibrant reflection on the water. The crane lights. Ren pulled something from under his jacket.

'Do you recognise this?'

He was going to touch it, could have said, 'Night blue with a black velvet pattern.' But Samos kept quiet. Just nodded.

The Denunciation

I embark on this poem in the hope its felicity of phrase will speed the boat towards St Pierre and Miquelon. I was practising how to type without looking at the keys. Copying a poem from an anonymous book that came to me in an envelope with no return address. We get lots of anonymous letters at the station. Mostly denunciations. You'd be surprised how many anonymous denunciations there are going around. In some of them, you can see the care they've taken with their handwriting. How it's been written and rewritten till the letters look elegant and pretty. Maybe the person writing it thinks this will make their denunciation more effective. Some of the poems in the anonymous book were in fact denunciations. True ones, against history, but I couldn't process them. They were good poems. The ones that attracted me the most talked of voyages through cod-infested seas to Terranova and Nova Scotia, even higher up, to the limits of Greenland and the Arctic. So my fingers were trotting happily along, driven by nostalgia for a didactic embrace from Catia, the teacher in the typing academy, when an alarm pulled them up. Without looking, I can tell a Fascist by the way he opens the door, since I work with Fascists. It didn't take me long to realise that the one who'd come in had a fire burning inside him. The sea breeze makes summers in Coruña cool, but suddenly, as if activated by the Hispano-Olivetti carriage return, the temperature rose by several degrees. I knew the man. He was a cold man. And yet now he was dying, burning, to find his wife. Invested with authority, he could have been wearing his gown, but despite controlling his words, he still couldn't extinguish the fire they caused to spread across his face and light up his eyes. Love? A red colour, I know, but I'd say there was a stronger type of fuel in that mixture. When he talked to me of 'wounded pride' and 'a question of honour', the way he said it, I knew he was chewing on hot coals and ashes.

At that time, when a woman of her class would never flee, I found the case enthralling, a strange present of amazement wrapped up in surprise. One of those moments you have the exciting sensation your badge has become a hunting permit for banned specimens. And as he discussed certain details, with lots of usury, I felt part of his hotness being passed on to me. He stopped before long. He had a problem. She had a problem. I had a handful of embers.

Paúl Santos leant out of the window. The year before, when he joined the station at around the same time, in the distance, beyond the swinging necks of the cranes, moored next to the yacht club, he could discern the solid presence of the *Azor*, Franco's recreational boat. The Head of State would sometimes arrive on it at the end of a fishing trip in the Bay of Biscay. But more often than not the boat arrived first, while the dictator travelled from Madrid by road. In his studies of physiognomy, Santos found a total, excessive, even grotesque correspondence between the Caudillo and his boat. The yacht was snub-nosed, simple in profile and heavy to sail. Any *bou* heading out for the Great Sole was more elegant. The most complete picture he had of the *Azor* was on the day it appeared in the bay towing a cetacean that had been shot dead. In the shimmering sea, the hard colours of dusk, Santos observed a violent tension in language. The only verb he could use to describe that act was 'gun down'. More than an aquatic machine, the *Azor* was a steamroller of water. As a boat, starting with the name, which meant *goshawk*, it was a paradox. An absurd reality. Santos knew this thought, even if it were never expressed, placed him on dangerous ground. The truth is the *Azor* was an imposing, intimidatory presence. That ugly, stunted boat dominated the port. Determined time. Altered measurements. And space.

Santos' mind had undergone a similar process to when he learnt how to type without looking at the keys. One thought led to another and these two to a third, which to start with caused him anguish (a voice that said,

'You'll think the worst'), as when he got trapped around the waist on a potholing expedition down a little explored passageway in King Cintolo's Cave, Mondoñedo. Having surmounted the difficulty, he found himself in a larger space. Which is what enabled him now to ignore the very idea of the Azor and observe the movement of the cranes loading logs on the Western Quay. Before entering the line of descent, they swung in the air. And he thought it was the stripped, shaken memory that caused the freshness.

No. The boat hadn't arrived yet this year. Something was up, no one quite knew what. The city had witnessed that strange event, an incident on the evening of 18 July, in the presence of all the authorities and National Movement's guests at a banquet to celebrate the mutiny that replaced the Republic with a dictatorship. Paúl Santos didn't need to work it out. The war had started twenty-seven years earlier. He'd been born almost nine months after 18 July. The war of wars. Omnipresent war. A war that stuck like another component in the air, oblivious of time. He didn't want to think about it. There it was, happy as Larry, thinking everyone's thoughts.

He had to think about specific things. His job as a scientific policeman. An outstanding detective in Crime. With two important cases on his hands. Different in size, but both affecting the city's very foundations. On the one hand, Manlle. Manlle's organisation. He'd been lucky, made lots of progress, had almost all the evidence he needed to expose this criminal empire. And now a kind of gift. He had to find an upper-class lady, a beauty of exemplary conduct, who'd just abandoned her husband, a judge with a promising career in front of him, who was well connected, influential, and about whom it was repeatedly rumoured he'd soon move on to higher things. Come on, think, Paúl Santos. Why did Ricardo the judge call at your office? He could have summoned me to the courthouse and I'd have gone running. He could have done it differently. But no. He came here and denounced his wife for abandoning the conjugal home and, he had reason to believe, committing the crime of adultery.

It must have been the station chief who told him to do this. They were testing him, right? Come on, Santos, think. Be more specific.

Paúl Santos walked over to a shelf where he had his reference books. Carefully read the articles in the Penal Code, and accompanying notes in Civitas, that had some bearing on the Vidal case. He never could have imagined his heart would beat faster on account of the Penal Code.

Adulterous conduct consists of carnal union between two miscreants that can be expressed by the terms: lying together, carnal access, copulation, cohabitation, leading a joint, intimate or marital life. It is essential that the lying together be evident or deduced from proven facts but, given the difficulty of surprising someone in the complete, material act, its existence can be deduced from facts that are more symptomatic, such as spending eighteen days in a hotel . . .

Eighteen days?

Why eighteen days?

Despite its absurdity, this law tested the imagination. The penalties were severe, involved imprisonment and related only to woman. According to the law, she could be convicted if she was surprised once with the other miscreant in bed. *Adultery is committed by a married woman who lies with a man who is not her husband, and by the one who lies with her, knowing her to be married, even if the marriage is then declared null and void.* Paúl Santos, however, was thinking about something else, not the judge or his wife. Eighteen days in a hotel room with the Tachygraphic Rose. He tried to trigger his imagination, but couldn't get past the first day. He was happy like this. Went back to the typewriter. Pressed a few keys. The word *cohabitation*. The word *miscreant*. The word *bed*. The metal bars got entangled and prevented the carriage return. He started again. Arms at right angles. The optic nerve connected to the fingers, but without looking. That's right. Have another go. *I embark on this poem in the hope its felicity of phrase will speed the boat towards St Pierre and Miquelon.*

The Notebook

'You can be present if you wish, Mr Samos.'

'No, it's better if you talk to him alone.'

Gabriel didn't talk. He read from his notebook. After saying goodbye to the docks, or on the boat to the Xubias, or when crossing Ponte da Pasaxe, or going inside the boat-houses, or taking the tram to Sada, or on the train to Betanzos, and once ('Surely not!' muttered Chief Inspector Ren), once it even happened on the upper deck of a trolleybus, one of those red trolleybuses from London, the number 2, Porta Real–Os Castros, there too they did it, made love or something, his hand up her skirt.

'Surely not!'

Yes, she'd been protected, covered by this city of Mist Pee, Fly Pee, Wind on the Side of Hunger, Widows' Wind, Night Enclosure, Sky with a Shell, with an Awning, Bramble Sky, Oza in a Thunderstorm, thunder and lightning, this city with its carnal, voluptuous, promiscuous sky.

Between thunder and lightning, when it cleared, thanks to Gabriel's tale, everyone began to see clips of Chelo Vidal kissing and loving the Portuguese architect. Or whoever it was. And in this third party's tale there was an enjoyment, a lingering, that acted like a sucker on the temples of all who listened.

Everything Gabriel said was noted down in shorthand or in handwriting no onlooker could read. But Santos wasn't looking at the strange note-book, he was watching the window, which was a moving picture of boats and cranes. Everything inside him was moving too. Rarely had he felt such excitement on account of language.

'In the sea?'

449

'Yes, they'd stay there for two, three, even four minutes and then emerge, blowing a siphon of water. In Canaval, when there was no one about, they'd wrap themselves in seaweed and roll in the sand.'

When he turned around, Ren was blowing smoke rings, which Mancorvo followed as they rose to the ceiling. The central table was empty, completely bare, except for Gabriel's notebook, which gave it the air of an incendiary device. The eyes, facial muscles, position of the body, suggest an initial critical reaction to the text. The line of the mouth, for example, is a type of pronouncement. They were satisfied to begin with. Both were in a stupor, but it was a victorious stupor. With his smoke signals, Ren seemed to be savouring this surprising tale like a triumph. Having this degree of information about a life doesn't just give you the power to dispose of it, it grants you access to a particular kind of enjoyment: the dissection of someone else's enjoyment.

'He's finished. How many meetings was that?'

When they looked at each other, Ren's face seemed to hide a complex thought after he'd blown so many smoke rings into the air. But what he said, with clearly universal connotations, was, 'Unbelievable!'

Mancorvo nudged him. 'Just as well the judge wasn't here!' Ren ignored him. He was reaching the same conclusion as Santos. The boy had laid a trap. A tale moored to reality. He was pulling their legs.

It was Santos who took the initiative. 'Tell us the truth, Gabriel. Everything you've written is a lie, isn't it?'

'Everything,' Gabriel replied with certainty.

'What's Durtol, Gabriel?'

'A sanatorium.'

'Have you been there? Why do you write from Durtol? What happens in Durtol, Gabriel?'

'Let's leave it,' suggested Santos.

'Katechon!' Ren exclaimed bitterly. He looked at Gabriel's unintelligible notebook. 'You know how to scrawl, don't you?'

A Load of Suspicion

'Judith?'

They could have enquired after anyone. But they go and ask about someone who doesn't exist. There are loads of names in these parts. Some people have three or four names. But, outside the Bible, I couldn't think of a single Judith. And even if I had, I wouldn't have told them.

'Police,' said the spindly one with a lack of enthusiasm. If you're police, I thought, you could at least act the part. Show a golden badge the way they do in American movies. No style! The spindly one looked like he had an invisible toothpick in his mouth. His hair was slicked back with brilliantine, he was a bit of a dandy. Maybe that was why he couldn't be bothered. The road had just been tarmacked, the tarmac was still fresh. The day was heavy, threatening rain. The dogs were barking. Soon as the car arrived, creeping along at that funereal pace, all the dogs started barking. They can't have liked that. So many dogs barking. Who can tell them to be quiet? The other was stocky, thickset, in an ashen suit and hat. He stood a little further back, leaning on the bonnet. What was he looking at? He kept staring at the load of washing.

'Judith. You ever heard of someone called Judith?'

I was going to tell them about the book in the Bible, but I could see them coming, they'd snatch at a loose thread and pull. A washerwoman talking about the Bible. What else do you know about the Judith in the Bible?

'No, never heard of her.'

The one who kept looking at my load could at least have told me to set it down on the bonnet. There they were, with their arms crossed, and me with that weight on top of my head.

451

'Do those clothes belong to the judge's wife?' asked the stocky one in the ash-coloured hat.

There he had me. There you could tell old gorilla features knew what he was up to. A voice inside me said I should tell them where to get off, why didn't they ask them, the judge and the painter? But Harmony stopped me. Harmony said, 'Let things go downriver and keep the load of washing well out of it.'

'The clothes belong to the judge's wife and to the judge. And to the boy too. To the whole house.'

'All right then. Set them down here, on the bonnet.'

I didn't like that. I'd been waiting for him to tell me to set them down there, because the tarmac on the road burnt like the fires of hell, but now he said it, I didn't want to.

'Set them down here.'

He felt the mass of clothes. Put his hand through the knot and rummaged inside. Pulled out the mags, which made the other stop chewing his invisible toothpick and quickly examine them, after threatening me, 'One move and you're dead!'

'They're old fashion magazines,' I said.

I was going to tell them I read them sitting on the toilet. It was a very peaceful moment in the day for me. But Harmony said, 'None of that. You stick to yea and nay.'

They kept flicking through the magazines.

'Orange vinyl suit! You're not thinking of wearing that, are you?' asked the big guy mockingly.

Harmony's voice, 'You keep quiet.'

They shook them. To see if anything would fall out, I suppose. And it was that movement, that flapping of pages in case anything fell out, that reminded me of the day Olinda set down her load next to Santa Catarina Fountain and a man came over with a white cloth, a large parcel, and said, 'You dropped this, madam.' And she said, 'Thank you, sir.' And I thought to myself, she didn't drop anything. But Olinda quickly put it, whatever it was, inside the bundle.

'How long you been washing for the judge's wife?'

'A dozen years, give or take. I started with my mother.'

'Where's your mother?'

'My mother's dead. And I'm going to leave it.'

'Why you going to leave it? Something happen?'

'They bought a washing machine. Washerwomen are a thing of the past.'

'What about your father?' asked the dandy. 'He alive?'

'Yes. He digs graves.'

'Good one,' said Harmony. 'That'll show them. Now look up at the sky. So they see it's going to rain.'

'What do you know about the Portuguese architect?' asked Ashen Hat.

There he had me. Judith. Portuguese architect. Ashen hat. Invisible toothpick. My heated voice told me, 'Pretend you're crazy. These people don't like dealing with nutcases. They move away, prefer not to know. Nutcases make them nervous. This woman, they'll say, has a screw loose. It's like she's possessed, one of those women who go to Pastoriza to get cured and, when they reach the church, start writhing about, spitting out iron coins that stick in the door. Pretend you're possessed. Spit out iron nails, breathe out fire.'

What about you, Harmony? And Harmony tells me I have to be clever. Cleverer than they are. 'They know who's crazy and who's only pretending. They'll take you down the station and give you a record. Once you've a record, you won't be able to get a certificate of good conduct. And without a certificate you won't be able to go abroad. They're searching for something, but they're not sure what it is. As well as you, they'll have questioned the other women who carry things on top of their heads. The women who appear in the paintings. It's obvious they don't know what they're after. And they don't like the orchestra of dogs.'

'What do you know about the Portuguese architect?' asked Ren.

And O replied straight off, without thinking, 'Tell me, sir, what's a Portuguese architect?'

'Go on, off with you,' said Ren. 'Before it starts raining.'

I don't know what it is today, what they see in me. Here's another car pulling up. Smaller though. It's a coupé.

453

'Good morning. I'm from the police. Can I ask you a few questions?'

At least this one bothered to show me his badge. He was handsome, though a little too sad for my liking. A little lost. Like he was searching for someone in a cloak in Santiago.

'Please don't worry. My name's Paúl Santos and I'm from the Brigade of Criminal Investigation.'

'You're from Crime?'

Hardly something to calm me down.

'You wash for Mrs Vidal, don't you?'

'I do, sir.'

When was the last time you saw her?'

Good question.

'Ages ago. I deal with the maid.'

'But there's a portrait of you in the sitting-room. The paint's still fresh, it's recent.'

Your legs. Hold on to your legs. What now, Harmony?

'I looked so ugly, sir. I was ashamed!'

'Does the name Judith mean anything to you?'

'Judith?'

Judith

'Now it's all starting to fit together,' said Mancorvo.

He acted as Ren's analyst and memory when Ren was confused, stuck in a kind of chronological niche. The subinspector made for a strange second. Tall and thin, with aquiline features, his hair held in place with hair cream, wearing fancy clothes, cufflinks and matching tie-pin, he was quite different from Ren. You only had to see how their handkerchiefs were folded in their jacket pockets. Mancorvo's was of immaculate triangular perfection, like a medal; Ren's was just stuffed in.

Paúl Santos had noticed another discrepancy. Mancorvo's hands were very fine, he kept them visible, his elbows on the table, moving his fingers in a constant manicure, as if filing and polishing his nails. Ren's characteristic gesture was to dig with the nails of one hand in the cracks of the other. He rarely took his hat off and, when he did, a coloured mark remained on his forehead for a time, as if the hat had been screwed on.

Together they made for a kind of catlike, alternative creature. A fearful creature, thought Santos.

From the way he talked, Mancorvo sounded like the more intelligent. But Santos knew he had to treat such impressions with care. Like his character, Mancorvo's intelligence was complementary. Dependent. Lacking in initiative. At the more difficult bits, he'd always seek the inspector's approval. He then came across as an affected lackey next to a coarse foreman who would answer his questions with a slight grunt. From time to time, he'd come out with a refrain of nostalgic resentment:

'So it was her. It had to be her!'

'We suspected her briefly,' said Mancorvo in his role as spokesman.

'But she was the first one we rejected. We looked into it, but reached the conclusion the hypothesis was absurd. The same thing happened with other women in her position. We followed clues to places you wouldn't imagine, where shit is gold. The higher you go, the more exciting is the darkness. There are classes in crime as well, why deny it? You're better off higher up instead of dealing with wild cattle. But there was nothing about Judith. Nothing. After a while, we thought she didn't really exist. She'd been invented by the enemy. That idea of an infiltrator, a perfect mole. A myth created in exile, both to feed the rebels and to waste our time and make us nervous.'

Mancorvo wasn't improvising. He kept consulting notes, some of which had been typed on light blue quartos.

'In 1936, she's in France with a grant to study Fine Art. Unlike the other students, who decide to stay abroad and take part in Republican propaganda, she returns at the start of 1937. Disembarks here, in Coruña. Now we've reason to believe it was then she was trained and made a network of contacts. Judith was born back then. She was meant to last. Very cleverly thought out. Smart as a red squirrel. In 1939, after victory in April, she joins a group of Carlist women travelling with a Galician aristocrat to the welfare service in Barcelona.'

'When did you start to suspect that Chelo Vidal, the woman who joined a Carlist trip to Barcelona, was Republican Judith?'

Ren cleared his throat. With his arms crossed, he leant on the table and hid Mancorvo from view. Stared at Santos. Seemingly surprised he'd used that professional tone with him here, in the police station.

'Shortly afterwards,' he replied. 'In 1940, when I joined certain special services it's not necessary to mention now. The war in Spain was over, but the Second World War had started. Officially we were no longer at war, but that was just an appearance. I don't suppose I need to explain myself, right?'

He paused. Inhaled. Santos didn't stop looking at him either. Seemed to be calculating the amount of air Ren consumed and pumped around his body.

'I knew Ricardo Samos,' continued Ren. 'Till then, from the moment she came back from her travels, they were formally engaged, but she kept putting off the marriage. She was very young and what have you. Samos was included in a group that would go on a training course to Italy and Germany, stopping in Paris, which was occupied. These were good times for the Axis. She was the one who asked him then to get married. She wanted to go on this trip. It would be their honeymoon. I didn't say anything to Samos, but I noted down that detail. In the end, women were ordered not to join the expedition.'

'And you noted that down?'

'In my head. You note these things down in your head.'

'I see.'

'The judge is taking it badly,' said the station chief. 'He's completely beside himself.'

'The judge is a fool!' exclaimed Ren. There was unusual bitterness in the way he talked about Samos. Paúl Santos decided his hidden gland of resentment was working very well and may have made him more intelligent.

'He was always a bit of a fool,' continued Ren. 'This is between us, right? I know him well. I've spent years putting up with his speeches. His lectures in Coimbra, his walks with D'Ors in Santiago, his trips with that Schmitt around Galicia to see tombs, his hunting exploits with the Minister. I know all of that from memory. And meanwhile all this was going on! Blasted keys of a Remington! You could see his horns even when he was wearing that cinnamon hat.'

'It's easy to say now, but you were there,' said Santos incisively. 'You visited their house.'

Ren's snort filled the station chief's office. He barely concealed the effort he had to make to endure his colleague from Crime. 'Listen here, Mr Scientist, I knew it wasn't possible. That woman didn't fit. Or fitted too well. Blasted eyesight! You only had to see her to understand she was Judith. The way she was there and not there. That vaporous presence of hers. Always so diplomatic. Blasted pluperfect! Now that I think about it, it's as if she had a star on her forehead: *I'm Judith, you fool!*'

'I'd like to know what's in the reports,' remarked Paúl Santos. He looked at the station chief. 'To tell the truth, sir, we still don't know exactly why Chelo Vidal has to be Judith.'

Ren thumped the table. 'Because she is!'

'When there's a drop of blood, it's our duty to analyse it,' said Santos, repeating one of his favourite examples. 'If we analyse it, it could turn out to be a person's or a duck's.'

'Let me tell you something,' growled Ren. 'I've no fucking idea what a drop of duck's blood is supposed to be like.'

Mancorvo spotted the station chief's gesture and took over in a neutral tone. 'In view of the current situation, many suspicions can now be considered proof that Chelo Vidal was, in effect, Judith. Reports? We had enough documents to drown in! They'll be here somewhere.'

'I looked and didn't find much. It's funny. There's no file on Judith.'

Mancorvo glanced at the station chief and then at Ren.

'You should know by now . . .'

He adopted a more conciliatory approach.

'You should know by now some things are in our domain. We're working for the security of the State. There were enough documents to drown in. They'll be here somewhere. Best not to worry.'

'We're talking about twenty years ago,' Ren intervened calmly and sarcastically. 'Things were different back then, Mr Unknown.'

Now he was the one shuffling papers. He opened a folder and pulled out another sheaf of light blue quartos. 'These are reports from 1937. Some of them you can't read so well. They're often carbon copies of reports requested by the military courts in summary trials of those who organised escapes by boat. In Coruña, there was an organisation, a secret network based on the union Maritime Awakening. It had its merit. This was no game. The city was in a state of war. People with a Republican background were . . . neutralised. But this network kept working. In two years, they organised twenty large-scale escapes on fishing boats. Most of them to France. How was this possible?'

Paúl Santos made as if to consult the light blue quartos, but Ren got there first and brandished them in the air. 'Lots of these reports talk of a strange, mysterious woman. Always dressed in black. Some of those questioned call her Carme, others Lucía, others Dolores, but from the description it appears the woman is always one and the same. Agents of investigation and vigilance even came from Burgos, from the Brigade of Special Services. And seem to have reached a single conclusion: this woman working for Maritime Awakening, rather than being an invention, could be a kind of . . . character in a novel. A myth those arrested and questioned believed in and passed on to each other.'

'What happened to this woman?' asked Santos. 'Did she disappear for ever?'

Ren fell silent. Seemed to be drilling his way through history.

'In the early 1940s, as Chief Ren already explained, she reappeared,' continued Mancorvo. 'The transport of wolfram to Germany was repeatedly sabotaged. A special group of German counterespionage arrived and managed to hunt down a guy who'd been hurting them, a man of a thousand faces, who turned out to be German, opposed to Hitler. But this spy's main contact slipped through their fingers. Theirs and ours. They were of the opinion that Judith did exist. A competent lot. Highly competent.'

He looked at Ren and the station chief. They were lost in thought. He was doing the job of remembering for them.

'There's a historical matter that won't have escaped your attention, my scientific friend. The Third Reich supported the cause of nationalist Spain. It wasn't just a few crumbs. A large number of weapons arrived by sea. Came in through these ports. Aeroplanes even, in pieces. Did you know the main radio station, Spanish National Radio, was here, in Coruña, on Mount Santa Margarida? It was a special, highly important present from the Führer to the Caudillo. Later, during the Second World War, as you can imagine, it was time to repay the favour. Some very special services were offered here.'

'We all know about the wolfram,' said Santos. 'And the radio station.'

'But the station wasn't just for transmitting radio programmes. The intricate Galician coast was used as a base for the control of sea and air traffic between continents. Also for shelter and repairs, especially to submarines attacking Allied convoys in the Atlantic.'

'I could imagine.'

'Not just shelter and repairs. Fundamental things like supplies. Minor things such as entertainment. The men, the officers, had to have a bit of fun . . .'

'That's enough of the history lesson, Mancorvo,' Ren intervened. 'What else is there?'

'Well, there came a time,' said Mancorvo, 'when every boat, every submarine, seemed to carry an invisible target. They were always being located, however well camouflaged.'

'Judith.'

'Yes, intercepted messages talked of Judith. But that's not all. Where there's collaboration, there are common business interests. 1942, for example, was a particularly good year . . .'

Ren started growling again.

'Well, these people also seemed to be located. Other things. There were escapes and arrivals we couldn't explain. People who slipped through our fingers. Imagine a complete security cordon. There was too much information.'

'But a single Judith couldn't be responsible for so much,' observed Santos. 'However skilful and active she was, this Chelo couldn't be everywhere at once. As far as I know, she was at home, painting.'

'There are nodes. Lots of scattered information converging on a node, like the astral orbits of a celestial sphere. The node has to be somewhere impossible. Judith was a node, the sphere.'

'You mean she only had to be here? Sit tight and wait.'

'Something like that.'

'Thank you, Mancorvo,' said the station chief. 'Now we know where we are in history. We're no longer dealing with ghosts.'

He'd been silent almost all the time. Santos thought he was a subordinate character in the presence of Ren. But now he was invested with authority. His tone was that of someone taking the initiative.

'We have to find Chelo Vidal,' he said. 'Right away.'

He surveyed the others in slow motion, 'All our heads are on the block.'

He stood up and went over to the window. He was in shirtsleeves and hooked his thumbs behind his braces. These days in the summer of 1963, when Franco delayed his holidays for no apparent reason, everyone looking out of the window seemed to be trying to glimpse the arrival of the *Azor*, the Head of State's yacht.

'This is a delicate situation,' murmured the station chief, with his back to them. He turned around and the verdict was more pronounced, 'Extremely delicate. It can't appear to be a political case. It can't appear in any shape or form. None of this can come out. Absolutely nothing. No leaks. I talked to the censor's office about dealing with the media. There'll be nothing about the incident on the 18th of July. The celebration was, as always, a success, a demonstration of popular support. That's what the newspapers will say. But the censors can't muzzle every single mouth.'

'Rumours are like the flow of a river,' said Santos. 'There's no stopping them.'

Ren growled intriguingly, 'Yes, there is. You create others.'

'The best way to stop rumours is for there to be no reason for them,' said the station chief less abstractly. 'We have to act fast. Locate Chelo Vidal. And not get nervous. Right, Ren?'

'Absolutely, boss. It's fallen to us and there's nothing we can do about it. And I always thought life in the provinces was meant to be peaceful.'

'Those are the orders,' concluded the station chief. 'No political case. Imagine the scandal at home, not to say abroad. The wife of a judge, one of the regime's most distinguished jurists, turns out to be a resistance hero. A clandestine myth from her youth. This scenario would please all our enemies. Make us an object of ridicule abroad. An international laughing-stock.'

Paúl Santos was thinking about that, the idea of being an international laughing-stock, when the station chief suddenly started talking obliquely, somewhere between light and shade, you could and yet you couldn't understand what he was saying. It took Santos a little while to react because he had to switch on the Spirit of Contradiction.

'Gentlemen, we're not going to let this situation get out of control. It's my job to make sure that doesn't happen. Everyone – that means everyone, Mr Santos – will have to contribute something.'

'Right you are, sir,' replied Santos. 'You can count on me.'

'Because we can't start groping in the dark, now, can we?' said the station chief.

'No, of course not.'

'We've spent too many years in the dark on this case. We have to find Chelo Vidal quietly, without turning the city upside down.'

In an attempt to understand the station chief's meaning, Santos decided to look into Ren's face as into a mirror. His expression was calm. Sarcastic.

'Someone's offered to collaborate,' said the station chief. 'We didn't go after him, he came to us. It's a service that on this occasion, however much it hurts us, we can't do without. I know one of you, namely Mr Paúl Santos of the Criminal Brigade, has been working with admirable courage, unprecedented steps of great intelligence, to unpick the criminal network it would seem is directed by a certain Mr Manlle.'

Paúl Santos froze. Amazed by what was coming. But his hands took a decision. They started to write, to transcribe what the station chief was saying in shorthand.

'What are you doing?'

'Taking notes, sir.'

'Then do it in your head. That's enough.'

The station chief's face was burning. His eyes were pouring out fire. Chief Ren was growing. Consuming and pumping most of the air in the office. He grinned at Santos.

'Listen to me. We're going to get this time bomb that is Samos' wife. I don't give a damn about the rest. The smuggling, the whorehouses, the intimidatory purchase of land, the gold business, the receipt of stolen goods. All of this is irrelevant compared to her. Compared to Judith. Got it? Everyone, from the top down, is after Judith's head. I received a call from the governor's office, they're sending people from the Special Brigade . . . What do they care about your progress with Manlle? Manlle won't go anywhere. He's part of the landscape. What we can't allow is the Azor to appear on the horizon while that woman's on the loose.'

'But you know how difficult it was to get where we are now, with absolute discretion, sir,' said Santos by way of reproach. 'We've got everything.

The structure of the empire and, for the first time, the witnesses we need to dismantle it. Let me try and get to Judith.'

'There's no time, Santos. It's a done deal. The Caudillo can't delay his holidays any longer. There are enough rumours. We're on one side and amphibians will take us to the other. Manlle's an amphibian. So you're going to leave him alone for a while. And he's going to help us.'

He was in his office. He decided to try and type it all up. He needed to see it in printed letters to understand that everything he'd heard was real. Pazos came in, the man he'd saved, the inspector in Crime he'd managed to pull out of the pit of scepticism. He dropped his jacket on a chair like someone shedding their last hope. Their final skin.

'There's no secret witness. Boa's dead.'

'What?'

'Yep, our number one witness. She was found with a shot in the head, holding a small revolver, a Bulldog. A hole in her temple. Another sewer in history. Apparent suicide. Bullshit.'

'Suicide? That woman would never have killed herself.'

Santos left, muttering, 'Not even for the prize of immortality would she have killed herself.'

The Whale's Belly

Sada to Dr Montevideo on the subject of boats, 'To think I could bring them here and not depart on them.' Suddenly his eyes blazed with St Elmo's fire. Montevideo knew the painter had just discovered how to enter the mural and perhaps leave for ever. He felt the wall and remarked in surprise, 'It's only a thin membrane.'

The Tachygraphic Rose

He'd been thinking about that moment for quite some time. He wasn't at all sure. He was used to observing people, watching them, examining the smallest details. A hair. The prints left by fingers or lips. To reading the writing bodies leave behind them in a space. The extraordinary information that can be contained in a bin full of rubbish. He thought about it one day. Writing poems, each of which was about a rubbish bin. It would be both biography and geography. It was one of the aspects of his job that most attracted him. He wouldn't tell anyone this. He'd tell her. A little later on. How the act of emptying a bin on a large table, sorting and arranging families of refuse, was a way of constructing a poetic place, a genuine, enthralling fiction. Catia was an intelligent woman. She'd be interested. For sure. In fact, being a policeman was like being a historian. And the search for clues, rummaging around in a rubbish bin, was a kind of archaeological dig. This position gave him security in front of the other, the one being observed, followed or watched. The biographee, so to speak. With Catia, he had the opposite impression. He was the one being studied. He was under her control, starting with her position in the class of speed typing. From the front, it was she who gave instructions that affected his whole body, who guided him with the invisible threads of words to achieve the goal of his fingers being as fast as his eyes. But it wasn't just in this time he spent as an automaton, sitting in a row with other pupils. When he stood up, before this woman who was younger and shorter than he was, he felt the mandate continued. His techniques of self-control didn't work. His desire to neutralise his muscles' spontaneous joy when, for example, she came to advise him on the position of his elbows actually caused extreme rigidity. It was the same with his speech. He was like a lopsided pair of scales. So when he finally took the step of asking Catia out one Sunday afternoon, after she'd twice agreed to have coffee with him in Borrazás during the break, and when Catia said yes, OK, she'd be there the day after next, at five o'clock in the Beach Club, his typewriter got stuck because he pressed several keys at once.

'You're a policeman?'

'Yes.'

'Why did you hide it at enrolment?'

'I have my reasons. Secrecy, a certain kind of secret, is a tool of the trade. More important than a gun.'

'Why are you telling me now? Better to have kept it a secret.'

'Right now I'm not a lawyer or a policeman. Or even a criminal. I'm just a guy who's nervous on a date with a girl he likes.'

'I'm not in the habit of ruining dates,' said Catia, 'but let me get something clear. I don't see a policeman or a lawyer or a criminal. I see someone who hides what he is.'

'Listen, Catia, we need the police. Call it what you like. They're here to protect people. And in my case a little secrecy is needed. I can't go around with a placard saying, "Long live people!"'

'It's not like that,' said Catia. 'Don't try and pretend we live in a normal country. I'm the one who has to be cautious.'

And she did speak cautiously, in a low voice, but what she said sounded very loud, incredibly loud, perhaps because it was unusual for the time and place, and seemed to spread as far as the eyes could see, which was a long way. As far as the lighthouse. She said, 'There's violence everywhere and it's fear because of you. Don't try and pretend this is a normal country. It's governed by . . .' She was going to say, 'It's governed by a dictator.' But she went even further. There was something in this man, Paúl Santos, that encouraged her to be bold. 'It's governed by the worst possible criminal.'

'Do you want me to arrest him and haul him up before a judge?' asked Santos with the voice of a detective in films. It was a quick, spontaneous reaction. And made Catia accept the joke. Smile for a second.

466

'Yes, I do,' she said.

'Then I'll do my best.'

That was all the humour Catia could take.

'What do you think of my uncle?'

'He's a great guy. An extraordinary intellect.'

'He's a wreck, isn't he?'

'No, I didn't say that.'

'I did. Did you know that Héctor Ríos, Dr Montevideo, was going to be a public prosecutor under the Republic?'

'No. You can tell he knows about law, though.'

'Actually he was a prosecutor when the war started. He'd passed all the exams. And was waiting to be posted. He passed with flying colours. He was passionate about literature and had a way of reading legal texts, even the dullest, most chaotic ones, as part of literature. As he says, literature with . . .'

'Implications.'

'Yes, implications,' continued Catia. 'Héctor Ríos wasn't even in the war. When it started, he'd just arrived from Madrid. He'd come to spend his holidays after those exams to be a prosecutor. During the first days of the war, he kept low. He went from the beach, the sun of the beach, to a hole. He finally managed to escape through Portugal. Lots of fugitives were detained by Salazar's police and returned to the border. He got to Lisbon and sailed for America. To start with, he was in Buenos Aires. He worked on a newspaper called *Crítica*. The owner's name was Natalio Botana. Lots of the heroes in his western novels are called that, Botana. He mentions them both, Botana and his horse Romantic. When I was typing up his novels, I always thought Botana and his horse were two fictional characters. But then, not long ago, while typing up a chapter on exile in that book he's so taken up with, *A Dramatic History of Culture*, I discovered that Botana and Romantic actually existed. They were responsible for saving the refugees on the *Massilia*. This boat, crowded with Spanish and Jewish fugitives, had left Bordeaux in October 1939. It reached Buenos Aires, but it wasn't exactly a good time in Argentina either. The *Massilia* remained in port, full of hungry people, being treated like a phantom ship by the authorities. Natalio Botana's horse, Romantic, had the courage to win the most important race at Buenos Aires' racecourse and the first thing Botana did was declare that the prize money was for the refugees on board the *Massilia*. This immediately drew attention to the boat. Thanks to a horse, the boat became a symbol.'

'That's why it's Romantic!' exclaimed Santos.

'Yes, he has these moments of optimism. He lived for years between Buenos Aires, Mar del Plata and Montevideo. He then had the idea of returning. Looked into it. There were no proceedings against him. No lawsuit. There was no reason not to return. Of course he couldn't be a public prosecutor, but he'd be left alone so long as he stuck to private activities. This is what the Spanish diplomats told him. It was a lie. I'm talking about six years ago, in 1957. Everything was a lie. No sooner had he arrived than they were after him. Which is when this guy turned up, claiming to be a civil servant. He could get them off his back. There was a way: by paying money. How much? All he had. They knew what his savings were. They were very well informed. And before he could even think of denouncing them, the guy got there first, "You're not going to denounce us, are you?" He showed him his own denunciation, one that he'd prepared against Héctor Ríos. My uncle was amazed. It contained everything. All his steps since a year before the Republic, since his participation in the Spanish University Federation. Even a short course in Esperanto he'd given at a cultural association. This also had been noted down. It was a terrible nightmare, as if a camera had been following him all his life. And then the extortioner mentioned the Law of Political Responsibilities. He could be tried not just for having Republican links. He could be tried, eighteen years after the end of the war, even for what he hadn't done. For the crime of passivity. He was ready to resist, but the following day two members of the Political Brigade came to carry out a search. They turned everything upside down and took away his passport. In the afternoon, the guy came back. I was present that day. He again insisted that everything could be arranged. I remember his gesture. He brushed against a keyboard and said, "Carriages won't go unless you grease them." That's what he said. He then hinted something about me and the academy. That's when

Montevideo gave in, I think. I didn't know he'd paid. He retired to his room, the cabin, as if into a second exile. And started writing non-stop. He hasn't stopped writing since. But you know that part.'

Yes, he knew that part. How he wrote western novels to earn a few pennies and then that work that filled his head day and night, *A Dramatic History of Culture*. He could hear the doctor, during a break in the class of advanced stenography according to the Martí method, asking him, 'Do you consider yourself brave, Mr Santos?' 'I think so,' Santos replied after pondering the question. It was then Montevideo said to him, 'I'm only a little brave when I write.'

The echo of the question came back to him. 'Do you consider yourself brave, Mr Santos?'

He could have guessed the ending to the story Catia was telling him since his incursion into the museum of horrors that was Ren's house. But Santos didn't dare say, 'I know.'

He replied, 'What you're telling me is awful. Things'll change, Catia. History will do justice. To Dr Montevideo as well.'

Shame about history, thought Paúl Santos. He also had a matter to settle with history. He was about to tell Catia something about the mystery of his biography, but his scientific gaze was stubborn. It was now examining colours. The various crimson shades of her lips, nails, knitted dress.

'I have to go,' she said, rising to her feet suddenly.

The knitted dress was cherry-coloured and had a black belt.

Paúl Santos stood up as well. He was going to protest, but he thought better and said, 'I'll go with you.'

'No, I'd rather be alone today.'

That adverb, the word 'today', struck him as a trail worth following. An adverb to be studied through a magnifying glass.

Before leaving, however, Catia turned and spoke to him at high typing speed, 'Do you know anything about two men in ashen suits who followed me down the street? Do you know why they were taking photographs?'

Paúl Santos picked up the chemical signals of imminent danger, but had no reply. He stopped seeing cherry colour and, looking into her eyes, shook his head. A scientific failure.

Ren's 'Museum'

The shutters were closed, the darkness thick and humid, a condition that seemed to belong to the house, a darkness incorporated, infiltrated, into the building, where the strange thing would have been light. But Santos picked out, with what he imagined was a mole's eyesight, the scent of outlines, regardless of the position of windows and lamps.

He lifted the torch very slowly, feeling it in his grasp. As a boy, he liked to think it was the light that moved, using his hand. This torch was his companion, his weapon, a continuation of his body. He knew he could trust Catherine Laboure the night he was caught in the Room for Secret Deliveries and his torch wasn't confiscated.

The whole of Ren's sitting-room resembled a history museum. At first glance, Santos didn't realise almost everything on display was recent. In the light of the torch, objects expressed mute surprise, helplessness. Even the swords.

Swords? Yes, swords. Swords with gold and silver embossed hilts and scabbards, decorated with ornamental or symbolic leaves. Lying on velvet, with labels held by a cord, they were swords that had lost their warlike function and seemed to be afraid. Santos took one with an attractively well-rounded hilt. 'Venerable Master's Sword', it said on the label. With the point, he touched the label of the most ornate one: '33rd Degree Sovereign Grand Inspector General's Sword'.

All the objects he found at first had to do with Freemasonry. There was even a mallet and 24-inch gauge. The mallet was similar to one he'd seen in the judge's office, in the Palace of Justice, which he'd identified as a judge's gavel. Now he understood what Ricardo Samos meant when he said, 'It has more history than it seems'.

The torch moved excitedly onwards, the light sniffing out great surprises. A glass cabinet contained the badges and devices of Galician and Portuguese Freemasons or *pedreiros livres*. The torch stopped at a pair of white gloves. Not exactly a pair. They were the same colour, but of different sizes, as if one of the gloves was for a woman's hand. Nearby there was an acacia-leaf brooch.

The torch went from one surprise to the next, travelling through history. A design on a matchbox from the First Republic. A peasant in a Phrygian cap saying, 'Don't call me Balthazar; I'm a citizen'. The Republican Madonnas Liberty, Equality and Fraternity, shown with wings, diffusely erotic in the darkness. The same or similar ones of modernist sensuality that appeared in the illustrated magazine of Coruña's Masons which the torch focused on now: *Brisas y Tormentas*, No. 1, Yr 1, Coruña, 15 April 1900. Paúl Santos took the torch in his left hand and passed his right hand over the magazine. It's true that, in secret vision, things emit what they say. 'Breezes and Storms'. Aprons, collars, embroidered in gold. One of the latter with a triangle and the number 33 in red thread inside it. A blue silk sash with white veins telling the years like tree rings. At one end, a jewel in the form of a key. On the label, it said 'Secret Master's Sash'. Santos focused the torch for a long time on that enigmatic key with the letter Z on the wards. He was passionate about keys and locks. Anything connected with this invention. Nobody in Charity Hospital had been able to explain how the boy got inside the Room for Secret Deliveries, to which only three people had access at any one time: the medical director, Mother Laboure and the woman who was due to give birth. And she entered through an outer door. She never saw or was seen, except when she was in that kind of camera obscura she came to give birth in. He got in there. Nobody knew how. He was found in the middle of the room, in the dark, with the torch on, inside his mouth, his cheeks acting as a pink lampshade.

He was now immersed with his torch, that light which was his fetish, in another secret place, a kind of study, where there was an hourglass.

The upper bulb was empty. The lower, full of sand. Santos did what anyone would do from childhood to old age. Turn the hourglass upside down. Set time in motion. He suddenly realised this simple, ancient object he'd never paid much attention to contained sky and earth. Was measuring his life. It depended on you whether or not symbols had meaning. This hourglass did. No, it didn't. He wasn't going to let symbols ensnare him.

Under the stairs was a small door painted black with the acronym VITRIOL in white letters. He remembered this was an old Rosicrucian motto, used by alchemists as well. Knowledge that was not derived from the indoctrination he'd received, despite specialising in criminology as opposed to the fight against subversion, which was the work of the Brigade of Politico-Social Investigation. Even so, they were always being asked to show their support for the cause and he knew that his had to appear unconditional, beyond suspicion. Another order drummed into them with the insistence of a hammer-blow to the head: no disaffection, but no indifference either. They couldn't be cold. When he heard this for the first time, without heating, Paúl Santos was appalled by the label. Being cold meant carrying the cold inside you. Actually liking the cold. The perfect school of adherence to the dictatorship in his case was Santiago Seminary. One of the coldest places in the world, a physical cold that got behind your eyes. You had to fight the cold. Franco's regime and the Church were united, the synthesis of everything, 'like body and soul', a continuation of the holy union of throne and altar discussed in a famous book by Archbishop Rafael de Vélez, founder of the seminary and author of an equally famous work, *The Sheath of Faith*. Santos recalled Vélez's portrait in the seminary's dark central corridor. He'd been painted holding that book for which he was famous, the title clearly visible, except that it'd been abbreviated to *The Sheath*. He also recalled the nervous, furtive laughter the sight of this title provoked in young men who'd only just discovered the comical treachery committed by words when least expected. As for their historical mission, they'd been told the spirit of reconquest and crusade should remain vigilant. As a mark of glory, the novices were reminded that the only time Santiago's seminarists had demonstrated politically was under the banner of traditionalism, which they'd used to beat the *negros*,

472

as the liberals of the nineteenth century were known. It was also the seminary that published the first panegyric on Franco during the war, in praise of a movement its protagonists didn't hesitate to call Fascist, starting with the author of the work, the priest Manuel Silva, who described in detail how the military uprising had been planned, how democratic inspectors and officers had been hoodwinked and all that machinery set in motion even before the elections, which the right was expected to lose, and who wrote with triumphal fervour about bloody acts, the rosary of crimes and human victims, necessary ritual sacrifices to see off not only the Republic, but also the heresy of centuries, anything at odds with the medieval empire of throne and altar. So it was that the Holy Year in Compostela, which should have been 1936, was prolonged for the first time in history so that Franco could be received as Caudillo in the cathedral, greeted with raised arms, led to the altar under a canopy and named Sword of God.

He turned the hourglass upside down. Earth and sky, sky and earth. His mind was going too fast. Paúl Santos had left the seminary, but not because he rebelled or lost his faith. Because of laughter. That clandestine laughter he was unable to suppress. One day, he opened the window of his room on the top floor of the seminary, with a view of Mount Pedroso to the west, and heard laughter. Another kind of laughter. Not at all clandestine. Seemingly provoked by the sun's tickling. And he knew he'd never resist a woman's laughter, however much he pored over The Sheath by Archbishop Vélez. So he went to the hospital in Coruña and spoke to Mother Catherine Laboure, his protector, who was drinking hot black coffee without sugar, who was smoking Celtas in the absence of Gauloises, because Romeo had got waylaid, and who was surrounded by children, a magnet for anyone with problems, anyone who felt unloved, because of her body, some part of her body, there they all were, he as well, a grown man, first up with his problem. He had a thing for laughter. That particular kind of laughter.

'Laughter never hurt anyone, God included.'

'What shall I do?'

'Leave the seminary,' she replied. 'Straightaway. You're not meant to be a priest. If you kill off laughter, you'll develop an illness in your intestine. I'll help you find a way.'

'OK, but what shall I do?'

In a few days, he'd gone from aspiring to be God's emissary to feeling completely lost.

'You wanted to fight against evil? Then fight against evil!'

She blew out a cloud of smoke, which she compensated for with a sip of steaming hot coffee. She was crazy, but Paúl Santos knew from experience she was almost always right. She was a courageous nutter in a place for taming. 'One thing's the Holy Spirit,' the chaplain had remarked about her sarcastically, 'another, the Spirit of Contradiction.' But she didn't care. She had two defences. Being crazy and never stopping still.

'If I could choose,' said Mother Laboure, 'I'd be a detective. I'd study Law followed by Criminology. I'd fight against real crime. Yep. That's what I'd be. And not a silly old Sister of Charity.'

She was the one who laughed when she saw Paúl's expression. Then she added in a hoarse voice and suspenseful tone, 'Instead of wiping noses, I'd be cleaning up the city's sewers.'

In the training he received, there was an inevitable section on subversive warfare. Information about the enemy, working constantly at home and abroad, in hiding and in exile, was hardly scientific. They were part of evil. They were anti-Spain. You had to know what they were doing, every step, how they breathed . . . but not delve into their thought too much. Know enough to apprehend them. Hate them. That was all.

But Santos' scientific mind couldn't stop finding obstacles. As with the laughter he heard from the seminary window, he couldn't block his ears.

He'd now got stuck on the R of VITRIOL.

He managed to pull out the first three letters from a corner of his memory: *Visita Interiorem Terrae*. But couldn't go any further. The training hadn't been scientific, pondered Santos. The study of Freemasonry, for example, was limited in practice to knowledge of special laws, the work of the Tribunal for the Repression of Freemasonry and Communism, and to the study of articles and a book signed with a mysterious name, Jakin

Boor, though he'd soon been warned this was a pseudonym of Franco, Spain's own Caudillo. Such an open secret immunised this pile of rubbish against any doubt or observation that might be classed as a criticism. With his innate ability to rise to the occasion when confronted with a mess, Paúl Santos extracted what he thought was the leitmotif: 'Freemasonry never rests'. Boor achieved something: Paúl Santos' interest in these conspirators who never let up. 'It's the Spirit of Contradiction!' joked a hoarse voice that could have been Catherine Laboure's. A sort of supreme assembly of international Masons met 'every working day in Geneva', from where they 'influenced the world's affairs and dictated orders to the majority of the universe'. They directed everything from liberal governments to PEN Clubs and the League for the Rights of Man. When their teacher asked for a summary of that volume that grew in size as you read it, Santos was crazy enough to raise his hand and reply, 'Freemasonry never rests'.

Everyone waited for him to continue, including Professor Novás, who gestured to him to expand on his thesis. Santos was known for his expositional seriousness. But something, a kind of filament, what Laboure called 'the root of a hair', tickled his way of thinking.

'Yes?' the teacher of doctrine urged him on.

'In the words of our expert, Jakin Boor, Freemasonry never rests, Mr Novás.'

He never thought he'd have so much success in an initiation class for future policemen on account of the indefatigable Boor. In this brief intervention, Santos adopted a serious, pithy tone, in the manner of an aphorism, and a grave look. Franco was often praised for his commitment. The Caudillo 'never rests'. To use a metaphor churned out by the propaganda machine, 'The light in the Pardo never goes out'. Recurring in the press, at any moment, for whatever reason, like the stuff of legend, this light in Pardo Palace that never went out had become part of the Spanish landscape. Did this light exist? Santos saw a man with thick eyebrows emerging from inside Franco every night in a green bathrobe and sitting down to write tirelessly next to the famous light. He had a hole in his right slipper, through which poked a toe in the form of a claw he used to scratch his left internal malleolus, the only compensation for being awake. This man was Jakin Boor. And what Santos saw was a figure with devilish traits. Childhood images aside, he'd always found it difficult to see or imagine what the devil would be like. He wasn't helped by his study of iconography at the seminary or by his reading of Vicente Risco's *History of the Devil*. So much erudition and, if he hadn't misunderstood, it seemed the closest thing to the devil in Risco's eyes was a university professor in Santiago. He realised this vision of Boor as the devil in disguise was fed by his conviction that the treatise on Freemasonry grew in size at night and represented a challenge to his mental control. He had to stop thinking about outlandish things, such as Boor's halitosis, albeit true, since they appeared clear enough in his vision and mental reconstruction of the character involved and he could see him pausing at his writing to breathe into a mirror and try to smell himself. Moments Santos could pinpoint in the text. When, for example, Boor distinguished varying degrees of perversity. He treated them as the enemy, but wrote about international Masons with all the rhetoric of a scholar, a supposed expert. When it came to Spain, however, he seemed to have to concentrate in order to crush some of the fearless insects that were about to collide with the Pardo lamp. In the case of Spain, anything that was not Catholic and absolutist was waste. 'The scum of society'. As he chewed on these words, Paúl Santos felt something fermenting in his mouth. The Spirit of Contradiction. He didn't know why there was a bitterness about this 'scum' he liked the taste of, like lemon rind. On Sundays, when they were allowed out of Charity Hospital, they'd sometimes invade the terraces of the marina, lively terraces with a view of the sea, when it was time for vermouth on the city's ocean liner. They'd jump in when the customers stood up and the waiters still hadn't cleared the empty table, the empty glasses, but there was the lemon rind with a hint of Cinzano. Miraculously they'd sometimes left the olive as well. Santos memorised phrases such as 'the scum of society', but could only repeat them by forcing a vision of Boor. Something he instinctively decided to avoid. A scientific mind was not incompatible with an awareness of evil. Boor's presence bothered him. If he wanted to be a policeman, albeit a criminologist, a scientific policeman, he had to swear allegiance to the National Movement's principles and declare his unconditional support for Franco. This is what he was going to do. You couldn't play with that, he knew. But he'd reached a private scientific conclusion he felt very proud of. If Jakin Boor was a pseudonym of Franco, the unknown quantity was not who was behind the character of Franco, but who was behind Jakin Boor. It was the book's fault. A bad book. He had to study it. Always fatter and emptier at night. An often quoted, though little read, author was Marcelino Menéndez Pelayo. One of his most famous quotes – 'Spain, scourge of heretics' – appeared at the front of one of their textbooks. Santos discovered one day this quote came from his *History of Spanish Heterodox Thinkers*. The title piqued his curiosity. The Spirit of Contradiction. It wasn't easy to find. This deepened his interest. When he finally had it in his hands and started reading, he felt a mental upheaval that spread to the rest of his organism. Every life he read about struck him as more charming. It was a history that seemed to have come out of the Room for Secret Deliveries. A history of Spain. Of hidden, mutilated, persecuted, burnt, expelled lives. 'And although there are not many Spanish freethinkers, we might well declare them to be the most impious lot to be found in the world', wrote Menéndez Pelayo. And yet without wanting to, with the intention of condemning them for eternity, cutting off their heads, he'd performed a monumental paradox, a remarkable three-point turn, that of preserving the stock of freethinkers from oblivion. So there were many nights Santos' light remained on, visited by moths. He couldn't stop smiling when he read, 'In this book, I've been pulling out thorns: it wouldn't surprise me if, through contact with them, some of their roughness stuck to me'.

'Freemasonry never rests, Mr Novás.'

'Why don't you take a rest, Santos?'

Santos' problem, as happened with other quotes that caught his fancy, was that he'd pull them out in quite different circumstances so that the quote became a sort of rejoinder he had to put in the same hiding place as 'God's hose' when he was rebuked by a superior.

It was a long time, not until he met Inspector Ren, before he repeated the formula 'Freemasonry never rests'.

⋆ ⋆ ⋆

He opened the door. The torch landed on an imitation skull with a bulb inside, a kind of graveyard souvenir. The light jumped up. There, hanging from the wall, was a skeleton, this time genuine, bones are never deceptive. On a wooden stool, acting as a table, was some sulphur and salt. This rustic table also contained a sheet of paper. Santos pointed the torch and read. It was a questionnaire:

> *What does a man owe to God?*
> *What does a man owe to himself?*
> *What does a man owe to society?*

Santos always tried to keep a cool head. An investigator's main weapon was his mental control. The mind had to be kept permanently running. He imagined situations of general panic and how he'd react. Mother Laboure's common sense could be summed up in the joke about a woman who, in the case of a fire, prayed for the Lord to intervene, to which a neighbour said, 'Tell God, if he's coming down, to bring a fire-hose'. Once, shortly after starting at the seminary, he told this joke at the end of some spiritual exercises for which the teacher had proposed the theme 'The Meaning of Prayer in Modern Society'. He just came out with what he thought would be an original response to the theme. He'd never forget their dumbfounded faces. It was as if they'd been listening to Luther once more nailing the Ninety-Five Theses to the wooden door of the Castle Church in Wittenberg. This anecdotal event was an important experience for him. He fully understood the meaning of the phrase *initium sapientiae timor Domini*. He had to know how to keep quiet or camouflage himself in the words of a superior. Yes, the fear of the Lord was the beginning of wisdom. But he also had to fit out a hiding place in his head where he could store the joke about God's hose. If he couldn't find that cranny, then he would lose his mind.

Scattered on the floor, as if they'd fallen off a snooker table, the torch lit up some black and white balls. Santos was about to take one. At least he'd have that as a memory. A black ball.

It was then he heard a noise. The front door opening and closing, foot-steps in the sitting-room. Whoever it was moved with fluency, though the way of walking and negotiating the furniture was that of a heavy, sluggish man. Probably Ren, the owner of the house. The one who'd turned his lair into a strange museum of spoils. In his dark room, simulacrum of the Chamber of Reflection, Santos lived out an initiate's experience, interpreting the movements outside (whoever it was struck a quick hand through a bundle of papers), but all the time thinking about the questions 'What does a man . . . ?' like waves crashing against his temples, without finding a suitable answer.

The visitor was in a hurry. He heard papers being shuffled, a cupboard door slamming. Followed by silence. Paúl Santos held his breath. He knew how to interpret this kind of silence. It was the silence of someone sniffing the air. Having a premonition. Waiting for something to creak. He had to be careful. Had Ren heard the hourglass? The last grain of sand would have fallen by now. The sky was on the earth. Ren closed the front door. Santos stayed still. Ren opened again, a surprise tactic. No, nobody here. False alarm. He left. The objects in Ren's museum had labels. There was an envelope on which it said 'Recovered Photos'. Santos opened it. There were three photos and the negatives. Promising. They showed smoking pyres in a scene he immediately recognised, the docks and María Pita Square. In all of them, there was a group making the Fascist salute. He couldn't work out what was burning, just embers on the ground. He carried on exploring. In one corner, there were flags, remnants of standards, a few artistic signs with an emery design on glass. In one, the torch followed the line of a wave and found the dorna boat floating on it. Read 'Maritime Awakening'. And, in smaller letters, 'Union of the Fishing Fleet'. The standards belonged to workers' associations. They had coloured ribbons, embroidered letters and occasional motifs relating to the profession. They reminded him of the banners carried by lay brotherhoods in processions. The union of carpenters 'Emancipation', of builders 'Social Aurora', of printers, of 'Light', of bakers 'New Union'. There were other smaller, more modest symbols, banderoles hanging from the wall, such as the union of barbers 'Fraternal', of net-makers 'Port's Progress'. In the case of the 'Union of Water, Gas and Electricity', he noticed a single boxing glove tied to the crossbar. Pictures of marine life. One showing Hercules defeating the giant Geryon. Sports trophies. An ABC with wooden upper- and lower-case letters by the Workers Press on Socorro Street.

Then there were books and leaflets, ordered not as in a library, but as in the display of confiscated goods. In gaps between the books, there were emblems, badges, slugs cast by a Linotype machine, typographical devices including a set of borders. In the light of the torch, they were like archaeological remains alternating with ancient parchments.

One leaflet caught the torch's attention. On the cover was a group of naked men and women bathers, wearing seaweed as a kind of natural dress. He opened it in the middle and read with the torch. There was a question. 'Is Man a carnivore? No.' Followed by thirty-five vegetarian dishes for the seven days of the week. He picked one at random. 'Thursday: rice with apple'. Closed his eyes. Acquired the two flavours on his palate. Thought of a pippin, cinnamon apple. He needed it. He'd been there long enough to hear things speak, the terrible murmur of imprisoned things, and he hankered after fruit. The booty of war, on display, which included a gold tooth. There it was. The size of a grain of maize, it seemed to have broken off a brilliant sentence arrested in mid-air. All the same, the wedding rings were the most impressive. They formed a fraternity of circles, of varying diameter and thickness, but with the natural complementary function of circular figures when placed or drawn together. One of them, which from the size must have belonged to a woman, was labelled with a date. In Ren's museum, '18 August 1936' was often repeated. The first 18th after 18 July. Santos knew the importance of dates in the history of crime. Dates that can be identified as the mark of a calibre on a missile. The imitation effect. The echo of a date resounding in mental cavities. But he'd never applied this basic criterion of criminology to the calendar. Seasons were important. Abrupt climatic vicissitudes. A leaden sky. He'd just been investigating a series of suicides in the district. The same week, the same early hour, people hanging from the same species of tree, the apple tree. Yes, the sky's weight. But from now on he needed also to study the history of days.

The stubborn torch persevered like another circle among circles. Awoke things. Unearthed them like a shovel of light. Over the years, how many eyes would have seen this, guided there by the Collector? He suddenly felt something he never allowed himself. Fear. He'd decided to forbid himself fear as others forbid themselves tobacco or alcohol. But now he felt fear. A fear with no exact location in his body. That affected neither his respiratory system nor his sweat glands nor his locomotion. That didn't belong to him, but alighted on him. A fear that sounded like a whisper. That issued from the intimacy of things. The experience of things. An exhibit's fear of being erased. Fear of disappearing. The torch took the initiative. Here, on a file like those used in a notary's office for keeping title deeds, a terse message: 'Castellana Bridge, River Mandeo'. As he took it, the cover gave way and out fell photographs that seemed to float on the table. That river. It could be said that river was the merriest in the whole of Galicia. It took the sea to the mountains. In the direction of the Caneiros festivities. Santos knew this. He'd gone there once with a group of Law students from Betanzos. He was so impressed he went to tell Catherine Laboure about it. She enjoyed music. That river was like a gramophone. The sailing of the boats, a stream of song. Of course this was no place for her. 'A nun in Caneiros?' she mused. 'Nuns bring bad luck to boats.' She liked these stories, to hear how people had fun. Listening to them, she'd smoke like a chimney. Not long before, as summer approached, Santos had thought about Catia and Caneiros. Upriver, rays of sunlight among alders. At dusk, the sun like a charred log in the water. Contact between boats, bodies carrying the day's enjoyment on rippling skirts and blazing shirts. What Santos saw now were corpses. Bodies thrown into the river from the Castile road. Among the photos he saw bobbing on the table, a woman's face. A small portrait, the edge of which matched the smile and teeth. An inscription on the back in well-rounded handwriting: 'Monelos Schoolmistress'. He'd never felt so confused. He thought of an unending debate, one of few possible, in the Law Faculty. That of the Plank of Carneades. Two shipwrecked sailors with a single plank. Not helping the other wasn't a crime if there was only one plank to save yourself. He'd vehemently taken the opposite side. It was a crime. It wasn't a question of codes. It was a question of conscience. The line between humanity and inhumanity.

'The thing about Carneades' Plank is that there'll always be someone to support, in theory, what you're saying,' the Professor with the Pimpled Nose remarked ironically. 'I'd like to see what you'd do with the plank if you were shipwrecked.'

He couldn't see himself abandoning or getting rid of the other sailor. So he failed to understand his own actions when he put down the photo of the Woman with Curls, stuffed the photos back into the file and returned it to the shadows.

His mind sought out an alibi. He wasn't at sea with a plank and another sailor. It'd already happened. They'd already drowned. This was something else. His attention was drawn to a bookshelf with various Bibles, different editions, most of them old and in several volumes. He leafed through one of the books the torchlight fell on, perhaps because of the golden letters on its spine. It was Bernard Lamy's *Apparatus Biblicus*, containing beautiful illustrations of animals and plants. There was another book on that shelf, *Ulysses*, a foreigner taken in by Holy Scripture. It was the book's foreignness that made him pick it up. Open it at random. There was an ex-libris with a geometrical design: 'This book belongs to Huici'. It was written in English. He turned the pages. Tried to translate something easy, but his eyes landed on a sort of medley:

> *Diddlediddle dumdum*
> *Diddlediddle . . .*

The torch headed urgently for the desk. Went straight to an artistic paperweight. A polished, oval shape. A black woman's head in ebony. Very pretty. Where'd it come from? He had to go. He'd been here too long. On the desk was a blue cardboard folder with a white label and a name: 'Judith'. He opened it, though he knew it wasn't necessary. From the weight, he could tell it was empty.

Blue Mist

'Here it is.'

A car driving slowly along Aduanas Esplanade. Just now, with the aid of two tugs, the cargo boat *Chemin Creux* started weighing anchor. The mist colours the night and makes land and sea machines act with animal caution.

Manlle gets out of his vehicle and comes over to the half-open window of the Opel where Ren, Mancorvo, Santos and Samos the judge are waiting. Deliberately seeks out the gaze of the new kid on the block in Crime, Paúl Santos is his name, sitting in the back with the judge, but talks to the chief of the Political Brigade. An old acquaintance. 'Here it is. She's in that car. I'll be off now, gentlemen. I've done my bit.' He doffs his hat in a mocking gesture. 'Lots to do tonight.'

Two women emerge. One of them is Chelo. The other is taller, walks stiffly. In a hat with veil.

'There they are,' says Ren. 'Chelo and the Portuguese architect.'

The judge is amazed. 'What architect? That's a woman!'

Mancorvo reacts fast, 'Not under her skirts she isn't!'

'Stay calm, your honour. Don't move. Don't rush into anything.'

They were arm in arm, two girlfriends out for a walk, but now they've separated. The two of them quicken their pace over the flagstones. There's an uneasiness, a bewilderment in their movements when they realise the *Chemin Creux* is being towed away from the jetty. The lights of the tugs are on, their powerful engines snort loudly in the night. But the cargo boat is like a phantom ship being dragged along in slow motion. The two women reach the edge of the jetty. Suddenly a shadow appears astern and emits flashes with a small torch.

The couple look at each other. Turn around. Head back towards the car. The driver is expecting this and has kept the engine running, though the lights are switched off. He turns and goes to meet them.

'Come on!' says Santos.

The judge grabs at the door. Trips and falls out, shouting, 'Chelo!'

The woman's name is the first cry to break out in the night. A commanding and yet anxious call. But no one replies. His intervention speeds up every movement. Only he stays still, petrified on the flagstones. The tragic balance of an intoxicated man.

'Stop!' shouts Santos. 'Police!'

Ren gets out of the car, but his behaviour is unusual. He gestures towards the dark, in the direction of the yacht club and House of Pilots, from where ambushed guards emerge. He gestures for calm, for them not to intervene.

Santos again tells them to stop. Measures the distance. If they don't heed him, and it looks as if they're not going to, he won't be able to reach them before they get in the car. He looks back. Come on, Santos, what's happening? You're the only one running after the fugitives. You should stop and think. This is what he does. He stops. His heavy breathing has more to do with the sudden agitation in his mind than with physical effort. As Chelo Vidal and the other fugitive get in the car, Paúl Santos turns around. Mancorvo hasn't moved. He's still at the wheel. The judge is on the ground, petrified, a white cravat around his neck like a luminous noose. Ren stares at him, at Paúl Santos, and nods mockingly when he gestures for the car to start, to follow him. Ren climbs in. The fugitives' car has already gone through the gears and is moving swiftly away, with a screech of tyres as it twists between the cranes, heading for the eastern exit.

The chase is on.

The car with Ren and Mancorvo, which has left the judge behind, approaches. Santos puts his weapon away and prepares to climb in. He won't be able. As they're passing, Mancorvo lowers the window. Says, 'It's our turn now, Mr Scientist!' Accelerates. He's grounded. Surrounded by blue mist.

* * *

484

His office is open. He's dozing with his head on the table. The night's dozing as well, on the blinds, the indirect sea, the collage of shadows in the city on the other side of the window. Finally he hears them arrive. They're greeted by the duty officers. Ask for a cigarette. It's as if he can hear everything. Including the sound of the smoke. Which is why, when Mancorvo starts typing and discussing the terms of the report with Ren, their voices and the sound of the keys reverberate inside his head.

So it was he learnt:

The driver of the vehicle being pursued performed a reckless manoeuvre on Hervés Hill, the car overturned on a bend and fell down the side. As a result of the accident, two occupants died: a woman identified as Consuelo Vidal Míguez and a man, the driver, as yet to be identified. A third person, also unknown, managed to escape, no doubt badly injured, judging by traces remaining on the scene.

And then:

The orders are, until further notice, not to provide any public information about these events, to avoid them being disseminated in the media, orders that will be duly passed on to the censor's office.

He could hear everything. Drying sweat, Mancorvo's handkerchief sounded like a paper blade, Ren's like the crackling of elytra in a light trap for insects.

'Where's Mr Scientist?'

'He'll be here somewhere. His door's open.'

'Give him time,' said Ren. 'He'll soon find out birds don't suck and pigs don't fly.'

The Arrest

It's a hot morning. Santos, the policeman, heads for the Tachygraphic Rose academy and finds it closed. A few pupils are standing around in confusion. It's the first time this has happened. 'Closed Owing to Bereavement'. They expect some such sign. But suddenly the door opens and Dr Montevideo comes out. It was he who opened. The one who was bedridden. Something extraordinary must have happened, something terrible or supernatural. The man exiled in his own room since he returned from his other exile ten or so years previously. They gaze at the ghost. Perhaps it's only a shell, empty on the inside. They'll soon find out when he turns around to lock the door. But no. On the contrary, he's very robust, not astral at all. A body, the memory of a body, wearing a coat and the coat's memory. When he entered the house, intending not to reappear, it was winter. This helped him. He entered like a shepherd driving a flock of dry leaves. Now the sea-blue coat gives him the air of a sailor emerging from a boat-house in another hemisphere, another season. He looks at the plaque: 'The Tachygraphic Rose, 2nd Floor'. Wipes the brass with his sleeve. 'The best polish for cleaning metals is and always will be Love. Love Polish.' An advertisement he remembers from his childhood. Another one, important for a reason that's become obscured, is the definition of Portland cement. The relationship between poetry and publicity is paradoxical. A verse quickly grows old when it takes the form of an advert, but a slogan that's presented as a poem lives on. For example . . . No, now is not the time to institute such proceedings. He wipes the plaque with his sleeve, a sea cloth. Says, 'Go back to the jungle, children. Classes are suspended.'

'Why, Mr Montevideo?'

The doctor looks back. His eyes rest on the policeman Paúl Santos. Speechless, shocked, suddenly fully aware of the outcome.

'What is it, Mr Montevideo?' asks Stringer.

'Nothing you can publish,' replies Héctor Ríos. 'A man descended into hell.'

Having said this, he heads quickly towards the pedestrian crossing. The road is flat, but he views each step as if it's an uphill climb.

'Has something happened to Miss Catia?' Stringer manages to ask out loud. He's conscious by now that the fact of asking could not only reveal a truth, but worsen it.

'She was arrested last night. They've taken her, Balboa.'

Stringer reiterates a long forgotten question, 'Why?'

'They say they arrested someone who had a photo of her. They searched his house and apparently found a photo of Catia with the name 'Judith' on the back. Nonsense. They then came here and turned everything upside down. They even tore my mattress and confiscated my papers. *A Dramatic History of Culture*. To see what it said. I told them I'd written it. They wouldn't listen. I was of no interest. They didn't want to arrest me, I think they thought I was too old. One kept looking at my teeth. I told him I had a new set which I'd lent to a friend working as a second-hand car salesman.'

He points across the road. 'For further information, ask the . . . lawyer.' Stringer turns to look at Paúl Santos, who's typing inside, has a problem, he's hit two different keys and the bars are entangled.

Popsy's Delivery

Pinche was watching TV. The owners had gone on holiday, so he was living like a king. All he had to do was keep the house warm. Those were his orders. He'd light the fires and then sit back to watch TV. That horse that could speak. Black Beauty. He understood everything after a few months. Spoke perfect English, like the horse. Who wouldn't? But as for me, I had to do the rest. The dogs. Look after the dogs. Besides watching that horse on TV, he could have taken care of the dogs. He said he would but, when it comes to dogs, who'd believe him? The only animal deserving of his attention was Black Beauty. So better to forget about Pinche. I like animals. When I told the lady of the house my mother had a donkey to carry the clothes called Grumpy, she almost cried with emotion.

'Grumpy!'

'That's right, madam. Grumpy.'

What I wanted was for her to talk to me in English, since I wasn't around for Black Beauty to teach me, but what she wanted was for me to talk to her in Spanish. She was an actress and had always dreamed of one day speaking Spanish. Sometimes, when Pinche and I spoke Galician, she'd listen in to our conversation. She obviously thought something funny was going on and we were trying to wind her up with a secret language we'd invented. She didn't know this language existed. She knew about Catalan and Basque. I explained it was a poor person's language, how could she know? But it wasn't something we'd come up with to annoy her. Thing is I couldn't talk Spanish to Pinche, it made me laugh. What, Spanish? No, Spanish didn't make me laugh, what made me laugh was talking it to Pinche and Pinche talking it to me. To her? No. Talking it to her didn't make me laugh. Why should it? 'All right, madam, you talk English to me in the mornings and in the afternoons I'll talk Spanish.' It seemed a good deal. She was almost always out in the afternoons. But, after that, she stopped going out. When the weather was good, we'd sit outside, chatting away. If I got paid for talking, I'd be rich by now. In the mornings, however, when she was due to speak to me in English, she'd fall silent. I'm not saying she wanted to save her words, keep them to herself. Though it would have been better for her if I spoke English well, then we wouldn't have had a problem when she asked me to 'clean the corner' and I understood *cona* or 'fanny', went all red, somehow managed to stop myself saying, 'Clean your own!' And she came up to me, what was wrong, was I offended? We laughed a lot after that, when I explained. Same thing happened when she asked me to 'collect the gateau'. What did she mean, collect the *gato*, the 'cat'? Ah, nonsense. After a while, you joke about it. Words like to play with us. The more serious we look to them, the more they play. I knew very well if she didn't speak much, it wasn't to save her words. No doubt she was outgoing enough in her time. She'd been an actress. They once showed a film on TV she'd worked on. A film a dozen or so years old. There we were, the four of us – her husband and her, Pinche and me – and it was all very funny to start with. She was good. But it faded after a while, as if the light on the screen had dwindled. No, she wouldn't talk much in the mornings. She'd hang anxiously around the phones and, if one rang, it was as if the cuckoo had sung after a long winter. She could be on the phone for hours.

He didn't like talking much. He'd been a pilot, he told me one day, a fighter pilot. Then commercial flights.

They'd insisted we shouldn't leave the dog alone. But I wasn't going to run after the dog all day long, with Pinche in the role of major-domo.

So there he was, watching TV. Ensconced in the armchair. A roaring fire in every fireplace. Like a lord, talking English to Black Beauty. And I ran downstairs to fetch him because, after all, a man is a man.

'Where is she?'

'On the bed.'

'Which bed?'

'The lady's. With six puppies.'

'What?'

I'd managed the birth. I'd been very nervous to start with because she'd climbed on to the bed. Unthinkable where I come from. That a dog should give birth on the bed, on top of a pink satin bedspread. A water bed, what's more. Brand name, Zodiac. I didn't believe the lady when she said it was a water bed. She told me to have a go and wouldn't let up until I did. She was right. Very strange to begin with. Then it was like lying on a river. How nice the way the water moved! You could close your eyes and just float. But now it was Popsy lying there, giving birth, her eyes on me. What did the bed, the pink satin, matter? I was fully aware everything would have been the same had I not been there, except for one thing. Her look. Which alighted on mine, light on light, shade on shade. Lots of looks meet in life. Your eyes take in what others see. At the end of the day, you might have been credulous, naked, saintly, raped, murdered, beloved, recognised, invisible, a kiss, a thorn, a harpy, an Amazon. One time I took Pinche to see the eye doctor, the doctor explained to me – or rather told me, the way he talked was like a tale – that inside each retina of the eye there are millions of tiny rods which gather the light. Each look we give each other must have its own rod. But the dog's look as she gave birth was different. A gift that required every single rod. Because it didn't meet mine, it landed on it. She left me her look. Such a beautiful thing, and she entrusted it to me.

I went down to fetch Pinche because she'd closed her eyes. It was her first delivery. She'd borne six pups and I was afraid she'd expire from the effort. I've seen that happen as a child. A dead cat whose kittens are still suckling. Apparently mothers have milk for a day after they die. Popsy was exhausted. But when we came back, she'd recovered some of her strength. There she was, on the pink satin bedspread, licking her puppies.

Pinche was annoyed.

'Little blighters, trust them to pick the weekend! I'll have to go for a sack.'

'A sack? What do you want a sack for?'

'What do you think? The sooner they go in the river, the better. She shouldn't grow too fond of them. The sooner, the better.'

I gave him the look Popsy had given me.

'No, Pinche, no more throwing dogs in the river.'

'Well, I don't mind. Or do you think I like drowning dogs? As far as I'm concerned, we can leave them where they are.'

He lit the fire in the bedroom. Got over his bad mood. Went to have a look at the litter and intoned, 'Boy, boy, girl, boy, boy, girl. How very considerate! You know what we're going to do? Pop down to the cellar and open one of those vastly expensive bottles of French wine.'

I was about to protest, but recalled something Polka used to say, 'Matter is neither created nor destroyed, it is simply transformed.'

The Lucky Gambler

It was the first time Alberte Pementa had gambled but, when he sat down, he had the impression that game of cards with Raúl Cotón had been foretold years previously. There was a strange sense of expectation in the bar in Brandariz. Fiz, the waiter, arranged the tablecloth as if for an autopsy and brought the cards with all the care of someone laying down a weapon. Cotón was playing and that spelt only one thing: disaster.

'These cards have got Morse on the back,' joked Pementa.

'I've no problem with them,' said Cotón.

'Then I haven't either.'

'Shut the door. Make yourselves comfortable. Gentlemen, we're outside the law. And bring us a bird,' Cotón told Fiz.

'A bird? Please not.'

'Don't grumble. We need to know the time.'

'There's a clock on the wall.'

'Bring us a bird. The bird is time.'

Fiz came back with a starling inside a cage. Placed it on the side of the table.

'What's its name?' Pementa asked.

'Figaro.'

'The last one was called Figaro,' Cotón remarked.

'Yes. But the last one died. Smoked to death in a cage.'

Cotón stopped shuffling and stared at Pementa. Offered him a cigarette.

'You'd better smoke. You know the condition?'

'What condition?'

'No one leaves till the bird is dead.'

Alberte Pementa was a lucky man. He'd always been lucky. The night he arrived at the bar in Brandariz, he opened the door, looked down at the ground and found a 500-peseta note. A blue note. Lots of money at that time. Some people had never seen a note that colour before. It was a Saturday night and the bar was full of men, almost all of them building labourers letting off steam after a week's work in the city. The smoke of Celtas gave conversations a structured consistency, though there was also the odd flourish of someone smoking a Tip Top, Portuguese blond. Each to his own, nobody noticed him. Until he bent down and stood up with that note in his hand like an oriflamme. The first look of congratulation gave way to a general feeling of resentment. Why should Pementa have found it soon as he came through the door? Why?

'Things look at us,' Pementa attempted a justification. 'We don't look at them.'

Pementa's remark was considered witty, but not without pride. At this late hour, on the back of several rounds, people were highly sensitive to signs. What was so special about Pementa that notes should look at him?

'It's just that the man is lucky,' said Fiz. 'That's all.'

Everyone understood that Pementa had been very lucky. But such luck should be shared around. It couldn't discriminate in this way, pull a fast one on people who'd always lived there. People who were from the place. Where'd Pementa come from? Another village, on horseback. All he'd done was arrive and fill up.

'Somebody might be missing that note, I dare say.'

The person who made this observation was Raúl Cotón, who egged the others on with his look.

Everybody checked their pockets, their wallets, but no one claimed back the note. They might have been resentful, but they were honest.

'Well, I say that note's as much yours as it's mine,' insisted Cotón. Pementa understood. His horse was outside, tied to the hitching-rail, and he'd only stopped for a drink to shake off the night dew. It would give him great pleasure to share his luck with those present, in a toast to the parish's deceased. There was a murmur of approval. Here was a gentleman, a tavern prince. But Cotón broke the accord. What was under discussion was not the note, an accidental factor, but the possession of Luck with a capital letter, which Cotón, in a hoarse, forceful, brandy-laden voice, raised to the rank of virgin or goddess, Our Lady of Luck, whose favour had to be decided here, this night and no other.

Pementa didn't mind playing for luck. He wasn't superstitious.

'You ever been unlucky?' asked Cotón, who seemed to speak not through his mouth, but through the weal across his cheekbone.

'I camp out under my own star. Where I do not run, I don't grow tired.'

'Well, I cut the air with a sickle. I'm fed up of treading shit and am going to unwalk the wheel. Let's see those cards! I'm going to get your three, Pementa! Understand?' growled Cotón in the direction of the Brandariz public.

They played and all Pementa did was lose.

First off, what he had to hand, the money. Then his horse at the door. His belt. His riding boots. Followed by his property. His mother's inheritance. Her jewellery, the toad necklace and filigree earrings, the bedhead made of chestnut wood and carved with roses. Finally the chest. 'You going to bet the chest?' 'I've still got something. St Anthony of Padua.' 'How can you bet poor little old Anthony? The saint everyone loves, the matchmaker, the one who looks after the herd.'

'He wants a bullet in his head,' remarked a parishioner. 'Betting St Anthony!'

'Anyone else can shut up or provide tobacco,' said Cotón.

The lucky gambler lost St Anthony as well. He was ashamed. Not just because of what the living would say, but because of what the dead might think. Enough. He'd lost everything.

'Your turn in the dance.'

'What?'

'You've still got your turn in the dance.'

'It's not a cow, I can't bet that.'

'I want your turn.'

Pementa knew very well what this meant. For months now, he'd been

494

dancing with the same girl in the fixed corner, where you didn't have to give way in the dance. It was a kind of preserve. In the rest of the room, you had to give way. However content the couple might be, in the rest of the room, a local boy's request to step in for the slow dance had to be granted without further ado. A round that is not over until the couple formalises their relationship. Makes it clear they're serious. The fixed corner was the preserve of seriousness. The obligation to make way is an arbitrary rule, often irritating, but it leads to surprises, constant traffic, so that there's much more hullabaloo, whereas in the territory of those 'on speaking terms' there is safety in silence. The most ardent lovers bend and bow, hope to reach the light without getting burnt, like moths around a lamp, and, if we glance in their direction, they're trying out new symmetries that show a willingness to exchange bodies. There's a moment at the end of the number when a fiery couple seems to have swapped facial and bodily features to such an extent that, being of a different size, they've suddenly acquired the same stature. This interchange is beneficial. They're both more beautiful after the dance. But there are some who, in the formality of their engagement, suddenly grow cold, like bronze poured into a mould. They dance to each tune with a correctness that makes them all the same, be it a bolero or a paso doble, as if they were in fact doing the housework. Alberte Pementa and his girl belonged not to these, but to the first kind. Being 'on speaking terms' should be understood in the widest sense. Because speaking to each other implied carnal knowledge. They were either engaged or on the way to being so. Which was not just a verbal undertaking, but a bodily promise.

'You going to bet your turn?'

'Shut it,' said Cotón. 'It's the right to dance.'

'He wants a kick in the balls,' said the parishioner.

After that, Pementa had only one thing left. Luck.

Time was running out. The starling in the cage was showing signs of suffocating amid so much smoke. Its death signalled the end of the game. And the bird seemed to know it. Motionless on its perch, it had a grave look, like an animal in a fable.

495

'I've nothing left,' said Pementa. 'Not even a horse. I'll have to walk.'

'Yes, you have,' said Cotón with the same voice, the same desire as in the first game.

'What's that?'

'Luck.'

'Go to bed, Cotón,' said a local, hoping to do him a favour. 'You've won everything. Don't weigh using the devil's scales.'

'Calamity, why don't you go and see if it's raining.'

They played for luck. Cotón concentrated harder than ever. He'd had a magnificent night. Game after game, he'd beaten Pementa. And now he was going to deprive him of luck.

From the first card, it was obvious the wind had changed. Luck loved Pementa, or it didn't love Cotón, one way or the other.

Which is why Alberte Pementa decided to leave. Ashamed at having betted love and kept luck. I don't know what happened that day, what mist got inside his head. But even his friends stayed away from him. He must have been lucky because, just before embarking in Coruña, Santa Catarina, he found a thousand pesetas on the ground. There were lots of people, some whose job it was to do just that, catch anything that might fall out, so to speak, but Pementa found the money as soon as he arrived. Though his head was bowed, his soul in the doldrums. This may have helped him.

Adela, the local soothsayer, with a black bandage over her eyes, said, 'Don't let that man embark! No one should leave a city who finds notes on the ground.' But Alberte Pementa thought differently. He thought the opposite. He thought he should leave at once.

'I don't believe a word of it,' said O.

And Pementa whispered in her ear, 'It's true, girl.'

Disguises

He wanted us to know. It was customary to pray, even the rosary's unending litany. And though we nodded when they asked, yes, we said the rosary at home, the only prayer was that of Polka reading us geography from Élisée's book, followed by me with an extract from *The Invisible Man*. He found this book very funny. He'd sometimes cry with laughter. Of the book with burnt edges, Olinda would say, 'Poor thing never thought it'd be so popular, sad though it is.' Polka also kept newspaper cuttings with mankind's chief inventions. The paper was yellowed. So old I thought inventions were the most ancient thing there was. Needless to say, the most important one for Polka, after aspirin, was electricity. He wanted Pinche to become an electrician. Or a painter. Because of the clothes.

In the field of construction, painters are the most stylish. Because of their shirts. They're the ones who wear the most elegant shirts. They're the only workers who go and buy them from Camisería Inglesa. Like musicians, they have that courage. Bricklayers and plumbers are the most modest. But a Coruñan painter, at the end of the day, changes on site and struts down the street like Valentino.

When Pinche worked as a sandwich-man for the Sherlock Holmes Museum, we sent Polka a photo so he could see a detective's style. He looked wonderful in his deerstalker and matching cloak. With a magnifying glass in one hand and calabash pipe in the other. We also sent him a photo of Pinche as a Beefeater, the summer he worked as a Yeoman Warder in the Tower of London. Very smart in his Tudor outfit. He had a go at everything, including executing tourists, but I didn't want to send Polka a photo of his son with an enormous two-edged axe, pretending to cut off heads.

'Don't be stupid,' said Pinche. 'Dad likes Carnival more than anything.'

'In this photo, you're an executioner.'

'Yes, but an English executioner. What an axe! What civilisation!'

What Pinche said was true. I remember, at carnival time, Francisco would completely disappear, change skin, leaving only Polka. It was forbidden back then to wear disguises in the street. Thing is they'd have had to post a policeman at every door. There came a time they did post one at the end of each street especially to stop men dressed as monuments, *femmes fatales*, reaching the city centre.

I can see them now. The monuments. It's very early. I'm with Amalia in Torre Street. Suddenly men dressed up as women start to turn the corners. Some of them are impressive. Sailors from San Amaro and Lapas looking like queens of the night. Hairy chests sprouting between pinnacled breasts. They have a taste for rouge, fishnet stockings and stiletto heels. 'Oh my, don't look, Amalia, don't look.'

'Hey O! Look, look, look, look. The one with a flower in her hair, isn't that your father?'

She would have to spot him of all people. There are dozens of monumental women, but she goes straight like an arrow to Polka in his print dress, short like a miniskirt, you can see his bulge, lace knickers containing that packet, how horrible, even a tutu would have been better.

'There, there! The one acting all innocent. He looks great!'

There's no shutting her up. She turns to me and points out a defect, 'His legs are like matchsticks.'

Lame, with legs like matchsticks. She's even impressed she noticed.

'Come on, let's go,' I say.

'What's wrong, O? You're all red. Hey, you're blushing! We have to greet him. We can't leave here without saying hello to your father. Polka, Mr France, Francisco!'

'Why don't you shut up?' I mutter, getting more and more annoyed.

And then he readjusts the padding in his bra and walks towards us. Completely ignores me. Says to Amalia, 'Miss, what's all this fuss about? I may not be La Belle Otero, but it's the first time someone calls me "Mr". Your desire for a man is making you see things.'

He'd disappear for three days and nights. First on his own, dressed as a monumental woman on Mount Alto, then he'd join the procession that left Castro on Ash Wednesday to bury the Carnival. By then, he was a bishop or cardinal. One year, they threw the dummy into the River Monelos. I didn't quite understand what was going on, but I know several men were beaten up by the civil guards. Fled cross-country. The guards then came to arrest them. To take their statements in the barracks. And they started with him, with Polka. Because they hadn't forgotten. Because he was important enough to have a record. As a child, I didn't know what this meant. I heard at home he couldn't get a job because he had 'antecedents'. And I confused 'antecedents' with 'ancestors'. Who were these ancestors that kept causing problems? Were they men dressed as monumental women? Were they carnival priests?

They were kept with the horses. They'd been taken to the stables underneath the barracks. And Polka used the term 'commander' to address a corporal, who didn't object to the sudden promotion, and explain, 'My commander, there's no need for us all to be conveniently interrogated.'

The corporal looked with suspicion at this freak wearing an alb on top of his work clothes. He was joking. Parodying the phrase always used in police reports and press releases: 'conveniently interrogated'.

'There's no need for us all to be conveniently interrogated, my commander, because I'm the one who's to blame. They simply responded to my invocation, my *Kyrie eleison*.'

'I like brave people, so I'm going to show you a kindness,' replied the corporal. He led him to a cupboard hanging from the wall, which he opened by pulling the handle with the tip of his rifle.

It was full of whips. Different makes and sizes. One with iron balls.

'*Domine, non sum dignus*,' murmured Polka.

'Between you and me,' said the corporal, 'it takes balls to do what you did. Throw a dummy of the Generalissimo into the river. With a bit of Latin to boot.'

'It was Carnival.'

'Doesn't matter.' He pointed to the cupboard with whips. 'You can choose one. You deserve it.'

In Polka's words, 'It became clear to me then that, deep down, he was a very liberal Fascist.'

'What a pig!' exclaims O as she recalls the story. 'Even made him choose a whip.' She looks at Pinche and the photo of him as an executioner at the Tower of London, about to crop a tourist at the neck. 'What the hell! Send it to him. He's sure to laugh. He sees the humour in everything.'

The Camden Town Fire-Eater

Some women carried fire on top of their heads, factory workers who sometimes placed oil lamps there on wintry nights, on their way to the factory, to play at being souls, though it may not have been a game, like this girl with the green crest ejecting flames through her mouth in Camden Town, having juggled torches while balancing a larger torch on her forehead, between her eyebrows, flames rising to the sky, that's what I call art, no need to put on an act, risk your neck, like Pinito del Oro, the trapeze artist who fell at Price Circus, set up in Riazor Field, slipped out of the sky without a net, only the arms of a man to break her fall, of course I'm sorry she fell but, since she fell, I'm also sorry not to have been there, it's all people talked about, seemed everyone was there that night to see Pinito del Oro fall, I don't have that bad dream about falling, they say it's a common nightmare, but I am afraid of fire, a form of fear to me, which is what happened to Mary of the Shells, the one with the long, blond hair, Polka told us one night, there was a shipwreck and the locals went to collect what the sea gave up, the gifts of tragedy, among which they found some bottles they supposed could be used, liquor or something, but, when they got back to Mary's, someone opened one of those containers, accidentally knocked it over next to the hearth, and the liquid rose in huge flames that licked the girl, she started running in the night towards the sea, Mary of the Shells, her beautiful locks burning in the storm, this for me was the image of fear, another that of the Morraza Vixen that could fly and projected flames through its mouth when it howled, be it true or not, what was true was that fire that burnt books in the city, real fear, a fire emerging from the mouth of hate, and the Girl with the Green Crest comes towards me, throwing flames through her mouth as if reading my thoughts, I can't leave, I'm not going to leg it now, having seen the whole show, though other people are about their business, no one stops, they're sure to think we planned it as she walks around me, spitting fire, me spell-bound, like an idiot, it's started raining and the flames are coloured, like a rainbow, they're sure to think I'm an advert, or her mother trying to persuade her of something, to come home, or the opposite, the fire suddenly goes out and the Girl with the Green Crest stands and stares at me, clenching her teeth, she looks furious, of course she would be, it's about time I loosened the purse-strings, I'd always planned to give her a coin, she deserves it, no one should be poor, especially those who cheer up our sad streets, musicians in the Underground, make lonely people feel safe, they should be paid a salary instead of being hounded by guards all day long, you need permission to sing or swallow fire, but not if you want to do nothing, you don't need permission for that, to do evil, no licence for that, point is I'm going now, I'll drop a coin on the plate the Girl with the Green Crest has left on the ground, drop it slowly so she sees it's a pound, not pennies, and I value her, the way she swallows fire, I wonder what state her teeth, tongue, lips are in, poor thing, any day a gust of wretched wind, ravenous wind, shadowed wind, that's the worst, girl, I know my airs, could suddenly turn the fire against you, your lashes, your crest, I didn't like it at first, now it's kind of funny, makes you look different in the night, an ancient being, wandering priestess, and up she comes, as if reading my thoughts, doesn't say anything, slowly, her teeth clenched, though her eyes are laughing, I've dropped the coin, these things help, not being there, at the show, for free, Marshal Mountebank used to complain about that when he was in Castro with the troupe, art is a risky business, and there he was, as if he had two bodies, one that worked, the other stiff on account of his spine, that's what he told Polka, two lame people meet, two classics, he said, though the art of parish gravedigger has a future, ours is uncertain, that box, the television, will finish us off, but he wasn't a moaner, so long as he was fit, he'd never abandon his sublime, artistic duty of supporting the contortionist, La Bambola was her name, holding her with the harness he tied to his shoulders and head,

which secured a bar with a small platform, tiny fulcrum so she could pirouette like an elastic woman, incredible dance in the air, the only man I knew to carry something on top of his head, the contortionist with her beautiful, long hair, one day she came to wash it in the river, dry it with a comb, I'd never seen hair like it, you could wear it as a tunic, but then in the evening, during the show, she'd fasten it in a ponytail, the moment came, the decisive moment, with a bugle call and roll on the tabor, when La Bambola tied her ponytail to the bar and started turning dizzily round and round, Benjamin, the Marshal of Deza, unmoved, with his Napoleonic coat and tricolour sash, that's how they'd met, La Bambola needed a broad-shouldered man, her husband, Homer, the ventriloquist, was skinny, an intellectual, though he did help with the naughty number, pointing with a stick at the anatomy of the contortionist wearing a bathing suit, sitting on a high stool, and asking where do women have most hair – on their head? – and the public would laugh and shout lower, lower, a number that gave them a few problems, once they ended up in jail, Benjamin covered the contortionist while she slept on a bench with his marshal's coat, and the jailer said every Napoleon had his Waterpolo, and Benjamin said something to La Bambola in French, the advantage of being on the road, languages stick to you, what he said was *Il est très dur de tête*, to which the jailer replied with the typical speak normal, or you'll know about it, the fool didn't realise how happy he felt protecting his fair lady, a circus artist's life is full of self-sacrifice, and then came the chance to join the Circus of Portugal, welcomed by a director who was extremely polite, tamed elephants, female elephants, though one was called Dumbo, treated everyone right, as if they were elephants, and theirs really was a very artistic piece, though the historical background was a bit confused, the central motif being a large whale, he was introduced as the knight Donnaiolo, who had to fight in order to get into the whale's mouth, which involved various trials, out of that mouth came, for example, a Samurai archer shouting halt, you bastard, twit, twat, or I'll have your balls for garters, which had a certain impact on Portuguese children, and shooting an arrow that stuck in his chest, which he pulled out with his own hands, applause, followed by an old, tame, half-blind lion, which Benjamin frightened by showing it a

live mouse, further applause, and so on until the magnificent moment when Donnaiolo finally made it inside the whale and came out with the contortionist La Bambola in his arms, standing ovation, placed her on the small platform secured with a harness, she climbed up on to the twister, the contortions began, figures in the air, a sublime elevation for which Benjamin was the support, everyone thought they were a couple, the contortions were so intimate, but no, there was no other kind of relationship between them, one was La Bambola, the other Benjamin, the Marshal, Donnaiolo, call me what you like, sometimes she'd even do a pirouette and land astride him, Polka said that must have been like cohabiting, Benjamin replied with a murmur it was more, a lot more than cohabiting, another thing was her husband, Homer, the ventriloquist, who also emerged from the whale, Benjamin muttered, he and the puppet – Manolo Pinzón! – the way he said it, it was obvious the puppet played a role, a pimp, that puppet, Benjamin affirmed, a real pimp, soon as he got on stage, he'd turn to the audience, shout wahey, anyone with purse-strings, hold 'em tight!

Yes, my girl, I know you've hidden the fire in your mouth. I'm not afraid of your fire. If only you knew the fire I carry inside . . .

Felicity of Expression

London, 10 January 1968

I can be bad as well. Thing is you can't pretend when it comes to clothes. You can't lie about the weight of clothes. If they're damp, that's worse for me. More weight. They say with washing machines clothes don't last so long. Who knows? I'd have thought hands are more delicate. Or both. Hands have to slap clothes against the washing stone. Twist them. Wring them out.

Clothes have eyes. Like worms. The eye doctor once told me worms can't see, but they can feel light and shade. Olinda used to wash the clinic's coats, sheets, towels, clothes. Pinche had a bad eye, not the evil eye, he saw badly out of one eye. How did we know it was only one eye? Because, when he looked through the keyhole, he saw fine. He told us this himself. He saw better when looking through a keyhole.

'What keyholes are those?' asked Olinda.

'Who cares?' replied Polka. 'The important thing is . . . the diagnosis.'

He was so happy to have found that word he smiled at me, repeating it like a gift, 'That's it, the diagnosis.'

Olinda mentioned it to the eye doctor and off I went with Pinche. It was very funny when he said Pinche had a lazy eye. The right sees less than the left. 'Why?' I asked. 'Well, to start with, because it doesn't want to. That's why we call it a lazy eye.' It was a pleasure talking to him. Most doctors never explain anything. They detect what's wrong, hand you the armament, but you never know what it is you're firing against in your own body. Dr Abril explained everything and I understood him straightaway.

Must be because we both work with the light. That's something machines don't do, leave the clothes in the sun. Bring them in when it's raining, stretch them out again when it clears. There are days the sun is lazy and then it clears, the sun peeps out of the clouds, a kind of grand absolution. Worms only have light and shade. The first way of seeing. Skin-sight. We're a bit like that. I love the sun. Seems to forgive everything.

'A lazy eye,' said Dr Abril.

Pinche kept quiet. His manner was contrite. If he had a lazy eye, he must be partly to blame.

'What are we going to do?' I asked.

'We're going to make it work. That's what you do with lazy eyes.'

I'd always thought eyes were the same, Pinche's or anyone's, except for Miraceu's, each of which went about its own business. But in the clinic I quickly realised not only eyes but also profiles were completely different. Which is why Pinche had two sides to him. He could be very brave and very cowardly. Very joyful and very sad. Very good and very bad. Maybe it was all because of his eye.

'What we're going to do,' said Dr Abril, 'is put a patch on the eye that sees OK. And leave the lazy eye as it is. I know, I know, it seems unfair. It is unfair. We're depriving one eye, the eye that wants to see, of the pleasure of seeing. But that's life. It won't be for long.'

Which may have been why Mr Sada's poet friend and I never met. Because of a lazy eye.

One eye didn't fight for him. That may have been it.

'What are you looking at?' asked Pementa.

'Nothing.'

I went red. This was in the Troubadour when Glenda, Pementa and I went out for a drink for the first time. Pementa had just started as a hospital porter. Before that, he'd worked in a psychiatric hospital in Epsom for years.

'I was lucky,' he told me. 'I found the job as soon as I arrived. They even gave me accommodation. I hardly ever left. The patients left more than me. What for? There was a good library, with books in Spanish and Portuguese. I'd never read before, I read like crazy. I learnt a lot there.

From the patients. Languages. How to play chess. How not to go crazy. I once went with a group of them to the races. A doctor said to me, "Mr Pementa, a group of patients has been invited to the Derby, would you care to accompany them?" They were all, we were all very elegant. The women in outrageous hats and dresses that looked like artistic grafts on the landscape. The men in suits, the suits of their lives. They'd been waiting for that moment for years. They soon caught the attention of people and the cameras, hats were as much centre-stage there as horses. And our group of Epsom aristocrats was the most visible. I was lucky to find that job. Then came that real lunatic with her government, shut Epsom's mental homes down. It wasn't paradise, but I was lucky.'

We were in the Troubadour and Glenda got up to buy another round.

'Why are you looking at me like that?' he asked.

'I'm looking at you with both eyes. The lazy one and the other.'

I'd been lucky too. I didn't want to come to London, to a general hospital. They're not like mental homes. They're much more complicated. More bizarre. Anything can happen. Mental homes are much more tranquil. People are polite and cultured. Here there's stress all the time, accidents, sirens at night.

Repartee. Before Glenda came back, I had to say something funny.

'I'm looking at you with both eyes. So that you don't get away.'

'Lucky me,' said Pementa. 'Ending up in this hospital.'

The night was hard. Pementa slept at the hospital, in a room for porters. No, he wasn't on duty tonight. So I loosened my tongue and said why didn't he come and sleep at my place? Tomorrow we'd go to the hospital together. Glenda protested. No way. Her place was much nearer. Besides, when we'd arranged to go out, she'd told Pementa – hadn't she, Pementa? – there was plenty of room in her flat. Reality was on Glenda's side. Her flat was half the distance. Less than half. A stone's throw away. Pementa in the middle. Each of us tugging at his arm, without touching. 'You're right, Glenda. I'll come with you! A night's a night.' Glenda, my soulmate, my fellow Godspellian Sunday mornings in Willesden Green, I feel so well with you, *Take my hand precious Lord, lead me home.* She pierced me with a look, silently cursed me. Jezebel, bitch. She would have killed me.

The two of us sleeping together, in bed. Pementa, on the sofa. Glenda and me with our backs to each other to start with. Embracing our own patch of darkness. Resentment sprawled in between. Pementa's whistles as he slept, lucky him, like a steamboat departing in the night. So I turned and sought Glenda's body. She moved away, but couldn't go very far. I inched closer.

'What is it?'

She spun around. Breathing heavily. Anger on her breath. She could have strangled me if she'd wanted. She was much stronger than I was. In life, she was a gentle, sensual creature. She taught me to appreciate sounds, colours, body postures. A second start in life. Rousing what was asleep. In return, I made her laugh. All those mantras, yantras, asanas, kundalini, latent energy, it's not that they didn't work, opposite, they worked far too well. Her body was excessively happy. Ticklish all over, including her eyes and thoughts. Glenda reaped much more than she sowed.

She was probably furious. I wondered what a furious woman would be like inside placid Glenda.

I whispered, 'I've an idea.'

'Will you leave me alone!'

Quietly, 'Listen, Glenda, we can share him.'

'What? You're crazy!'

In a low voice, 'One day for you, one day for me.'

I knew she'd laugh. When she laughed, her whole body shook. Without stopping. A reverse Negro spiritual.

Take my hand precious Lord, lead me home.

Finally that Sunday in winter arrived. It was freezing. We arranged to visit Kew Gardens and saw a rose despite the cold, a white rose, like the ones on the road from Castro to Elviña. There it was, a tiny white rose, next to the ground, opening like a memory in the frostbitten earth. 'Snowdon', it said on the sign. That day, the flower, reminded me of a compliment a stranger once paid Amalia, which left us amazed.

'Your beauty is intolerable!'

Though she was quick enough to reply, 'And you haven't really seen me!'

508

He was more or less blind, despite having a good eye, because he was unable to turn back. Some people are afraid of being lucky.

Lucky me, I thought, next to winter's solitary flower.

Lucky I wore stilettos that were killing me, chafing my skin, freezing my toes. Even when I'm naked, I won't take them off. Till the pleasure is too much and they fall off.

Lucky all the cafés shut their doors in our face. A moment ago, I'd have given anything for a hot cup of tea and a cloud, lucky, but now I keep quiet because we're hugging and kissing, next to the iceberg, and everything's in motion, there's pleasure in the world's navel, which is good for the circulation, and hot air that goes to your head, the warmth of chestnuts roasted in their own burs.

Lucky the Underground carriage was empty to start with, a nuptial carriage that Sunday afternoon, rocking, taking us from corner to corner.

Lucky I kept the fire inside my mouth. The fire the girl from Camden Town gave me.

Lucky we opened the red door. Lucky we climbed the stairs. Lucky we entered the room, embraced in front of the window. Lucky there's someone to take you from cold to heat. To the other side of the wind, but still inside it.

From the room, we can see the small gardens with their trees. We can't set foot inside them. Our key is for one floor only. But now we're able to run across them, jump over the hedges, come and go with the wind. Pictures are fine, but there's nothing like a window. Windows are better for framing an embrace. Everything we see belongs to the embrace. The railway, the hoarding, the barbed wire, keep out, the plastic bag lifted up, up, but then falling, nostalgic for its weight, as if searching for what it carried.

The wind is one and the same, but each tree has its own. They move in different, sometimes opposite directions. Look. Even the branches of a single tree move differently, as if they've torn off bits of wind. The birch shakes, is embraced, more than the others. That plane tree still has a few leaves. Another mystery. Almost every tree has a few leaves that don't fall. They're there the whole winter and don't fall. Why not? The rain as well.

I mean the rain is one and the same, but each tree, each bush, has its own. The fatness, the gleam of the drops is quite distinct. See how the drops hang after it's rained. How they settle on the branches, the buds, the tips of the buds. Settle like notes in a score. Not just the trees. Each house has its own rain. Each window. This window.

Lucky.

Lucky wind.

Lucky rain. Notes sliding down the windowpane.

'Lucky you,' they told me for finding someone like Pementa.

'Lucky,' murmured Pementa when he found the mole on my back. Lucky. Rocking like a boat on the water bed, he found the mole on my back, the circle of his lips around it, a sucker, his tongue whispering, writing. Lucky. A murmur I heard through my skin, which resounded in the cavern of my chest, alongside my heart, climbed my throat and emerged like a sloe. The black mole opening, 'Snowdon', Kew's rose, the white rose on the way to Elviña, blue wellies, stiletto heels, with the one I like, everything, tossing and turning, black mole, white rose.

Lucky.

The Medal

He was about to open the back door of the house by the marina when someone got ahead of him and opened from inside. That nightmare he sometimes had. Gabriel had seen her only once. They could have been the same age. Except he was the father's son and she was the wife. Her hair in a bob, smooth and coppery, matched her skirt. Golden locks that were like a continuation of the letters printed on the invitation to the wedding he didn't attend. Gabriel the Odd sent a cold, irreproachable telegram. *Katechon* came into his mind. The one who holds back the years, though they're still there, riding an invisible merry-go-round. 'No, Ricardo's not at home. He's too busy. He had a pressing engagement followed by an important lunch with the directors of the Academy of Political and Moral Sciences, who, as you should know but don't, are visiting, a token of their appreciation, quite unusual really, despite the fact we live in Madrid. The session will be here, during the summer. They're to pay him a tribute in the provinces. You can imagine the state he's in, having just received the Raimundo de Peñafort medal.'

'Yes, apart from the medal, how is he?'

He shouldn't have asked this question she was waiting to answer with one of those fateful punches you get in a clinch in the ring.

With a youthful spirit. Like an ox. Living a second spring. Any one will do.

'Unbearable,' she said with a triumphant smile, as if she meant a little child. 'He won't stop.'

Yes, in this meeting, she was giving him a good hiding with the back of her tongue. He'd come in search of sin, the stain of history, but it wasn't going to be cheap as far as she was concerned.

Another punch.

'He's in fine fettle. Gets up early every day, when it's still dark, does his exercises on the bearskin, as you know, works in the study and then attends first Mass. Won't hear about a siesta. Before lunch, he has a quick doze, a few minutes, what he calls the ram's sleep.'

He's waiting to be asked in. *Would you like to come in?* But no. She says, 'I'm sorry not to invite you in, but I was just on my way out. And next time don't act like a terrorist. Use the front door!'

She raised her index finger, an apparently spontaneous movement that is aimed at poking out the other's eye. 'I'm in a hurry! Ricardo and I are due to have lunch with the board of honour of the Academy of Political and Moral Sciences in recognition of a whole life devoted to Law and Justice. Work that has always been solid, discreet, rigorous, never political or biased. The work of an exemplary civil servant. I'll tell him you called.'

Purple Rain

In La Boîte de Pandora. People betting around the aquarium. Twin dragons fighting. Small fish, large jaws. Destroyed in seconds. The host introduces new combatants with the seriousness of a croupier dealing out cards. Zonzo offers him the house speciality. A drink called Purple Rain. She's there, singing fados. The reason he came after so long, at nightfall. The effect of her voice: a brush running over his hand, painting a souvenir, walking on soft grass near the cliff face.

'So you're a judge?' asks Zonzo.

'Yes. That's my job.'

'It's a good job. Meting out justice and all that. But you have to be stricter. The world's in a terrible state. No moral principles. No authority.'

'How did Manlle die?'

'I don't know. Don't know the details. Seems he died in his own way. Slowly.'

'People don't usually die because of a harpoon.'

'Why not? He was by the sea.'

Gabriel Samos thinks the conversation will end there. He remembers Zonzo. He's capable of closing in on himself like a mollusc. There's no point insisting.

'He shouldn't have gone,' says Zonzo surprisingly. 'But then you know what he was like. No, you don't. How could you? He wanted to be in all places at once, do everything. What was he doing combing the beach for a lost shipment? Someone had got a hold of the bales, OK, and so what? I heard rumours. Remember that Bible full of banknotes I showed you? He went with it to buy a woman in Brussels central station. A woman from the east. Why'd he have to go? He didn't. He found out later the woman was missing a toe. Wanted to try her out in a small *pension*. At his age, he still wanted to do everything. And saw she was missing a toe. He should have let it go. It's a way women for sale are sometimes branded. So he went back to the central station, wanted to reverse the agreement, to get the Bible back with its banknotes. He'd been buying a woman who was whole. He wanted to do everything. Ended up with a harpoon stuck in his chest. I don't know who it was.'

'Your mother sings better than ever.'

'She comes from time to time.'

'I remember she was always at the window.'

'Still is. Watching out for boats.'

'Customs patrol boats?'

'No.' Ironically, 'yachts.'

Coccinella septempunctata

Gennevilliers National Theatre, spring 1994

He was awake the whole night. Couldn't get the bill out of his head. Read the reviews, which were favourable, some of them enthusiastic. The woman with the hoarse voice was playing King Lear. Three hours on stage, six days a week. He was actually quite grateful not to have got a ticket the first few days. He'd use them to see other things in Paris without the stifling heat. He remembered one August when he'd managed to survive a trip to the Botanic Gardens and Père Lachaise Cemetery. He thought he could still see the acrylic memory of those touristic footsteps sticking to the pavements. But most of all he viewed the delay as a kind of mourning. He took the most sensitive evidence out of his suitcase: the books with burnt edges and a survivor's vitality. Then a copy of a document with lists of confiscated and imprisoned books. Incomplete lists since disappeared, burnt books, deceased books, had not been included. Several postcards from Durtol Sanatorium. A magnifying glass. The books he'd brought had not been chosen for their literary or bibliographical value. He'd let his hand pick them out. The first books he'd read in the section of charred remains. The start of his secret induction. He planned to tell her how the books from 12 Panadeiras Street had resisted. Lots had fallen. But some had survived the flames, the dampness of the dungeons, the robbers in the Palace of Justice. The books he'd brought had something else in common: Santiago Casares' stylish signature, an elegant calligraphic portrait. Anthropomorphic.

He went to 168 Rue de Vaugirard and tried to glimpse the sixth floor.

He was tempted to climb the stairs and ask who was living in the dovecot, the garret that was their first home in exile. But he checked his detective's instinct. Then, at midday, took a taxi and decided to visit the Rue Asseline.

He made a mistake.

He passed in front of her house. Thought he heard the sound of the news on television. But couldn't see anything from the street. There was a window with a net curtain and a thicker cloth curtain behind. He could ring the doorbell, but he didn't have the books with him. It'd been a furtive incursion, a strong wish to visit the Rue Asseline and see where 12 Panadeiras Street had got to, where the dramatic corridor of history led to. He'd left everything back in the hotel. It'd be ridiculous to turn up now and stammer out a story with nothing to support it. What would she think? She'd be suspicious of someone arriving out of the blue, stirring up the embers. A judge, son of a Francoist judge, who'd come to talk about extant books. Maybe not. Maybe she'd have a taste for such surprises. Someone who in her twenties had played Death in Jean Cocteau's *Orpheus* and in her seventies still had it in her to play King Lear had to be brave.

He entered a Portuguese eating-house on the corner. Most of the customers were building labourers or mechanics, depending on their work clothes. He fancied eating in a place like this, wine served in a jug, not in a bottle, oilskin tablecloths. He sat down next to a window. And then saw her. Saw her approach the Portuguese restaurant. His mistake was not to stop looking. Most of the workers glanced at her when she came in. Some of them probably knew her. Though there was nothing about her to draw attention. Just herself. She was wearing ankle boots, trousers and a dark blue jersey. Hair cut short, grey. She entered with discretion, but her eyes came on stage. The presence of a woman it wasn't necessary to ask if she was alone. A wild, roving look.

Which is why Gabriel Samos made the mistake of staring at her. Not deliberately. He simply didn't realise. She did. She realised. Gave him a serious look while lighting a cigarette, perhaps so she wouldn't have to address the ogler. He became embarrassed. Instead of taking a step forwards, tried to hide it. Without saying a word or moving a piece, opened the pit of the intruder.

The performance of *The Tragedy of King Lear* at Gennevilliers National Theatre was sold out for this night and the next. A woman, María Casares, was playing the legendary king. The reviews had been highly favourable. Talked of her energy, her hoarse voice, her face carved out on the stormy stage. She'd acted in *A Midsummer Night's Dream* and *Macbeth*. Lear was waiting. And now she was Lear, the king named after a Celtic sea-god. María always thought in terms of nature for a role. The sea was strong and melancholy, impulsive and sweet, brutal and loving. She found her ideal of mature beauty in the weather-beaten faces of those who inhabited Atlantic shores. Since she couldn't be in Galicia, she was sorry not to live in Brittany. But the theatre itself was a Finisterre, a windy outcrop. In her early seventies, she'd finally acquired the look of an old sea lady.

The books her family had taken on their last trip from Coruña to Madrid, which had accompanied her into exile, included volumes of works by Shakespeare, Valle-Inclán, Manuel Curros Enríquez. This had been her father's favourite poet. A memory that goes with her everywhere. Not a relentless ghost, but a place made of voice she returns to when necessary. The feeling is warm and strange. An exile within an exile. To send her to sleep, her father recites *Galician Melody*. Recites fragments from Curros' *Airs of My Land*, verses he knows off by heart, which seem to come not from the memory that plays with elevated notes, but from another corner, a deep cave.

'Another beakful?'

'Go on then!'

He calls each stanza this, the amount of food a bird carries in its beak for its chicks. María thinks it's the verses that remind her of him, of Santiago, as he murmurs them next to her bed in the twilight. When she was a girl, her father had periods of frenetic activity followed by bouts of illness. The *Melody*'s verses are like lines drawn on a face that takes shape as they're spoken. Lines that contain the mystery of life: what's hidden behind the eyes. As when she went with her mother to visit him in Madrid's Modelo Prison. She was eight. He'd been arrested for participating in the clandestine Republican government during Berenguer's regime, which supported the monarchy. She was horrified. What she saw was the ghost of her father. A bag of bones suffering from consumption and imprisonment. Everything had changed. There was no warm home. The only thing that remained was what was hidden behind the eyes. Which is why the *Melody* doesn't rock her to sleep, it makes her more alert, keeps her company. The *Melody* remembers for her. Wherever she may be. In the dovecot on the Rue de Vaugirard. In La Vergne, her house in Charente. On the Rue Asseline. On all her artistic tours, in the loneliness that follows her artistic triumphs. She has photos, postcards, letters, small personal belongings she keeps like talismans or relics. But nothing like those verses that escaped the burning, the pillage. Something no murderous tyrant or governor can imagine. A *Melody* protected by the mouth's dampness or, as her father, Santiago, would say, kept in a corner of the occipital ark. A *Melody* that talks of the siren (who has song), the snake (who has breath) and God (who has hell).

> You have enough
> with what is hidden
> in those eyes of yours.

Shakespeare was fortunate to make that journey from Coruña to Madrid when her father was appointed minister. He stayed alive. Then accompanied them into exile. Was now on the main bookshelf in the house on the Rue Asseline. She needed to have those books always in sight, within reach. She liked the way they weighed like arks or flagstones. They contained all the others. All the deceased books from 12 Panadeiras Street. When she agreed to act the part of King Lear in her early seventies, she reread the play in one of the volumes that had been saved. Ran her finger along each line. In Madrid, her father had a secretary who read books she loved like this, churning up words with her long varnished fingernail. Her finger ploughed the furrow of words as if she were reading not only with her eyes, but also by touch. María had heard her father mention a captain in the army who learnt Braille so that he could read in the dark when on campaign. She felt darkly pleased when they suggested she represent King Lear. The same feeling she had during the end-of-summer storms, when the rafters of the sky over Paris gave way. Finally the clouds of the Atlantic carrying the sea were here. Écoute, Paris! She was carrying the storm on top of her head. The unsettling joy of the first downpour after the drought. It'd been more than fifty years since she left Madrid and went into exile. The first thing she did was pull down the volume and run her eyes along the rail of her index finger:

> The weight of this sad time we must obey;
> Speak what we feel, not what we ought to say.
> The oldest hath borne most: we that are young
> Shall never see so much, nor live so long.

María can see the faces in the audience, faces determined to believe in the truth of the legend, convinced that what's been said has something to do with the times they live in.

The audience? She always chooses a face. Her mark, she calls it.

Gabriel's convinced she's looking at him. Some actors use this method. Seek out a reference point, a face they can address in the audience. But why him of all people? He's sitting in the third row. Is tempted to look away. Perhaps it's a false impression. Perhaps María Casares' look deliberately has this vague precision. Is able to take in each and every face in the audience. That must be it. But no. She's looking at him. He's sure of it. He can feel the parcel on his thighs, under his folded coat. A small package containing three books and the report written in 1955 by the Inspector of Archives for the Northwest, a civil servant who seems punctilious, but omits his name. All he needs is for the contents to move, to give off smoke. In the hotel, he went over everything. In preparation for the symbolic return.

She, Lear, stares at him:

> Thou art the thing itself:
> unaccommodated man is no more but such a poor bare,
> forked animal as thou art. Off, off, you lendings!
> come unbutton here.

That night, as she left Gennevilliers National Theatre, María Casares was handed several letters and notes from spectators. And a parcel. It could be said she had a premonition, but not enough time to give it shape. The first thing she saw, in large letters, was the return address: '12 Panadeiras Street'. And, by way of stamp, a drawing of a ladybird.

Working for Eternity

'You've a visitor, Francisco!' shouted Aphrodite from the door. She and the porter wheeled a bed into the other half of the room. Polka saw everything in large blots verging on diffused clarity, exactly the opposite of what he'd always imagined blindness to be, a progressive and definitive sinking into darkness. What he perceived of his new hospital companion was a white head and nothing else. Then Aphrodite, as he called the nurse, that woman who had the grace to be cheerful and pleasant, drew a curtain between the two beds, creating two compartments.

'He's a bigwig,' the nurse whispered to Polka, 'a judge. Had a heart attack too. Has just come out of Intensive Care. Will soon get his own room. He has influence. He's a chosen one.'

Polka fell silent after hearing this but, when the nurse made to leave, said in a loud voice, 'If you need a gravedigger, here I am, girl! Working for eternity.'

He wasn't sure if the gesture the nurse made from the door was one of farewell or another kind of message. He did think she smiled, though.

'Why'd you say that?'

Polka was surprised the man behind the curtain spoke so soon. He'd just fallen into a mid-afternoon stupor as he tried to sew together the rags of white and grey blots. Put them in order for when his daughter arrived. She still didn't know he'd lost his sight. Couldn't read. Couldn't even dig graves. At least, he wasn't the one who shovelled earth or sealed niches. He could still play the bagpipes, though, when asked to do so. A march. *Mother*, or *Ancient Kingdom of Galicia*, or *St Benedict*, or *Laíño*, the one he liked so much, it always sounded good, from cradle to grave. At night, he'd listen to the radio. He enjoyed moving the dial, listening to stations broadcasting in foreign languages. Words sound wonderful when you can't understand them. Animal electricity. He could barely read, but occasionally he'd open the pouch and hold the books in his hands. Feel their electricity. He recalled Jaume Fontanella, *Joan Sert*, his fellow prisoner, the Catalan architect who fled on a Portuguese passport and studied Braille so he could read at night. Polka copied that movement. He didn't know Braille, but he could imagine. His fingers ran over the paper's geography, relief. He felt the excitement, the way the words bristled under his touch. He could rattle off the whole of *The Invisible Man*.

'Say what?'

'That you work for eternity.'

'I make graves, sir, houses that last till doomsday.'

'Anyone knows that's Shakespeare!' declared the judge.

'Matter is neither created nor destroyed, it is simply transformed.'

'Nonsense!'

His reaction was a way of decreeing silence and Polka was only too happy to obey. He had too much to do, was far too busy to worry about calming down an angry man. On the way back, reviewing his life, he'd got into a discussion with the priest. As far as he could remember, it was the only time in his life he'd come out on top. He had to persuade him he could be the new gravedigger, he'd be good at it. He wasn't wanted on site or at the Dairy or at Coca-Cola. A lame, old man bearing antecedents. The sun had surely gone past his door by now. The ants climbed his legs, occupied his body, especially in winter. Olinda carrying bundles of clothes. He had to bring in some money. He was lame, he'd been a victim. But he wasn't considered as such. Ex-combatants were the victors. He'd only been imprisoned, so he must have done something. Those who accused him of having done something had no idea what he'd really done. The secret he shared with Olinda. Couldn't even imagine how the two of them had helped to derail trains loaded with wolfram, sink boats transporting the mineral to Nazi munition factories. He must have done something. Of course he had. More than they realised. Now he had to convince the priest he'd make a good gravedigger. He was going over that part of his memory.

The priest apologising, a historic step, for having forced O to count up to 666 chestnuts, the number of the devil. He may have been bad-tempered and a bit bald, said the priest, but not like that vindictive prophet in the Bible. They then moved on to discuss the wedding in Cana. The first of Christ's miracles. With the wine. He knew the Gospel from memory, word for word, as he did the Latin Mass. And he'd always been greatly intrigued by this chapter. There was something enticing, mysterious, about it. He found what was left unsaid as charming as what was mentioned. Christ didn't want to perform his first miracle. He may never have wanted to perform miracles. But he had to make a compromise. It was a question of family honour, of Mary's insistence. What difference does it make? said Jesus' mother. Get us out of this fix. Whoever heard of a wedding without wine? What'll people think? This stingy lot count their beans, won't give bones to the dog. Mary was right. She knew the score. But Polka suspected Christ was always a little resentful of his mother for making him turn water into wine.

A grunt came from behind the curtain. The hidden man was breaking the silence. The grunt was a conciliatory one.

'What you said before was obviously a tribute to Shakespeare. I'm glad. We need culture. I wondered where I might find it and here it is. In a ward in hospital.'

His heart was pumping again. Aphrodite had told him you get this ecstatic reaction in people who've suffered a heart attack. A false sense of power. Life coursing back into their body. Reserved people who suddenly loosen their tongue. Yes, misery guts had suddenly become chatty. Extremely polite. 'How wonderful,' said the hidden man, 'to find someone who really knows their Scripture.'

'His tongue loosened, mine got stuck,' Polka told the nurse. 'You should have seen me in the good times. *Verbum caro factum est et habitavit in nobis* . . .'

'You'd have made a good Holy Father, Francisco.'

'Call me Polka. When I was young, everybody called me that. And I've already been Pope. During Carnival. It's a miracle I wasn't martyred.'

She'd been wanting to talk about that. The doctors were amazed by what they'd found in Polka's heart. Nothing to do with an ecstatic recovery.

523

His was slow, gradual. Rather they were amazed he'd lasted so long. He had other complications. Polka knew he had other complications. But the thing with his heart was surprising. A clinical case.

'I don't want to be a clinical case,' he said mistrustfully. 'What's wrong with my heart?'

'Your heart is a book,' replied Aphrodite. 'You had two heart attacks before this one. It's obvious from the scars. The doctors can't understand how you managed to survive without medical attention. Don't you remember anything? You should have felt something like the thread of life being severed.'

'Once or twice, I did forget to breathe, yes.'

'And what did you do?'

'I drew on my resources. Drew on my resources and tore death's horse-shoes off my face.'

So all that had been written in his heart? After that business with the books, his right arm had been numb for days. He had no memory of the pain. He felt lethargic, resistant. Remembered what Holando used to say, always playing with words. He said *traballo* – 'travail' or 'work' – came from *tripalium*, a tool used to restrain a horse while shoeing it. He'd felt he was being tortured. But who could distinguish between what was happening inside and outside the body? He never complained. As he was afraid of being afraid, so the possibility of complaining caused him such unease it made him laugh. He'd heard of the thyroid, a gland that made you grow. Perhaps his made him laugh. He'd certainly forgotten to breathe, but realised in time. His skin changed colour. Everything around him acquired a crimson glow, on the verge of going out. The other time he forgot to breathe was when he was invaded by ants. He had high fever. Was convinced he was underground. The ants came in through his bullet wounds and all his other orifices. He'd once had a nightmare that insects were invading his body. The first to arrive were death flies, which laid eggs out of which came larvae, etc. His body was there for the taking. But on this occasion the ants were burdened with seeds, tufts, breadcrumbs. One ant carried a drop of duck's blood. Another, the head of a matchstick with red aniline. There were groups carrying even larger things. A cricket they insisted on introducing through his mouth. Fragments of *The Invisible Man*. His body was to be a deposit. Until, that is, he remembered to breathe. So all that had been written in his heart?

He didn't stop. Polka let him speak.

'Some people focus on his great genius as a comedian and tragedian, or the way he controls the passions, but I'm fascinated by the way he chronicles power in action. Each sentence is imbued with decisive power. I have to admit that, in questions of power, even my admired Machiavelli is like a pettifogger next to this friend's royal musculature.'

'I've buried more books than I've read,' said Polka finally, without a hint of irony. He was being enigmatic.

'Books? You're a strange kind of gravedigger.' There was now an obvious tremor in the voice of the man behind the curtain.

'That's right. It was the first time I dug graves. My apprenticeship, so to speak. I buried books. Most of them were dead. Reduced to cinders. They'd been burning for two days. But some were still alive. Still bubbling. You threw earth on top and, after a while, the tips of pages stuck out like thorns. A shame. Most of us were simple labourers with little or no education. This was the first time some of us had opened a book. Oh, it was terrible, sir, *a drop of duck's blood*.'

He came out with this phrase whenever he felt uncomfortable, afraid of being afraid. It was his way of describing the indescribable.

'Terrible, sir, *a drop of duck's blood*.'

The hidden patient, the man behind the curtain, fell quiet, but wasn't exactly silent. He made a noise with his body, an expression of malaise. It seemed he was trying to stand up. They'd both been through Emergency, where time became detached from bodies, to Intensive Care, where time floated about, clinical appliances emitting underwater sounds. Now time was saline, dripping back into their bodies. He spoke in a torrent. Kept talking about duck's blood. May have wanted to use Shakespeare to make fun of him. But he acquitted himself well. He was not uneducated. Common, thought the judge, but not uneducated.

'What books, what books did you say you buried?'

'All kinds. It was at the start of the war. Right here, in the city. Lots of people find it strange. Some things I don't talk about. So as not to be thought mad. He's a screw loose, that's what they say. Terrible, sir, *a drop of duck's blood.* There was even a book on the city's coat of arms. You know the city's coat of arms is the lighthouse. Well, on top of the lighthouse was a book. This book was also removed, never made it back on to the shield. As if they were burning stone and bronze as well. You're not young. You must have heard about it. The way they burnt books.'

'No,' lied the judge. 'I wasn't here then. Listen. I'm greatly interested in books, you've no idea how much. I swear few things in life interest me as much as books. Perhaps you can help me.'

'I already said I'm not a man of books.'

'Tell me about the ones you buried. You must recall the odd title. Try and remember.'

He remembers. Letters hovering over the ashes like samara wings. That piece. That wafer. *A drop of duck's blood.* The horror. The nails, bones, entrails of books. An unmistakable stench that won't go away.

'There were loads of books. Whole libraries. The best. Those belonging to cultural associations. To Germinal. To Casares Quiroga. You've heard of Casares, haven't you? He also was erased. They even wanted to tear his name out of the register of births. Lots of people suffered the same fate as that book on the city's coat of arms and were erased.'

'Listen to me. What books were those that stuck out when you were burying them? What books caught your attention?'

Polka could feel the stench of the smoke that day in his nostrils. Estremil was right. It was like being at the mouth of hell. The whole of Germinal's library burnt. A good one, that. Because there were things that were extremely learned, but practical as well. He would have explained this to the man behind the curtain, but didn't quite like the way he asked questions. His impatience. Polka sifted through time, raked time into piles. Remembered and felt. Didn't want to lose direction. Germinal had books for trades, for getting up to date in a profession. Most of the people who went there were workers. Elegance and culture in this city were a popular fashion. On the whole, people with money were brutes. No, Olinda, don't

526

worry, I won't say that to him. You're right, it's best to be prudent. You never know who you're talking to.

'Yes, sir, matter is neither created nor destroyed, it is simply transformed. I learnt this from a young boxer by the name of Arturo da Silva, who worked as a plumber. This idea did me good, did me a service. Such a simple thing and yet so true, don't you think?

'The first time I entered Germinal, Holando told me that to get a book I had to go to Minerva. "Minerva?" "Yes, the librarian." He'd come out with these lyrical excesses to hide his shyness. "That's Aphrodite and she's Athene." And they ended up making fun of me. Was I crazy? "Her name's Minerva," Holando kept telling me. So off I went with my scrap of paper. "Excuse me, Minerva . . ." And I thought now she's going to give me a sarcastic look with those large black eyes of hers and say in a hoarse voice, because her voice was a bit hoarse, "Are you also crazy?" But she didn't say anything. She read the scrap of paper: *Galvani and Animal Electricity.* Holando and the others were crying with laughter. Very funny. So what? I could have chosen something else. But this caught my attention. Don't know why. Or perhaps I do. Once, when I was little, I watched my mother cut a duck's neck. She was brave enough to do this, to kill an animal with her bare hands. My father was as strong as an ox, but couldn't do it. Couldn't even kill a mouse. What's more, he once bumped into a mouse on the staircase and shouted so loud the poor animal died of fright. So there's my mother, with her sleeves rolled up, holding the duck, cutting its neck, when something happens and the duck pulls loose, flies over us without a head. My mother explained, "That's because it had a lot of electricity stored up inside." I told Minerva this story and she seemed very moved. "Animals shouldn't be killed for eating," she said. "I agree. We all agree. Just the other day, we were reading the ten commandments of naturism." "Who read them?" "Holando. Holando's the expert." And Holando comes over. Starts chatting to Minerva, of course he's pleased. She's working on a new dictionary. "A dictionary of usage," she said. "By word families." That's nice, I thought. Word families. Holando was one of the first to get killed. Together with the champ of Galicia. They went for the best of them.'

527

'Get to the point, will you? The books! What about the books?'

'Electricity is an amazing thing. You have electricity. A tree has electricity. When life runs out, electricity goes to earth. That book about Galvani and animal electricity must have burnt as well. Though I looked for it among the carnage.'

'The carnage?'

'The remains. The remains of books. They stank of flesh.'

'Some of them were probably bound in leather. It'd be the leather.'

'I suppose so. It happened right here, a short distance away, in the docks and María Pita Square. They brought loads of books to be disposed of. The pyres burnt for two whole days. I was a park and garden employee at the time and was assigned to clean up the ashes. It was during the summer. August, the 19th of August. Some things you never forget. My body still sways with that blasted lorry, I can feel my teeth chattering. The whole ground was covered in ash, but some were only half burnt. The lorry had to make several trips. We buried them in a waste tip in Rata Field, on the other side of San Amaro. We worked with rakes, it was like scraping away the skin, revealing flesh. Some people vomited, chucked their guts up. After we'd covered them, I could still feel them bubbling under my feet. I threw earth on top, pressed it down as hard as I could, but still felt the bones under my galoshes. I was fired after that. Apparently I was on a list for belonging to the union. That wasn't all. Half a year later, I was arrested. I was married, my wife about to give birth. Some nativity scene!'

Polka waited for the other to laugh at his irony. It was a pretty sad story, but the man didn't have much of a sense of humour. He cleared his throat and asked, 'Was there a copy of the New Testament? It's not the kind of thing you just forget.'

'It was like treading on bones, you bet. Point is I was then arrested. Do you know why? For playing. Doesn't sound very serious, does it? Well, I was arrested for playing music. Someone denounced me because I was due to play on a union excursion. The cultural associations had organised a special train to attend the Caneiros festivities. Upriver. I was a gardener, but played the bagpipes as a hobby. I played for the union, but for the feast of Our Lady of Mount Carmel as well. You see, one piece does as well for a wedding, a baptism, a funeral, as for a union march or a procession. But that train never departed. Had it left, it'd have been empty. Understand? It's as if they came and asked for our tickets. In a short time, we'd all been arrested. Those who didn't flee were killed. I was lucky. I was imprisoned to start with and then sent to a labour camp, a wolfram mine. I was a slave, but that wasn't the worst of it. Do you know what the worst of it was? Knowing, when you dug up that mineral, it was for fattening the beast. Do you understand or not?'

'Excuse me,' said the man behind the curtain. 'What you're saying's all very interesting. But I was thinking about the books. The day you buried the books. You said some of them were still alive.'

'In a manner of speaking. Ashes are ashes. But some were almost intact.'

'You mean they were asking for a hand.'

'I suppose you could say that.'

'So you took some.'

'You could get killed for doing that.'

'Even so, you took some. You took some of those books. There was one. A copy of Scripture dedicated to Antonio de la Trava, the valiente of Finisterra.'

'The valiente of Finisterra? No, I didn't take any books.'

'You couldn't help yourself. You felt sorry. I can see it now. You're a good person. You felt sorry for that book and hid it under your shirt. Am I right or not?'

'Nothing of the sort. I didn't take anything. I buried the lot. Even those sticking out.'

'I'm sure you kept one or two. Sure you've still got them. Trust me. I can pay you a fortune for that book.'

Polka felt for the switch. Found it and rang insistently.

'What is it, Francisco? What do you want?'

'Aphrodite, what time does one eat around here?

'That's not the best part, girl. Do you know what happened next? He seemed to calm down when the nurse came in. Lunch was served soon after. Hake with potatoes and peas. Followed by yoghurt. You know what I think of yoghurt, but still I ate it. He didn't eat a thing. Carried on deliberating. I could hear him deliberating. I swear the conspiracy in his head was as loud as the sounds emitted by clinical machines. I know that sound. It's the beep of troublemakers. Up to him if he didn't eat. I can be at death's door, I still won't leave peas on my plate. "*Bon appétit*," I said and fell into a doze. It was a way of bringing the matter to a close. But when I woke up, he was there. Not in bed. He was standing. Clinging to the end of my bed. Staring at me. Tall and strong. In a cloak.'

'A cloak?'

'OK. A very smart dressing-gown with a velvet collar over his shoulders, on top of his pyjamas. My God! He looked like General Primo de Rivera. A light in his eyes like that of the one who played Dracula, set the screen in Hercules Cinema on fire, left two holes like cigarette burns. First thing I did was close my eyes. To slow my heart more than anything. What the eye doesn't see, the heart doesn't grieve over. I had to think. And I thought I knew that man from somewhere. He belonged to another class. The skin on his face, his hands, hadn't weathered. And off he went again.

'"I can offer you a fortune for that book."

'I swear he had the same light in his eyes as the actor Bela Lugosi. He was turning into a nightmare.

'"You don't have to worry about a thing. Nobody will know. I'll make you an exact copy, a facsimile. It'll be like having the original. And a mass of money. You can name your price."

'"Let me think," I said, hoping this would calm him down. But it had the opposite effect. That man was like a horse. We'd obviously not been treated by the same doctor. He came up to me with emotion, took my hands. His look was – how shall I say? – Eucharistic.

'"So you do have the book dedicated to the valiente of Finisterra?"

'I said, "Yes, sir, I have it."

'"Borrow's New Testament?"

'"The very same."

'"You have to sell it to me!"

'"We'll talk about that later."

'"Later?"

'"Yes, now I need to sleep."

'What was I supposed to say, O? The guy was crazy. It hurt me to look at him. He was boring a hole in my head.'

'The truth,' said O. 'You could have told him the truth. That you had another book, Elisha's book, as you like to call it.'

'No, I couldn't have said that.'

'Why not, Papa?'

'That's my business. I still have to return it.'

O had already discussed this with him. She'd been the repository of a secret, but couldn't believe he was still feeling guilty.

'Who are you going to return it to, Papa? That book's yours. It belongs to you more than anyone.'

'There'll be somebody. Somebody'll have the key. Maybe even Minerva. Women live longer than men. And they're more careful about keeping things.'

'If that guy's so crazy, he'll bring it up again. You should have told him about The Invisible Man. Told him the truth.'

'What for? He didn't want to listen. He could have killed me then and there. I could see he was capable of such a barbarous act for the sake of a book. Capable of killing for a copy of Scripture.'

Bigarreaus

As he sits on the terrace of the Dársena Café, things move in and out of his glass of amber and ice cubes. For example, he's convinced the cloud of starlings drawing a protective bird in the sky, a bird composed of dots like a pop cartoon, wasn't there before. He decides to count them. A hundred thousand, give or take. Nor was the puppet there before, standing in front of him, in front of his eyes.

Leica stirs in his chair. This is a man who doesn't want to know anything about anybody except those moving in and out of his glass. He no longer argues with customers. Today he was even polite. A woman came to his studio. The doorbell made him nervous, particularly edgy, to start with he'd fidget about. Who can it be? Why are people still interested in having their portrait done?

'What is it?'

'I've come to have my portrait done.'

'Why?'

Yes, why? Were they not able to spot impending disaster? Were they not aware of the world's structural ugliness? No. They were optimistic! Sufficiently optimistic to want an immortal portrait.

But Leica had changed. He'd had some terrible years trying to get rid of himself. He used to say he was afraid of his own body, which is why he didn't dare destroy it. Who knows how that brute will respond? he used to think. He hated it so much, was so bored of it, this carcass holding on to him, so afraid, he couldn't even pluck a hair from his nose. He imagined it spewing a jet of blood. What a ridiculous way to die, to empty like a barrel. The nightmare of stepping in his own blood and wandering off, like a ghost, leaving acrylic footprints on the pavements. He longed not to be. From time to time, a student of local culture would refer to a Coruñan brand of existentialism. Coruña, despite the persecutions, kept up an international beat, the systole-diastole of new tendencies, etc., etc., and when existentialism was needed, well, there it was. Among them, Leica the photographer, our own Robert Doisneau, our own Henri Cartier-Bresson. What a shame! They hadn't even bothered to find out if he was still alive, had ever really existed. Only the selfishness of cells, the irrational tenacity of organs, the stubborn functionality of the respiratory system, explained his inopportune presence in this world.

'Why what?' asked the woman. Her tone of voice matched her eyes, which darted about a little.

'Why do you want a portrait?'

Leica almost always achieved his goal. To make the person who'd come for a portrait take in the studio, suddenly aware they may have fallen into a murderous psychopath's lair. The old curtain at the back showing the lighthouse had acquired sombre tones, filled with black clouds. A storm was trapped inside it. Then there was the wooden aeroplane. The seat looked every bit as if it wasn't for sitting in, but for denouncing the absence of children who'd sat there previously. And all the tools. The cameras.

'I've got a cold. My nose must be like a beetroot. That can be arranged, right?'

'There's no need. Your nose is extremely . . .'

He looked at her, afraid something was happening in his mouth.

'Greek,' he said finally. 'Classical.'

'Like one of those statues missing a nose?'

They laughed. And he breathed in. On any other occasion, he'd have been enraged by the suggestion he might retouch a photo. He was quite direct with customers about it. 'If you want to look pretty,' he'd shout at them, 'go visit a surgeon . . . or Mago Photos!' But now there really was something happening in his mouth.

'Excuse me. We'd better get on with it right away,' he said with sudden urgency. 'I have to go out. Photograph a wedding.'

'A wedding?'

Why was she laughing? Everything struck her as funny. She must have been about fifty years old, though it was difficult to be sure. Curly hair, swimmer's body. What Sada the painter called a nautical age. Against the current. You advance in time, not time in you.

'A wedding so late?'

'Nowadays people get married at night.'

'With malice aforethought.'

He laughed at the woman's comment. His mouth. What was going on in his mouth? He swallowed. His saliva had a strange taste, of grass. He realised he hadn't spoken in ages.

He asked her to stand on the stage, with Hercules Lighthouse in the background. There was a small table with a plant, a begonia that miraculously also advanced in time and not the other way round. She instinctively drew near the plant. He was now concerned about her face. The light on her face. He ignored her swimmer's body. Forgot about asking her if she was the Sea Club's Esther Williams. Saw her face out of the water. Her curls intertwined with seaweed.

Her beauty was *intolerable*. When and where had he read this? He thought alcohol acted like bleach on the memory. Ended up erasing everything. The imagination. Dreams. Culture. All that nonsense.

His mouth. That was it. Something in his mouth tasted of seaweed. Never mind!

'Are you sure you want one of my portraits? I don't do colour, you know. I paint the photo. So don't tell me afterwards you're not happy.'

She gazed at him in silence for a minute. The sitter now studying the lack of light on the artist's face.

'I've been walking past here for years. I always wanted to have my portrait done. A painted portrait. Then today something strange happened. I thought the studio would be closed. You no longer existed.'

'You say you come past here every day?'

'Every day. I'm the fruitseller. You used to buy bigarreaus. At the start of summer, you'd always buy a cone of bigarreaus.'

'They're a little harder than cherries. That's why I like them. Because they're just that little bit harder than cherries.'

'Absolutely.'

'And they don't have a stalk.'

'No.'

'Why don't bigarreaus have a stalk?'

'I already told you that a thousand times.'

'Did you?'

'Yes, whenever you bought a cone. Bigarreaus don't have a stalk because they let go of it when they're gathered from the tree. Like lizard tails.'

He fidgeted about, glancing in all directions, seeking a memory, but without taking his eyes off her.

A memory! My memory, like a bigarreau, has lost its stalk. One moment if you please!

There was just enough light. There, on the hat-stand, was the body that contained it, had kept it until now.

'Put this on if you would.'

She draped the night-blue shawl over her shoulders. Positioned her arms as if holding and protecting it. Behind her, the trapped storm gathered momentum.

'Every day?'

'I used to. Almost every day.'

He sits on the terrace of the Dársena Café. Looks at the camera. Can't bear the camera's look because it tells him the truth. Is aware the best photographs were its decision. To hear it better, he has to take it in his hands and look through the viewfinder. He seems to be taking photos of boats, but he isn't. He's listening to the camera. To see what it has to say.

'How could you let go of those photos?'

'Don't start that again. What was I supposed to do?'

'Photos of dead friends. You had to protect that film like a roadside shrine.'

'You know what happened. They were after the other photos, but they were all mixed up. The photos of friends the day we went to Ara Solis together with the photos of burning books. They were on the same film. Too much pressure. Having them was like putting a bullet in your head.'

*   *   *

His eyes are on the glass. He sees the puppet's reflection.

'Shall I tell you a joke, sir?'

'No.'

He was about to say he didn't like jokes or jokers. I despise jokers even more than jokes. He kept quiet. He could have spoken, but he'd renounced the art of conversation. It didn't seem reasonable to have to explain himself to a puppet. On the other hand, he didn't have the energy to lift his head and observe the puppeteer. If he had to speak, he preferred to speak to the puppet.

'Have you seen a boomerang go past, sir?'

'No, not today.'

'Thank you, sir,' said the puppet. 'Did you know you're flying low? *The weight of the silent dagger.*'

He looked at his flies. It was true. They were open.

'Thank you. Much obliged.'

'Don't mention it, sir. Manolo Pinzón at your service.'

It left. He was sorry now. Really a very interesting puppet. Sharp-witted. And not at all boring. He went back to his glass. Who knows? Perhaps, if he followed it, he'd come to a city beyond the sea. They'd go down street after street until suddenly the puppet started moving him. He'd be the one hanging on strings. They'd stop in front of a building with a shop sign on which was written *Invisible Remedy*. The puppet would say, 'Now, Leica, raise your head. Look up there, at that window on the third floor. It's her.'

'Impossible! I can't see anything.'

'Don't be daft, Leica. It's her!'

He sits on the terrace of the Dársena Café, his eyes sunk in a glass of amber. Liquid photos. Curtis goes by with the horse Cariri. Leica recognises them, but is not sure why. They must be coming from the lighthouse, Hercules Lighthouse. He sometimes thinks people coming down from Mount Alto are amphibian and also aerial creatures. They stop. The travelling photographer greets him with affection. He likes creatures that give you a wave and then carry on. They leave a wake in the amber and that's all. Farewell, friend. Farewell, horse. Farewell.

You I Can

Today he won't listen to an extract from *The Invisible Man*, as he usually does. Today he'll be late. Who knows what time he'll turn up? After funerals, the men invite him for a drink. And he has to go. Says it's part of his duty to toast the souls. Give them one last push.

He has his very own toast for bars: 'Matter is neither created nor destroyed, it is simply transformed.' He always says this, with feeling, and the deceased's relatives are grateful because it sounds convincing. Scientific. Like a commandment. 'Another round?'

It's what he says when Olinda tells him off for drinking too much.

'A fine state you're in!'

'Matter is neither created nor destroyed, sweetheart, it is simply transformed.'

When Polka drinks too much after a funeral, he sings hymns to everything. You can tell he's drunk by the way he opens the door. Today scientific proof, as he'd say, because when he opens the double door, the upper leaf bangs against the wall. He's always telling us to open the door slowly so the upper leaf doesn't bang against the wall and spoil the paintwork. Pinche makes him suffer every time he bangs the door when he comes in. So whenever he opens the door and there's a slam, Olinda and I know that Polka, in an attempt to dissemble, is going to shout out some *vivas* – long live electricity, long live Carballo bread, long live fillets of cod and cauliflower, long live the Umbrella Maker's whistle – and then sing 'The moth alights in a very pretty way'. He pops into our bedroom in the hope that Olinda will go back to sleep and forget about her invisible man. Sits next to my bed and murmurs the refrain: 'Till it finds a flower, it never wants to alight'.

He sings the one about autumn leaves.

'This is no time for singing!' shouts Olinda from bed.

He likes that song a lot. I like it when he sings it. 'We're two autumn leaves'.

'We're out of time, girl.' Then he asks me one of his scientific questions, 'Why do leaves change colour?'

'To save light.'

'Why?'

'To live longer. There's less light in autumn and the leaves change colour to make the most of it.'

What he wanted was for us to be knowledgeable. What I wanted was for him to carry on talking. Because of what he said and to watch the way his Adam's apple moved.

He hasn't shaved for days. Darkness has gone to sleep, so the light of the table lamp concentrates on his face. You can see him better than during the day. Polka's so skinny, instead of a double chin, he has a hollow that arches the roof of the grotto where his amazing Adam's apple holds stage. His beard's a bit ancient. Roots sticking out through cracks in the stone. A laborious renaissance of thickets among crags, stalks with colourful spikes you couldn't see before his beard went grey.

He was tired that night.

'I dug the grave and saw myself on top of a palm tree. Felt dizzy again. The body's memory is such a strange thing.'

'What were you doing on top of a palm?'

'Pruning and climbing. It's the only place in the world you cut and climb.'

'You used to prune palm trees?'

'I did. I pruned the palms in Recheo Gardens.'

'Were they very tall?'

'They were of a certain height. And I made them taller.'

'You did?'

'That's right. You have to make palm trees. Like building a staircase in the sky.'

I stayed silent because there was a wounded note in Polka's response as if the pruning had affected his body. I imagined him clambering up the palm tree's old cuts to reach the branches he still had to saw.

'Pruning a tall palm is very different from pruning any other tree. It's like cutting wings. The whole leaf shakes as you're sawing. Though they're not really leaves. More like spines. Skeletons.'

His glistening eyes also lived in holes. Polka's face was an inhabited rock. Not round, a succession of stone slabs with caves where shiny-skinned, expressive creatures darted about. I watched him with my face on the pillow, Pinche having been rocked to sleep by his flowing tones, and it seemed to me his apple was a pendulum moving his lips and the scent of words brought his eyes out, his eyes and his memories, since they illustrated the story he was telling. Polka's mechanism, set in motion, went in the other direction to night. He was able to resist it. Olinda knew this and called him to bed.

'Skeletons?'

'Spines of big fish. Swordfish.'

With my face lying on the pillow, in the mist of sleepiness, I could see him up there, on top of a palm, sawing the skeletons of swordfish. Polka is shaped like a spine. Never had much flesh. He had a friend, Celeiro, whose skeleton alone weighed a hundred and twenty kilos. At death's door, he said to him, 'Polka, death doesn't want you, you've nothing to gnaw on.'

Now Polka's lying down and O is standing next to his bed. Polka's feet are cold, the rest of him is warm. His ribs are becoming more and more visible, even under the sheet. A body assembled on a palm leaf. The creatures living under the stone slabs of his face seem to be quiet tonight. Except for his eyes. His eyes are wide open and look at her in surprise. Suddenly he blinks as if trying to clear a mist. O doesn't want to stop talking, maintains the flow of her voice. She may be watching him on top of a palm tree, sawing swordfish spines. Sawing and climbing.

Before falling asleep, O hears Olinda calling to Polka, 'A lot of hare your mother must have eaten when she was pregnant with you!'

It's true. He sleeps with open eyes.

539

O wakes up with a start. Sweating. Has the sensation the imitation leather on the hospital chair has been grafted on to her skin. She was asleep for a few minutes, but saw herself descending one staircase in Polka's arms, and climbing another, holding him.

'What do you do in that hospital?'

'The laundry, Polka.'

'Are you your own boss?'

'Mine and the washing machines,' replied O ironically.

'That's good. The washing machines kicked you out of here and now you press their buttons. Let the machines do the work, damn it!'

'Before going to London, I worked in the house I told you about. In Sussex, invisible man country.'

'I don't suppose you saw him,' said Polka.

'No. I was the one who became invisible.'

'You said you liked it there. You wrote and said you were happy. It was all fun and games.'

'What was I supposed to say? When I write, my sorrows stay inside. The others saw me – Mr and Mrs Sutherland, Pinche, Popsy the dog. But I didn't. They were very kind to me, but I lost sight of myself. All that peace was finishing me off. So I decided to leave.'

'I always said the countryside is good for a visit,' remarked Polka. 'For what the Portuguese call a *pickenick*.'

'Pinche's the one who likes it. To start with, he came with me to London, but couldn't get used to it. He even worked as a sandwich-man for a time. Dressed up as Sherlock Holmes to advertise the detective's museum. He also worked as an executioner of tourists. That photo . . .'

'The uniform didn't suit him,' observed Polka. 'He didn't look very comfortable with the axe.'

'No. He went back to Sussex, far-flung Chichester. He loves it there. Mr Sutherland, Lena's husband, the pilot, lives for his fuchsias. He's a breeder. Mixes them, obtains new colours. Produced one so white, virtually albino, he called it Miss Griffin. Shame the invisible man didn't find his invisible mate. Another time. Mr Sutherland barely speaks, but chats away to his flowers. Gets on very well with Pinche. Says he has green fingers, a way with plants. One day, he'll be the best at fuchsias.'

'There'll be something else in Pinche's life apart from fuchsias.'

'He's a girlfriend who rides a bike.'

'Bike woman!' exclaimed Polka. 'I thought so.'

Yes, O thought, they passed each other so often they fell in love. Passed each other every day without speaking. Started to communicate with the calligraphy of their bikes. She once performed an unexpected 180° turn, ended up facing him. And so on. The most important day was when the wind tried unsuccessfully to push them over. He gazed at her admiringly. She was older than him. Perhaps twice his age. Until then, he'd seen very few women on a bike. The first was called Miss Herminia, who was said to be mad. Now he thought it wasn't like this, she was probably pedalling against her madness. He fell in love with the cyclist who stood up to the wind. Their outings got longer. When he thought she was about to leave, he'd draw another phrase on the road. This made him happy, drawing circles around her. When he told O, she burst out laughing, 'She's much older than you!' 'The bike, you mean,' he replied. Winked. And walked off.

'I didn't tell you,' said O to Polka, 'but before I found that job in the hospital, I was a waitress. Wasn't much fun. I had an argument, that's why I didn't tell you. The owner was on my back all the time. One of those guys who do their own work badly, but are always watching what others are up to. I went after some people who'd forgotten to pay. When I came back, he told me off for leaving the café without his permission. So I grabbed him by the neck, lifted him clean off the ground, and he said something no one's said to me before, "You are a half-man!"'

'What did you do?'

'I yelled at him, "Not half, I ain't."'

'Well said, that girl!' cried Polka.

'You're at home. You'll be better here than in hospital.' Polka keeps quiet. He knows what this means. He'll be better for as long as he lasts. But there's nothing he can do about it. What amazes him is the bed.

'And this bed?'

'It's orthopaedic,' said O. 'Goes up and down. Has a little engine.'

'Well, give it a go! That's brilliant! Does it go any higher? Make it go higher.' Then, looking worried, 'It must have cost a lot . . .'

'Social Security paid for it.'

'Did they?' he asked with mistrust. 'Well, we may as well make the most of it. Move it up and down.'

In this way, whenever he had a visit, Polka would ask to be lifted aloft and from up on high would greet the visitor with the gesture of a carnival minister:

'*Sursum corda!*'

One day, with the bed raised, he tells her he can't see.

'What is there to see, Papa?'

'I thought I'd see better from up here. But I can't see a thing. Here or there. A bit of mist, that's all.'

'Mist?'

'Dust. More like dust. Like dots on the television screen when there's no signal. I struggled with that television you sent me. Not because of me. I'd got used to the dots. I wanted it to be ready for your arrival. I tied the aerial to the top of the eucalyptus tree. But eucalyptuses grow very quickly and the trunk half swallowed the aerial. It was like having a metal branch. When crows landed, broken lines. Starlings, little black dots.'

'Now what can you see, Papa? Lines or black dots?'

'Nothing. The quality's gone.'

She shows him things. 'It's Élisée's book. Can't you see?'

'Here, let me touch. Books are so well made, damn it! It took them a while to get the hang of it. But now it's as if they're natural, like grafts on hands.'

'What about my hands?'

'I can't see anybody's hands, girl.'

She strokes his cheek. 'But you can feel them, right?'

He falls silent. Everything on his face acquires a subtlety of movement.

'What about me, Papa? Can't you see me?'

'You I can, girl. You I can.'

Something Special

The judge had a serious relapse. Gabriel went with Sofia to the house by the marina, intending to pick up some of his things. He hadn't been inside for a long time. Was surprised by the suspended animation, the watchfulness of things. The spectral attention of the begonias, which had extended their vegetal forms into the semi-darkness, giving the shadows a withered smell. He set Grand Mother Circa going. The house's heartbeat. Time that didn't leave, a present that remembered. Gabriel opened the shutters. The light went after them. Caressed them. A warm command they obeyed. The sensation they weren't making love, love was making them.

The front doorbell rang. Insistent and energetic. An old man who more than ever resembled Inspector Ren, with his supplier of Bibles' suitcase.

'Is Mr Samos in?'

'No, he isn't.'

Gabriel recognised the large, ill-tempered body's reaction, on the verge of ripping his ashen suit asunder. The voice as well, the way he chiselled his speech, 'You're the son, right? Yes, you're the son. Gabriel. Katechon! So how's the judge then?'

Gabriel's own voice surprised him, 'Come in, Mr Ren. The judge insisted you leave whatever you brought with you.'

'He said that?'

'With great interest.'

Ren looked doubtful. He knew about the old disagreement between father and son. Glanced at the suitcase with metal rivets. 'I've brought the judge something very special.'

Gabriel's voice carried on and he decided to let it, 'I'm sure you have. That's what he's expecting. That's what we're expecting. Something special.'

He invited him into the study. For old times' sake. Ren alighted on the mahogany table, opened the suitcase very slowly, as if something might escape. Gabriel Samos wondered what effect a handful of *Coccinella septempunctata* might have, carrying seven little dots on their wings. The tic in his hand had gone, the way it opened and closed.

'Here it is.' Ren's face was red. His cheeks, inflamed.

'Borrow's book. The New Testament. Here, look at the signature. The dedication written with a quill. A wild goose quill, I dare say.'

For Antonio de la Trava, the valiente of Finisterra.

'See! Look at the date: Madrid, 1837.'

'Is it very valuable?' asked Gabriel Samos with a show of indifference.

'Very valuable, you say? You've no idea how much work a thing like this can give. Your father's been after this book for years. But I told him, "For books, you needs must wait."'

The pimple, the spot on his nose, was also inflamed.

'Like this one. See, it's in English. A first edition. *Ulysses.* Now I'm no expert, but I have a rough idea of the value of things. And this is worth a lot.'

'That's strange!'

'What is?'

'That you should find it now. Here.'

'What's strange about that, Master Samos? Here there were always highly cultivated people. And good libraries. Even workers had libraries. No, Master Samos, this is not the back of beyond.'

To start with, Gabriel thought he might be teasing him. The way he called him 'master'. The way he praised workers' ransacked libraries. But then he realised he wasn't. He was being serious.

'It's not easy to find what you're looking for. And I'm in no fit state to rummage around. If I made an effort now, it was because of your father. He called me from hospital the first time he was admitted. He was excited. Very excited. Had a lead. So old Ren here got back on his feet.'

544

He flourished *Ulysses*. 'It would seem half the world would go crazy for this book. It has only one little defect, apart from the fact you can't understand it. A flyleaf is missing.'

Gabriel anxiously flicked through the pages. Muttered, 'I wonder if it has an ex-libris.'

Ren was sweating. Took off his hat and laid it on the suitcase. Wiped his stunted head with a handkerchief. Breathed in through his nose. Seemed to be sniffing a new scent that had found its way into the house. A scent sewn to the plants.

'It may have. I don't know, nor do I care.'

'It'd make it more valuable,' said Gabriel.

'More valuable? I doubt it. Who the heck cares about ownership? These pieces are of incalculable value.' He whispered the word again, like an echo, 'Incalculable.'

'How much is incalculable, Ren?'

Ren dried his hands on the handkerchief and stuffed it, withered and hanging, back into his jacket pocket. Said, 'Let's see. These objects are difficult to value. Some things are just priceless. Your father would have paid well. Extremely well. In this case, I'd have said the payment would have been splendid.'

'How much?' asked Gabriel again.

Author's Acknowledgements

The author wishes to thank the following:

The staff of Coruña and the Archive of the Kingdom of Galicia's libraries. Xan Carlos Agra, Xesús Alonso Montero, Cleudene Aragão, Mimina Arias, Pedro and Pepe Barrós, Manuel Bermúdez Chao, Vicente Boquete Tito, Fermín Bouza, Manuel Bragado, Euan Cameron, Picco Carillo, Esther Casal, Xosé Castro, Ramón Chao, Xosé Chao Rego, Cheni, Antonio Conde, Juan Cruz, Isaac Díaz Pardo, Pilar Diz, Antón Doiro, Jonathan Dunne, Amaya Elezcano, Xaime Enríquez, Guillermo Escrigas, Manuel Espiña, Carlos Fernández, María Estrela Fernández and the family of the murdered Coruñan book-collector Eirís, Benito Ferreiro (son), Xosé A. Gaciño, Víctor García de la Concha, Beatriz Gómez (from Silva), Benito González, Xesús González Gómez, Henrique Harguindey, Juantxu Herguera, the tailor Mr Iglesias, Luis Lamela, Xurxo Lobato, Lola from Lume, Antón López, Alberte Maceda, Santiago Macías, Bernardo Máiz, Danilo Manera, Xosé Luís Martínez, Carlos Martínez-Buján, Xosé Mato, Serge Mestre, César A. Molina, Enrique Molist, Xulio Montero, Eirín Moure, Serafín Mourelle, Xosé Manuel Muñiz, Antón Patiño, Dionisio Pereira, Nonito Pereira, Carlos Pereira Martínez, Gabriel Plaza, Xulio Prada, Miguelanxo Prado, Xesús María Reiriz, Manuel Rodríguez, Ana Romero, Josep Maria Joan Rosa, Andrés Salgueiro, Carme Salorio, Manuel Sánchez Salorio, Antón de Santiago, Sito Sedes, Felipe Senén, Xavier Seoane, Xurxo Souto, Celia Torres Bouzas, Dolores Torres París, Olivia Tudela, Alberto Valín, Elvira Varela, Ánxel Vázquez de la Cruz, Mari Vega, Graça Videira, Manuel Vilariño, Dolores Vilavedra, Elke Wehr, Manuel Zamora.

Iria, Gastón, Miguelón, César Carlos Morán, the group Jarbanzo Negro and Rómulo Sanjurjo.

Pedro de Llano.

His uncle Francisco and aunts Manola and Pepita.

Paco, Sabela and Felicitas.

Sol and Martiño.

Isa.